Richard Laymon wrote over thirty novels a~~~ ~~~ May 2001, *The Travelling Vampire Show* won ~~~ Best Horror Novel, a prize for which Lay~~~ shortlisted with *Flesh*, *Funland*, *A Good, Secre*~~~ and *A Writer's Tale* (Best Non-fiction). Laym~~~ books of the Beast House Chronicles: *The Cella*~~~ *~~~* and *The Midnight Tour*. Some of his recent novels ha~~~ *got in the Lonesome October*, *No Sanctuary* and *Amara*.

A native of Chicago, Laymon attended Willamette University in Salem, Oregon, and took an MA in English Literature from Loyola University, Los Angeles. In 2000, he was elected President of the Horror Writers' Association. He died in February 2001.

Laymon's fiction is published in the United Kingdom by Headline, and in the United States by Leisure Books and Cemetery Dance Publications. To learn more, visit the Laymon website at: http://rlk.cjb.net

'A brilliant writer' *Sunday Express*

'Stephen King without a conscience' Dan Marlowe

'This is an author that does not pull his punches . . . A gripping, and at times genuinely shocking, read' *SFX Magazine*

'In Laymon's books, blood doesn't so much as drip as explode, splatter and coagulate' *Independent*

'No one writes like Laymon and you're going to have a good time with anything he writes' Dean Koontz

'Incapable of writing a disappointing book' *New York Review of Science Fiction*

'One of the best, and most underrated, writers working in the genre today' *Cemetery Dance*

Island

and

Quake

headline

ISLAND first published in Great Britain in 1995
by HEADLINE PUBLISHING GROUP

QUAKE first published in Great Britain in 1995
by HEADLINE PUBLISHING GROUP

First published in this omnibus edition in 2007
by HEADLINE PUBLISHING GROUP

A HEADLINE paperback

1

ISBN 978 0 7553 3178 9

Typeset in Janson by Avon DataSet Ltd, Bidford on Avon, Warwickshire

Printed and bound in Great Britain by
Mackays of Chatham plc, Chatham, Kent

Headline's policy is to use papers that are natural, renewable and recyclable
products and made from wood grown in sustainable forests. The logging and
manufacturing processes are expected to conform to the environmental
regulations of the country of origin.

HEADLINE PUBLISHING GROUP
A division of Hachette Livre UK Ltd
338 Euston Road
London NW1 3BH

www.headline.co.uk
www.hodderheadline.com

Island

This book is dedicated
to
Frank Coghe
A legend in his own time.

When they made you, Cog,
they broke the mold.

The Journal of Rupert Conway, Castaway

Today, the yacht exploded.

Fortunately, all of us had gone ashore to have a picnic on this island, so we didn't get blown to smithereens. All of us, that is, except Prince Wesley.

Prince Wesley wasn't actually a prince. He was actually an asshole. Sorry about that; you're not supposed to speak ill of the dead. But he was a royal pain in the butt and I wouldn't be at all surprised if the explosion was his fault. He probably picked the wrong time and place to light up a cigarette.

Kaboom!

Now he's fish nibbles.

I'm sorry he's dead, but he *was* a ridiculous, arrogant jerk. He was a grown man; all of thirty, I suppose, but he went around all the time wearing one of those stupid white yachting hats. And you never saw him that he wasn't strutting around the deck with his ivory cigarette-holder hoisting up a Marlboro in front of one eye or the other. Oh yeah, he wore aviator sunglasses, too. And an ascot, more often than not.

Anyway, that was Prince Wesley. He's dead, so I won't spend any more time running him down. His actual name, for the record, was Wesley Duncan Beaverton III. He died today, April 1, 1994, which is not only April Fool's Day, but also happens to be Good Friday. What a day to go.

He is survived by his wife, Thelma. Who ought to consider herself lucky to be rid of him, but instead seems to be terribly upset.

Wesley and Thelma didn't have any children, but they'd only been married for about a year.

Personally, I think he married her for her money.

He sure didn't marry Thelma for her good looks. Her

sister got all of them. The sister, Kimberly, is about twenty-five and a knockout. To think I'm marooned on a tropical isle with a babe like Kimberly . . .! Whoooey!

Not that anything much is likely to come of it. Aside from the fact that I'm a few years her junior and here as the guest of her half-sister, Connie, she's married. Her husband, Keith, is one of those incredibly handsome, bright, sincere and capable guys who makes ordinary jerks (like me) look like we got stalled somewhere low down on the evolutionary ladder. I'd hate him, but he's too nice to hate.

The other male with us here on the island is the sire of all three gals, Andrew (never Andy) Collins. His first wife, mother of Thelma and Kimberly, bit the big one in a snow skiing accident at Lake Tahoe. He subsequently married Billie, and together they had Connie.

This little yacht excursion in the Bahamas was a gift from the children to celebrate the twentieth wedding anniversary of Andrew and Billie. (Wesley came down to Nassau a week ahead of everyone else to set it up – scout the situation, check up on the hotel reservations, rent the boat, and so forth.) Andrew is probably in his mid-fifties. He's retired Navy, rich because he invested in some sort of oil scheme that paid off huge, and a pretty decent guy. If you're going to get marooned, he's probably a good fellow to have along. A straight arrow, smart, and tough. He treats me okay, sort of, even though I'm sure he suspects I've been 'putting it' to Connie.

Connie's mother, Billie, is only a couple of years older than Thelma. In other words, she's young enough that you'd logically take her as one of Andrew's daughters, not his wife. She's a lot better looking than Thelma, though not quite as hot as Kimberly.

She and Connie look more like sisters than like a mother and daughter. They both have dark tans and golden hair, and wear their hair in the same short, pixie style. Connie is slightly taller. Her mother is a lot fuller in the chest and hips, and of course looks older in the face. Actually, Billie is quite a bit more attractive in many ways than her daughter.

(I'd better make sure none of these folks gets a chance to read what I'm writing here. I've only just now started working on this journal, and I've already thrown in some stuff that could get me in trouble.)

My plan, by the way, is to keep a detailed account of things, and use it as the basis for a 'true adventure' sort of book. Which won't pan out if we get rescued too soon. I'm hoping we'll have to spend a while here, long enough for there to be a few more dramatic events. For the record, the reason I brought my writing pad when we came to the island is that I've been working on some short stories. I plan to win the Belmore fiction writing contest . . . Man, what an optimist! Maybe none of us will ever get off this island, in which case I might as well forget the writing contest. And a few other things.

Never mind.

Gonna depress myself, if I don't watch out.

Anyway, back to the introductions.

Connie, daughter of Billie and Andrew, is my 'girlfriend'. We're both freshmen at Belmore University. That's how I got to know her. We kept being forced together by the alphabet: she being a Collins, I a Conway. At a university, you can't remain strangers for long with the person who immediately precedes you in the ABCs. Soon, we began talking to each other. After a while, we started going out. Before I knew it, she was inviting me to spend spring break with her family on a yacht in the Bahamas.

You don't turn down an offer like that.

I don't, anyhow.

I decided to postpone the inevitable – breaking up with her – until after the excursion.

Now, there might not *be* an 'after.' Yee gads, stuck with her for life. No no no. Won't happen. We'll probably be rescued shortly. There's just no way this can turn into some sort of Robinson Crusoe deal. At most, we might spend a few days here. More likely, we'll be picked up before dark; that's if somebody heard or saw our boat explode.

It was one hell of an explosion.

For a while, crap kept falling out of the sky and plopping into the water. Pieces of the boat – and undoubtedly Wesley. (I expected to see a foot or a head or a big looping coil of entrails coming down, but nope.) Many of the pieces were on fire. They got snuffed out when they landed in the water. Nothing came down on the beach, luckily.

Then there wasn't much left but a bunch of junk floating on the water, and a smudge of drifting smoke.

At the time it went up, we couldn't spot any aircraft or boats. We sure did look. Some of us did, anyhow. Not Thelma, of course. That's when Thelma clutched the sides of her head and started shrieking, 'No! No! Oh, my God, no! Wesley! My poor Wesley! No!' And like that.

After a few seconds, Kimberly put her arms around her. They stood there hugging each other, Kimberly patting her sister's back and murmuring to her. Kimberly was wet. She'd gone in the water for a little swim after our picnic lunch on the beach, and had just waded ashore a minute or two before the explosion. Her black hair was matted against her skull and hung in a sheath down the nape of her neck. Her back was golden and smooth and dripping. She wore a white bikini. The pants of her bikini hung a little crooked, lower on one hip than on the other, showing more of the top of her right buttock than her left. And the middle of the seat had a crease in it . . .

Enough of that.

She looked damn fine, that's all. I couldn't help staring. But I also spent my share of time looking out across the water. The cloud of smoke had moved on and thinned out. I could see a couple of islands, way off in the distance. But not much else except water and sky.

Kimberly led her sister away from the rest of us. They sat shoulder to shoulder on the blanket where we'd had our picnic.

'Poor thing,' Billie said, watching them.

'Splendid move on Wesley's part, blowing up our boat.'

'Andrew!'

'Fumes in the engine compartment,' he went on. 'The

idiot *knew* they could blow us to hell and gone. My mistake. Shouldn't have let him stay on board, nobody there to keep an eye on him. Should've known he'd fuck up the works. The bastard. He was too dumb to live.'

'Andrew!'

'At least he blew *himself* up with the boat. That's the silver lining.'

'Don't let your daughter hear you say such things. She loved him.'

'He sure as shit didn't love her. Anyhow, good riddance. Rest in pieces, Wesley.' And he hocked a wad of spit onto the sand at his feet.

After that, Andrew and Keith went out on the dinghy to see what they could find at the scene of the explosion. I offered to go along, but they said it wouldn't be necessary. Typical. Maybe it's because they think of me as a useless kid or because I'm not part of the family. Maybe there's a reason I don't know about. Even though they're generally nice to me, they treat me like an outsider. I get excluded a lot. I'm sort of used to it by now, having spent several days with this bunch.

Anyway, they left me behind with the women while they puttered out and started picking up nearly everything that was still afloat.

Connie stood on one side of me, her mother on the other.

'They won't bring back Wesley, will they?' Connie asked, making a face like the one she'd given me once when we talked about eating beets.

'We should give him a proper burial,' Billie said.

'He's probably in chunks,' I added.

'They'd better not bring back *chunks* of him. God! That's just what we'd need.'

'If we're stuck here very long,' I said, 'we might want to eat him.'

'Rupert!' Billie gasped.

'God!' Connie snapped. 'I can't *believe* you sometimes. That's disgusting!'

'We'd have to jerk him right away,' I said, 'so he doesn't go bad on us.'

7

Billie shook her head at me. She was smiling slightly. 'You're demented,' she said. 'Just don't say anything like that around Thelma.'

'I wouldn't,' I assured her.

She swayed sideways and bumped me a little with her shoulder. 'I know,' she said. 'You're demented, but sensitive.'

'That's me.'

'Cut it out, huh?' Connie said. I think she meant both of us. I'd noticed before how it seemed to annoy her when Billie and I talked or goofed around. Come to think of it, just about everything about Billie seems to annoy her. Maybe it's one of those competition things, and she knows she doesn't measure up. I mean, her mother has her whipped in every department: looks, brains, sense of humor, compassion, you name it.

Must be hard on Connie. I'll have to be more understanding.

After she told us to cut it out, we just stood there silent as the 'men' gathered floating treasures.

The sand of the beach was almost white. The water lapped in gently – no big combers, I guess, because of the reef. (There'd been some pretty good waves right after the explosion, but they didn't last long.) The water, pale blue, was a little murky. It had been incredibly clear until the boat blew, and would probably be that way again in a while. There was a soft, warm breeze taking away the worst of the heat. And there were the gals.

Man oh man.

It's a shame that Prince Wesley had to go (I'm sure), and it's too bad that Thelma is taking it so hard, but I couldn't help thinking how lucky we were to be stranded in a place like this.

At least for a while.

The longer the better, as far as I'm concerned.

Not really. But I wouldn't mind a couple of weeks, as long as we don't starve (no need to worry about fresh water, because of the stream).

After a while, Andrew and Keith returned with a boat full of odds and ends – including some packets of food, but no bits or pieces of Wesley. I'm sure Connie was relieved.

'Is his body out there?' I asked.

'Bet on it,' Keith said.

'We're going back out,' Andrew said. 'We've gotta salvage what we can.'

'I could go with you, this time, if you need an extra set of hands.'

'That's all right, chief,' Andrew said. 'Somebody's gotta stay here and watch out for the ladies.'

Chief. He calls me chief quite a lot. It's like a thing with him. I'm almost nineteen years old, and he calls me chief like I'm a kid.

Oh, well, maybe it's quaint.

'Whatever you say, skipper,' I told him.

He hoisted an eyebrow.

Anyway, Thelma and Kimberly came over. Thelma had stopped crying, and seemed groggy. They pitched in, and everyone helped to unload the boat. Then Andrew and Keith cranked up the dinghy's motor and took off to scour the inlet for more loot.

The gals got to work on the goodies we'd just unloaded, so I went over to our picnic area to get my notebook and a pen. They were in my book bag along with a couple of paperback books. Instead of taking them out, I just swung the bag onto my back and took the whole thing with me.

I called out, 'I'll be back in a while.' Before anyone could ask questions or offer to accompany me, I hurried off.

I walked alongside the stream, figuring to follow it into the jungle. Keith and Kimberly had gone exploring before lunch while the rest of us dinked around on the beach, and they said the stream led to a great little lagoon, complete with a waterfall – if you hiked inland far enough.

My impression was that they took the hike to get away from the rest of us. They probably skinny-dipped in the lagoon, and I'd bet a million bucks they screwed.

I sort of wanted to see it and maybe take a little dip, myself – but I was more interested in sitting beside the lagoon and getting to work on my journal.

When I started into the jungle, it looked pretty dense and

creepy. No telling what sort of creatures might be lurking there. The open beach seemed a lot safer. So I gave up on following the stream, and went along the sand toward a big tower of rocks on the point.

The inlet is shaped like a large U, with the stream running down its center to join up with the salt water, and rocky points at each tip. The one ahead of me was higher than the other. It would give me a good view and all the privacy I needed.

The climb to the top winded me, but was worth it. The summit was probably forty or fifty feet above the water. When I got there, I took a while to look around. I could see the gals down on the beach. Also, I saw 'the men' on the dinghy, hauling crap out of the water.

In places, the water was clear enough that I could see to the bottom. Mostly, though, it was still cloudy because of the explosion. I turned away pretty quick – afraid that I might spot some leftover Wesley.

On the other side of the point, there's a lot more beach and jungle. No docks, no houses, no roads, no telephone poles, nothing to indicate the island has inhabitants.

I studied the sky and ocean. No aircraft, no boats.

After a check of our beach to make sure nobody was coming my way, I found myself a nice, sheltered nook in the rocks, sat down and started to write.

It's been very nice. No one can see me here. An overhang keeps the sun off me, and there's a wonderful breeze. All I can see is a bit of ocean and the sky.

Now, I'm caught up to the present.

I feel like I've been at it for at least an hour, maybe a lot longer. I didn't keep track of the time. My butt's a little sore. I'm about ready to head back down and see what's going on.

Maybe I should leave my journal up here. Hide it in the rocks.

No, I'd better take it with me. If I leave it here, might be tough to retrieve it in case we suddenly get rescued. Also, something could happen. Some sort of wildlife might attack it – I don't want my precious pages getting munched by an iguana or ending up as insulation for a bird nest. I'll keep it in my book bag, and take it with me everywhere so nobody will have a chance to lay eyes on what's written in here.

That's all for now.

The First Supper

I'm back.

It's early evening, and we're still here. Looks like we probably won't be going anyplace tonight.

Andrew and Keith spent most of the afternoon making trips to the scene of the explosion to salvage things. Keith even did some diving and brought up stuff that had sunk. They managed to retrieve quite a lot of items that should make our stay on the island more endurable: food and clothes and utensils, not to mention a few bottles of booze that had somehow survived the blast and some fresh fish that hadn't. But they came back without anything *really* major – such as a flare gun or transmitter – that we could use to alert rescuers of our position.

Andrew, a great hand at everything, cleaned the fish. He is not only retired Navy, but an Eagle Scout. He is nothing if not prepared. Just as I never go anywhere without my writing implements and reading material, he is forever equipped with a slew of useful items, including a Swiss Army knife and a butane lighter for his pipe.

While Andrew gutted the catch of the day, the rest of us trooped over the beach and gathered driftwood for our fire. It is plentiful. In about ten minutes, we had a pile six feet high.

Done with the bloody work, Andrew built a tidy little fire about twenty feet from our huge stack of driftwood. He used his butane lighter to ignite it.

Keith had recovered a skillet during one of his dives.

Billie did the cooking. We didn't have any grease for the skillet, so she opened one of the liquor bottles and cooked up the fish in bourbon. It wasn't bad.

This is sort of like being on a camping trip. A trip where you messed up and left most of your supplies behind – a trip where you don't necessarily have a way to get home. Those are the negatives. On the other side of the coin, this is better than any camping trip I ever went on because this one includes the gals.

I've had a hard time keeping my eyes off Kimberly in her white bikini. And Billie isn't any slouch, either. Her black bikini is a lot bigger than Kimberly's, but seems smaller because there's so much of her that it doesn't cover. She was really something to see, crouched beside the fire and shaking the skillet. The skillet wasn't the only thing that shook. She seems to like showing off what she's got. I try not to let Connie catch me looking at her.

I'd be looking at Connie, but there's not much to see. She's spent most of the day wearing an extra large T-shirt over her swimming suit. Also, even though she has a decent build, she looks scrawny compared to her mother. And unlike her mom, she doesn't seem to have any tendencies toward exhibitionism.

As for Thelma, she's sort of cute in a thick, blocky way, but nothing much to look at. I don't mean to be unkind. She's a pretty nice woman and I actually like her quite a lot most of the time. The whole trip, I haven't once seen her in a bathing suit. She always wears a big floppy straw hat, a loose blouse that she doesn't tuck in, baggy shorts, white socks and Reeboks.

I probably shouldn't be writing this stuff about the women. It'll be embarrassing if someone happens to read it. Also, it sort of makes me look shallow and creepy. As if all I care about is how a gal looks in her bikini.

That isn't *all* I care about.

The thing is, it's probably easy to be nonchalant about gorgeous, semi-nude babes if you're a handsome, confident guy who has nailed about fifty of them. But I'm eighteen, short and skinny and zitty. My name is RUPERT, for God's sake. (I was named after Rupert Brooke, the poet. He was a great poet, and I love his stuff, but if my parents had to pick a poet's name for me, why not Robert Frost, Carl Sandburg, or Walt Whitman? Rupert? Please! I guess I should count my blessings; at least they didn't name me Wilfred, Ezra or Sylvia.)

Anyway, I'm basically a shrimp with a dumb name and an attitude. Connie goes for me – to the extent that she does – because I'm nonthreatening, she thinks she generally controls me, and she often finds me amusing. There might be other reasons, but those are the most obvious.

I think there are always *other reasons* for everything. Invisible reasons. Sometimes, they're so well hidden that nobody knows about them at all.

There might be some deep, dark reason why I've been going out with Connie. I hope so. Otherwise, it's just because she's the only gal at school who has ever shown the slightest interest in me. It certainly isn't her glamorous looks or her winning personality.

Among other things, she's a real prude.

I mean, I've gotten nowhere with her in the romance department.

Which is about as far as I've gotten with most girls, which might explain why I'm so interested in *looking* at people like Kimberly and Billie.

Or maybe there are hidden reasons.

It's almost too dark out here to see what I'm writing. I'll quit now and go over to the campfire, where everyone else is.

Day Two

A Mysterious Disappearance

Keith is missing.

It must've happened while he was standing watch.

Right after I joined the bunch sitting around the campfire last night, we had a discussion about whether we ought to take turns on guard duty. Most of us were against it. Why bother, since we'd been on the beach since late morning and hadn't found any reason to consider ourselves threatened? But then Andrew said that, even if we didn't seem to be in any danger, it's better to be safe than sorry. Also, he thought we shouldn't let the fire go out.

'We ought to keep it going day and night till we're picked up,' he said. He was packing tobacco into his briar pipe as he spoke. 'Don't need to get caught with a dead fire when a search plane comes along. Besides, we let it go out and we'll wind up lighting new ones all the time. That'll get a bit more difficult after my Bic runs out of juice. I've stopped using it to light my pipe, of course.' As he said that, he pulled a stick out of the fire and sucked its flame down onto the tobacco in his pipe. He puffed to get things stoked up. Then he explained that the men should take turns staying up to keep watch and feed the fire.

There were three of us, and he figured about nine hours till morning. That meant that we would each have to stand a three-hour shift. (Finally, I get to participate as one of the guys! Thanks a heap, skipper.)

Then Kimberly asked why the women weren't being included in the guard duty. 'Do ovaries disqualify us?' she asked.

Which made me laugh. Which won me some points with Kimberly and Billie, but didn't seem to be appreciated by the others.

17

There was a general discussion. It stayed friendly, and the decision was made that the women could be responsible for watch duty on the second night, if we're still here by then. That ended the complaints.

Andrew was supposed to take first watch, then wake up Keith, who would do his three hours and then wake me up at about four in the morning to keep an eye on things for the rest of the night.

With that settled, we all turned in except Andrew, who remained by the fire.

The night was warm and nice. We each made up our beds with assorted blankets, clothing, and whatnot that we'd either brought with us when we came for the picnic, or that Keith and the skipper had retrieved from the water. (Everything was dry by then.)

All of us stayed in the general area of the fire. Couples made their beds together. Not Connie and I, though. We helped each other build separate sleeping places – side by side, but with a space between us. Which was fine with me.

She gave me a goodnight peck on the mouth, then we retired to our rag piles.

There was method in her arrangement.

Billie's bed was only about ten feet away. Once we were lying down, however, I couldn't see her; Connie blocked my view.

I might've been able to see Kimberly in the other direction, but she and Keith had insisted that Thelma share their quarters. It was nice of them. Otherwise, Thelma would've had to spend the first night of her widowhood alone.

Kimberly, unfortunately, stretched herself out between Thelma and Keith. Which ruined any chance I had of watching her.

Thwarted on both sides, I shut my eyes and let my imagination take over.

The next thing I knew, someone was shaking me by the shoulder. I opened my eyes. It wasn't Keith waking me up. And the sky wasn't dark anymore.

At first, I didn't recognize the guy squatting over me.

It was Andrew, of course. The skipper. But he was wearing nothing except his khaki shorts. I'd hardly ever seen him when he didn't have on a T-shirt, sunglasses and ballcap. He had a gray fur all over his chest, his eyes looked sort of pale and bare, and he was bald and shiny on the top of his head. He seemed older than usual, and not as tough.

'What's going on?' I asked.

'You tell me.' He didn't sound angry. Concerned, though. 'Why aren't you up and standing watch?' he asked.

I had to think about that for a minute. Then I said, 'Nobody woke me. Keith was supposed to, wasn't he?'

'And he didn't?'

'No. He was supposed to, though. Yeah. When he was ready for me to relieve him at four.'

'That was the plan.'

'If he didn't wake me up, it's not my fault. I mean, I haven't got an alarm clock.'

I sat up to see what was going on with Keith. Thelma and Kimberly were sleeping side by side, but Keith wasn't there.

I gave the whole area a quick scan, and didn't see him anywhere.

'Where is he?' I asked.

'I don't know.'

'Uh-oh,' I said.

'*You* don't know?'

'Huh-uh. I fell asleep right away. You were over by the fire, and Keith was with Kimberly. That's the last I saw of anybody till now.'

'I never took Keith as the sort to desert his post,' Andrew said.

'If he had a good reason.'

'Such as?'

'I don't know, a bad case of the trots?'

'He should've gotten you up three hours ago,' Andrew said, making a point of the *three hours* part.

A mighty long time to spend squatting in the jungle.

'Maybe he decided to let me sleep...' I looked over at where the fire used to be. Only a smokeless pile of ashes remained. Obviously, nobody had fed the thing for hours.

I suddenly got sort of a sickish feeling in the pit of my stomach.

'What's the matter?' Connie asked, sounding groggy. With a yawn, she pushed herself up on one elbow. Her hair was a messy tangle, in spite of being almost as short as mine, and her T-shirt hung off her shoulder. She actually looked sort of cute that way. This was the first time I'd ever seen her wake up in the morning.

Andrew explained to her about Keith. 'Did you notice anything last night?' he asked.

She yawned again and shook her head. Then she added, 'I bet he went jogging or something. He's such a fitness freak. Probably on the other side of the island by now.'

'Maybe,' Andrew said, but I knew he didn't buy it. I'd noticed before how he sometimes agreed with his daughters and wife even when they were obviously wrong. It was just his way of keeping the peace.

Anyway, our discussions were getting nowhere fast.

So Andrew went over to Billie, bent down and shook her. She seemed to be quite a heavy sleeper. She moaned and rolled onto her side. She'd gone to sleep in her bikini, and wasn't covered by anything else. Looking between Andrew's legs, I saw that her upper breast had gotten dislodged a little. About half the nipple showed. I kept watching, hoping her entire breast would fall out. But then Andrew turned around, so I had to look the other way quick.

'Honey, go on over and wake up your sisters, would you?'

Connie groaned like it was a chore, but she followed orders. While she was on her way to where Thelma and Kimberly were sleeping, I got to my feet. I checked on Billie. She was sitting up and rubbing her eyes. One of her elbows was in the way, so I couldn't see much of her bikini top.

I turned my attention to the others. Connie nudged Thelma with her foot and said, 'Guys, wake up.'

Thelma, flat on her back, blinked up at her and scowled.

Kimberly was covered to the shoulders by a blue blanket.

(It wasn't the good one that we'd brought with us to spread on the beach for our picnic. Andrew and Billie claimed that one.) Kimberly's blanket had been retrieved from the inlet. A survivor of the boat explosion, it was missing a corner, had a rip down one side and a bunch of burn holes with dark, charred edges. I could see her skin through some of the holes.

She didn't move when Connie said, 'Guys, wake up.' Then came, 'Keith's disappeared.'

Kimberly threw the blanket aside and sat up fast. Frowning, she swung her head from side to side as she got to her feet. She was still in her white bikini. She looked terrific. She also looked worried.

Andrew and Billie were already striding toward her. (Billie had straightened her bikini top so nothing showed that wasn't supposed to.)

Kimberly said, 'Dad, what's going on? Where's Keith?'

'We don't know, honey. He was supposed to wake up Rupert at four, but he didn't. From the look of things, he's been gone a long time.'

Kimberly suddenly shouted 'Keith!' toward the jungle. She got no answer, so she cupped her hands to the sides of her mouth and belted out, 'KEITH!'

Then we all started yelling his name.

We even tried calling out in unison. That was Billie's idea. She counted to three, and we all yelled 'KEITH!' at once.

Then we waited, but no reply came.

'Do you have any idea where he might've gone?' Andrew asked Kimberly.

'No. Are you kidding? He wouldn't go anywhere, not when he's supposed to be keeping watch. Not Keith. Except maybe for five minutes, if he had to go to the john. He wouldn't take off for *hours*. No way!'

I'd never seen her this upset. She wasn't hysterical, though. She didn't cry, but her voice sounded tight and she had a frantic look in her eyes like she wanted to scream for help.

'Something's happened to him,' she said. 'He's had an accident, or . . .' She shook her head. 'We've gotta go and find him.'

21

We might've started a general discussion about the various possibilities, but Kimberly didn't hang around. She picked up her shoes and started running toward the jungle.

'Kim!' Andrew yelled. 'Wait for us.'

Still running, she glanced back over her shoulder.

'Stop!' he ordered.

She quit running, turned around, and walked backward toward the jungle.

'Somebody should stay here,' I suggested. 'You know, in case Keith shows up. If he comes back and everyone's gone . . .'

'Good idea,' Andrew said. 'You wanta stay?'

'No, but . . .'

'I'll stay,' Connie volunteered.

'I don't want you here by yourself,' her dad said.

'Rupert'll stay with me.'

'I want to help search for Keith,' I said.

The skipper pointed at me. 'Stay with her.' He dug into his pocket, came up with the lighter, and tossed it to me. 'Get the fire going, Rupe.'

'Aye-aye, sir.'

Andrew, Billie and Thelma spent a couple of minutes picking up odds and ends such as shoes, hats, and sunglasses. Then they hurried to catch up with Kimberly.

Before long, they vanished into the jungle. Connie and I stood by ourselves on the sand.

'He'll turn up,' Connie said.

'I hope so.'

She frowned the way she does when she wants you to know she's concentrating hard. 'What do you think happened to him?'

'He went out in the jungle to take a dump last night, and the local headhunters nailed his ass.'

'Ha ha ha. Very funny. You're sick if you think that's funny.'

'Maybe not headhunters,' I said.

'I should think not.'

'Maybe a snake got him. I bet something did. Might've been one of those giant spiders I heard about – they're indigenous to these islands. They have this special venom that turns your blood to acid so you burn up from the inside out.'

'Yeah, right.'

'Really.'

'Get fucked,' she told me, then spun around and walked off toward the water.

'By you?' I asked.

'In your dreams,' she said, not even glancing back.

Not in *my* dreams, I thought. I didn't say it, though. I'd already said enough, pretty much.

She went in for a swim, so I built a new fire in the ashes of the old one. When the fire was going good, I fetched my pen and journal and got to work.

The search party still hasn't returned.

Connie's been leaving me alone.

After swimming around for a while, she went climbing on the rocks at the point. (Good thing I didn't leave my journal hidden up there. She probably would've found it and read it, and then I'd be in some real trouble.) Later, she climbed down and swam some more. Then she sprawled out on the sand. She's acting like I'm somewhere else.

We didn't exactly have a model relationship *before* this trip, but it started to really deteriorate as soon as the others entered the picture. I think she considers it a big mistake that she asked me to come along.

Oh, well.

I'm having a good time, mostly, in spite of her.

On the negative side of things, it's not a good sign that the search party has been gone so long. I'm afraid something bad might've happened to Keith.

I sure hope *they're* all right.

Shit! What if *they* don't come back?

I don't want to think about that. Besides, it isn't very likely.

So long for now. I've got a few personal matters to take care of while I've got the place pretty much to myself.

Keith Turns Up

Oh, man. Oh, shit.

The search party hasn't come back yet. No wonder. They're still out there looking for Keith, probably.

I found him.

I didn't have to look far, either. Just *up*.

Here's what happened. Since there was nobody around, and I'd been holding things in for a while, I decided to take advantage of the privacy to answer nature's call. I took a paperback book with me. Not for reading purposes. I figured I could start ripping out pages from the first half, which I'd already read. (It's not that great a book anyway.)

I went wandering over to the area that our group has been using since our arrival yesterday – in the jungle and a pretty good distance south of the stream. It wasn't very far to walk, and the foliage in there was thick enough so that you could disappear after just a few steps.

Most everyone had gone in, at one time or another.

It was the first place that Kimberly and the others had searched, too.

But they'd missed him.

I didn't stop at the first likely trees, but went in a little deeper. After all, no telling when the searchers might return.

I found a good place, and did my business.

I had taken off my swimming trunks to make the job easier, so then I had to put them back on. The problem was, I *hadn't* taken off my shoes. When I stood on one foot and tried to slip the other into the leg hole of my trunks, the heel of my Nike got caught and I lost my balance. I hopped and tried to work my foot loose. All of a sudden, though, I was out of control. My shoulder slammed into the trunk of a tree in front of me. The blow turned me, and I landed flat on my back.

Which is when I found Keith.

I'd crashed into *his* tree.

It wasn't a palm tree, by the way. The jungle here was full of regular, non-palm trees of maybe a zillion different varieties. This one looked like a normal tree – the sort that has a thick trunk, branches starting about ten feet up, and normal-sized leaves instead of fronds.

Keith was a little higher than the first set of branches.

All I saw, at first, was the bottom half of a naked man dangling almost directly above my face.

I pulled my trunks on, fast as I could, then got out from under him.

He was up there so high that I couldn't see enough of his face to recognize him. There was no doubt in my mind, though. This was Keith. He'd lost his flip-flop sandals. He'd also lost his trunks. What he still wore was his bright green, blue and yellow Hawaiian-type shirt. It was fluttering in the breeze up there. And he was swaying just a bit from side to side.

I was pretty sure he'd been hanged, even though I couldn't make out the rope.

Suicide didn't seem real likely.

Which meant someone had *done* this to him.

I got the hell out of there.

Connie was down near the shore, stretched out on the sand. Sunbathing, maybe asleep.

I went back to my journal, and here I still am.

I'm still pretty shaky. This stuff is barely legible. It isn't every day you run into a murder victim. He was a nice guy, too – unlike Prince Wesley.

Now we've got two dead husbands. And two widows.

Poor Kimberly. It's sure going to be tough on her.

I could keep it to myself about finding the body, but that won't really solve much. I mean, it's not like Keith got lost in the jungle and if we wait around long enough, eventually he's going to turn up. All he's likely to do is rot.

Besides, everybody needs to know we have a killer out there.

One or more killers.

Savage natives?

Who knows?

Maybe one of us did it. Possible, but not likely. Andrew's probably the only one strong enough to hoist Keith up a tree like that. Unless a couple of the women teamed up to do it. No motive for anything like that, though, as far as I can see.

Oh, shit. The search party is coming back.

Gotta go.

We Deal With It

They came out of the jungle with Andrew and Billie supporting Thelma. She was hobbling along between them, putting almost no weight on her left leg. Her left ankle was wrapped with Andrew's black leather belt.

Kimberly brought up the rear. She kept turning around and looking back into the jungle.

All of them were flushed and sweaty.

As they walked closer to me, Andrew shook his head.

'No luck?' I asked.

'He could be anywhere out there. No sign of him at all. I take it he hasn't put in an appearance around here?'

'Nope,' I said. Then I asked Thelma, 'What happened to you?'

'I'm such a klutz,' she said. 'I slipped and twisted my ankle.'

'Could've happened to anyone,' Billie told her.

'We'll go out looking again,' Andrew said. 'Needed to bring Thelma back, and we ought to get some food in us.'

They lowered Thelma onto the collection of rags and towels that she'd shared last night with Kimberly and Keith.

Kimberly kept walking. 'I'm going in to cool off,' she said

as she passed us. She was scratched, shiny with sweat, dirty, and had bits of green sticking to her skin.

'Did something happen to her?' I asked, when she was a fair distance off.

'There wasn't any stopping her,' Andrew said. He shook his head as he watched her stride toward the shore. 'She crawled into tight places, went through bushes, scampered up rocks. Wore me out just watching her. What a kid – all I could do to make her come back with us. Keith better have himself one damn good excuse if he turns up okay.'

'He won't,' I said.

Andrew, Billie and Thelma all suddenly looked at me.

'He won't what?' Andrew asked.

'Turn up okay. I found him. Just a few minutes ago. He's been killed. Hanged, I think.'

Thelma's mouth fell open and she started to blink at me very rapidly.

Billie murmured, 'Oh, my God.'

Andrew mashed his lips together and shook his head. Then he said in a low voice, 'Better show me. You two stay here,' he told the gals.

'What about Kim?' Billie asked.

I turned my head just in time to see Kimberly, up to her thighs in the clear blue water of the inlet, raise her arms and dive under.

'No point in telling her anything until we're sure,' Andrew said. 'Jesus wept. What is there, some damn conspiracy to turn all my daughters into widows?'

When he said that, Thelma started to cry.

Kimberly surfaced and began to swim, her back flashing sunlight.

'Let's go, chief.'

We hurried. As we went, he asked how I'd discovered the body and was I sure it was Keith. I left out the part about falling down, but told him the rest. As for being sure of the identity, I pointed out that Keith was the only guy who had disappeared and the body in the tree was wearing a shirt exactly like Keith's, so I figured it was a pretty good bet.

'Don't be smart about shit like this,' he told me.

I apologized.

'That's my girl's husband you're talking about, and he was a good, decent man. Unlike that fuckhead who blew himself out of the water yesterday.'

When we got into the jungle, we had to wander around for a while, but finally I found the right place. The crumpled pages of a paperback book marked the spot, so to speak. That wasn't Keith's tree, but it worked as a landmark. I took a few strides away from it, looked up, saw Keith and pointed.

'I reckon that's him, all right,' Andrew said.

'I think he probably came out here during his watch,' I said. 'You know, figuring it'd be a good time to take care of business, everybody else being asleep. Only someone was out here waiting for him.'

'Or followed him when he left the beach,' Andrew added, and gave me a look. I couldn't see his eyes too well, his sunglasses being in the way, but I knew what sort of look he was giving me.

'If you think I did it, you're nuts. Why would *I* do it?'

'You've got the hots for Kimberly, so you take Keith out of the picture . . .'

'You're nuts!'

'You can't take your eyes off her.'

'Bull. And anyway, I'm not dumb enough to think she'd fall into my arms just because Keith isn't around. What kind of a moron do you think I am? And how in hell do you think I could possibly hoist a guy Keith's size that high into a tree?'

'It could be done,' Andrew said.

'With a winch, maybe.'

'A block and tackle.'

'Have you seen me running around the beach with a *block and tackle* hanging outa my trunks?'

'Steady there, chief. Don't blow a gasket, I'm just speculating.'

'Well you can quit speculating about me. How do I know *you* didn't kill him? I bet you could hoist a guy up there *without* a block and tackle.'

'What's my motive, Sherlock?'

'You tell me.'

'Shit. He was the salt of the earth, that boy. Shit!' Andrew suddenly jabbed a finger toward the body. 'Get up there and cut him down. Kimberly sees we're gone, she might get suspicious and come looking.'

'You want *me* to climb up there . . .?'

'You betcha, chief. I'm a sixty-year-old man, for God's sake.'

'Sixty?'

'Bet yer ass.'

'You're in better shape than me, anyway.'

'I know that, and you oughta be ashamed to admit it.' He dug the Swiss Army knife out of a front pocket of his shorts, and tossed it underhand to me.

I fumbled it and had to bend down to pick it up.

'Get up there. Haul yer ass. Kimberly comes along and sees him swinging up there with his dick in the wind, she'll have nightmares the rest of her life.'

I figured that Andrew was probably right about that.

My swimming trunks didn't have a pocket and I wasn't wearing any shirt, so I kept the knife shut and slid it down the top of my right sock. Then I started climbing the tree.

It wasn't my idea of a good time.

For one thing, I was worried about falling. For another, I was on my way up to a dead guy. I'd had about as much experience with dead bodies as I'd had with live gals. Basically, none. And I would've liked to keep it that way. (Not about the gals, about the corpses.)

If being dead wasn't bad enough, he was as good as naked. There's just about nothing I'd rather see less than some guy without any pants on. Especially the front of him, which is the section that was turned toward the tree trunk – and me.

I made sure not to look at him, and kept my eyes on the tree while I climbed. After a while, his bare feet showed up in my peripheral vision.

I turned my head and saw where the rope was tied off. I didn't look up to see where it came from. Obviously, though, it went upward from around his neck, was looped over a limb above his head, then came down – sort of behind him. It was wrapped and knotted around a limb just a little distance below his feet.

Which meant I could cut him down without climbing any higher, if I was willing to squirm out on the limb. The idea didn't appeal to me. To get within reach of the rope, I would need to go under Keith – and nudge his feet out of my way. If that wasn't bad enough, what was going to happen when I cut the rope? He would fall on me, that's what.

I wanted to be out of harm's way when I cut him loose.

So I turned my face to the tree again, and kept on climbing.

Even trying not to look, I couldn't help but see a lot more of Keith than I liked. You just can't *avoid* taking glances, now and then, when you've got something like that hanging next to you.

For instance, you want to make sure you aren't about to bump into him, or something.

And you want to know if he's got something on him that might, say, leap across the gap. I mean like a snake or other beast.

Anyway, it made me feel pretty sick, the way he looked. The whole business disgusted me, especially that he didn't have any pants on. But then I got up high enough to see his face, and things got a hundred times worse.

I won't even get into what he looked like.

'It's him for sure?' Andrew called.

'I think so.'

'Do you think so, or know so?'

'He's all wrecked up. His face. But I guess I'm sure.'

'Hung?'

He meant 'hanged.' Hung meant something very different, also applicable to the situation. I was in no mood to make any cracks, though. I said, 'Yeah. But he's got blood all over his hair and face. It looks like maybe someone whacked him on the head, *then* strung him up.'

'Go ahead and cut him down.'

'Just a second.'

I checked out the rope. It didn't look very new, and was a

little thicker than an ordinary clothesline. It had an actual 'hangman's knot'. I counted thirteen coils. They were tight against Keith's right cheek, and the thickness of the knot had shoved his head sideways. From the top of the knot, the rope went straight up to a limb several feet above his head. It looped over the limb, then stretched down behind his back, straight as a rod to where it was tied off on the limb below his feet.

He'd probably been hauled up by someone standing on that lower limb.

Maybe he'd been killed first, or at least knocked out.

'What're you doing up there?' Andrew called. 'Cut him down!'

I wondered if there might be a way to lower him.

If he could be hauled up, why not lowered?

Because, looking down, I could see that there was no extra rope at the lower limb. After tying it off, the killer must've cut off any excess.

I hated to just cut him loose and let him drop.

'Damn it, Rupert!'

'He'll fall,' I called back.

'So what? He's dead. He won't feel a thing.'

'Okay, okay.'

I climbed a little higher. Hugging the tree with my left arm, I brought up my right leg and pulled the knife out of my sock. I used my teeth to open the blade. Then I reached out over the top of Keith's head and pressed the edge of the blade against the rope.

Andrew's knife must've been awfully sharp.

One slice, and the rope popped.

Keith dropped.

It was worse than I expected.

He hit the limb underneath him, all right. But it went in between his legs and slammed him in the crotch. The whole limb shook. He sat there for a few seconds, head hanging. In his bright shirt, he looked like a flamboyant cowboy who'd fallen asleep in the saddle. Then he slumped over sideways. He fell the rest of the way head first.

Andrew let out a grunty noise and pranced backward to get out of the way.

Keith hit the ground with the back of his head. His spine seemed to bend in half. His legs shot down and his knees struck the ground on both sides of his face. For a second, he gazed up at me from down there like some sort of mutant that was half-face, half-ass. Then he tumbled over sideways.

I pushed my face against the tree trunk and sort of trembled for a while.

Pretty soon, Andrew started telling me to quit stalling and climb down – and bring the rope with me.

I did it. I had to climb out on that lower limb to get the rope. My hands shook too badly for me to untie the knots, so I used Andrew's knife to cut it loose. Then I just let it fall.

On the ground, I gave back Andrew's knife. He'd already picked up the rope and coiled it.

'What're we going to do with him?' I asked.

'Kimberly can't see him this way.' He handed the rope to me, then crouched by the body and took off Keith's noose. 'She'll want a look at him, though. We can't get around that. If she doesn't see his face, she'll never believe he's really dead.'

At that point, Andrew pulled and tugged at the body until it was stretched out flat on its back.

'Where's his damn trunks?'

'The killer must've taken them.'

'Look around.'

I did, but couldn't find Keith's swimming trunks, sandals, or anything else.

'Wanta give him yours?' Andrew asked.

'No way. Are you kidding? Not mine. You want to go around volunteering pants, volunteer your own.'

He gave me a smirk. 'Run on back to camp, then, and grab a beach towel . . . a blanket . . .'

'Maybe we should cover him with leaves or something.'

'Do what I told you.'

So I did, even though it seemed like a mistake.

When I came out of the jungle, Kimberly saw me. She must've just waded out of the water. She was striding up the beach toward Billie and Thelma, but then she spotted me and broke into a run.

Maybe I should've run off. I thought about it, but just couldn't. She's too nice for me to run away from.

'You found him,' she said. She must've figured it out from the look on my face. 'Oh, God. Where is he?'

'Your dad's with him. He doesn't . . .'

'He's dead, isn't he?'

'Your dad's fine.'

'Keith.'

Before I could think of a good way to answer, she dodged past me and raced for the jungle. She must've seen where I came out, because she was headed straight toward it.

'Wait!' I yelled. 'Kimberly, don't! Just wait!'

She didn't stop. She had too big a headstart on me, so I didn't try to chase her down. Besides, what was I supposed to do, tackle her?

Andrew shouldn't have sent me back to the beach. I'd warned him not to. But he'd insisted.

Anyway, I still had a job to do. I took my time, though. Walked slowly to our camping area, picked up a blanket, answered a few questions from the women, then made my way back to the jungle.

When I got there, Kimberly was sobbing in her father's arms.

He was just in his white briefs.

He must've heard her coming, and had enough time to make Keith less indecent. He'd covered the lower parts with his own khaki shorts, and he'd draped a white handkerchief over the poor guy's face.

While he was busy consoling Kimberly, I went ahead and covered the body with the blanket. Then I reached under and plucked out Andrew's shorts and hanky. I stood off to the side, holding his stuff, and waited for them to get done.

The Funeral

After Kimberly stopped crying in her father's arms, she insisted on giving Keith a close inspection. (All our worries about covering him up seemed a little absurd.) Andrew tried to stop her, but she ignored him and pulled the blanket off and crouched beside the body.

She was awfully grim. She didn't say a thing, but she didn't cry, either. She actually lifted Keith's head, turned it from side to side, and searched through his hair with her fingers. (I think she was trying to figure out what killed him.)

After a while, she unbuttoned the front of his shirt. She asked us for some help, so we lifted him into a sitting position and Kimberly pulled his shirt off. She put it on right away, over her bikini top, but didn't fasten the buttons.

Then the three of us, working together, wrapped Keith in the blanket. Andrew wound the rope around it, so that the blanket would stay put. The result was a tidy, man-shaped bundle. Tidy except for the fact that Keith's feet stuck out the end.

Andrew slung Keith over his shoulder. With him in the lead, we made our way back to the beach.

Billie, Connie and Thelma were waiting for us at the campsite. They were all pretty much in tears. When we showed up, they gathered around Kimberly, shaking their heads and sobbing, hugging her and muttering. Kimberly seemed to be taking things pretty well. She was grim, but didn't fall apart. Something about the way she stood there, being really brave and wearing Keith's festive shirt, got to me so that I choked up, myself.

We had a discussion about what to do with Keith's body. Since we don't expect to be castaways for any great length of time, we didn't want to dispose of it in any sort of permanent way. We wanted it handy and easy to recover.

We let Kimberly make the final decision. She chose to

bury Keith (*store* him, more like it), over where the rocks jutted out to the south side of the beach. The place was close enough so we could keep an eye on it and get to the body easily in case of rescue. It was also far enough away so that the thing wouldn't exactly be living with us. I'm hoping we won't be able to smell it.

Bad enough that we can see it.

Not the body. It's out of sight. But every time I turn my head in that direction, I can't help but look at the pile of rocks covering it. Not to mention the cross. Kimberly made the cross out of driftwood, this afternoon. She stood it up at the head of Keith's 'grave.' It's gnarled and twisted and as white as bleached bones.

That's getting ahead of things, though.

First came the decision about where to put Keith. Then we all trooped over there, Andrew marching inthe lead with the body slung over his shoulder. (Thelma came with us. Her ankle injury had been pretty minor, and she was able to hobble along okay without help by the time we had our funeral procession.)

Kimberly picked exactly the spot where she wanted the grave to be. Then Andrew and Billie and I helped her to clear some rocks out of the way.

Thelma stood by and cried like a maniac.

Connie didn't help, either, but acted strange; she stood rigid and watched, had this far-off look in her eyes, and rubbed her upper arms as if she was cold. Personally, I don't think she was grieving over Keith. I think she was scared witless.

After we'd cleared a depression in the rocks, Andrew and Kimberly loaded Keith inside it.

Then Billie said, 'Someone should say something.'

'Let's bow our heads,' Andrew said. We did. In a low and steady voice, he said The Lord's Prayer. Knew it by heart, which came as a surprise to me. I wouldn't have taken him for the religious sort.

While everybody still had their heads down, I broke into 'Danny Boy.' God only knows what possessed me. I've got a pretty good tenor voice, but I'm not a guy who goes around singing in public. It was a sappy thing to do. The guy's name wasn't even Danny.

But I'd liked him, and I felt so sorry for Kimberly . . .

When I got into 'Danny Boy,' the waterworks were a sight to see. *Every*body cried.

Even Kimberly teared up. After the song was done, she came over to me, wet-eyed and sniffing. She put her arms around me and hugged me.

I'm hoping she'll do that again sometimes, under more favorable conditions.

Fat chance.

She was too overcome with emotion to know what she was doing.

Anyway, I'm glad I went nuts and sang 'Danny Boy'. She wouldn't have hugged me, except for that.

When it was time to finish the burial, she asked everyone to leave. 'I'll take care of it,' she said. So we all left her there.

Away from the rocks where Kimberly was working, Andrew called the rest of us together.

'I don't want anyone to go straying off alone,' he said. 'Keith didn't have an accident. He was murdered.'

Thelma let out a high-pitched, squealy sound. She seemed embarrassed by it, and plastered a hand across her mouth.

Connie started to shake.

Billie, frowning with concern, put an arm across Connie's shoulders. 'It's all right, honey,' she said.

'We think it happened out in the jungle where we found him,' Andrew went on. 'Someone knocked him on the head, and then hung him. That's how we figure it.' He glanced at me.

'It was probably just one person who did it,' I added. 'I mean, the sneaky way it was done.'

'Somebody strong enough to hoist Keith's body fairly high up in a tree,' Andrew said.

'What'll we do? Billie asked.

'I'm not sure yet. Need some time to think things through. Let's figure on a pow-wow later on. For now, we'll probably be all right as long as nobody goes off alone. I don't think the killer'll come after any of us out here on the beach in plain sight.'

'What about . . . when we need to relieve ourselves?' Billie asked. 'Do you want us to do it right here on the beach?'

Connie joined the party. 'Not me. Huh-uh.'

'We'll work something out,' Andrew said. 'For the time being, we can keep on using the same area as before. But not without an escort. Let me know, and I'll go with you.'

'Oh, charming,' Connie said.

'I changed your diapers, babe. But don't worry, I won't peek.'

'This really sucks,' Connie said.

Andrew suddenly looked steamed. 'You've got two sisters whose lives have been blown all to hell in a matter of less than twenty-four hours. There's an asshole out there who'll probably try and kill more of us the first time he gets a chance. What we do not need at this particular juncture is any kind of adolescent shit from you. We *know* you're deeply inconvenienced by all this, but . . .'

'Go to hell!' she blurted. Bursting into tears, she whirled around and ran toward the water.

Thelma, by the way, was already on her knees, sobbing into her hands. This had happened at about the time Andrew made the remark about the two sisters whose lives had been 'blown all to hell.'

Billie scowled at Andrew and shook her head. 'That was really uncalled for, do you know that?' She didn't wait for an answer, but went hustling after Connie.

I was the only member of the group still standing in Andrew's presence. He seemed to be glaring at me from behind his sunglasses.

'*I* didn't say anything,' I told him.

'Don't be a smartass,' Andrew said. And stalked off himself.

I was left on my own, so I got my bag and came up to my tower. (Violating the new rules about straying off, I suppose, but nobody called me on it.) There was a lot of journal to catch up with. Instead of going to the place I'd found yesterday, I picked a spot in the rocks where I had a view of our beach.

When I arrived, Kimberly was still busy on the other side of the inlet, picking up rocks and gently arranging them on top of her husband. After she finished with that, she took care of making the cross. (I've been keeping an eye on her while I write. The others are down there, too, but they haven't been doing anything worth mentioning.)

For a while now, Kimberly has been sitting on the beach. She is still wearing Keith's bright, Hawaiian shirt. Her legs are out in front of her, her knees drawn up, her arms around her shins. She seems to be gazing out at the water. A breeze is stirring her hair, and fluttering the shirt a little behind her back.

She looks so beautiful and alone.

I wish there was some way to make things better for her.

The important thing, now, is to make sure that the killer doesn't get any more of us.

Pow-Wow

We ate supper early. Billie did the cooking again. It was a mixture of noodles and beef from some foil packets that Andrew and Keith had gathered out on the inlet, yesterday. We also had some canned peaches, and bread from a loaf that had gotten through the explosion with its cellophane bag intact. We drank stream water, pouring it into our plastic cups from a pot that we passed around.

None of us had eaten anything all day, as far as I knew.

I, for one, was pretty hungry.

We sat in the sand around the fire, eating, passing the water pot around, and not saying much. Everyone seemed pretty upset.

Afterwards, Billie asked me to help her with the dishes, and I agreed. Glad to get away from the group, for one thing.

The 'dishes' were a mix of things: a couple of metal pots rescued from the bottom of the inlet by Keith, plus plastic plates, cups, knives, forks and spoons that we'd brought ashore for our picnic.

We didn't want to mess up our beach with food scraps, so we carried everything out to the north point – leaving the beach behind and stepping carefully from rock to rock until we reached the very end (forty or fifty feet below the place where I like to work on my journal). We went around the tip, just a bit.

There was nothing to see on the other side. Just more water, beach and jungle.

Billie sat on a rock and dangled her legs in the water. She washed her dishes by bending forward and dipping them into the water between her knees. When I knelt near her and tried to scoop up some water in a pot, she shook her head. 'Just put it down. I'll take care of washing these things. I just wanted you along for the company.'

'I'll help.'

'Don't be ridiculous. There isn't enough here to worry about.' She had brought a rag with her. Also, back on the beach, she'd scooped up some sand in one of the pots. While I watched, she rubbed the dishes with sand, wiped them with the rag, and leaned forward to rinse them with a dip in the water.

She didn't seem to be in any hurry.

I sure wasn't.

I liked being out there with her. For starters, Billie is great to look at. She had some major cleavage showing, and her breasts wobbled and shook because of the vigorous way she was washing the dishes. And then there was the way she kept bending forward to rinse things . . .

It wasn't just her looks, though. Also, she's a cool lady. She has always been very nice to me (too nice, if you ask Connie), she treats everyone decently, she has a sense of humor, she isn't prudish (she's almost immodest), she doesn't fly off the handle every two seconds, and she seems to have loads of common sense.

Unfortunately, she didn't pass on many of these traits to her daughter. Connie has some of Billie's looks, but apparently didn't inherit much of her temperament.

Anyway, it was very nice to be out there on the point with her. I tried not to stare at her *all* the time.

Each time she finished cleaning an item, she twisted sideways and reached up and handed it to me. I made a neat pile on a slightly higher rock.

We were almost done when she gave me a plastic fork, looked me in the eyes and said, 'I have a feeling it might be Wesley.'

Her words took me completely by surprise, but I knew right away what she meant.

'It's occurred to me, too,' I said. 'He blew the boat on purpose?'

'Some kind of timing device, so he'd have a few minutes to swim clear before she went up.'

'I've seen that sort of thing done in some movies,' I said.

'And so, I'm sure, has Wesley.'

'Do you think he'd have the guts?'

'Never underestimate the guts of a weasel,' she told me. She patted the rock beside her, so I sat down. 'I haven't mentioned this to Andrew, yet. Not to anyone else, either. Wanted to see what you thought of the idea. You're not an actual member of the family, for one thing. And you're a good, sensible guy.'

'Well, thanks.'

'Look at the whole deal as an elaborate set-up,' she said. 'Whose idea was it to give Andrew and I this boat trip for our anniversary? Wesley's. Who made all the arrangements? Wesley. Who came down in advance to look things over? Wesley. Who picked this island for our little picnic yesterday? Who stayed on board while the rest of us came ashore? Who got blown up – supposedly?'

'He might've actually *chosen* this island as the place to stage the accident,' I suggested. 'Maybe he toured around last week till he found a nice, uninhabited one.'

'Exactly,' she said. 'He would've needed not only a deserted island, but one that's out of the way – where we're not likely to get found immediately.'

'Or at all.'

'And while we're on *that* subject,' Billie said, 'he could've left a trail of false information to make sure nobody misses us – or knows where to come looking.'

I nodded. I'd been nodding fairly regularly since the start of our talk.

'I bet he even came ashore,' I said.

'Here?'

'Yeah. He must've brought in a bunch of supplies and hidden them somewhere. For his own use, you know? Whatever he's got in mind for us, I'll bet his plan doesn't include screwing himself out of stuff to eat and drink.'

'And what,' Billie asked, 'do you suppose his plan might be?'

'What do *you* think?' I asked her.

'I asked you first.'

'Okay.' I took a deep breath. 'For starters, Wesley wouldn't do any of this if he really loved Thelma.'

'I agree. And he didn't. I think he could barely tolerate her.'

'So why did he marry her?'

'She's very rich. As are we all, thanks to Andrew.'

'Yeah. Okay. Is there a way that this business of marooning us might make Wesley rich?'

'Sure. If he's the only survivor.'

We looked at each other, and we both grimaced.

'What would he inherit?' I asked.

'What wouldn't he?'

'Jeez.'

'So that's his plan. Kill us all.'

'Maybe,' I said. 'He's gotten off to a great start – killed the toughest male in the group.'

'I don't know about that.' She smiled. 'Andrew's a pretty tough *hombre*.'

'He's probably next on the list.'

41

She shook her head. 'Won't let that happen.'

'We'll have to talk to the others about this.'

'That'll certainly endear us to Thelma. We'd better leave her out of it.'

'Talk to them one at a time,' I suggested.

'Yeah.'

'We might be completely wrong, you know. I mean, this is all guesswork – sort of farfetched, too.'

'But it all fits,' Billie said.

'Yeah. The only thing is, sometimes things *are* the way they seem. Maybe Wesley *did* get blown up with the boat.'

'And Keith was killed by . . .?'

'A restless native?'

A corner of Billie's mouth turned up. 'Maybe Gilligan did it.'

'Or the Howells.'

Billie smiled and shook her head.

I suddenly felt a little guilty for kidding around about Keith's death. Getting serious, I said, 'In a way, it doesn't matter *who* did it. What matters is that it happened and the killer's probably still out there. Whether he's Wesley or someone else, it's pretty much the same deal.'

'Except I'd sure like to know who we're dealing with.'

'Yeah,' I said. 'Me, too.'

'It isn't quite as scary when I think of Wesley out there trying to knock us off. At least he's not a complete stranger. If it's *not* him, it might be someone ten times more dangerous.'

'Better him than some sort of deranged jungle-man.'

'I'll say.'

'So, what are we going to do about our theory?' I asked.

'You don't see any major holes in it?'

'No. I think there's every reason to believe it is Wesley – except that maybe he was blown to bits yesterday.'

'Or maybe he wasn't.'

'Nobody found any bits,' I admitted. 'Which doesn't mean he *wasn't* blown up . . .'

'I've picked up one lesson from many long years of watching crappy TV mysteries,' Billie said. 'Here it is: if the body isn't found and identified beyond a shadow of a doubt – then the person ain't dead. It's almost always a ruse, and the "dead" guy is up to no good.'

'I've noticed that, too,' I said. 'But that's TV. TV ripping off Agatha Christie. Or maybe . . . is there a Holmes story where a "dead" guy is a perpetrator?'

Billie frowned at me. 'I wouldn't know, Rupert. Do you think it *is* or *isn't* Wesley?'

'Might be.'

She slapped the side of my arm, but in a sort of playful way. 'Don't be difficult.'

'Sorry.'

'What I'm getting at . . . should we tell the others about our suspicions?'

'We'd better.'

'Good. That's what I think, too.'

'But maybe we'd better bring it up in front of everyone,' I said. 'Including Thelma. Otherwise, what'll happen if he *is* the killer, and she runs into him?'

'You're right,' Billie said. 'We'd better let everyone in on it.'

With that settled, we gathered the dishes and returned to the beach. I was all set to work on my journal. Before I could get started, though, Andrew called everyone together for a group discussion.

We all sat around the fire.

Everyone seemed solemn except for Connie, who gave me dirty looks from the other side of the fire. Odds are, she's put out with me for disappearing around the point with her mother. She probably thinks we were making out.

'There are things that need to be said about our situation here,' Andrew began. 'And we need to make some decisions about how to proceed. This time yesterday, our only real concern was how long we might have to wait before being picked up by a rescue party. Now, Keith has been murdered. That changes . . .'

Thelma raised her hand like a schoolgirl.

Andrew gave her a nod.

'I've been thinking,' she said. 'About Keith's murder and . . . about Wesley.' Her chin trembled. She pressed her lips together. After a couple of seconds, she went on. 'Doesn't anybody find it funny that Keith got killed so soon . . . It was just yesterday the boat exploded and . . . you know. Wesley. What I'm trying to say . . . you all think the boat was an accident. But maybe it *wasn't*, though. I've been thinking about all this, you know? Maybe somebody blew up the boat on purpose. What I mean is, maybe *Wesley* was murdered, too. Not just Keith. Maybe they blew up the boat to kill Wesley and strand us here. Maybe the idea is, they want to pick us off one by one. Or maybe they only just want to kill off all the men.'

'If that's the plan,' Kimberly said, 'they're halfway home.'

I didn't much like the sound of that, me being part of the remaining half.

'What "they" are we discussing here?' Andrew asked. He seemed a little annoyed. 'I'm not aware of any "they." '

'Whoever's behind all this,' Thelma told him.

'You think we're the victims of a conspiracy?'

She stuck out her lip. 'You're just *so* sure Wesley got careless . . .'

'If he didn't blow up the boat by accident,' Andrew said, 'then why *did* it explode?'

'I don't know,' Thelma said. 'Anything's possible. Maybe it got hit by one of those rocket things. Or somebody might've swum up to it underwater and attached a bomb to it. You know?'

'Who would do such things?' Andrew asked.

'Drug dealers? Maybe we've stumbled onto a nest of drug dealers, and they need to eliminate us. Or maybe there's a secret military base on the island.'

'Maybe it's Dr No,' I suggested.

Nobody seemed amused. Not even Billie, who sort of cringed when I said it.

'We'll have no more of that,' Andrew told me.

'Yes, sir.'

'All I'm trying to get at,' Thelma went on, 'is that in my

opinion I think Wesley didn't get killed because he did something stupid on the boat and blew everything up. I think he got murdered, the same as Keith.'

Staring toward the fire, her voice very calm, Kimberly said, 'Has it occurred to anyone that maybe Wesley isn't dead, at all?'

Billie's eyes latched on mine.

'Suppose he arranged for the boat to explode – after he got off it?'

'What do you mean?' Thelma asked.

Kimberly grimaced at her. 'I'm sorry. It has to be said, though. I think there's a chance that Wesley's alive, and that he might be the one who murdered Keith.'

Then she spelled it out. The whole scenario, just as if she'd been listening to Billie and I out on the point. She used nearly all the same reasoning, but presented her argument in a more logical, concise way than we'd done. About the only thing she left out was my theory that Wesley visited the island in advance and hid a cache of supplies for his own use.

Through the whole thing, Thelma sat there looking stunned, betrayed, aghast.

When Kimberly finished, Thelma said to her, 'You're out of your fucking mind.'

'If she is,' Billie said, 'so am I.'

'Me, too,' I said.

Thelma turned her gaze to Connie, looking for an ally.

'Don't ask me,' Connie said, then went right on and added, 'All I know is that I've always thought Wesley was a pig . . .'

'Constance!' Andrew snapped.

She flinched, but went right on. 'So it wouldn't exactly come as any big shock if he pulled something like this. I mean, I don't wanta hurt your feelings, but I thought you were nuts to get involved with him in the first place, much less marry him.'

Andrew glared at her.

'Well,' Connie said in a whiny voice, 'she asked.'

Thelma looked as if she'd been slapped silly. She turned to Andrew. In a sad, pathetic voice, she said, 'Dad?'

'You know good and well how I felt about Wesley. But I'm on your side in this.'

'There aren't sides,' Billie put in.

'Whatever. Thing is, it makes a cute theory – Wesley set us all up and faked his own death. But I'd say it's too cute. He didn't have the smarts or ambition or guts to pull off a stunt like that.' Andrew stuffed some tobacco into the bowl of his pipe.

'Maybe we never knew him,' Kimberly said.

'You didn't,' Thelma blurred. 'None of you knew him. He wouldn't . . . *do* something like this. You don't know how sensitive he could be.'

Andrew took a burning stick from the fire. As he sucked the flame down into his pipe, Billie said, 'I think most of what we saw from Wesley – including you, honey – was false. I don't know that we ever saw an honest emotion from the guy.'

'Slick Wesley,' I said.

'*You* shut up,' Thelma snapped at me.

After a few puffs on his pipe, Andrew said, 'There's the matter of the rope. It didn't come from our boat; I would've seen it. Which leads me to the conclusion that the rope was on this island before we got here. More than likely in the possession of the fellow who used it on Keith.'

'And that lets Wesley off the hook?' Kimberly asked.

'In my opinion.'

'Suppose he had the rope in his luggage?'

'He didn't.'

'How do you know?'

Andrew blew out a pale plume of smoke, then said, 'I inspected his luggage.'

Thelma's eyes bulged. 'You *what?*'

'Settle down, honey. It was as much for your protection as ours. Just wanted to see that he hadn't packed anything worrisome. Drugs, a firearm . . .'

'Dad!'

'Who else's stuff did you search?' Connie asked. She looked ready to blow her lid.

'Nobody's. Just Wesley's.'

'Yeah, I'm sure.'

'It isn't any wonder that he felt like everybody was always against him,' Thelma said. 'I just thought he was being overly sensitive, but . . .'

'We're not against him,' Andrew said.

'Like fun.'

'*I'm* not, anyway,' he told her. 'I'm saying the rope didn't come from the boat. If it didn't come from the boat, where could Wesley have gotten his hands on it? He's innocent. Keith was murdered by a stranger. A stranger who had access to that rope.'

'Wesley might've brought in a load of supplies last week,' Billie pointed out.

'That's right,' Kimberly said, nodding eagerly. 'If he set things up to maroon us, he almost *had* to lay in supplies for himself.'

That was my idea, of course. But I was happy to let them take credit for it. Seemed as if I'd already opened my mouth once too often.

I had to open it again, though. With a look at Thelma, I said, 'Whether it's Wesley or some stranger, there probably is a bunch of supplies hidden somewhere on the island. I mean, the rope came from *somewhere*, right? Tomorrow, we oughta go and try to find where the stuff is being kept.'

'What we oughta do tomorrow,' Connie said, 'is climb into that dinghy and haul our asses out of here before we *all* get killed. I mean, isn't that the smart thing to do? Just leave? Whoever this guy is, he won't be on the dinghy with us. We just trot ourselves over to a *different* island, where there isn't some lunatic trying to wipe us out. I mean, you look out there and you can *see* those islands.'

'They're farther away than they look,' Andrew pointed out.

'So?'

'We'd run out of gas before we got anywhere close to them. Then we'd be stuck on a dinghy with limited amounts of food and water . . .'

'But nobody trying to kill us,' Connie pointed out.

'We're a lot better off here, believe me. We've got everything we need to sustain life. We could spend our entire lives here in relative comfort, if it came to that.'

'Swiss Family Collins,' I said. Couldn't help it.

'God save us from *that*,' Billie said.

'Wesley'll murder us all first,' Connie said.

'It's not my Wesley!' Thelma cried out.

'Well, whoever!'

'Stop it,' Andrew said.

I'll have to stop pretty soon, myself. Gotta hurry things along; it's almost too dark to see what I'm writing.

The upshot of the pow-wow was that either Wesley or a stranger killed Keith and might be after more of us or all of us. We won't try to get away in the dinghy tomorrow, but we might keep it in mind in case things get worse. We'll probably spend tomorrow exploring the island. We are posting double guards tonight: first Andrew and Thelma; then Kimberly and Billie; and finally me and Connie. Obviously, nobody is supposed to go off alone.

After the pow-wow, we all ran around and gathered a whole bunch of firewood. We also picked up rocks to use as weapons. Then I had a chance to sit by myself and start writing. I've been at it for a long time. Almost done, though. If I don't hurry, I'll have to finish tonight's entry in Braille.

While I've been working on the journal here, Thelma has been pouting. Connie has been sitting by herself, over near the dinghy, gazing off into space. Andrew, Billie and Kimberly have been putting together a nice little arsenal: aside from a pile of throwing rocks, we've now got spears, clubs, and makeshift tomahawks. We'll be in great shape if we end up in a pitched battle with Fred, Wilma and Barney.

I shouldn't joke about it. I like the idea of having weapons. What'd I'd *really* like, though, is maybe an M-16.

Oh, well. Castaways can't be choosers.

Day Three

What Happened
With the Dinghy

Here's what happened.

Some time during the night – we don't know whose watch it was – he got the dinghy.

No big trick. Though we'd kept it beached above the high-tide line, it wasn't close enough to keep an eye on. For one thing, the beach had a slight downward slope from where we camped. For another, the area where we left it was beyond the reach of the firelight.

Nobody was really paying attention to it, anyway. We were worried about each other, not the boat.

What he must've done was sneak in from a side, staying close to the shore, and drag the dinghy into the water. Then he probably swam away, towing it by the bow line.

Connie and I started our watch at four in the morning. We sat so we faced each other across the fire. That way, between the two of us, we had a 360-degree view and nobody could approach without one or the other of us spotting him.

It was Connie who suggested our positions. Not only were we beyond touching distance, but we couldn't carry on a conversation without raising our voices. So we stayed silent, for the most part. Fine with me.

Even though we just sat there, looking around and not talking, neither of us noticed anything wrong. Maybe the dinghy was already gone by then.

An hour or so into our watch, I got up from the fire and went over to the rocks and took a leak. I must've walked within twenty feet of where the dinghy was supposed to be. I don't recall seeing it, but I don't recall *not* seeing it. More than likely, it had already been taken. But I can't swear to that.

A little later, Connie headed toward the same area – for the same reason I'd gone there. I started to get up and go with her, but she said, 'I don't need an audience, thanks all the same. Anyway, I can take care of myself.' She was holding one of the spears, and gave it a shake. 'You just stay here and mind your own business.'

So I stood with my back to the fire and watched her. After she left the firelight behind, she was just a dim shape. All I could see was her T-shirt, because it was white. It seemed to float above the beach as she walked. Then it started to rise, which meant she was climbing the rocks. When she got up into them, the T-shirt sank out of sight.

At the time, I thought how it would've served her right if she'd gotten nailed right then and there.

She didn't, though.

Pretty soon, she came back.

'Real nice,' I congratulated her.

'Sorry. I'm sure you would've loved to watch.'

'Guess who would've gotten the blame if our resident Thuggee had taken the opportunity to kill your ass while you were over there? Me, that's who. Your dad thinks I'm worthless, as it is. There'd be no living with him if I let you get killed.'

'Ha ha ha. I'm sure you wouldn't mind, otherwise.'

'You think I want you to get killed?'

She let out a huff. 'You wouldn't exactly consider it a great loss. All you care about is my mom – and Kimberly. I don't exactly stack up, do I?'

'Well, no.'

'See?'

'That doesn't mean I'd like you to get killed. What I'd really like is if, by some miracle, you stopped being such a bitch all the time.'

She gave me a sneer and said, 'Oh, isn't that cute.' Then she strutted over to her side of the fire. She sat down, crossed her legs, and lay the spear across her thighs. 'Don't even look at me,' she said.

So I didn't look at her.

Not for about half an hour, anyway.

But she drew attention to herself by raising the spear overhead. Just as I turned my eyes to her, she threw it.

At me.

It flew over the top of the fire, its whittled point coming straight for my face. I whipped an arm up just in time, and knocked the spear aside.

'Real nice!' I told her. 'Shit! You could've *hurt* me with that thing!'

'That was the general idea.'

'Try it again some time, and maybe I'll forget to be a gentleman and shove it . . .'

'Fuck you.'

'Just shut up before we wake everybody up,' I said. Then I muttered, mostly to myself, something about her being a 'crazy fucking bitch.'

'What did you say?'

'Nothing. Shut up, okay? We're supposed to be keeping watch.'

Oddly enough, our quarrel didn't wake anybody up. At any rate, nobody yelled at us to knock it off.

Connie and I didn't say anything to each other for the rest of the night. I tried not to look at her again, but couldn't help it. I had to make sure she wasn't about to hurl a weapon at me. Whenever our eyes met, she never failed to give me a dirty look.

Dawn finally came.

Andrew woke up and came over to the fire. He was shirtless, barefoot, and wearing his khaki shorts. He said, 'Lovely morning, eh, kids?' Then he did a couple of quick knee-bends, arms forward for balance. Then he rubbed his hands together. 'How was the watch? No trouble, I take it?'

'What're *you* so peppy for?' Connie said.

'Ah, the child's in a snit, and it's barely sun-up. Lover's quarrel?' he asked.

'Give me a break.'

'Tell you what, a good brisk swim oughta set things right. I'll race the both of you.' Grinning and rubbing his hands together, he looked toward the inlet. 'We'll make it a race to the . . .' His face changed. Something was wrong. As I stood up to see what it was, he said, 'What's *that* doing out there?'

A boat was floating on the water, maybe four hundred yards out. For a second, I thought that rescuers might be on the way. But then I checked the beach and saw that our dinghy wasn't where it ought to be.

Connie stood up, too. She studied the situation, then made a face.

Andrew turned on me. 'What do you know about this?'

'Nothing,' I said.

'Connie?'

'Don't ask me.'

'You two were supposed to be keeping watch.'

'We didn't notice anything unusual,' I said.

'Well something unusual sure as hell *happened*. That dinghy didn't just get up and *walk* off the beach.'

'No, sir.'

As if the three of us all wondered the same thing at once, we turned suddenly toward the sleeping areas. Billie, Kimberly and Thelma were where they ought to be: none of them had snuck past us and taken the boat out for an early-morning excursion.

'And you are sure you two don't know anything about it?' Andrew asked Connie and me.

We both shook our heads.

'We obviously had a visitor last night,' Andrew said. 'He slipped right past you and set our boat adrift. Did you fall asleep?'

'No, sir,' I said.

'You?' he snapped at Connie.

'No.'

'Mess around?'

'With *him*?' She wrinkled her nose. 'Get real.'

'We didn't do anything,' I said.

'Apparently, that includes keeping watch. Good thing our friend didn't decide to slit a few throats while he was in the neighbourhood.'

Connie cringed and looked a little sick.

'A couple of terrific sentries you two are,' he said.

I considered pointing out that the visit might've occurred during someone else's watch – even his – but decided not to bother. After all, we should've at least noticed that the dinghy was missing.

Connie didn't try to give the skipper any excuses, either. The way she looked, I bet she was thinking about how she'd gone over to the rocks, all by herself, to take her leak last night. I bet she was wondering where the killer might've been while she was there.

'What's all the fussing about?' The question came from Billie. We looked over at her. She lay on her side, propped up on one elbow. Her upper breast seemed about ready to fall out of her bikini, but so far it was staying put.

'Our friend,' Andrew explained, 'snuck in here last night right under the noses of our two sharp-eyed sentries and set the dinghy adrift.'

Frowning, Billie thrust herself up to a sitting position. She was wonderful to watch – all that shifting flesh barely contained by her black bikini. Nothing came loose, though. Once she was on her feet, she took a few moments to adjust her top and bottom. While she fiddled with the bikini, she frowned out at the dinghy.

'Maybe a wave just came in and took it off,' she suggested.

'Not a chance,' Andrew said. 'This was done on purpose. By a person. By the man who murdered Keith, more than likely.'

'What'll we do?' Billie asked. 'We aren't going to just let it go, are we? What if we decide we want it? Even if you don't think we should try for another island . . .'

'It isn't going anywhere,' Andrew said.

'It's almost gone *now*.'

'I'm going out to get it.'

She looked at him. She gazed at the boat. 'No, you're not.'

'Yes, I am.'

'You can't swim that far.'

'Of course I can.'

'I don't mean you *can't*. I mean you're not *going* to. You're sixty years old, for Godsake.'

'Don't give me that age crap. I can outswim anyone here.'

I raised my hand a little – like a schoolkid who thinks he might know the answer but isn't quite sure. 'I'll swim out and bring it back,' I offered.

'Don't make me laugh,' Andrew said. 'I've *seen* you swim – if one can call it that.'

'Maybe we should just let it go,' Billie said. 'It's not worth . . .'

'No!' Connie blurted. 'It's our only way out of here! We've got to get it back!'

'She's right,' Andrew said. He unbuckled his belt.

Billie put a hand on his shoulder. 'No. Come on, now. Kimberly's the swimmer of the family. She should be the one to go, if anyone.'

Kimberly appeared to be asleep. She was face down in her nest of rags, sprawled limp, one leg out to the side and bent at the knee. One arm was under her face. The other stretched away from her as if she were reaching for something.

Maybe reaching for Keith.

She still had his Hawaiian shirt on. The gaudy fabric rippled in the breeze. The shirt had gotten mussed in her sleep, so it let some of her back show above her bikini pants.

Man, she looked great.

'I'm not going to wake her up for this,' Andrew said. 'No, sir. Not me.' He took off his khaki shorts, handed them to Billie, and stood in front of us wearing nothing except his white briefs. They were sagging a bit, so he tugged them up. (Like Thelma, Andrew had come to the picnic with no intention of swimming. They both left their suits on the boat.)

Billie was frowning. 'Andrew,' she said. 'Don't . . .'

'For Godsake, woman.'

'Don't make *me* a widow,' she told him.

He narrowed an eye at her. 'The day I can't swim out as far

as that dinghy, I might as *well* be dead.' He winked, then grabbed her upper arms, pulled her against him and planted a big kiss on her mouth. 'That'll have to last you till I get back.'

'I wish you wouldn't go.'

'Christ, now, you're gonna jinx me!' He smacked her on the rump.

Hard enough to make her flinch and wince.

'Back in a flash,' he said.

Then he whirled around and marched with a jaunty swagger toward the water.

'The idiot,' Billie muttered. Even though she was annoyed, she seemed proud of him.

'He'll be all right,' Connie said. 'He can swim that far without even getting winded.'

'He *is* in great shape,' Billie admitted.

The way he was wading through the knee-deep water, I thought he looked rather like an old, bow-legged monkey. But I kept the observation to myself.

'Should I go with him?' I asked Billie.

'Get real,' Connie said.

'I wasn't asking you.'

'He wouldn't like it,' Billie told me, not taking her eyes off Andrew. 'He thinks he's perfectly capable of doing everything.'

'Made me climb the tree and cut down Keith yesterday,' I said.

Billie shook her head. 'Did he? He isn't fond of heights.'

'Dad'll be fine in the water,' Connie said.

The water of the inlet was very shallow. Andrew waded out nearly as far as the point before he began to swim. Because of the reef, there was no real surf. Just small, calm waves that shouldn't give a swimmer any trouble at all. He moved along smoothly, taking his time. The dinghy kept drifting farther away, but he was slowly gaining on it.

The next thing I knew, Kimberly stood beside me.

'Hi,' I said.

'Hi,' she said. 'What's happening?'

'Your father's swimming out to get the dinghy.'

'That's our dinghy out there?'

'Yeah.'

'How'd it get away?'

'We don't know,' I said.

Billie joined in, saying, 'Andrew thinks the killer snuck in and set it adrift last night.'

'Jesus,' Kimberly muttered. She put a hand against her brow to shade her eyes. 'It sure is far out there.'

'We were going to have you go for it,' Billie said, 'but your father insisted on doing it himself.'

'He didn't want to wake you up,' I added.

'Figures,' Kimberly said. Then, without asking for advice or permission, she flung off Keith's shirt and bolted for the water. She didn't jog, she sprinted. It was great to watch. She dashed over the beach, shiny black hair flowing behind her, arms swinging, long legs striding out, feet kicking up sand, then water. The water flew as she splashed forward. It sparkled in the sunlight. It gleamed on her dark shoulders and back and legs.

'He doesn't *need* her,' Connie whined. 'God! She always has to butt in and take over.'

'It's fine,' Billie said.

'Yeah, sure. What's the point, anyhow? She isn't even gonna catch up to him in time.'

I'd been watching Kimberly splash through the water, but now I looked past her. It took a few seconds to spot the dinghy. And there was Andrew, closing in on it.

I got my eyes back to Kimberly in time to watch her dive. She vanished under the waves for a few moments, then surfaced and began to swim with quick, sharp strokes.

Man, she was fast!

Not fast enough, though.

She was only about halfway there when Andrew arrived at the dinghy.

'He made it,' Billie said.

Way off in the distance, he reached up out of the water with both hands. He grabbed a gunnel near the bow. Then someone stood up in the dinghy.

I thought I'd have a heart attack.

Connie made a gasp.

Billie cried out, 'My God!'

We couldn't see who it was. We couldn't even see whether it was a man or woman. Just that it was a person, and that it came up suddenly out of the bottom of the boat and raised an object overhead with both hands.

The object looked like an ax.

It swung down and appeared to strike Andrew on top of his head. He let go of the gunnel.

He vanished under the water.

I felt like I'd been kicked in the stomach.

Connie went nuts. She started shrieking, 'Dad! Dad!'

But Billie kept her head. Like me, she must've known it was a waste of time to cry out for Andrew. If we'd seen things right, he was past help.

Kimberly was the one in danger, now.

She was still swimming toward the dinghy. Hadn't she seen? Maybe she *had* seen, and planned to do something about it.

Billie shouted, 'Kim! Kim! Watch out! Get back here!'

'What's happening?' Thelma called. I glanced around and saw her staggering toward us.

Billie ignored her and kept yelling at Kimberly.

Connie was on her hands and knees, head up, staring out toward the scene of the murder, shrieking, 'Dad!'

I flung my shoes away and hit the water at a run.

God only knows what I hoped to accomplish.

Save Kimberly, I guess.

As I splashed my way forward, I heard the sound of a motor. So I stopped running. In water up to my thighs, I saw the dinghy start moving away to the right. The killer sat hunched over low at the stern, steering.

Maybe it was Wesley.

Could've been almost anyone.

The boat picked up speed.

Kimberly kept swimming, but the boat was long gone by the time she reached the place where it had been.

Three Down, One to Go

I'm the only guy left. On the surface, that might be an enviable position. Here I am, the lone male marooned on a tropical island with four women.

There's one big drawback, though.

The other three males have been killed in quick succession. (That's if you include Wesley, who is dead unless he's the killer.)

The women are still here, intact.

Makes me think it isn't safe to be a man on this island.

In other words, guess who's next?

I'm not sure what to do about it. I can't exactly *leave* – the killer made off with our dinghy. No telling where it might be, by now. The last I saw, it was heading toward the north end of the island. Kimberly and I had just dragged Andrew's body onto the rocks around the end of the point. (About where Billie and I did the dishes last night.)

Now that I've seen the wound, there's no doubt that the weapon was an ax. It chopped Andrew's head pretty much in half all the way down to his jaw. The back of his head was still intact, sort of. But the front was split open wide – including his face. Bloody yuck was slopping out when we pulled him onto the rocks. I've never seen such an awful mess in my life. You wouldn't even know who he was, if all you had to go by was his face.

It was terrible for Kimberly to see her father that way. Ironic, too. He'd tried like mad, yesterday, to protect her from the shock of seeing Keith's body. Now here *he* was, ruined a lot worse than Keith – and he couldn't do anything about it.

I threw up.

Not Kimberly, though. After we hauled him out of the water, she sat on the rocks with her back to both of us. She was facing out to sea, her legs bent, her arms around her shins. It was the same way she'd sat for a long time yesterday on the beach after she'd finished with Keith's body.

The dinghy, by then, was almost out of sight.

I thought about sitting down with Kimberly and maybe putting an arm around her. I sure *wanted* to do that. Comfort her. But it might look as if I was trying to put moves on her, so I gave up the notion.

After a while, I said, 'What should we do?'

She shook her head.

'We don't want the others to see him like this,' I said, figuring that's what Andrew would've said if he'd been able to talk.

She just sat there, staring out to sea.

'Maybe I should go and get a blanket or something,' I suggested.

'Yeah,' she said.

'Will you be all right out here?'

She nodded.

But when I turned to go, she said, 'No, wait.' Then she got to her feet and turned around. She was crying softly. She wiped her eyes and sniffed. 'Just a second, okay?'

'Sure.'

'I'll be all right . . . just a second.'

I tried not to stare at her. It made me feel guilty, because a guy shouldn't be paying attention to how great someone looks in her bikini – not when her father is sprawled on the rocks three feet away with his head hacked open.

She wiped her eyes again. Then she said, 'Thanks for helping, Rupert.'

I shrugged.

'You're right, what you said. About how he shouldn't be seen this way. God knows, I wish I hadn't . . . He'd want to be remembered the way he was. You know?'

'That's why I thought I'd go back and get something. To cover him with.'

'I'm going to tow him out beyond the reef.'

'What?'

'Bury him at sea. That's what he always wanted.'

'Don't you think we should, maybe, put him over with Keith? So we can take him back with us when we're rescued?'

Kimberly shook her head. 'It's different with Keith. Dad would want it this way.'

'Shouldn't Billie have a say?'

'Bring her out here. Connie and Thelma, too. Have them all come out. I'll wait with Dad in the water.'

'Do you want a hand?'

'No, go on back.'

I had a choice of swimming, or walking along the rocks. Since I was shoeless, I swam. Billie and Connie were still sitting on the beach, Billie with an arm around her daughter. Thelma stood nearby, watching me and shaking her head and sobbing.

Nobody objected to Kimberly's plan. Apparently, Andrew had made it quite clear to Billie and his daughters that he desired to be buried at sea.

I put on my shoes, and the four of us made our way out along the rocks to the point.

Kimberly hadn't gone far. She was treading water, thirty or forty feet away. Andrew's body floated beside her. In spite of the water being crystal-clear, you couldn't see what a mess he was in. There was the distance. Also, Kimberly had him face down. The main thing, though, was probably the way the sunlight glittered on the water's surface – it was almost blinding. All you could see really well was Andrew's gray, furry back. And his right arm.

The arm was stretched across the water because Kimberly had it by the hand.

'I'm going to tow Dad out,' she said. 'Is that all right with everyone?'

Connie and Thelma were both sobbing like crazy.

Billie wiped her eyes, then said, 'I want to come, too.' Then she stepped down off the rocks into the water and swam out to Kimberly and Andrew. She went to the other side of Andrew, and came up with his left arm.

They both started swimming away, towing him between them.

It was a hell of a thing to watch. I ended up crying, myself – and I never even liked the guy very much.

That was a couple of hours ago. We all returned to the beach after the 'burial at sea.'

It's mighty gloomy around here.

Billie, Kimberly and Thelma have all lost their husbands (one way or another) since we came to this island a couple of days ago. If that isn't bad enough, Kimberly, Thelma and Connie lost their father today.

I'm the only one who hasn't lost one or two loved ones, and I'm worried about the killer coming for me next.

I've been writing in the journal, here on the beach. It doesn't exactly take my mind off our plight, but at least it gives me a chance to think about something other than how much danger *I'm* in.

There's no doubt that I'm next on the hit list, is there?

He kills me, then there won't be any more men to stand in the way.

In the way of what?

The women.

He wants the women.

We'd better figure out something before it's too late.

We Hatch a Plan

It was only mid-morning, but I was feeling hungry by the time I finished catching up with my journal. Nobody else had eaten any sort of breakfast. The way things looked, it might be a while before they got around to thoughts of food.

It seemed like bad castaway etiquette to eat by myself – which might be looked upon as trying to sneak more than my share. I didn't want to bother any of the women, though. They were busy mourning.

I felt like more of an outsider than ever, since I was the only person who hadn't lost a husband or father (or both). I hadn't lost anyone I really cared much about. They were going through these huge, awful changes, while I was unscathed.

I actually resented it, to some extent. Maybe because I was keenly aware that I might be the next person to get killed. Also, because I was hungry and they seemed too wrapped up in moping around to care.

As far as they were concerned, I didn't even exist. That's how I saw it, anyway.

I figured nobody would miss me anyway, so why not take a hike? I'd been wanting to see the lagoon – and swim in it – ever since hearing about it from Keith and Kimberly. Now seemed like a good time to visit the place. So I put the book bag on my back, picked up one of the spears, and started striding toward the jungle.

I was fearless.

If any jungle creatures came after me, they'd better watch out.

As for the killer – I counted on him being too far away to nail me. Even though I had no idea how large the island might be, and he'd had about three hours to make his comeback, I was convinced that he must still be miles away.

Anyway, he was bound to kill me sooner or later.

And nobody would likely give a damn, anyhow.

I was still on my way through the sand, striding with bitterness and determination toward the place where the stream entered the jungle, when Kimberly called out from behind me, 'Rupert! What are you doing?'

I glanced back. 'Just thought I'd check out the lagoon.'

'Are you nuts? Get back here.'

'I won't be long.' I started walking backward. All four of the gals were looking at me.

'Rupert!' Billie yelled.

'You can't go off by yourself,' Kimberly called to me. 'If you *have* to go to the lagoon, we'll all go.'

'I don't *have* to.' I suddenly felt a little bit like a jerk. Pleased that somebody cared, after all – but a jerk for being so self-centered and making myself a nuisance.

'I think we all oughta have something to eat,' Thelma said. 'What do the rest of you think? 'Cause, I mean, I'm kind of starving here.'

'Good idea,' I said.

As soon as I started back, all the gals quit paying attention except for Kimberly. She didn't take her eyes off me. I pretty much kept my eyes on her, too.

She stood in the sand with her feet apart, her Hawaiian shirt blowing behind her in the breeze, her hair blowing, too. Her left hand was planted on her hip, which was bare except for the thin band of her bikini pants. Her right hand held a spear. With its end in the sand by her foot, the spear was higher than her head.

I wish I could've taken a picture of her.

Andrew did bring a camera with him. (Which I'd forgotten about until seeing Kimberly in such an awesome pose.) It should be in the picnic basket. As far as I know, nobody has taken it out since the boat exploded. I guess I'll leave it there. For one thing, the camera doesn't belong to me. For another, I'd look pretty creepy trotting around shooting snapshots on a day like this.

We should've taken photos of the bodies.

Nobody thought of it. Everyone else must've forgotten about the camera, the same as me.

Photographs would've been a really good way to show the authorities how Keith and Andrew were killed. (Andrew is out to sea, but we could still unearth Keith and get some shots. I'm not about to suggest it, though.)

Anyway, my mood underwent a major change because of Kimberly calling me back – not to mention the way she looked.

We gathered at the supply pile (preferring to avoid the campfire with its heat), and sat on the sand around it. As usual, Billie took charge of the food. We ate crackers and cheese left over from the picnic. There was sharp, Swiss cheese, and smoked Edam. She sliced the cheeses with Andrew's Swiss Army knife. She also popped open a bottle of wine that Keith had brought up from the bottom of the inlet. It was a Glen Ellen Cabernet Sauvignon. Though warm, it tasted awfully good. We passed it around, and took sips while we ate our cheese and crackers – and talked.

There was 'small talk' at first. About the food and wine and weather. Like everyone wanted to avoid mentioning the nasty stuff. After about ten minutes of that, Kimberly said, 'I saw who did it.'

Wham.

Silence.

Everybody stopped chewing and stared at her.

We knew she meant the killer.

She'd been swimming out toward the dinghy with her head down, most of the time, so I think the rest of us assumed she hadn't gotten a look at him.

We waited for her to say the killer's name.

But her face told us who she'd seen.

Thelma said, 'No.'

'I'm sorry,' Kimberly said. She looked terribly solemn.

'Wesley's dead!'

'He isn't. I saw him plain as day.'

'No, you didn't!'

'I'm sorry, Thelma. It was him. He's the one I saw. He's the one who murdered Dad.'

'You're lying!'

Kimberly shook her head. 'I thought long and hard about whether I should tell. I almost decided to pretend I hadn't seen who did it. Pretending wouldn't do us any good, though. I know it's tough, but you've got to face it. Wesley's alive, and he's killing us.'

'No!' Thelma blurted. 'It's a lie!' She started to blubber. She still held a half-eaten cracker with a slab of half-eaten cheese on top. I expected her to throw it. Instead, she shoved it into her mouth. Then she flopped over and scurried away from us on her hands and knees. When she was clear of the group, she staggered to her feet and trotted away.

Kimberly started to get up.

Billie raised a hand and shook her head slightly. 'We've gotta make some plans. She'll be all right.'

Kimberly stayed.

Thelma stopped just short of the water's edge, then sat down on the sand, her back to us.

With Thelma out of earshot, a change came over Kimberly. She let her anger out. 'The dirty bastard. I *knew* it had to be him. He's gotta be the one who killed Keith, too.'

'He probably plans to kill us all,' Billie said.

'Guys first,' I added.

'What're we gonna do?' Connie asked. She seemed more frightened than her mother or Kimberly.

'We can't just sit around and wait for him to make the next move,' Billie said.

'That'd be me,' I said.

Though Billie nodded in agreement, she said, 'It might just be the next person he happens to catch off guard. I realize he started with Keith, then got Andrew, but . . . he couldn't possibly have known who'd be going after the dinghy this morning.' She hesitated. 'When I think how close we came to letting it go . . .'

'If I'd kept my big mouth shut,' Connie said.

'It wasn't that,' I told her. 'Andrew wasn't about to let it go.'

'I could've stopped him,' Billie said.

'Nobody's to blame,' Kimberly said. 'Nobody but Wesley.'

'He's awfully damn sneaky,' I said. 'We'll really have to watch ourselves.'

'We'll have to do more than that,' Billie said.

Kimberly nodded. 'We need a plan of action.'

'I still think we oughta get off the island.' That was Connie, of course.

'No,' Billie said. 'Your dad was absolutely right about that: we've got food and water here. We can survive indefinitely.'

'Yeah, right. Look what happened to him.'

'Wesley did that,' Kimberly said. 'What we've gotta do is eliminate Wesley.'

'Or eliminate ourselves,' I suggested.

Billie asked, 'What do you mean?'

'He can't kill us if he can't find us.'

'You mean we should try to hide?'

'It's just a thought. The thing is, we'd have to *find* him before we could do anything to put him out of action. That might be a pretty good trick. But he knows exactly where we are. We're almost always in plain sight, here on the beach. All he has to do is hang back in the jungle and spy on us till he spots an opportunity to strike. But what if he comes looking for us and we aren't here?'

'He'd find us,' Connie said. Always the optimist.

'Not necessarily.'

Frowning, Kimberly said, 'I'm not too crazy about playing hide and seek with the bastard. I want to take him out. Hunt him down and kill him.'

'Why not *draw him in* and kill him?' Billie suggested.

'How would we do that?' Kimberly asked.

'Pull a disappearing act,' Billie explained, giving me a nod. 'Lure him in and ambush him.'

I liked the sound of that.

From the look on Kimberly's face, so did she. 'How would we pull it off?' she asked.

Billie shrugged. 'We'll have to figure something out.'

So we sat there talking about it, tossing schemes back and forth as we passed around the bottle of wine. We were in agreement on the general principle of the thing, but kept running into the same snag; we had to figure that Wesley might already be watching us. How could we possibly pull off a vanishing act (especially one that would allow us to hide nearby and attack him), right in front of his eyes?

Even in the middle of the night, with the fire out, the beach wouldn't be dark enough to completely hide our activities. The sand was too pale, and too much light came from the moon and stars.

'We need to keep the fire going,' Billie said. 'It'll screw up his night vision.'

'But if we don't put it out,' Kimberly said, 'he'll be able to see us in the firelight.'

'Maybe we can figure a way to make that work *for* us,' I suggested. 'You know? Make him see what we want him to see. And while he's watching that, the rest of us might be sneaking to our positions.'

Billie nodded. 'Distract him.'

'Right,' I said. 'If, say, one of us creates a diversion he can't take his eyes off of, the rest of us could do just about anything.'

'What sort of diversion do you have in mind?' Connie asked. From the look on her face, she must've already suspected what I had in mind.

I shrugged and said, 'I don't know. We could stage a fight, maybe.'

Not what I really had in mind, but I would not be the one to suggest a striptease.

'A fight would take at least two people,' Billie pointed out. 'That only leaves three to maneuver around and jump him.'

'It's just the first thing that came into my head,' I explained. Right.

'Three could be enough,' Kimberly pointed out. 'I want to be one of them, that's all.'

'Connie and Rupert,' Billie said. She glanced at each of us, then met Kimberly's eyes. 'They can have a quarrel during their watch tonight.'

Typecasting.

Billie didn't stop there. 'A real knock-down drag-out fight.'

'A quiet one,' Kimberly added. 'They don't want to wake us up.'

'Right. And while they're at it, we'll slip out of our beds and hide.'

'Hide where?' Connie asked.

'You'll be out in the open, fighting with Rupert.'

'I don't mean me. Where'll *you* go, where Wesley won't be able to see you? The rocks are too far away.'

'We'll do some digging this afternoon,' Kimberly said. 'Make ourselves a hidey-hole or . . .'

'He'll think we're digging a latrine,' Billie said.

'So,' I said, 'Connie and I get his attention by having a big fight. You guys sneak over to your ambush positions. But how do we get Wesley to come out of the jungle?'

'You and Connie split up,' Billie suggested.

'She runs off,' Kimberly elaborated.

These two women made quite a team.

'She runs to the water to get away from you,' Kimberly continued.

'Leaving you alone and upset by the fire,' Billie added.

'We should have him walk toward the jungle,' Kimberly said to Billie.

'Right. After all, he's the one Wesley probably *really* wants to kill next.'

'Let's not make it too easy for him,' I suggested.

'Don't worry,' Kimberly told me. 'We'll be right there, just out of sight. When he comes for you, we attack.'

'What if he's got that ax?'

'He won't get a chance to use it,' Kimberly said.

'We'll kill him before he gets close enough,' Billie said.

Connie raised her hand. She had a bit of a smirk on her face.

Our plotting sure had pulled these gals out of the doldrums. They were acting as if they'd forgotten all about Keith and Andrew being dead. Apparently, scheming vengeance is a great cure for the blues.

Anyway, Connie had a little problem with our plan. 'What makes you so sure Wesley's gonna be in the jungle while all this is going on? I mean, I'm supposed to go running down to the water, right? Just suppose that's where *he* is? And there I am, all by myself, while you guys are waiting for him all hell and gone over here.'

Billie grimaced. 'You're right.'

'Why does she have to leave the fire?' I asked.

'So you'll be alone,' Kimberly said.

'I'll be alone, anyway, when I walk to the jungle.'

'Connie can't be watching,' Kimberly explained, 'or Wesley won't make a try for you. He'll be afraid she might see what's going on and raise the alarm.'

'He'll be thinking the rest of us are asleep in our usual places,' Billie said. 'If Connie yells and wakes us up, we might come running to help you. He doesn't want that.'

'He *has* to think he's got you alone,' Kimberly added.

Connie started up again. 'If you think I'm gonna go running off by myself . . .'

'Wesley'll probably be in the jungle,' Kimberly said.

'Like last night when he took off with the dinghy?'

'I know how we can do it,' I said, meeting Connie's frown. 'We're having our big fight by the fire, okay? Now, suppose I really land one, and knock you out?'

'Oh, terrific,' she said.

'It's pretend,' I told her. 'I wouldn't actually hit you, but you'd go down and stay down. Like you're unconscious. That way, you'll be safe and sound by the fire, in plenty of light and not very far from help. But you'll be out of the picture, as far as Wesley knows.'

'Sounds good to me,' Billie said.

'Yeah,' said Kimberly. 'I don't see any problem with that.'

Connie wrinkled her nose. 'I don't know,' she muttered.

'What's the matter?' I asked.

'It seems . . . kind of corny.'

'Corny?' I asked. 'This guy killed your father.'

Wrong thing to say.

'You think I don't know that? Fuck you!' She flung a handful of sand at me.

At least it wasn't a spear, this time.

I turned my head away, shutting my eyes and mouth. The grains of sand stung my cheek. They got in my ear, too.

'That's enough, Connie,' Billie told her.

'He's such a creep!'

'Just calm down, honey. The thing is, we've got to do whatever we can – whether it's corny or not. It isn't just that he killed your dad and Keith; he'll kill us all if we don't stop him.'

'Maybe, maybe not.'

I said, 'Maybe everything'll turn out wonderful, and he'll stop after he nails *my* butt.'

Connie glared at me. 'Yeah, maybe so.'

A smile actually lifted the corners of Kimberly's mouth. 'You guys oughta be able to pull off a very convincing fight.'

'Only why don't you save it for tonight?' Billie suggested.

Connie was sort of snarling. 'Yeah, yeah,' she muttered. Then she turned her head and looked over at Thelma. 'What about her?'

We had a brief discussion about that. The upshot was, we decided to keep the plot to ourselves. For one thing, Thelma wasn't in good enough physical shape to be much help in eliminating Wesley. For another, she's his wife. She apparently loves him, even if he did chop her father's head in half.

After deciding to leave her in the dark, we figured out where to construct our ambush site.

The 'latrine' would go about two-thirds of the distance from our campfire to the edge of the jungle, then off quite a way to the south of the stream that cuts down through the middle of the beach. (The route to be taken by Kimberly and Billie shouldn't cross the fire. Diversion or no diversion, we don't want them backlit as they sneak to their position.)

For the next couple of hours, we dug in the sand with our hands, with our spears, and with cups and pots. Thelma wondered what we were doing. We explained that we were making a latrine so that we wouldn't have to risk our lives by going into the jungle. She seemed to think that was a good idea, and she even helped.

While digging, we came up with the idea of adding an enclosure. So we made a couple of frameworks out of branches, then went to the edge of the jungle and gathered foliage. When we were done, we had a double-sided stall with two walls about four feet high. They ran parallel to the edge of the jungle, so Wesley wouldn't be able to see in – not if he was watching from the general area where we expected him to be.

The make-believe latrine should provide a great hiding place for Kimberly and Billie, if they could just get to it without being spotted.

A problem came up, though, a while after we finished. Thelma wanted to use it.

I had already started to write, but I was sitting within earshot. Kimberly intercepted her. 'What are you going to do?' she asked.

'Well, what do you think?' Thelma said.

'That wouldn't be a good idea.'

'What do you mean?'

'You can't use it.'

'I helped build it.' She was indignant. 'What're you talking about?'

'Nobody can use it till tomorrow.'

'Why on earth not?'

'It has to set,' Kimberly explained.

Thelma frowned and looked confused. 'What?'

'The sand needs time to set. Otherwise, it'll all fall in and fill up the hole.'

'Are you crazy?'

'No, it's true.'

She shook her head. 'I've never heard of such a thing.'

'It's true,' I chimed in. 'You never use a sand latrine the first day. I thought everyone knew that.'

Thelma wrinkled her face. She looked quite perplexed, and vaguely suspicious.

'Where am I supposed to go, then?' she asked her sister.

'The same place as always.' She nodded toward the jungle. 'I'll get Billie and Connie. We'll all go together, from now on.'

'What about me?' I asked.

Thelma narrowed her eyes at me. Kimberly, though, is always a sport. She knew I was mostly kidding. 'I think you'll be fine right here. We won't go far.'

'Don't you think you might need a guy along for protection?' I asked.

'We'll be fine, Rupert.'

'Have it your way.'

So all the gals went trooping off into the bush without me. I stayed where I was, but quit working on the journal for a while. I didn't want any distractions, in case Wesley might pop up out of nowhere and make a try for me.

73

Even though I felt vulnerable, I was fairly safe. I was surrounded by stretches of sand, for one thing. For another, I was fairly well armed – a spear, a club and a selection of rocks within easy reach.

Also, the gals never went very far. They only pushed into the jungle far enough so I wouldn't be able to see them. I could hear their voices, though, so I knew they'd be able to hear me if I had to yell for help.

Nothing happened.

It's been pretty uneventful, since then. I've just kept working on the journal here, taking my time, keeping an eye on the gals. Kimberly and Billie went in swimming for a while. Connie went for a climb on the rocks, but never wandered out of sight. Thelma has mostly just sat around and napped.

I'll probably try to take a nap, myself.

It may turn out to be a long night.

Day Four

The Diversion

Thelma turned in, last night, shortly after dark. That seemed to be a good thing, since we needed her out of the picture. She'd worried me, the way she had spent so much of the day sleeping. I was afraid she might be wide awake, ready to stay up all night, and manage to wreck the ambush we had planned.

I said as much to the others, after she'd gone off.

'It's not uncommon at all,' Billie said, 'for people to sleep a lot more than usual when they're going through tough times emotionally. It's a way of escaping from the pain of the situation.'

Billie had been a high-school teacher before marrying Andrew. She'd taught English, but you have to learn a lot of psychology to become a teacher – at least in California. That's probably how she picked up the stuff about escaping with sleep. Or maybe she picked it up watching Oprah.

Kimberly said, 'Sleeping's about the *last* thing I feel like doing.'

'You're a lot stronger than Thelma,' Billie said.

'A lean, mean, killing machine,' said I.

Which earned a friendly smirk from Kimberly, a roll-upward of the eyeballs from Billie, and a snarl from Connie. (You can't please all the people all the time . . .)

Anyway, we kept sitting around the fire and talking about this and that for another hour or so. We mostly avoided the topic of the ambush, but I bet it was the main thing on all our minds. We were talking about trivial stuff to keep ourselves from dwelling on it.

I felt awfully shaky, and even got goosebumps from time to time. Not because there was a chilly breeze, either. There was a breeze, but it was warm and felt good. It felt so good that I'd taken my shirt off, just after sundown.

I'd started wearing a shirt, now and then, especially during the hottest times of the day – to keep from getting a sunburn. It wasn't so much a shirt as a blouse, actually. A bright pink silk blouse that belonged to Billie. It had been retrieved from the inlet, along with so many other things, by Andrew and Keith. The lower back of the blouse had gotten burnt off, but otherwise it was fine.

Billie is the one who picked it out for me to wear. That was way back on the day after the yacht blew up. (Seems like about ten years ago.) It was the best of the lot. I said she might want to keep it for herself. She told me, 'If I need it, I'll know right where to find it.'

So far, she hasn't asked for it. She's been happy just going around all the time in her bikini. (As I might've written way back at the start of all this, she is sort of a borderline exhibitionist. We'd be seeing a lot more of her, I bet, if her daughter wasn't around.)

Billie uses some pretty heavy-duty sunblock. When she runs out of that, maybe she'll start wearing more clothes. I'm not looking forward to it. I like her attire just the way it is.

The way things are going, however, we'll probably all be dead long before we need to worry about running out of sunblock.

Never mind. I don't want to think about what the future might hold for us.

Back to a subject I can write about with a certain amount of pleasure – the wardrobe.

Kimberly has continued to wear Keith's bright and flowery Hawaiian shirt most of the time. She never buttons it. The shirt is always open, often blowing behind her in the breeze, giving me a wonderful view, whenever I look, of her bare brown skin and her skimpy white bikini.

Connie wears her own skimpy bikini. Hers is orange. But she keeps her T-shirt on nearly all the time. The T-shirt is white, large and loose. Sometimes, it hangs off one shoulder or the other. It covers her all the way down to about mid-thigh, like a short dress. The material is so thin that you can see through it.

Thelma has continued to wear the same . . .

Thelma.

I guess I'd better stop wasting time, and get to what went wrong.

I'm not real eager to do that.

Procrastination, thy name is Rupert.

'We'd better get on with it,' as Billie said last night by the fire.

We had been doing some procrastinating, ourselves.

'Is everyone about ready?' she asked.

Kimberly didn't say a thing, just made a single nod with her head.

'Are we really gonna go ahead with this?' Connie asked.

'Unless you have a better idea,' Billie told her.

Connie wrinkled her nose.

'He hasn't left us any choice,' Kimberly said. 'It's him or us.'

'Are you two really gonna kill him?'

'If we can,' Billie said.

'You've got the knife,' Kimberly said to her hip. The

Billie had Andrew's Swiss Army knife on her hip. The thick plastic handle was tucked down the waistband of her bikini pants, all the blades and tools folded in.

'Do you want to be the one to use it?' Kimberly asked.

The two women stared at each other, the firelight flickering in their eyes.

'You want to, don't you?' Billie said.

'Yes.'

They were not exactly beating around the bush.

'Okay,' Billie said. She pulled the knife out, leaned sideways and passed it to Kimberly.

Kimberly shut her hand around it, and pressed her fist against her belly.

Billie glanced from me to Connie. 'Do either of you have any questions?'

'Guess not,' Connie said.

'I'm ready,' I said. 'Just don't let him kill me, okay?'

Kimberly got to her feet.

So did Billie. 'Good luck, you two,' she told us. 'Make it look good.'

'We will,' I promised. 'You be careful out there.'

Side by side, carrying their spears, they walked away from the fire. I was facing the fire (and Connie on its other side) so I had to look over my shoulder to watch them. They went to the stream – the usual routine – drank from it and brushed their teeth (using fingers). Then they wandered over to the rocky area at the north side of our beach. As they started to climb, Connie snapped, 'Quit watching. Jerk.'

'I can't see anything,' I said.

'Not that you aren't trying.'

I faced front – to be on the lookout in case Connie chose to throw her spear at me. 'I'm *not* into watching ladies take a leak,' I explained. 'Maybe *you* are, but . . .'

'Fuck you.'

'Give it a rest, okay? Why don't you just sit quietly and try to work on your vocabulary?'

'What a wit.'

I looked back over my shoulder, but couldn't spot Billie or Kimberly.

'This is such a treat for you,' Connie said.

'Really.'

'A dream come true.'

'Right.'

'Trapped on an island with a band of women.'

'And a maniac who wants to kill me. It's a blast. Why don't we save all this for our big fight scene, okay?'

She didn't come back with a crack, so maybe she liked the idea.

After a while, Billie and Kimberly reappeared. They climbed down from the rocks and came across the beach. After crossing the stream, Billie waved and said to us, 'Night, now.'

'See you in the morning, people,' Kimberly said.

They split up and went to their own sleeping nests – beds, as Billie calls them. Billie lay down alone. Kimberly, a few yards away, eased down into her place beside Thelma.

From where I sat, not much could be seen of them. They weren't completely beyond the glow from the fire, but the light that reached them was pretty dim and murky. Just the way we wanted things.

'Let's wait a little while,' I said to Connie.

'Your wish is my command.'

I sighed.

'What?' she asked.

'Nothing.'

'Yeah, sure.'

'Okay. First off, we're in a real mess. You know? People have died . . .'

'Tell me about it,' she muttered.

'I just think that, under the circumstances, it'd be nice if we didn't have to fight among ourselves. I mean, my God, it's pretty weird to be bickering with each other about a load of insignificant crap when there's a guy out there killing us off. I know you're upset and scared, but that doesn't give you any excuse to go around making everyone miserable.'

She showed me her teeth. 'Do I make you miserable?'

'You make me want to smack you silly.'

'Well, two can play that game.'

'Why the hell did you even ask me to come on this damn trip? All you've done the whole time is dump on me.'

'Maybe I *like* to dump on you,' she said.

'Sure.'

'You're such a fucking loser.'

'Why did you ask me to come? I don't get it. Did you just want to show your family what a loser you've got for a boyfriend? That doesn't exactly make sense. Not that I ever exactly *expect* you to make a whole lot of sense, but . . .'

'Up yours.'

'Why am I here? Why did you invite me? You needed someone your own age to pick on?'

She sneered at me. 'What was I supposed to do, come by myself? I figured, better you than no one.'

'Oh, thanks a heap.'

'Well, you asked. Besides, I used to think I liked you.'

That one actually sort of hurt.

'I thought I *loved* you,' she said.

That one stunned me so much I wondered if it was a lie.

'If you loved me,' I said, 'you had a funny way of showing it.'

'What, because I wouldn't jump into bed with you?'

'No!'

'I happen to be very particular about who I jump into bed with, buddy. It's a very select few, as a matter of fact. I have to be one hundred per cent sure of a guy . . . and I had my doubts about you from the start. Thank God, I didn't give in. But maybe you'll have more luck with my mom . . . or Kimberly. It's so disgustingly obvious that you'd rather fuck one of them . . .'

'Knock it off,' I said. 'Man! Your father got his head chopped in half this morning; how in hell can you be talking like this?'

'Maybe it's time for a little honesty, that's how. Why go around lying and being a phoney about everything if we're all gonna get killed anyway? You know? Screw it. From now on, I say what I think.'

'You mean, you haven't been? Could've fooled me. But you know what? I don't see more honesty here; all I see is that you're getting more energetic in your nastiness.'

'Fuck you.'

'That's original.'

That was apparently the final straw.

Or she just figured it was time to start the show.

She started it by twisting her face so she looked like a maniac. Then she hissed through her teeth and she leaped at me. Didn't bother to go around the fire – sprang over it, instead. I didn't even have time to stand up before she crashed down on top of me and slammed me backward into the sand.

She seemed to be all knees and elbows and fists.

Next thing I knew, she was sitting on my stomach. The knees and elbows no longer jabbed into me, but her fists kept smacking me in the face.

I put up my arms to block them.

And gasped things like, 'Stop it! Shit! That hurts! Hey!'

I knew better than to think she was simply trying to make our fight look good for Wesley; she was trying to inflict damage on me.

And succeeding.

I've got a thing about hitting girls.

The thing is, I don't do it.

If you aren't some kind of a pervert or shit, you've got a deep-down revulsion when it comes to hurting a female.

So even though Connie was pounding me pretty well, I couldn't bring myself to slug her. I tried to defend myself by blocking her blows. Then I managed to catch hold of her arms. She lurched and twisted.

'Stop it!' I gasped.

She kept trying to jerk her arms free, so I bucked and threw her off me. We rolled, and I got on top of her. I sat across her hips and leaned forward and pinned her arms down. She wouldn't stop squirming, though. Afraid she might throw me off, I stretched her arms up past her head and put as much weight on her as I could. We were belly to belly, chest to chest, face to face.

Pretty soon, she quit struggling. She lay under me, gasping for air.

We were so tight together that I could feel the pounding of her heart. I also felt the push of her breasts against my chest. And her breath on my lips.

'Get off,' she said.

I stayed.

She was between my legs, and our groins were pressed together. She had sort of a mound down there that pushed against me.

'Get off, damn it!'

I'd never been this close to her before, never had so much actual contact. It started having an effect on me.

'Oh, terrific,' she muttered.

She'd noticed.

'Get off me, for God's sake. We're supposed to be *fighting*. Leave it to you . . .'

'Sorry.' I let go of her wrists and shoved against the sand and started to push myself up.

'Get it over with,' she said.

'What?'

'What do you mean, what? Slug me, knock me out.'

'Shouldn't we get on our feet first?'

'What, so I get a chance to fall down? I'm already down. Go ahead and do it.'

'This isn't the right way. It won't look right.'

'Okay,' she said. And her right arm shot up. She punched the side of my face so hard that I toppled over sideways. I flopped onto my back. She stood up.

'This how you want it?' she asked.

'Yeah,' I said.

She wasn't playing the game I expected, but at least she was on her feet, up where Wesley could get a good view of her. When I tried to stand, she rushed in and kicked me over. On my second try, I blocked her kick and staggered up.

More like it.

We started circling each other, hunched over, hands out like a couple of disarmed knife-fighters. She made a lunge as if to grab me. I leaped out of reach.

Suddenly, she pulled her T-shirt off. She tossed it to the sand. 'This better?' she asked.

I couldn't believe she'd done it. Miss Prude. Up till then, she hadn't even taken off the shirt to go swimming. She had a tan, though. She must've gone without it sometime, just not in front of me.

She didn't look bad.

'Think I've got his attention now?' she asked.

'Probably.'

'Yeah? Just probably?'

Her right hand darted out.

Slapped my face.

Not a hard slap. It didn't hurt as much as her punches, but it stung my ego. It was a humiliating taunt, just as she'd meant it to be.

I pressed a hand to my face.

She slapped the back of my hand, then pranced backward. 'They're on the move,' she said.

'Huh?'

'Your girlfriends. Remember? The plan?'

I started to turn my head.

Connie stopped me. Stopped me dead by crossing her arms and grabbing the front of her bikini top with both hands and tugging it up. Her breasts seemed to spring out from under it. And there they were, right in front of me. Loose all of a sudden, they jiggled. They lifted and nearly went away, turning into small slopes, as she raised her arms and shucked the bikini top off over her head. When she put her arms down, her breasts came back out.

They looked so *naked*. They weren't tanned at all, but had a pinkish hue from the firelight. The nipples looked big and dark.

'Think he's distracted now?' she asked.

I didn't even try to answer.

Letting out a huff of laughter, she tossed her orange top aside with one hand and slapped my face with the other. Before I could do anything about the slap, she leaped out of range.

We went back to circling each other.

She was wonderful to watch – the way she was bent over with her arms out, naked except for the waistband and meager orange front panel of her bikini pants, her skin ruddy and shimmering in the firelight, her hair golden – and how her prancing, lurching movements made her breasts bounce and bob.

For me, it was like something in a wild dream.

For Wesley, it must've been pretty exciting, too.

The absolute perfect diversion, just so long as the guy you're trying to distract isn't dead, blind or gay.

If our campfire was in view of Wesley's hiding place, his eyes were glued to Connie. Not a shadow of a doubt about that.

Connie darted in and slapped me again.

I didn't mind.

It was a good, sharp smack, but the view was stunning.

'Do it now,' Connie said, circling again.

'What?'

'Knock me out.'

I shook my head. 'Too soon.'

'Isn't. They're there.'

'Are you sure?'

'Damn it, Rupert! Quit stalling.'

'I can't hit you.'

'It's pretend, remember? My Christ, this was *your* plan in the first place. Let's do it! I'll come in at you.'

'I don't . . .'

'Now!'

'Okay, okay.'

She charged straight toward me, arms out as if she wanted to give me a bear hug.

I threw a roundhouse in the general direction of her chin. She ran right into it.

Honest. I never intended my fist to connect with her. It was an accident. Really and truly.

But what a punch! The blow snapped her head sideways. Her cheeks flopped, her lips almost jumped off her face, and a glittering banner of spit flew toward the fire. Her legs kept coming, but the rest of her body stopped fast and started on its way down. Her back struck the sand, *whup!* Her breasts flattened as if mashed against her chest by invisible hands. An instant later, they were springing up. Then her legs landed.

She lay sprawled on the beach, motionless.

Scared, I hurried over to her and dropped to my knees. Her eyes were shut. Her mouth drooped open. My punch had taken her out, no question about that. She was breathing, though. I could see the rise and fall of her chest, so I hadn't killed her.

I looked around.

Thelma appeared to be asleep. Kimberly and Billie were nowhere to be seen, but they might be watching me. Wesley was probably watching, too. So I didn't allow myself to spend much time enjoying the view of Connie. Also, I kept my hands to myself.

On my feet, I went over to my place by the fire and picked up my 'tomahawk.' The weapon, made by Kimberly, consisted of a sturdy, Y-shaped limb with a rock at the forked end. The rock was wedged in and strapped secure with strips of denim cut from some jeans that had been salvaged after the explosion.

I looked back at Connie. She was still sprawled on her back. I grimaced. I'd *really* nailed her. Which made me feel guilty, but secretly pleased. Also, I felt sort of pleased about my self-control; I'd wanted to feel her up so badly it hurt, but hadn't done it. What restraint! I deserved a medal.

Actually, restraint didn't have much to do with it. I was just afraid her mom might see me. I sure wouldn't want Billie to know what a horny degenerate I really am.

Anyway, I gave Connie one last, long look. Then I turned away and headed for the darkness beyond the firelight.

The Ambush

Thelma lay on her bed of rags where she belonged. Curled on her side, she slept with an arm under her head for a pillow.

Kimberly and Billie had left human-shaped mounds of sand covered with scraps of cloth at the places where they usually slept. A pretty lame trick, really. The sort of thing a kid might do before he sneaks out his window at night.

In fact, our entire ambush plan seemed to be made of lame, childish tricks.

Tricks that didn't stand much chance of fooling a reasonably intelligent adult.

(In spite of the opinions of Andrew and some others in our group, Wesley isn't stupid.)

As I walked away from the firelight, I got a terrible feeling that we hadn't even come close to outsmarting him. He hadn't been distracted by Connie. He'd watched Billie and Kimberly sneak to the fake latrine. Maybe he'd already silently killed them both.

About halfway between the fire and the latrine, I stopped walking. The area ahead looked so damn dark. I needed time for my eyes to adjust.

That's what I told myself, anyway.

Actually, I stopped because I was suddenly scared to keep going. I wanted to be back at the fire, safe in its light, with Connie. (Even out cold, she'd be better company than nobody.)

I couldn't turn back, though. I'd look like a chicken.

So I forced myself to start moving again. It seemed to take forever, but finally I reached the latrine.

From the side, I saw the dim shape of someone low down in the darkness between its walls. There seemed to be only one person. I couldn't tell who it was. Or whether it was a woman.

I stood there, staring.

The person hiding in the latrine didn't make a sound.

I told myself: This has to be Billie or Kimberly.

Unless it's Wesley.

The way the body kept so still, I thought it might be one of the gals, but dead.

I started to feel like running away.

Which, of course, would've blown everything.

Finally, I choked out, 'Who is it?'

'Rupert?' A hoarse whisper. But it seemed to be Billie's voice.

'Yeah.'

'Thought it must be, but . . .'

'Where's Kimberly?' I whispered.

'Get in here,' Billie said, rising up slightly higher in the darkness.

We hadn't exactly rehearsed this part. I stepped in between the bushy walls. They were about as high as my waist. Billie seemed to be standing below me in the hole, her face level with my knees.

'What am I supposed to do?' I asked.

'Pretend you're taking a whizz.'

Great, I thought.

But I saw the point. After all, the whole charade was for Wesley's benefit. If I was going to visit the latrine, I should appear to be using it.

So I clamped the tomahawk under my arm, then started going through the motions – as if I'd just stepped up to a urinal.

Of course, I didn't haul anything out.

'What happened to Kimberly?' I whispered.

'She went off. Thought we ought to split up.'

I looked around, but couldn't spot Kimberly. The beach between me and the jungle looked gray and desolate. Beyond the line of trees, the jungle was black. Turning my head the other way, I checked on our campsite. The sleeping area looked like a field of dark lumps. Connie was still sprawled on her back near the fire.

'Do you know where she went?' I asked.

'The jungle.'

'She out of her mind?'

'She wants you to go there. If Wesley doesn't attack you here.'

'Oh.'

'If the attack happens here, she's gonna come in and take him from behind.'

'I don't think it'll happen here,' I said.

'Let's give it some time.'

'It doesn't take all that long to . . . you know, take a leak.'

'Stop looking around.'

'Okay. Sorry.'

'Wesley hasn't got a stopwatch on you. I'm sure he isn't keeping track of the time.'

'I don't know. I'd be done by now.'

Her arms came up, barely visible in the darkness, and I felt her hands curl softly against my calves. 'Just stay for a while,' she whispered. 'Give him a chance.'

'Okay.'

Her hands glided up and down a little, caressing me. 'How are you holding up?'

'So far, so good.'

'I don't know what we'd do without you.'

'Thanks,' I said. 'I hope you don't get a chance to find out.'

She patted one of my legs. 'Wise guy.'

'How are *you* doing?' I asked.

'Getting along. I'll fall apart later. After we've dealt with Wesley.'

'Must be awfully hard on you.'

She was silent, and her hands went motionless on my legs. Then she said, 'I've still got Connie.'

'Yeah.'

'I saw some of what happened with her over there.'

'You did?' Apparently, the low wall of bushes at the front of the latrine wasn't as thick as I'd thought. I felt my face go hot. 'What did you see?' I asked.

'Oh, her little strip show.'

'Ah.'

'She's a beautiful girl, isn't she?'

'Takes after you,' I said, which was more flattering to Connie than to Billie, and untrue.

'Bet she surprised you with that.'

'I'll say.'

'She's got spunk.'

'Yeah.'

'She sure knew how to get Wesley's attention.'

And mine, I thought.

'She shouldn't have slapped you, though.'

Billie had seen that, too. My face flamed up again. 'Like you say, she's got spunk.'

'She can be a real bitch, sometimes. But she's a good kid. Under it all. You probably know that already.'

'Yeah,' I said.

Yeah, my ass.

'You just have to stand up for yourself. Don't take any crap from her, you know?'

'Didn't you see me punch her lights out?' I asked.

'You what?'

'It was an accident.'

'You mean you *hit* her?' Billie sounded concerned, but not angry.

'Weren't you watching?' I asked.

'I must've been looking away when that happened. All of a sudden, I looked back again and Connie was on her back. I thought . . .'

'No, it wasn't any act. I mean, it was supposed to be, but she walked right into my fist. She's okay, though.' I looked. Connie was still spread out on the sand. 'I bet she's conscious by now. She knows better than to get up.'

'Well . . .'

'I'm sorry. It really *was* an accident. I would never hit her on purpose.'

'I hope not.'

'Honestly.'

'Okay.'

'I'd better get going,' I said. 'I've been here way too long. Wesley'll know something's up.'

'Yeah.' She squeezed the backs of my legs, then took her hands away. 'Kimberly'll be at the regular place. Go slowly and keep your eyes open.'

'Okay. See you later.'

I stepped backward away from the latrine, hitched up my trunks a bit, then took the tomahawk out from under my arm and started walking toward the jungle.

I got more and more scared. It helped, though, to tell myself that Wesley might not even be there. For all we really knew, he could be miles away. Or maybe the dinghy had gone down with all hands aboard. Maybe he'd fallen off a cliff. Maybe he'd been dropped by an aneurism or a coronary. Maybe he'd run afoul of a man-eating critter, a poisonous snake, a headhunter, or Dr Moreau.

Endless ways he could've met a demise.

But I figured that he was probably lurking among the trees, watching my approach and fully intending to lay me to waste.

The only thing that kept me going was Kimberly.

Wishful thinking aside, *she* was probably in there lurking among the trees, watching my approach and fully intending to jump the bastard when he made the try for me.

Unless she'd already been jumped by him.

My legs were shaking pretty good, but I kept going.

I was half a dozen strides from the edge of the jungle when the whole deal went to hell.

A shout came from Thelma. 'HELP!' she yelled. Then, 'WHAT'S GOING ON?'

I turned around fast.

She was on her knees beside Connie's sprawled body, her arms raised and spread out wide as if to show us all the size of her confusion and fear.

'RUPERT!'

She'd spotted me.

I flapped an arm, signaling her to stay put.

But she scurried to her feet and started running straight toward me.

I muttered a curse.

She was ruining everything.

I kept waving her back, but she kept coming, chugging closer, her bosom leading the way, her head thrown back. If her bra had broken during the charge, her leaping breasts would've torn open her blouse, whammed her in the face and probably knocked her over backward.

When she came to a halt in front of me, I considered whamming her in the face.

I'd like to have done it with my tomahawk.

But I don't hit women.

Anyway, she didn't *know* she was ruining everything. All she knew was that she'd woken up to find herself alone – and to find Connie unconscious and topless.

Wasn't Thelma's fault she went nuts.

Wasn't her fault she'd wrecked our whole scheme.

Wasn't her fault I suddenly hated her guts.

She staggered to a halt in front of me and stood there, huffing for breath, her mouth hanging open.

'What's . . . going on?' she gasped out.

'I've gotta take a dump,' I said.

'*What?*'

'You know.'

'I don't know. You're . . . way over here. Connie's *out cold*. What's the matter with her?'

'I slugged her.'

'You what?'

'We had a fight.'

'A fight? What kind of a fight? How come she's half naked? Did you do that to her?'

'No!'

'Where's Kimberly? Where's Billie?'

'I don't know.' Not exactly a lie. I wasn't entirely sure where they were – mainly, I wondered why Billie hadn't hopped out of the latrine to intercept Thelma.

Suddenly, I was worried about her.

'Billie!' I called. 'Are you okay?'

'Yes.' Her voice came from the direction of the latrine. It didn't sound joyful.

'You might as well come on out.'

A few moments later, Billie crawled out from between the dark, leafy walls. She stood up and walked slowly toward us, shaking her head.

Thelma said to her, 'What *is* all this? What were you doing in there?'

'I was using the facility,' Billie explained. 'Is that all right with you?'

Thelma's mouth fell open. 'It isn't supposed to be used till tomorrow!'

'What?'

'It has to set. The *sand* needs time to set.' She turned to me for support.

'That's right,' I told Billie.

'None of us were supposed to use it till tomorrow,' Thelma protested.

'Oh.'

'Now you've probably ruined it.'

'We forgot to tell you,' I said to Billie. Then I faced Thelma and said, 'See? *I* knew better than to use it. That's why I was heading for the jungle.'

'By yourself?' Thelma asked.

'Who am I supposed to take with me?'

She opened her mouth as if to give me a suggestion, but then she grabbed Billie's shoulder and shook it. 'Did you see what he did to your daughter?'

Billie nodded.

We all looked toward Connie. She was still stretched out in the sand near the fire, but not on her back. While nobody was watching, she must've rolled over.

'Guess she's okay,' I said.

'Rupert attacked her,' Thelma explained.

'I did not.'

'Bull!' she snapped at me. 'You tried to tear off her clothes.'

'Settle down,' Billie told her. 'Connie took off her own top.'

'No, she didn't. Why would she do that?' Thelma glared at me. 'And what did you do with Kimberly?'

'Nothing.'

'Then where is she?'

Billie and I shared a glance. She shook her head; I shrugged.

'If we don't tell her the truth,' Billie said, 'we'll be making up stories till Hell freezes over.'

'Yeah. I know. But look, the thing is, I've got a little, uh, chore to take care of. Why don't you two go on back to the fire. See how Connie's doing, and you can tell Thelma all about our plan. I'll be back in a few minutes.'

'Where's my sister?' Thelma demanded.

'I'll see if I can find her,' I said. Without waiting for any more trouble, I turned around and headed for the jungle. When I was just about there, I looked back. Billie and Thelma were walking slowly away, side by side. They seemed to be talking, but I couldn't make out the words.

I was so annoyed and frustrated, thanks to Thelma, that I forgot to be afraid.

A short distance into the trees, I looked back and couldn't

see much of the beach anymore – just a little flicker from our fire.

The bit I'd told Thelma about 'taking a dump' had been a fib. I truly did need to pee, though. Right where I stood seemed like as good a place as any.

Nobody seemed to be nearby.

Of course, Wesley or Kimberly might've been standing three feet away without being seen. Awfully dark in there.

I told myself, *If I can't see them, they can't see me.*

I half believed it, too.

My trunks don't have a fly. I got clear of them by tugging the crotch up and sideways, which gave me a window of opportunity through the left leg hole. I kept the trunks out of the way with my right hand, and kept the tomahawk in my left.

One more glance around, then I started to go.

It promised to be a long one.

Which didn't thrill me. I wanted to get it done with and *amscray* back to the beach.

Also, I wasn't thrilled by the noise I was making. A loud, papery, splattery sound. Obviously, I was hitting leaves or some other variety of foliage. It's damn near impossible to take a silent leak in a jungle. I tried swiveling from side to side. The noise changed directions, but not volume.

It was just starting to taper off when I heard someone take a step. At first, I didn't *know* it was a footstep. I didn't know for sure until I heard the second one.

Then came the third, closer to me than the others.

By that time, I had shut down my irrigation project and stowed the equipment.

I switched the tomahawk to my right hand.

Then I stood still and held my breath.

And wished to God I had stayed on the beach where I belonged.

The footsteps stopped.

Maybe two yards away?

I strained my eyes to see who was there, but all I could make out were different shades of dark gray – and a lot of black.

It's probably Kimberly, I told myself.

But what if it isn't?

I knew, really, that it had to be her. She'd heard me and started to come toward me, then stopped, afraid I might be Wesley.

We were both standing there, trying to convince ourselves that the other person *wasn't* Wesley.

Suddenly, I had a bad thought.

What if she decides I'm Wesley, and attacks me?

She wouldn't do that. After all, I was supposed to come out here and act as bait. She was *expecting* me.

But she also expected Wesley to show up.

It was actually possible that she might goof and kill me by mistake.

Anyway, we couldn't just stand here all night.

In a quiet voice, I said, 'Kimberly? It's me. Rupert.'

The voice came back, 'Rupert? It's me. Wesley.'

Close Shaves and Rescues

Wesley, being the asshole that he is, apparently couldn't resist the chance to scare the hell out of me. If he'd just kept his mouth shut and snuck in closer and used his ax, I'd be a dead boy right now.

But he had to answer me back.

My reactions surprised me.

I didn't scream and whirl around and make a mad dash for the beach. Which is what I would've *guessed* I'd do, if anyone had asked.

Maybe everyone isn't like this, but I seem to have at least two different people inside of me: one is timid and plays by the rules; the other is a little nuts – and the nut pops up at odd, unexpected times.

I was standing there, scared half to death even before Wesley answered – my knees shaking, my heart slugging. Then he said, 'Rupert? It's me. Wesley.'

Instead of having a panic attack, I heard myself greet the guy. 'Hey, Wesley, how's it going?'

'Having a ball.'

'Glad to hear it.'

'What was this supposed to be, tonight? Some sort of trap?'

'Yep.'

'Guess who got caught in it?'

'You tell me.'

I hoped to God he wasn't about to say, 'Kimberly.'

Wesley said, 'You.'

'Sure thing,' I said.

He laughed.

I threw my tomahawk at the sound. Threw it hard. It went smashing through bushes. I didn't wait for the outcome, but made a one-eighty and ran.

Behind me, Wesley let out a yell. He sounded more angry than hurt.

Then I heard him come charging after me.

I dodged between a couple of tree trunks, rammed my way through a bush, and raced onto the beach.

I almost collided with Kimberly.

What a sight! I'll never forget it as long as I live. She stood only a few strides in front of me, bare and dark except for the white of her bikini. (Not wearing Keith's Hawaiian shirt, for a change.) Her feet were planted in the sand, legs apart and slightly bent, one foot forward. Her left arm was stretched out toward me, her right arm cocked back near her ear – the spear all set to throw.

'Hit the deck!' she commanded me in a quick, loud whisper.

I dived for the sand, pounded against it chest first and slid toward Kimberly's bare legs. About to plow into them, I threw myself sideways. Did a half-roll and looked up just as she hurled her spear.

It shot straight forward.

Snapping my head around, I kept track of it.

The spear raced toward Wesley as he came charging out of the jungle.

This was the first I'd seen of him since the explosion.

He appeared to be stark naked. His skin gleamed black in the moonlight – some sort of camouflage, I guess, for sneaking around at night. (He hadn't put the stuff on his backside, I discovered pretty soon.) He held his ax in both hands, raised high over his left shoulder, ready to split me like a log.

His grin was big and white.

The grin went away when he saw Kimberly – and the spear speeding at him.

His mouth opened wide.

He yelled, 'YAAAH!' and tried to dodge the spear, giving himself an awkward half-twist to the left in the moments before it struck.

The whittled point of Kimberly's spear caught him in the chest area. He was a husky guy, and he had pretty good boobs on him. The spear hit him in the left one. He was partly turned away, though, so all it did was poke through one side of his tit and come out the other side, just behind his nipple and maybe half an inch under his skin.

He squealed. Dropping the ax behind him, he grabbed the shaft of the spear with both hands and stumbled and fell to his knees. Though he clutched the spear, he didn't try to pull it out.

I think he was afraid to pull it out.

Afraid of the pain.

He held on to it the way he did, I think, to keep the weight of the spear from dragging open his wound. If he'd just let go, it probably would have split the front of his boob wide open from one side to the other.

Anyway, I scurried over to where the ax had fallen.

While I did that, Kimberly rushed Wesley and reached for her spear.

'No!' he cried out. 'Don't touch it!'

Kimberly touched it, all right.

She grabbed its end and tugged. On its way out, it must've hurt him pretty good. He screamed so hard I thought my ears might bleed.

He fell onto his side and curled up and squirmed and whimpered.

I picked up the ax.

When I looked at Wesley again, he was on his hands and knees. Trying to crawl away.

Kimberly rammed the spear into his bare ass.

It missed his anus (the likely target), but jabbed into his right buttock. He squealed again, and flopped down flat.

Kimberly pulled out her spear and planted it in the sand by her feet. Then she pulled her father's Swiss Army knife out of her bikini pants. She flung a leg over Wesley and sat down in the middle of his back. With both hands, she worked on prying open one of the knife blades.

'Look out!' Billie yelled from a distance. 'Watch it! Thelma!'

We both turned our heads and saw Thelma coming at us. Billie was chasing her. (Connie stood by the fire, watching. She'd put her T-shirt back on. She hugged her chest and rubbed her upper arms as if she had a chill.)

Billie was faster than Thelma, but Thelma must've had a good headstart. Too good a headstart. Billie wasn't likely to catch her in time.

'Don't let her interfere,' Kimberly told me. 'I've gotta finish him off.'

Thelma must've heard that. She cried out, 'No! Don't you dare! Leave him be! Kimberly, leave him be, damn it!'

Kimberly muttered, 'Yeah, right.'

I put myself in Thelma's way, the ax at port-arms. I had no intention of hurting her, of course. I planned to block her, that's all, and give Kimberly the time she needed.

Coming at me, growling, stocky as a bulldog, she gave me a bad case of the creeps. This woman, normally so plain and innocuous and rather dumpy, had somehow changed into a raving lunatic.

At the last second, she veered to avoid me.

A quick sidestep put me into her path again.

'Stop!' I yelled.

The rock in her hand came as a surprise. She hurled it, point blank, at my face.

It almost missed.

Nicked my cheekbone and cut a hot path all the way back to my ear. I stayed on my feet, but staggered a little – enough to let her slip by.

Billie made a flying leap for Thelma's feet.

She came up short and plowed a furrow through the sand.

'Shit!' Kimberly shouted.

Stumbling, I saw her still sitting on Wesley's back. She had the knife open in her right hand. Her left hand clutched Wesley by the hair. The way he was thrashing and whimpering, though, I knew she hadn't gotten a chance to use the knife. Her torso was twisted sideways as she watched her sister.

'Stay back!' she shouted.

Thelma snatched the spear out of the sand. With a bellow that gave me goosebumps, she swung the spear at Kimberly. It whistled as it cut the air. Kimberly flung up her right arm to block it. The spear lashed in underneath her arm and whacked against her side.

'Leave him be!' Thelma shrieked, and raised the spear overhead to strike again.

Kimberly was already tumbling off Wesley's back.

With a leap, I put myself in front of Thelma. I blocked her spear's downward stroke with my ax. When it crashed against the haft of the ax, it broke in half.

Half of it flew off into the darkness.

Thelma still held the other half. She rammed it in low, shoving its sharp, broken end into my belly. It didn't go in. Not very far, anyway. But it felt red-hot and rammed my wind out. I staggered backward, tripped over Wesley's feet, and fell.

Fast as I could, I raised my head.

Wesley was starting to crawl away.

Billie was on her knees, trying to get up. Thanks to her

skid through the sand, her breasts had come out of her bikini. (Normally, I would've been thrilled by such a development. Not then, though. I noticed, but didn't much care.)

Thelma smacked Billie across the face with what remained of the spear. Down went Billie.

'Get up!' she yelled at Wesley, who was still crawling. 'Get up and run!'

She kept shouting as she rushed over to where Kimberly was struggling to stand up. She kicked her sister in the side and knocked her over, then kicked her again – this time in the stomach. I heard Kimberly grunt.

Wesley, whimpering and sobbing, scrambled to his feet.

I still had his ax.

He didn't come for it, though. He started to run, in a lurching jog, toward the jungle.

Thelma yelled, 'Run! Run! Go!'

She followed him like some sort of rear guard, twisting and turning to keep her eyes on us.

I used the ax handle to push against the sand and keep myself steady as I got to my feet. When I was up, I glanced at the others. Billie lay on her back, holding her face and moaning. Kimberly, curled on her side, made wheezy sounds as she tried to breathe.

Connie was now dashing toward us, a spear in one hand. She must've decided to join the fray when she saw Thelma slam her mother in the face.

She was still too far away to do a lot of good.

None of the three gals on my team was in any position to stop Wesley's escape.

It'd be me or nobody.

I'm not exactly a hero-type, but I sure as hell didn't like the idea of letting him get away. So I hefted the ax with both hands and went after him.

I would've caught him, too.

And hacked him to death, probably.

But Thelma, guarding his rear, turned on me and blocked my way. I should've gone through her. That's just what I would've tried, if she'd been a guy. But instead, I cut to the

101

right and tried to dodge past her side. She leaped and got in the way again. Head up, arms out, hunched over at the waist, she looked like some kind of butch sports-fiend determined to stop me from scoring.

'Get out of the way!' I yelled in her face.

I dodged to the left, but she sprang in front of me again. 'No no no no no,' she said. 'You think you're getting him? No no no. Think again, shithead.'

Meanwhile, Wesley had almost made it to the jungle.

I'd wanted to nail him while he was still on the beach, but the chance for that was gone.

'Get out of the way or I'll chop you down!' I shouted.

'Like fun.' Suddenly, she dropped her arms and stood up straight, her eyes wide with alarm at something going on behind me. 'NO!' she yelled.

I whirled around.

Connie, in mid-stride, launched her spear. Its long, pale shaft soared through the night high above our heads.

I think they call such a throw, in football, a 'hail Mary'.

It flew over us and kept on going like a Tomahawk missile homing in on the naked, pale back of Wesley as he lurched closer and closer to the darkness.

Thelma yelled, 'Wesley! Look out!' She bolted after him.

Wesley twisted sideways and looked back. He stumbled. He fell sprawling. A moment later, the spear zipped down and planted itself in the sand – probably ten feet to his right.

Behind me, Connie yelled, 'Fuck!'

I glanced back at her. She had quit running – must've thought the spear would take care of business. She looked disgusted and punched at the air with her fist.

I spotted Wesley again, just in time to see him vanish into the jungle.

Thelma was chasing him.

'Wait up!' she called out, and waved a thick arm. 'Wait! Wesley! I'm coming with you!'

A couple of seconds later, she was gone, too.

Battered Angels

Nobody went in after Thelma and Wesley.

Would've been too dangerous, for one thing.

For another, our ambush had turned into a disaster. We were stunned, disappointed, angry, confused – and injured.

Mostly thanks to Thelma.

After the end of the mess, we stood around together on the moonlit beach where it had happened. I had the ax resting on my shoulder. Billie, hands on hips (and breasts back inside her bikini), frowned toward the jungle. Connie was bent over, hands on knees, still trying to catch her breath after racing almost to the edge of the jungle to retrieve the spear she'd thrown at Wesley. Kimberly shook her head and shut the blade of her Swiss Army knife.

We must've all been thinking about Thelma.

'How could she do it?' Kimberly said.

Billie made a snorty sound. 'She loves the guy.'

'But he killed *Dad*. My God! Her own father! I can see how she might not turn on him for a little thing like killing *my husband*, but he murdered *Dad*.'

'Oh, her dear Wesley wouldn't do *that*,' Connie said. 'The dumb bitch.'

'She knows he did it,' Billie said. 'She might not be a genius, but she's not *that* stupid.'

'I think she just went nuts,' I said. 'All this stuff the past few days – and then seeing her father get whacked this morning – it unhinged her.'

'You might be right,' Billie said. 'This sure wasn't the behavior of a rational person, tonight.'

'We knew she might cause trouble,' I reminded everyone. 'That's why we didn't let her in on the plan.'

'Never thought she'd do something like *this*,' Kimberly muttered. 'Jesus H. Christ.' She tucked the knife down inside her bikini pants. 'We should've tied her up.'

'Thought she was asleep,' I said.

'Well. Nothing we can do about it now.'

'Let's go on back to the fire,' Billie suggested.

So we turned our backs to the jungle. We walked side by side, me with the ax on my shoulder, all of us battered (me the only one bloody). We must've been a sight to see – if anyone was watching.

Charlie's Angels and the Tin Woodsman.

All messed up and nowhere to go.

Or whatever.

I'm starting to lose it. I've been writing for hours, trying to get down all of last night's events in this journal. My hand is turning into a claw – my mind into mush. Anyway, I've got to finish about last night.

Before something else happens.

If I let the journal fall behind, I might have real trouble catching up.

On second thoughts, I'm going to take a break.

Hello, I'm back. Took a nice swim, then sat around with the gals for a while.

Maybe it was a mistake, but I finally admitted that I'm keeping a journal. I'd been telling everyone, before, that I was working on a series of short stories. But it was finally time to trust them with the truth. I mean, there's only three of them, now.

I wanted them to know about it. To know I'm not just fooling around while I'm sitting by myself for hours. To know there's a record of our ordeal being kept. (Maybe it'll be important for them to know that, at some point. Especially if something happens to me. Yuck. Made me feel squeamish, writing that little line.)

We had quite a long talk about the journal. They wanted to know what I've written about them (which made me sweat big-time), but I explained that I wouldn't be able to write truthfully if I had to worry about pleasing an audience. Finally, they promised to respect my privacy and make no attempts to sneak a peek.

They'd better stick to their promises, or there will be some mighty embarrassed and angry people on this beach. (I couldn't stand to face any of these gals, knowing they're aware of certain things I've written about them.)

Shit. They gave their word. If they read this stuff, they deserve what they get.

Maybe I shouldn't have told them.

Seemed like the right thing to do at the time.

Anyway, now that I've rested and shot off my mouth to the ladies, I'm ready to knock out the conclusion of last night's events.

I left off when we were on our way back to the camping area.

Okay.

We got into the firelight, and the gals suddenly noticed my wounds. They seemed pretty concerned – even Connie. In fact, she's the one who insisted on tending to me. She told her mother and Kimberly that they should try to get some sleep. She would fix me up, then she and I would stand watch for the next few hours.

I urged them to go along with it. I mean, they both seemed worn out and hurting.

While Billie and Kimberly settled into their sleeping places, Connie grabbed a couple of rags. She went to the stream, dipped them in, and came over to where I was sitting by the fire. She made me turn so the firelight would shine on the wounded side of my face – the right. Then she knelt in front of me.

The firelight lit up the swollen left side of her jaw.

Where I'd punched her.

'I'm sorry about that,' I told her. 'It wasn't supposed to connect.'

'Wasn't, huh?'

'I swear.'

She started dabbing at the raw trench that Thelma's rock had torn in my face and ear. She was gentle about it, but every touch ignited pain. 'I had it coming,' she said. 'I got in my shots, you got in yours.'

'It was an accident.'

'Sure.'

'I never would've hit you on purpose.'

She smirked. 'If you say so.'

'It's the truth.'

'What'd Thelma get you with, anyway? It sure fucked up your face.'

'A rock.'

'Look at this.' She pulled back the rag and showed it to me. It was red with my blood. The other cloth was still clean. She used it to mop off the blood that had run down my face and neck and right shoulder and arm. Then she wrung out both the rags, squeezing and twisting them. Bloody water spilled onto the sand between us.

She scowled at my lower wound.

Thelma's broken spear had gouged me just above my belly button. The hole wasn't deep, but it had bled a lot. The front of my swimming trunks was soaked, and trickles had even made their way down my thighs.

Connie shook her head. 'We'd better just go over to the stream.'

She took the rags with her. I carried the ax.

Gaining possession of the ax was the best thing to come out of our disastrous ambush. Next to a gun, you couldn't ask for a better weapon. Now it was ours, not Wesley's. I planned to keep it close by.

Connie led the way to the stream. We stepped down its shallow, sandy bank and waded in. The water felt great – slightly cooler than the night air.

The stream is basically so narrow that, during most of its course from the jungle to the inlet, you can jump across it without much trouble. It is also fairly shallow. Ankle-deep in many places, knee-deep in a few.

Connie and I entered one of the deeper areas. She faced me. We were out of range of the firelight. 'You can put down the ax,' she said.

I swung it underhand, and let go. The heavy, steel head thumped onto dry sand near the shore. The haft dropped toward me, and splashed into the stream where it would be easy to grab in case of an emergency.

Crouching in front of me, Connie rinsed the bloody rags. She stayed down. After draping one of the cloths over her knee, she reached up with the other and began to wash my wound. To hold herself steady, she clutched the waist of my trunks with her left hand, over near my hip.

I couldn't help but feel the backs of her fingers in there.

Couldn't help noticing how she'd tugged my trunks down a good inch – just by virtue of hanging onto them.

Not to mention, her face was straight in front of my groin.

I tried not to let these things affect me.

They affected me quickly and obviously.

'Not again,' she said when my trunks started sticking out.

'Sorry,' I told her.

She stopped patting the wet cloth against my wound. She lowered that hand, but the other stayed. 'Don't apologize, make it go away.'

'Huh?'

'You heard me. I'm trying to help you, and here you've got your *thing* in my face.'

'I don't have a lot of control over it. You know? It just . . . responds. To things like you.'

'Things like me.'

'Yeah, you. The way you look. Your hand there. The water. It all . . . adds up.'

'So then, it's *my* fault?'

I smiled. 'Pretty much.'

'I'm supposed to be flattered, or something?'

'Maybe,' I said.

She looked up at me and didn't speak for a few seconds. Then she said, 'You had one when we were fighting, too.'

'Yeah. When I was on top of you.'

She dipped the rag in the stream, then lifted it and began mopping the blood off the area between my wound and the top of my trunks. 'And when I took my top off,' she said.

'You noticed that?'

'Of course.'

107

'Thought maybe you were too busy slapping me,' I said.

'Ha ha, very funny.'

She dipped the rag again. As it came up soaked, her left hand plucked the waist of my trunks away from my belly. She mashed the sopping cloth against my skin, and a flood washed down. It drenched my works, then spilled out through the leg holes of my trunks and streamed down my legs.

Keeping my trunks pulled out, she dunked the rag into the stream again. She swished it around. 'Would you like me to take my top off again?' she asked. 'I could do it, you know. Right here, right now. You want me to?'

'Sure.'

'Or would you rather have me pull your trunks down?'

All I could think of to say was, 'You're kidding.'

'Take your pick.'

'How about both?'

'One or the other.'

It wasn't a very difficult decision. 'My trunks,' I said.

'Why?'

'Sort of tight in there.'

'I'll bet. Why else?'

I thought about that for a second, then said, 'It'll make it easier for washing the blood off me.'

'Lousy reason. Give me another.'

I shrugged. 'Well, I've already seen . . . you know, seen you topless.'

'And once was enough, huh?'

Woops.

'No,' I protested. 'But it's too dark here. I wouldn't be able to see.'

'You could touch.'

'Really? You didn't say that before. Okay, I pick that.'

'What?'

'Taking off your top.'

'Too late. You already made your choice.'

'Can't I change my mind?'

'No.'

'Okay.'

'You sure give up easy.'

'I just don't want to argue.'

'You just really don't want to see me topless again. Don't worry, pal – you won't.'

With that, she pulled at the waist of my trunks as if she wanted to see how far the elastic would stretch. She drew it out about half a foot, then let go. It shot in and snapped me.

And it hurt.

I staggered backward to get out of her reach – not knowing what to expect next.

She stood up. 'Fuck you,' she snarled. 'You're such a pathetic fucking loser. You really thought I'd pull your trunks down? Or take off my top? No way. Not a prayer. Last thing I want is your stupid cock in my face. And the only reason I let you see my tits back at the fire was to let you take a good look at what you're never gonna see again.'

I doubted the truth of that. Fact is, I doubt that she *ever* says what's really going on in her head – maybe doesn't even *know* what's going on in there.

But she was looking for trouble, so I gave her some. Not a smart move, but what I said was, 'I figured you took off your top 'cause you wanted to show off your boobies – such as they are – to Wesley.'

Her mouth fell open.

A moment later, she blurted, 'That's the thanks I get for trying to be nice to you.'

Whatever that meant.

I was afraid she might go for the ax. She didn't, though. She stomped through the water and ran up the bank and didn't stop till she reached the sleeping area. There, she flopped down on her usual assortment of rags.

I was left standing in the stream, a bit confused about what had gone wrong.

She'd been getting pretty friendly there for a while.

Unless it had been an act.

When it comes to Connie, it's just mighty damn awful hard to tell what's real from what isn't.

All I can be sure of is that she is never likely to react the way I'd expect a person to react. Not like Billie or Kimberly, for instance. You can make sense out of them. Unlike Connie.

Could it have to do with the fact that she's still a teenager? At eighteen, though, you'd think she might be past the usual adolescent crap.

Doesn't seem to be.

She reminds me of a cat I used to know. One time, I was petting its head. The cat was really into it, eyes half shut, its purr rumbling away. But all of a sudden, God knows why, it went nuts and shredded my arm.

I was thinking about that sort of stuff while I finished at the stream. What I did there was kneel in the water, wash the blood off my body as well as I could, then work at getting my trunks clean. Finally, I waded out, picked up the ax and returned to camp.

Connie was probably not asleep. I considered going over to her and trying to make amends, but that didn't seem like such a hot idea. I might just end up setting her off again.

So I went to the fire and sat down, figuring I might as well keep watch – even though sentry duty didn't seem very necessary.

Our ambush hadn't been a complete failure – Kimberly had delivered a couple of nasty wounds to Wesley. They were probably not fatal (barring infection), but they were pretty sure to keep him in major pain for a while.

And out of our hair.

Though I didn't expect an attack, I stayed awake and kept watch. There was plenty to occupy my mind. My plan was to stay up all night, so that the gals could get plenty of sleep. A while before dawn, though, Billie woke up and came over to the fire.

She sat down next to me. The side of her face was swollen and discolored by the blow from Thelma's spear. 'How's it going?' she asked.

'I don't think there's much chance of them bothering us tonight.'

'There isn't . . . How about you? How are your wounds doing?'

'Connie washed them off for me.'

'Let's see.'

I leaned back and turned toward her. Looking at my injuries, Billie grimaced. 'Must hurt.'

'How about you?'

'I'll live.' She put a hand on my leg. 'Why don't you go on to bed, now?'

'I'm not that tired.'

'Sure you are. Go on.'

'Why don't I stay and keep you company?'

'Thanks. But you know what? I'd rather be alone for a while. You know?'

I wanted awfully badly to stay with her – not to keep *her* company, but because I felt sort of lonely, myself. When it comes right down to it, I'd rather spend time with Billie than with anyone else I can think of.

But she probably wanted time to sit by herself and think about Andrew. I said, 'Sure. See you later.'

Then I went over to my sleeping place.

Before you know it, I was out like a light.

Odds and Ends

So much for last night. This is still day four, and I've spent the better part of it working on my journal here.

I'm just back from another break.

It's late afternoon, now. This has been a fairly uneventful day. Thank God.

I already went into how I took the earlier break from my writing and told the gals about the journal.

There are a few other matters worth mentioning.

For instance, we've started using the latrine as a toilet. Laid some branches across the hole, to stand on.

Also, Billie and Kimberly, with some help from me, constructed a couple of shelters. We made them like the walls of the latrine, by lashing bushes and fronds to frameworks of sticks. Instead of being walls, though, these are roofs. We set them up on poles, near our sleeping area. The purpose is to have places where we can escape from the sun. I'm using one, now. Though the sun hasn't been terrible (the heat is fairly moderate, and there's usually a pleasant breeze), I really enjoy being able to sit in the shade while I write.

Billie and Kimberly also made new weapons to replace the ones that were lost or broken last night.

Connie has spent most of the day by herself. She's hardly spoken to me since our squabble at the stream. The few times she's been near me, she has thrown narrow-eyed glares my way.

The good part is, she spent hours fishing. This morning, she borrowed the knife from Kimberly and used it to whittle a special point on the end of her spear. The point is very long and thin, with three barbs carved into its side. They look like small, sharp limbs, and sweep back at an angle away from the tip. The one nearest the tip is the smallest. They get bigger as they go. The obvious purpose for the barbs is to stop fish from falling off, once they've been speared.

It's a wicked-looking piece of work, though. Sure hope she doesn't get into a tiff and decide to use it on me.

Anyway, she stood in the inlet for hours, way out where it's waist-deep. Must've taken a long time to get the hang of using the spear. Every once in a while, I heard her yell 'Fuck!' Finally, she yelled, 'Yes! Gotcha, you bastard!' I looked up and saw her hoisting a big, silvery fish toward the sky on the tip of her spear. Everyone cheered, including me. She brought the fish ashore. Kimberly went running to her with our biggest pot, scooped it full of salt water, and Connie tossed in the fish.

She ended up with four of them.

We'll be having a real feast, tonight.

That's about it for today's events. So far, so good.

We've done pretty well when you take all the circumstances into account. Yesterday, we'd had to deal with the killings of

Keith and Andrew. Today, on top of that, there was the failure of our ambush to think about and the defection of Thelma – plus all the injuries from last night.

In the injury department, I'm the worst off, if you don't count Wesley.

Kimberly is probably the most beat up, after me. Her skin didn't get broken, but she has a horrible bruise on her ribcage, just below her right armpit. She also has bruises on her stomach and right hip from Thelma kicking her.

Billie and Connie have bruises on their faces. The swelling went away, leaving behind dark smudges that almost look like dirt. Billie's is on the left cheek, Connie's on the left side of the jaw. Billie got dealt a much meaner blow from Thelma's spear than Connie got from my fist.

I'm going to knock off now, and help prepare the fish for supper.

The fish was great. Billie fried it up on the skillet with bourbon – her special method. We also passed the bottle around, and had a few nips to help our finny friends go down smooth.

One thing really struck me during the meal.

The size of our group.

Or the lack thereof.

Four of us.

Jesus.

There used to be eight of us. Eight is a fair number of people, a pretty good crowd.

Four is measly.

And I've got to say, four looked a lot like three, from where I sat. I'm sort of like a movie camera, you know? I don't see myself, most of the time. I see Billie, Kimberly and Connie. One, two, three. That's all.

We've been whittled down considerably.

We didn't talk much while we ate. About the time we finished, though, Billie said, 'We'd better do something, tomorrow.'

Connie looked offended. 'Hey, *I* did something today. You just ate it.'

'We should've gone hunting,' Kimberly said, 'not fishing. Hunting for Thelma and Wesley.' She met Billie's eyes. Pressing her lips together in a tight line, she shook her head. Then she said, 'I just didn't want to deal with it today.'

'Yeah,' Billie said. 'I know. Neither did I.'

'Not after last night,' I added.

Connie gave me a quick, sour glare.

'But we'd better go looking for them tomorrow,' Billie said. 'We can't give Wesley time to recover. He's gotta be in bad shape after last night. If we find him while he's still laid up, he'll be a lot easier to finish off.'

'What'll we do about Thelma?' I asked.

'Save her,' Billie said.

Connie let out a snort.

Ignoring it, Kimberly said, 'Yeah. He'll probably kill her, sooner or later.'

'Maybe not right away,' Billie said. 'He'll want her around to take care of him, at least till he gets better.'

'You're both nuts,' Connie said. 'He isn't gonna kill Thelma.'

I decided to stay out of it.

'Why not?' Kimberly asked her.

'For one thing, she saved his bacon last night.'

'You think he'll spare her out of gratitude?' Kimberly asked.

'He's got no *reason* to kill her. She's on *his* side, you know?'

'He might not see it that way,' Billie said. 'Maybe he just sees her as an obstacle.'

'In the way of what?'

'Why is he doing any of this?' Billie asked. 'That's the real question. In my opinion, he set up this whole operation in order to make himself rich. Most of the family wealth is in Andrew's name. And mine. With both of us dead, you two girls and Thelma inherit everything. With the three of you dead, your spouses would get it. Connie hasn't got a spouse . . .'

'And he killed mine,' Kimberly muttered.

'Right. So that leaves Wesley. He stands to make a pile if he's the only survivor.'

'I'd bet he's also got a life insurance policy on Thelma,' Kimberly said. 'So you can add that to his take.'

Connie had a sick look on her face. 'I think you've all been watching too much *Murder, She Wrote.*'

'Why do *you* think he's doing all this?' Billie asked her.

She wrinkled her nose and shrugged. 'Because he's nuts?'

'He's nuts, all right,' Kimberly said. 'Nuts if he thinks he's gonna survive. First thing in the morning, I'm going after him.'

'We'll *all* go after him,' Billie said.

Day Five

War Dance

I didn't have to stand watch last night. The women took turns, and let me sleep.

I woke up on my own. The sun had risen over the tops of the jungle trees, and threw warm gold across our beach. It sure felt good. I wanted to just keep lying there, enjoying it.

Billie and Connie were asleep nearby, but I couldn't see Kimberly. After a while, I raised my head to look for her.

She was about midway between the campfire and the shoreline, swinging the ax. Exercising with it. Or practicing. She was as graceful as a dancer, twirling and smiting the air, springing forward to cut down an invisible enemy, taking swings to one side, then the other. She was a little spooky to watch. So smooth and graceful, yet wielding such a vicious weapon. The head of the ax glinted like silver in the sunlight. Her thick dark hair flowed and shook like the mane of a stallion.

She wore her dead husband's Hawaiian shirt. Unbuttoned, as usual, its gaudy fabric flew out behind her like a cape when she lunged or twirled. Her white bikini flashed. Her bronze skin gleamed with sweat.

She was spooky, elegant, primitive, beautiful. It made me ache, watching her. I couldn't force my eyes away.

Being stuck on this island *is* the best thing that's ever happened to me. By that logic, of course, I ought to be thanking Wesley, not trying to kill him. Except that I hate him for bringing grief to Kimberly and Billie. And I hate him for what he might do to them, if he gets the chance. (I'm not tickled by the fact that he wants to kill me, either.)

Anyway, Kimberly was spectacular to watch.

Until she noticed me watching. I felt like a peeping Tom who'd been caught in the act, but I smiled and waved. She waved back. I sat up, gave myself a couple of minutes to calm down, then got to my feet and wandered over to join her.

'Preparing for the big battle?' I asked.

She rested the ax on her shoulder, and smiled. She has a spectacular smile. 'Just fooling around,' she said. 'Getting a little workout.'

'You must be part Viking,' I said.

'That's me, Nordic through and through.'

She was making sport of me, but I liked it. 'I wasn't referring to your complexion,' I explained. 'It's the way you swing that ax. Like you've got battle-axes in your blood.'

'Ah. That might be my Indian blood.'

'You're Indian?'

'Injun. Part Sioux . . . Lakota.'

'You kidding me?'

'I swear.' With her free hand, she drew a quick X in the middle of her chest. 'On my mother's side. Her grandfather fought at Little Big Horn.'

'You're kidding.'

'I have it on good authority that he *personally* scalped Custer.'

'Really?'

She grinned. '*That* was kidding.'

'Glad to hear it, because I don't think Custer *got* scalped.'

'I don't really know if my ancestor scalped anyone at all. He was there, though. That's a fact.'

'My God.'

'So I guess maybe things like tomahawks, spears and knives might run in my blood. I'm also part Sicilian.'

'Sioux and Sicilian. Man! Red blood *and* hot blood. That's a dangerous combination. Remind me not to make you mad at me!'

'Yep. Watch it. I'm hell on wheels.' Her smile died and her eyes went dark. For a while there, she must've forgotten about the murders of her husband and her father. But she had just remembered. I could see the pain in her face. And the anger.

Wesley had made a very big mistake, killing people Kimberly loved.

He's already paid for the mistake, but I've got a feeling that his torments have hardly even started.

Wanting to take her mind off her grief, I said, 'Boy, I didn't think we'd be stuck on this island more than a day or two, did you?'

'An *hour* or two,' she said. 'I thought for sure somebody must've seen the explosion. And even if nobody *did* . . . My God, it's like a century too late to be getting marooned on an island.'

'Just goes to show, anything can happen.'

'Especially when there's a devious bastard scheming to *make* it happen.'

'He *must've* filed a false itinerary,' I said. 'Or, what do they call it, a float plan?' It was something I'd thought about and mentioned before, but now I felt certain of it. 'That's about the only way I can figure why we haven't gotten rescued yet. Nobody's looking for us. Either that, or they've been tricked into searching in the wrong places.'

'At this point,' Kimberly said, 'I don't even *want* to be rescued.'

Her words stunned me.

They echoed my own feelings on the subject.

This was the start of our fifth day on the island. In some ways, it seems like we'd been here for years. Mostly, though, it seems like much too short a time. Thanks to all our troubles with Wesley, we haven't even explored the island, yet. There's no telling what we might find, or what adventures we might have over the coming days – or weeks. Or even months.

Rescue would put an abrupt end to all the fabulous possibilities.

I figured that Kimberly must feel the same way, but then she said, 'I'm not leaving this island till I've taken care of Wesley.'

'You already got him pretty good.'

'I'm going to kill him.'

The way she said it, and the way she *looked* when she said it, gave me a shiver up my back.

Preparations

I did some quick catch-up on the journal while the gals got ready for our jungle excursion.

Our hunt.

Our mission to rescue Thelma and finish off Wesley.

Before leaving, we had a small meal and discussed what to do about the fire. So far, we'd followed Andrew's advice about never letting it go out. But we figured we might be gone all day. If we wanted to keep it burning, we would almost have to leave someone behind to tend it.

We were not about to leave anyone alone.

But if we let two stay behind to guard each other and watch the fire, that would leave only two for the hunt.

Which, we all agreed, would be ridiculous.

We decided to let the fire burn out.

Anyway, we still had Andrew's lighter.

Billie went over to her sleeping area and looked for it. She found Andrew's khaki shorts, picked them up, and searched the pockets. She emptied them as she went along, pulling out such things as his pipe, tobacco pouch, billfold, keys and the white handkerchief that he had placed over Keith's dead face. Soon, she came hurrying back with the shorts in one hand, the lighter in the other.

She tested the lighter. A flick, and the flame leaped up.

She had brought the khaki shorts over to us because she thought someone ought to wear them. 'They've got such great, deep pockets,' she explained.

Obviously, we could use something for carrying odds and ends.

Aside from Andrew's shorts, the only pocket in sight was the one on the chest of Kimberly's Hawaiian shirt – a pocket so loose and flimsy that she didn't even trust her Swiss Army knife to it.

There was my bag, of course. I'd hidden it under some

rags over at my sleeping place, for safe keeping. I planned to leave it there, because I sure didn't want to spend the day hiking through the jungle with *that* on my back. (It's the home of my journal, which is a big thick spiral notebook – probably weighs at least two pounds.)

'Who wants to wear them?' Billie asked, holding up Andrew's shorts.

Nobody volunteered.

Probably because the shorts would be too bulky and heavy and hot, especially for gals who were used to going around in scanty bikinis.

'You wear 'em,' Connie told me. 'They're men's shorts, and you're the only guy around here.'

'I don't want to wear them,' I said. I remembered how Andrew had taken them off and spread them over the lower parts of Keith – who'd been naked down there and dead at the time.

'Just put 'em on over your trunks,' Connie said.

'That'd be too hot.'

'I'll wear them,' Kimberly offered.

She didn't sound eager, and I didn't like the idea. In fact, I didn't want to see *anybody* wearing them – but especially not any of the gals. 'That's all right,' I said. 'I'll put 'em on.'

I took them from Billie, bent over, and raised a foot to step into them.

'No,' Billie said. 'Get your trunks off, first. You'd smother in all that. Besides, your trunks are a mess.'

They aren't a *mess*. I'd gotten most of the blood off them, so they were only a little bit gory.

I looked around for a place to change.

'Just do it here,' Kimberly said. She was pretty matter-of-fact about it.

I shook my head. 'I can go over to the rocks . . .'

'Don't be silly,' Billie said. 'Just do it here. We won't peek.'

Connie smirked. 'Who'd *want* to?'

I sighed. Then I said, 'Well, okay.'

After their backs were turned, I pulled my trunks down and got them off. It felt weird. I was naked on a beach in broad daylight, and the three gals were almost near enough to touch. They weren't wearing much, themselves – but more than me.

I got enormous, all of a sudden. I stepped into Andrew's shorts and pulled them up as fast as I could.

'You decent?' Billie asked.

'Almost.'

I shoved myself inside the fly and got the zipper shut. The shorts were big and loose, drooping well below my waist. But I hitched them higher and got the belt cinched.

'All set?' Billie asked.

'Uh, yeah.'

She turned around. They all did.

I bent down fast and picked up my trunks. When I straightened up, I held them in front of me.

Connie said, 'Good God, Rupert.'

I shook my head. I felt as if my face might burst into flame. 'What's the matter?' I asked.

Big mistake.

'Your *hard-on*'s the matter, you fucking degenerate.'

'Connie!' Billie blurted.

'Well, look at him!'

'He doesn't need you pointing it out to everyone,' Billie scolded her.

'It's *already* pointing out to everyone,' Kimberly said, smiling.

I think I moaned. I think I muttered something like, 'Oh, man.'

In the meantime, Kimberly's comment had cracked Billie up. Even Connie was laughing about it.

The object of their amusement, meanwhile, was shrinking like an icicle in Hell.

I stopped trying to hide behind my trunks. 'Yeah, well,' I said. 'These things happen, you know?'

'Happen to *you* all the time,' Connie said.

'It's nothing to be ashamed of,' Billie told me, being sort of solemn now that she'd finished laughing. 'Don't worry about it, honey.'

Honey?

Kimberly said, 'Looks like the big fella's out of commission, anyway.'

'Do we have to talk about it?' I asked, feeling awfully squirmy inside.

'You're the one who brought it up,' Kimberly said. She gave me that smile again. That spectacular smile.

I actually laughed, myself.

'Okay, okay,' I said. 'Now, can we get on with things?'

'Here.' Billie tossed me Andrew's lighter. 'You've got the pockets.'

I dropped it into a front pocket of my shorts, and felt it way down against my thigh. 'How about the knife?' I asked Kimberly.

Normally, I avoided looking at it.

This gave me an excuse, though.

It was tucked into the front of her bikini pants. The thickness of the plastic handle made the flimsy white triangle purse out. I could see bare skin down there.

Kimberly's open right hand suddenly covered it all.

Patted it.

'I'll hang on to the knife. It has an appointment to keep with Wesley.'

Over at the supply pile, we gathered a few items so that we'd have something to snack on. The food went into the pockets of Andrew's shorts. (My shorts, now.) Then we gathered our weapons.

I volunteered to carry the ax.

'It's awfully heavy,' Kimberly said.

'I can handle it.'

'Let's take turns.'

'Okay,' I said.

'You start out with it, if you want. Just let me know when you get tired.'

'Okay.'

The ax required two hands. I wanted to have a back-up weapon, though, so I loosened my belt enough to slip a tomahawk under it, by my right hip.

Billie watched me do that, then pushed her tomahawk down the side of her pants. The waistband couldn't take the weight. 'Woops!' The pants were at about a forty-five-degree angle by the time she grabbed the weapon.

'Mom!' Connie blurted. 'For God's sake!'

'Oh, calm down.' She pulled out the weapon, hooked a finger under her waistband, and corrected the slant.

'You did that on purpose.'

'Don't be an idiot.'

At that, Connie glared at me as if I were somehow to blame.

I just gave her a goony look and shrugged. 'I wasn't even looking,' I said. Which was a lie, and she knew it.

Billie, still determined not to carry the tomahawk in her hand, came up with the section of rope that had been around Keith's neck. Someone had untied the hangman's noose, so she had four or five feet of rope to work with. As all of us watched, she knotted the ends together and made a sling for her tomahawk. She slipped the loop over her head and put her right arm through it, then adjusted the rig so that the rope crossed her chest like a bandolier, the weapon hanging at her hip.

'I oughta do that,' Kimberly said.

As it turned out, Kimberly and Connie both did it. They used sections cut from the main length of the hanging rope, which we'd kept coiled with the rest of our supplies.

It took a few minutes. Worth the wait, though. They each had a spear. Would've taken both hands just to carry their weapons if they didn't have the tomahawks suspended by the rope slings.

We didn't burden ourselves with water bottles. For one thing, we wanted to travel fast and light. For another, we figured that we would never stray very far from the stream.

At last, we were ready.

Kimberly led the way. I went second. Connie followed me, and Billie took the rear.

We left the beach behind at the place where Wesley and Thelma had escaped into the jungle.

The Hunt

At first, we tried to follow the trail of Wesley's blood. Kimberly moved slowly through the bushes, often stopping, sometimes crouching for a closer inspection.

Even though Wesley must've bled plenty from his chest and buttock wounds, it wasn't easy to find the places where he'd left dabs of it behind. The jungle was so dense, in most places, that you couldn't see for more than a few feet in any direction. Also, not a lot of sunlight made it down to our level. We spent most of our time trudging through deep, murky shadows.

We probably would've had no luck at all finding traces of Wesley's blood, if Kimberly hadn't been so persistent. Or talented. Or psychic. She often seemed to know, by instinct, where to look.

Maybe it's the Sioux in her genes.

In spite of her uncanny abilities in the tracking department, we eventually lost all trace of the blood. By then, however, Kimberly had determined the general direction of his travels.

'He's going for the stream,' she whispered to us.

'That makes sense,' I said. 'He's gotta have fresh water.'

'Why didn't we go there in the first place?' Connie said. 'We could've skipped all *this*. This place blows.' With that, she smacked a mosquito that had landed on the side of her neck. She said, 'Yuh!'

Today was the worst mosquito trouble we'd had so far. They'd mostly left us alone, on the beach. They hadn't even been a major nuisance during the few times I'd ventured into the jungle.

But today they were awful.

We had no *6–12*, no *Cutter's*, no *Off!*, no nothing. The insect repellents had come on the sea voyage with us, but had been left aboard the yacht when we set out on our picnic. An oversight that we paid for today.

We'd been slapping mosquitoes ever since leaving the beach.

Some of us had been, that is.

Kimberly didn't let them bother her. Basically, she ignored them.

I tried to follow her example, but couldn't stand the way the little monsters hummed around my ears and the way they tickled wherever they landed. They seemed especially fond of the injured area on the side of my face and on my ear. (Apparently, they dig scabs.) I was very glad that I'd worn my shirt – the pink blouse on loan from Billie. Also, Andrew's big old shorts probably gave me more protection than I would've gotten from my swimming trunks.

Connie was wearing her usual T-shirt, but it was so thin and clingy that the mosquitoes nailed her right through the cloth. Her only safe areas were those protected by her bikini. If I haven't mentioned it before, hers is the skimpiest of the three. (Why Connie, who likes to act the prude, would wear such a revealing swimsuit is beyond me. But then, when it comes to Connie, what isn't? Maybe the T-shirt is her way of maintaining an appearance of decency.) Anyway, the top of her bikini consists of twin orange triangles and a few thin cords. Its bottom is what they call a 'thong' – with a slightly wider strip in front than the one that goes up her rear. In other words, only a few very private inches of her body were safe from the attacking mosquitoes.

Billie, as usual, wore only her bikini. No shirt, and the swimsuit didn't cover much. Even though hers had at least three times the fabric of Connie's, there's a lot more flesh to Billie. She seemed to have acres of bare skin, all of it shiny and dripping with sweat. She looked like a wonderful hot meal for the little bastards. But they left her alone.

I noticed this when we stopped in a sunny clearing to rest on our way to the stream.

'Aren't they eating you alive?' I asked her.

'Nope. They never do.'

'What's your secret?'

'When I was about five, I saved a mosquito's life. Word got around. They haven't touched me ever since.'

'She told *me* that story when *I* was five,' Connie said. 'It's such bullshit.'

Billie gave her daughter a big understanding smile. 'Think what you like, dear.'

'I think they leave you alone 'cause they don't like your smell.'

'You're such a sweetheart.'

'You smell fine,' I told her.

Hell, I thought she smelled great.

'Thank you, Rupert,' she said.

'Whatever your secret is, I wish I had it. These things are driving me nuts.'

'All they want,' Kimberly said, 'is a little of your blood. They aren't asking much.'

'I'd just as soon keep my blood,' I told her. 'You're just *letting* them have at you?'

'Trying to fight them off is a losing battle. I accept what I can't change.'

Connie smirked. 'The bullshit's thicker than the mosquitoes around here.'

I smacked a mosquito on my forehead.

After a while, we got moving again and came to the stream. We gathered along its shore, and looked both ways as if we'd come to a highway and were worried about getting struck down by a speeding truck.

No sign of Wesley or Thelma or anyone.

The stream flowed along at a pretty good clip, splashing over rocks, coming down from the high ground to our right. Looking to my left, I saw it running downhill toward our beach. I couldn't see our beach, though. Or the ocean. Just trees and bushes and hanging vines – and birds swooping here and there. Not much of the stream was visible, either. About thirty feet away, it curved out of sight.

'Hold this for me,' Connie said. She thrust her spear into her mother's free hand, then climbed down into the stream. She knelt, bent over, and cupped some water into her mouth.

Then she started splashing and rubbing herself, apparently to soothe the itch of her mosquito bites.

The way she acted, it must've felt really good.

The rest of us still stood on the bank.

'How are you doing with that ax?' Kimberly asked me.

'Fine.'

'Want me to take it for a while?'

'No, really.'

'I'm pretty sure we're just below the lagoon.' She stepped down into the water. Billie and I did the same. 'It'll be an easy hike from here,' Kimberly said, 'but we'd better keep our eyes open.'

We crouched and took drinks, then just stood in the stream to wait for Connie to finish. I sort of felt like rolling in the water and rubbing my itches, too. But it was only a few inches deep here. I preferred to wait for the lagoon.

Connie took her time, as if she enjoyed making us wait. I didn't mind much. It was just fine with me, watching her flop around all shiny and wet in her transparent T-shirt and her feeble excuse for a bikini.

Finally, she stood up. Billie returned her spear, and we got moving again.

We made our way single file up the stream bed. Sometimes we walked in the water, sometimes on dry rocks alongside it. It was much easier than trekking through the jungle. As we went along, though, the terrain got steeper. The stream tumbled down, loud and frothy. We had to climb, and sometimes leap from rock to rock. Luckily, things never got to steep that we needed our hands.

Kimberly had said it would be 'an easy hike' to the lagoon.

For her, I suppose it was.

The rest of us had to stop a few times along the way.

Our last halt was called by Kimberly, which surprised me. Had she finally gotten worn out enough to need a rest?

Nope.

She sat on a rock. As she waited for the rest of us, she set her spear aside, took off the tomahawk hanging by her hip, and slipped out of Keith's gaudy shirt. When we arrived, she said, 'We're just about there. I'll go on up. You guys wait here, okay? I want to take a look around.'

'You shouldn't go alone,' I said.

'I'll be in plain sight. Just up there.' She turned her head and nodded toward the higher rocks. 'I want to make sure the coast is clear.'

We agreed to stay behind.

Kimberly climbed the rocks to the right of the stream. Just below the top, she scurried part way up the face of a large slab that was at about a forty-five-degree angle. Then she sank to her belly and squirmed the rest of the way.

She lay flat, her head up. For a long time, she didn't seem to move at all. Then her head made small, slow turns from one side to the other.

The three of us watched her from below, and said nothing for a long time.

After maybe ten minutes, though, Connie muttered, 'What the hell's taking her so long?'

'Maybe she sees something,' Billie said.

'Maybe she just wants to make sure nobody's there,' I suggested.

'This is stupid, waiting around.'

'A few more minutes won't hurt anything,' Billie told her. All patience and calm. 'Just relax.'

A few more minutes passed. Connie spent them sighing and shaking her head and rolling her eyes upward.

It annoyed me. 'You late for an appointment?' I finally asked.

'Fuck you.'

Billie said softly, 'Cut it out, Connie.'

'He doesn't have to be such a fucking wise-ass all the time.'

'Would you please watch your language?'

'Oh, yeah. Take his side, why don't you?'

'I'm not taking any sides. I just think you should settle down, all right? You're not improving the situation. And it seems like all I've been hearing out of you lately is "fuck" this and "fuck" that. You wouldn't be talking that way if your father was around.'

131

'Well, he isn't.' She said that in a very snotty fashion.

'No, he isn't.' Billie said that in a sad way that made me get tight in my throat.

And Connie suddenly started to cry.

Her mother tried to put an arm around her, but Connie shoved it away and blurted, 'Don't touch me. Leave me alone.' She turned her back on both of us, and buried her face in her hands. She didn't make much noise with her crying – just a gasp or sniffle now and then. But she was crying pretty good. I could tell by the way her back and shoulders kept jumping.

As much as I sometimes can't stand Connie, it hurt to watch her crying. It sort of made *me* want to cry. It also made me want to comfort her. I knew better than to try a thing like that, though. So I kept my distance and silence.

She'd finished crying, but still had her back to us, by the time Kimberly climbed down.

Kimberly frowned at her. 'You okay?' she asked.

'Fuck off,' Connie muttered.

Which didn't seem to faze Kimberly. 'Sure. Whatever.' She turned to Billie and me. Crouching in front of us, she said, 'Doesn't look like anyone's up there. We shouldn't count on it, though. We'll have to be really careful, and watch our backs.'

'Wesley might be too weak to attack anyone,' Billie said.

'Good chance of it,' Kimberly agreed. 'But there's no telling what Thelma might pull. I think she'll do *anything* to save him.'

'Stands by her man,' I said.

Kimberly came very close to snarling. 'What a gal,' she muttered.

'We shouldn't blame her too much,' Billie said. 'She never could see straight, as far as Wesley was concerned. She probably *still* refuses to believe he killed Andrew and Keith. If she's even . . . still in the picture.'

Kimberly slipped the rope sling over her head and adjusted the tomahawk so it dangled by her right hip. 'I'd say it's ten to one she's still alive. And on his side. If she attacks, though . . .'

Shaking her head, Kimberly squeezed her lower lip between her teeth. Then she said, 'We have to defend ourselves. I don't want her hurt, though. Not if we can help it. She's still my sister.

'You're my sister, too,' she said, turning her head to look at Connie. 'I'm not going to leave you sitting there, no matter how much you might prefer to spend the rest of the day sulking.' She took her spear and stood up. 'So get on your feet, all right? It's time to go.'

'Sure,' Connie muttered. 'Your wish is my command.'

'You better believe it,' Kimberly said, and smiled.

I'll have to quit writing, pretty soon. I went to work as soon as we got back to the beach, this afternoon. They let me stick with it while they prepared dinner. Then I took a break to eat, and came back to the journal. I'm going to run out of daylight before I run out of things to write about yesterday.

I'll be backed up pretty good.

What I really need to do is stop trying to write about every damn thing that goes on. Well, actually, I'm not writing about *every*thing. I've been leaving plenty out. There are a million little details that I haven't mentioned, and some might even be important.

You don't know what's important until later, sometimes.

For want of a nail, the shoe was lost. For want of the shoe, the horse was lost. For want of the horse, the battle was lost. I don't know what's coming, so I might not even mention the lost nail. Does that make any sense?

Maybe that's why I try not to leave out any details that I think might turn out to be important. Since I don't know how things will turn out . . .

Maybe if I stopped wasting time and paper with stuff like this, I'd get further.

I'd *better* cut down somewhere. At this point, about half of my notebook is filled up. I've been writing on both sides of each page, but it looks like I might run out of notebook before I run out of story – at least if things keep going on for very many more days.

I'll try being more careful about what I include. And from now on, I'll write *really small*.

What if I end up running out of paper because I spent too much space writing about running out of paper?

Life and its ironies.

Back tomorrow. I hope.

Day Six

The Hunt (Part Two)

Here we are, at the start of our sixth day as castaways.

It's dawn.

We agreed for me to take the final watch of the night, so that I would have daylight for working on my journal. A few minutes ago, Kimberly woke me up to relieve her. She has just gone over to her sleeping place. Billie and Connie appear to be sound asleep.

It is very pleasant and peaceful, sitting here alone by the fire at sunrise. I hear the gentle swishing sounds of the waves. The fire crackles and snaps. Off in the jungle, a few birds are squawking.

I'd better get down to business.

Yesterday, and our hunt for Wesley and Thelma.

When I left off, we were just about to reach the lagoon.

We climbed the rest of the way, and found ourselves standing within a few feet of its shore.

The lagoon turned out to be larger than I'd expected – maybe fifty yards across and twice that size in length. I'd also expected its entire shoreline to be in sight, but there were so many curves and points and coves that fairly large portions of the lagoon and its banks couldn't be seen from where we stood.

It was a lovely sight, though. The surface was so still that it had hardly a ripple except where the waterfall splashed down directly across from us.

The water of the falls looked like a curl of silver where it slid over the rock edge about ten or fifteen feet above the lagoon. It hung down the face of the rock, shiny and transparent. At the bottom of its drop, it splashed softly.

The rest of the lagoon was like a dark mirror. It cast a

perfect, upside-down image of the rocky shores, the bushes and towering trees.

We stood for a while on the shore, looking around.

As expected, there was no sign of Wesley or Thelma. It was hard to believe that any human had ever been here before – even though I knew that Kimberly and Keith had visited the lagoon on our first morning at the island, before the boat blew up. The place seemed so remote and primitive that I wouldn't have been surprised to see a dinosaur wading through its water. Like in *The Lost World* or *King Kong*. Or *Jurassic Park*.

The only wildlife I could see, however, was of the winged variety. Bugs and birds. And not a pterodactyl in sight.

'I'm going in,' Connie said. She set down her spear and tomahawk, and started to take off her shoes.

'We'd better not all go in at the same time,' Kimberly said. 'Someone should stay on the bank with . . .'

Connie dived in.

'. . . with the weapons.'

'I'll stay,' I volunteered.

'We'll take turns,' Billie told me. 'I'll come out in a few minutes and take over for you.'

'Fine,' I said.

'Let's give ourselves about half an hour,' Kimberly suggested. 'Then we'll scout the shores, see if we can find any traces of my sister and Wesley. Maybe we'll be able to pick up their trail.'

'If they were even here,' Billie said.

'This is where *I'd* come, if I were Wesley. I'd have a hiding place somewhere near the lagoon, here. A base camp.' To me, she said, 'So keep a sharp eye out.'

'Don't let anyone sneak up on you,' Billie said.

'And watch us, too,' Kimberly added. 'We'll be sort of vulnerable out there.'

That was like our cue to look for Connie.

She had made it to the other side, and was standing under the waterfall. As we watched, she took off her T-shirt, wadded it into a ball, and started to rub her face with it.

'I sure wish she'd shape up,' Billie muttered.

'She's having a tough time,' Kimberly said.

'We all are. That's no excuse.'

'Come on, let's go in.'

They piled their spears and tomahawks on the shore, along with the rope slings, the Hawaiian shirt, the Swiss Army knife and their shoes. Then they entered the water.

Kimberly dived in. Did a much cleaner job of it than Connie had done – darting into the water with hardly a splash. I watched her slide along under the surface. She was long and sleek, black hair flowing down her back, the white seat of her bikini pants slipping through the gloom like a bright, winged fish. With the reflection on the water above her, she seemed to be gliding beneath a translucent landscape painting.

Billie, less athletic and more cautious than Kimberly, climbed down to the water and waded in. She made her way slowly, as if worried about what she might step on. When the water reached her thighs, she leaned forward, turning her body, and eased into a side-stroke.

Connie, still at the falls, was rubbing the wadded T-shirt up and down an arm.

At the moment, she was the most vulnerable of the three gals. Nobody appeared to be sneaking up on her, though. I looked around to make sure no one was sneaking up on *me*. Then I added my tomahawk, shirt, shoes and socks to the pile. I also emptied the pockets of my big old khaki shorts, since I planned to wear the shorts when I went in for my swim.

Then I climbed onto a good-sized boulder that stuck out into the lagoon, sat down on it and lay the ax across my lap.

It was sort of like being the lifeguard at a public swimming pool. All I needed was a whistle and some white goop on my nose.

I could've focused completely on any one of the gals. They were all worth watching, all exciting for one reason or another.

Connie, in spite of her attitude problems, had a slim, fine body and such a skimpy swimsuit that she almost seemed to be naked.

Billie, more appealing than her daughter from the get-go because she's so nice, also had the most fabulous body: wide shoulders, large breasts, a flat belly and full, firm buttocks.

Kimberly, gorgeous enough to be on the cover of a fashion magazine, was dark and slender and hard, an athlete and a warrior. Her body looked as if it had been carved from wood and polished to a high gloss.

Each was sort of a masterpiece, in her own way.

I could've spent all my time watching just one of them. All three were my responsibility, though. I had to force myself to turn my eyes from Kimberly to Billie, then force myself to abandon Billie for Connie. I could've lingered on Connie for an hour, but made myself look away to make sure Kimberly was all right. And on it went.

With me as the observer and guardian, each followed her own whims in the lagoon.

Kimberly swam the crawl. Back and forth, back and forth across the middle of the lagoon. Low and quick in the water, she swam for speed, not pleasure.

Billie luxuriated. She moved slowly, doing a languid sidestroke for a while, then rolling face down and breast-stroking, later flipping over and paddling along on her back. She never stayed long in any one position. She seemed to relish rolling over, sloshing. And I relished watching her. Which is putting it mildly.

Connie hardly did any swimming at all. She stayed in the waist-deep water below the falls, rubbing herself with the wadded ball of her T-shirt. Apparently, this was to relieve the itching of her mosquito bites. That's what I thought at first, anyway. Until, after a while, she took off her bikini. She put her back to me, *then* took it off and sidestepped away from the falls and tossed it onto a big, flat-topped block of stone. Keeping her back to me the whole time. And never letting the water level drop below her waist.

After ridding herself of the bikini, she returned to her place beneath the falls and resumed rubbing herself with the T-shirt. Always with her back toward me.

What a bitch.

I knew I should be keeping an eye on Billie and Kimberly, but Connie had me hooked. I couldn't look away from her.

She must've thought she would taunt me by keeping her back turned, so she would've been disappointed to find out how much the view of her bare back thrilled me: her delicate shoulders, the moving curves of her shoulder blades, the way she tapered to her slender waist, then flared out at the hips. Not to mention that I could see her buttocks, the crease of her ass, and the backs of her legs – all of which were perfectly visible below the surface of the water.

She also had me hooked because she kept rubbing her breasts with the wadded shirt. And rubbing her belly. And rubbing between her legs. It was very obvious *where* she was rubbing herself – she made sure of that.

What a charmer.

While she was at it, though, my time on guard duty ran out.

I hadn't been keeping track of time, hadn't even given much thought to going into the lagoon. But Billie had apparently noticed Connie's antics.

She rose to her feet in the waist-deep water just in front of me. At the sight of her, I almost immediately forgot about Connie.

Billie's short hair, clinging wet, looked golden. She was dripping and shiny and breathing hard. Her breasts, as brown as bread loaves, moved up and down, barely contained by her black bikini. From my position above her, I could see a strip of light at the bottom of her cleavage.

She said in a quiet voice, 'I'll take over. Jump on in and pay her a visit.'

'Who?'

'Who do you think? Connie.'

'You're kidding.'

'She needs a little visit.'

'Not from me.' A drop of water fell off the tip of Billie's nose. It vanished into the crevice between her breasts.

'Go on,' she said.

141

'I'll go in the water,' I said, 'but I'm gonna stay away from her.'

Billie shrugged. 'Well, it's up to you.'

'It's up to me?'

'Sure.'

'In that case,' I said, 'why don't I stay here and keep *you* company? You're not as likely to dump on me. And you're better to look at.'

She smiled. 'Is that so?'

'Yeah. And you know it.'

'*She's* the naked one.'

'Big deal,' I said.

Which brought a quick, soft laugh from Billie. 'A big deal, all right. You'd better get over there, or she'll *really* hate you.'

'Oh, she really hates me *now*.'

'Only it'll be more so if you stick around with me while she's doing everything in her power to drive you nuts.'

'Think so?' I set the ax aside, and stood up. 'Hey, Connie!' I called.

She looked over her shoulder at me. She did not turn around. She scowled. 'What?' she snapped.

'Is that waterfall big enough to share with a friend?' I asked.

'Fuck you!' she yelled.

I smiled down at Billie, who still stood in the waist-deep water in front of my rock. She shook her head. 'You *like* to piss her off,' she said.

At the other side of the lagoon, Connie was now side-stepping toward the place where she'd left her bikini.

She didn't plan to take any chances.

'I'm *coming* for you!' I called.

'Just try it, and see what happens!'

Billie grinned. 'Clearly an invitation.'

'Should I take off my shorts?' I asked Billie.

'That might be pushing your luck.'

'I wouldn't, anyway.'

'I know. Now quit wasting time and jump in.'

Across the lagoon, Connie was bending over. On the nearby

rock, her bikini had been replaced by the sodden wad of her T-shirt.

She straightened, pulling up her bikini pants. (To tell the truth, the addition of the thong didn't make much of a change to her rearview appearance.)

'What are you waiting for?' Billie asked.

'Nothing,' I said.

A few moments later, Connie finished putting on her top. Only then did she turn around. She gave me a smug little smile, and a wave.

Not wanting to look like a jerk in front of Billie, I refrained from giving Connie the finger. I just shook my head. Then I waited for Kimberly to swim by. When she was out of the way, I dived in.

The water felt great – cool enough to be refreshing, but not chilly. It slid against my skin like satin. No wonder Billie had rolled and wallowed in the luxury of it.

When I came up for air, I couldn't find the bottom with my feet. So I trod water, blinked my eyes clear and spotted Connie straight ahead. She was on her way back to the falls.

'Do you mind if I come over?' I asked.

'It's a free country,' she said, sounding like a six-year-old.

'You sure of that?' I asked. I started to paddle toward her with a modified breast-stroke that kept my face above the water. 'I mean, what country *is* this?'

'Don't be such a wise-ass.' She turned her back to me and stepped into the gleaming curtain of water. Her body seemed to cut its own likeness into the falls. She spread out her arms and tipped back her head.

'I bet that feels good,' I said.

She didn't answer.

About six feet away from her, I was able to stand up. The water reached the middle of my chest.

'That was a nice show you put on,' I said.

She lowered her head and arms, then turned around. The turning around, I'm sure, was to give me a good look at her snotty smirk. 'Glad you liked it,' she said.

'Your mother was *very* impressed.' I hoped that Billie

couldn't hear us. We were probably safe – at least if we kept our voices down.

'Good for Mom.'

'She's the one who sent me over here.'

'No kidding. Why did she do that?'

'She thinks you *want* me.'

Connie blew out a big puff of air. 'That's how much Mom knows. I want you like I want a hole in the head.'

'The feeling is mutual.'

'Yeah, right,' she said. 'Like you weren't *aching* for me to turn around.'

'Yeah, right,' I said. Two can play that game.

'Fuck off,' she said, and shut her eyes.

Instead, I stood there. If she'd really wanted me to fuck off, she wouldn't have shut her eyes.

Anyway, I couldn't just leave. Not with Billie watching. Besides, the view was too good.

The waterfall was splashing Connie behind her shoulders, but missing her head completely. After a few seconds, she leaned backward. Her head made a hole in the liquid sheet. Water spilled down over her ears and face, splattered the tops of her shoulders, ran down her chest.

Maybe she really did want me to leave, and now she was trying to shut me out. Or maybe this was part of the game: her way of letting me look her over, unobserved – possibly to gain a full appreciation of what I would never be allowed to see naked, or touch.

Unless, as Billie might see it, this was Connie's bizarre method of trying to seduce me. Fat chance of that, in my opinion.

Since Connie had her eyes shut, I moved closer to her.

I watched how the water slid down her chest and the tops of her breasts. Her breasts were about half the size of Billie's. Each was partly covered by a clinging orange triangle, pulled taut by thin strips of elastic.

Her nipples were sticking out big and hard against the flimsy triangles.

Maybe Billie was right about her motives.

After all, Connie knew I hadn't gone away, knew I was standing close enough to touch her, knew I must be giving her a close-up inspection, knew what I was seeing and the effect it would have on me.

I suddenly wondered if she wanted me to touch her.

Maybe pull her against me and kiss her.

Prove to her that *she's* the one I care about – not Billie or Kimberly.

We *used* to kiss, back before we embarked on this excursion that somehow turned her into a monster. Kissing was *all* we used to do in the sex department. Hug and kiss, but no feelies below the waist, front or back, and her chest area was totally off limits. It got to be enormously frustrating and annoying.

I'd been all set to dump her, but then she'd invited me on the trip.

Now, she seemed to be waiting for me to *do* something.

Frankly, I didn't much want to kiss her.

You have to like somebody for that to be any good.

What I *wanted* to do was hook my fingertips under each of her breasts and give the elastic strip a big tug toward the sky so they'd leap out like they did by the campfire the night of the ambush.

With or without Billie watching, I couldn't pull a stunt like that.

Connie opened one eye slightly, to see what I was doing.

I said, 'See ya,' and started to back away.

Both eyes open, she took a small step forward and muttered, 'Yeah, go on and run away like a . . .'

'I'm just fucking off. Isn't that . . .?'

'LOOK OUT!' Billie shouted.

The Hunt (Part Three)

As Billie shouted her warning, a rock the size of a coconut came straight down as if carried over the falls by the stream's current. I saw it an instant before it hit Connie. It struck the side of her head, then crashed onto her left shoulder.

The way her head jerked when the rock hit it, you'd think she'd been swatted by a baseball bat. Her hair flew. Her face shook. When the rock pounded her shoulder, she was knocked to the left. Half a second later, she dropped under water.

Billie and Kimberly were both yelling, but I'm not sure what they said.

I ducked and grabbed Connie under the armpits and hauled her up. She felt limp. Her head lolled sideways and water slopped out of her mouth. Her eyes were open, but rolled upward so that only the whites showed, mostly. Blood mixed in with the water running down the left side of her head.

I dragged her through the water, over to the place where she'd put her T-shirt. Then I thrust her up and backward, trying to sit her on the slab of rock. I couldn't get her high enough for that. But she started to slump backward, so I let go of her sides and hugged her around the thighs and hoisted her again. This time, I got her rump up there.

Kimberly arrived. 'Stay with her,' she gasped, then hurled herself out of the water and went scurrying up the rocks. She rushed for the top of the falls.

She didn't have a weapon.

I stood in the water, holding Connie by the legs so she wouldn't slide back into the lagoon. Before I had a chance to think about what to do next, Billie showed up. She brushed past me and climbed onto the slab. Kneeling by Connie's side, she leaned over and pinned her down by the shoulders. 'Got her,' she gasped.

Kimberly, near the top of the falls, raced out of sight.

146

I boosted myself onto the rock.

Kneeling on both sides of Connie, her mother and I lifted and dragged her until she was flat on her back. 'That's fine, that's fine,' Billie said. She sounded almost calm. 'You're gonna be fine, honey. Everything's fine.'

I wasn't so sure about that.

Connie was out cold, and bleeding from the side of her head. She was alive, though. Breathing. With so much bare skin showing, you couldn't miss all the parts of her that rose and fell. Here and there – at the side of her neck, just under her sternum – I could even see her skin throb with her heartbeat.

'What'll we do about her head?' I asked.

'There's her shirt.'

I was almost kneeling on it. I snatched up the sopping T-shirt, folded it into a big, thick pad, and pressed it against the bloody side of Connie's head.

She moaned and started to turn her head away.

Billie put a hand against the other side to hold it steady. 'That's all right, honey,' she said. She began crying softly. With relief, I guess, because Connie had moaned – a good sign. 'You'll be fine, honey.' She sniffed a couple of times. 'You had an accident, but you'll be fine.' With the hand that wasn't holding Connie's head, she wiped her eyes. She said to me, 'Do you think her shoulder's broken?'

The top of Connie's shoulder had a nasty abrasion. She looked as if she'd skidded across a sidewalk on it, rubbing it raw. The shoulder didn't appear to be swollen much, though, or knocked out of shape.

'I don't *think* it's broken,' I said. 'Not that I've had that much experience with broken bones.'

Connie squeezed her eyes tight and bared her teeth and moaned again.

Billie clutched the girl's good shoulder. 'You're gonna be fine, honey.' To me, she said, 'Thank God you were with her. She might've drowned.'

I shook my head. 'That rock was just there, all of a sudden,' I said. 'I didn't have time to *do* anything about it. If I could've

147

pushed her out of the way, or something . . . I just stood there like a jerk.'

'You were great,' Billie said. 'It happened too fast, that's all.'

'Did it just *fall*, or what?' I asked her. 'Did you see?'

'It rolled off the edge of the falls.'

'By itself?' I asked.

'Not hardly. I don't think so, anyway. I think somebody threw it – or rolled it. Somebody up at the top of the falls, but far enough back to stay out of sight.'

'Wesley or Thelma.'

'I should think so.'

'How is she?' At the sound of Kimberly's voice, I raised my head and saw her trotting down the slope.

'She's banged up pretty good,' I said. 'She's coming around, though.'

'She'll be fine,' Billie said.

'What'd you find up there?' I asked.

'Nothing.' Kimberly squatted down for a better look at Connie, and her bare arm rubbed against mine. 'How are you doing, Con?'

The answer she got was a groan of pain.

'She's so thick-headed,' Kimberly said, 'the rock probably didn't even dent her.'

Connie murmured, 'Fuck you.'

With that, I'm sure we all figured Connie was well on her way to recovery.

'You didn't find *anything* up there?' Billie asked.

Kimberly shook her head. 'I didn't do much searching, though. Just took a quick look around, then tried to see if I could find any footprints. Nothing. I wanted to get back and see how Connie was doing. And I didn't want to get myself jumped. There must be about a million hiding places up there. I didn't have anyone to watch my back, so it didn't seem smart to hang around.'

'I could go up with you,' I offered. 'The two of us could do a search.'

'Not gonna leave Billie and Con. Anyway, all our weapons

are over there.' She nodded toward the other side of the lagoon. 'We've taken enough casualties for one day. What we've gotta do now is get ourselves back to the beach.'

Which is what we did.

We waited a few minutes for Connie to recover some more. Then we helped her sit up. We needed a way to keep the bandage (her folded T-shirt) in place against the side of her head, so Billie volunteered my belt. While I held the bandage against the wound, Kimberly wrapped the belt around Connie's head – making passes over the top and under the chin, then fastening the buckle.

Then we lowered Connie into the water. We floated her across the lagoon on her back, and helped her out on the other side.

I was only half a help; my belt being otherwise occupied, I needed one hand to keep my shorts from falling off.

We found our stuff where we'd left it. I removed one of the tomahawks from its sling, and used the rope as a belt for my shorts. Then I refilled my pockets. (We hadn't touched the food yet, but nobody wanted any.)

It was agreed that Billie and I would work together on helping Connie back to camp, and Kimberly would take care of whatever weapons we couldn't manage. I put on my pink shirt, and stuck a tomahawk down the side of my rope belt.

Kimberly ended up in her Hawaiian shirt, with her chest crossed by rope slings, a tomahawk at each hip, her Swiss Army knife tucked down the front of her bikini pants, four spears hugged against her side with her left arm, and the ax in her right hand.

I took one side of Connie; Billie took the other. We held her by the arms.

With Kimberly in the lead, we started downstream.

Connie whimpered and groaned and sometimes cried. With Billie and I holding her steady, though, she was able to stay on her feet and support her own weight, most of the time. Every now and then, she sagged and we had to struggle to keep her from going down.

149

We stuck to the stream; it was easier going than the jungle, and seemed like the most direct route back to the beach.

Sometimes, the stream was too narrow for the three of us to walk side by side. We always managed to keep Connie up, through places like that.

We only had real trouble once. That happened when we were making our way down a fairly easy slope. We would've been fine, but some damn bird suddenly flapped up out of nowhere and crossed right in front of us. It startled the hell out of us. Billie yelped. All three of us, I think, flinched and jumped. But then Billie had a foot slip out from under her. We tried to hold each other up, but we all fell down, splashing in the shallow water and landing on the rocks of the stream bed.

Only Kimberly, a few strides ahead of us, got away unscathed.

The rest of us weren't scathed in any major way – not from that. It just added several new sore places to each of us.

Soon after that stupid fall, we hobbled out of the jungle and onto the clear, bright sand of our beach.

The big hunt was over.

We hadn't found our prey, but we'd been preyed upon.

Connie is mighty damn lucky to be alive.

All that was yesterday.

Andrew's lighter, in my pocket at the time of our fall into the stream, got soaked and stopped working. This had us very worried. A couple of hours in the sunlight yesterday afternoon dried it out, though, so we were able to get our campfire going again.

Connie is doing fairly well. The gash on the side of her head isn't large. It bled a lot for a while, then clotted and hasn't reopened. She's got quite a lump there, under her hair. She complains of fierce headaches and shoulder pains, but nothing serious has happened so far. I mean, she hasn't fainted or had dizzy spells or blurred vision.

We think she'll probably make a full recovery.

Agony, by the way, has improved her personality; she's in too much pain most of the time to be a bitch.

Also, she seems to be busy feeling sorry for herself and wanting everyone's sympathy. At least when she's awake.

She didn't have to do any guard duty last night. Kimberly, Billie and I took turns, with me taking the morning shift so I could work on my journal here.

Been writing like a madman, ever since dawn.

A while ago, Kimberly woke up. She came over to the fire and we said 'Good morning' to each other. She asked how the journal's coming along. I said, 'Fine. I'm just about caught up.'

'I hope you're making it clear that Wesley's behind all this,' she said. 'Wesley Duncan Beaverton the Third. So there won't be any doubt about who murdered Keith and Dad.'

'It's all here,' I said.

'And he's probably the one who dropped that rock on Connie yesterday.'

'Yeah.'

'You got that?'

'Sure do.'

'Good.' She shook her head. 'I'd sure hate for him to get away with this. If he ends up killing all of us, maybe that diary of yours'll be the only way anybody ever finds out the truth.'

'My God, I hope it doesn't come to that.'

'It probably won't,' Kimberly said. 'Anyway, I'm going in for a swim. Can you hold down the fort for another ten or fifteen minutes?'

'Sure.'

So then she jogged down to the shore and charged into the water.

She came out of it a few minutes ago. When she first came out, she did some push-ups on the beach. Then sit-ups, knee-bends, etc. She just now walked over for the ax. I guess she plans to swing it around, the way she did yesterday. I'm going to watch. So long for now.

Thelma's Story

And who should wander out of the jungle this afternoon but Thelma?

At the time she put in her appearance, nobody was actually keeping watch.

Billie and Kimberly were out in the water, trying to spear some fish for supper. Kimberly was going after them with Connie's special spear, while Billie stood by with the pot. They'd just finished nailing their second fish when Thelma came toward our campsite.

Connie was asleep under one of the shelters. We'd let her drink a few slugs of bourbon after lunch to ease her aches and pains. It must've helped considerably, because she zonked out. She'd been snoozing for a couple of hours by the time Thelma showed up.

I was stretched out on my back beneath the leafy roof of the other sun shelter, my head propped up by a mound of sand, my paperback held above my face with both hands. I'd been reading, watching Kimberly and Billie, reading a bit more . . .

Thelma's shout of 'Help!' startled me so much that I flinched and the book jumped out of my hands.

I flipped over onto my belly.

The paperback had landed in the sand about four feet away.

Thelma was about fifty feet away, walking slowly toward me. More of a stagger than a walk, actually. Small, stiff steps. She was bent over a little, as if cramped. Her arms hardly moved at all. She carried herself like someone who'd recently fallen down the cellar stairs, or something.

She had some pretty good damage to her face, including a shiner and a fat lip.

One sleeve was missing entirely from her blouse, leaving her right arm bare to the shoulder. The blouse was filthy, spotted with blood, and untucked so it hung down in front of her shorts.

Even though her blouse was buttoned up, I saw right away that she'd lost her bra. You couldn't miss it. She has *large* breasts. Un-leashed, they swayed and bounced, making the front of her blouse leap around as if she had a couple of wild animals trapped inside.

One bare knee had an abrasion similar to the one on Connie's shoulder.

Her hands were empty.

There was no sign of Wesley. I figured he might be nearby, though, using Thelma as a diversion while he snuck in.

Also, Thelma had given us a taste of how dangerous she could be *without* any help from Wesley.

I reached out and grabbed the ax. Hanging on to it, I crawled out from under the shelter and stood up.

She raised an open hand.

I twisted around. Kimberly and Billie were still busy fishing. Apparently, they hadn't heard the shout.

'Hey!' I yelled. 'Billie! Kimberly!'

Their heads turned. Because of the slope of the beach, I doubted that they could see Thelma. They could see me, though. I gestured for them to come out, and added, 'Hurry! Thelma's here!'

I looked over at Connie. She was curled on her right side, the same as before, to keep the pressure off her wounds. The shouting must've woken her up. Her eyes were open, watching me.

'Thelma's here,' I told her, even though I was repeating myself.

She didn't say anything. She barely moved. But her upper lip twitched slightly.

Kimberly and Billie were sloshing toward shore.

For at least a while, it would be just Thelma and me. And Wesley, if he was trying to pull off a sneak attack.

Thelma was still coming.

'Stop,' I said. 'Don't take another step.'

She stopped.

'Put both your hands up. Put 'em on top of your head.'

She obeyed. Her breasts lifted. So did her entire blouse, a little bit.

I thought about frisking her.

Not just so I could feel her up, either: the way her blouse hung down, big and loose, there was plenty of room for hiding weapons.

The other two gals would be here soon, though, so I gave up the idea of checking her.

'Do you have any weapons?' I asked.

'No,' she muttered. She had a dull, sullen look in her eyes. 'I didn't come here to cause any . . .'

'Thelma!' Kimberly blurted. I looked back and saw her break into a run. Billie hurried after her. Over at her shelter, Connie didn't want to miss out. She was getting to her hands and knees.

Kimberly raced past me, then slowed, then stopped a few strides from her sister.

Thelma started to lower her hands.

'Don't.' Kimberly jabbed out with the spear, prodding her in the ribs.

'Ow!'

'Stay put.' She held the spear in both hands, its point an inch or so away from Thelma's chest.

Billie arrived. Both of us moved in and stood with Kimberly.

'Can I put my hands down, now?' Thelma asked.

'No. Don't move. Billie, you wanta search her?'

With a nod, Billie stepped forward. She went behind Thelma. Using both hands, she started at the armpits and worked her way down Thelma's sides.

'I haven't got anything.'

'We'll see,' Kimberly said.

Billie patted the pockets of Thelma's baggy shorts. After checking around the waist, her hands moved up Thelma's front. She stayed outside the blouse, but pushed in the fabric until she met flesh. She rubbed up and down, lifted and shoved Thelma's breasts this way and that as she checked underneath and between them.

Thelma grimaced while this went on. She also winced a lot, as if she were being hurt.

'Does *he* have to watch this?' Thelma wanted to know. Meaning me.

'Make him look the other way.'

'Shut up,' Kimberly told her.

Squatting, Billie squeezed Thelma's rump, patted the legs of her shorts, and shoved a hand up between her legs. When the hand jammed against her crotch, Thelma gasped and went to her tiptoes.

'Nothing,' Billie announced.

'Okay, you can put your arms down.'

She lowered her arms.

Billie came around to the front, and stood beside me. A second later, Connie joined us. This was the first time since the attack yesterday that she'd been up and walking without any help. But she seemed to be on the verge of falling over. She leaned against her mother.

We all stared at Thelma.

Her chin was trembling. She sniffed. 'I . . . I know you're all mad at me. You have a right to be, I guess. I shouldn't have . . .'

'Cut the shit,' Kimberly said. 'Where's Wesley?'

She struggled to speak. When her voice came out, it sounded so high it was almost a squeak. 'Dead.'

'What?'

'Dead!' she blurted. 'He's dead!'

'Yeah, right,' Connie muttered.

'He is!'

'When did he die?' Kimberly asked.

'Yesterday.'

'When yesterday?'

'Morning.'

'Who did that to Connie at the falls?' Billie asked.

Thelma blinked and shook her head.

'Did you do it?'

'Do what?'

'Throw that damn rock over the falls?'

155

'No! We . . . We weren't at any falls.'

'Where were you?' I asked.

'His place. Wesley has this . . . secret place. It's past the falls. It's nowhere near the falls.'

Billie glared at her. 'If you didn't throw the rock, who did?'

'I don't know!'

'Did Wesley throw it?' I asked.

Before Thelma could answer, Kimberly said, 'He was dead by then, remember?'

'That's right,' I said.

'Which means *you* did it,' Kimberly said, and gave Thelma another quick poke with the spear.

'Ouch! Don't!' She grabbed the hurt place.

'*You* did it,' Kimberly said, and jabbed the back of her hand. The spear put a pale dent in it.

'Stop that!'

'Tell the truth.'

'Wesley made me!'

'What do you mean, he made you? He was already dead.'

'No. He wasn't. We were there. We were watching you all. We were up there above the falls, and spying on you, and he wanted to, you know, kill *him*.' She nodded at me.

'Me?' I asked.

'Yeah, you. I told him we shouldn't. I didn't want anybody else getting killed, but Wesley said he'd kill *me* if I didn't do it. What could I do? He would've *killed* me. So I went and snuck down to the stream and did it.' She glanced at Connie. 'It wasn't supposed to hit you. It was supposed to hit *him*.'

'Stupid bitch,' Connie muttered.

'I'm sorry. What can I say? I couldn't see what I was doing. Just a quick little peek or two. Somebody would've seen me up there watching, so I just had to throw it blind, and it got you by mistake.'

'Sure,' Connie said.

'It's the truth! If you think I hurt you on purpose . . . I *never* would've done it on purpose. Look what Wesley *did* to me!' She raised both hands, open fingers trembling toward her face. 'He beat me. Look how he beat me! All because I hit *you* instead of that *boy*!'

That boy.

Nice.

'He didn't want *you* getting hurt. And he wanted *him* getting killed – so when I hit you instead, he blamed me for screwing up everything. He . . . he beat me and . . .'

'Pretty damn active for a dead guy,' Kimberly said.

'He wasn't dead then.'

'Ah. So you were lying when you said he died yesterday morning.'

'It was after you all left the lagoon and everything.'

'He beat you up, and *then* he died.'

'Must've taken a lot out of him,' I said.

Glaring at me, she blurted, '*I* killed him!'

The rest of us went silent. I think we were stunned.

'What did you all think, he died from those old spear wounds? They were nothing. He was getting *over* them. *I'm* the one who killed him. You have *me* to thank for it, and nobody else.'

Kimberly looked her in the eyes and said, 'I don't believe you.'

Thelma's mouth dropped open.

'You wouldn't harm a hair on that asshole's head. He can do no wrong, as far as you're concerned. He's your god.'

'He hurt me!' she blurted. 'After I hit Connie with the rock, look what he did to me.' She gestured to her battered face again. 'And *this*!' She fumbled with the top button of her blouse, then stopped and said, 'He has to turn around.'

Kimberly gave me a nod.

I turned my back to Thelma.

A few seconds passed. Then she said, 'See? See what he did?'

Kimberly murmured, 'Jesus.'

I took a look over my shoulder.

Thelma's head was down. She had her blouse off.

Her huge breasts were striped with scratches, smeared with livid bruises. Some of the bruises were shaped like fingers;

others were crescents. From the look of her breasts, she'd been lashed by a switch, slapped around with open hands, and bitten.

Sobbing, still not raising her head and noticing me, she turned around. 'And *this*!' Her back didn't look as if anyone had slapped or bit it – just whaled the crap out of it with a switch. Her skin was streaked with threads of dry blood. She must've taken fifty lashes back there.

'And that isn't *all*!' she blurted. Keeping her back to us, she started to put her blouse on. 'I'm not gonna show . . . not gonna pull my shorts down . . .'

I took that as my cue to turn away.

'But he . . . he made me strip . . . take off everything . . . and then he beat me and beat me . . . all because I dropped that rock on *Connie* by accident . . . He didn't want her damaged. But oh, God, he was sure the hell happy to damage *me*. And he got all turned on, beating me, so then he . . . he did other things to me.'

'He raped you?' Kimberly asked. She sounded upset.

'That was . . . yeah, and worse, too.'

I looked over my shoulder again. Thelma had her blouse on, and was trying to fasten its buttons. Her eyes were red and wet, her nose was runny and her hands trembled so much that she was having real trouble with the buttons. She saw me watching, but didn't complain about it, so I went on and turned around.

'What else did he do to you?' Kimberly asked her.

'No. I can't . . . I won't tell. It's too awful. But at least . . . It wore him out. That's the good part. When he was done, he was so tired he couldn't stay awake. He fell asleep and that's when I killed him. I bashed his head in. There was a rock nearby and I grabbed it and I *bashed* his head in.' One of her hands fluttered away from her blouse. It held an imaginary rock. She raised it and hammered it down. '*Bashed* him till there was nothing left of his head but a big bloody pile of *crap*!'

Kimberly shoved her spear into the sand. She opened her arms and Thelma staggered into them. They hugged each other and Thelma bawled her head off.

Thelma on the Hot Seat

After Thelma finished her story and finally got done crying her eyes out in Kimberly's arms, we went over to the shelter where I'd been reading, and sat down on the sand. We couldn't all be in the shade, but Billie and Kimberly prefer the sun, anyway. Thelma, Connie and I got to be under the roof.

Thelma crossed her legs the best she could, and wiped her eyes. She sniffled. Then she said, 'I've just gotta tell you all how sorry I am. I just went crazy the other night.' Meeting Kimberly's gaze, she said, 'I should've let you kill him, right then and there.'

'That's for sure,' Kimberly said.

'I'm sorry.'

'I'll just bet,' Connie muttered.

'I *am*.' She glanced at the rest of us. 'Maybe I deserve getting punished for what I did. I was wrong, and stupid, and I hurt *all* of you.'

'Fucking right you did,' Connie said.

'I know, I know. But . . . I paid for it, didn't I? Wesley saw to that. He hurt me a lot worse than all of you could ever come *close* to. And I . . . even though I rescued him, *I'm* the one who bashed his brains in. So I think . . . I think I paid for my mistakes.'

'You're very forgiving of yourself,' Billie told her, perfectly calm. 'You nearly killed my daughter. You *did* mess her up badly. God only knows how long she'll be in pain from that stunt you pulled.'

'I'm sorry,' Thelma muttered.

'Sorry,' Connie said. 'Big deal.'

'What am I *supposed* to do?'

'We'll figure out something,' Kimberly told her. 'We can't just forget what you did. My God, you not only attacked us and injured us, you *betrayed* us. You went over to the enemy.

159

He's the guy who killed Dad and Keith, and you *helped* him. You're a traitor to your own family.'

Thelma started crying again.

'We can never trust you,' Kimberly went on. 'Never.'

'But . . . But I made things right. I killed him.'

'Did you?' Kimberly asked.

'Did I what?'

'Kill him.'

'Yes!' She sobbed a couple of times. 'What do you think, I'm *lying*? I made it all up?'

'It's crossed my mind.'

'You . . . you saw what he did to me!'

'That's no proof you killed him.'

'What kind of . . . proof do you need? Do you wanta see his body?'

'Until I *do* see his body,' Kimberly said, 'I'm assuming he's alive.'

'This is the same guy,' I pointed out, 'who tried to make us think he'd blown himself up with the yacht.'

'It smells like a trick to me,' Billie said. 'I don't think she killed him.'

'She didn't,' Connie said. 'No way.'

Thelma wiped her eyes and uncrossed her legs. 'Let's go,' she said. 'I'm ready.' She sniffed. 'I'll take you there now, and you can see for yourselves. You'll . . . you'll see I'm not a liar.'

'Not a liar?' Kimberly curved a corner of her mouth. 'Give me a break. You lie like a rug. Do you think I've got amnesia? I grew up with you. My Christ, you lied every chance you got – even when you didn't have any *reason* to lie.'

'You're full of it,' Thelma said.

'The question isn't whether you're a liar, the question is whether you're lying about Wesley being dead. And the consensus is, yes.'

'Well, you'll just *see*.' She scooted backward to get out from under the shelter. 'Let's go. Come on. You'll see.'

'No hurry,' Kimberly told her.

'Well, maybe *I'm* in a hurry.' No longer crying, she now seemed to be in a huff. 'Nobody's gonna believe me, and you're all gonna keep on treating me like some kind of a leper till this is settled.'

'Nobody's treating you like a leper,' Kimberly said.

'You're not a leper,' Billie said.

'You're a traitor,' Connie said.

'That's exactly right,' Kimberly said. 'A traitor. But we're giving you the benefit of the doubt because you're my sister.'

'What benefit of the doubt?'

Kimberly paused a moment, then said, 'We probably *ought* to execute you.'

'What!'

'Kill you. The way I see it, you committed a capital offense when you helped him escape from our ambush. If you weren't my sister – and Dad's daughter – I would've probably killed you by now.'

Thelma suddenly looked as if she might throw up. 'You're kidding,' she murmured.

'Do you think so?'

Connie smirked and said, '*I* don't think she's kidding.'

'We're being easy on you,' Kimberly went on. 'We're giving you a second chance. But you'd better not be lying about Wesley.'

'He's dead and I killed him! I'm not lying about that! If you don't believe me, let's go right now!'

'Maybe tomorrow,' Kimberly said.

Which took us all by surprise.

'Or the day after tomorrow,' she added.

We all stared at her.

'Shouldn't we get it over with?' I asked. 'I mean, it'll be really nice to know for sure. If he *is* dead, we won't have to worry about him sneaking up on us . . .'

'*I'd* sure like to know,' Billie said.

Thelma brightened. She obviously had the impression we were on her side. 'See?' she said. 'They're for going now.'

'We haven't heard from Connie yet,' Kimberly said.

Connie grimaced. 'I'm not going anywhere. Are you kidding me?'

'Is it okay if we leave you here?'

'Alone? I can't stay here alone. This whole deal might be a trick. Maybe the minute you're gone, Wesley comes out and *gets* me.'

'Don't worry,' Billie told her. 'We won't leave you by yourself.'

'I'm *not* going with you looking for his body. I can't. I'm too . . . I feel like shit.' She fixed her eyes on Thelma. 'Thanks to you, you stupid fuck.'

'I'm sorry.'

'Sorry. Can't *tell* you how much "sorry" helps the throbbing *pains* in my head and neck and shoulder and arm and . . . I'm one big fucking pain from head to toe, thanks to you. So don't give me "sorry". Piss on you.'

Kimberly held up a hand. 'We won't make you come with us,' she said. 'Not in your condition. And it'd be stupid to leave your mom or Rupert behind to protect you. We don't want to be splitting up our forces like that. What I suggest is that we stay put. We wait a day or two before we go out and . . .'

'A day or two!' Thelma blurted. 'That's ridiculous!'

Kimberly raised her eyebrows. 'He isn't going to walk away, is he?'

'No! Of course not!'

'If you hadn't busted up Connie with that rock, we could go right now.'

Thelma scowled.

'So we'll wait until Connie can travel?' Billie asked.

'Yep.'

Billie smiled. 'That sounds like a pretty good idea.'

'Thanks.'

Connie, an oddly sly smile on her face, added, 'It'll give Wesley time to die.'

We all looked at her.

'We don't really believe she killed him,' Connie explained, 'but we *know* he's badly hurt. Maybe he's *not* getting better. Maybe he's getting weaker all the time, and has some infections setting in. I mean, that could happen to me, you know? Which is what made me think of it.'

'It won't happen to you,' Billie told her. 'You're going to be fine.'

'Yeah, I guess. I'm not too worried. But I have all you guys sort of taking care of me. Wesley doesn't have anyone. We've got Thelma, so she isn't there to help him. Long as we've got her, he's on his own. If we give him enough time, maybe he'll just waste away and die without us ever having to touch him again.'

'That's right,' Kimberly said. 'But even if he isn't wasting away, it might screw him up if we don't come looking for him right away.'

'He'll think something went wrong,' I added.

Billie grinned. 'Something *did* go wrong.'

'You're all crazy,' Thelma said. 'He's dead.'

'He'd better be,' Kimberly said. 'That's another thing about our waiting period – it'll give you time to reconsider. Maybe you'll want to change your story.'

'There's nothing to change.'

'You'd better think about that. If you *didn't* kill him, you'd better let us know before we pay a visit to his body. If we get there and find out you've led us into a trap, there's gonna be hell to pay.'

'I'm not lying.'

'In the meantime, we can't exactly treat you like one of the gang. Go get some rope, Rupert, would you?'

'From the tomahawks?'

'No, we'll need to keep using those. Bring over what's left of the hanging rope.'

'What're you gonna do?' Thelma asked.

I'd started to scoot out from under the shelter, but I didn't want to miss anything, so I stopped.

'Tie you up,' Kimberly answered.

'Tie me *up*?' Thelma sounded shocked.

In a calm voice, Billie explained, 'You're his accomplice. What do you expect?'

'I *killed* him.'

'Yeah, right,' Connie said.

'Rupert,' Kimberly said. 'The rope?'

'Oh. Okay.' I went ahead and left them. I ran across the sand, found the remaining length of rope among the supplies, snatched it up and hurried back toward the shelter.

Approaching it, I heard Thelma complaining, '. . . stayed out in the jungle by myself, if I'd known you were going to treat me like a criminal.'

'Maybe so,' Kimberly said.

'You should've,' Connie said.

'You want to do the honors?' Kimberly asked me.

'Sure.' I ducked under the roof.

'Go ahead and tie her hands in front, for now. We'll see how it goes. If she gives us any trouble at all, we'll put 'em behind her. Do you hear that, Thelma? You don't want them behind your back, do you?'

'No.'

'Then you'd better cooperate.'

I knelt in front of Thelma. She glowered at me and held out her hands. I bound them together, wrapping the rope around her wrists, going in and out between them in a figure-eight pattern. I made it tight enough to keep her secure, but tried to avoid cutting off her circulation.

When I was done, a lot of rope was left over.

I picked up the hanging tail. 'What about this? Should we cut it off? I could tie it around her feet, or . . .'

'Maybe just let it hang,' Billie suggested. 'That way, we'll have something to grab hold of if she tries to run.'

'A leash for the bitch,' Connie said.

'You're all just horrible,' Thelma said. 'How can you do this to me? I know I made a little mistake, but . . . I'm all beat up. It isn't fair. You saw what he did to me. How can you tie me up? I saved you. I saved you all from Wesley, and . . . you're treating me this way. You're horrible.'

'Why don't we put a gag on her?' Connie suggested.

'No!'

'Then do yourself a favour,' Kimberly said, 'and stop whining.'

Thelma shut her mouth and turned its corners down.

Soon after that, we broke up. Thelma wanted to lie down,

so Kimberly, Billie and I led her over to her sleeping place. We helped lower her onto the bed of rags. She curled on her side. With her tied hands up close to her chin, she looked like she was about to start praying. But then she plucked up the end of a beach towel – one of the several towels we'd brought along on the picnic – and covered her face with it.

'Don't get up without asking,' Kimberly told her.

'Go away and leave me alone,' Thelma said through the towel.

Kimberly crouched beside her. 'Look,' she said, 'cut the attitude. We're being damn nice to you, under the circumstances.'

'Like fun you are. Am I supposed to be grateful . . .?'

With the flat of her open hand, Kimberly smacked her on the side of the head.

Thelma let out a startled yelp.

In a slow, steady voice that wasn't like anything I'd ever heard from her before, Kimberly said, 'You brought Wesley into our lives, sister. We warned you about him. You wouldn't listen. You thought he was *so* damn wonderful. Now, my husband is dead. Dad is dead. It's all because of Wesley – and Wesley is because of you. Do you get it? *You* did this to us! *You!*'

She gave Thelma's head another slap.

Billie put a hand on Kimberly's shoulder.

Kimberly raised her head. Her eyes were brimming with tears. As she looked up at Billie, she blinked. Tears spilled out and trickled down her face.

It's amazing to see Kimberly cry. She is so tough, most of the time. But when she weeps, it's like watching a heartbroken kid trying to act brave.

I choked up, myself, at the sight of her tears.

It made me remember Keith's funeral, and how I'd sung 'Danny Boy' like some sort of idiot, and how she had hugged me afterward.

The best hug I've ever had. All sloppy and sentimental, but coming from the most beautiful woman I've ever known – not to mention that Keith's shirt was open so I could feel all that bare skin against me, and the soft push of her breasts through her bikini.

I wonder if I'll ever get another hug like that from her.

Who knows? There's always hope, I guess.

I'd really like a lot more than a hug. I'd like her to fall madly in love with me, and seduce me.

Fat chance of that happening. I'm not much of a prize. Gals who look like Kimberly don't give guys like me a second glance.

Though, who knows? As long as we're marooned on this island, anything is possible. I am, after all, the only living male. (If you don't count Wesley.) Maybe, eventually, all three of the gals will get after me.

Who am I kidding?

Anyway, it's nice to imagine. Except that the fun of imagining such things has sharp edges that hurt.

With me as the only guy on the island, these gals would probably turn to celibacy or lesbianism before they'd throw themselves at my feet. That's the kind of luck I have with babes.

What got me started off on this tangent, anyway?

Kimberly crying.

I would've liked to kiss the tears off her eyes.

Licked them off her cheeks.

Licked her *everywhere*.

I just stood there watching. She'd hardly begun to weep before she stood up, brushed the sand off her knees, and wiped her eyes. 'Keep an eye on her, Rupe,' she told me.

'I will.'

Billie still had the hand on her shoulder.

Together, they turned away and headed for the water. They went back to spear-fishing. Connie had already returned to her shelter, and was lying down. I went to mine, took out my journal, and got down to business.

I started to write about Thelma coming out of the jungle.

But I was facing the inlet, which put Thelma behind my back. So I changed positions, turning sideways. Now, I've got Thelma off to my left, Kimberly and Billie in the water to my right, and Connie straight in front of me.

Connie is lying on her side, like before.

Facing me.

She is probably suspicious of the fact that I turned myself in her direction. It would never occur to her that I did it in order to keep Thelma in sight. She is sure to think I'm ogling her.

Every so often, she has opened her eyes and sort of gazed across the sand at me.

She hasn't said anything, though.

No 'What're *you* looking at!' No 'Fuck off!'

Getting beaned by Thelma's rock really took the starch out of her.

I ought to give Thelma my thanks.

Anyway, I'm all caught up, now.

Day Seven

My Visitor

With Connie out of commission and Thelma as our prisoner, the watch duty last night was being divided among me, Billie and Kimberly. Last night, they gave me first watch.

I stayed by the fire. After everyone else went to bed, I had nothing to do except sit there, sometimes toss in some driftwood, and keep watch.

I sat with my back to the inlet. That way, nobody would be able to come out of the jungle and sneak up on the gals without me spotting him.

I kept wondering if Wesley was really dead.

He had sure done a number on Thelma, no question about that. An awfully good reason to kill a guy, even if you weren't especially bothered by the fact that he had murdered your own father.

I sure hoped she'd done it. If Wesley was dead, I could stop trying to spot him sneaking through the dark toward where the gals were asleep. I could stop glancing over my shoulder every few minutes to make sure he wasn't creeping toward my back.

I kept wishing we'd gone ahead and checked on the body, right after Thelma came in and told us about it.

Then we'd know by now, one way or the other.

On the other hand, some of us might be dead right now. Especially me.

I'd always figured I was next on the list. It stood to reason, considering that Wesley had killed off both the other males almost as soon as we got to the island. But now we'd had it confirmed by Thelma. Over at the falls, Wesley had given her orders to nail *me* with that rock.

Sitting there by the fire, though, I wasn't especially worried about myself. The danger to me didn't seem as important as my duty to watch over and protect the women. I felt very protective of them.

While they were asleep and I was on guard, they were my flock.

I occupied my mind, now and then, with some gallant fantasies about rushing to their rescue. With other fantasies about them, too. I won't get into that stuff.

Anyway, about an hour into my watch, Thelma came over.

When I first saw her getting up, I thought she might be making an escape attempt. Instead of running for the jungle, though, she stepped cautiously away from the sleeping area, and walked toward me. The leftover rope hung between her legs and dragged behind her.

None of the others stirred. Which convinced me that they were asleep. Kimberly would've raised holy hell if she'd seen Thelma up and around. The same goes for Billie and Connie.

Looking back on it, that's what *I* should've done – raised holy hell.

It's what I *almost* did.

My first inclination, when I realized none of the others would be putting a quick end to the situation, was to shout for Thelma to halt.

A shout would bring the whole gang running. (Except maybe Connie.)

But I kept quiet.

No need to wake everybody up. I can handle this on my own.

That's what I told myself.

It wasn't the whole reason I didn't shout, though. There was also the fact that I was curious. What did Thelma have in mind? Why was she coming to me? I wanted to find out.

As she walked closer, I grabbed the ax, stood up, and stepped around the fire so it wouldn't be in the way if I needed to get at her. I held the ax in both hands, at waist level, to let her see that I meant business but didn't have any immediate plan to chop her.

Neither of us said anything until she was just a few paces away. Then she stopped and said, 'I couldn't sleep. I mean, I *was* asleep, but I woke up a while ago and . . . I couldn't get comfortable.' She raised her bound hands. 'I don't guess you'll untie me?'

'No, I can't.'

She shrugged and winced a bit. 'I didn't think so. No harm in asking, though. *You* oughta try to sleep with your hands tied together like this.'

'Did you try sleeping on your back?' I asked.

'On *my* back? Have you seen my back? No, I guess you haven't.'

I didn't correct her.

'Wesley whipped me. My back is so sore and tender . . . *everything* is. He really hurt me, Rupert. He hurt me *everywhere*. There *is* no comfortable position to lie in. It's a wonder I was able to fall asleep at all.'

'I'm sorry about that,' I said.

'It's not your fault. I'm the one that was fool enough to marry him.'

I said, 'Well . . .'

'Anyway, that's all over and done with, now. The thing is, would you mind a whole lot if I just stayed here for a little while? I won't cause any trouble, I promise. I just *can't* go back there and lie down. All I do is toss and turn . . . it's just so miserable. Can I stay with you? Please?'

A. She *had* to be in a lot of physical discomfort. She wasn't lying about that.

B. What could she do to me? Her hands were tied and I had the ax.

C. I could always shout if she tried to pull a stunt.

D. I was *still* curious. Did she have some sort of secret reason for coming over? Did she have a trick up her sleeve? Just exactly what *would* happen if I let her stay? Maybe something interesting, or even exciting.

Not to mention that I really wanted to ask her about a few things.

'Okay,' I said. 'You can stay, but just for a while.'

'Thanks, Rupert.' She sounded sincere. 'You're sure a life-saver.'

'One condition, though,' I told her.

Some of her friendliness suddenly evaporated. 'What's that?'

'You have to answer me, no matter what I ask you.'

She blew out some air. 'Oh, forget it. I thought you were different from them. You're just like them, aren't you? For once, I thought somebody was being nice to me around here.'

'All I want to do is find out a few things. What's the big deal?'

She took a deep breath and used it to form a long, annoyed sigh. 'Everybody wants to give me the third degree.'

'Maybe you'd better just go back to bed,' I said.

'No, no, no. I'll talk. Whatever you want. Lord knows, why should you be any different from the bitches? What do you want to know?'

'Let's sit down,' I said.

I went back to my place at the other side of the fire, sat down, crossed my legs and rested the ax across my thighs. I told Thelma where to sit: in front of me but over to my left, facing the fire. That way, we didn't have the fire between us. Also, it would be easy to give her a nudge with the head of the ax, if she caused trouble.

'For starters,' I said, 'did Wesley tell you why he did all this?'

'Did what?'

'Blew up the boat, marooned us here, killed . . .'

'He *didn't* blow up the boat. I asked him all about that. What happened is, he smelled gas and jumped overboard just in the nick of time. He was almost killed. He no sooner got off the boat than it blew sky-high.'

'That's what he told you?'

'Yes.'

'And you believed him?'

'Why shouldn't I?'

I could only think of about a *million* reasons. 'If that's what happened,' I said, 'then how come he didn't swim in to the beach? We were all there. He knew we were there. He obviously wanted us to think he'd been blown up.'

'Well, that was the whole idea.'

'What? What are you talking about?'

'He *had* to disappear. He was afraid he'd get all the blame for the explosion. Which is *just* what happened. You heard my dad. It was all Wesley's fault.'

'And that's why Wesley pulled his vanishing act?'

'Sure. Lord only knows what you all would've done to him.'

'Yeah, Lord only knows – somebody might've called him an idiot.'

'You don't know anything.'

'Was he afraid Andrew might make him walk the plank? Or keel-haul him? Whip out the cat-o'-nine-tails?'

'There's no telling.'

'Nobody would've done anything to him, not for having an accident.'

'You haven't got a clue. You have no idea how *cruel* Dad could be. How vicious. If you knew half the things he's done . . . what he used to do to me . . . and to Kimberly, too.' She shook her head.

I suddenly found myself very interested.

'Like what sort of things?' I asked.

'Do you have any idea how *uncomfortable* it is, having your hands tied like this?' She held them toward me. 'Kimberly made the rope too tight.'

Before turning in for the night, Kimberly had freed Thelma's hands for a visit to the latrine – then had retied them.

'You knew the right way to do it,' Thelma told me. 'When you tied me, the rope didn't cut in this way. Kimberly did this to hurt me.'

'No, she didn't.'

'Look. Just look, why don't you?'

I leaned toward her and checked. The rope did appear to be awfully tight. It was making grooves in her wrists.

'Can you make it looser for me? Please?'

'I don't know. Maybe Kimberly had a reason . . .'

'She had one, okay. She just loves to hurt me. It turns her on.'

'Sure,' I muttered.

'If you make it looser,' she said, 'I'll tell you whatever you want to know.'

Naturally, I was suspicious of her motives. I couldn't get around the fact, though, that the rope was digging into her wrists.

'I'll redo it,' I told her, 'But you'd better not try anything.'

'I won't. I promise.'

I put the ax out of reach behind me, then moved in close to Thelma on my knees and picked open the knot. When the knot came apart, I began to unwrap the rope from around her wrists.

She suddenly pulled her hands free.

I was left holding empty loops of rope.

Before I could do anything, she swung both her arms around behind her back and started shaking her head. 'Please. I'm not doing anything. Don't tie me up again, okay? Please? Give me a break. I can't *stand* having them tied. Just give me a few minutes, okay? Please?'

'No. Come on, you promised.' I glanced over at the sleeping area. The gals were still down, thank God. I faced Thelma. 'You'll get me in all kinds of trouble.'

'They don't have to find out. I won't tell them if you don't.'

'Damn it.' Dropping the rope, I leaned forward on my knees and reached out and grabbed Thelma's upper arms. They were thick, but not flabby. They felt strong. Squeezing them, I tried to pull her arms out from behind her.

She struggled not to let me. After a few seconds, though, she said, 'Stop it or I'll scream.'

I let go fast.

It took a while to catch my breath. Then I said, 'Come on. If somebody wakes up and your hands aren't tied . . .'

'You'll get in more trouble than me.'

'We'll *both* be in trouble. Come on.'

'I'll make you a deal,' she said.

I picked up the rope. 'Like what?'

'Just let me stay untied for a while, okay? Just while we sit here and talk, and then – I'll let you tie them up again, I promise.'

'Somebody might wake up. And besides, you tricked me. You took advantage of me trying to do you a favor. So just give me your hands.'

She shook her head, and kept them behind her back.

'Come on,' I said. 'Please. I'll make it really loose.'

'I thought you wanted to ask me a lot of stuff about Wesley. And about Kimberly? Don't you wanta know about how Dad used to abuse her?'

'He *abused* her?'

'He used to do all sorts of things to her. To both of us.'

'Really?' I glanced over at the sleeping area. So far, so good.

'You're so worried, we'll just *pretend* I'm tied.' Thelma offered her hands. I wrapped the rope around them a few times to make it look good, but left it loose and unknotted. 'There,' Thelma said. 'Now you're covered if anyone comes snooping.'

'Just don't try anything,' I warned her. Then I went back to where I'd been sitting, sat down and put the ax across my thighs. 'What did he do to her?' I asked.

'To both of us,' Thelma said.

'Okay.'

Family Ties

'It's ... awful nasty. Sick. Are you sure you want to hear about it?'

I nodded. Already, I was feeling a little shaky inside with a mixture of dread and excitement.

'Well, okay then. You asked for it. Don't blame me if you don't like what I have to tell you.'

'I won't. I promise. Come on.'

'One thing was, he used to make us strip naked and then wrestle on the floor. We'd *all* be naked. Me, Kimberly and Dad.' She spoke in a quick, hushed voice, as if she were sharing a very juicy bit of gossip. 'He'd start off by making just me and Kimberly go at it, while he watched from the side and . . . like cheered us on, gave us orders. He'd try to get us to hurt each other. And do perverted things. Then, after a while, he'd join in.'

'Jeez,' I muttered. 'How old were you?'

She shrugged, shook her head. 'I don't know. It went on from the time I was nine or ten, all the way through high school.'

'What about Billie? They were married for . . . twenty years? She let all this . . .?'

'He never did anything in front of her. But she worked, you know. Dad found plenty of time to be alone with us.'

'Wasn't he away at sea a lot?'

'Not that much. Not *nearly* enough, if you ask me. And when he did come back from sea tours, he was worse than ever. He had all sorts of games. The wrestling was just one of them. But it was his favorite, I think. He wanted to do it whenever he had us alone. He used to get these holds on us, and make us scream. We'd be screaming and crying, squirming around with him on the floor and he'd – you know, stick his fingers in us. And his tongue. And he'd bite us.'

'Billie didn't know any of this was going on?'

'No, huh-uh. It was our dark little secret. Dad said he'd kill us if we ever told on him.'

'What about Connie?'

Thelma shrugged. 'I don't know. I stopped living at home when I went away to college. I mean, that's like twelve years ago. Connie would've only been like . . . how old?'

'She's eighteen now.'

'So that would've made her only six when I left. I know he kept it up with Kimberly after I was gone. We never talked about it, but I knew. I mean, they weren't *about* to stop. But I don't know if they got Connie doing it. It sure wouldn't surprise me, though.'

'"Weren't *about* to stop"?' You almost make it sound like Kimberly was . . . a willing participant.'

Thelma blew a huff of air out her nose and mouth. 'Kimberly *didn't* go away to college. What does that tell you? An honor student, class president, you name it, she could've gone to Princeton or Yale if she'd wanted to. But what did she do instead? Enrolled at the community college and lived at home.'

'You think she kept on *doing* things with him?'

'Hell, yes. She really got into it. The whole pain thing. Delicious pain. That's what Kimberly always called it, *delicious* pain.'

'Really?' I was a bit dumbfounded by all this. 'She hasn't got any scars. Not that I've seen, anyway.'

'No, no. Of course not. Scars are a dead giveaway. She's always been very careful not to let herself get hurt in any ways that show. You don't want people knowing about your nasty little secret life. They'll think you're a degenerate, a sicko. You know what I mean?'

'What about her and Keith?' I asked. 'I mean, she married the guy. If she was having this thing with Andrew . . .?'

'Keith was the same way.'

'*He* liked to hurt her?'

'Sure, he did. I walked in on them, one time. This was just before I got married to Wesley. I had to go to Dad's house to pick up . . . a book. I needed Billie's etiquette book for my wedding plans. And I walked into the house without ringing the doorbell. I thought nobody was home. But I heard noises upstairs, so I snuck up to see what was going on. I was afraid there might be a burglar, or something. It wasn't any burglar, though – it was all three of them in Kimberly's bedroom.'

'All who?'

'Kimberly, Keith, and Dad.'

'Having *sex*? All three of them?'

'Yes, having sex. *And* torturing her.'

'Torturing Kimberly?'

'She was strapped down to her bed, spread-eagled, and . . .'

'Never mind,' I said.

'Dad was in her mouth.'

'Cut it out. I don't wanta hear . . .'

'Keith was kneeling between her legs. He was reaching up with pilers in each hand, working on her nipples, while his mouth . . .'

'Shut up! I don't believe you. You're making it all up. Kimberly wouldn't . . . She *said* you're a liar. This is all a load of bullshit.'

'Anyway, Wesley knew all about Dad and Keith. You see? He knew what a couple of sick degenerates they were. So when the boat blew up . . . he was afraid they'd blame him and he knew how they liked to torture people. He was terrified. Not just for himself, either. He was terrified for me and Billie . . . *all* of us. Can you imagine being stranded on an island with a couple of sadistic bastards like them? He *had* to kill them.'

'So why did he want to kill *me*? I never tortured anybody.'

A strange smile tilted up one side of Thelma's mouth. The other side, dark and swollen from the beating Wesley had given her, didn't move. 'You'd like to, though, wouldn't you?' she said.

Which wasn't exactly what I'd expected her to say.

'Like to what?' I asked.

'Torture somebody.'

'You're nuts!'

'Somebody like Kimberly,' she said.

'No!'

She smirked at me. 'Who are you trying to kid? It makes you hot, just thinking about it. You'd just love to take her nipples and pinch them till she wept and squirmed and begged for mercy.'

'You're nuts.'

'Or bite them.'

'It's time for you to go,' I said. I set the ax aside, picked up the rope again, and shuffled over to her on my knees. 'Put out your hands.'

'Look at you,' she said.

She was looking at the front of my shorts.

'So what. Hold out your hands.'

Instead of holding them out, she started to unbutton her blouse.

'Stop that,' I said.

'You can pretend I'm Kimberly,' she said, and pulled her blouse open. The firelight shimmered on her huge breasts. 'Here. Feel. I know you want to. You're *aching* to.'

'No. Stop it.'

She reached under her breasts and lifted them, raised them toward me. 'Here,' she said. 'They're all yours. You want to squeeze them, don't you? And slap them around? Make them swing and bounce? Wouldn't you love to take my nipples and twist them till I cry out for mercy?'

'No.'

She lowered her breasts, but only to free her hands. Then she started to finger her nipples. She pinched them, pulled at them, twisted them. While she did it, she clamped her lower lip between her teeth. She breathed through her nose, air hissing in and out her nostrils.

I watched.

'You do it,' she gasped. 'I know you want to. You'd *love* to.'

I had to admit, I was tempted. This was sort of like the kind of thing I'd been hoping for. But only sort of. Thelma was the only woman on the island who'd never figured in my fantasies.

I couldn't help being aroused, though. She'd been talking dirty, getting me all turned on with that stuff about Kimberly, and now she was showing me her breasts. They were huge, covered with bruises and welts and scabs. They excited me, anyway.

Frankly, I was pretty disgusted with myself. And with Thelma.

I felt like, if I took her up on the offer, I'd feel very guilty and very dirty. I'd want to wash my hands afterward.

'Come on,' she gasped. 'Come on.'

'Thanks, but no thanks.'

'I'm Kimberly. Just shut your eyes, and I'll be Kimberly for you. Come on. Take my tits, and I'll unzip you and . . .'

'Forget it,' I said. 'Now stop it. Button up and hold out your hands.'

'Okay, okay. Just a minute.'

She started to get up.

'Wait. What are you doing?'

'I just want to be on my knees, that's all. I don't wanta be sitting down. It's too hard to get up once your hands are tied.'

That made sense. I waited until she was kneeling in front of me, then said, 'Give me your hands, now.'

Instead of obeying, she smiled at me, rubbed her hands down her thick belly and started to unbuckle her belt.

'Don't.'

She didn't stop. 'I'll show you what *else* Wesley did to me.'

'I don't want to see.'

'Sure, you do.'

She was right, of course.

I knew I should stop her. In some ways, though, I didn't really want to. Also, I didn't know how. If I tried anything Thelma didn't like, she might yell. The *last* thing I wanted right then, was for one of the other women to wake up and find us like this.

So I just knelt there, watching while she unbuckled her belt, un-fastened the waist button of her shorts, and pulled her zipper down.

The shorts dropped to her knees.

I expected to see panties, but didn't.

She had no pubic hair, to speak of. Just a bulging triangle with dark whiskers like a guy might get on his jaw if he goes a day or two without shaving.

Is *that* what she'd wanted to show me – where Wesley'd shaved her?

Maybe there were injuries to see, but I didn't keep looking. I turned away fast. Off beyond the fire, there was no sign of movement at the sleeping area. I thought, *Thank God*.

Somehow, I had to make Thelma stop all this.

I had to do it on my own.

Things had gone way too far. I never should've untied her hands. One thing had led to another, and now I couldn't see how to end it. Not without shouting for help.

What would they think, if they found us like this?

What I *ought* to do, I thought, is back off, get away from her, grab the ax and stand up and order her, point blank, to pull her shorts up and . . .

Something tipped me off.

I still had my head turned and was staring toward the sleeping area. I had no intention of looking in Thelma's direction again until I'd backed away. But something happened. I don't know what. Maybe I'd heard a quiet sound that didn't belong. Maybe I'd caught a movement in my peripheral vision. Sensed a change in the air. Something.

I turned my head.

Glimpsed Thelma's hand lurching up toward my belly with a straight razor.

No fooling, a *straight razor*. The kind with a blade that folds into its handle – the kind of thing that nobody in his right mind would even *own*, except a barber. Because they're so damn nasty, and it's too easy to cut yourself by accident if you try to shave with one, and you can't help but think about the sort of damage a crazy woman might do to you if she got her hands on it.

I don't know where the hell Thelma got it.

All I know is that all of a sudden I found her with the damn thing in her hand, and she was about to run it up my belly and split me open.

I let out a yelp and threw myself backward off my knees.

She missed.

I didn't feel anything, but saw her razor-wielding hand sweep up past my face as if she still had hopes of dividing my nose in half.

Then I flopped against the sand.

I shoved myself up with my elbows, not sure whether to kick at her or try scurrying away on my back.

For the moment, she wasn't coming at me. Her head was turned aside.

Was Kimberly getting up?

I didn't waste time trying to find out what Thelma was looking at. She was distracted, at least for a moment. That's what counted.

An extra second to put some distance between me and that blade.

I dug in my elbows and heels and started scooting myself across the sand on my back.

Right away, she noticed.

The instant her eyes shifted in my direction, I cried out, 'Help! Help!'

She came waddling toward me like someone whose legs had been chopped off at the knees. Her shorts were still down. They had her trapped, so she couldn't move very fast. Not fast enough to catch me as I kept scooting away.

She was a real vision.

Lurching and flopping flesh, too well lit by a long shot, in spite of the shadows – her bruised, swollen face *grinning*. She waved both arms overhead as she kneed her way after me. The razor in her right hand flashed firelight.

'You stay put!' she gasped. 'Stay put, you little cocksucker!'

I kept shouting for help.

Then I spotted the ax in the sand, not far from my left elbow. I hauled it toward me by its haft.

'Thelma!'

Kimberly's voice, an angry shout.

Thelma glanced in the direction it had come from. Gasped. Then flung herself at me.

I swung the ax as hard and fast as I could.

The flat side of its steel head struck her in the forearm.

The right forearm.

She cried out and the razor leaped from her hand.

She landed on me. Her head knocked me in the crotch. A second later, though, she rolled off. Making grunty noises, she rolled over a few times and got to her hands and knees. As she staggered to her feet, she snatched up her shorts. Holding them up with both hands, she ran for the inlet.

Kimberly went sprinting after her.

Lean and quick, dark except for the white of her bikini.

At the water's edge, she leaped and reached with both hands for Thelma's shoulders.

A great flying tackle.

Except that Thelma twisted around and smashed her elbow into the side of Kimberly's face. The blow deflected Kimberly. And dropped her. She smacked down on the water, and Thelma kept going.

I was on my knees by then, in spite of the bash to my nuts. I turned to look for the others.

Back at the sleeping area, Connie was sitting up and staring in my direction. Of course, she was too battered to come running to the rescue. And Billie didn't dare leave her behind. Billie, on her feet, a spear in her hands, was standing ready to fight in case Wesley should spring an attack on her and Connie.

I got to my feet and hurried toward the inlet.

Thelma was lunging through thigh-deep, black water. I couldn't see her very well. Suddenly, I thought she was coming *back*. Which scared the hell out of me. I stopped short. I fought with an urge to turn around and make a run for it.

If I ran, she would finish off Kimberly.

I had just decided to go back for the ax and fight to save Kimberly when I realized that Thelma was smaller than before. Nothing showed below her waist – because she was in deeper water. She wasn't returning. She'd been wading away, the whole time.

I hurried to help Kimberly.

She was on her hands and knees, head hanging, her face a few inches above the surface of the water. When I reached her, she didn't look up.

'Are you okay?' I asked.

She didn't answer.

'Kimberly?'

'Go and get her,' she muttered. 'Don't let her get away.'

I looked for Thelma. At first, I couldn't find her. Then I spotted a dim shape way out near the point.

'She's awfully far away,' I said.

Kimberly muttered, 'Damn it, Rupert.'

'I wouldn't be able to catch her.'

She groaned.

'Can I help you up?' I asked.

'Don't touch me.'

She sounded disgusted.

'I'm sorry,' I said.

'You're sorry, all right. Jesus H. Christ.'

'I almost got killed.'

'That would've been a big loss.'

Man. I was beginning to wish Thelma *had* killed me.

'Okay,' I said. 'I'll go after her. If that's really what you want. What do you want me to do if I catch up to her? Am I supposed to try and bring her back? Or do you want me to try and kill her? Maybe I'd better take along a knife, or something. Can I have your knife?'

Head still hanging, Kimberly said, 'Forget it. Just forget it. Go to bed, or something. Shit.'

I'd never felt so low. I mean, you could tell she was completely disgusted with me and thought I was a waste and a loser.

Which is true. I am.

I decided to follow her advice, and go to bed. The problem with that, though, was Billie and Connie. They were there waiting for me, and I was crying pretty good by then. I just couldn't help it.

'What happened?' Billie asked. She didn't sound disgusted with me. She sounded like she cared.

'I'm sorry,' I said. 'Thelma got away. I let her get away.'

'Neat play,' Connie said.

'Hush up,' Billie said. Then she poked her spear into the sand and came over to where I was standing and put her arms around me.

It was one of the nicest things anyone has ever done.

She was all soft and warm and gentle, stroking my hair with one hand and my back with the other while I cried against the side of her neck. She kept murmuring, 'It's all right, honey. It's okay. Everything's fine.'

She's the best woman I've ever known.

I calmed down pretty soon, thanks to Billie. Then Kimberly came along, so I got out of Billie's arms and turned around to face the music.

'Are you okay, Rupert?' she asked.

'No. I really screwed up.'

'You're not hurt, though?' I shook my head.

'How the hell did she get loose?' Connie asked.

'I . . . I untied her hands.'

'You outa your fucking mind?'

Billie put a hand on the back of my neck, and rubbed me.

'We'll talk about it in the morning,' Kimberly said. 'Everybody go back to sleep, now. I'll keep watch.'

'I'm sorry,' I told her.

'What's done is done,' she said. Then she turned away and walked back to the fire.

That's about it for last night.

More than enough, if you ask me. Aside from the fact that so much happened – good stuff and bad stuff and some very weird stuff – it's taken me most of the morning to write it down.

And I'm not even caught up yet.

The Inquisition

Anyway, I had all last night to worry about explaining the fiasco with Thelma. I wanted to make up a good story about it, so I wouldn't look totally stupid and gullible and perverted.

Also, there was a whole lot I didn't want to talk about.

But I couldn't concentrate very well. I was lying there on my 'bed,' trying to focus on coming up with a good lie, but all I could think about was what had *actually* happened. I kept reliving everything in my head. Not just remembering, but sort of *feeling* most of it – the confusion and fear and excitement and revulsion and arousal and terror – though in milder forms than when all of it was going on for real. And in jumbled order.

I couldn't even get away from Thelma by falling asleep. My nightmares were *worse* than what had really happened. I don't remember much about them, just that they had a lot to do with sex and razor blades, and that they were awful.

I was glad when morning came, so I wouldn't have to suffer through any more nightmares.

After everybody was up, we gathered around the fire and ate the last of the canned ham for breakfast.

Have I mentioned the canned ham before? It was one of the things Keith and Andrew salvaged after the explosion. We got into it for the first time a few days ago when we didn't have any fish. Anyway, now it's gone – and we're starting to get low on things to eat.

We'd started off on the trip with a *lot* of stuff, a great deal more than eight people could hope to finish off during a week at sea. The explosion happened when we still had four days left, and I guess that Keith and Andrew recovered about half of the food that was left. Including some good stuff like the canned ham.

They didn't fare nearly so well with the drinks – we must've had enough soda, beer and hard stuff on the boat to keep an army happy. All that survived the explosion, though, were a few bottles of booze. (Nothing carbonated – soda, beer and champagne – survived the explosion. They all blew.)

Anyway, I'd say we were pretty lucky to end up with as much as we did.

For most of the time here, there have been only four or five of us to share it. We eat fish whenever possible. So we've stretched out our food supply pretty well. It should last a few more days, if we're careful. Then we'll have to concentrate on fishing, hunting, gathering edible fruit and vegetables from the jungle, etc.

That shouldn't be much of a problem, except that we have

to contend with Wesley and Thelma. With them out there, getting enough food isn't exactly on the top of our priority list.

Man, this was a lengthy digression. I think I'm loopy from so much writing today.

After we finished the ham, it was time for the Inquisition.

'You want to tell us what happened last night?' Kimberly asked.

'Not especially,' I said.

Nobody appeared amused.

I sighed. 'Where do you want me to start?'

'Why did you untie her hands?'

Relief. An easy one. 'I had to. You know how you untied her before she went to the latrine last night? Well, when you tied her back up again, you made the rope too tight. It was digging into her wrists.'

Kimberly frowned at me. 'That's nonsense.'

'It isn't. I checked. The rope was way too tight.'

'Not when *I* tied her up. I was very careful . . .' She glanced from Billie to Connie. 'Did either of you retie her last night?'

Billie shook her head.

'If I was gonna do anything with her rope,' Connie said, 'I would've strangled her with it.'

'Maybe *she* tightened the rope,' Billie suggested. 'Did it herself, so she'd have a reason for asking Rupe to untie it.'

'How could she do that?' Connie asked.

'With her teeth?' Billie said.

'I guess it's possible,' Kimberly admitted. She frowned as if thinking for a few seconds, then said, 'Shit, it sounds *exactly* like something she might pull. She goes around acting like a lame-brain, half the time, but she can be . . . crafty. Very crafty. She used to be, anyway. Maybe she's changed, but I doubt it. Once a sneak, always a sneak.'

'What sort of things did she do?' I asked. I was somewhat interested in hearing about Thelma's sneaky ways, but mostly I hoped to delay the interrogation.

'She was always doing stuff. But . . . one time when she was pissed off at me, she chopped up her *own* Barbie doll – cut off

189

its hands and feet and head – and hid them under *my* mattress. Then she acted all innocent, went around and asked Dad if he'd seen her Barbie doll anywhere. When it finally turned up, I caught living hell.'

'From your mother?' Billie asked.

Kimberly shook her head. 'From Dad. This was after Mom had died, and before he met you.'

'Did he beat you?' I asked. I was suddenly breathing harder than a second ago, and my heart was thudding.

'Who?' Kimberly said. 'Dad?'

'Yeah. You said you caught living hell.'

'Right.' She looked a bit offended. 'He didn't *beat* me, though. Are you kidding? Dad? He gave me a *talking to*. Which made me feel lower than a snake, and I hadn't *touched* the damn doll. You should've seen Thelma. She was so proud of herself for pulling it off and getting me in hot water.'

'Did you get even with her?' I asked.

Kimberly gave me an odd look – as if she suspected that something was up. 'Yeah. What're you getting at?'

I could hardly force the words out, but I managed. 'She said you used to beat her up.'

'What?'

'That you'd . . . you were always forcing her to wrestle with you. You'd throw her down on the floor and put head-locks on her . . . make her cry out for mercy . . . stuff like that.'

Kimberly smirked and shook her head. 'She would've liked that.'

'You didn't wrestle with her?'

'She's five years older than me. She always outweighed me. And she had a cruel streak. There's no way I ever would've wrestled with Thelma. The one time we actually had a fight, I pulled her hair and she stabbed me in the arm with a pencil. It went *in*. I had to go to the doctor and get shots.'

'She said you used to wrestle with her all the time.'

'Really?'

'Yeah.'

'Maybe in some alternate universe.'

I was tempted to go on and explain that they'd been naked and their father had joined in – that the matches were supposed to be some sort of sadistic sexual romp.

Already, though, I figured Thelma must've made up the whole wrestling business.

'So you two were over here last night talking about make-believe wrestling matches between me and Thelma?'

'Yeah.'

'Why did she tell you that stuff?'

'I don't know. We were just talking.'

I felt sort of cornered, and wished I hadn't brought up the subject. It was a relief, though, to discover that Thelma'd been lying. If she'd lied about the wrestling, it stood to reason that the torture and incest stuff probably hadn't really happened, either.

I felt a little cheated, a little disappointed. Part of me had gotten sort of excited, picturing Kimberly mixed up in that sort of thing. Mostly, though, I was relieved.

'She must've had a motive,' Kimberly said.

'Not that I . . .'

'I know,' Connie said. She gave me one of her snotty looks. 'I bet Thelma was trying to get him to wrestle with her.'

I almost denied it. But the idea seemed to have some merit. I sure didn't want the truth coming out. 'Well . . . That's sort of . . . She *did* want me to have a wrestling match with her.'

'What on earth for?' Billie asked, half of her mouth rising in a crooked smile as if she were amused but baffled.

'She made it a challenge,' I explained. 'If she won, I'd have to let her get away. If I won, she'd let me tie her hands back up. See, she'd pulled them away when I tried to loosen the rope for her.'

'That's when you should've called for help,' Kimberly said.

'Sure, and have everyone think I was some kind of a worthless jerk for being dumb enough to untie her.'

Kimberly grimaced a bit. She lowered her eyes and looked ashamed. She didn't actually apologize, but she regretted being so sharp with me last night. You could tell.

'Boy,' Connie said, 'that Thelma read you like a book.'

I looked at her and didn't make the mistake of asking, 'What do you mean by that?' I kept my mouth shut, but it didn't help.

Billie asked, 'What do you mean?'

'She knew just which buttons to push. Amazing. Rupert's got sex on the brain. There's no way in the world he's gonna miss out on the chance to wrestle with a woman.'

I felt like my face might go up in flames. I said, 'That's bull. We're talking about *Thelma*. God Almighty, she's the *last* woman I'd ever want to wrestle with.'

'Yeah, right.'

'She's disgusting.'

'As if you'd let a little thing like that get in your way.'

'Yeah,' I said, 'look at you.'

'Go fuck yourself.'

Kimberly raised a hand. 'Let's not get sidetracked here, kiddies.'

Connie sneered at her and gave her the finger.

Kimberly ignored it. To me, she said, 'So, did you agree to have this wrestling match?'

I frowned and tried to decide on the best way to answer. After a while, I said, 'Well . . . she pushed me into it. She called me a chicken, and said I was too much of a wimp and a loser to beat her in a fair fight.'

'So you went for it?' Kimberly asked.

'I had to.'

Billie sighed. 'You didn't have to prove anything to Thelma. She was just manipulating you.'

'I guess . . . Well, not all the way. I mean, at first I agreed to wrestle her. But then she started to take off her clothes. She wanted us doing it naked.'

'You figured you'd died and gone to Heaven,' Connie said.

'I did not! I told her no. I said the deal was off, there wouldn't be any wrestling match, and I wanted her to hold out her hands so I could tie them. She wouldn't listen, though. She didn't pay any attention, and started taking off her clothes. It was like we were going to wrestle, no matter what I said. Before I knew what was happening, she had her blouse wide open and her shorts down. I didn't know what to do.'

'Probably had a boner on you the size of the Washington Monument.' Connie said that. Who else?

'I did not.'

'Yeah, right.'

'Leave him alone,' Billie told her.

'The thing is, that's when I knew it had all gone too far. I started backing away from her. I was planning to go for the ax, and *make* her quit messing around, but all of a sudden she attacked me with a straight razor. She almost killed me.' I met Connie's narrow eyes. 'If you don't believe me, we can probably find the razor. I knocked it out of her hand. It's probably in the sand around here someplace.'

Kimberly, who was wearing Keith's Hawaiian shirt this morning, slipped her hand into its left breast pocket and pulled out the razor. She flipped the blade open.

Billie pursed her lips and made a 'Whuuu' sound.

I grimaced, myself, getting a good look at it in daylight and realizing how close it had come to slicing me up the middle.

'Has anyone ever seen this before?' Kimberly asked. She held it between her thumb and forefinger so that we could see the handle – which looked like mother-of-pearl.

Connie shook her head.

Billie said, 'Wicked-looking thing.'

'Do you recognize it?'

'Me? No. I haven't seen a razor like that in years. My father had one that folded like that, but his had a green handle.'

'How about you, Rupert?'

'I saw it last night. When she came at me with it.'

'It's probably Wesley's,' Connie said.

Kimberly nodded. 'Maybe. It might even be Thelma's, for that matter.'

'She didn't have it when I frisked her,' Billie said. 'I couldn't have *missed* a thing like that.'

'Well,' Kimberly said, 'she sure got hold of it somewhere.'

'Why didn't she just *use* it?' Connie asked.

'She tried,' I pointed out.

'No, I mean to cut herself loose?'

'Maybe she couldn't get to it while her hands were tied,' I suggested.

'But she must've gotten her hands undone *before* she came over to you,' Billie said. 'If we're right that she'd retied the rope to make it too tight, she would've probably had to *un*tie it first.'

Connie scowled. 'This is getting too complicated.'

'Yeah,' I said. 'We've got her untying her hands so she can tie them more tightly so she can come over here and trick *me* into untying them for her. That doesn't make any sense at all.'

'Yeah. It does.' Kimberly nodded and nibbled her lower lip for a few seconds. Then she said, 'Yeah, it makes a lot of sense. We've been looking at it wrong. This wasn't about Thelma getting herself untied so she could escape. This was about killing Rupert.'

'Terrific,' I said.

She raised a finger. 'Here's what I think happened.' Looking at me, she said, 'Back at the lagoon, Thelma tried to kill you by throwing that rock over the falls. She missed you, and hit Connie by mistake.'

'That's according to *Thelma's* version of what happened,' Billie pointed out. 'Might not be the truth.'

'Whatever Wesley has in mind, he wants all the men dead first. That's how I see it,' Kimberly said. 'The thing is, he was too injured to try for Rupert, himself, so he ordered Thelma to do it. She screwed up and hit Connie. Then – her story – Wesley trashed her, so she killed him and came back to join up with us. I don't think so.'

'You don't think he *trashed* her?' Billie asked.

'Somebody sure did,' Connie said.

Kimberly nodded. 'Yeah, Wesley probably did it to her. Or some of it. I bet most of it was self-inflicted.'

'Would she *do* that?' Billie asked.

'Beat herself up? Maybe. I don't know. It wouldn't surprise me.'

194

'You think she's a masochist?' Billie asked.

Connie snorted. 'She's gotta be, she married Wesley.'

'She couldn't have *bitten* herself in all those places,' I pointed out.

'Not in all of them,' Kimberly said. 'I think it was probably a joint effort. The beating was supposed to be Thelma's excuse for killing Wesley, so it had to look good. She almost *had* to do some of it, herself. The beating was just too severe for Wesley to manage it by himself. In his condition? He might've given her some bites, but he couldn't have slapped her around and whipped her like that. She had to do that to herself. Most of it, anyway.'

'Sick,' Connie said.

'It was her ticket into our camp,' Kimberly pointed out. 'She could come in, show us those terrible wounds, and we'd be all set to believe she'd paid Wesley back by killing him.'

'But we didn't believe her,' I pointed out.

'No. Not entirely. I had my doubts all along that Wesley could've done that to her. But what *I* suspected – and I think the rest of us did, too – was that she'd been sent in here to set us up. If we believed her about killing Wesley, we'd let our guard down. That'd leave us open for a surprise attack. We also suspected that she might try to lead us into an ambush when we went looking for Wesley's body.'

'Right,' Connie said.

'But we were wrong. Completely wrong. She didn't come in to distract us or lead us into a trap so Wesley could nail us. You know what it was? From the very start? It was a one-woman mission to take out Rupert.'

'Kill me?'

'Right.'

'What does it mean?' Billie asked.

'Means, for one thing, Rupert's a very lucky fellow.'

'That's me, lucky.'

'Also means that Thelma's in this all the way with Wesley. She's perfectly willing to commit murder for him. She's a lot more dangerous than we thought.'

'And trickier,' I said.

'I always knew she was tricky,' Kimberly said. 'I just didn't know she was homicidal.'

Billie, frowning, shook her head. 'Do you think she was in on it with him?'

'In on what?'

'Setting us *all* up. Blowing up the boat. Trapping us here. Is it possible that Thelma helped Wesley plan it? I mean, I'm beginning to wonder. For that matter, maybe this whole thing was *her* idea.'

'I tend to doubt it,' Kimberly said. 'She might be a hell of an actress, but I think she really and truly believed that Wesley got killed in the explosion. She didn't know what was going on. She just got into this whole mess when she found us trying to ambush her husband. That's the way I see it, anyhow.'

'If Thelma *wasn't* in on the plan,' Billie said, 'then all this was Wesley's idea like we thought in the first place. So how does Thelma fit into it?'

I saw where she was heading. 'If we're right about Wesley's motives,' I said, 'she'll be killed like the rest of us.'

'He can't possibly let her live,' Billie added.

'That'll be her tough luck,' Kimberly said. 'But he won't kill her as long as he has uses for her. And maybe he doesn't intend to kill her at all. We *suspect* he's doing all this so he can be the sole survivor and inherit and so forth, but we don't really know *what* the hell his reasoning is. Or what to expect from him.'

'I expect he'll try to kill me again,' I put in.

'I suspect you're right,' Kimberly said, and smiled at me. 'We'll try not to let that happen.'

'Thanks,' I said.

'So, what do we do?' Connie asked.

'Nothing,' Kimberly said. 'Not today, anyway, You're in no condition to go on another hunt for those two. I'm sure Rupert has a lot of writing to do in that diary of his.'

'Big deal,' Connie muttered.

'It is a big deal,' Kimberly told her. 'I want him to keep current with it. I want there to be *something* – a record of what's happened here. In case we don't make it.'

'That's a laugh. I'm *sure* Wesley's gonna kill us all and then let Rupert's little *diary* incriminate him. Are you kidding me? He'll burn it.'

'Thanks, Connie,' I said.

'Oh, get real.'

'Anyway, I'm not planning to get killed. I'm gonna make it out of here – I hope we all do. And then I'll find a publisher. We'll be famous. I'll make a ton of money. And everybody who reads my true-life adventure book will see just what a bitch you are.'

'Maybe I'll burn it myself.'

'Just try, and see what . . .'

'Knock it off,' Kimberly said. 'Both of you.'

'And *you* leave Rupert's diary alone,' Billie told her daughter.

Her daughter said, 'Yeah, right, take *his* side, why don't you?'

That was pretty much the end of the conference. It hadn't turned out so badly, after all.

Being the intended target of Thelma's hit, I came out of things looking a lot better than expected. I was now the survivor of an assassination attempt, not the dork who'd let Thelma escape.

I couldn't help feeling a little scared, though.

It's one thing to have somebody pull a razor on you because she's your prisoner bent on making a getaway. It's a whole different ballgame if she dropped in on us with a battered body and a load of lies just so she could get close to me, late at night, and rip me open.

I'm damn lucky to be alive.

Day ?

Anybody's Guess

Musings on My Return
to the Journal

It's where I left it. So I've opened it. So now I'm writing again.

I don't know why I'm bothering.

Except, like Kimberly said, we've got to have a record of what's been happening here.

Maybe the cops'll get their hands on it, someday.

Yeah, right.

Do they have cops in this goddamn armpit of the universe? Do they have *anyone*?

I know one thing: I don't ever want to see this thing get published. Not anymore. Not after what happened.

'After *what* happened?' you ask.

I don't *know* what happened.

It has been a few days since my last entry in the journal. I think. I'm not sure how long it's been.

I just now turned back a couple of pages to read what's there and refresh my memory. It's almost like somebody else wrote them. Wrote them a long time ago. Years ago. So much has changed.

I'm embarrassed to see what I wrote.

Example: *I expect he'll try to kill me again.* The placement of *again* makes it sound like I've already been killed once. But that isn't the real problem. (One can't be held accountable for the grammar of dialogue, right? And who gives a rat's ass, anyway?) The real problem is my cavalier, jaunty fucking attitude. Ah, yes, my good Wesley? He'll likely make another try for me. Tut, tut. Have to be on my guard, won't I? Have to remember to duck.

Well, here's news.

It wasn't me he got.

It was them.

Kimberly, Billie and Connie.

They're gone with the fucking wind, and I'm not. I'm here, back at the beach, writing in my journal, alive and well and alone.

I'm not planning to get killed.

Another gem from my previous entry.

Talk about arrogance.

Talk about being the prime asshole of the world.

Talk about prophetic.

Of course, I don't actually know if the women have been killed. I think it's likely, but I'm not sure. I know some of what happened, but not everything. They were still alive when I went down, but what happened to them afterwards?

I don't know.

I know they're gone, though.

I can't handle this. I'm going for a swim. Maybe I'll be lucky and a shark'll eat me for dinner.

War Party

This is the next day.

I was too messed up to do any more writing yesterday. I went for a swim, like I said. The sharks didn't get me, though. I didn't see hide nor hair of any sharks.

I did consider suicide, though.

One of those really cool, melodramatic suicides like you've seen in a billion crappy movies – where some idiot goes swimming off into the sunset. The deal is, I guess, you keep swimming away from shore until you get too pooped to make it back. So even if you eventually change your mind, you're history.

There are several reasons why I didn't do it.

A. Drowning sucks.

B. Being dead sucks.

C. Being the lone survivor is *not* a fate worse than death.

D. I'm not one hundred per cent sure that all the gals are dead.

E. If I kill myself, I won't be able to do any of the things that I want very badly to do to Wesley and Thelma.

F. Like it or not, I do feel a certain obligation to play Ishmael and tell thee, to be the Horatio of our noble, lost band and report our cause aright to the unsatisfied. Other than *not* kill myself, what I did yesterday is of little consequence. I swam, I ate, I wept, I slept.

Today, I'll tell what happened to us on day eight.

As much as I know, anyway.

Day six was when Thelma returned, battered and claiming that she'd killed Wesley. That night, she went at me with her razor. Then she escaped by swimming away.

Day Seven, we did a lot of talking about what had happened on Night Six. And I did a lot of writing about it. Other than that, nothing of consequence happened. Connie's injuries were the main reason why we didn't take any action. She seemed to be getting better, though.

Nothing happened that night.

Day Eight, Connie was still sore but she was ready for action. We all were. We knew it was time to go after Wesley and Thelma.

We hoped that Wesley was already dead.

We were fairly sure that Thelma had lied about killing him, just as she'd lied about nearly everything else. We thought there was a good chance, however, that Wesley had died from the wounds he got on the night of our ambush. Kimberly had put her spear through his left tit, and she'd rammed a hole into his ass. As a result of those wounds, he could've died from blood loss or from infection.

If he wasn't dead, we figured he might at least be incapacitated.

On the other hand, maybe he'd recovered enough to be a real threat to us.

We'd discussed every possibility that we could think of.

We'd concluded that *anything* was possible, but that we were more likely to have trouble from Thelma than Wesley.

We set out at mid-morning.

Kimberly wore Keith's Hawaiian shirt over her white bikini. She carried her tomahawk on its rope sling. The Swiss Army knife puckered out the front of her pants. The spear was in her left hand.

Billie wore her same black bikini and no shirt, of course. Her chest was crossed by ropes. The single line of the tomahawk sling swept down from her shoulder to her right hip. The remains of the hanging rope (which we'd used for tying Thelma's hands) crossed her from the other shoulder. It was long enough to make three loops. We'd decided to bring it along in case we took a captive.

Though Kimberly was the one with Indian blood in her

veins, Connie looked more the part. Because of her headband. She wore it to hold the bandage in place against her wound. The bandage was a pad of cloth made from her old T-shirt. The T-shirt had been ruined, anyway, so Billie had washed it in the stream and cut it up.

Connie also wore a vest. She'd made it herself, using my razor on day seven to cut it out of a beach towel. It had yellow and white horizontal stripes. Even though it didn't weigh much, it helped to hold a bandage down against her left shoulder. It also protected her shoulders and upper back from the sun, though it had no sleeves and was so short that it left her arms and lower back exposed. Not to mention her rump, which was as good as naked in that thong.

Before we set out, I offered to spread some of Billie's sunblock on her butt. She told me to fuck off. (Like I said, she was feeling better.)

The vest couldn't be shut in front, but the towel panels covered her breasts – her *real* reason for making and wearing the thing, more than likely. To keep them out of my sight. To taunt me and punish me.

Logically, she should've made herself a skirt, too. But she didn't. Did she think I had no interest in her lower regions? It didn't make any sense, really. But then, you could go crazy trying to make sense out of Connie.

She was sure good to look at, though. They all were.

To think that I might never see any of them again . . . It isn't fair. I know this is a terrible thing to write, but I feel cheated.

They're dead, and *I* feel cheated.

Sooner or later, maybe one of them would've . . . either fallen for me or gotten so desperate . . .

Maybe not. We'll never know.

What is for sure, though, is that they aren't here to *look* at, to daydream about, to talk with, to sometimes hold.

Which makes me realize that I've had hugs from all three of them, at one time or another.

I've seen Billie's breasts and Connie's, but never Kimberly's. Now, I never *will* see hers. Along with all the other things I'll never . . .

* * *

I had to stop writing for a while.

It depressed me too much – to put it mildly. I miss them so much. I can't stand the thought that they are dead.

I don't know for sure that they *are* dead.

A big mistake, around here, to assume that *anyone* is dead.

What I need to do is find them. I need to know whether they are dead or alive. If they're alive, they are almost certainly being held captive. Maybe I'll be able to rescue them. If they're dead, I'll . . . I don't know what. In either case, though, I have to kill Wesley and Thelma.

I should be out searching for them right now, not sitting here on the beach.

But I want to bring the journal up to date first. That way, in case I don't come back, there will be a record.

Back to the story.

I'd been telling about Connie's towel-vest. Because of the injury to her left shoulder, she wore the rope of her tomahawk sling on her right shoulder. The rope crossed her chest, and the tomahawk hung by her left hip. In her left hand, she carried her spear – the special, wicked one she'd made for fishing.

As for me, the day seemed too hot for Billie's pink blouse, so I went without it. I wore Andrew's khaki shorts. I haven't worn my swimming trunks since the day I started wearing Andrew's shorts. I like having the pockets, and the shorts are so big and roomy that they give me plenty of freedom. I wore shoes and socks, too, by the way.

I haven't written much about footwear. That's because it doesn't interest me much, and so far it hasn't been of any great importance. We all had shoes to wear. Sometimes we wore them; sometimes we went barefoot. Not much else to say on the subject.

For weapons, I had the ax in both hands, a tomahawk at my hip (stuck under my belt, which I'd gotten back after the loan to Connie), and Thelma's straight razor. Kimberly thought I should get to keep the razor. For one thing, it was the weapon I'd almost gotten murdered with. For another, even though Kimberly had actually found the razor where it had fallen in the sand, she pointed out that I'm the one who'd knocked it out of Thelma's hand.

Besides, Kimberly had her Swiss Army knife, Connie didn't even want to *touch* the razor, and Billie thought I should keep it because I was obviously the one in the most danger.

Wrong.

We were so damn wrong about that.

Anyway, I had the razor safely folded inside the right front pocket of my shorts, along with Andrew's lighter and Billie's plastic bottle of sunblock. (My other front pocket bulged with chucks of fish that we'd smoked overnight and wrapped in some leftover cellophane.)

So that's pretty much the way we were – how we were dressed and armed and so on – when we set out on the morning of day eight to hunt for Wesley and Thelma.

We'd agreed to try our luck at the lagoon. It seemed the most likely place to find them.

But Kimberly said, 'This way,' and started walking toward the inlet.

We went after her.

'Where are we going?' I asked.

'We shouldn't look like we're on our way to the lagoon,' she said.

'Are you kidding?' Connie asked. 'Who do you think is *watching*?'

'Probably no one. But maybe Wesley or Thelma.'

'Give me a break.'

'We'll just go up the shore for a while, make them think we're off to explore the island.'

'Then what?' Connie asked. 'Sneak around *behind* the lagoon?'

'Yep,' Kimberly said.

'Fabulous.'

'I think it's a good idea,' I said.

Connie gave me a sneer. 'You would.'

'Look what happened last time,' Billie told her. 'We don't want to repeat the same mistake. If we come in from the back, maybe we'll take them by surprise.'

'I think it's stupid,' Connie said. 'We'll probably get lost.'
She was outnumbered.

With Kimberly in the lead, we climbed the ridge of rocks just to the north of our beach, made our way down to the other side, and hiked along the shoreline.

Connie glanced back, now and then. 'How far are we gonna go?' she asked.

'Let's make it around that point,' Kimberly said.

It was pretty far off.

Connie wrinkled her nose.

'If anyone's watching,' Kimberly explained, 'they'll think we're trying to circle the island.'

'Maybe we *should* circle the island,' I said.

'Some other time. First, we've gotta take care of Wesley and Thelma. They're too big a threat. After we've killed them, we'll be able to explore the island to our heart's content. What we'll do, as soon as we get to the other side of the point, is take cover in the jungle and make our way back till we're sure of our bearings . . .'

'Why don't I just wait for you here?' Connie offered.

'You're not helping matters,' Kimberly said. 'We know you're hurt, but . . .'

'But you're gonna make me walk a few extra miles, anyway.'

'What *about* trying to circle the island?' Billie asked Kimberly. 'It might not be a bad idea.'

'It's a *fine* idea,' Kimberly said. 'For some other day.'

'No, hold on. Except for a couple of short little trips into the jungle, we've been cooped up on that beach ever since we got here. We don't know *what* we might find.'

'Probably the dinghy,' I said.

Connie stopped glowering. 'Yeah! If we find the dinghy, we can get outa here.'

'This might not even *be* an island,' Billie said. 'How do we know we didn't land on . . . the end of a peninsula, or something?'

'It's an island,' Kimberly said. 'Dad was showing me the charts the night before we got here.' She nodded. 'We're nowhere near any mainland. Nothing for miles around but scads of little islands.'

'Well, that was just . . . I *know* we aren't on a continent or something. But we don't know *what* island this is, or how big it is. It might very well be inhabited. We might even find some sort of town.'

'And police,' Connie said. She was perking up. In spite of her injuries, she would apparently be delighted to walk for miles in search of the dinghy or a precinct house.

Billie nodded. 'It couldn't hurt to just keep going on the beach and *see* what . . .'

'Be my guest,' Kimberly said. 'I'm not interested. The rest of you wanta bail out on me, that's your problem. I don't care if there's a metropolis around the corner, I'm going into the jungle after Wesley and I'm not coming out till I've got his head.'

I couldn't help it. I gave her a buggy-eyed stare and said, 'His *head*? You mean, like, figuratively speaking?'

She just looked at me.

Which was all the answer I needed.

I muttered, 'Jesus.'

Billie had that look on her face – a mixture of amusement and disbelief. 'You're not *really* planning to cut off Wesley's head?'

'He killed my husband and my father. You know how we towed Dad's body out? I'd like to swim out to exactly the same place with Wesley's head, and let it sink there in the same place so Dad'll see that I took care of business.'

I didn't like the sound of that.

I wanted Wesley dead, too, but it disturbed me to find out that Kimberly had come up with such a bizarre, grisly plan. She'd obviously given it a lot of thought.

It seems she had depths of creepiness I had never even guessed at.

Connie, too, seemed impressed. With a look on her face as if she'd just encountered a little green man, she did a brief rendition of *The Twilight Zone*'s music – 'Doo-*de*-do-do, doo-*de*-do-do.' I'd heard her do that before, but never an impression of Rod Serling (or anyone else, for that matter). 'One Kimberly Dickens, cheerleader, prom queen, loving daughter and faithful wife. She came to a tropical island in search of a picnic, and found instead that she had slipped into a netherworld of primitive . . .'

'Knock it off,' Kimberly said.

'Hey, you're talking about de*capi*tating someone.'

'You have a problem with that?'

'Not with that, with you. I mean, you're creeping me out. You start talking about taking a guy's head off – even *his* – and it starts making me wonder if you've lost a few screws.'

Kimberly frowned at her, then shrugged. 'You're probably right, I shouldn't go around saying stuff like that.' She glanced at each of us. 'I guess maybe I got carried away. I'm not missing any screws. A couple of them might be slightly *loose*, but . . . don't worry, I haven't gone crazy.'

'I've had some pretty horrible thoughts, myself,' Billie said. 'Things I'd like to do to Wesley. Some of them are a lot worse than chopping his head off.'

'Me, too,' I said.

'Well, so have I,' Connie admitted. Meeting Kimberly's gaze, she said, 'The difference is, *you* mean to do it.'

'I don't know,' Kimberly said. 'I guess we'll see, won't we?' With that, she turned away and continued walking.

Billie, Connie and I gave each other looks.

Kimberly had spooked all three of us.

None of us talked much, after that. Connie didn't even raise any more complaints.

Our silence must've bothered Kimberly. After a while, she frowned over her shoulder at us. 'What's the matter with you people?'

Billie just shook her head.

'Nothing,' I said.

'Nope,' said Connie, 'nothing wrong here.'

Kimberly turned around and walked backward. 'You people! For God's sake, I was *kidding*. Okay? Christ! You'd think I was foaming at the mouth! I'm not gonna cut off anybody's head, okay? I didn't *mean* it. I never should've said it. Now you all think I've flipped out. Anyway, as a matter of fact, *so what* if I wanta cut off his head? You think he hasn't got it coming? He chopped Dad's head *in half*. In my book, anything he gets is better than what he deserves. If we're lucky enough to catch him alive, what we *oughta* do is skin him. We oughta spend a few days killing him a little bit at a time, make him scream till he's hoarse, make him beg for death. If you think cutting his *head* off is extreme, just wait and see what I do to him *before* I take his head. He's gonna pay big-time for murdering Dad and Keith. If you think I'm mad now, just wait and see. You've got no *idea* what I'm capable of.'

The three of us gaped at her.

She suddenly swung out an arm as if trying to bat away a trio of pesky flies. 'Get out of here. Leave me alone. *I'll* take care of Wesley and Thelma. I don't need the three of you hanging around . . . You're all useless, anyway. None of you has got the stomach for what's coming, so get outa my face. Go! Get outa here!' She swung her arm again, then spun around and took off running.

'Don't!' Billie yelled. 'Hey! Wait up!'

'Ah, let her go,' Connie said.

'Kimberly!' I shouted.

She kept running.

Billie took off after her.

'Mom!'

Billie didn't stand a chance of catching up with Kimberly, so I joined the chase. Even lugging the ax with me, I was able to gain on Billie. But Kimberly, faster than both of us, kept drawing away. And I could tell that she wasn't even running full tilt.

Connie shouted at our backs, 'Damn it! Come back! Are you *all* out of your fucking minds?'

Billie, still slightly ahead of me, glanced over her shoulder. So did I.

Connie just stood where she'd been. We were leaving her quite a distance behind us.

Billie stopped running.

I dodged to keep from crashing into her.

'Leave the ax,' she gasped at me. 'Get her. This is . . . gotta stop her.'

I let the ax fall to the sand. Then I put on all the speed I could muster. As I dashed after Kimberly, I yelled, 'Quit it! Come on! We're with you! Slow down! You're not crazy! Please! Stop running! Please! We wanta go with you!'

A lot of good my shouting did.

It was a waste of breath, so I quit yelling.

Soon, I found myself gaining on her.

She must've been *allowing* me to gain on her.

Not to catch her, though.

She let me approach to within about three strides behind her, but no closer.

I watched the way her black hair streamed behind her. I watched how the seat of her bikini pants, visible under her flapping shirt tail, moved with the flexing mounds of her buttocks. And how her slender legs strode.

As she ran, she held the spear low by her left hip, its shaft parallel to the sand, while her right hand held the tomahawk against her side to stop it from flinging about and pounding her right hip.

Though she didn't pump at all with her arms, she raced along swiftly enough to stay ahead of me.

After a while, she said, 'Give it up, Rupert. Go on back to them.'

'I'm coming with you.'

'Forget it.'

'Just stop and wait,' I gasped. 'You're the one . . . always against us . . . splitting up. We . . . gotta stay . . . together.'

'You'll get in my way,' she said.

'No. Please.'

'I'm gonna do Wesley *my* way. Don't wanta hear you guys whining about it.'

'We . . . won't whine.'

'Forget it. You had your chance. *Adios, amigo.*'

She started to pour it on. I made a dive for her.

My fingertips brushed the flying tail of her shirt. Moments later, both my hands buried themselves in the sand. They shoved ditches into the beach as I flopped on my chest and skidded.

The landing knocked my wind out.

I lifted my head and watched Kimberly sprint up the beach. Spear raised high, she pumped it up and down as she dashed along like a Zulu on the attack.

Missing People

On my hands and knees, I watched Kimberly until she vanished around the point. Then I stood up, brushed the sand off my body, and started trudging back to Billie and Connie. Billie was a couple of hundred yards away from me, Connie another hundred yards or so behind her mother.

The way we were separated, any one of us could've gotten picked off. Keeping an eye on the edge of the jungle, I quickened my pace.

Connie made no attempt to join us. She just stood where she'd stopped, and watched.

When I got within speaking range of Billie, I started shaking my head.

'You almost had her,' Billie said.

'It only looked that way. She slowed down to let me get close.'

'I can't believe she just ran off and left us.'

'She wants to go on by herself.'

Billie handed the ax to me. 'We can't let her.'

'We can't stop her,' I pointed out.

'But we can join her.'

'I guess so. If we can find her.'

'She's on her way to the lagoon,' Billie said. 'We'll just go there.'

We started walking toward Connie.

'What route should we take?' I asked.

'What do you think?' She wasn't being sarcastic; she was asking my advice.

'Well, we could circle around through the jungle, but that's what Kimberly's probably doing. I don't think we'd have any luck intercepting her, either. It'd be too easy for her to sneak past us. So maybe we oughta just go ahead and make a direct approach to the lagoon.'

'Go straight up the stream?'

'Yeah. That'd be the quickest way to get there. We might even reach the lagoon ahead of her.'

Billie made a rueful smile. 'Ahead of her? Think we wanta do that?'

'If we're careful.'

'I'd hate for us to get attacked without Kimberly around to help.'

I shrugged. 'We can probably handle it. I mean, we're talking about Wesley and Thelma. Unless they take us completely by surprise . . .'

'What gives?' Connie called to us.

'Kimberly doesn't want us in her way,' I explained.

'Is she still going to the lagoon?'

'Guess so.'

'Good. We can go back to camp now, right?'

'Sort of,' I said.

'What do you mean, *sort* of?'

'We'll go back,' Billie said, 'but then we're heading straight up the stream.'

'Oh, really?'

'That's the idea,' Billie told her.

'I've got a better idea,' Connie said. 'Let's *not*, and say we did.'

We reached Connie. Then the three of us started walking back toward camp.

'I mean,' Connie said, 'Kimberly obviously doesn't want us with her. Shouldn't we do what she wants, and stay out of it?'

'She'd be outnumbered two to one,' I pointed out.

'That's just assuming Wesley hasn't already bought the farm.'

'Even if he *has*, what's to stop Thelma from jumping her?'

Connie smirked at me. 'You think Kimberly can't take Thelma?'

'Sure, in a fair fight. But maybe she gets jumped from behind. Thelma almost nailed *me*. She isn't that easy.'

'Well, she knew which buttons to push on you, didn't she?'

'There's no point arguing,' Billie broke in. 'We're going up to the lagoon, and that's final.'

'Is it?'

'Yeah, it is.'

'We'll see about that.'

Billie gave her an annoyed glance, but said nothing. For a while after that, none of us spoke.

We were nearly back to our camp when Connie said to her mother, 'It sure is nice to know you care more about Kimberly than you do about me.'

'Don't give me that,' Billie said.

'I've got a splitting headache – and my shoulder's killing me. I'm an absolute wreck, but you're gonna make me hike all the way up to the lagoon just to help Kimberly – who doesn't even *want* our help.'

'But maybe she needs it.'

'Shit, she ran *away* from us. Why should we wipe ourselves out when she doesn't even . . .?'

'You know why,' Billie told her.

'I do? Really? That's news to me.'

'She's your sister, for one thing.'

'My *half*-sister.'

'Oh, that's nice. Very nice. If your father could hear you say that . . .'

'Well, he can't. And I don't appreciate you throwing him in my face all the time.'

'He's your father *and* Kimberly's.'

'Big deal.'

'If you don't come with us,' Billie said, 'I can't go. I'm not about to leave you by yourself.'

'Fine.'

'You *have* to do this for her.'

'Yeah? Do I? And what'd she ever do for me?'

They glowered at each other.

'Practically *raised* you, maybe?' Billie said.

'Oh, for God's sake . . .'

'Stayed *home* instead of going away to college. Because of you.'

'She didn't have to do that.'

'No, she didn't *have* to. She wanted to.'

'Didn't wanta miss out on all those fine opportunities to boss me around.'

I couldn't help it. I asked, 'Why *didn't* Kimberly go away to college?'

'She wanted to stay with the family,' Billie explained. 'She never came straight out and said so, but that was the reason. We certainly could've *afforded* to send her anywhere, and she had the grades. I think it was almost entirely because of Connie.'

'My fault.' Connie raised her hand.

'Not your "fault." You were . . . ten or eleven at the time. When Kimberly was just about your age, a year or two older, maybe – that's when Thelma went off to college. Kimberly always . . . She loved Thelma so much. It hurt her so much when Thelma left home.' Billie's eyes filled with tears. She sniffed, wiped her eyes, and said to Connie, 'She just couldn't . . . put *you* through that. You two were so close. She knew how you would miss her.'

Now, tears began to glimmer in Connie's eyes. 'So it *was* my fault.'

'Don't be silly. She loved you, that's all. She didn't want to leave you without your big sister. And she would've missed *you* too much.' Billie looked at me and wiped her eyes. 'That's why,' she said.

I came out with a lame, 'Oh. Just wondering.'

Billie was done crying, but Connie kept it up for a few more minutes. When she finished, she sniffed and rubbed her eyes and said, 'I *still* don't think Kimberly needs any help from us, but I'll go along. I mean, what choice do I have, anyway? It's not like you're gonna let me stay here by myself while *you* two run off to save her bacon. As if her bacon *needs* any saving. I just hope we don't screw things up for her, that's all.'

The surprising thing is that, after all her complaints, Connie ended up taking the lead. She seemed to be in a hurry, too.

Billie's talk must've gotten through to her, somehow – reminded her that Kimberly was more than just a young woman put on this earth to annoy her, boss her around, and turn the heads of her boyfriends.

Leading us upstream through the jungle, it was as if Connie had magically forgotten to be self-absorbed – as if all that mattered was the bond between her and Kimberly.

She could be a wonderful human being for short periods of time.

I'd seen it before. It wouldn't last. But it was nice to see, on the rare occasions when it happened. I found myself actually *liking* Connie again.

Not that I'd ever stopped liking her body. From the neck down, she'd always been really fine. Her face wasn't bad, either. Behind her face is where the troubles lurked – inside her mouth, and in her brain. Her words and her thoughts. And, of course, the actions that came from the thoughts.

I liked *all* of Connie, though, as she led us up the middle of the stream that day.

And she actually did stay that way.

She never got a chance to revert.

The self-centered, whiny, pushy, obnoxious bitch had taken her last bow.

In a way, I almost wish she *hadn't* turned into a caring, decent person for her last hour or so. Might be easier. Maybe I wouldn't miss her so much, now. On the other hand, it's sort of nice – even wonderful – that she wasn't being a shit toward the end of things.

God, I miss her.

I miss her almost as much as I miss Billie and Kimberly.

No, not really. Who am I trying to kid?

I miss Connie a lot, but I miss Billie and Kimberly worse. It kills me to think that I'll never see them again.

And yet, here I sit.

Writing in my journal instead of going to find them.

Why is that?

Simple. If I go looking, I might get killed. God knows, I barely escaped with my life last time.

I'm fairly safe here.

Wesley and Thelma probably think I'm dead. At least for the time being.

Also, there's one other thing.

I really do not want to find any of my women dead.

Which is what might happen if I go looking.

I'd hate that.

It's better, not knowing. This way, I can at least hang on to the possibility that they might not be dead.

Or not *all* of them.

If even just one of them is still alive . . .

If I had to choose one, I wonder which would it be? Not Connie, I'm afraid; she was a bitch too much of the time. Not nearly as attractive as her mother or half-sister, either. She was better than plain, but both of them were beautiful.

So it's between Billie and Kimberly.

It would be sick for me to choose which of them should die. So let's say this: which would I rather have living with me till we get rescued from here?

(If we ever *do* get rescued, which is seeming less likely all the time. God, what if I have to live the rest of my life on this island without any of them? Just me. Never mind. I want to go on with my game of who to pick.)

Kimberly or Billie?

Not an easy choice.

Kimberly is a hothead, sometimes. She can be awfully tough and scary, and would definitely take charge of everything. She would run my life. Which might not be such a bad thing.

Billie is more easy-going and sensible. She's sweet, cheerful and compassionate. She wouldn't push me around. We'd be like great friends. We already are – were – awfully good friends, I think.

Obviously, the smart pick is Billie. We'd be great together. Making love with her would be incredible, too. She has a fabulous body, and knows it, and would probably relish the chance to share it.

I'd give anything, though, for just one time with Kimberly.

Who am I kidding? How about one time with *anyone*?

Losers can't be choosers.

Speaking of losers, I should stop playing games and go out and try to *find* Kimberly, Billie and Connie.

Not yet. I can't go and look for them until I've caught up on my journal. It might be the only way anyone will ever be able to learn what has happened here.

And it gives me an excuse to stay put.

Also, the writing of it helps me to remember them. I describe what they did, what they said, what they wore and how they looked, and it's almost as if they're with me again.

I have them with me whenever I write about them.

Hey, here's a thought. Maybe I'll *never* stop writing about them. When I catch up to the present, I'll just start making things up. Just to keep going.

My journal can turn into the literary equivalent of the Winchester House. I just keep going, building more rooms for my ghosts.

Not a bad idea, but I don't have a hell of a lot of paper left. When I run out, I'll start writing in the sand.

Here lies one whose name was writ in sand.

That was somebody's epitaph, I think. Keats?

This is far off the track, and getting weird. I'm too tired and way too depressed to go on any more right now. Anyway, it's almost dark.

I'm going to quit now.

Tommorrow will be plenty soon enough to finish off what I can remember about how we got creamed. Then things will be up to date, and then I'll have to figure out what to do next.

Build a staircase to the ceiling, perhaps???

Oh, God.

I wonder if they *are* dead.

If not, what the hell is happening to them – being *done* to them – while I sit here lonesome on the beach fucking around with this stupid journal???

Night Journey

This is the next day.

Last night, I got brave. Or, more likely, just desperate.

So this chapter won't be about our 'last stand', after all.

Fine with me. I'm not exactly looking forward to the task. I will get to it, but not right now.

Instead, this chapter will be about what happened last night.

After dark, I snuck upstream for a look at the scene of the crime.

It started out as a way to stop feeling like such a worthless loser. I was taking action. I would stalk the night, revisit the places that held such horrible memories, *face* what had happened to us, and search for answers.

Maybe I would find my women alive, and rescue them.

Maybe I would find their bodies.

Maybe I would come upon Wesley and Thelma, and slit their throats.

I had my razor.

I was Rambo.

I was Rambo until I left the beach behind. The moment I waded upstream into the shadows of the jungle – and out of the moonlight – I stopped being Rambo and became Chicken Little. I could see almost nothing, just a few pale speckles and scattered tatters of dim light that somehow made it down through the trees.

I was tempted to turn back. If I went on, I would probably fall in the dark and bust open my face.

I went on, anyway. Taking tiny steps. Hunkering down low so I wouldn't have so far to fall. Keeping both my arms forward to catch myself.

That way, I made slow progress up the stream.

I fell several times, banging up my hands and knees but not getting hurt in any serious way.

Frequently, I stopped to rest, stand up straight, and stretch to get the kinks out. Then I'd bend over again and continue on my way. In spite of the rest stops, all the bending tired me out and made me ache. I finally decided to take my chances and walk upright.

It felt good, walking tall.

I had farther to fall, and the falls hurt more, but I felt sort of proud of myself. I stayed high and even quickened my pace.

Sometimes, I felt as if Billie, Kimberly and Connie were walking with me through the night. I couldn't see them, but they were there. In front of me, behind me, wading by my side.

Other times, I felt alone.

Worse than alone. There can be comfort and peace in being truly alone. The bad kind of alone is not when you're all by yourself, but when your only company is an unseen stranger, imagined or real, creeping toward you in the dark. You have nobody to help you. There's no safe place to run. All you can do is keep going and hope for the best.

That sort of aloneness gives you goosebumps scurrying up your spine. It makes your scalp crawl. It makes you feel like someone has shoved an icy hand against your crotch.

That's the way I felt, off and on, while I was making my semi-blind way up the stream last night.

Off and on.

Coldly spooked when I felt the loneliness.

Warm and safe when the women seemed to be with me.

Off and on. I knew it was only my mind playing games, but I couldn't control it.

Sometimes, I nearly screamed with fright and ran like hell. Other times, surrounded by my phantom ladies, I loved the darkness and warmth of the night.

I felt the good way as I approached the lagoon.

Raising my eyes, I saw the moonlit slab of rock where Kimberly had stretched herself flat, days ago, to scan the lagoon for signs of Thelma and Wesley. I climbed onto it. I lay down on it, in exactly the place where Kimberly had been. The warmth of the rock seeped through my shirt and shorts.

She was with me. Her heat was in me.

That's how I felt, anyhow. It was only in my mind, but maybe that's no great reason to discount it.

Lying there, I slowly scanned the lagoon.

In places, it sparkled with points of silver moonlight. Mostly, though, it looked black.

This was not a *forbidding* blackness.

The opposite. One look, and I wanted to be in it. Could hardly wait.

I told myself that I hadn't come up here for a dip in the lagoon; I'd come to look for the women.

To search for them beyond the far side of the lagoon, above the waterfall and farther upstream where we'd last been together. I wouldn't find them here. Maybe not there, either, but that was the place to start.

To get there, I needed to cross the lagoon.

On my feet, I looked all around. No glow of firelight was anywhere to be seen. Nor did I see a sign of anyone's presence. I listened. The only sounds were birds and bugs, plus some of the usual jungle shrieks and jibbers (God knows what they came from), and the quiet splashing sounds of the waterfall on the other side of the lagoon.

Bits of moonlight lit the falls. Otherwise, they were black except for a few dim, gray streamers of froth at the bottom.

I wanted to feel the waterfall spilling onto me. I wanted to feel the *lagoon* and the night air. I wanted to be gliding through the black water, naked.

I took off my shirt and shoes and socks.

Then I took off my shorts. Naked, I crouched and set

them down. I pulled the straight razor out of the right front pocket.

Though I wanted complete freedom in the water – nothing to carry – I suddenly found myself reluctant to leave the razor behind. Someone might steal it. Or I might chance upon Wesley or Thelma. Without the razor, how would I defend myself?

After giving the matter some thought, I put on my right sock and slipped the razor down inside it against my ankle.

Which was exactly the same way I'd carried Andrew's Swiss Army knife up the tree to cut down Keith. I started to remember about that. It was more than a week ago, but seemed like it had just happened. I could *feel* the tree against my body, *see* Keith hanging . . .

'Don't think about it,' I said. Even though I spoke in a whisper, the sound of my voice unnerved me a little.

Who *else* might've heard it?

Standing up straight, I looked around. I stood motionless and listened. And started to feel very exposed and vulnerable. I began imagining that someone was out there, hidden in the darkness, spying on me, creeping closer.

As fast as I could, I climbed down the rocky bank and eased myself into the water. My legs vanished. A moment later, everything below my waist was gone, as if I'd been sawed in half by a magician.

Right away, I felt safer.

It would be no trick, at all, to disappear entirely.

My chills began to fade. My goosebumps started to go away. My tight muscles relaxed. A pleasant warmth seemed to be spreading through my whole body.

I felt even better as I waded into deeper water. When it reached my neck, I looked down and there was none of me left to see.

I had become invisible.

Except for my head, of course. Even though I couldn't see it, I knew that it showed.

If anyone was watching.

So I ducked below the surface to make my head invisible.

Now, I was completely gone. Completely safe. I was all alone in the warm water, surrounded by a jungle where my enemies might be lurking . . . I felt wonderful. I was not only safe, but invincible.

Staying below, I swam. The water flowed along my body, warm and smooth. After a while, my lungs began to ache. I stayed below, anyway. Soon, I heard the shooshing and plottering of the waterfall.

Underneath the falls, I found footing on the rocky bottom. I turned around and came up slowly. The curtain of dropping water pattered on top of my head, ran down the sides of my face, splashed softly into the water still covering my shoulders.

My head was no longer invisible.

I didn't feel frightened, though – maybe because it would be so easy to disappear again.

I stood up straight.

And shivered as I did it. This was no shiver of fear, though. This was excitement. I felt daring and powerful as more and more of my body came out of the lagoon and into full view of anyone who might be watching.

How different this was from my last time here! Only a couple of days ago, I'd stood battered and aching and desolate beneath these very falls. I'll have to write about that in more detail. Soon. Not now, though. For now, I want to tell about last night.

And how I continued to rise up under the falls.

When I was bare down to my waist, I shut my eyes. The falling water splashed onto the top of my head, onto my shoulders and outstretched arms. It slid down my body like warm oil.

This was where Connie had stood, naked, rubbing herself with her wadded T-shirt. She'd stood with her back to me.

In my mind, I turned her around.

I became her.

I was Connie standing under the waterfall, arms out, trembling as the water spilled down my naked body, showing myself to an imaginary Rupert.

Which sounds a trifle odd, now that I try to write about it.

Let's just say I let my imagination run wild for a while, there at the falls last night. I had so many different emotions swarming through me, I'm lucky I didn't go nuts entirely and stay that way.

After a while, though, I remembered my reasons for coming up to the lagoon.

Namely, to search for Connie, Billie and Kimberly.

Not for their spirits, but for their bodies – alive or dead.

And to see if I could get some idea about where Wesley and Thelma might be.

To kill them, if I could.

So I waded over to the flat rock where we'd taken Connie after she'd been knocked out. I boosted myself up, got to my feet, and climbed to the top of the falls.

Even though I'd finally gotten back to business, I still felt strange. I was dripping wet and shivering – trembling from head to toe. My *jaw* even shook. The night probably hadn't turned any colder while I'd been in the lagoon, but it felt as if the temperature had dropped about twenty degrees. Also, I was gripped by a weird mixture of fear and excitement.

At the top of the falls, I stood in a patch of moonlight and gazed down at the lagoon.

My lagoon.

It seemed like a wonderful place just then, and all mine. It was my own private swimming hole, a place where I could be completely free and completely safe, where I could dwell in my memories of Kimberly, Connie and Billie – where they would come alive in my fantasies.

Better to have imaginary friends and lovers than none at all.

In some ways, they might even be an improvement over the real thing. If they only exist in your mind, they can't get killed.

Plus, they cooperate better than . . .

(That's me, going off the deep end again. Maybe I was having – *am* having? – a slight encounter with a touch of mental breakdown. Could that be? Tee hee hee. And I ain't even gotten to the BAD part yet. The bad part about last night, that is – as opposed to the bad part when we got attacked several days ago and all three of my women . . . Never mind. That's for later, too. I should get back to last night.)

I'll skip over some of the weird shit I was feeling and thinking, etc., while I roamed the jungle naked with the razor in my sock. I've got so much to write about, anyway, without dwelling on stuff like that. (Not to mention that I've already filled up more than three-quarters of my notebook. I have about a hundred empty pages left, and that's counting both sides of the paper.)

Here's how it went last night. From the top of the falls, I followed the stream uphill, climbing through the shadows and the moonlight toward the place among the rocks where we'd found Kimberly on the day I think of as 'the last stand.'

I wanted to see where it had happened.

That would be the best place to start my search.

The Calm Before the Storm

Before I go on with the rest of what happened last night, I'd better tell what happened to me and the women at the chasm. Last night will make more sense that way.

When I left off, we were wading upstream, Connie in the lead. Earlier, Kimberly had run away from us on the beach. She was afraid we might try to tone down her vengeance, so she wanted a crack at Wesley without us.

We were afraid that, going after him alone, she might get herself killed.

We hurried up the stream. Though we splashed quite a bit, we didn't speak.

Connie and I slapped mosquitoes, now and then. They

weren't as bad as they'd been on the day we made our first trip to the lagoon, but plenty of them buzzed around us and settled on us and sucked our blood and tickled, so we both worked at smacking them flat. (The critters didn't bother Billie, of course. My theory is that they didn't want to spoil her fabulous body by marking it with little red bumps.)

Anyway, we waded up the stream at a good, quick pace, and didn't speak at all for quite a while. We were afraid of giving away our position. None of us, I think, looked forward to a premature encounter with the enemy. If it came to a fight, we wanted Kimberly to be with us.

About halfway to our destination, though, Billie broke into song.

'Once a jol-ly swagman . . .!'

Connie twisted around. 'Mom!'

'What?'

'Shhhh!!!!'

'Let's all sing,' Billie suggested.

Connie's attitude had improved so much that she didn't blurt out, 'Fuck you!' Instead, she asked, 'What on earth for?'

'It's a great day for singing.' Billie looked over her shoulder at me, and smiled. 'Don't you think so, Rupert?'

'They'll hear us,' I said, and whacked my neck to mash a mosquito.

'That's the idea,' she said. 'Let's get their attention, if we don't already have it.'

Connie lifted her eyebrows. 'So they'll worry about us instead of Kimberly?'

'Exactly,' Billie said. 'It might not even occur to them that Kimberly isn't with us.'

'As long as they don't *see* us,' I added.

Billie grinned. 'If they're busy watching us, they aren't watching Kimberly.'

'Okay,' I said. 'But we'd better be ready for them.'

'What the hell,' Connie said.

'Let's do it,' said Billie.

Off we went, marching up the stream, the three of us singing 'Waltzing Matilda' at the top of our lungs. Billie and

Connie seemed to know the lyrics by heart – Andrew, the Navy lifer, had probably learned the song on shore leave in Australia, or something, and taught it to them. I knew most of the words, myself. (I've made it a point, since I was a little kid, to memorize song lyrics, poems, all sorts of quotes that impress me.) We sounded damn good, bellowing it out.

Even though the song is mostly about death and ghosts, it's so jaunty that I felt great singing it.

We were flaunting ourselves, taunting Wesley and Thelma if they were near enough to hear our cheerfully defiant marching song.

After 'Waltzing Matilda', we sang 'Hit the Road, Jack'. I didn't know the words at first, but caught on after listening to Billie and Connie. Then we sang, 'Hey, Jude', which we all knew most of the words to.

For our next song, I suggested, 'We're off to See the Wizard'.

Billie laughed. 'Oh, that's rich.' Rich, mostly, because I was lugging an ax. 'You make a cute Tin Woodsman,' she said. 'I'll be the Cowardly Lion.'

Cute. She'd called me cute.

'Gimme a break,' Connie said. 'We're choosing *parts*? What does that leave me, the Scarecrow? Fat chance. What was he looking for, a brain? Thanks, but no thanks.'

'You can be Dorothy,' I told her, smiling.

'What if I don't *want* to be Dorothy? Dorothy's a woos.'

'That leaves Toto,' Billie said.

'A dog. Thanks a heap, Mother. If we're gonna sing the damn song, let's just get on with it, okay? You guys can pretend to be whoever you want, just include me out.'

'Party pooper,' Billie said.

'You and the horse you rode in on.'

'Cowardly Lions don't ride horses,' I pointed out.

Connie gave me a narrow look, then smiled. 'And doughnut holes don't fly,' she said, 'but maybe you can take a leap at one, anyway.'

'Let's sing,' Billie said.

Without any more discussion, we started in on 'The Wizard of Oz'.

Turned out, none of us knew the words very well. We made an energetic botch of the song, then quit when we reached the flat, slanting rock just below the lagoon.

This time, nobody went sneaking up the rock to take a look around. Connie leading the way, the three of us climbed its face. We stood at the top in full view of anyone who might be watching.

We saw nobody.

'Now what?' Connie whispered.

'Kimberly was planning to come in from the rear,' Billie said. 'She'll probably be over on the other side.'

'Somewhere upstream,' I added.

'So I guess we swim across,' Billie said.

'Not me,' I said. 'I can't swim anywhere with this ax.'

'Leave it here?' Billie asked.

'Somebody might swipe it. Besides, what if we need it?'

'Guess you're right,' she said. 'Maybe we'd better walk around to the other side.'

I expected Connie to say, 'Be my guest,' then dive in and swim across. I wouldn't have blamed her, either. *I* wanted to dive in. The water looked wonderful. Also, it would've been very soothing on our mosquito bites.

Connie surprised me, saying, 'I'll go first.' Then she turned to the left and began to make her way along the shoreline. Billie followed her, and I took up the rear.

It wasn't easy going. A lot of climbing. A lot of ducking under branches. A lot of squeezing through tight places. A lot of tricky footwork, crossing ledges and steep slopes and deadfalls. A lot of huffing and sweating.

I felt responsible. After a while, I said, 'Are you two sure you wouldn't rather go on and swim across? I can meet you on the other side.'

'This is the *last* place we oughta start splitting up,' Billie said.

'You got a death wish?' Connie asked me.

'I just feel bad about making you do this.'

'You're doing *us* the favor,' Billie said. 'Hell, you're hauling around our major piece of weaponry.'

She was right about that.

And very sweet to point it out.

They both seemed to accept this rough haul as an unavoidable part of our mission to hook up with Kimberly, and didn't blame me.

We stayed as close as possible to the water. That way, we had a good view of the lagoon and most of the opposite shore, including the waterfall. We kept our eyes open for Kimberly. And we watched for any signs of Wesley or Thelma.

Being at the rear, I watched our backs.

I couldn't help, from time to time, also watching the backs of Billie and Connie.

Billie's close-cropped hair, dripping with sweat, clung to her head in dark ringlets. Her back, richly dark from the sun (sunblock only goes so far), gleamed as if she'd been dipped in melted butter. Her back was crossed by the single rope of her tomahawk sling, and by the three coils of the long rope. The tomahawk bounced and swayed against her right hip as she walked. The seat of her black bikini pants was packed with her full, firm buttocks. I remember thinking, as I followed her, how I would've loved to see her wearing a thong like Connie's.

As for Connie, her short, blond hair looked almost exactly like her mother's. But that's where the resemblances stopped. She didn't have the broad shoulders, the wide back, or the impressive hips and rump. From behind, she looked like skin and bones while her mother looked like flesh and blood.

She wore the towel-vest, which covered most of her back. Below the rear of the vest, she was naked except for a waistband and a strip of orange fabric that descended (and very nearly vanished) between her buttocks. Her cheeks were brown and shiny, but had a few red bumps from the mosquitoes.

Both women were wonderful to watch.

For about an hour, I worked my way along behind them, struggling with the weight of the ax, keeping an eye out for trouble, and for Kimberly, and savoring my views of Billie and Connie.

I'm glad that I didn't try to be a perfect gentleman and avoid looking at them; pretty soon they would be gone and I might never have another chance to see them.

I didn't know that at the time.

I only knew that we were together on a mission, that I could admire them from behind to my heart's content, that I loved them both, and that this was one of those few, special times I would always look back on with fondness and sorrow.

The great times are often that way.

In the middle of everything, you suddenly realize that you're having a perfect, golden experience. And you realize how few they are. And how this one is bound to end too soon. You know that it will always be a wonderful memory, that the loss of it will give you a soft ache in the heart.

This was one of those times.

It had begun, I realize now, with 'Waltzing Matilda.'

It ended upstream, in the rocks beyond the lagoon, at the edge of the chasm.

By the time we reached the other side of the lagoon, we were drenched with sweat and gasping for breath. Instead of pausing to rest, however, we climbed the rocks alongside the waterfall.

We no sooner reached the top than Kimberly shouted, 'Over here!'

We spotted her standing on a boulder by the side of the stream, waving her arms back and forth. She was uphill from us, about a hundred feet away. Her spear leaned against the boulder, close enough for her to crouch and grab in case of an emergency. But if she fell on it . . .

The idea made me grimace.

While we approached her, she climbed down.

Didn't fall and get skewered.

Scooted on her rump down the face of the rock, then jumped to the ground.

'Was that you guys singing?' she asked.

'Who else *would* it be?' Connie said.

She smiled. 'I couldn't believe my ears. You're coming to my rescue belting out songs?'

'You obviously didn't require rescuing,' Billie said.

'It's the thought that counts.'

'We would've sung "The Gary Owen", I told her, 'but I don't know the words.'

'The Gary what?' Connie asked.

Kimberly wrinkled her nose. 'Is that the Seventh Cavalry song?' she asked.

'Right.' I hummed a few bars.

Billie grinned. She said, 'Ah, John Wayne.'

'George Armstrong Custer,' I said.

'That would've been choice,' Kimberly said.

'You being part Sioux, and all . . .'

'Anyway, I'm glad you came.'

'We thought you might be able to use some help,' Billie told her. 'Even if you *didn't* want us getting in your way.'

'Hey, I'm sorry about that. I got a little carried away down there. Anyway, as it turns out, you don't have to worry about me going nuts and torturing the hell out of Wesley. The bastard's dead.'

'Whoa!' Connie said. (I think she meant it to mean, 'Wow!')

'You found him?' I asked.

She nodded. 'Let's go. I'll show you.' She started leading us through the strange terrain to the right of the stream.

'What about Thelma?' Billie asked.

'No sign of her. But at least we don't have to worry about Wesley anymore.'

We followed Kimberly on a zigzag route through a maze of boulders, bushes, trees, and rock piles that jutted up like miniature mountains. Though we walked through patches of shadows, there was more sunlight than we'd seen since the beach. A gentle breeze blew. It cooled my sweat, and kept the mosquitoes away.

'He's through *here*?' Connie asked. 'How did you ever find him?'

'Took a while. This is upstream from the falls, like Thelma said.'

'But conveniently close to the falls and lagoon,' I pointed out.

'Yep. To me, it seemed like just exactly the right sort of area. You could hide an army through here. So I scouted around for a while. I climbed that.' She pointed at a tall cluster of rocks, not far ahead of us.

'You must've been here a while,' Billie said.

'I hurried. I was pretty sure you guys would come after me, sooner or later, and I wanted a chance to find Wesley before you got here. *Thought* I'd find him alive.'

'That's what we were afraid of,' Connie told her. 'That's how come we tried to hurry.'

'What took you so long?'

'We had to go around the lagoon,' I explained. 'We couldn't swim across because of the ax.'

'I'm glad you showed up when you did.' She smiled. 'Better late than never.' She seemed quite cheerful. 'Anyway, I was up there when I spotted something that looked like a pair of red panties on the ground. I figured they must be Thelma's. So what I did, I climbed down and went over to check them out. They were right by the edge of a chasm. I sort of peered over the edge, and there he was, down at the bottom. I could hardly believe my eyes. It was Wesley, all right.'

'And he's definitely dead?' I asked.

'I'd say so. You'll see.'

'So,' Connie said, 'now we only have to worry about Thelma.' She glanced nervously at several nearby places where the gal might be lurking.

Billie said, 'Don't worry. She isn't likely to jump all four of us.'

'I can't figure her out,' Kimberly said. 'Looks like she told us the truth, after all, about killing Wesley. His head's bashed in, just like she said. So how come she went for Rupert with the razor? I mean, we figured Wesley must've. sent her. That idea doesn't quite work anymore.'

'She must've had some other reason,' Billie suggested.

'You try putting moves on her?' Connie asked me.

I blushed and blurted, 'No!'

Connie smirked. 'Not your type?'

'Not even close.'

'She must've had some kind of reason,' Billie said, frowning slightly as if puzzled.

Kimberly smiled. 'We'll just have to ask her when she shows up.'

'I'm hoping she *doesn't*,' I said. 'If I never see her again in my whole life, it won't be too soon.'

'She'll show up.'

'What makes you so sure?' I asked.

'You've got her favorite razor.' As Kimberly said that, she gave me a look and a smile that not only let me know she was kidding around, but somehow made me feel as if everything would turn out fine and dandy.

God, how I would love to see that look again, that smile. Nevermore.

I shouldn't say that. I shouldn't give up hope. Not till I've seen her dead body with my own eyes. And even *that* might not make anything certain.

Plenty around here is not what it seems to be.

I've started drifting again. Procrastinating. The problem is, I just don't want to tell about what's coming. I've got to, though.

The Last Stand

We arrived at the chasm.

Maybe 'chasm' isn't the best word to describe it – this wasn't the Grand Canyon. It was actually a long, narrow space between a couple of neighboring rock formations. I would guess it was thirty feet long, and about six or eight feet from edge to edge at the place where we were approaching it. At one end, the gap narrowed down to nothing. At the other end, it stopped at the open air of a drop-off.

Striding toward the gap, Kimberly tossed her spear to the ground and rid herself of the tomahawk. She didn't halt, though, until she reached the very edge. There, she bent over as if taking a bow, and planted her hands on her knees.

The rest of us held back.

'He's down there?' Connie asked.

'Yep. Come and take a look.'

'I'd just as soon not, if it's all the same.'

Kimberly straightened up. Swiveling at the hips, she looked back at us. 'Doesn't anyone want to see him?'

I raised my hand.

'Well, come on over here.'

'I'll hold the ax for you,' Billie told me, so I gave it to her.

Then I forced myself to step forward. The last thing I really wanted was to look at another dead guy. God knows, two were more than enough. But I needed to see for myself that Wesley was down there, and that he wasn't alive.

I couldn't force myself to walk all the way to the edge, as Kimberly had done. When I got close to it, I went down on all fours. I crawled the rest of the way.

The chasm wasn't nearly as deep as I'd feared.

Deep enough, though. Fifteen or twenty feet, probably, with very steep walls on both sides. The bottom looked like a flat but slightly tilted slab of rock. A few bushes sprouted here and there out of crevices in the walls and floor.

The whole time I was busy inspecting the dimensions and general appearance of the chasm, I was trying *not* to see the body.

It was just to the left down there.

I kept seeing it in my peripheral vision while I studied everything *except* the body.

I finally had to look, though.

He was sprawled face down. At first glance, he might've been a guy who'd drifted off to sleep while doing a bit of nude sunbathing. But his skin was a bad color. And he had a hole in his ass where there shouldn't be one – in the middle of his right buttock. And the back of his head was a ruin of mashed, black mush. Also, his left leg showed a lot of bone from the knee down; some sort of animal must've been working on it – an animal a lot larger than the ones I saw crawling on him and buzzing over him.

'You don't get much deader than that,' Kimberly said. She was by my side, bent over, her hair hanging down so I couldn't see her face. It's just as well that her face was out of sight. It must've worn a look of delight. Because that's what I heard in her voice. 'There's a fine example of what we call "dead meat," ' she said.

'Guess so,' I muttered, unable to work up much enthusiasm.

When she stepped back, I crawled away from the edge and stood up.

'Nobody else interested?' she asked, and took off Keith's shirt as she walked over to where she'd left her tomahawk and spear.

'I can live without seeing him,' Billie said.

'Let me have your rope,' Kimberly said.

Billie frowned. 'What for?'

'I'm going down.'

'You're kidding,' I muttered. 'You don't want to do that.'

'Sure I do.' Kimberly had *never* seemed so perky. It was scary. 'Have to make sure it's him.'

'Of course it's him. Who else could it be?'

'Gilligan?' she suggested. 'The professor? D.B. Cooper? Who knows? Could be almost anyone.'

'It's Wesley,' I said.

Connie scowled at her. 'You *told* us it's Wesley.'

'I'm sure it *is* him. I'm just not *sure* sure. That's why I need to go down and turn him over.'

Turn him over?

'Oh jeez,' I said. 'Don't. You don't want to *touch* him.'

She gave me a strange smile and said, 'Sure I do.'

'Be my guest,' Billie said. Nose wrinkled, she lifted the

coils of rope off her shoulder and swung them over her head. She held them out to Kimberly, who took them.

'There's really no reason to go down there,' I protested. 'Really. I mean, you know and I know that it's Wesley, so . . .'

'Maybe *you* know, bucko.'

'*You* know, too.'

'I know no such thing.'

'It's not funny!'

'Am I being funny?'

'You're being *strange*.'

'He's right,' Connie said.

'How about we just call it quits and go back to the beach,' Billie suggested.

The quirky grin vanished from Kimberly's face. 'I'm gonna do what I'm gonna do. What I'm gonna do is go down and pay a visit to our dead friend because if he's *not* Wesley, I wanta know it and if he *is* Wesley . . .' She shrugged.

'What?' Billie asked.

'Nothing. I just have to know for sure it's him. That's all. You know what? I'm not so sure, anymore. The more I think about it, the more this guy doesn't look *big* enough to be Wesley.'

'That's a crock,' I said.

Without another word, Billie walked to the edge and peered down. Then she made a sound. 'Uhhh.' After about a minute, she turned around and came back to us. She looked ill. 'It's gotta be Wesley,' she muttered. 'Who else *could* it be? Anyway, I think people are *supposed* to look smaller when they're dead.'

'*You* think he looks smaller?' Connie blurted.

'Well . . . sort of. Wesley was a pretty big guy . . .'

'The dead guy's big,' I pointed out.

'I'm not sure he's *as* big.'

Connie muttered, 'Jesus.'

'He's got Kimberly's spear hole in his ass,' I said. 'And his head's caved in, just the way Thelma . . .'

'Making him conveniently difficult to identify,' Kimberly said. 'And anybody could've poked a hole in someone's butt.'

'In *whose* butt?' I blurted. 'Who else *is* there?'

Kimberly's smile returned. Not her spectacular smile – her bizarre and gleeful one. 'Remains to be seen, Watson.'

With that, she twirled around and made her spritely way to the edge of the chasm. Holding one end of the rope, she let the rest of it fall over the edge. Then she faced us and shook her head. 'Not long enough. We'll have to add on the tomahawk ropes.'

By that time, we were all ready to cooperate. We hadn't had much faith in Kimberly's judgment, but Billie's doubts had turned the trick. *She* wasn't one hundred per cent sure the body belonged to Wesley, so we really needed to make an absolutely positive ID.

While I stood guard with the ax, the women took apart their tomahawk slings.

Billie tied the knots. The three shorter pieces added at least twelve feet to the length of the rope.

Kimberly held one end and tossed the rest of it over the edge. 'Reaches,' she announced.

I looked around for a good place to tie off the upper end. A tree trunk, for instance. Or a solid jut of rock. There was nothing of the sort near enough to the edge. 'I guess we'll have to lower you,' I said.

'Nope. I'll just climb down.'

Apparently, she'd already figured out what to do. She took the ax from me, carried it toward the edge, and turned the ax so its haft pointed away from the chasm. Then she squatted and shoved the blade into a crack in the rocks. Standing up, she stomped it deeper.

She tied a loop at her end of the rope and slipped it down the haft until it stopped against the steel head.

'That should do it,' she said. 'Rupe, how about hanging on to the ax handle? Just keep it pushed down, and try not to let the head pop out of the crack.'

I nodded. 'Okay, but . . .'

'Or stand on the ax. Whatever.'

'Okay.' Crouching, I clutched the wooden handle just below the loop of rope. 'Got it,' I said.

'Good guy,' she said. She gave my shoulder a gentle squeeze, then moved around in front of me. Briefly, we were forehead to forehead. Then she crawled backward, the rope on the ground between her knees.

'Be careful,' Billie said.

'For God's sake, don't fall,' Connie said.

They both moved in closer. Billie stood near my left side, while Connie sank down to one knee on my right. They were ready to help if anything should go wrong.

So far, Kimberly hadn't even taken hold of the rope. Hands pressed against the edge of the chasm, she lowered her legs. Then she stopped. She held herself there, braced up with stiff arms in front of me, the ledge pushing a long dent across both her thighs. Her shoulders and arms, usually so slender and smooth, bulged with curves of muscle. So did her breasts. They swelled, smooth and round, ballooning the pouches of her white bikini. Her dark skin dripped sweat and glistened.

'Rupe,' she said.

I met her eyes.

'I'm gonna lose my knife.'

I looked at it.

I'd been trying to avoid looking there.

As usual, the Swiss Army knife was tucked in between her bare skin and waistband at the very front of her bikini pants. Its top end stuck up more than usual — about half an inch. The thickness of the handle held the pants away from her body, and made a bulge all the way down.

I saw her problem right away; if she tried to lower herself any further, the rock ledge would push at the bottom end of the knife, thrusting it up and out.

'Take it,' she said.

'Uh . . .'

She sort of rolled her eyes upward. 'Just do it. Please.'

'*I'll* get it,' Connie said, sounding annoyed. Up on one knee, though, she was too far away. She started to put her other knee down.

'Never mind,' I said. Leaning over the ax, I planted my left hand on the ground to hold myself steady while I reached for the knife with my right hand.

I found myself gazing nearly straight down into wedges of open space on either side of the knife handle. Twin triangles formed by red plastic, white spandex, and bare skin. Smooth, flawless, private skin and curls of black hair.

The view sucked my breath out, made my heart start to slam, and sent a quick surge through my groin. I grew hard as I reached down to rescue the knife.

I tried to pinch the tip of the handle where it jutted out above her waistband.

Not enough there to get a firm grip on.

So I slipped my thumb and forefinger down inside. By accident, they brushed ever so softly against her skin. I felt the smoothness, and moaned. I murmured, 'Sorry,' in a shaky voice.

I was taking too long.

I squeezed the sides of the handle between my thumb and forefinger, and slowly lifted. The knife slid upward. I could feel the tightness of it, trapped like it was. But it came up smoothly. When it was nearly all the way out, I stole a glimpse down deep inside the gaping front of her pants.

Then the elastic snapped back. Her pants shut like a mouth.

'Got it,' I murmured.

'Thanks,' Kimberly said.

Thank you, I thought. Didn't say it, though.

I raised my head and forced a smile. The look she gave me, she knew what had happened. She'd *intended* it. Or maybe I just read that into her look, and all she'd really intended was to have me stop the knife from falling out. Who knows?

'If you need any help down there . . .' I said. The words were out before I realized they could be taken in a couple of different ways.

I expected Connie to pop out with a nasty crack. She didn't, though.

Kimberly said, 'I might want you to lower the knife to me. We'll see.'

'Sure. Just let me know.'

She bent her arms. The stone edge rubbed its way up her thighs, her groin and belly. Propped up on her elbows, she grabbed the rope with one hand.

I took my position beside the ax. Keeping the knife snug inside my right hand, I held the ax handle down with my left. By the time I looked at Kimberly again, only the top of her head showed. A moment later, it vanished below the rim.

With Kimberly out of view, I focused on the ax and the rope. They looked fine. The ax seemed to be solidly planted in the crack. The rope, taut and stiff, vibrated slightly.

Connie was still beside me on one knee.

Billie still stood near the edge, watching Kimberly's descent.

Someone yelled, *'YAHHHHHH!'*

The noise of it almost stopped my heart. For an instant, I thought Kimberly'd fallen. The yell didn't sound like her voice, though.

Sounded like a man's voice.

I raised my head.

He came at us from the other side of the chasm, yelling as he charged. He didn't look like Wesley. He *was* Wesley, though. And he *was* bigger than the guy in the chasm.

Even though I only saw him for a few seconds, I remember every detail as if I'd snapped a photo of him. Or caught him on videotape, to be more accurate – they're *moving* pictures. Often, I see them in slow motion.

Somewhere, Wesley had gotten hold of a blue cap. He wore it backward, the plastic adjustable tabs across the middle of his forehead so he looked like some sort of fat, white gangsta rapper.

He also wore Thelma's large, red brassiere. He seemed to be using it as a harness to hold a bandage in place against his left boob; the red cup on that side was stuffed to bulging. The right cup had been cut away, so his hairy tit bulged out through the frame, bouncing and flopping as he dashed toward the chasm.

Since the night of the ambush – the last time I'd seen Wesley – he had also found a leather belt. If he'd come upon a pair of pants to go with it, though, he'd chosen to go without. He wore the belt around his waist, and hunting knives in leather sheaths at each hip.

On his feet, he wore a pair of high-topped sneakers.

He wore nothing else except his own sweat, hair, and hard-on.

He was pretty damn funny-looking, in a way.

But there wasn't much amusing about how he ran at us yelling like a madman and waving machetes overhead with both hands.

Even though I'm able to see him in slow motion, everything actually happened very fast. He had almost reached the far edge of the chasm by the time I raised my head and saw him coming.

Connie made a squeaky little noise.

Billie let out a loud gasp.

Wesley was in mid-leap before any of us started to move. Connie started trying to get off her knee. Billie began to turn and take a step backward. On my knees, I opened my hand and glanced down at the shiny red plastic handle of the Swiss Army knife, the silvery edges of the blades and tools that were safely folded away.

No chance of getting a blade out in time.

I started trying to get off my knees.

Billie, glancing over her shoulder, flinched and gaped. Her arms began to rise as she continued to twist around. Something about her expression and posture reminded me of a football player lunging for an interception.

In that instant, I knew Thelma must be attacking from the rear.

I heard Wesley's sneaker whap close by. Still in a crouch, I turned my head and glimpsed him on our side of the chasm – but not directly in front of me. Off a bit to my right. Charging straight at Connie.

I tried to stand up faster.

Connie had managed to get up. She was in the midst of turning her back to him, flinging her arms forward as if reaching for help.

That's where it stops.

That's all I remember about our 'last stand.'

Just at that point, I imagine, Thelma must've nailed me from behind.

Perchance to Dream

Here's my guess. While I was out cold from a blow to the head, someone 'disposed' of me.

That is, threw or shoved me over the edge of the chasm.

My guess is also that the fall didn't finish me off because I landed on the dead guy.

Lucky me.

My buddy, Matt.

Short for Mattress.

I slept on him for a long time, in a condition known as 'dead to the world.'

What's the difference, I wonder, between being in a coma and simply being knocked out cold? Just that one lasts longer? I don't know, and it doesn't much matter.

At some point, I 'came to' in the night.

I opened my eyes, saw a starry sky above me, wondered vaguely where I was, decided I must be on a camping trip, then faded out again.

I came to again with the sun baking me. I wished someone would make the sun go away; it felt way too hot, and made my head throb. Then the sun went away and stopped bothering me.

Bugs bothered me, off and on. Mostly, I ignored them.

Sometimes, I found myself enjoying how they tickled.

I must've had a hundred dreams. I could write to the last page of this notebook, and not be able to finish describing all the dreams that rambled through my sore head (many of which I'd like to forget, but can't) while I was sprawled there at the bottom of the chasm.

They were much more vivid and realistic than regular dreams.

Some of them were extremely erotic. Those mostly featured Kimberly, but I had some doozies with Billie and Connie, along with various combinations of the three.

Thelma found her way into some of my dreams. Those were usually sexy, but in a nightmarish way. Often her razor played a part. The Thelma dreams were really sick and perverted and repulsive.

The same goes for most of my other nightmares.

Horrible.

In one, for example, I was climbing the tree to cut down Keith's body after he'd been hanged. Which was lousy enough in real life. In my dream, though, it got worse. He suddenly swung toward me by his neck and embraced me – wrapped his arms and legs around me – and started to chew off my nose.

That one was nasty, but brief.

I had several nightmares that seemed endless.

Of those, one that I remember vividly involved a group of women who came walking up the beach toward me on a beautiful, sunny day. I didn't know who they were at first. For one thing, they were naked so I couldn't tell them apart by what they wore. For another, they didn't have their heads. Their necks ended at pulpy, bloodless stumps.

I was pretty turned on, but also spooked.

They said I could save them, if I wanted to badly enough. (This in spite of having no heads.) I was eager to save them, and asked how. They said, 'You have to match us up.'

That's when I realized that each woman was holding something out of sight behind her back.

They brought their arms around to the front.

Each woman was carrying a head.

Among the heads, I recognized the faces of Connie, Billie, Kimberly, Thelma, Wesley, Miss Curtis (my fifth-grade teacher whom I'd had a terrible crush on), Ardeth Swan (a girlfriend from high school – never got to first base with her), and a total stranger (I think) who looked sort of cute except for all the rings and bolts and pins sticking out all over her face and ears.

The last head belonged to my own mother. God knows what it was doing there, but it sure added to the creepy weirdness of the nightmare.

Right off the bat, it was clear to me that none of the ladies was holding on to her own head.

Wesley's head explained the rules of the game. 'If you wanta save us, you've gotta match up our heads correctly before sundown. Think you can do that, little buddy?'

'I wouldn't save you if I could,' I told him.

Besides, Wesley's body wasn't even there. Of the nine decapitated bodies standing in front of me on the beach, each and every one appeared to be a properly equipped female.

I took Wesley's noggin out of the hands of a heavy-set gal, and tossed it down the beach. Then I rushed over to Thelma's head, plucked it out of the hands of a slim gal I suspected of being Connie, and hurried with it over to the stocky gal who'd been holding Wesley's head. I plonked it down on her neck stub.

Thelma, now properly assembled, smiled and wiggled her fingers at me.

I won't go through the whole nightmare. I don't want to even *think* about some of what happened, much less write it down. So I'll skip the worst parts, and just tell about the stuff that isn't quite as disturbing.

Through the whole dream, whether I was laughing or feeling horny or confused or disgusted or terrified, I always had this terrible, heavy feeling of dread. Nobody'd explained what would happen if I failed to match the heads correctly with the bodies before sundown – aside from the obvious, that I wouldn't 'save' the women. But I had a feeling that my fate might be something too creepy for words.

Sundown was fast approaching.

So I raced back and forth, snatching heads out of hands,

rushing this way and that, shoving them down onto neck stubs.

It wasn't as simple as it might sound.

I'd taken care of Wesley and Thelma right off the bat. Two down, seven to go. I'd seen enough of Connie and Kimberly to recognize their bodies, so they presented no problem (except when I dropped Connie's head and it rolled away and I had to chase it down the beach). Four down, five to go.

I tried to do Billie next, figuring she'd be a cinch. After all, she'd been running around forever in nothing but her bikini, and I'd seen her breasts completely naked the night she tried to tackle Thelma but ended up diving through the sand. (I remembered, even in my dream, about how they'd looked looming out loose over her bikini top.)

I grabbed Billie's head from the hands of a body I didn't recognize, then hurried it over to the broad, lush figure I knew to be her.

When I plonked it onto the neck, Billie's mouth said, 'Dumb move, Rupert. You don't know your own mother when you see her?'

Yuck!

Down the line, I spotted an identical body.

To me, they both looked like Billie.

Whoa, Nelly. Here comes Freud, Oedipus leering by his side.

The hell with it. This is no time to start worrying about what might be lurking in my subconscious. Screw id.

Anyway, I was shocked by that part of the dream, but the mistake had a silver lining. I quickly matched two heads to the proper bodies: Billie's and my mother's.

Next, I went for the head of the stranger.

Its ears, nostrils, lips, and even eyebrows bristled with all manner of metallic ornaments. I took her head out of Kimberly's hands and rushed it down the row of ladies to a pale, skinny gal who had rings dangling from her pierced nipples, clitoris, etc. Easy.

That done, only two heads remained.

My cute blonde fifth-grade teacher, Miss Curtis. And my high-school girlfriend, Ardeth Swan.

Unfortunately, *three* headless bodies remained.

That's because my first move of the game had been tossing away Wesley's head.

It wouldn't have matched any of the three remaining bodies, anyway.

Off on the horizon, the sun was sinking slowly into the sea.

Miss Curtis and Ardeth gave me no trouble.

Miss Curtis had a petite, slender body with a nice tan, cup-sized breasts with turgid dark nipples, and a shiny tuft of blond hair between her legs.

Ardeth Swan, a freckled and pimply tub, had lost her head but not her modesty. She kept an arm across her huge breasts, a hand clamped to her crotch.

When I put Miss Curtis's head on her neck, she gave me a warm smile and said, 'You always were such a fine young man, Thomas.'

I didn't know who the hell Thomas might be, but I thanked her anyway.

After returning Ardeth's head, I simply smiled at her. She said, 'Fuck off, meatball.'

Even in my nightmares . . .

Only a small curve of orange sun remained above the horizon.

I faced the final headless body.

I had no head to give it.

Thinking I might spot a head I'd missed, I looked around.

Everyone had vanished.

Everyone was gone except me and the lone, headless woman. We stood close together on the empty beach, facing each other. (She wasn't 'facing' me, of course, as she didn't possess one.)

What she did possess was an absolutely fabulous, incredible body.

Her skin gleamed all over with a tawny, golden tan.

She was at least six feet tall, from neck to toe. She had long, slender arms and legs, broad shoulders, breasts that were high firm mounds with stiff jutting nipples. Her hips were wide and smooth, her belly flat. Lower, she had a glossy curve without so much as a trace of whiskers – as if she'd never grown any hair at all down there.

'I don't know what to do,' I told her. 'I'm out of heads.'

She shrugged her shoulders, which made her breasts lift and descend wonderfully.

'Do you know where your head is?' I asked her.

Again, that lovely shrug.

I checked the horizon and saw the last sliver of the sun easing out of sight.

Fast as I could, I snatched off my own head and shoved it onto her neck.

'There!' I yelled in triumph.

The yell didn't come from *my* mouth, though. I was looking at my mouth, my face, my head, on top of that gorgeous body.

Not a match!

In my haste to provide a head for her, I'd forgotten that the rules called for a match.

Not just any old head would do.

But *mine* did!

Figure that one out.

Anyway, I watched my own face give me a very nice, friendly smile.

Then my dream woman said, 'Thanks, Rupert.' (Not my voice, I'm glad to report. It sounded more like Lauren Bacall in *To Have and Have Not*, and a lot like Billie.) 'You won,' she told me. 'You saved us all, do you know that? You should be very proud of yourself.'

It made me feel really good.

'Of course,' she said, 'now *you* don't have a head.'

'Oh, that's okay.' I can be quite the gallant fellow, sometimes. 'I don't need it that much,' I told her. 'I'm just glad I was able to match everyone up.'

'Do you know what you get for winning?'

I shook my head. (Well, maybe not. I thought I did, though.)

248

'You get me,' she said.

'Oh boy!' I said.

She came forward. She took me in her arms, and I felt her body against me. Unfortunately, she had my face. When she tried to kiss me, I turned away.

'What's wrong?' she asked.

'I don't know about this. I don't think I wanta be kissing my own face.'

'Okay. That can be fixed. Whose do you want?'

'You can change your face?'

I watched myself give me a knowing smile. 'Sure. Just tell me who you want me to be.'

'Yourself,' I said.

'I *am* myself. I'm your dream lover. I'm whoever you want me to be.'

'I sure don't want you being me.'

'Who, then?' she asked.

'Can it be anyone?'

'Anyone you'd like.'

'How about Kimberly?'

'Excellent choice,' she said. Immediately, the face of my dream lover stopped being me and became Kimberly.

Then things really sizzled.

Somewhere along the way, my nightmare had gotten left behind, leaving me with a fantastic erotic dream. Probably the best dream I've ever had.

It stayed great, too. The worst thing about it, from the moment after I saved her with the donation of my head, was when I woke up very suddenly and the dream ended.

I remembered her (Oh, God, did I ever!), but she had fled, along with my sleep, and I couldn't bring her back.

I would gladly let myself get knocked out today, if I thought she would return.

Of all the dreams and nightmares that came to me at the bottom of the chasm, though, she only put in the one appearance.

* * *

In my last dream down there, I found myself on the beach in a wheelchair, trying to get away from someone. I couldn't turn my head around to see who was chasing me, but I was plenty scared. I kept shoving at the wheel rims, trying to pick up speed, but the wheels were bogged down in the sand. They kept sinking deeper and deeper, until my chair wouldn't move at all.

Finally, screaming in terror, I hurled myself out of the chair and started to run away. My legs worked fine. What the hell had I been doing in the wheelchair? Elated, I sprinted for safety. But my feet started sinking in the sand.

With each step, I sank deeper. Pretty soon, the sand reached my waist. No matter how hard I tried, I couldn't wade any farther. I was trapped. It hugged me like tight, heavy trousers.

I was terrified.

Now, *he'd* catch me. He would come running up behind me with his ax or machete or . . . chainsaw.

It'll be a chainsaw, I suddenly realized.

I couldn't hear it, though. Not yet.

Had he given up the chase?

I listened. Ocean sounds, bird sounds, bug sounds, but no cough, sputter and roar of a chainsaw.

I smiled with relief.

All of a sudden, down deep in the sand, hands caressed my legs.

I woke up with a yell of fright and a splitting headache, and that was the end of my odyssey through a hundred dreams and nightmares at the bottom of the chasm.

Some of my worst nightmares, though, were more pleasant than what I found on my return to reality.

I was sprawled on my back, my head pounding with pain. I felt as if every bone in my body had been hammered. In some places, I felt numb. In others, I itched. In still others, sharp pains stabbed me.

Above me, swarms of flies and other winged bugs zipped this way and that. Some landed on me, while others were happy to circle.

A vulture suddenly flapped up into my line of vision, startling me.

I saw the chasm walls towering above me on both sides.

The gray sky above the chasm held a promise of sunrise – or night.

Beneath me, I felt Matt.

Waking Up is Hard to Do

Matt felt like lumpy, warm goo.

I shouldn't complain, though. Without him, *I* would probably be lumpy, warm goo.

Still, he disgusted me.

I had been napping for at least a couple of days, probably longer, on top of a naked, decomposing corpse.

I, at least, wasn't naked. Thank God, I had my shorts on. Where my bare back pressed against him, we seemed to be stuck together. My skin, there, itched like crazy. Also, I felt squirming, crawling things; various critters that had apparently gotten sandwiched between us.

Let's not dwell on all that.

I won't even *mention* the smell.

The moment I realized where I was – and what was under me – I let out a cry and rolled off him.

It made quite a sound when we came unstuck. You might get a similar effect by dropping a large, hot pizza on the tile floor of your kitchen and letting it stay there for a couple of hours before you peel it off.

When you peel it off, that's when you get the sound.

Rolling off Matt, I took some of him with me. I could feel gop and stuff glued to my back.

I started to crawl away from him. Then I threw up. Then

I crawled farther. It's a wonder I could move at all. Aside from all my other complaints, I felt like a passenger on a twilt-a-whirl. I kept crawling, though, wanting to put miles between me and Matt.

I probably made ten feet before I collapsed.

I lay there groaning, sleepless and full of agony.

The next time I lifted my head, the chasm was dark. I sat up and leaned back against a curving surface of rock.

The full moon, directly overhead, shone pale light down between the steep walls. It lit most of the chasm's floor. Including Matt.

My silent partner.

He seemed almost like an old friend.

A long-lost buddy I might've shared some good times with once, but who had recently undergone some major changes for the worse – especially in the personal hygiene department.

I had no idea who he might be.

Gazing at his moonlit corpse over there, though, I found myself fancying him as an old prospector. He was Walter Huston. I was Bogart. We'd run into some tough luck – his a lot tougher than mine.

'Reckon we won't be buying no rabbit farm, Lenny,' I said to him.

Wrong movie. Wrong characters. But it's what I said, anyway.

'Shit happens,' I told him.

I thought about crawling over to him and taking a look at his face. For all I knew, I might recognize him.

Could he be Keith?

Maybe Wesley and Thelma had disinterred Keith, brought his body here to trick us . . .

No.

Matt was too large to be Keith.

He couldn't possibly be Andrew, either. Again, wrong size. Besides, they would've had to fish his body out of the sea.

So who the hell *was* he?

Or she? Matt might be a female. After all, I'd never seen the body's frontal areas. She couldn't be a woman from our group, though; all of ours had been up at the top while the body was down here.

Not that I'd actually seen Thelma up there. But I figure it must've been Thelma who attacked us from the rear.

Anyway, Matt seemed too large to be Thelma, and his shape was all wrong.

His shape seemed wrong, in fact, to be any woman at all.

Not that he *couldn't* have been one. Kimberly and Billie had looked at him, though, and they'd assumed he was a man: Wesley, in fact. Though we'd had doubts about his identity, none of us had doubted that the body was a *he*.

I wondered, though.

Matt was probably no Matilda, but I was curious.

Would I recognize him – or her?

Only one way to find out.

I didn't want to move, though.

I especially didn't want to take a good, close look at the stiff.

A. It stank.

B. His or her face was bound to be a wreck.

C. He or she was a critter magnet.

D. If I got any closer, I might start getting the creeps.

E. Or throw up again.

F. All of the above.

So I stayed put.

Then I squinted up at the top of the chasm and wondered what had happened.

Obviously, I'd been knocked out cold and dumped into the chasm. What about the women, though?

They hadn't won the battle, that was for sure.

If they'd won, I wouldn't have found myself waking up at the bottom of the chasm, days later, alone except for a corpse.

They would have taken care of me.

Not necessarily, I told myself. Suppose they won the fight, but only *after* I'd gone over the edge? Someone climbs down to check on me. Kimberly. She mistakes me for dead, so they go off and leave me here.

That didn't seem likely.

Not being an idiot, Kimberly would've noticed that I was alive.

Thinking about Kimberly, I recalled the last time I'd seen her. She had been climbing down a rope into the chasm. She'd just dropped out of sight below the edge moments before the attack came.

She wasn't down here, now. I had already looked around. Nobody was down here except for me and the corpse. I scanned the moonlit bottom again, anyway. No sign of Kimberly, or anyone else.

She'd most likely scurried back up the rope to join the fight. A losing fight, almost for sure.

The last I saw, Wesley had been hot on Connie's tail. Seconds after I went down, he'd probably whacked her head off with one of those machetes. Then he and Thelma had probably made quick work of Billie.

So Kimberly, late in joining the fray, would've found herself standing alone against those two.

She was tough enough to win.

If she'd won, though, where was she? Why had she left me down here?

They're dead, I thought. *All of them. Kimberly, Billie and Connie. Dead.*

Then I almost went nuts, but I kept a grip on one thin thread of hope: that they had somehow won the battle. They'd thought I was dead; and left me. And they'd gone on back to our camp at the beach. If I could get out of the chasm, I would find them there, alive and well.

God, they'd be so glad to see me!

Not half as glad as I'd be, though, to see them.

We would have a great celebration.

I knew they were dead.

Sometimes, though, kidding yourself isn't the worst course of action. Instead of self-destructing, I got myself out of the chasm.

For starters, I struggled to my feet. Then I roamed back and forth, checking in the shadows and bushes to make absolutely sure that Kimberly wasn't down here.

I found no one.

I found no heads or other parts.

I found nothing worth finding.

Not even the rope. After the end of the battle, someone must've pulled it up. (Why leave behind a perfectly good rope?)

Not that it would've done me much good. I could barely hold myself upright, much less climb out of the chasm on a rope.

I did try to climb out without one.

I never got very high, fortunately, because I kept falling.

I fell three times.

Then I made my way to the open end of the chasm.

It overlooked a steep drop-off.

I studied the situation for a minute or two. The darkness hid most of what I wanted to see. But I did notice that the treetops beyond the cliff were *above* me. Very encouraging: I was somewhat lower than the treetops.

A fall might not kill me.

That was about all I really cared to know.

I lowered myself over the edge.

Braced up with stiff, shaking arms, I remembered when Kimberly had paused in almost the same position and asked me to rescue her Swiss Army knife.

What had happened to the knife?

Just before being taken out of the picture, I'd seen it in my hand.

Had I somehow slipped it into a pocket of my shorts?

Not in my seat pockets, that was for sure. I'd spent plenty of time on my back and would've felt it pushing against my butt. It didn't seem to be in my front pockets, either; they held the straight razor, Andrew's lighter, Billie's small plastic bottle of sunblock, and a pack of smoked fish. The way I was braced up against the face of the cliff, I could feel them all being pressed into my thighs.

No Swiss Army knife there. No big surprise.

Maybe the knife had ended up at the bottom of the chasm, though. If I'd still been holding on to it when I went over the edge . . .

I scrambled back up, got to my feet, and staggered over to the area where I had landed.

The area included Matt. Or Matilda.

Which goes to show how much I wanted the knife.

A good knife like that could make all the difference.

Also, it held memories.

I wanted it badly.

After sinking to my knees – perhaps a yard from the body – I dug Andrew's lighter out of my pocket. I gave it a flick. A small spear-head of flame leaped from its top.

By the shimmery yellow glow, I searched the ground. Staying on my knees, I circled the area, sweeping my gaze back and forth, trying not to look at the body.

Looking at it anyway, from time to time.

After a while, you get used to anything.

Desperate to find the knife, I finally considered the possibility that the corpse might be hiding it. The knife couldn't have fallen *underneath* the body, but it might've dropped out of sight in any of several places.

My lighter was little use on some of them.

I had to reach into the darkness under the chin and on both sides of the neck. I fingered the spaces under the armpits. I traced the entire body, crawling around it and running my fingertips along the crevice where its skin was pressed against the rock floor. I spread the legs apart and searched between them.

That's when I confirmed that the body was not a woman, after all.

But I didn't find the knife.

So then I turned the body over. (In for a penny, in for a pound.) As he rolled out of the way, I felt almost positive that the knife would show up, at last.

Kidding myself.

It wasn't there, of course.

And, of course, I couldn't stop myself from gazing at the front of the body.

The man had a pulpy ruin where his face should've been. Also, the left side of his chest was split open.

My guess is that Wesley and Thelma couldn't be sure whether he would land face up or face down when they gave him the old heave-ho into the chasm. They wanted to make sure he would pass for Wesley, either way, so they didn't spare any efforts in mutilating him.

Who was he, though? He certainly wasn't Keith or Andrew. Where in hell had they gotten their hands on a spare man to use for their trap?

Giving up my search for Kimberly's knife, I put away the lighter and returned to the open end of the chasm. I eased myself over the edge, and began to make my way down the sheer wall of rock.

I made it to the bottom in record time.

No bones got broken, though. Nor did I find myself unconscious. I was able to pick myself up again and get moving a few hours later, a while after the sun came up.

I found my way, without much trouble, back to the lagoon. I came upon its shoreline near the south end. After emptying my pants pockets on a rock, I took off my sneakers and socks. (How great it felt to have bare feet!)

I climbed down into the water and washed my hands the best I could, then cupped water to my mouth.

Delicious!

Cool, clear water, just like the song. (Not very cool, as a matter of fact, but it tasted wonderful anyhow.)

After gulping down quite a load of it, I waded out until most of the lagoon came into sight.

Nobody else seemed to be there.

I submerged myself. The water felt like a soothing ointment on my battered, bruised and bitten skin. Staying under, I rubbed my face. I rubbed my shoulders, arms, chest, sides and belly, using my hands to wipe away the layers of filth.

Then I took off my shorts and worked for a while at scrubbing them. They certainly didn't come clean, but I got rid of the worst of the mess. Done with them, I waded toward shore and tossed them onto the nearest rock. Waiting no longer, I bent over and rubbed all the itchy, sore, grimy places from my waist on down to my feet.

Later, I swam to the waterfall. I stood underneath it, the water splashing on my head and shoulders, running down me, spilling down me, flooding down me, washing off the last of the sweat and blood and whatever bits of Matt might still be clinging to my back.

I must've stood under it for half an hour.

Then I returned to the south end of the lagoon and climbed out. Nearby, I found a large slab of rock with a fairly flat surface. I crawled onto it and lay down.

I slept. If dreams came, I don't remember them.

Later that day, I walked out onto our section of the beach.

By then, I'd stopped kidding myself; I knew the women wouldn't be there.

The camp looked as if it hadn't been touched since our departure, some days earlier.

The fire was dead.

But I found my book bag, opened it up, and took out my journal and one of the pens.

My journal – my only companion, now.

I sat down in the sand, crossed my legs, placed the journal on my lap, and opened it. After riffling through the great thickness of it, I came to a blank page.

I wrote, 'Day? Anybody's Guess.' I turned that page and wrote on the next, 'Musings on my Return to the Journal.'

When a Body Meets a Body

It took one hell of a long time to write all that. Yesterday morning, I started to write about my hike upstream the previous night. I was only about half done with that when I realized everything would make better sense if I went back in time and told the whole business about our 'last stand'.

I can't seem to be brief about this stuff. Next thing I know I'll spend all day writing – and still have plenty left to go.

I haven't been building fires since my return to the beach (trying to stay inconspicuous), so writing after dark is out of the question. I had to call it quits before I'd even gotten myself off the top of Matt.

This morning, I finished about the chasm, and brought myself back to the beach.

Now, I'm ready to tell the rest of what happened when I went upstream (two nights ago, now) to search for the women. I'd made my way about halfway through before breaking off to backtrack. But I need to get to the bad part, and get it over with, before I'm free to stop writing and do whatever comes next.

I was last seen above the waterfall, running naked through the jungle with the straight razor in my sock.

I found the place where Billie, Connie and I had joined up with Kimberly. Without her to lead the way, though, I had a difficult time finding the chasm from there. I became lost. More than once, I arrived at a boulder or tree that I recognized because I'd recently walked past it. I was roaming in circles.

It didn't bother me. I was in no hurry to reach the chasm. I didn't *want* to reach it, in fact. But the chasm (the area above it, actually) was the place where I needed to go, so I kept searching for it.

Eventually, I got there. Peering around a corner of rock, I scanned the scene of our battle.

No bodies littered the moonlit field.

I murmured, 'Thank God.'

Then I burst into tears. I couldn't help it.

I'd fully expected to find the remains of my three women on the ground near the top of the chasm. If not all of them, at least one or two.

Relief overpowered me.

The relief lasted about as long as my tears. I no sooner

recovered from the crying than things came back into perspective; the absence of their bodies was an excellent sign. It didn't, however, guarantee they were still alive.

Wesley and Thelma might've killed my women and dragged them away: buried them, burned them, sunk them, tossed them off a ledge, hauled them off somewhere to play nasty games with – God only knows.

Or they might've taken my women away alive – as prisoners.

Stepping into the open, I wondered if I might be walking into another trap. After all, this was enemy territory and we'd been ambushed here before.

I crouched, drew the razor out of my sock, and flipped open its blade. Then I made my way slowly toward the area where we'd been attacked. I crept along, turning, checking to my rear and sides, glancing in every direction.

Not far from the edge of the chasm, I found Connie's beach-towel vest. The last time I saw her, she'd been wearing it. Now it lay crumpled in shadow beside a block of stone. I clamped the razor handle between my teeth, then crouched and picked up the vest. I spread it open and studied it. The stripes looked like different shades of gray in the moonlight.

The vest appeared to be free of blood – another good sign.

I couldn't leave it behind. I wanted to keep my hands free, though. Wearing the vest seemed like the best solution, so I put it on.

And felt closer to Connie. As if the vest was a living part of her, keeping company with me. (This explained a lot about why Kimberly had gone around almost constantly in her dead husband's Hawaiian shirt.)

While still crouched in the place where I'd found the vest, I spotted a wadded rag and picked it up. Though it was dark with dry blood, I wasn't alarmed. It appeared to be the piece of old T-shirt that Connie'd been using as a bandage for her shoulder. She must've lost it along with the vest.

I dropped it, took the razor out of my teeth, stood up and continued my search.

I probably looked like a madman, roaming through the night with my wicked straight razor – and wearing not a stitch except for the vest and one sock. A demented Crusoe. A castaway Sweeney Todd.

Anyway, I continued my search of the battlefield.

The ax and rope were gone. I found none of our makeshift spears or tomahawks, either.

Nor could I find the Swiss Army knife.

I looked very carefully for that, not only walking a grid pattern over most of the area, but getting down on all fours to study the ground in the vicinity where I'd last been holding it.

The knife wasn't there. Except for Connie's vest and bandage, it appeared that nothing had been left behind. Someone must've carried away everything that had fallen (including the women?).

I didn't find blood on the ground, though. Which gave me more reason for hope. If Wesley had used his machete on anyone, vast quantities would've gotten spilled. Even though several days had gone by and I was doing my search by moonlight, a mess like that should've been easy to spot.

Unless someone had cleaned it up.

I pictured Thelma on her knees with a bucket and scrub brush. Ridiculous.

In some other setting, dirt and leaves might've been spread around to cover telltale blood. Not here, though. Most of this area was bare rock.

If blood had been spilled, much of it would've remained for me to find.

Nobody'd been chopped or slashed or stabbed to death, not on our field of battle.

Before leaving, I crawled to the edge of the chasm and peered down.

Nothing at the bottom except Matt.

He appeared to be on his back, the way I'd left him.

Staring up at me.

He was *not* staring up at me; he had no eyes. Down there after turning him over, I'd gotten a good look at his face. It had been smashed apart: nose flat, cheekbones and mouth demolished, nasty little craters where his eyes should've been.

But I *felt* him staring up at me. My skin crawled.

What if he gets up and starts climbing out?

A dumb thought, but mine.

It creeped me out plenty.

The moment I was sure that nothing new had been tossed into the chasm, I backed away from the edge.

One more quick look around the scene of our 'last stand,' then I scrammed.

For a while, I couldn't get Matt out of my head. We'd been almost like buddies when I was down at the bottom with him. But now I felt as if he hated me. Maybe because I'd gone off and left him?

I pictured his mutilated, rotten corpse scurrying up the chasm wall, coming after me.

Stupid. But you know how it is. You get some sort of spooky crap into your mind, and it's hard to get rid of.

Trying to get away, I got lost and went in circles for a while. I half expected to rush around a boulder and bump into Matt. Didn't happen, though. Finally, I came to the stream.

By then, I figured I'd given him the slip. (I know, I know, I'm nuts. I was spooked. So sue me.)

Anyway, I felt better and better as I followed the stream downhill toward the lagoon. An irrational relief at leaving Matt behind. More than that, though, I felt a growing sense of elation about my women.

Sure, they might be dead.

I doubted it, though.

No bodies at the scene of the fight. And no blood.

It now seemed more likely than not that they'd been taken alive.

If you take people alive, you probably want to keep them that way. Otherwise, why not just go on and kill them in the first place? Save yourself the trouble of tying them, taking them somewhere, risking an uprising or an escape.

By the time I reached the top of the waterfall, I felt certain that I would be able to find my women alive, and rescue them.

I felt great!

So great that I had an urge to leap off the falls – in spite of knowing the water at the bottom was only waist-deep.

Already wrecked enough from various plummets, I fought off the urge and made my way down to the lagoon by foot. I stopped on the flat rock by the side of the falls and made sure the razor was secure in my sock. Then I took off Connie's towel-vest and rolled it into a bundle.

After lowering myself into the water, I raised the vest overhead with one hand. I kept it dry all the way to the other side of the lagoon. Not climbing out, I tossed it onto the same rock where I'd left my shorts etc.

Then I spent about fifteen minutes having a very pleasant time: floating on my back, sometimes swimming, just relaxing in the smooth warmth of the water, relishing the way it slid over my body, always very aware that it was like a magic vanishing fluid: I could make parts of me, or all of me, disappear at will.

For a while, I felt as if I'd found a wonderful new home.

I would abandon our camp at the beach, and live at the lagoon.

Over near the north end, I saw a place where a slab of rock the size of a dining-room table slanted down into the water. I had probably seen it before, but paid no attention. This time, though, it caught my eye. Though the rest of the shoreline was either dark or dappled with specks of moonlight, the special rock was brightly illuminated. It must've been aligned perfectly with the moon and a break in the treetops. It looked pale and smooth like a patch of snow.

I wanted to climb on.

I wanted to lounge on that glowing white slab and bathe in the moonlight.

I swam most of the way over to it, then waded.

When I first started wading, the water came as high as my shoulders. With each step, the level lowered a little. It was waist-deep when I stepped into something soft and squishy that wrapped around my foot and tripped me. I fell headlong with a splash, and my foot pulled free.

Whatever had grabbed my foot, it wasn't like anything that I'd ever stepped on before.

I didn't know *what* the hell it might be.

Standing again, I turned around. Nothing to see except black water and a few shiny coins of moonlight shimmering on the surface.

I had my ideas about what had tripped me.

I needed to find out for sure.

So I took a deep breath and bent down into the water, reaching toward the bottom with both hands. At first, nothing. I walked slowly, moving my arms.

Instead of finding the thing with my hands, I bumped it with my right foot. I kept my balance, though, and didn't fall. After coming up for air, I went down again, bending and crouching, and explored it.

A naked woman.

She was split wide open from sternum to crotch.

She had a load of stones where her guts should've been.

When I figured it out, I screamed or something. I'm not sure what I did, exactly, but I took in a mouthful of lagoon. I popped up choking. I *would've* screamed my head off then, except that I couldn't breathe. I could only cough and gasp for air and cough some more.

When I was breathing again, I just stood there and shook.

I wanted to be miles away.

But how could I leave without knowing who it was?

I'd touched her enough to know that she was a woman, that she'd been gutted and stuffed with rocks – probably to keep her down. I hadn't explored her well enough, however, to identify her.

So down I went again, quickly, before I had time to change my mind.

The first part I found was a shoulder. I held on to it with one hand, and explored with the other.

I started with her face, feeling it with my fingertips but

trying to keep away from her eyes. I did *not* want to touch her eyes; they might be open – or gone.

Her mouth was open. I fingered her lips, touched the edges of her teeth, and tried to imagine the face that went with them. Which of the women had nice, straight teeth?

In my memory, all of them.

I ran my fingers through her hair. It felt limp and slippery and very short. Kimberly had much longer hair than this, so she was ruled out (unless someone had cut it). Thelma, Connie and Billie all wore their hair very short.

I had my hopes pinned on Thelma – though she seemed unlikely, being Wesley's ally.

After surfacing to take another breath, I went down again.

I wasn't exactly thrilled about touching the breasts of a corpse, but I figured the size of them would tell me plenty. So I took them in my hands. (My first time ever to actually handle bare breasts, and it has to be like this.) They were too large for Kimberly or Connie. Though big, they didn't feel enormous like Thelma's. They seemed to be about Billie's size.

Billie.

God, I sure didn't want it being her. But it *had* to be Billie. Nobody else had breasts the right size.

In a frenzy of despair, I went at the body with both hands. I felt her wide shoulders, and how her sides tapered in, then flared out at the hips. I felt the solid thickness of her thighs.

Not just the breasts had Billie's shape and size.

She felt like Billie all the way up and down.

No!

I went a little nuts and straddled her and dug into her split torso with both hands and started snatching out the rocks that someone had packed in to keep her down.

Someone?

Wesley!

Wesley-fucking-Duncan Beaverton III.

How could he do it to her! How could he kill my Billie? How could he ruin her this way?

I suddenly thought, If Billie's like this, why not the others?

Why not Kimberly and Connie? Maybe they, too, were sprawled on the bottom of the lagoon, hollowed out and stuffed with stones.

I kept digging rocks out of the woman under me.

When I ran out of breath, I flung my head up out of the water and yelled at the top of my lungs, '*Wesley! You fucking cocksucking load of shit! I'm gonna kill you! I'm gonna cut you to pieces and make you EAT 'em, you motherfucking asshole!*'

I cried while I yelled.

And I kept on yelling.

I yelled a lot of things that don't even bear repeating.

With all the yelling and crying, I wore myself out. Finally, I quit. Then I just stood in the waist-deep water, panting for air.

It took me a long while to calm down enough to let me hold my breath and go under again.

She still held plenty of ballast.

Instead of unloading the rest of it by the handful, I crouched beside her, took her by the upper arm and the back of her thigh, and lifted.

Turned her over.

Dumped her out like a canoe.

Right away, she began to rise. I kept hold of her arm, and stood up. There were soft lapping sounds when she broke the surface. I could see, just barely, the dim, pale shape of her. In a few places, the moon put white marks on the skin of her back and rump. The patches of light scooted down her body as I floated her toward shore.

I climbed onto the tilted slab of rock.

Squatting at its edge, I lifted her by the arms. I staggered backward and dragged her up with me. She made sloshy sounds like someone rising out of a bathtub.

I let go of her arms, but stayed kneeling above her head.

The moon shone down like a spotlight onto us. A white spotlight, dimmed for gloomy atmosphere.

Bright enough, though, to let me see a few things.

She'd been beaten. Her back and buttocks were stained in places with gray blotches that appeared to be bruises. They were also criss-crossed with stripes as if she'd been whipped.

She'd also been stabbed in the back many times. Each wound was a narrow slot, more than an inch long, with puffy edges. (Probably made by a blade about the width of the knives that I'd seen on Wesley's belt when he leaped across the chasm.) I had a difficult time finding all of them – some were hidden among the lash marks. So I crawled alongside her body, searching them out, studying and counting them.

I found eighteen stab wounds in her back.

I found none in her buttocks.

But I made a startling discovery there – something I might've noticed right away if my attention hadn't been focused so completely on her injuries.

Bruises and lash-marks aside, her buttocks were the same pale shade of gray as her lower back and her thighs.

Where was her tan line?

Billie, I knew, had stark borders between her tanned skin and the parts covered by her bikini. Where she wasn't tawny, she was as pale as milk.

With her black bikini pants gone, she would certainly look as if she'd changed into a new, white pair.

She shouldn't be all one shade, like this.

For a few moments, I knew this wasn't Billie. Then doubts came.

Not enough time had passed, since I'd seen her last, for her tan to fade so completely. But several days had gone by. If she'd spent them naked in the sun, the white of her buttocks might've darkened enough to match the rest of her.

And what about being submerged in the lagoon? Over a period of time, the water might've done something to her skin color.

She hadn't been in it very long, though.

Not very long at all.

From the start, I'd been vaguely aware that she seemed to be in decent shape for a dead person. I hadn't given the matter much thought, though, except to be thankful that she wasn't as repulsive as she might be. That is, she didn't feel slimy or stiff or rotten.

(Compared to Matt, she was a regular Sleeping Beauty.)

Suddenly, it dawned on me that she was *extremely* fresh.

I picked up one of her hands. Holding it close to my face, I studied the fingertips. They were pruned, all right. But not that much.

I compared them to my own wrinkled fingertips.

I'm no damn forensic pathologist, but it was suddenly obvious that she hadn't been in the water for more than about an hour.

She had probably still been alive while I was above the falls trying to find our battleground.

If I hadn't gotten lost up there (twice) . . .

If I hadn't spent so much time looking around . . .

I might've returned to the lagoon in time to find her being murdered, gutted, stuffed, sunk.

Maybe I could have saved her.

Or maybe I would've gotten myself murdered, gutted . . .

Life and death, a matter of destinations and delays.

Only they don't tell you the right or wrong place to be, or when.

I couldn't bear the thought that I might've missed a chance, by such a slim margin, to save Billie's life.

I turned the woman over.

Glimpsed the terrible chasm down the middle of her torso. Looked a bit longer at her breasts: bruises, welts, scratches, but no stab wounds. Then made myself gaze at her face.

It was gray in the moonlight, etched and pocked with black shadows.

Enough of it showed, though.

This was not Billie's face.

This was the face of a woman I had never seen before, not even in my dreams.

I swam back to the place where I'd left my stuff, found Andrew's lighter, and returned to the body. Kneeling by her side, I studied her by the lighter's small, shaky flame.

She was definitely a stranger.

Physically, she bore a lot of resemblance to Billie. They

268

seemed to be similar in age, size, build, and hair color. Even their faces had much in common. I could see that this wasn't Billie, but it would've been hard to describe the differences. This woman's face had obviously been attractive, even beautiful, before her death.

Her face, by the way, showed no signs of injury.

(Wesley hadn't wanted to spoil her looks, more than likely – just torture and murder her.)

Before leaving, I dragged her a small distance away from the lagoon. I hid her in among some rocks – so I'd be spared the sight of her, maybe, if I should return to the lagoon in the near future.

Speculations

I'm now nearly caught up to the present. A good thing, too, because I've only got a few pages left in my notebook.

I've had plenty of time to think about things.

I think the dead woman was probably linked, somehow, to Matt. I think they lived together, here on the island, before our arrival. My guess is that they were married to each other.

Wesley murdered Matt first – probably just before Thelma came into our camp and told us she'd bashed Wesley's brains in. He would've expected us to go looking for his body as soon as we heard the news, so it would've been in position at the bottom of the chasm on Day Six, waiting for us. That was two days before I got thrown down on top of Matt's remains.

Wesley kept the woman alive, abusing her, and didn't get around to killing her until shortly before I found her body in the lagoon two nights ago.

Obviously, Thelma had a hand in things, too. They're in it together. Partners, allies, accomplices.

Some of this is just speculation, of course.

But it makes sense to me.

I wonder about a lot of things, though.

If I'm right about Matt and the woman being inhabitants of the island, did they live in a house? Is their house the place where Wesley got his hands on such things as the ax and rope?

Where *is* their house?

If I find it, will I also find Kimberly, Billie and Connie?

I think so.

I think so, yes. If they are still alive, I'll probably find them at the house.

Last Words

Okay. I'm up to date with my journal, now. In fact, I'm done with it. I have no more reason to procrastinate. I can't build my Winchester House of words; there's no more room for words – or hardly enough to matter.

Tomorrow, I'll set out to search for my women. I don't expect I'll be returning to our beach. I plan to travel light; wearing Connie's towel-vest, Andrew's shorts, and my own socks and shoes. I'll carry the lighter in my pocket, of course. And I'll take along Billie's sun-block, mostly because it reminds me of her and it smells good. My only weapon will be Thelma's straight razor.

I'll take my journal with me in the book bag, along with a couple of pens that haven't yet run out of ink (in case I should stumble upon paper but no writing implement), my swimming trunks (though I haven't worn them since acquiring Andrew's shorts), the pink blouse that Billie gave me (though I now prefer to wear Connie's vest), and a few remaining items of food.

I'll leave just about everything else behind. Including Andrew's camera. I haven't used it yet, so I can't see a good reason to lug it around.

The less I have to carry, the better.

I do wish that I had something of Kimberly's, though. Her Swiss Army knife (Andrew's before it came into her possession) would have been a great treasure. I haven't been able to find it anywhere, though.

I have nothing of Kimberly's to carry with me.

Only my memories of her.

With luck, though, I'll be with all three of my women soon.

If I can find the mystery house, they'll be nearby. I'd bet on it.

Whether or not I find them alive, I'll take care of Wesley and Thelma.

I'll make it hard for them, too.

Very hard.

Bet on it.

I'll make them pay for every hurt they've done to my women.

Which sounds like a mean-spirited, brutal way to end my journal. But so be it.

Obviously, I'll tell the rest of my story if I'm able. To do that, I'll need to find a new source of paper. And I'll have to still be alive.

Both good tricks.

So long.

The Rest of the Story

My Quest For the Mystery House

I've gotten hold of a new notebook.

A lot has happened since my last entry.

I'll take my time, though, and tell about it in the proper sequence – starting with the morning when I went off to hunt for the house.

The island obviously had no shortage of vacant beachfront property, so nobody in their right mind would've built a house somewhere deep in the jungle. You'd want an ocean view. You'd want easy access to the water.

If I just followed the shoreline, I was almost certain to spot the home of Matt and the dead woman.

I started out early in the morning. After a light breakfast of smoked fish, I filled an empty booze bottle with water from the stream (just in case), put the bottle in my book bag, shouldered the bag and set off, heading north.

This had been our route on the morning of the 'last stand,' until Kimberly ran off without us.

Now, I was alone as I hiked the beach.

Though I started my journey with eagerness, sure of success, my optimism dwindled along the way. There might not *be* any house. Its existence was nothing more than a theory of mine.

For all I knew at the time (I've found out plenty since), Matt and the woman hadn't necessarily been residents of the island. They might've come to it for a brief visit – parked their boat and come ashore to do some exploring, have a picnic, who knows? Or they might've been castaways:

survivors from a boat wreck or airplane crash. If so, I was searching for a home that didn't exist.

No, no, I told myself. There *has* to be a house. If not, where did Wesley get his hands on the ax, the rope, the machetes, the sheath knives he wore on his belt, the belt itself . . .?

That argument comforted me for a while.

But then I remembered how, within a day or two after being marooned, Billie and I had come up with the theory that Wesley must've made a prior visit to the island.

He had obviously toured the region to search for a good island to use. Just as obviously, he would've taken steps to avoid becoming a victim of his own plot. That is, he planned to maroon the bunch of us, but he sure didn't want to find himself trapped on an island without the means to ensure his own survival.

So we had figured out, way back at the start of the whole mess, that he must've come ashore earlier and hidden a load of supplies.

Supplies that might've included the ax, rope etc.

By the time I'd spent a few hours hiking along the shore, I had pretty much convinced myself that I wouldn't be finding any house. The house was a phantom, thrown together by bad logic and wishful thinking.

It would've been too convenient, too easy.

Find them all in a shack by the shore. Go sneaking in late at night, commando-style . . .

No, it wasn't going to be that simple.

I would probably need to hunt for them in the jungle. In the region above the lagoon and in the areas beyond where I'd never been before. Who knows? Maybe they had a cave.

The problem was, I didn't want to go looking for them in the jungle.

I wanted to stay on the beach, where I could feel the sun and the soft breezes, where I had a fine, open view in all directions and nobody could sneak up on me.

Besides, the house *might* exist.

Even if it didn't, there were plenty of good reasons to

continue along the beach. No telling what I might find. We'd always intended to explore the boundaries of our island, but had never gotten around to it. Thanks to Wesley, there'd always been more urgent matters to deal with first.

I was finally getting around to it.

I decided to keep at it, too. Any journey into the jungle would have to wait for a day or two, or however long it might take me to circle the island.

I felt as if I'd been granted a reprieve.

Then I found the house.

Some time earlier, I had rounded the north end of the island and started back along the eastern shore. I'd been hiking southward for quite a while when I came to a cove.

From a distance, the cove had been out of sight. I'd seen nothing ahead except more beach – ocean on one side, jungle on the other. Though my view had been obstructed, here and there, by rocky areas, I assumed that I was approaching a continuous shore-line.

I was climbing over a low spine of rocks when I first noticed a break in the beach ahead.

Seeing my forward progress blocked by water, I felt frustrated and annoyed; it was an inconvenience that would force me to walk a lot farther than I'd expected. Within a few seconds, though, my curiosity took over.

I could see across the water to where the beach started again, but very little of what lay to the right. The trees at the edge of the jungle got in the way. What seemed to be ahead, however, was a small bay, or cove, that looked at least five times as large as our little inlet on the other side of the island.

Hurrying down from the rocks, I ran through the sand. With each stride, more of the cove's opposite shore came into sight. More and more.

Nothing but sand and rocks; jungle further back.

When the boat loomed into view, it scared the shit out of me. I dived for the sand.

Stretched out on the beach with my head up, I gazed at the vessel.

There'd been no need to panic; it wasn't under way, as I'd thought.

I saw anchor lines stretching down into the water.

I saw nobody aboard.

It was a big white cabin cruiser – about a forty-footer.

Matt's boat, I figured.

And our ticket out of here.

Now all I've gotta do is find my women . . .

That's what ran through my mind, for a few seconds. I was elated. Then scared, realizing I might've already been seen. Just because the boat *looked* deserted . . .

I stared hard at it, and wondered if Wesley or Thelma might be staring back at me through a window or port.

No sign of anyone.

I scurried on my belly for the edge of the jungle. In the shelter of the bushes and trees, I got to my feet. Then I snuck through the thick foliage until the cove came into view again.

From my new position, I had a full, wide view.

Off to the right, perhaps a hundred yards beyond the anchored cabin cruiser, a dock jutted out from the shore. Floating at the end of the dock were two dinghies. One of them had probably been used to transport people (Matt and the woman?) ashore from the anchored cruiser. The other looked a lot like *our* dinghy.

I'd last seen it heading north, Wesley aboard, when he was making his getaway after splitting open Andrew's head.

He must've brought our dinghy here, and docked it.

I hardly got a chance to think about the dinghies, though, because the house suddenly caught my attention.

For my high-school graduation present, just last summer, my parents took me on a special trip.

It started with spending a week in Memphis, Tennessee.

There, I almost got trampled to death by a mob of spectators in the lobby of the Peabody Hotel when I tried to catch a glimpse of the damn ducks that march through twice a day. I almost got *scared* to death when we visited the Civil Rights Museum at the old Lorraine Motel where Martin

Luther King got shot. My white parents and I were pretty much the only people of that shade roaming through the museum, which seems to be a monument to the evils of the white man.

Memphis wasn't all bad, though. It had delicious barbeque and fabulous music. Every night, we walked from our hotel to Beale Street, where the blues were born. Beale Street was great.

While staying in Memphis, we also visited Elvis's home, Graceland.

The house on the cove didn't remind me of Graceland.

No, this house was what I'd *imagined* Graceland would be like: a huge plantation-style mansion.

Graceland had turned out to be smaller, more modern than I'd expected. But I had a chance to see plenty of actual plantation houses after leaving Memphis.

My *real* graduation present wasn't the visit to Memphis, but a trip down Old Man River on an authentic paddlewheel steamboat, the *Mississippi Queen*. (For one thing, I'm a big fan of Mark Twain.) We spent six days and nights on the river, and ended up in New Orleans.

Along the way, we stopped at places like Vicksburg and Natchez. And visited God-only-knows how many ante-bellum homes. These were plantation houses built in the period before the War Between the States. Big old hunchers, usually three storys high, full of narrow stairways and tiny rooms, their outsides loaded with columns, balconies and verandas.

They were very interesting until you'd been through about two of them. After that, they mostly looked alike. (Mom is big on antiques and Dad is a Civil War buff, so they were happy as pigs in slop. My fondness for Mark Twain didn't extend far enough, though, to cover endless, dreary tours of mansions.)

The deal is, the white mansion beyond the cove looked as if it had been plucked off the grounds of an old cotton or tobacco plantation on the Mississippi, and plonked down here.

I gaped at it, stunned.

What the hell was an ante-bellum mansion doing on a little lost island like this one?

My imagination told me that a Southern Gentleman had settled here, long ago. Maybe he'd lost his original plantation house during the War Between the States (most of them went up in smoke, though you wouldn't think so if you ever got pushed into touring them), so he'd sailed to this island to start over again – far from the Yankees – and built this home in the image of the one he'd lost.

Sort of a romantic notion, and probably wrong.

Maybe it was built in the 1980s by a rich guy with a weird fondness for Scarlett O'Hara (or Rhett).

I kept staring at it from my hiding place at the edge of the jungle.

I would've been pretty thrilled to find any house at all.

But *this*!

I felt as if I'd taken one small step into *The Twilight Zone*. All I needed was Connie to give me the 'doo-*de*-do-do' music and her Serling intro – *One Rupert Conway, eighteen, took a little walk along the beach one day in search of his missing ladies. Instead of finding the ladies, he found himself venturing into a strange land ruled by the limits of the imagination . . .*

I stared at the mansion for a long time.

It had probably been the home of Matt and the woman I'd found in the lagoon. Just as the cabin cruiser and one of the dinghies must've been theirs.

Theirs until Wesley came along.

He had taken everything from them: their home, their boats, their lives.

And then he'd taken over.

All his, now.

Maybe he'd brought us to this island – killed our men and captured our women – because he wanted belles for his cotillions.

Or servants for his mansion.

Or slaves.

Recon

After watching for a long time and seeing nobody, I made my way through the jungle. I moved cautiously, stopping often to check around and listen. Usually, I stayed away from the cove. Every so often, though, I snuck closer to it for another look.

I saw nobody: not on the cabin cruiser, not on the dinghies or dock, not in the water or along the shore, not in or around the mansion. Nowhere.

Nor did I hear any voices or other sounds, such as pounding, that would tell of people nearby. Of course, it would've taken some major noise to reach me through all the squawks and squeals and shrieks from the birds and other animals. (Some of the shrieks sounded almost human, but I figured they probably came from birds.)

Finally, when I took a left and snuck toward the cove, I came to a lawn instead of the shoreline – a broad field of grass that led to the rear of the mansion. The lawn looked as if it had been well-kept until recently. It needed a mowing.

At the far side of the lawn was a red tractor mower. It didn't seem to belong there. The way things looked, someone might've started to cut the grass, but quit before getting very far and never got a chance to put the tractor away.

Off beyond it, past the side of the house, were a couple of brick outbuildings. One had an open door large enough for the mower to fit through.

I couldn't see what was inside. Just a small, empty space near the front – probably where the mower should go.

In places where you keep your lawn mower, you usually store other equipment and tools. Things like shovels, picks, pruning shears, hammers, saws ...

Axes.

My heart pounded a little faster.

This could be the place where Wesley had gotten hold of the ax.

Maybe the rope, too. The rope he'd used for hanging Keith.

He'd strung Keith up during our first night on the island. So he must've come here immediately after blowing up the yacht. Is that when he killed Matt and the woman?

No. Impossible. Neither of them had been dead that long. Matt had probably been alive for most of the first week – killed only when they needed a body to double for Wesley. And the woman must've been killed the very same night I found her body in the lagoon.

Wesley had probably held both of them captive from Day One until their deaths.

Where had he kept them?

In one of the outbuildings?

Aboard the yacht?

Inside the mansion itself? Maybe in a bedroom or attic or cellar?

Somewhere else?

The place where Matt and the woman had been kept was, almost for sure, the prison where Wesley now held Kimberly, Billie and Connie.

If they're still alive.

He took them alive. Otherwise, I would've found their bodies at the battlefield.

He took them alive, and he's *keeping* them alive.

I had to believe that.

I had to hang on to that belief, no matter what. It was like a rope over the edge of a chasm – only not a shallow chasm like the one beyond the falls.

One so deep I would fall for a mile. If I lost my hold, down I'd go, screaming all the way to the bottom.

They're alive, I told myself. I just need to find where Wesley's keeping them, set them free, and take Wesley and Thelma out of the picture.

Not necessarily in that order.

What should I do first? I wondered.

Find someone. If not my women, at least find Wesley or Thelma.

Get up and go, I told myself.

But I stayed put.

I just couldn't force myself to break cover.

That's because Thelma and Wesley were almost sure to be nearby. If one of them should spot me sneaking around, I'd lose any chance of taking them by surprise.

Then I'd probably lose my life.

If that happened, I'd not only be dead (which I hoped to avoid for as long as possible), but I would pretty much cease having a chance to rescue my women. If *I* couldn't save them, who would?

More than likely, I was their only hope.

Barring some sort of miraculous rescue by outside forces, they would remain at Wesley's mercy for weeks, months . . . maybe even for years.

Maybe for the rest of their lives.

For their sakes (not just for my own), I needed to be extremely careful, take no chances; under no circumstances allow myself to be captured or killed.

What I oughta do, I thought, is get the hell off the island and bring back help.

It sounded like a chicken way out.

But it also seemed like the smartest move – by a long shot.

Take the cabin cruiser to the nearest inhabited island, get in touch with the authorities, and come back with a rescue team.

For a while there, it seemed like the perfect solution to my problem.

I could wait for dark, then swim out to the cabin cruiser, cut the anchor lines, start the engine . . .

Start it with what key?

Even if Matt and the woman had been trusting or stupid enough to leave the boat's key in the ignition, Wesley wasn't. He would've gone out there, at some point. Checked the vessel from stem to stern. Taken whatever he felt an urge to take.

Not much chance he would've left the starter key behind.

Not a crafty bastard like Wesley.

And I'm not exactly the kind of guy who knows the first thing about how to hotwire an Evinrude or Johnson, or whatever. Without the key, I had no chance in the world of starting the engine.

Where would I find the ignition key?

Probably in Wesley's pocket.

Great. If I could hunt down Wesley and take the key off him, I wouldn't *need* to run off on the boat and go for help.

So much for fleeing on the cabin cruiser.

Just as well. It would've been the 'smart' thing to do, but I sort of hated the idea.

I don't really think I *could've* done it – left the island without knowing what had happened to my women, whether they were even still alive. And if I *had* found them alive, I couldn't have gone off without rescuing them.

Sometimes, you just can't do the 'smart' thing because it leaves out the heart.

That sounds sort of sappy.

The deal is, those three women had gotten to mean a lot to me. (Not just that they made me horny, either.) I couldn't abandon them, not even if that would've been the best way to save them.

I *could* make them wait, though.

They'd been captured (if captured) at least five or six days ago, maybe longer. A few more hours shouldn't matter very much to them. The hours might make plenty of difference to me, though.

I needed to wait until dark.

Darkness would hide me, so I'd be able to move about without so much risk of being spotted. Also, somebody might put on a light.

I *really* hoped for a light; it would give me a location.

It might even light my way to Wesley and Thelma.

Night, however, was a long time off.

I crept away from the edge of the lawn. When I was surrounded by jungle so thick I could see no trace of the lawn or mansion, I lay down on my back to rest. I used my book bag for a pillow.

There seemed to be little hope of falling asleep. I was too nervous and excited. Also, I ached nearly everywhere from my injuries. The plan was simply to rest and wait for night to come.

Shutting my eyes, I thought about my plans. Soon, I began daydreaming about the women. The next thing I knew, I found myself waking up in the dark.

Not knowing where the night might take me, I decided against leaving my book bag behind. I sure didn't want to lose it – not with the journal inside. The only way to make sure it stayed safe was to keep it with me.

I made my way back to the edge of the lawn. The windows of the mansion – those within sight – all looked dark. There was no light anywhere except for what came from the moon and stars.

Staying hidden, I kept watch for a long time. Nobody appeared. No lights came on.

Maybe I had the wrong house.

Maybe this house had nothing to do with Wesley, and was simply deserted.

No, no. Our dinghy was at the dock.

This had to be the right house.

But maybe Wesley wasn't using it. He might've simply raided the place, taken what he wanted (including the man and woman who lived here), and returned to some secret base camp in the jungle.

If he wasn't here, I'd already wasted hours upon hours.

I suddenly couldn't stand the thought of waiting any longer, so I broke cover and dashed across the lawn. Nobody yelled. Nobody shot at me. Nothing happened. I stopped at the side of the house, near its rear corner. Leaning against the wall, I tried to catch my breath and calm down.

So far, so good.

I'll just walk around the whole building, I thought. Check to see if there are any lights on.

If the place is dark, I'll try to get in.

The Game

I was about to push myself away from the wall when a fluttery, dim glow seemed to drift out the window just to my left and hover in the darkness. The murky light was so faint, at first, that I wondered if it might be a trick of the moonlight – or my imagination.

It grew brighter.

I gazed at it, stunned. For a while, I couldn't move. Then I forced myself to sneak toward the window.

I was afraid of what I might find, but I *had* to look. My heart slammed. My stomach trembled. My legs felt weak and unstable.

The fact is, I was shaking all over by the time I reached the window and peered in.

The room on the other side was lit by candles and several kerosine lamps with glass chimneys. Thelma, walking about with a candle in her hand, ignited more candles while I watched.

She wore a glossy, royal blue robe that looked like satin. It was too short for her. She had to reach high, now and then, to light wall sconces. Each time she did that, the lower half of her ass showed. Not a pretty sight. Her big buttocks, ruddy from a sunburn, looked dimpled and lumpy. They were bruised, too, and striped with red marks from being lashed.

Her legs also looked banged up – a lot more so than they'd been the last time I'd seen her.

When she turned in my direction, I saw that her robe wasn't shut all the way. She was bare down her middle – except for the loosely tied sash that crossed her belly. The opening was too narrow to let me see much. Only that she'd gotten a sunburn all the way down.

I realized she was coming straight toward me, so I dropped to a crouch.

Directly above my head, the window scooted upward. Thelma sighed.

What if she leans out!

She can't, I told myself. A screen's in the way.

I wondered if she could see me, anyway. Screen or no screen, she might be able to spot the top of my head if she looked downward.

Or she might hear my slamming heart.

No sounds of alarm came from her, though. Just that one sigh. A few seconds later, I heard her bare feet thumping away.

Up again, I put my face to the window screen.

Thelma seemed to be gone. The room she'd left behind was bright with tiny flames. She had lit perhaps twenty of them with her candle, but those twenty were caught and doubled by a mirror that stretched the length of one entire wall – the wall way over to the left, not the one straight across the room from me, so I'd probably not been reflected in it.

Attached to that mirror wall, at about waist-height, was a wooden rail. It looked like the sort of rail that ballet dancers use during practice.

Dance practice would also explain the long, full-length mirror.

In one corner of the room stood a baby grand piano.

In another corner was a sound system. It appeared to have a turntable, radio, twin speakers, the works.

I saw light fixtures on the ceiling.

Lamps with cords snaking across the floor to wall outlets.

So the mansion came with electricity, after all.

I wondered if there might be a generator, somewhere, that had broken down on Wesley and Thelma. Or maybe they just didn't know how to work it.

Possibly, they'd made a choice not to use any electricity. Maybe they feared it would give them away, somehow. Or perhaps they simply preferred candlelight.

Most of the floor was empty. To give the dancers plenty of prancing space, I suppose.

The room was more than a dance studio, though. Apparently, it doubled as a reading room, or library. It had a few small tables, lamps, and some thickly padded chairs over near the wall to my right. A wall of floor-to-ceiling bookshelves.

Movement in the mirror suddenly caught my eyes.

It reflected the doorway near the middle of the bookshelf wall.

I saw Wesley before he even came in.

If I can see him in the mirror, he can probably see me.

I ducked and waited, my heart hammering.

A few quiet sounds came: bare feet, wood creaking, a noise like a chair being scooted, the *snick* of a striking match. Then Wesley said, 'What would you like if you win tonight, my dear?'

A voice murmured, 'Nothing.'

'Oh, you must want something.' Wesley sounded very cheerful. 'What'll it be?'

'As if she's gonna win, anyhow,' Thelma said. 'Hasn't got a chance.'

'Of *course* she has a chance. There's always a chance.'

'Yeah, sure,' Thelma said. 'There's a *chance* I'll get struck by lightning.'

'Name your prize, my dear.'

I eased myself higher until I could see in.

The girl stood with her back to me, facing Wesley. She was slender and several inches shorter than Thelma. She had blond hair in a ponytail. She wore a short-sleeved white blouse, a tartan kilt that seemed mostly green and blue, forest green knee socks, and no shoes. The mirror, off to her left, gave me a side view of her face.

I had never seen her before.

My guess was that she might be thirteen or fourteen years old.

Matt's daughter? Daughter of the lagoon woman with the rocks in her belly?

I wanted her to be Kimberly, Billie, or Connie. I'd come here to find them, not some stranger. Where were *my* women?

My mission wasn't a complete failure, though; at least I'd found my two enemies.

Thelma, off to the girl's right, was facing Wesley.

Wesley sat in a padded armchair, grinning at the girl. He

wore a square white bandage on his chest. It reminded me of a pirate's eye patch, the way it covered only one side while his other boob bulged out, bare.

Because of how he sat deep in the chair, with one leg crossed, he looked naked. I'd had that glimpse of him in the mirror, though, while he'd been coming in from the hallway. He'd been wearing a belt, two sheathed knives, and some sort of blue bikini-style shorts – briefs or a swimming suit, I couldn't tell which. The way he was seated, I couldn't see any of that.

Except for his bandage, he looked like an acre of bare, hairy skin. (He even had hair on the tops of his shoulders.) He had a dark tan.

Other than his chest wound, he didn't have any signs of injury. Nobody'd been whipping him, slapping him, punching him, kicking him, biting him. (I'm aware, of course, that he was sitting on a good wound. I couldn't see it, though.)

Pinched between Wesley's thumb and forefinger was the long, silver tube of a cigarette holder – but not the one I'd seen him using on the yacht. (That had been ivory.) A cigarette was plugged into the end of it. A thin, pale stream of smoke climbed the air in front of his face.

'Your prize, Erin?' he asked again.

The girl's shoulders shrugged slightly. A moment later, she muttered, 'Doesn't matter.'

Wesley seemed amused. 'Of course it matters! Certainly! You must have an incentive. We can't have you giving up too easily, can we?'

The way Erin looked from behind, she had already given up.

'What would you like more than anything else in the whole world?' Wesley asked. 'But no fair asking for your mother and father.'

After a few moments, Erin said in a soft voice I almost couldn't hear, 'Let us go?'

Thelma gave a snort.

Wesley said, 'Let who go?'

'My sister and I.'

'Good try! I'm afraid that's out of the question, though. Name something realistic.'

'Like what?'

'How about a Pepsi?'

Thelma snorted again.

'Okay,' the girl said. 'But one for Alice, too.'

'Alice can win her own.'

'If she can't have one, I don't want one, either.'

Wesley blew smoke at her. 'Have it your way. I'm trying to be nice, offer you a prize. Where's your gratitude?'

Erin said nothing.

Wesley took a puff, then gave a nod to Thelma.

She stepped up behind Erin, reached around her, and ripped open the front of her blouse. She peeled the blouse off the girl's shoulders and down her back. Then she stepped aside and tossed it to the floor.

Erin was bare down to her kilt. She had narrow, fragile shoulders. Her back was smooth and tanned, and looked as if it might've had a few days to heal since her last beating. It had seen a lot of abuse, though. Along with livid blotches, there were several old, fading yellowish bruises. Along with numerous crusty brown scabs that criss-crossed her back, she had pale, shiny pink stripes where older scabs had come off.

She just stood in front of Wesley, arms hanging by her sides, not even trying to cover herself.

The mirror gave me a side view of her breasts. They came to points and looked like small, soft cones. They were almost as tanned as her back.

'Lovely,' Wesley said. 'You're a very lovely girl, Erin.'

She didn't respond.

'When someone gives you a compliment, you're supposed to say thank you.'

'Thank you,' she mumbled.

'I'd like you to put up a good fight, tonight,' he told her. 'No slacking, like last time.'

She just stood there, limp, her head and arms hanging.

'Let's start the fun,' he said.

Thelma's blue satin robe fell to the floor. She looked as if she'd watched a lot of television wrestling, the way she stomped toward Erin.

But this was no 'gorgeous lady of wrestling.'

This was a monster, battle-scarred, growling, hunched over, arms open, fingers hooked like claws. She attacked from behind, hugged Erin, hoisted her up, swung her around and hurled her.

Flung her in my direction.

The girl came toward me, feet first. Under her kilt, she was bare all the way to her waist.

In midair, she made a frightened noise as if she suddenly realized she had a long way to fall.

She hit the hardwood floor, thudding and bumping as she tumbled, letting out whimpers and grunts, her skin squeaking as she skidded. When she came to a stop, she just lay there on her back and sobbed. Her kilt was up around her hips. I had a hell of a view. I felt guilty, looking. I couldn't *help* looking, though.

I mean, the way she was sprawled out on the floor with her feet no more than about two yards in front of my window.

It ran through my mind that I ought to help her.

But what could I do? I'm not a big guy. I didn't have a gun. My only weapon was the straight razor in the pocket of my shorts. If I just tried to Rambo my way in and save the day, Thelma would wipe me out. She probably wouldn't even need Wesley's help.

I watched her storm across the floor, her huge breasts swinging and flopping. Her eyes were fixed on Erin.

Who didn't even try to get up or defend herself.

'Fight, ya little twat,' Thelma gasped. She clamped the girl's head between her ankles and hopped. Erin's trapped head was jerked up off the floor, then slammed down.

Then Thelma dropped on top of her.

A lot happened, after that – nasty stuff I don't want to write about.

I'm ashamed of myself for watching. Looking back on it now, I know that I should've done whatever I could to stop it. But I was enthralled. Horrified and disgusted, but entranced.

I'd never seen anything like this before. As much as I felt sorry for Erin and wanted to help her, I couldn't force myself to stop watching the spectacle.

I told myself there was nothing I could do, anyway.

Which was pure shit. I could've stopped it. One way or another.

Didn't want to, that was the thing.

The girl never did put up any struggle.

Thelma didn't let that stop her. She stripped off Erin's knee socks, wrestled her, squeezed her, tugged the kilt down Erin's legs, kissed her and sucked her and bit her, pinched her, twisted her, slapped and probed her.

They were a rolling tangle of bare flesh. Both of them gasping for air. Both of them groaning and whimpering. Both shiny with sweat and spittle and God-knows-what.

I watched from my window.

Wesley watched from his chair across the room, puffing cigarettes, leaning forward, eyes fixed on the action. He squirmed around a lot. Sometimes, he licked his lips.

I only glanced at him from time to time. Mostly, I watched Thelma and Erin.

By the time I noticed that Wesley had gotten out of his chair, he no longer had his shorts on. His belt was gone, too. He wore nothing but his bandages. His cigarette holder jutted upward from between his teeth, and smoke drifted into his right eye as he strolled toward the women.

His penis led the way, big and solid, pointing at the ceiling.

From his right hand dangled a length of electric cord. (I don't know where it came from – hadn't noticed it before.) Its end trailed along on the floor beside him.

When he got to where Thelma was working on Erin, he began to use the cord on them. He didn't seem to care whether he hit Thelma or the girl. Either of them seemed fine with him.

He started off by casually flicking them with the cord. Toying with them. Slowly, though, he worked himself into a frenzy. He became like a madman. Wild-eyed, huffing for breath, slobbering down his chin, he pranced around them, swinging the cord so hard it whistled. It cracked against their skin. Made them jerk rigid with pain. They writhed and shrieked and bled on the floor.

Through all of this, Thelma never stopped holding on to Erin. Never stopped offering the girl's body to Wesley's lash. And never stopped hurting Erin with her own hands and mouth.

Again, I don't want to dwell on all the nasty details.

I'll skip to the finish.

This is how it ended – with Thelma on her back on the floor, Erin on top of her.

Thelma used her arms and legs to pin the girl to her – face up and spread-eagled. They were both very bloody from the whipping and other things that had been done to them. But now, with Thelma holding Erin helpless, Wesley dropped on top of them both.

He raped Erin.

While he did it, Thelma went nuts on the bottom as if *she* was the one getting screwed.

Then it was over.

They unpiled. Thelma and Wesley took Erin by her arms, helped her up, and walked her out of the room.

I sank down against the wall under the window, shaky and exhausted. Dazed by what I'd seen.

I wished I hadn't watched.

Also, though, I wished I could get to see it all again.

I know, sick.

The thing is, you don't get a chance to see something like that every day.

Like a car accident.

Only better.

Never mind. I know I shouldn't have watched. I should've risked my life to stop it. But I didn't. How come?

A. I'm a miserable, horny pervert.

B. I didn't even know the girl.

C. Thelma and/or Wesley would've killed me.

D. I owe my allegiance to Kimberly, Billie and Connie, not to some stranger.

E. All of the above.

After the Game

After they left the room, I didn't know where they might be. I figured they would probably return pretty soon, though, if only to gather their clothes and put out the candles and lamps. You don't leave flames untended, not for long. Not unless you want to burn down your house.

I could burn the place down!

Standing up, I peered through the window.

Nobody'd come back into the room, yet.

All I needed to do was remove the window screen (or slit it with my razor), climb in and spread around some kerosine, toss a candle . . .

And maybe burn up Kimberly, Billie and Connie – not to mention Erin and her sister, Alice.

As far as I knew, they might all be locked inside the house, somewhere.

Maybe others, too.

I couldn't take any sort of action until I knew where they were being kept.

I'd missed a great opportunity to find them, I realized. While Wesley and Thelma were busy brutalizing Erin in the dance room, I should have gone exploring. I probably could've searched the whole house – with no danger of being caught. Instead, I'd just planted myself at the window and gotten my kicks watching the show.

I'd blown it.

Maybe I'd blown my single, best chance to find and save my women.

All because I'm a low-life, horny pervert.

On the other hand . . . I didn't know in advance that they'd be spending an hour or more messing with that girl. If I *hadn't* stayed and watched, maybe I would've been in the house when they got done. I might've bumped smack into them and gotten myself nailed.

Being a low-life, horny pervert might've saved my life.

Might've saved my women, too, since there was nobody to rescue them except me.

You just never know.

Maybe it was a good thing that I stayed and watched.

While I stood outside the window, peering in and thinking about all that stuff, Thelma came back into the room. She was still naked, but no longer bloody. Apparently, she'd gone off somewhere to wash up.

She hurried about, crouching to pick up what they'd left behind: her robe, Wesley's pants and belt, Erin's kilt and blouse and knee socks. Clutching them to her bosom, she circled the room and blew out the candles and lamp flames.

When she finished, the room was dark except for faint light from the doorway – and its reflection in the mirror. The mirror showed her backside as she hurried down the hall. Then she disappeared.

I decided to climb in through the window and try to catch up with her.

The only safe way to play: keep my eyes on Thelma and Wesley. So long as I never let them out of my sight, they wouldn't be able to take me by surprise.

Also, they were sure to lead me to my women. (Unless my women were dead, which I couldn't allow myself to believe.)

The window screen was attached to the sill by small hook-and-eye catches. A simple flip of two hooks, and the screen should swing out for me.

But the hooks were on the inside.

At the bottom of the screen, just above one of the hooks, I sliced a small flap with my razor, I pushed against it with the tip of my forefinger. The flap lifted inward. I inserted my finger to the second knuckle and shoved the hook sideways. It was tight in the steel eye. But it suddenly popped out.

I started to work on the screen above the other catch. When the flap was made, I put away my razor. Then I poked my finger in. I shoved at the hook. It slipped free.

The screen went loose at the bottom.

I stuck my index fingers into both the flaps.

I started easing the screen toward me. It came easily.

But all of a sudden, a door banged shut somewhere to my right – in the direction of the front of the house. The sound, though not very loud, startled the hell out of me. I jumped. I felt as if I'd gotten zapped by lightning – a hot current sizzling through my heart and every vein and artery.

I damn near fell down.

Somehow, though, I kept my hold on the screen. I eased it gently back into place, in spite of my quaking hands. Then I let myself collapse.

I lay on the ground, head up, eyes on the grounds by the front of the mansion. I no longer sizzled from the sudden fright, but my heart wouldn't slow down. It whammed like a madman. I had a hard time catching my breath, too. I was a wreck.

Nobody walked into view.

I heard voices, though. Probably Wesley and Thelma, but the sounds were soft and masked by a thousand jungle noises. I didn't have a clue about what was being said.

After a few seconds, the voices faded out completely.

I pushed myself off the ground and ran alongside the house. Glancing around the corner of the veranda, I found my quarry; Wesley and Thelma, walking Erin toward the jungle.

They had their backs to me.

Thelma's right hand clutched Erin by the arm. She carried a flaming torch in her left hand. It lit the three of them with an aura of shimmering gold.

Thelma wore shoes, and nothing else. Erin wore nothing at all. Wesley, holding her by the right arm, wore his knife belt, a bandage on his right buttock, and high-top sneakers.

Erin limped along between her two captors. She'd been cleaned so that she no longer looked as if she'd been rolling in blood. But I could see a mad pattern of stripes on her back and buttocks.

Her head hung. She looked hugely weary.

They led her away from the mansion, following a dirt pathway that curved to the left and vanished into the jungle.

I watched until *they* vanished into the jungle. When all I

could see was the haze of Thelma's torchlight, I broke cover. I dashed past the side of the veranda and across the front lawn (book bag whapping against my back), and didn't slow down until I came to the dirt path.

Crouching low, I crept forward. With bushes in the way, I could no longer see the glow of Thelma's torch. But she and the others couldn't have gone far. They had to be just a short distance ahead.

I snuck around a curve in the path.

And found them.

Found them on the path, no more than fifty feet in front of me.

Loading Erin into a cage.

A cage the size of a small room, bars on all sides, bars across the top, a door of bars in front.

At the fading edges of the torchlight, I could just barely see a second cage. A space the width of a sidewalk separated it, from Erin's cage – enough distance to stop the prisoners from reaching each other, touching.

A girl stood in the second cage, her face pressed between two of the bars. She was poorly lit. She looked too small, though, to be any of my women.

I guessed she might be Alice, Erin's sister.

Wesley shoved Erin through the door of the first cage, then swung it shut and locked it with a key.

He had a whole bunch of keys. They hung on a ring the size of a bracelet. After locking Erin in her cage, he slipped the key-ring over his right wrist.

I figured he and Thelma might turn around soon, to start back, so I scurried off the path and crawled in among the bushes and tree trunks. I'd just gotten myself turned around when they came down the path.

I couldn't see them, so they couldn't see me, either.

I saw the glow of the torch, though. It drifted slowly by, no more than six feet in front of me but high off the ground.

Wesley and Thelma weren't talking. I couldn't hear their footsteps, either. All I heard was the soft jangle of the keys.

The light moved on and vanished. The jangle faded away.

I didn't move.

What if it was a trick? Maybe Wesley stayed behind to spring a trap on me. He could've given the key-ring to Thelma.

Don't be ridiculous, I told myself. They almost certainly think I'm dead, and they *sure* don't know I've tracked them down.

Unless they do.

Unless they spotted me somehow. Somewhere. When I followed them over here to the cages. When I spied on them through the window. Or earlier. Maybe they'd even spotted me before dark.

No.

They don't know I'm here. They think I'm dead. Wesley didn't stay behind to jump me. He and Thelma are on their way back to the mansion.

Probably.

I sure hoped so.

I couldn't see myself staying put all night, hiding there in the bushes on the off-chance that Wesley might be waiting to jump me at the cages.

So I crawled out.

On hands and knees, I looked both ways – up and down the path.

No sign of anybody.

I couldn't see the light of Thelma's torch, either.

Nor could I see the cages. They'd been eaten by the darkness.

Getting to my feet but staying low, I hurried down the path to where it opened with a view of the front lawn and mansion. Thelma and Wesley had almost reached the veranda.

As I watched, Thelma stepped over to a bucket by the side of the veranda stairs. She swept her torch down and plunged its blazing end into the bucket.

No more light.

At least it seemed that way for a few seconds. But then I saw – or thought I saw – Wesley and Thelma climb the veranda stairs. Vague, moving blurs, not quite as dark as the darkness that gave them shape.

One small, pale bit was slightly more distinct than the rest. I figured it must be the bandage on Wesley's ass.

All traces vanished at the top of the stairs, killed by the shadows from the veranda's roof.

Then a door bammed.

They'd gone inside the mansion.

I hoped.

Waiting no longer, I turned around and rushed up the path toward the cages.

Caged Birds

In the absence of Thelma's torchlight, I couldn't see the path. I couldn't see anything at all except for a few different shades of darkness that were flecked, here and there, with dabs of white from the moon.

I remembered Andrew's cigarette lighter. I could feel it in the right front pocket of my shorts, along with the straight razor and Billie's sunblock. They bumped and brushed against my thigh as I walked.

I dug the lighter out. Got my thumb ready to flick it. Then changed my mind.

In the darkness, I was almost invisible.

I *like* being invisible.

You're so safe and powerful when nobody can see you.

I slipped the lighter down inside my pocket, then made my way slowly forward, watching and listening.

Soon, I heard voices. Girl voices, softly spoken, coming from ahead and over to my right. I crept toward them. When I was near enough to understand the words, I crouched down and listened.

'Don't be dumb,' one girl said. 'We aren't old enough.'

'You're the dumb one.' This sounded like Erin's voice, though it seemed more lively than the other times I'd heard it. 'It isn't how old you are, it's whether you're having periods yet.'

'Who says so?'

'Dad.'

'How come he didn't tell me?'

'Maybe you never asked.'

'Mom never said so.'

'Mom never said anything about *any*thing. Not that sort of stuff. That's how come I asked Dad.'

'You asked him when you can start having babies?'

'Sure.'

'How come?'

'Just wondered.'

'So if you already know, how come you're asking *me*?'

Erin didn't answer at first. When she spoke again, she sounded more like the timid kid I'd heard in the room with Thelma and Wesley. 'It's just . . . do you think he's gonna make us have babies?'

'Jeez, don't ask me.'

'That's what's gonna happen, I think. You know?'

'I honestly don't think you can have a baby till you're eighteen.'

'Eighteen? You're nuts. You don't have to be any eighteen.'

'Do, too.'

'Ask Connie.'

Connie!

My heart gave a quick lurch.

'No way. Are you kidding? I'm not gonna wake her up just to ask her some dumb question. She'd kill me.'

'Would not.'

'I'm not gonna.'

'Well anyway, I happen to know for a fact you don't have to be any eighteen. You only gotta be old enough to be having your periods, because that means you've got eggs going. Once that's happening, you can have all the babies you want.'

'No. Huh-uh. You've gotta be eighteen.'

'You're out of your mind.'

'Am not. I read it someplace.'

300

'Eighteen must've meant something else.'

'Like what?'

'How should I know? I didn't read it. I just think we're all gonna end up having babies if we keep letting Wesley screw us.'

'Who's *letting* him?'

'He's doing it anyway, isn't he? I mean, how many times have *you* ever stopped him?'

Alice didn't answer.

For a little while, neither of them spoke. Then Erin said, 'I wonder how many times it takes.'

'For what?'

'You know. To make you pregnant.'

'You tell me. You know everything.'

'I don't know that,' Erin admitted. 'I wonder if you have to do it, like, twenty times or something.'

'I wouldn't know. You should've asked Dad.'

'Very funny. But don't you think we'd maybe be pregnant by now if it only took once or twice or something?'

Alice sighed. 'I guess so.'

'But we aren't, right? He did us both the day he showed up for the first time. Then he got me twice more before he went away. So that makes a total of three, all the way back then.'

'Twice for me,' Alice said.

'But we had our periods since then, so obviously it wasn't enough. So how many *does* it take?'

'Who knows?'

'At least it's not *us* all the time, now that he's got everyone else.'

Everyone else!

I couldn't keep silent any longer. 'Excuse me,' I said.

They both gasped.

'It's okay,' I told them. 'Don't be scared. I'm a friend. I'm here to rescue you.'

Erin said, 'Rupert?'

I couldn't believe my ears.

'Yes,' I said. 'You know who I am?'

'Just a guess. They told us all about you. Where are you? I can't see you.'

I crept closer. No moonlight, at all, made it down to where the cages were. I could see nothing. Not the cages, not the girls, not even my own hands. It was like being shut up at night in a closet.

Reaching out with one hand, I touched bars. 'I'm at your cage.'

'I can't see you,' Erin said.

'I can't see you, either,' I said.

'Are you sure?' Alice asked. 'You can't see either one of us?'

'If we can't see each other *or* him,' Erin said, 'how is he supposed to be able to see us?'

'It's possible. It all depends.'

'Alice is just worried 'cause we don't have much on.'

'That's okay. I can't see a thing.'

'She's Alice, by the way. I'm Erin. We're Alice and Erin Sherman. We're fourteen, and we're twins.'

'Identical twins?' I asked.

'No,' Alice said.

'Yes,' said Erin.

'We are not.'

'In the technical sense, we are. Only we just don't look exactly alike, that's all. Alice thinks she's prettier than me.'

'Liar.'

'But *I'm* actually the pretty one,' Erin said. I imagined her smiling as she said that.

'You're so full of crap,' Alice said, 'it's not even funny.'

I started moving sideways, following the bars. They felt warm in my hands. They were at least an inch thick. The gaps between them seemed to be about four inches across.

'What're you doing?' Erin asked. 'Rupert?'

'I'll get between your cages so we won't have to talk so loud.'

'Have you been here long?' she asked.

I blushed, but nobody could see it. 'No,' I lied. 'Just got here.'

'Everyone thinks you're dead.'

'The reports of my death are greatly exaggerated,' I explained – Mark Twain had said it first.

'Boy, this is great,' Erin said. 'You being alive.'

'And not in a cage,' added Alice.

I found the corner of Erin's cage, and crawled around it. To make sure I was between the cages, I stretched out my arms. I touched bars to my right and left. So I sat down and crossed my legs. 'Okay,' I said.

From both sides came quiet sounds – rustling, sliding, breathing, a couple of small moans – as the girls moved in closer. The moans had come from my right, from Erin. After the beating she'd taken in the room, it probably hurt her a lot to move.

'Are you there?' she asked.

As quietly as I could, I slid myself toward Erin's cage. I stopped when my upper arm touched a bar.

'Can you get us out of here?' Alice asked.

'I sure hope so. One way or another. Is there any way to open these things without a key?'

'Nope,' Erin said. Her voice was much closer to me than Alice's. I thought I could feel her breath on my arm. Though I couldn't see even a hint of her, I pictured her sitting cross-legged, leaning forward, elbows on her thighs, the tips of her breasts almost touching her forearms, her face only inches from the bars.

I wished I could see her.

I thought about the lighter in my pocket.

I didn't go for it, though. Better for us all to stay invisible, at least for the time being.

'You can't get in or out,' Erin said, 'unless you've got keys. These're really strong cages.'

'They were made to hold gorillas,' Alice explained.

Monkey Business

'*Gorillas?*' I asked.

'This used to be a gorilla zoo,' Erin said.

'Before we moved here,' her sister added.

'Yeah, a *long* time before we moved here. We've only been on the island a couple of years.'

'It'll be two years in June,' Alice said.

'The gorillas were all dead before we ever got here. *Long* dead. Like before we were even born. This guy massacred them all. How do you like that? The same guy that brought them here.'

'To save them,' Alice added.

'Yeah,' Erin said. 'There was some sort of revolution going on some place in Africa. Like back in the sixties? And this guy was afraid all the gorillas might get killed off.'

'He was a naturalist,' Alice explained.

'You know, like that *Gorillas in the Mist* woman. Sigourney Weaver?'

'Dian Fossey,' Alice said.

'Yeah,' Erin said, 'like that.'

'He lived right here in the big house when he wasn't running around places like Africa.'

'So anyway,' Erin said, 'he captured like a dozen of these gorillas and shipped them over here to this island. He had the cages built especially for them. Made himself a nice little private zoo.'

'It wasn't really a zoo,' Alice pointed out.

'Not if you wanta get *technical*,' Erin said. 'It wasn't like a *public* zoo. He kept the apes for himself, like pets. Then one day he slaughtered them all.'

'Killed them?' I asked. 'Why'd he do that?'

'Maybe he got tired of them,' Alice suggested.

'Or they done him wrong,' Erin said. Again, I pictured her smiling.

304

'Nobody knows why,' Alice said.

Then Erin went on. 'He must've gone nuts, or something. He chopped them all up in their cages with a machete, and then he shot himself in the head. Anyway, that's how come the cages are here.'

'We weren't permitted to play in them,' Alice said.

'Now we gotta *live* in them,' Erin said.

'Who else is here?' I asked.

'In the cages, you mean?'

'Yeah.'

'Connie and her mother, and Kimberly.'

All of them!

I started to cry. I tried to be quiet about it, but couldn't help letting out a few little noises. Erin and Alice didn't say anything. It was like they were both sitting in their cages, listening to me.

Then something rubbed the top of my head.

I flinched.

'It's just me,' Erin whispered.

Her hand gently stroked my hair, then eased down along my cheek. Petting me.

I'd started crying out of relief at the news my women were here and alive. With Erin caressing my face, though, I started crying for her, for what had been done to her.

And for myself because I'd allowed it to happen.

I'd enjoyed watching.

'It's okay,' she said softly. 'They're fine.'

'Are not,' Alice said.

'They're as fine as *we* are.'

'You call that "fine"?'

In a softer voice, Erin said to me, 'They're really gonna be shocked. They thought you were dead, for sure. You fell off a cliff or something?'

I nodded. I tried to stop crying.

'That was *after* Thelma got him in the head,' Alice reminded her.

'Yeah,' Erin said. 'Anyway, they were awfully upset about you getting killed. They thought you were the greatest.'

'Me?'

'Yeah. They're gonna go nuts when they see you.'

'They're in . . . some of the . . . other cages?' Even though I was getting better, I could only talk between sobs.

'Connie's in the one next to mine,' Alice said. 'Then's Kimberly. Billie's cage is on the other side of Kimberly's. And then the rest of 'em are empty.'

I said, 'Maybe I'd better . . . go over now, and . . .'

'No.' Erin's hand dropped to my shoulder and squeezed it. 'Don't go yet. Please? They're probably all asleep, anyway. Can't you just stay here and talk to us for a little while more? Please?'

I didn't much want to go over and see my women, anyway, until I'd completely finished the crying. Besides, I wanted to find out a lot more about what had been going on. I said, 'Okay. I won't go yet.'

'Thanks,' Erin said.

'How long . . . when did they get here?'

'Connie and the others? About a week ago.'

'This is their seventh night,' Alice said.

'What about you two?' I asked.

'It's night twenty-four,' Alice said.

I gasped, 'What!'

'Yeah,' Erin said. 'Twenty-four.'

'My God!'

'Wesley put us in the day he got here.'

'The *first* time he came,' Alice pointed out.

'He knew about the cages,' Erin said.

'He'd read about them.'

'Yeah. An article in some old *National Geographic* magazine, or something, and he wondered if they were still here, and could he see them.'

'He said maybe he'd buy them if they were in good enough shape.'

Erin's hand glided down my arm. She found my hand, and took hold of it. Then she continued with the story. 'Anyhow, Alice and I were off swimming, so we weren't around when he came along. Mom and Dad had to fill us in. I guess they were showing him the cages, and all of a sudden he grabbed Mom and put a razor to her throat. So then Dad was afraid to do anything, 'cause he didn't want Mom to get her throat slashed. Wesley made them both get in cages, and locked them in. Then Alice and I got back home and he put us in cages, too.'

'We could've gotten away,' Alice said.

'Yeah. It would've been a cinch. There was only Wesley. He didn't have a gun or anything, either. But he said he'd kill Mom and Dad if we didn't do everything he told us.'

'And he told us to get in the cages.'

'So then he ended up killing them, anyhow – only not right away.'

'Maybe not Mom.' Alice sounded a little offended.

'If he didn't kill her, where is she?'

I figured I knew where she was, but I kept my mouth shut.

'I don't know,' Alice muttered.

For my benefit, Erin explained, 'He kept Mom in one of the cages just like the rest of us. Dad, too, but they took him away a long time ago. With Mom, she was here the whole time till she got away.'

'When was that?' I asked.

'A few nights ago.'

'Four,' Alice said. 'Counting tonight.'

Four. That would've been the night I hiked upstream, searched our battlefield, and found the woman at the bottom of the lagoon.

'Yeah,' Erin said. 'They were bringing Mom back to her cage after . . . it was her night for going to the house. She hadn't ever tried anything before. Because of us, you know? What Wesley said he'd do to us if she ever tried to escape. But she figured we didn't stand any chance *unless* she made a getaway. Then she could sneak back, you know? And save us. So she waited till they were trying to put her back inside her cage, and then she shoved free and made a run for it. They both went chasing after her, though. And they got her.'

'Maybe they did, and maybe they didn't,' Alice said.

'They got her.'

'Just because they said so . . .'

'Come on, Alice. You think they would've been acting like that if they *hadn't* caught Mom? You know darn well.'

Alice went silent.

I thought about asking more questions. What time had their mother made her break? Were they familiar with the lagoon? How far was the lagoon from here?

But I didn't have to ask.

The dead woman I'd found in the water *had* to be their mother. Who else could it be?

And Matt, I'd already figured out, was their father.

Wesley had made orphans out of these kids.

One of his many crimes, and one of his worst.

'Anyhow,' Erin said, 'back to what I was saying. The day Wesley got here? We all ended up in cages. Then he hung around for a couple of days. He never did anything to Dad, but he like . . . took turns . . . fooled around with the rest of us.'

'He likes to hurt people,' Alice muttered.

'He'd take us out of our cages. Just one at a time. And make us do stuff.'

'Awful stuff,' Alice added.

'And if we didn't do everything just right, he'd make someone else pay for it. Like he wanted me to . . . do something to him. I wouldn't. So then he put me back in my cage and took Mom out. He whipped her right in front of us, then made *her* do it to him. 'Cause I'd said I wouldn't.'

Erin's hand felt hot and sweaty, holding mine. I gave it a gentle squeeze.

'Anyhow,' she said, 'he did that sort of stuff to us right from the start, when he was here the first time. He didn't stay very long, that time. When he went away, he left us in our cages with some food and water, and said he'd come back.'

'But not when,' Alice added.

'Yeah. After a while, we started to think he wasn't gonna come back at all. We got really low on the food and water. Before it was totally gone, though, we heard this huge explosion.'

'Our yacht going up in smoke?' I asked.

'Yeah. And next thing we knew, he was back. He came in from the jungle, all smiling and happy.'

'And not wearing a stitch,' Alice added.

'He hardly ever does,' Erin said. 'Like he thinks everybody wants to be looking at his *thing* all the time.'

'Which they don't.'

'Not me.'

'Did he say how he blew up the yacht?' I asked.

'Sure,' Erin said. 'He bragged all about how easy it was. He used that razor of his to cut open a fuel line. Down in the engine compartment? Then he made a fuse out of a bedsheet. After he lit it, he snuck overboard and swam away underwater.'

'He was laughing about it,' Alice said. 'He thought he was so smart.'

'He outsmarted us, all right,' I told them. 'We all thought he blew it up by accident and got himself killed.'

'That's what he wanted you to think,' Erin explained. 'Billie says you figured it out pretty quick, though.'

'Well, we guessed. After people started getting murdered. I mean, who else *could've* been doing it? As far as we knew, the island was uninhabited. We didn't know there was a whole family . . . Are there any others?'

'Other what?' Erin asked.

'People. Families. Houses. Do you have neighbors?'

'We're it.'

'Nobody here but us,' Alice said.

'We had the island all to ourselves. It was great. Until Wesley came along.'

'Mom and Dad brought us here so we'd be safe,' Alice said. 'That's a good one, huh?'

'We lived in Los Angeles,' Erin said. 'We moved when the riot happened. That was the last straw, you know? They were afraid we'd all get killed, or something. They wanted to take us someplace where we wouldn't need to worry about stuff like crime and drugs.'

'And look what happened,' Alice said.

'We *know* what happened,' Erin told her. 'But it was great

while it lasted.' To me, she said, 'We did home study. No school. Mom and Dad taught us. She used to be a school-teacher, and Dad was a writer. It was great, not going to some awful school full of nasty kids. And we went swimming and fishing almost every day. It was the greatest, till Wesley came along and ruined everything.'

'I wish we'd stayed in Los Angeles,' Alice said.

'No, you don't.'

'Mom and Dad'd still be alive.'

'Maybe. But you never know. Maybe the quake would've killed us all.'

'Would've been better than this.'

'No, it wouldn't have been.'

'I'd *rather* be dead,' Alice blurted. 'I'd rather be dead any day of the week than get . . . Rupert, you don't know what he does to us.'

'Huh-uh,' I said.

I wasn't about to let on that I'd watched him and Thelma with Erin. It would've been too embarrassing. And it would've made the twins wonder what was wrong with me – how come I watched them mess with Erin, but didn't try to help her?

'They *play* with us,' Alice said. 'It's bad enough we've gotta stay in these *cages*, but it's a lot worse when they take us out. They take us out to *play* with us. They play *dress-up* with us. They play *house* with us. They make us eat with them and dance for them and fight with them. Anything they can think of, they make us do. And it always ends up the same way, with getting beaten to a pulp and getting fucked.'

'Hey,' Erin said. 'You don't have to get crude about it.'

'It *is* crude. Everything *about* it is crude! I *wish* I was dead!'

'No, you . . .'

'Hey! Knock it off! Jesus H. Christ, it's the middle of the night. Some of us are trying to *sleep* around here, thank you very much.'

'Connie?' I said.

Silence.

Then she asked, 'Who said that?'

'Me.'

More silence.

Then, 'Rupert?'

'That's my name, don't wear it out.'

'Holy fucking shit! Rupert!'

Reunion

'Rupert?' Now Billie had joined in, obviously awakened by Connie's excited voice. 'Is that you?'

'Yeah. How are you?'

Instead of answering, she sort of gasped, 'Oh, my God' in a shaky voice.

'Haul it over here so we don't have to yell,' Kimberly greeted me.

'Hi, Kimberly,' I said.

'You're a little late for arriving in the nick of time,' she said, 'but better late than never. Come on over here.'

I whispered, 'I'd better go. But don't worry, I'll take care of everything.' I eased my hand out of Erin's.

'You'll get us out of here, won't you?' Alice asked.

'Yeah. Somehow.'

'Just be careful,' Erin told me. 'And come back to our side of things when you get a chance, okay?'

'Sure. Thanks.'

'We don't even know what you look like,' she said.

I thought about the lighter in my pocket. She'd pretty much invited me to strike it up. I wanted to do it. The flame would give me a close-up look at her, sitting there in her cage. I'd get a chance to see her twin sister, too.

Both of them probably naked.

A good way to find out whether they were really identical. But they'd already been badly treated – to put it mildly. I didn't want myself adding to their troubles by lighting them up and embarrassing them.

So I kept the cigarette lighter in my pocket.

I said, 'You want to know what I look like? I'm so gorgeous I make Tom Cruise look like he got hit by an ugly-stick.'

Soft laughter came from Erin.

'Really?' Alice asked.

From farther away, Connie said, 'What kind of shit are you handing those girls, Rupe? Tell 'em the truth! You look like a fucking chimp! An albino chimp that lost all its hair!'

She was sure in fine form.

'I don't, either,' I said to Erin. 'Chimps have tails.'

'You'd better go,' Erin said, 'or she'll start saying *really* bad stuff about you.'

'Okay. See you later. You, too, Alice.'

I made my way out of the space between their cages. I got to my feet in front of Alice's cage. Running a hand along its bars to keep myself oriented, I hurried toward the cages where Connie and my other women were waiting for me.

'What've you got, nine lives?' Connie asked when I was in front of her cage.

'Just lucky.' I kept moving slowly, following its bars. 'Something broke my fall.'

'You must've been hurt,' Kimberly said. Her voice came from a distance ahead of me. 'It was a long way down.'

'Got banged up pretty good. That's why it took me so long to get here. I was out cold for a couple of days or so, then I was too messed up to do much.'

'We're lucky you're alive at all,' Billie said from her cage on the far side of Kimberly's.'

'And lucky that you finally *found* us,' Kimberly added.

'Yeah.' Connie sounded a little annoyed. 'Better late than never.'

Reaching out, I felt no more bars. I'd apparently arrived at the corner of Connie's cage. Leaving it behind, I crossed an open space. My searching hand bumped against steel.

And got grabbed around the wrist.

'Stay.' Kimberly's voice. Her hand clutching me.

It felt strong and warm. Heat from it seemed to flow up my arm and spread through my whole body.

'You've gotta get us out of here,' she said.

'I will. Are you all okay?'

'Yeah, right,' Connie said. 'They've had us for a *week*. All they wanta do is figure out new ways to fuck us over.'

In a low voice, Kimberly said, 'They've raped all of us.'

'Even you?'

'Yeah, even me.'

'How?'

'What do you mean, how?'

'You're so . . . tough.'

'They make you go along,' she muttered.

'It's my fault,' Connie said. She sounded different, suddenly. Quiet and upset. 'They use me. If Mom or Kimberly don't go along, *I'm* the one who gets it. They don't want me getting wrecked, so they . . . keep cooperating. No matter what Wesley wants.'

'You've gotta get the keys away from him,' Kimberly said. Her hand tightened around my wrist.

'I will,' I said. 'Are you all okay, though? I mean, I know you're not *okay*, but . . .'

'We're fucked,' Connie said.

'We're fine,' Billie said.

'We *are not*.'

'Our injuries aren't too serious,' Kimberly explained. 'Superficial stuff. We probably don't need a hospital, nothing that bad.'

'I had you all figured for dead,' I told them.

'Hate to disappoint you,' Connie muttered.

'I couldn't find your bodies, though. I went back to where we had the fight. I thought . . . you'd all still be there. But when I couldn't find your bodies . . .'

'We gave up,' Kimberly said.

'Thanks to me,' Connie said. 'My fault. I plead guilty.'

'Wesley got her down,' Billie explained from her distant cage. 'You were already out of it, by then. Thelma'd clobbered you in the head with a rock. You never even saw it coming.

Next thing I knew, Connie was flat on her face.'

'I was still on the rope,' Kimberly said. 'By the time I got to the top, Wesley had a foot planted on her back. He was all set to kill her with a machete. We *had* to give up.'

'Glad you did.'

'You wouldn't be so glad,' Connie said, 'if *you* had to go through this shit.'

'Rupert?' Billie asked. 'Do you remember all our talk, those first few days, about Wesley's motive? How we figured he wanted to kill everyone?'

'Yeah, for the money.'

'We were wrong. It didn't have anything to do with money. He wanted *us*. The three of us. He had this fantasy about trapping everyone in a remote place, killing the men, and keeping us as his prisoners.'

'He admitted it?'

'Yeah. Told me all about it. He had me alone – Thelma'd wandered off somewhere – so I started asking questions. He happened to be in a talkative mood. Real pleased with himself. He'd just finished . . . having a fine old time with me. So I found out a lot. For starters, we were all together the first time he met Thelma. So right from the beginning, he knew what we looked like. Me, Connie and Kimberly.'

'Three hot babes,' Connie muttered.

Billie said, 'He told me that he'd never in his life scored with anything but bow-wows. Women like us would never even *think* about going out with him.'

' 'Cause he's a fucking loser,' Connie threw in.

'From then on,' Billie said, 'everything was a set-up. He started by going after Thelma. She was easy.'

'Being also a fucking loser,' Connie added.

I half expected Kimberly to speak up in her sister's defence, but she kept silent.

Billie said, 'What Thelma didn't know is that he only wanted her as a way of getting at the rest of us. He figured he would have plenty of access to us if he married her. Then – surprise, surprise – it turned out she was as kinky as he was.'

'A match made in Bedlam,' Kimberly muttered.

'Both of 'em a couple of fucking sadists,' Connie said.

'Was Thelma in on everything?' I asked.

Billie answered. 'She sure didn't know her loving husband had the hots for every other woman in her family. He kept that to himself. Along with his big plan to blow up the boat and maroon us.'

'He knew the cages were here,' Kimberly said.

'He did *research*,' Billie explained. 'My God, he hadn't even gone on an actual *date* with Thelma before he started studying up – trying to find just the right place for his little caper. He thought about cabins in the mountains, ghost towns, abandoned factories, warehouses, barns – every sort of place he could imagine where nobody'd be likely to get in his way. Where he could keep us for as long as he wanted, and do anything to us that suited his fancy.'

'Fucking degenerate,' Connie said.

Billie ignored her. 'It wasn't long before he realized that an uninhabited island would be perfect. You're cut off from everyone. You've got the run of the place, so you don't have to keep your prisoners hidden away. Nobody around to hear them scream. And it's tough for them to escape.'

'Tough, all right,' Kimberly said, her voice low. 'Look what happened to Dorothy.'

'Who?' I asked.

'Their mother. Dorothy. She made a break for it – Christ, just a few nights ago – but they ran her down and nailed her.'

'I heard about it,' I muttered.

'Those poor children,' Billie said, keeping her voice quiet, not wanting Alice and Erin to hear her. 'They've been through worse than any of us. They've been in the cages for almost a month. They've lost their mother *and* father. And . . . Wesley and Thelma do such *awful* things to them. My God, they're only kids.'

'Kids with tits and . . .'

'Knock it off, Connie,' Kimberly snapped. In a softer voice, she said, 'Billie, go ahead and finish what you were saying about Wesley looking for an island. Rupert oughta hear this.'

'Yeah,' Connie said. 'So he can put it in his fucking journal.'

'You still keeping it?' Kimberly asked me.

'I ran out of paper.'

'Aw, ain't that a shame,' Connie said.

'Finish it after you save us,' Kimberly told me. 'And put in how Wesley planned it all, how he picked which island, and everything. It'll help show he had premeditation.'

'Like he's ever gonna stand trial,' Connie said.

'However it all turns out,' Kimberly said, 'it'll be a good thing if Rupert has a detailed record of the whole situation. It might be the only way anyone ever finds out what happened here.'

'If I'm dead anyhow,' Connie said, 'I'm not exactly gonna *give* a rat's ass.'

'Billie, go ahead and tell him the rest.'

'Okay. Let me see.' She was silent for a few seconds, then said, 'Wesley decided an island would be the perfect sort of place, so he started doing research. At first, he thought mostly in terms of islands in places like Wisconsin and Michigan. You know, on lakes and rivers. He concentrated on the Midwest. Probably because he was raised in that area. Grew up near Chicago. The minute he broadened his horizons, though, he realized that the Bahamas would be ideal. Beautiful, tropical islands with great weather. Conveniently located off the coast of Florida. Handy airline service. The best part was, he found out that there're hundreds of uninhabited islands in the area.'

'He didn't pick an uninhabited one,' I pointed out.

'That's because he read about the cages. He ran across an old magazine article . . .'

'Erin and Alice told me about that.'

'When he saw the bit about gorilla cages . . .'

'Thought he'd died and gone to Heaven,' Kimberly said.

'In case you haven't noticed,' Connie said, 'we're in Wesley Heaven.'

'Everything seemed to be falling into place for him,' Billie explained. 'It was almost uncanny. First, he finds the absolutely perfect place for fulfilling his nasty little daydreams about us. On paper, anyway. Then, it turns out that Andrew

and I are about to have our twentieth wedding anniversary.'
With mock eagerness and an edge of bitterness unusual for
her, Billie proclaimed, 'Why not celebrate it with the whole
family aboard a rented yacht in the Bahamas?'

'It did sound great,' Kimberly admitted.

'It *was* great . . . until . . .' Billie stopped speaking. I heard
her start to cry.

For Andrew, her husband. That's what I figured. Or maybe
she was crying because of everything. Not only had she been
made a widow during her twentieth anniversary celebration,
but she and her daughter were locked in cages, kept like
slaves for the amusement of a couple of demented perverts.
She might've been crying for the others, too. Kimberly's
husband had also been murdered, and Kimberly'd ended up
in a cage. The twins, too – Erin and Alice.

All five of them had lost people they loved. All five had
been toyed with by Wesley and Thelma – beaten, whipped,
raped, and God-only-knows what else.

It's a wonder that they weren't *all* bawling their heads off.

You can't cry all the time, though. This was Billie's time for
it.

Kimberly still held my wrist.

'Let go,' I whispered.

Her fingers opened. I slipped my hand free, then felt my
way along the front of her cage. I crossed the open area and
came to Billie's cage. She was still crying.

'Billie?' I asked.

'Rupert?'

I pressed my body against her cage and reached through
the bars with both arms. 'Over here.'

She found my arms and moved in between them. We
hugged each other, bars sandwiched between our bodies. She
sobbed quietly. The sobbing and gasping made her shake. I
started to caress her back, but the smoothness there was
broken by ridges – welts and scabs from the beatings she'd
taken. She twitched slightly when I touched one.

'I'm sorry,' I whispered.

'It's okay, honey.'

Then I was crying, too.

I stopped caressing her back, afraid of hurting her. As I lowered my arms, she said, 'No, hold me. Don't stop.'

So I put them around her again, but very gently.

Jealous Dogs

'What the hell are you two doing over there?' Connie called out.

'Shut up,' Kimberly told her.

'We aren't doing anything,' I said. Which was true. We were only embracing each other while Billie continued to cry.

'Thank God you're all right,' Billie whispered. Her breath tickled my lips. Then she had her mouth there, wet and open, pushing against my mouth. It was a kiss, but not like any kiss I'd ever had before. She was still sort of crying while we kissed. It was strange, but awfully nice.

I'd been trying to ignore the fact that her bare breasts were pressed against me. You don't want to notice that sort of thing when a woman is crying in your arms. But now that she'd begun kissing me, it seemed okay to think about them.

They were pushed out between the bars, soft and springy against my chest.

While we kissed, I squirmed so I could feel them slide on me. We were both sweaty. Our skin was slippery as if we'd been oiled. Her nipples were stiff, and rubbed against my chest like little tongues.

I tried to pull away so Billie wouldn't feel how hard I was getting. But she held me tightly, so I couldn't.

Her kiss was astonishing and wet.

By the time it ended, Billie didn't seem to be crying anymore. We were both gasping for air, though. And she didn't let me go. She kept her arms around me, just like before the kiss. We stayed pressed together.

'Thank you, honey,' she whispered.

'My pleasure.'

She made a quiet 'Hmmm' sound, but didn't say anything.

'Are you okay?' Kimberly asked.

'A lot better, now,' Billie said.

'I'll bet,' Connie called.

'Why do you always have to be such a snot?' That one came from Erin – the first I'd heard from either of the twins since I'd left their cages. I grinned.

'Up yours,' Connie yelled at her.

'Same to you and many more.'

Alice got into the act. 'Erin! Shhh!'

'She's such a bitch.'

'*You're* a shit-eating little twat!' Connie shouted.

'Cut it out, children,' Kimberly said. 'Let's not fight among ourselves.'

'Blow it out your ass,' Connie told her.

Kimberly laughed.

Billie, still in my arms, called out, 'Connie. Stop it. What the hell is the matter with you!'

'Oh, nothing. What could possibly be wrong? My mother's over there in the dark, bare-ass naked and messing around with my guy . . .'

'We're not messing around,' Billie said.

'My *former* guy. My *ex*-guy. My worthless fucking loser of a wimp . . .'

Very quietly, Billie whispered to me, 'You should go over to her. Give her a hug.'

'You've gotta be kidding.'

'I mean it. Go.'

'I don't think she'd like that at all.'

'Sure she would. Go on over to her, let her know you care about her.'

'I want to stay with you.'

'I know.'

'Don't you want me here?'

'Sure. But Connie . . . she's really hurting. Go over and be nice to her.'

'She hates me.'

'No, she doesn't. When she thought you were dead . . . she was devastated.'

That was fairly hard to believe. 'Really?'

'Yes, really. I've never seen her so upset. Now, go over to her. Please.' She kissed me again. This was a quick one, a thanks-and-get-going sort of kiss. Then her arms went away from me.

'Okay,' I said. I felt almost sick with disappointment, but I had to do what Billie asked. Whispering, 'Is it okay if I come back later?' I slid my hands all the way down her back. I was gentle about her wounds.

'Sure,' she told me. 'Later. But help Connie first.'

She wore nothing around her waist. My hands curved down over her buttocks. She didn't try to stop me.

But she kissed me once more, and whispered, 'Go on, now.'

I stopped caressing her and brought my hands back through the bars. As I stepped away from the front of her cage, I said fairly loudly, so everyone could hear and stop wondering what was up, 'So, what about Thelma? She didn't know anything about Wesley's plans?'

'Not a thing,' Billie said, sounding a little surprised about the return to that subject. 'She actually believed he'd blown himself up.'

'Why didn't he tell her?'

Billie was probably wondering why I was still standing near the front of her cage, instead of heading for Connie's. The truth is, I wanted to please Billie, but wasn't very eager about confronting her daughter.

Connie was not in one of her finer moods.

'He planned all along to kill her,' Billie explained.

'What?'

'Wesley intended from the start to murder Andrew, Keith, you and Thelma. That's what he told me.'

'Why Thelma?'

'You ever take a good look at her?' Connie called out. 'Oh, yes. Forgot. Sure you have. But apparently *you* found her so attractive you wanted to wrestle naked with her. You got this thing for older women, don't you? Thelma, my mom, Kimberly. Bet you'd like to wrestle naked with . . .'

'Knock it off,' Kimberly told her.

'Wesley hated Thelma,' Billie said, speaking loudly and firmly. 'He hated everything about her, but most of all that she was so much like him.'

'Bet he didn't tell you *that*,' I said.

'You're right. That was a personal observation. But he did say he hated her. Called her ugly and disgusting. He fully intended to kill her as soon as he'd finished off the men. He'd had enough of her. He didn't want her getting in the way. He only wanted *us*.' She lowered her voice. 'And the twins, too. He didn't know about them. He picked this island because it had the cages; the twins were a special bonus for him.' Lowering her voice even more, she whispered, 'Go and see Connie. Go on.'

'I will,' I whispered back. Then I asked in my normal voice, 'Why *didn't* he kill Thelma?'

'Because she saved his ass,' Kimberly said.

'When we tried to ambush him at the beach?' I asked.

'Right,' Billie said. 'It went sort of like we thought: he was wounded so badly that he needed her help. After they got away, he put on a big show of breaking down and confessing. He basically admitted everything.'

'Not that he hated her, though,' Kimberly added.

'No, not that. He kept that to himself. Claimed he loved her. Said he'd done all this for *her*, because he knew how much she despised us.'

'How could she possibly despise you?' I asked.

'For one thing, we tried to kill her husband.'

'She didn't take kindly to that,' Kimberly added. 'Also, she just hates our guts on general principle.'

' 'Cause she's a jealous fucking dog,' Connie called out.

I heard a bit of grim humor in Kimberly's voice as she said, 'Apparently, we make Thelma feel ugly.'

'Make her feel like the worthless loser she is,' Connie said.

'And she's been making us pay for it,' Kimberly explained. 'She's been having a great time with us.'

Billie said, 'She's worse than Wesley.'

Connie let out a harsh laugh. 'At least Thelma hasn't got a dick.'

'She makes up for it,' Billie said.

'They're a hell of a team,' Kimberly said.

I knew that. But I didn't say anything. Nobody was supposed to know I'd watched them in action with Erin.

'Does that about cover it?' Billie asked.

I didn't know who she was asking.

'That's the important stuff,' Kimberly said. 'He doesn't have to know everything.'

'I bet he'd *enjoy* hearing all the juicy details,' Connie said. 'He can write all about 'em in his diary. Isn't that right, Rupe?'

'I ran out of . . .'

'Oh, yeah, right. But you wanta hear it all anyway, don't you? Wouldn't you just love for us to tell you how they raped us? Which orifices Wesley preferred, and how Thelma . . .'

'Shut up!' Kimberly snapped.

'Connie?' Billie sounded worried. 'What's the matter with you? Stop that.'

'Come on over *here*, Rupert,' Connie said. 'I'll tell you the *good* stuff. I'll give you an earful.'

'Thanks, anyway,' I said. 'I don't . . .'

'You wanta know what Thelma did to Kimberly with a stick yesterday?'

'You'd better shut your mouth,' Kimberly said.

'Come on over, and I'll tell you all about how Mom sucked Wesley's cock.'

'Rupert,' Billie said. She sounded upset, but still fairly calm. And she wasn't whispering. Apparently, it was all right now for Connie to hear what she had to say. 'Go on over to her,' she told me. 'Quick, okay? She's sounding . . . I don't know, I'm afraid she's about to lose it.'

'*Lose it?*' Connie blurted. 'You're afraid I'm gonna *lose* it? Ho ho ho! Surprise, surprise! It's lost!'

I started to hurry in the direction of her cage.

'Connie?' I asked.

'Over here, Rupert. Right over here.' The mocking, coaxing tone of her voice gave me the creeps. 'I'm *waiting* for you.'

'Hey,' I said. 'Take it easy.'

'You miss me?'

'Sure.'

'Bet you missed my mother more.'

Right on the money, I thought. I said, 'No, I didn't.'

'Liar, liar, pants on fire.'

From the direction of her voice, she seemed to be straight in front of me. I stopped walking, and faced her cage. Reaching out, I moved my hand from side to side.

The cage was too far away to touch.

Just the way I wanted it.

'How about Kimmmmm-berly?' she asked. 'Bet you missed herrrr.'

'I missed all of you.'

'Bullll. Bull, bull, bull! You missed her more than me. You missed 'em both more than me. Admit it. You wanta fuck 'em, don't you! Or maybe you've already done it. Have you? Huh? Have you fucked my mom yet, Rupie? Or the fabulous Kimmmm-berly? Have you? How were they? Were they good and . . .?'

'And you called *Thelma* a jealous dog?' I said.

Which was not the best thing to say, just then.

Connie screamed.

Not a fright-scream like you hear in the movies. This was a rage-scream, a shrieking snarl. '*RAHHHHHHHHHHH HHHHHHH!!!*'

She sounded nuts.

My skin crawled.

I dug the lighter out of my pocket, raised it in front of me and thumbed it. A yellow flame spurted up.

'Kill that light!' Kimberly gasped.

I didn't.

I kept it going, and stared at Connie.

Still shrieking, she clung to the bars of her cage about halfway up the front. Her feet were planted wide apart, her knees bent, her back hunched. She jerked her body back and forth, up and down, as if she were trying to shake apart the cage.

Which didn't budge.

I'd expected her to be filthy, for some reason. She looked clean, though. Clean, but shiny and dripping with sweat.

'Rupert!' Kimberly snapped. 'Put that light out! They might see it from the house!'

My thumb stayed, holding down on the gas lever. The flame stayed up.

Connie stopped all her jerking and shaking. She stopped the shrieking, too. But she didn't climb down. She clung to the bars, panting for air, and grinned at me.

She was too high on the bars for me to see her old shoulder injury from the time Thelma had thrown the rock over the falls. Her short blond hair was wet and clinging to her scalp, but there wasn't any blood on it that I could see.

Her face looked okay.

If you forget about the wide, mad eyes and peeled-back lips. If you ignore the fact that she grinned at me like a maniac.

Which is to say, they'd been careful not to wreck her face.

From the neck down, her bare skin was a map of bruises, raw abrasions, scabs, welts, scratches and cuts.

The usual handiwork of Wesley and Thelma.

I groaned at the sight of her.

I muttered, 'My God, Connie.'

'Pretty as a picture,' she said. She tilted her head to one side, and licked her lips. 'Gimme a little kiss?'

Kimberly said, 'You'd better get out of here, Rupe. They might've heard the screams. If they looked out and saw your light . . .'

'Come here,' Connie said. 'Come, come, come.' Leering, she thrust her pelvis toward the bars. Somebody had shaved her. Instead of public hair, she had smooth, glistening skin. 'Come and gimme a little kiss. Gimme a little kiss on the lips.'

As if to punish me for looking, for seeing what I shouldn't, my lighter suddenly died.

Blackness clamped down on us all.

I let up on the gas lever and got ready to strike the lighter again.

'Go!' Kimberly said. 'Get going!'

'No, no no,' Connie said. 'Come. Come right over here, Rupie. I got something for you.'

'Rupert,' Billie called from her distant cage. 'Leave. Right now. Run. If *they* get their hands on you, we're all finished. We won't have a hope.'

Turning away from Connie's cage, I scanned the darkness. In the jungle and down the trail, I saw a bit of moonlight – and nothing else but black and vague shapes of gray. No sign of the house. No sign of anyone.

I heard plenty.

Jungle noises.

Nothing that sounded like anyone approaching us.

If Wesley and Thelma realized I was out here, though, they wouldn't come dashing after me, yelling and waving a torch. They would come in darkness and silence.

It might already be too late for me.

'I got something for you, Rupie. Come a little closer. Or are you scared? You aren't scared of me, are you? I won't hurt you. Promise. I'll make you feel *real* good.'

'Bye, everyone,' I said.

'Oh, no you don't!' Connie cried out.

I hurried away from her cage. Behind me, she shrieked and raged and called me horrible names.

Into the Lair

I stumbled through the jungle, feeling my way in the darkness, until I came to the edge of the mansion's grounds. Staying in the bushes, I crouched low and peered out.

After the nearly complete blackness near the cages, the moonlit lawn and house seemed amazingly bright.

No sign of Wesley or Thelma.

I'd last seen them entering the house. Were they still inside?

Off behind me, Connie continued yelling things like, 'You bastard, come back here!' Billie and Kimberly were talking to her, trying to calm her down. Their voices, and Connie's wild shouts, got mixed in with the usual squeals and squawks of jungle creatures.

I doubted that they could be heard inside the house. Even Connie's first and loudest raging shriek had probably gone unnoticed by Wesley and Thelma. They might've caught the noise if they'd been standing, quiet and listening, near an open window in one of the front rooms. But the chances were against it. In a huge house like that, they were more likely *not* at a front window.

They probably weren't standing quiet, either, straining to hear sounds from outside. More likely, they were *doing* something in there. Moving around, talking, sleeping, whatever.

It was unlikely that they'd heard Connie.

There seemed to be a better chance that they'd noticed the glow from my cigarette lighter. For one little dab of flame, it had really knocked a hole in the darkness. A fairly narrow strip of jungle separated the cages from the mansion's lawn. If the foliage wasn't really thick, the light might've been visible from the mansion.

It would've gone unnoticed, though, unless Wesley or Thelma happened to be watching from a front window.

After a while, I reached the conclusion that we'd overreacted. I could have stayed with the gals.

Better safe than sorry, though.

I *am* their only chance.

Besides, it's just as well that I got away when I did. Things had gone a little haywire with Connie. No telling what might've happened.

My departure improved the situation with her. After a while, she quietened down. Within about fifteen minutes, no more voices were reaching me.

By then, too, it was obvious that nobody had shown up to check on the prisoners.

I tried to figure out what to do.

There seemed to be three choices:

1. Do nothing.
2. Sneak back to Billie's cage.
3. Sneak into the mansion.

Doing nothing sounded pretty good. It held the least risk of unpleasantness – or death. As long as I remained hidden in the jungle, I stood a good chance of staying alive. It might also be the smartest course of action, since I didn't know exactly where Wesley and Thelma might be.

I was very tempted, though, to sneak back to Billie's cage. If I could do it with complete stealth and somehow get her attention without any of the others catching on . . . My God, no telling what might happen. I got excited, just thinking about it.

But why restrict myself to Billie? I could sneak over to *any* of the cages.

Wouldn't want to get near Connie, of course.

How about Kimberly? Man!

No. Kimberly'd be all business. She might grab my hand, but she wouldn't want to mess around.

What about paying Erin a visit?

I liked Erin.

She seemed to like me, too.

She's too young, I told myself. You can't *do* anything with her.

Who says so? She's only four years younger than me. That isn't so much. When I'm thirty, she'll be twenty-six.

But she's only fourteen now.

So what? In some cultures, people get married *when they're fourteen.*

I imagined myself over at Erin's cage. Touching her in the dark. Both of us exploring each other through the bars. In my mind, I could almost feel the smoothness and warmth of her small, pointy breasts.

The more excited I got, the more guilty I felt.

I couldn't let myself sneak back to the cages.

If I went to Billie, I might end up going to Erin.

Which would be a very wrong thing to do, in spite of the arguments I could give myself in its favor. How could I even *think* about trying to mess around with Erin? I'd be no better than Wesley.

I was angry at myself.

Maybe I wanted to punish myself for being so tempted over Erin. Or maybe the awful urge to take advantage of her – the wrongness of it – sort of shone a spotlight on the *right* thing that needed to be done.

I'll go back to the cages, all right. I'll go back when I've got Wesley's key-ring in my hand.

And not before.

There weren't three choices anymore.

Only one.

Number three: sneak into the mansion.

Staying in the jungle's darkness, I made my way along the perimeter of the lawn until I came to the area that faced the side of the house.

Then I gazed out.

Directly ahead of me, a short sprint away, was the window where I'd watched their vicious abuse of Erin.

The window was dark.

No light showed anywhere.

I saw no sign of Wesley or Thelma. Most likely, though, they were someplace inside the house. I'd seen them go in. There was no reason to believe they'd left.

But they might've left.

They might be almost anywhere.

Just waiting to nail me.

I broke from cover and dashed through the long grass. I was so scared that I did that thing where you separate into two people: one of them doing this crazy and dangerous thing while the other watches, astonished, from a distance – sort of cheering on the fool.

I thought, *Oh, man, you're asking for it.*

But I kept running, and didn't stop until I reached the side of the house. I leaned my shoulder against the wall. I gasped for air. It didn't take long to get my breath back, but my heart wouldn't slow down. It pounded like mad. Because it knew what was coming.

The dash across the lawn had been the safe part.

I stepped over to the window. Pressing my face against the screen, I peered in.

Saw nothing.

Actually, I could see a lot. This wasn't the sort of blackness I'd found at the cages. The room seemed to be filled with a dim mist – moonlight that had spilled in from the window and spread itself around.

Enough to show me that the room was cluttered with darkness.

Plenty of darkness to hide two people – or twenty.

Exploring the bottom of the screen, I found the pair of flaps that I'd made earlier with my razor.

What if Thelma found them?

I wished I hadn't thought of that. If she or Wesley had spotted my handiwork with the screen, they'd *know* a prowler had paid them a visit. They'd be ready and waiting.

But they probably hadn't spotted it.

They probably hadn't so much as entered the room after Thelma's return visit to pick up the clothes, blow out the candles, and so forth.

I poked my index fingers through the flaps, bent my fingertips downward and swung the screen toward me.

A few seconds later, I had my head inside. Without the screen in the way, the view was much better.

I could see the darkness a lot more clearly.

I stood there, the screen pressing against the back of my head while I scanned the room.

Black blotches all over the place.

Nothing appeared to be moving, though.

There was a lingering, somewhat foul odor of cigarette smoke. I smelled candles and blood, too. Or thought I did; those might've only existed in my imagination.

I pictured Wesley and Thelma sitting cross-legged in the middle of the floor, smiling as they patiently waited for me to enter their lair.

With the moonlit outdoors behind me, I would be easy to see. Like a black bust of Pallas perched upon the windowsill.

I went ahead and started to climb in, anyway.

The 'other' me seemed to stand back and shake his head and warn me, *It's gonna be your ass.*

The book bag on my back caused some trouble. I had to elbow the screen up out of its way. Finally, though, I got myself over the sill and into the room.

Sidestepping away from the window, I put a wall to my back.

Then I just stood still and listened to the house. The only human sounds came from me: my own breathing and heartbeat – and my stomach gurgling now and then.

Too long since my last meal.

I had food with me, but this was no time to pause for a snack.

I dug into the right front pocket of my shorts. First, I took out the lighter. I switched it to my left hand, then reached down again and brought out the straight razor.

I kept its blade shut.

Wanted it ready, but not *that* ready.

Then I tried to make myself flick the lighter.

The Bic was slippery in my hand. My thumb didn't want to move.

Go on and do it, I thought. What've you got to lose? If they aren't in the room, they won't see it, anyway. If they *are* here, you're already a dead duck and just don't know it yet.

I struck the lighter.

So did a guy standing off to my left in the corner of the room.

I jumped. I gasped, 'Yah!'

Then I realized the guy over there was a mirror-made duplicate of yours truly.

(I know, I know, I'm an idiot.)

I killed the light and stood in the darkness for a long time, waiting for someone to come and investigate my odd little yell.

Nobody came.

I ignited the lighter again. This time, the guy in the mirror didn't scare me. In fact, I appreciated him; he doubled the brightness.

We both stood motionless and scanned the room.

It seemed to be deserted, except for us.

I started walking slowly. He and his flame followed me.

When the floor suddenly went slick under my foot, I skidded but didn't fall.

I turned around and bent over to see what I'd stepped in. On the floor was a wet, reddish smear. This was where Thelma and Wesley had finished their fun with Erin. Thelma had come back into the room for their clothes and to blow out the lights, but she hadn't bothered to wipe up the blood, sweat, and so on.

Now, I'd made skid marks in it.

After taking a step backward, I found a clear imprint of my sneaker's tread pattern.

I killed the flame. I dropped the razor into my pocket. Holding the lighter in my teeth, I slipped the book bag off my back and brought it around in front of me.

Inside, I found the towel-vest that Connie had made. I held it between my knees while I put the pack on again.

Standing in the dark, I lifted one foot, wiped the bottom of its sneaker, stepped backward, wiped the other, and repeated the process. Then I got down on my knees and lit the lighter. My mirror-double and I crawled forward, mopping away our tracks. We stopped at the edge of the wet, blood-smeared area. The skids could stay; since they didn't show tread marks, they might've been made by someone barefoot.

We stood up and walked backward slowly. No new tracks were being made.

In darkness again, I rolled the towel-vest and returned it to my book bag. This took a while. Also, the towel made my hands wet and sticky. I had to wipe them on my shorts.

When I lit the lighter, my double reappeared. He didn't last long – only until we got close to the doorway and I killed the flame again.

Keeping the lighter in my left hand, I took out my razor and stepped through the doorway into the corridor.

Sleeping Dogs

Room by room, corridor by corridor, stairway by stairway, I searched the enormous house. Last summer's long, boring tours of ante-bellum mansions along the Mississippi paid off: the general layout of this mansion was similar to many of those I'd seen. I felt as if I'd been here before. Much of the time, I sensed what was coming.

Though I held on to the lighter, I didn't use it.

I searched in darkness, creeping along, often stopping to listen.

After a while, I put the razor back into my pocket; I needed a free hand for feeling my way.

The house seemed terribly silent.

Except for the thousand times its floors moaned and squawked under my footsteps.

I made very little sound, myself. My breathing and heartbeat *seemed* noisy, as did the frequent growling of my hungry stomach – but they were quiet compared to the outcries of the wood under my feet.

The flooring of the house seemed to be in cahoots with

Wesley and Thelma. Sure it is, I thought. It *likes* those naked bodies tumbling around on it, enjoys the feel of all that bare skin, loves having its planks oiled with blood and sweat and semen. I was here to put a stop to such things. So, of course, it wanted to cry out warnings.

(You think odd thoughts at times like that. It gets you, being alone in the darkness, never knowing if you're about to stumble and fall down, or crash into a wall, or knock over a lamp, or bump into someone who wants to slit your throat.)

It would take me hours to write about every stumble and collision, fright and false alarm I had while searching the mansion – the nightmarish scenarios that fumbled through my mind – the terror I felt each time I crept around a corner or entered a new room.

The searching seemed to take hours.

I expected the sun to come up.

To be realistic about it, though, I probably spent no more than an hour sneaking through the place before I found Wesley and Thelma.

I was beginning to think that they weren't in the house, after all. Maybe they spent their nights on the cabin cruiser. But then, as I climbed the stairs to the third and final story, I detected a quiet, grumbly sound. I stopped moving, and listened. The sound went away, but soon came again. Again, there was silence. Then came a harsh snort.

Some sort of animal snuffling around?

After listening a while longer, I realized that the sounds were probably being made by someone asleep.

Asleep and snoring.

Ever so slowly, I started climbing again. I set my feet down gently and eased my weight onto each tread. Most of them squeaked, anyway. Every time that happened, I cringed, stood still and listened until I heard the snoring again.

At last, I reached the top of the stairs.

I found myself in the middle of a hall, surrounded by walls with open doors. From where I stood, I could see into four moonlit rooms – one near each corner.

The snoring sounds, more distinct than ever, seemed to be

coming from the doorway in front of me and over to the right. I stopped beside the newel post, and faced the sounds.

The doorway looked vaguely pale in the darkness.

I snuck carefully toward it.

This had to be Wesley and Thelma's quarters.

With the entire house at their disposal, why had they chosen to sleep in such an out-of-the-way room? It seemed very strange, especially considering Wesley's wounds. Why climb three flights of stairs when there were plenty of fine, comfortable rooms on the ground floor?

I stopped at the doorway. I peered in.

The two windows at the other side of the room were bright with moonlight.

Of course!

This is the room with the view.

From this height, they could probably look down through gaps in the foliage and see the cages.

Watch the women.

From here, they probably could've seen the glow of my cigarette lighter.

But only if they'd been looking.

The way things sounded, they *hadn't* been looking. If they'd seen my light, they sure wouldn't have gone ahead and turned in for the night.

Along with the snoring, a sound of deep, slow breathing came from inside the room.

Both of them were in there, both asleep.

Apparently.

In a way, I was glad I'd finally found them. The mystery of their whereabouts, at least, was solved.

But part of me wished I hadn't found them.

What the hell was I supposed to do, now?

I could think of only two possible courses of action.

1. Get the hell out of the house.
2. Enter their room.

To be honest, I *ached* to get out of there. If I stayed, bad stuff was bound to happen.

I thought about getting out and setting fire to the house.

It would be a fairly safe, effective way to kill Wesley and Thelma.

Not a half-bad idea.

Trapped this high up, their chances of escape would amount to zilch.

There was only one drawback.

(Seems like there's *always* a drawback.)

Wesley had probably taken the cage keys into the room with him. If I burnt down the house, what would happen to the keys? For starters, I might not be able to find them in the rubble. For enders, what if they melted in the heat? I'm no expert on the melting temperature of gorilla cage keys. After going down with the blazing house, they might be reduced to puddles – or at least distorted enough to be useless.

In which case, how would I get the cages open?

If that's the only drawback, I thought, then what you've gotta do is sneak into the room and find the keys. Take the keys, *then* get the hell out of the house and set it on fire.

It seemed like a very good idea.

It had only one drawback: to get my hands on the keys, I would have to enter the room and look around.

And how could I hope to find them in the dark?

Into my head came a voice that sounded like Kimberly. It said, 'Quit thinking about all this shit. Just do it.'

She was right.

Or *I* was right, since the voice wasn't really Kimberly's, but mine.

I didn't want to do it.

But I'd found Wesley and Thelma. They were sleeping. Asleep, they were helpless. They were in my power. This might be the best chance I would ever get. If I chickened out, I would hate myself forever.

If I blew it, the women would be the ones to pay.

Before entering the room, I slipped the razor out of my pocket. I thumbed open its blade.

By then, I was doing that schizo thing again: standing outside of myself, a critical and worried observer.

You must be outa your ever-lovin' mind, I thought.

I stepped over the threshold.

The floor squawked.

One of the sleepers snorted. (Wesley, I think.) The other continued to take those long, easy breaths.

They're dead to the world, I told myself.

Unless they're faking it.

And then I thought, *What you oughta do is slit their throats right now.*

I knew I couldn't do that, though. You'd have to be damn cold-blooded to murder people in their sleep. And even if I could bring myself to nail Wesley that way, Thelma was a whole different story.

Being a woman.

How could I slit the throat of a woman?

I couldn't, that's how.

(But I could burn her by setting fire to the house? Apparently. Even while deploring the notion of slitting throats, I fully intended to burn the house down around those two monsters. Go figure.)

Stopping just inside the room, I saw Wesley and Thelma sharing a bed. At least, I supposed it must be them.

I couldn't see them very well at all.

On each side of the double bed was a lamp table. The lamp tables and the bed stood against the wall between the windows, so they were bypassed by most of the moon-light.

Wesley and Thelma (at that time, I could only assume it was them) lay side by side – vague, dark shapes on the white sheet.

The body on the left side of the double bed appeared to be larger than the one on the right. The snores came from there. Also, the body had a patch of white that I took to be Wesley's chest bandage.

Which put him on the left, Thelma on the right.

I made my way toward Wesley's side of the bed. He was the keeper of the keys. If I were him, I would've placed them on the lamp table, where they'd be within easy reach.

I needed a free hand. I wanted to hang on to my razor, though, so the lighter went into my pocket.

Both the sleepers continued to make their usual noises while I crept closer and closer to Wesley's lamp table.

When I got there, I turned sideways so I could keep my eyes on them.

If you stare at people, though, they seem to feel it.

One or the other of them would wake up, for sure.

So I looked toward the doorway, instead, while I gently patted the top of the lamp table.

Not gently enough.

Searching blindly, I nudged the key-ring with my fingertips. It moved, scraping against the wood. A few of the keys must've bumped into each other. They made two or three clinking sounds.

Wesley snored on.

Thelma popped up off her back.

I froze.

She sat there on the mattress on the other side of Wesley, not moving, not saying a word.

I couldn't tell which way her head was turned.

She *had* to be staring at me, though.

Could she see me?

I didn't move. I tried not to breathe.

Maybe I can wait her out.

If she couldn't see me, and if I made no sounds, she might relax after a while, lie down and go back to sleep.

Pretty soon, I had to breathe. I did it slowly. She probably couldn't hear me over Wesley's loud snores.

She still sat there.

I was turning into a wreck. I felt as if I couldn't get enough air. My heart raced. My whole body trembled – including my hands.

The key-ring was pressed against the tabletop by the fingertips of my left hand. If my trembling got much worse, I might not be able to stop myself from giving the keys another jangle.

I thought about lifting my hand.

But taking it away might cause a jangle.

Maybe I oughta just snatch them up and run like hell.

No no no no no!

Wait her out, I told myself. Any second now, she'll lie down. Before long, she'll be sound asleep.

'Come here, Rupert,' she whispered.

I flinched and gasped and clutched the keys. They clanked together for a moment before my hand squeezed them silent. Wesley made a choky-sounding snort. Moaning, he rolled onto his side. Which put his back toward me, his face toward Thelma. She stayed silent. After a few seconds that felt like an hour, Wesley resumed snoring.

I stood by the bed, the keys in one hand, the razor in the other.

I stared at Thelma.

Though I couldn't see her eyes – or even which way her head was turned – I knew she was watching me.

Slowly, I began sidestepping toward the foot of the bed.

She'll think I'm coming, I told myself. Right up to the instant I bolt for the door.

At the foot of the bed, however, I didn't bolt.

One step in the wrong direction, and Thelma would let out a shout. I knew it. I didn't have the slightest doubt. Her outcry would wake up Wesley, and they'd both come after me.

Deal with her alone, or deal with them both.

Also, I was curious. It seemed very strange that she'd whispered, *Come here, Rupert*. Why had she done that instead of yell?

She continued to sit upright while I crept past the foot of the bed. Wesley continued to snore.

When I rounded the corner, she eased herself sideways and lowered her legs. She sat on the edge of the mattress and waited for me.

A pace or two away from her, I stopped.

She grabbed the front of my belt. Not resisting, I let her pull me until I was standing in front of her. She pulled me closer to her. I stepped in between her knees. Her legs rubbed against mine.

Still gripping me by the belt, she whispered, 'Give me the keys.'

This time, her whisper didn't seem to disturb her husband. He kept snoring, and he didn't move. The way I towered over Thelma's head, I had a fine view of him. I just couldn't tell whether or not his eyes were open.

'I don't have 'em,' I whispered.

'Wesley?' Not a whisper. Not terribly loud, either, but enough to make him sputter and give out a moaning noise that sounded like a question.

I had the keys in one hand, the razor in the other.

One quick slash with the razor . . .

Even if she deserved such a fate – and she did – I couldn't do it to her. Not this way, surprising her in the dark. For one thing, she was a woman. For another, it would've been cold-blooded to kill her except as a last resort, to save myself.

Wesley's snoring had stopped.

Instead of slitting Thelma's throat, I pushed my left fist against her body. It met warm, yielding skin. Her hand fumbled with my fingers. I opened them and she took the keys. They jingled a few times, then went silent.

'Mmmmm?' Wesley asked.

'Nothing, honey.'

'Mmm.'

A few seconds later, he was snoring again.

I heard a couple of quiet clinks – Thelma setting the keys down somewhere, I suppose. Maybe on the mattress behind her.

Still clutching my belt with one hand, she used her other hand to rub the front of my shorts. Then she slowly slid my zipper down. She reached in.

Something like that should've gotten me hard really quick. But I was damn scared, and Thelma wasn't quite in the same class as the other gals. In fact, I might've been just as horny if she'd been Wesley. I was shrunk up so small I'm surprised she could find what she was hunting for.

She found it, though.

And started working on it.

I remembered the time by the campfire, and how she'd tried to split me with a razor.

The same razor I was holding in my right hand while she squeezed and stroked and pulled on me.

I knew she didn't have a weapon, this time. Not in her hands.

One hand held me by the belt, the other by the dong.

Reaching out with my left hand, I found the top of her head. I caressed her short, damp hair. I slid my fingers in and held on. Then I felt along the side of her head with the wrist of my right hand.

I located her ear.

I put the razor against it – in the valley between the top of her ear and the side of her head.

The hand inside my pants quit trying to arouse me.

It took hold.

'Let go or I'll cut you,' I whispered.

'I'll rip your cock off.'

'Just give me the keys, and I'll get out of here.'

'In your dreams, dickhead.'

Wesley was still snoring.

'I won't hurt you,' I whispered. 'I'll just go.'

'Fuck me,' she whispered. 'Fuck me, and maybe I'll let you have 'em.'

You've gotta be kidding, I thought.

'Right now.' She gave me a gentle tug.

'I can't. Not with *him* there.'

'Want me to wake him up?'

'He'll wake up anyway if I . . . do what you want.'

'Who knows? Let's find out.'

'How about somewhere else?' I suggested. 'If we go to a different room . . .'

'Here. Right here beside him.'

'Just let go of me and give me the keys. Please?'

'That my razor?' she asked.

'Yeah.'

'Wanta shave me?'

'No.'

'You sure? I haven't had a nice, close shave since I lost it.'

'Since you tried to kill me with it.'

340

'If you aren't gonna give me a shave, how about putting it away?'

'I'm going to cut off your ear if you don't give me the keys.'

She made a quiet, laughing sound. 'Go on ahead, then.'

As I started to think about doing it, she said, 'If you had the guts to go around cutting people, me and Wesley'd be dead right now with our throats slit open. You're just too nice a fella for that sort of shit.'

'Think so, do you?'

'I know so. And anyhow . . .' She gave me a squeeze. Not hard, but hard enough. It made me flinch, gave me a sick feeling. 'I got you by the nuts, boy. You're gonna do what *I* say. Now, take that razor away from my ear, or I'll scramble your eggs for you.'

I hesitated.

She squeezed harder.

Maybe I should've gone ahead and sliced off her ear when she did that. Instead, I groaned and bent over a little, trying to ease the pain.

'Okay,' I whispered.

I lifted the blade away from her ear.

The hand holding my belt let go. It brushed against my belly. 'Give,' Thelma said.

'What?'

'The razor.'

'How do I know you won't cut off my whang?'

She laughed softly. 'You won't be much good to me without it.'

'Okay,' I whispered.

I could hardly believe that Wesley was sleeping through all this. My luck wasn't likely to continue forever, though.

I tried to concentrate on what I needed to do.

'The razor,' Thelma said.

'Let go of me, and I'll give it to you.'

'Think I'm an idiot?'

'It'll be a fair trade,' I whispered.

'Long as I've got hold, you're gonna do whatever I say.'

'You'd better let go,' I said.

'The razor.'

I let go. I'd been holding a lot more than the razor. It seemed like about a gallon. I opened up on her.

She still clutched me for a second or two. Probably not sure what was going on – what was that hot liquid squirting all over her hand and up her arm? Then she must've figured it out. She went, *'Yuuuuuh!'* Her hand leaped away. *'You bastard!'* she shouted.

I was probably catching her in the chest, so I reached down and gave myself some elevation.

'Wesley!'

She got his name out. A moment later, she began to sputter and spit as I hosed her face.

I backed off fast.

Wesley sat up in bed. 'What . . .?'

'Get him!' Thelma squealed. She sounded as if she'd lost her mind. *'Kill the little shit!'*

I couldn't wait around to finish what I'd started. I couldn't manage to quit, either. So I whirled around and ran for the door, still squirting.

The Chase is On

From behind me, I heard thuds and voices.

'Who?' Wesley asked. He sounded mighty damn scared. 'Who was it?'

'Rupert!'

'He's dead!'

'My ass!'

Just outside their door, the wet floor sent my feet sliding. I gasped and flapped my arms. My legs flew out from under me. My butt whammed the floor.

Behind me, Thelma was still talking. 'He snuck right in here. Had my razor. Gonna slit our throats!'

'You sure?'

'*Yes!* He *peed* on me, the little cocksucker!'

I was *still* peeing. My shorts were drenched.

My feet stuck out into space. I pushed myself forward. My legs lowered. My feet found a plank of flat, slippery wood, which I figured to be the second stair down from the top.

'The keys!' Wesley blurted. 'He got the keys!'

'I got 'em,' Thelma said.

'You sure?'

I switched the razor to my left hand, reached up with my right, grabbed the banister, and pulled.

'Right in my hand,' Thelma said. 'He *had* 'em, but I got 'em away from him.'

On my feet, I looked back toward the doorway. Thank God Wesley and Thelma had decided to have a discussion instead of a hot pursuit.

'Good going,' Wesley said. 'Here, give them to me.'

The way they were thumping around in the room as they talked, I figured they must be grabbing stuff. Not just the keys, either. Weapons, more than likely.

What if they've got flashlights?

I took a step down. My feet skidded on the wet stair. I might've fallen again, but I kept a good grip on the banister. In the meantime, I was still going. You can't just shut things down at the drop of a hat, not if you've been holding it a while, and especially if you're scared. Anyway, I'd probably only been at it for half a minute or less even though it seemed like ages.

Somewhere along the way, my tool had gotten out of alignment with my open fly. Which meant I'd been splattering the insides of my own shorts. A lot came back at me, the rebound drenching my groin and spilling down my legs and soaking my socks.

'Come on, come on,' Wesley said.

'You ready?'

'Yeah. Here, take these.'

343

I hobbled down the slippery stairs, my sneakers squelching. From above and behind me came the thuds of quick footfalls.

I tried to move faster.

I wished I could see where I was going.

Suddenly, I could.

They'd turned on the lights!

The mansion had its power on, after all.

I suddenly missed the darkness. The darkness seemed like an old friend that used to hide me in its closet.

Now I was out in plain sight.

But at least I could see, and move faster.

I was about three steps up from the bottom of the stairway. I leaped. The book bag sort of lifted off my back. A second after I landed on the floor, the pack swung down and gave me an extra shove. As I stumbled, a spear shot by. (Connie's special fishing spear with the carved barbs.) It missed me by inches. It clattered and skidded on the hardwood, and went scooting down the hallway.

I thought about chasing after it.

Which would mean leaving the stairs behind.

Which would mean a fight, not an escape.

Two against one.

The spear wasn't worth it.

From the sound of things, Wesley and Thelma were already rushing down the stairs.

Not daring to look up at them, I made my turn-around and lunged for the next stairway. About to start my race down, I heard someone cry, *'Yeeee!'* Then came some quick thuds.

I looked.

Wesley seemed to be poised on top of his head, about halfway from the bottom of the stairs. He was barefoot, bare-ass, bare everything. Except for the soiled white squares patching his boob and butt, all he wore was a belt around his waist.

I glimpsed an empty leather sheath at one hip as his legs and rump slammed down. The hunting knife was in his hand.

He held onto it all the way as he somersaulted and crashed down the rest of the stairs.

He came to a stop on his back.

He was all sprawled out.

He looked unconscious or dead.

Up near the top of the stairway, he must've slipped on my pee.

And now he was out of the picture.

Now there was only Thelma . . .

Maybe she'll fall, too.

She came sliding down the banister like a demented swashbuckler – legs wide apart, rail squeaking between her buttocks, a strange and terrible grin on her face, both arms raised, a machete in each hand.

She didn't seem worried about the wooden knob atop the newel post at the bottom of her banister.

I was tempted to stick around and watch, but didn't dare.

I turned away and started leaping down the stairs toward the manison's ground floor.

Somehow, Thelma dealt with the newel post. I heard thumps, but no outcry. Seconds later, I looked over my shoulder just in time to see her start down my stairway. This time, not sliding on the banister.

Pounding her way down the middle of the stairs, machetes waving above her, sweat (and maybe some of my urine) flying off her hair and skin, jowls and arms and thighs shaking, her enormous breasts hopping up and down, swinging every which way.

Each heavy step sounded like a battering ram trying to demolish the stairway. I felt the tremors through my own feet as I raced for the bottom. I also felt air coming in through my fly, and realized I'd finally run out of piss.

About four steps from the bottom, I jumped.

I landed on both feet. The book bag whapped my back. I plunged across the foyer, staggering more than running toward the front door. The razor would do me no good – not against Thelma's machetes. Afraid of hurting myself with it, I whipped its blade shut on my way to the door.

345

I put on the brakes. Skidded. Not able to stop in time, I twisted sideways and slammed against the door. As I reached for the handle, I glanced back.

Thelma, chugging her way down, had about three steps to go.

I lurched backward, jerking the door open.

The veranda was brightly lit by a couple of spotlights on the front lawn. It surprised me. I wished they'd been off. Wesley or Thelma must've activated them, somehow, the better to chase me down.

It worked both ways, though. *I* could see better, too.

On my way out the door, something struck me in the back. It felt like a fist slugging my book bag. A punch, but no real pain.

The moment I got outside, I dodged to the right. As I raced for the end of the veranda, I took a quick look over my shoulder.

Thelma didn't slow down enough. After charging onto the veranda, her momentum swung her out wide. Yelling '*Wahhh!*', she crashed a shoulder against a front column. The blow knocked her to a quick halt. The way her tits swung, I half thought they might fly off and land in the front yard. But they stayed attached and rebounded as she bounced off the column. She couldn't stay on her feet after that.

I watched her crash onto the floor of the veranda.

She hit it hard with her right side.

I quit running as she skidded and rolled onto her back. By then, however, I had almost reached the railing at the end of the veranda. A fine distance for my escape. But a bad distance for any hope of rushing back and jumping Thelma; she would have plenty of time to recover and get up.

Even as I watched, she rolled off her back and raised her head and met my eyes.

She had a machete in her left hand. Her right hand was empty.

She started to push herself up.

I suddenly spotted her other machete. It lay on the veranda floor about midway between us.

How had it gotten there?

I remembered the blow to my back.

But that had happened while I was still in the doorway.

My guess (later confirmed by gashes in my book bag and journal) is that Thelma had thrown the machete at me. It must've penetrated my book bag and had probably been sticking out for a few seconds while I dashed along the veranda. Then, shaking loose, it had fallen to the floor.

Thelma saw me looking at it.

She glanced at it.

We looked at each other.

I suddenly felt as if I'd become the star of a Sergio Leone film. We're just waiting for the music to stop. That'll be the signal. With the final note, we both break into mad dashes for the machete – in slow motion.

But there was no music.

This was no film.

Neither of us waited.

There was no slow motion, either, but I can play it that way in my mind. When it happened, though, it happened fast.

As I sprinted for the weapon, Thelma scurried forward and onto her feet. She already *had* a machete. And she raised it high, ready to chop me.

I had the greater speed, though. My chances looked good for reaching the other machete first.

By maybe half a second.

Then I'd have to swoop down and snatch it off the floor and swing it up in time to stop Thelma from whacking my head off.

The distance between us closed fast.

She wasn't even *paying attention* to the damn machete.

Her eyes were on *me*.

She knew she had me. *I* knew she had me.

This was just me. Rupert Conway, not Clint Eastwood or Bruce Willis, Arnold Schwarzenegger or Mel Gibson. This was real life, not a scene in an action movie. These were real machetes.

I was about to get myself killed.

Thelma, threatening the veranda floor with each thundering stride, yelled, '*Yahhhh!*'

I yelled, '*No!*' and swerved away from our collision course and dived over the white-painted railing. I smashed through some bushes. They scratched me, but broke my fall.

Thelma didn't leap the railing. She must've gone ahead to the second machete, picked it up, then run back to the veranda stairs.

Which gave me a little time.

I used the time to pocket the razor, shuck off my book bag, stuff the bag under the bushes for safe keeping, scramble to my feet and get a start on my dash for the corner of the house.

When I looked back, Thelma was charging down the veranda stairs. She turned toward me and broke into a run, pumping her two machetes.

Now that we were out in the open, I figured she didn't stand a chance of catching me.

Not unless I fell down and broke my leg, or something.

I'd never broken a leg in my life, so it didn't seem likely to happen tonight.

After turning the corner of the house, I slowed down a little. No point in wearing myself out. Anyway, I needed to think.

For a while there, my survival had looked iffy.

Now that I'd gotten out of the mansion alive, I had to make up my mind about what to do next.

I wanted the keys to the gorilla cages.

They were probably still inside the house.

I could hardly go after them with Thelma on my tail.

Wesley might not remain out of action for long. It had looked like a very nasty fall, though. It could've put him out of commission for hours, or days, or for ever.

So Thelma seemed to be my main problem. Sure, I could outrun her. I could hide, or run circles around her. But I didn't want to fight her. Not while she had those machetes.

They were my real problem.

She had to be disarmed.

Bet she can't swim with them, I thought.

The lagoon crossed my mind, but I rejected it. For one thing, how do you get there from here? For another, the ocean was dead ahead.

Swim out to the boat, I thought.

I remembered the two dinghies tied at the dock.

Can't leave either of them behind.

Dealing with them would take a while.

Suddenly, I wished I hadn't slowed down. I poured it on and sprinted at top speed for the shore.

How the Chase Ends

If I'd had another ten seconds, maybe I would've had time to slice through the mooring line of the second dinghy. As it was, I only cut through one.

My plan, formed as I dashed for the cove, had been to cut both the dinghies loose, hop into one, and tow the second away from the dock. Which would force Thelma to swim after me, leaving her machetes behind.

Probably not such a terrific plan, anyway.

But I didn't get a chance to find out, because Thelma came pounding onto the dock before I even had a chance to *start* cutting the second rope.

I dropped the line of the first dinghy, sprang up and ran like hell for the end of the dock.

My sneakers clumped on the planks. Thelma, barefoot, slapped and thudded after me, wheezing for breath.

Again, she didn't stand a chance of catching up.

On my way to the end of the dock, I flipped the razor shut and dropped it into my pocket.

I raced to the very edge, then dived.

My dive carried me way out over the water. I hit the surface flat out with a whop that hurt. Then the water shut down on top of me. I stayed under and kicked hard, trying to pick up speed.

No big splashing sound came from behind me. I kept waiting for it. My headstart hadn't been much; Thelma should've already reached the end of the dock.

Obviously, she'd decided not to jump in.

Needing air anyway, I kicked to the surface. As I filled my lungs, I looked back.

I was closer to the dock than I'd expected or hoped. The shoes had probably slowed me down – as had my big, baggy shorts. Even though I wanted more distance between myself and Thelma, I began treading water.

The shoes made it tough, but I wasn't about to kick them off and lose them. Pumping my feet as if I were racing a bicycle, I managed to keep my head above the surface.

Thelma, pale in the moonlight, was stepping down into the first dinghy. She held her arms out for balance. Beyond her hands, the blades of her machetes gleamed like silver.

She set the weapons down inside the boat. Then she bent over the outboard motor.

For a few seconds, I could only see her rump and the backs of her thighs. Then the drifting dinghy gave me a side view. Thelma had already planted one hand against the motor's cowl. With the other, she jerked its starter cord. Her breasts swung like crazy. The motor coughed but didn't start. She gave the cord another pull. The motor sputtered and caught.

Next thing I knew, she was sitting down and steering the boat in my direction.

I started swimming like mad for the cabin cruiser.

In this race, Thelma had the advantage. The dinghy was no speed-demon, but it moved faster than I could swim.

I had a fair headstart.

Not good enough, though. At the rate Thelma was coming, she'd overtake me long before I'd reach the cruiser.

I swam as fast as I could, and didn't look back. The growing noise of the motor told me all I needed to know.

From the sound of things, Thelma was straight behind me, coming on, probably planning to run me over and chop me with her propeller blades.

I caught a deep breath and plunged for the bottom.

The motor sounded like a tinny, grumbling buzz as the dinghy passed over me. Abruptly, the pitch lowered. My guess, Thelma'd throttled down.

The noise faded, then swelled.

Thelma had turned around.

She's going to stay up there, I realized. Circle and wait me out. Knows I can't stay down forever. When I come up for air, she'll try to nail me.

Rolling onto my back, I looked up and saw the moonlight shining on the water. I also saw the dark underbelly of the dinghy. It glided over the surface like a shadow.

I had a shark's-eye view of the dinghy.

Inside my head, I started hearing the theme music from *Jaws*.

If I were a Great White, I could shoot straight up and ram the dinghy hard enough to capsize it. In the water, Thelma'd be at my mercy.

Ramming the dinghy wasn't likely to work, though, me being a little guy and having nothing to push off against. If I shot up like that, playing shark, I might rock the dinghy a little bit. Mostly, though, I'd simply end up shoving myself downward off its hull.

While I considered these things, the boat slowly circled above me. And my lungs began to burn from holding air too long.

Getting some fresh air shouldn't be terribly difficult. I could probably surface a safe distance from the dinghy, grab a breath, and have enough time to submerge before Thelma could reach me. Just a matter of picking the right moment to pop up. And being quick about it.

A fresh breath would give me extra time, but it wouldn't solve my main problem.

If I could keep going up and snatching breaths . . .

Doing that, I might swim all the way to the cruiser. Or back to the dock.

What would that accomplish? She'd be right there, ready to chop me.

Sooner or later, she'll run out of gas.

At first, the idea thrilled me.

No gas, no motor. The dinghy would be useless to her. She'd end up drifting around aimlessly. She'd either have to sit there and hope for the best, or start swimming.

Perfect!

But I had no idea how empty her tank might be. For all I knew, the gas might last for an hour.

An hour of me bursting to the surface, every minute or two? No way. I might be able to pull off a stunt like that three or four times, but then she'd catch on. I wouldn't last ten minutes.

Unless the dinghy was already running on fumes . . .

Not much chance of that.

But maybe I could think of a way to kill her motor. Something that didn't involve an endless wait.

By the time I'd gotten that far with my thoughts, my lungs ached so much that I could no longer think straight. I looked for the dinghy.

Damn!

It had just reached the far curve of its circle – as far away as it was likely to get. With each passing moment, now, it would be moving closer to me.

I rushed for the surface, jabbing my arms up, kicking hard. I went up so fast that I almost lost my shorts. I felt them slipping, but didn't dare make a grab for them.

When they were down around my thighs, I remembered the razor in my pocket.

If I lost the shorts, I'd lose the razor.

So I reached down, grabbed the waist with one hand and held on. An instant later, I burst up out of the water. I gasped for air. With both hands, I pulled up my shorts.

Thelma's head suddenly jerked sideways. She'd spotted

me. She shoved the steering arm. The bow swung sharply and pointed at me. The motor noise swelled to a roar.

I dived.

A near miss. I felt the shivering water of the prop-wash against my back.

That'd be one way to stop the motor, I thought. Let it hit me.

Which probably *would* stop it. But the price seemed a bit steep.

During family vacation as a kid, I'd spent enough time in outboard motor boats to have them quit on me any number of times. Not always because of a fuel problem. If the prop hit a large rock . . . got tangled with weeds.

Yes!

Staying as deep as possible, I shoved a hand into my pocket and dug out the razor. I slid the razor under the top of my right sock. Then I tugged the shorts down and off.

After missing its chance at me, the boat had slowed down and resumed its casual circling.

I wadded the shorts.

Holding them in both hands, I started toward the surface.

Probably lose a few fingers, I thought.

Might be worth it, if it works.

I watched the gliding black belly of the boat. Slowed my climb. Watched. Waited. Felt the push of water as the bow passed over my head.

And suddenly shot both arms up, ramming my shorts into the propeller. In an instant, they were ripped from my grip. I jerked my arms down.

Fingers and hands intact.

Above me, the motor groaned, coughed and quit.

Yes, yes, yes!

Motor dead, the dinghy glided on by. I started swimming underwater to stay with it.

In a few seconds, I managed to get underneath it again.

A few seconds after that, the dinghy wobbled. Then the entire submerged portion of the motor swung up and broke the surface – taking along the remains of my shorts.

You can swing these outboard motors up on their hinges to get at the props. I'd done it myself a few times. So I knew that Thelma had to be standing at the stern, bent over the motor, both her hands busy.

A good, precarious position.

I lunged for the surface.

Reached high.

As my face cleared the water, I grabbed the gunnel with both hands and jerked down on it like a guy desperate to climb aboard.

My side of the dinghy lurched downward.

The other side jumped up.

Thelma, looming above me, was bent over the raised motor just as I'd hoped. Both her hands were on it. By the time I saw her, she had already turned her head to see what had gone wrong.

Already lost any chance of staying on her feet.

Crying out with alarm, she flung up her arms. She swayed sideways, shoulder first. For a moment, she stood on her right leg while her left leg lifted like a boy dog about to wet a tree. But her left leg kept rising higher. Then she was plunging down over the side of the dinghy. The gunnel jerked out of my grip and the dinghy scooted off. I kicked to keep my head up.

Thelma's right shoulder struck the water.

The rest of her followed.

Then came a concussion that buffeted me, shoved at me, and slapped a load of water into my face.

Blind from the drenching, I began to swim after the dinghy.

My goal was to reach it, climb aboard, and take control of the machetes. Once I had them, Thelma wouldn't dare give me any more trouble.

I'd have nothing more to fear from her *or* Wesley.

As I swam, I blinked the water out of my eyes. The dinghy was about twenty feet away.

No sweat.

I glanced back. No sign of Thelma. She still hadn't come up. Though glad she wasn't hot on my tail, I felt a twist of worry.

Maybe she'd drowned.

I actually thought about going back to see if she needed help. Which sounds nuts. But I had this idea that she might be grateful, might even change her tune and decide to stop fighting me. Maybe we would join forces, be a team . . .

She grabbed my left ankle.

Stopped me cold and jerked me down.

When her other hand clutched the back of my right leg, it gripped me *above* the top of my sock – missing the razor, thank God.

I felt myself being dragged backward.

A hand released me, grabbed me higher on the leg.

Knowing Thelma, she'd be going for my nuts. So I squeezed my legs together to stop her from reaching between them. Just in the nick of time, too.

She shoved a hand between my thighs. As she drove it in, prying her way deeper into the crevice, I suddenly tried to fling myself over. Her one hand stayed trapped between my thighs. Her other let go of my calf. I twisted, flung myself about, and kicked with both legs. In seconds, Thelma no longer had me.

I clawed to the surface. Gasping to fill my lungs, I whirled around as her head popped out of the water. She sucked in a single big breath. Then I clutched her shoulders with both my hands and drove her down.

She didn't go *straight* down – she went over backward, me on top.

She fought me. When I lost hold of her slippery shoulders, she wrapped her arms around my back. She gave me a hug as if trying to crush my ribcage. My arms were free, so I grabbed her by the hair and one ear, and twisted her head.

Both of us kicked and squirmed.

I quickly lost track of who was on top – or where the top might be. We both stayed underwater, though. Neither of us could breathe.

And neither of us let go.

We stayed in our clinch as if each of us figured we had the upper hand.

It seemed like hours that we struggled under the water in that fierce embrace. It might've been as long as a minute.

Finally, Thelma seemed to tire out. Her thrashing and writhing and kicking slowed down. Her arms no longer squeezed my ribcage so hard. Soon after that, she ceased all her struggles. Her arms loosened their hold, then slid away from my back.

I let go of her ear. With the hand that clutched her hair, I eased her away from me.

She seemed limp.

Unconscious, maybe dead.

Maybe faking.

Keeping my grip on her hair, I rose to the surface. I breathed, but held her head under – at arm's length, just in case she was playing 'possum.

I had to tread water furiously to keep my own head up. With so much motion on my part, I might not be able to detect movements by Thelma. Until it was too late.

Unnerving.

I felt like a murderer *and* a sitting duck.

It became very difficult to keep on holding her down. I thought she might already be dead. But I also half expected to feel her suddenly slide the razor out of my sock. Scared of both things, I gave her head a shove backward and let go.

A few seconds later, her head popped up. I glimpsed her face in the moonlight – eyes abulge, lips tight. I felt sure she must be alive, after all. But she didn't start gasping and huffing for air. In silence except for the slurping sounds of the water, her head tilted back and the rest of her body came sliding to the surface.

The next thing I knew, she was floating on her back. Sprawled out loose and open, arms spread, legs wide. She looked as if she'd maybe zonked out while relaxing in her back-yard swimming pool.

She sure didn't look dead.

It was uncanny.

It gave me the willies.

Treading water, I watched her for signs of life.

She just drifted lazily, being lifted and turned a little, now and then, by the motions of the water under her back. After gazing at her for a while, I noticed she was farther off than before.

I didn't want her to get away.

Not yet.

I wasn't about to *swim* after her, though. So I twisted myself around and swam to the dinghy.

I made a stop at its stern. Reaching up, I spent a minute or two untangling my shorts from the propeller. They'd gotten torn up pretty good. I tossed them into the boat, anyway. Then I managed to throw myself aboard without capsizing the thing.

While I put on the shredded remains of my shorts, I checked on Thelma. She was pretty far off, but still spread out on her back, the same as before.

It didn't seem right.

If I'd drowned her, she should've sunk. If I *hadn't* drowned her, she ought to be either swimming somewhere or floundering in the water, gasping and coughing.

Just didn't make any sense for her to be floating like that, as if asleep.

I lowered the outboard back into the water and got it started. Keeping it throttled down, I turned the dinghy toward Thelma. I puttered toward her very slowly.

The prow was aimed between her legs.

I steered to the side a little earlier than I needed to, just to avoid temptation.

I tried to miss her completely.

But the port side of the dinghy gave her left foot a gentle nudge. She didn't so much as flinch. She simply remained sprawled on her back, and began to swivel counter-clockwise.

She reminded me of the knife thrower's assistant in a circus act. The beautiful gal in a skimpy outfit who gets strapped to a wheel, gets twirled, gets the fun of being the knife target.

Except Thelma wasn't beautiful and she didn't have a skimpy outfit on. She was naked. Her huge breasts, shiny and pale in the moonlight, sort of drooped off the sides of her chest like a couple of seasick voyagers getting ready to woops.

The bump by the dinghy made her spin half a turn.

She appeared to resume spinning when I started to circle around her with the boat.

The waves of my wake made her tilt and bob.

She seemed oblivious of it all.

Reaching down between my knees, I grabbed one of the machetes. I picked it up and waved it overhead. 'Hey!' I shouted. 'Thelma! Look what I've got?'

She just lay there in the middle of my wave-circles.

I threw the machete at her.

It was supposed to be more of a toss, really. A gentle, underhand toss – the way you might throw a ball to a little kid.

Intended to startle her, make her flinch or try to dodge out of the way.

It wasn't even meant, actually, to hit her.

For some reason, the toss went haywire. For some reason, I swung my arm up with more force than I'd planned on. Instead of making a shallow arc through the air so it would fall fairly harmlessly on or near Thelma, the machete went high.

Maybe all 'Freudian slips' aren't verbal.

Maybe this was a slip-of-the-arm.

Who knows? Maybe there was no subconscious intent, and it just happened because my coordination was loused up from all the running and swimming and stuff.

Anyway, I was surprised and shocked to see that I hadn't given the machete such a gentle toss, after all.

It flew almost straight up, tumbling end over end.

I said, 'Oh, shit.'

As it flipped higher and higher, I had no idea where it might come down. For all I knew, it might land on me.

We're talking a very large knife, built for whacking its way through sugar cane or jungle or something. The blade didn't have much of a point, but it must've been two feet long – broad and heavy.

It tumbled blade over handle on the way up.

To a height of at least thirty feet.

At the very top, it made a tight U-turn. Then it started down, still tumbling.

Right away, I saw that I was no longer in danger of being Ground Zero.

Thelma was.

'Thelma!' I shouted. 'Watch out!'

She didn't react – just floated spread-eagled on her back like a naked and unlovely knife thrower's assistant.

She's dead, I told myself. Don't worry about it.

But I yelled 'Thelma!' again, anyway.

And watched the machete fall, whipping end over end.

Maybe it would miss her, after all. Or maybe she would be struck by its handle, not its blade.

It struck blade first. It caught her just below the navel. It sank in almost to the handle.

Thelma screamed.

She was punched underwater by the blow. Her scream went gurgly, then silent.

She vanished, swallowed by the black.

My own scream ended when I ran out of breath. Gasping and whimpering, I gave the motor full throttle and sped away at top speed – which seemed way too slow.

I glanced back.

No sign of Thelma.

After that, I didn't look back any more. I was scared of what I might see.

I sort of thought she might be swimming after me.

One to Go

I took the other machete with me, climbed onto the dock, and tied up the dinghy. Still feeling creeped out, I wouldn't look behind me at the cove as I hurried to the foot of the dock. Nor when I walked through the thick grass at the rear of the mansion.

The whole thing had been too damn weird.

Also, I'd never killed anyone before.

I felt pretty strange about killing Thelma.

It was bad enough that I'd ended the life of a human being. But she was a woman, too. You're not supposed to hurt women, much less kill them. Also, she was Kimberly's sister; I didn't feel good at all about that.

On the other hand, it wasn't as if Thelma hadn't deserved what she got. She'd thrown in with Wesley, who'd murdered her own father and her own sister's husband. Along with Wesley, she'd done some vicious, sick things to Billie, Connie and Kimberly. To those kids, too – Erin and Alice – not to mention helping Wesley murder their parents.

If that weren't enough, she'd tried to kill *me* a few times – including the attempt at the lagoon that had nearly wiped out Connie. I was damn lucky to still be alive.

Also, it wasn't as if I'd murdered her in cold blood. Our struggle in the cove had been self-defense, on my part. I'd only been trying to stay alive.

And the final deal with the machete had been sort of an accident. Which wouldn't have happened if she hadn't been playing dead, or whatever the hell she'd been up to.

She had nobody to blame but herself.

In a way, I felt sort of angry at Thelma for making me kill her.

In another way, though . . .

Maybe I'd better not write it.

Oh, why the hell not? Who am I trying to impress? The

whole idea is to tell what happened – accurately, without any phoney stuff . . .

It's not that I didn't feel sort of rotten in some ways about killing Thelma. Especially because she was Kimberly's sister, and I hated the idea of causing Kimberly any more grief.

But here's the deal.

There was part of me that felt absolutely *great* about killing Thelma.

We'd gone one-on-one, her or me, a fight to the finish, and I'd wasted her ass.

Sure, I felt sort of horrified and disgusted and guilty and spooked and *very* tired – but holy Jesus I was so excited by it that I felt all trembly inside. As I walked through the grass of the back lawn, I clenched my teeth and pumped my machete at the sky and hissed, 'Yes! Yes! Yes!'

One down, one to go.

And with any luck, the 'one to go' might already be out of the picture. Wesley'd taken a major fall down those stairs. At the very least, he'd been injured so badly that Thelma'd gone after me without him. Maybe he'd broken a leg. Maybe his neck.

In a way, I hoped the fall hadn't killed him.

Just busted him up enough to make him easy for me.

Even from the back yard, I could see light in a few of the mansion's windows. Wesley or Thelma had turned on some lights to help them chase me down. From the look of things, nobody'd gotten around, yet, to turning them off.

A good sign.

It might mean that Wesley was at least disabled.

I planned to enter by the front door, so I walked through the yard alongside the house, past the window where I'd watched Wesley and Thelma brutalize Erin, and on past the corner of the veranda. The front area was still brightly illuminated by the spotlights.

On my way to the veranda stairs, I spotted my book bag under the bush where I'd left it. It could stay there until I'd finished with Wesley.

I also happened to catch a look at myself. My shorts had

been so demolished by the outboard motor that they no longer had pockets. I'd lost Andrew's lighter, Billie's sunblock, and the snacks of smoked fish that I'd never gotten around to eating. A good thing I'd transferred the straight razor to my sock. The razor was still in place.

So little remained of my shorts after their run-in with the prop that they'd hardly been worth putting back on. Andrew's belt was scarred but intact. Most of the area below the belt, however, was either shredded or completely missing. A few flaps hung here and there. Otherwise, there was nothing much save fringe and gaps and me.

Which I sort of liked.

I wouldn't want to walk down Broadway wearing them, but hell, this was a tropical island. A wilderness. Nobody here but me and my women.

And Wesley.

Can't forget Wesley.

Not quite yet.

Machete in one hand, razor still in my sock, I trotted up the veranda stairs. The front door stood wide open. Was that how Thelma had left it? Of course. She sure hadn't slowed down to shut it after her mad dash onto the veranda.

I stepped through the doorway.

Looked all around, fast, to make sure nobody was coming.

Then turned my attention to the stairway. I could see to the top of it. But not to the place where Wesley had landed after tumbling down from the top story.

I sure hoped he was still there.

Very slowly, I made my way to the foot of the stairs.

There, I stopped and listened. My heart was thumping awfully loud and fast. That was about all I heard other than the outside sounds – the usual jungle noises – squeals and screeches and twitters and stuff.

Nothing inside the house.

Nothing that might come from Wesley.

I switched the machete to my left hand so I could use my right to hold the banister. Then I started to climb. I set each foot down with great care. Silently. Once in a while, a stair creaked under my weight. Each time that happened, I halted, waited and listened.

Nothing from Wesley.

Maybe he *is* dead, I thought.

Or just sleeping.

No, not sleeping. Not where I'd last seen him. I should've been able to hear his snores.

Which left three possibilities:

1. He was dead where he'd fallen.
2. He was too hurt to move, lying very still and silent, aware of my approach.
3. He was gone.

Number one would've been okay with me, but I was pulling for number two. Still pumped from my encounter with Thelma, I looked forward to dealing with him.

I did *not* want possibility number three.

But that's what I got.

After all that slow sneaking up the stairs, I finally climbed high enough to see the next floor. I wanted – expected – really thought for sure that I would find Wesley's naked body sprawled out there on the hardwood floor.

Crippled, but alive.

Or dead would've been just fine and dandy.

But not this.

I groaned and clutched the banister. Shivers scurried up my back.

He might be anywhere.

I twisted sideways and glanced down the stairs.

Thank God, he wasn't sneaking up behind me.

Thinking that perhaps he'd managed to crawl a short distance from where he'd originally landed, I climbed the final six or seven stairs.

No sign of him.

He might've gone into one of the rooms off the hallway, or back upstairs, or downstairs . . . or anywhere.

Now what? I wondered.

Easy. I'll find him, or he'll find me.

I thought about doing a room-by-room search. But quickly

gave up the idea. A search like that would be scary, dangerous and time-consuming. Possibly a *waste* of time, too.

He might not even be in the house.

He might've gone over to the cages.

What if he's with the gals, right now? Doing things to them?

Whatever he might be doing, he wasn't attacking me at the moment. He wasn't available for me to deal with. I needed to figure out my next move.

Go to the cages?

No, no, no! Find the keys, and *then* go to the cages.

Wesley hadn't seemed to be carrying the keys when he fell down the stairs. Which meant they were probably still in the upstairs room, unless he'd returned for them.

I dashed up the stairs. Most of them were pretty wet, so I kept a hand on the banister, ready to catch me if I should slip. But I reached the top without any trouble.

Though the hallway was lit, the bedroom was dark. I rushed in and searched the wall near the doorway until my hand hit the switch. An overhead light came on.

No keys on the rumpled white sheets of the bed. I snatched up both the pillows. Still no keys. Nor could I find them on the floor or nightstand or dresser. After scurrying around the room, I even dropped to my knees and looked under the bed.

Not a completely thorough search.

No luck. By then, however, I wasn't *expecting* to find them. Wesley had returned to the room, all right. He'd either hidden the key-ring, or taken it with him.

Taken the keys to the cages?

I rushed to one of the windows.

Seeing little more than my own reflection in the upper pane, I crouched and peered out through the screen.

Out beyond the moonpale front lawn, a small area of the jungle shimmered with an orange-yellow glow of firelight.

It gave me a nasty sinking in my stomach.

I muttered, 'Oh, jeez.'

And ran from the room.

Return to the Cages

On my way down, I took a fast detour and grabbed up Connie's fishing spear.

Spear in one hand, machete in the other, razor in my sock, I trotted the rest of the way downstairs and raced out of the mansion. I leaped down the veranda steps. I sprinted across the front lawn, leaving the lights behind.

From ground level, I couldn't see the fireglow. Too much jungle in the way. I was certain the glow had come from the area of the cages, though.

And wondered if I might be running into a trap.

Wesley seemed good at traps.

Maybe he wanted to play it safe just in case I should win against Thelma. Maybe he'd even watched us, and knew I'd taken her out.

And figured I'd be coming after him next.

Just his style, he might light a fire to draw me into position. But he wouldn't be *at* the fire. He'd be nearby, instead, waiting to ambush me.

With that in mind, I changed course. Instead of heading straight for the cages, I veered to the left and ran to a far corner of the lawn before entering the jungle. I went in fairly deep, then turned to the right and started making my way back.

I was quick about it. If Wesley had gone to the cages for some reason other than to ambush me, he needed to be stopped fast. There wasn't much need for quiet, either. With all the regular jungle noises, he wasn't likely to hear me crashing through the bushes. Not, at least, until I was very close to him.

When I spied the glow in the distance and off to my right, I slowed down. It seemed to come from a strange height, shining on leaves and limbs about ten or fifteen feet above ground level.

I couldn't recall any hills near the cages. Had Wesley climbed a tree and planted a fiery torch among its branches?

Reminding myself that he was probably *not* at the torch, I hunkered down and crept closer to the area. I listened for voices, but heard none.

I figured Wesley would probably jump me at any moment.

The last time I'd seen him, he had been holding one knife and wearing a belt with one empty sheath. There'd probably been a second sheath on his other hip, holding his other knife.

So I could expect him to be armed with two hunting knives.

At least. No telling what else he might've grabbed before coming over to the cages.

Not the ax, I hoped.

I hadn't seen the ax since our 'last stand,' when we'd used it as an anchor for the rope. Hadn't seen the Swiss Army knife since then, either.

Wesley or Thelma must've taken both those weapons.

The Swiss Army knife didn't worry me much. Though wickedly sharp, my razor was sharper. And the little pocket knife was outclassed, big-time, by my machete.

The ax was a different story, though.

If Wesley snuck up on me with the ax . . . or some major weapon I didn't even know about, such as a chainsaw . . . or even a gun . . .

No gun, I told myself. If he'd found a usable firearm, he would've started using it a long time ago.

Probably.

But God only knew what other sorts of weapons he might've found. If he'd looked in those storage buildings behind the house . . . A family that keeps a tractor mower might own a vast assortment of nasty tools: a chainsaw, a scythe, hedge-trimmers, a pickax, a sledge hammer.

Most of those, I figured, wouldn't be much worse than the ax. The ax had to be somewhere. Not in his hands, I hoped.

I'd seen, close up, the damage it had done to Andrew's head.

The ax really scared me.

Scared the living hell out of me until the moment I found out what Wesley *did* have.

Then I *wished* he'd had the ax instead.

Wait, wait. Time out. That was jumping ahead. The last thing I want to do is jump ahead – bring myself closer to when I need to write about what's coming, anyway, much too soon for my taste.

I wish I could just skip the whole business.

I've come this far, though. I've already written about all sorts of nasty shit that hurt to write about because it was so disgusting or horrible or personally embarrassing. What's coming is worse than anything else, so far. I'd love to stop writing, right now, and avoid the rest.

That'd be chicken, though.

It's not as if I haven't known what's coming. For days, ever since I first started to write 'The Rest of the Story,' I've known how things turned out at the cages that night. I've known how painful it would be to write about. Now that the time is just about here, I can't just call it off. Even though that's exactly what I'd *like* to do.

I mean, it's the end of the story. I've gone through several ballpoint pens, my entire spiral notebook and most of a smaller notebook that I found in Erin's bedroom (everything is on Erin's paper since 'Last Words' at the end of my journal) all to keep track of what has happened from the time Wesley stranded us on this island. I've probably spent some seventy to eighty hours writing. I didn't go to all that trouble just to go yellow and quit before telling how things came to an end.

So, here goes.

Sneaking toward the fireglow, I found myself in the bushes behind one of the seven gorilla cages. From where I crouched, the cage was only a dim, black shape. It appeared to be empty, but I couldn't be sure. The fire was still a good distance off.

Keeping the spear and machete in my hands, I crawled between the bushes and scurried across a strip of open ground toward the back of the cage. Before I got close enough for the bars to interfere with my spear, I turned to the right and hurried to the cage's far corner. I slipped around that corner. As I crept along the side of the cage, I looked through its bars.

The fire came from that direction. It was high and far away, as if Wesley had flung a blazing torch on top of one of the cages. The back-light let me see that the cage beside me was empty. So was the next cage down. The torch seemed to be directly above the third cage.

Much farther away than it might sound.

Each cage was shaped like a rectangle, about twelve feet high, fifteen feet wide and maybe twenty-five feet long. There was an open space of about five feet between cages. So the torch must've been some seventy or eighty feet away from me.

Because of the distance, my angle of vision and all the bars in the way, I couldn't see if anyone was up on top of the cage with the torch.

But I could see a woman inside the cage. Her face was anybody's guess. I recognized her figure, though, in spite of the distance, bars, and murky light. She stood near the middle of her cage, almost directly under the torch, her naked body half-concealed by shadows but unmistakably Billie.

She didn't walk anywhere, but turned around slowly as if looking for someone.

Maybe looking for me.

Facing my way, she seemed to stare at me. She probably couldn't see me, though, in the heavy darkness at my end of the cages.

So where's Wesley? I wondered. Up on Billie's cage with the torch, or waiting to jump out of the jungle and take me from behind?

I needed a clear look at the top of her cage.

If I could climb *this* cage . . .

No. I might've been strong enough to shinny up the bars, but I sure couldn't do it without setting down my spear and machete.

Which weren't going to leave my hands. Not, at least, unless I knew for sure that Wesley wouldn't be jumping me.

Keeping hold of the weapons, I retraced my way into the jungle. In among the bushes and trees, I watched the glow of the torch and took a route parallel to the row of gorilla cages. I stayed far enough back to keep the cages and the blaze of the torch out of sight.

For a while, I planned to sneak in near Billie's cage and try to see if Wesley was on top.

But if I could spot him, he could spot me.

I hit upon a better idea.

Don't look for him – ask.

Sticking to my route, I continued through the jungle. Past the torchlight. And on, and on, leaving the glow farther and farther behind me.

When I judged that I'd covered enough distance, I started sneaking to the right.

I thought I had probably overshot Erin's cage, and would need to backtrack and search for it. Luck was with me, though. I came out of the jungle behind the middle of her cage.

After a quick look from side to side, I started crawling across the strip of open ground.

Erin didn't seem to be aware of my approach. She stood at the door of her cage. Though she was merely a dim shape in the darkness, she appeared to have her back toward me. Her hands were raised to about the height of her head, and seemed to be gripping the bars of her door.

Pausing, I looked to my right and saw Alice's cage. The girl was hunkered down – as if cowering or trying to hide – at the back corner nearest to Erin's cage.

I couldn't see anyone inside Connie's cage. Which was closer to the torchlight, but a fair distance away from me. I figured she must be in it – just out of sight. Maybe lying down.

The next cage was Kimberly's. The light was better, way over there. Not so much darkness as a shivery glow. What with the distance and my angle, though, I couldn't exactly tell where Connie's cage left off, Kimberly's began or ended, or Billie's began.

Someone seemed to be roaming around down there, in among the confusion of bars. I supposed it must be Kimberly, but I couldn't be sure.

I tried to spot the torch.

Couldn't, though. Not the torch, just its glow.

At the other end of the cages, I'd been a lot closer to it. From my new position, the bright aura of torchlight might've been coming from on top of Kimberly's cage. I figured the torch was probably still above Billie's, though.

Anyway, I stopped inspecting the place and finished crawling across to Erin's cage. When I was almost there, I turned myself sideways. I lay down flat, mashing the tall grass on the ground alongside the bars. The grass was maybe six inches high, so it would help to conceal me. It felt cool and wet. I put the spear and machete by my sides, and propped myself up on my elbows.

Erin still stood at the door of her cage.

I called out to her. It was a whisper, really. She didn't respond, so I whispered her name more loudly. The pale blot of her head jerked. Her hands fell away from the bars. The width of her body narrowed, then widened, as she turned around.

'Erin,' I whispered again.

She started walking toward me. She had a slight hitch to her gait – a limp.

Which gave me a sudden, harsh reminder of what I'd watched them do to her. Wesley and Thelma. In the downstairs room. How they'd brought Erin in wearing a white blouse, a cute tartan kilt, and knee socks. How they'd stripped her, brutalized her, done such horrible, sick things to her . . . All while I watched, guilty and aroused. It made me feel strange, just thinking about it. I had to squirm a little in the dewy grass.

'Rupert?' she whispered.

'Yeah.'

She stopped at the bars and lay down on her side of them, matching my position, her head turned, her face close to mine.

'How are you?' she asked.

'Okay. What's going on here?'

'Wesley came.'

'Where is he?'

'Up on top of the cages. I think so, anyhow. It's kinda hard to keep track of him all the time.'

'Is everybody okay?'

'Rupert?' Alice's voice, her whisper loud.

I turned my head and found her. She was still at the corner of her cage, but no longer in a hunched position. She was poised there on all fours like a dog, her face to the bars. 'Don't leave me out of everything,' she said.

'You were asleep, anyway,' Erin told her.

'Was not.'

'We'd better keep our voices down,' I said. 'Come on,' I told Erin. I picked up my two weapons. Then she and I crawled, side by side, the bars between us.

I wished there was more light. I wanted to be able to see her and Alice. But this was better than last time, when the darkness had been almost total. This time, at least I could make out their shapes – sort of. Basically, they weren't much more than pale blurs without any distinct features.

At the corner of her cage, Erin halted. I crawled around it, turned myself so I faced the rear, put down my spear and machete, and sat in the grass between the two cages.

Alice on my left, Erin on my right.

Like old times, except this time we were gathered at the back of the passageway, not the front.

'I thought you were asleep,' I told Alice. 'That's why I didn't . . .'

'It's okay,' she said. 'I'm sure glad you're back.'

'Is everybody okay?' I asked.

'All depends,' Alice said. 'What do you . . .?'

'We're fine,' Erin said. 'I mean, you know. Not exactly fine and *dandy*, but we're the same as before.'

'He hasn't been *at* us,' Alice explained.

'Where'd you go?'

'Over to the house, for starters. I went looking for the keys, so I could come back and let everybody out.'

'Did you find them?' Erin asked.

'Wesley doesn't have them?'

'I don't think so.'

'I *know* he hasn't got them,' Alice said.

'Well, he didn't unlock any cages.'

'He walked *by*. You could *see* what he had and didn't. And he didn't have any keys. Not if they weren't, like, stuck up his kazoo.'

'He couldn't *fit* them up his kazoo,' Erin pointed out, sounding a trifle annoyed. 'That big brass ring? No way.'

'It was a figure of speech, stupid.'

'Anyway, I guess she's right. We would've seen the keys if he'd had them.'

'What did he have?' I asked.

'A boner,' Alice said.

'Very nice,' Erin said.

'Well, he did.'

'I'm sure Rupert wants to hear all about it.'

I was blushing, but the darkness kept it hidden. 'What sort of weapons did he have?' I asked.

Erin said, 'Two knives. Does the torch count?'

'I guess.'

'Okay, then the torch. And a can of gas.'

'*A what?*'

'A can of gasoline.'

'We keep *tons* of it around for the generator,' Alice explained.

'For a lot of things,' Erin added.

'Mostly for the generator, though. We've got *tons*.'

'Wesley has about two gallons,' Erin said. 'He took the can up with him.'

'He says he's gonna incinerate us,' Alice said.

Me and the Twins

'He won't do it,' Erin said. 'It's just a threat. If he burns us up, he won't be able to mess around with us any more. It'd wreck everything for him.'

'Yeah? Well just suppose he only burns *some* of us?'

Erin didn't have a quick answer for that.

'He's already doused Billie,' Alice added.

I felt my stomach sink and shrivel. 'Are you sure?'

'It was the first thing he did,' Erin explained. 'He showed up, I don't know, like maybe an hour or so after you took off? With the torch and gas.'

'And no pants on, as per usual,' Alice added, sounding disgusted.

'So he parades by our cages, and says how we're all going to help him set up a surprise for you.'

'He called you a chickenshit motherfucking asswipe,' Alice explained.

'Real nice,' Erin said. 'You don't have to tell him *every-thing*.'

'*I'd* want to know it, if somebody called me . . .'

'Doesn't matter,' I said. 'What about the surprise?'

'He said you paid him a visit at the house, and that you ran away, but Thelma'd gone after you. He said Thelma would probably kill you . . .'

'Nail your puny little butt,' Alice elaborated.

'But just in case she *didn't* get you, he wanted to have a surprise ready. He said you'd probably come over here to the cages, first thing. So we should be expecting you, and we'd better not yell and try to warn you off.'

'He said he'd toast our twats.'

'Alice! Stop it!'

'I'm just telling what he said.'

'Well, don't. For Godsake. You don't have to be so *crass*.'

'You talk just as bad. Only not around *Rupert*.'

'Hey, girls. Come on.'

'She's got the hots for you, Rupert.'

'I do not.'

'Like you'd ever admit it to *him*. But she does, Rupert. Trust me. She told me so.'

'Liar.'

'You're the liar.'

'I never said I had the *hots* for him.'

'Maybe not in those exact words, but . . .'

'Can't we talk about it some other time?' I suggested. 'I mean, if I don't take care of Wesley . . . Does he ever come over to this end of things?'

'Hasn't yet,' Erin said. 'The closest he's come is Kimberly's cage. He hasn't gotten on top of Connie's or ours.'

'Not that he couldn't,' Alice said.

'Yeah, he could if he wanted to. If he didn't want to move the ladder, he could always just go ahead and jump. It isn't that far between . . .'

'What ladder?' I asked.

'*Our* ladder,' Alice said.

'He got it at our house,' Erin explained. 'Like everything else, just about. He's been keeping it handy ever since he put us in the cages. It's one of his things. He climbs up on top of the cages and sort of . . . messes around. You know, looks down at us. Teases us. He keeps a box of stuff up there. Things he can drop on us whenever he feels like playing "bombardier." '

'Mostly books,' Alice said.

'He drops *books* on you?'

'Yeah,' Alice said, 'and they can hurt. Even a paperback hurts if it catches you with its spine.'

'Especially a *corner* of the spine,' Erin added. 'The deal is, Wesley doesn't want to bomb us with anything we might use against him. He figures we can't do much damage with a book.'

'Sometimes, he bombs us with pages,' Alice said. 'He'll rip one out and wad it up, then set it on fire and drop it through the bars.'

'You can usually dodge them,' Erin said. 'He just likes to hear us scream.'

'And watch us try to get out of the way. He *loves* to make us jump around. You know, because we aren't wearing a stitch of clothes, or anything.'

'He dumps buckets of water on us from up there, too.'

'All kinds of stuff,' Alice added.

'It'd take all night,' Erin said, 'to tell you *every*thing he drops on us. I mean, he's had a lot of time on his hands with nothing to do but mess with us.'

'His favorite thing, he lies down and dangles his dong through the bars. Then he'll . . .'

'God, Alice. That's not . . .'

'I'm just trying to tell what he does.'

'Rupert doesn't need to hear it. You know? Jeez!'

I decided to bring us back to the subject. 'So Wesley got this ladder, tonight, and used it to climb up to the top of Billie's cage?'

'Right,' Erin said.

'Then what?'

'Then he pulled it up after him. And he put it across the gap between Billie's cage and Kimberly's to make it easy for him to cross back and forth. He can just use the ladder like a bridge, you know? Instead of having to jump.'

'That's why he hasn't come over here,' Alice said.

'I don't think he's real eager to jump. It'd be pretty tricky. There's nothing up there but bars.'

'And the ladder,' Alice added.

'He can get around pretty well, walking on the bars. He's had a lot of practice.'

'He's part ape,' Alice said.

'Thinks he's King Kong,' Erin said.

'*Thinks* he's King Dong.'

'You'll have to excuse my sister,' Erin said. 'She isn't usually like this.'

'It's all right,' I said.

'See?' Alice asked. 'I *told* you it was okay with Rupert.'

'He's just being polite.'

I stayed quiet at that, not wanting to get involved in their little squabbles. The thing is, I didn't really mind Alice's language. It's hard to be offended by stuff like that when you've got a guy like Wesley nearby. It's hard to be anything except scared. But I did find myself a little bit amused, now and then. And sometimes embarrassed.

And turned on. I mean, there I was, sitting on the ground between Erin and Alice. They were stark-naked. I might as well have been naked, too, considering the condition of my shorts.

Even though I couldn't see the girls, I sort of knew what they looked like. After all, I'd had time to study every inch of Erin when she'd been in the room with Wesley and Thelma. And Alice was her twin sister. What I couldn't actually see because of the darkness, I had no trouble imagining.

On top of all that, Alice's talk about things like twats and dongs and boners only made things worse – or better, depending on how you look at things.

Plus, I couldn't quite stop thinking about Erin having the 'hots' for me. Apparently, she hadn't used that exact word. Whatever words she might've used, though, she'd made it clear to Alice that she liked me.

Interesting news. Incredible news. Wonderful news.

Too bad it had to come at a time when everyone was in so much danger that I figured we probably wouldn't all make it through the night.

Anyway, that sums up what was going on with me, and why I said that I didn't have any problem with Alice's language. I wasn't being polite, I was being truthful.

Trying to get things on track again, I said, 'So you think Wesley won't try to jump from cage to cage?'

'I haven't even seen him try *that* in broad daylight,' Erin answered.

'Doesn't mean he *can't*,' Alice pointed out.

'If he wants to come this way,' Erin said, 'I bet he'll bring the ladder with him. Put it down across each gap. We'd hear that, if he tried it.'

'The ladder's aluminum,' Alice explained.

'So we don't need to worry about him sneaking over,' Erin said.

'Unless he *does* jump the gaps. We'd hear him when he lands on *this* cage, but . . .'

'He's too smart to try it.'

'Or unless he gets down off the cages,' I suggested. 'Then he could sneak over here on the ground . . .'

'Kimberly's gonna warn us if he climbs down.'

'She's *supposed* to,' Alice corrected.

'Yeah. We sort of set up a few tricks of our own. If Wesley does anything we need to know about, Kimberly's gonna pass the word to Connie, and Connie'll tell Alice.'

'Except Connie's asleep,' Alice said.

'Maybe she is and maybe she isn't,' Erin said. 'Anyway, he won't climb down. He's right where he wants to be, up above everything where nobody can get at him.'

'I have a spear.'

The girls were silent for a second or two. Then Erin asked, 'Can you hit him with it?'

'I don't know.'

'You'd better not even try,' Alice said. 'Even if you get him, he'll probably still be able to set Billie on fire. All he has to do is drop the torch.'

'What if I wait till the torch goes out?' I asked.

For a couple of seconds, nobody answered. Then Alice spoke up. 'I don't know.'

'It might be a really long wait,' Erin said. 'And when it does burn out, he'll just dip it in the gas and light it back up.'

'With what?' I asked.

'Huh?'

'How would he relight it?'

'Oh, he's got a couple of Dad's cigarette lighters. Keeps them in the box up there for lighting his paper wads.'

'And cigarettes,' Alice said. 'The creep smokes like a chimney. That's something *else* he uses on us. His butts. He gets a big charge out of flicking them at us.'

'He doesn't have to be on top of the cages for that,' Erin explained. 'He mostly does it from the sides. Yells "incoming" and fires the things through the bars. They aren't as easy to dodge as the paper balls.'

'They can really sting, too,' Alice said.

'That's horrible,' I muttered.

'It isn't half as horrible as *some* of what he does to us.'

'Rupert doesn't want to hear about it.'

'And Thelma's even worse than Wesley,' Alice went on. 'She comes right into the cages with us, sometimes and . . .'

'Knock it off,' Erin said. 'I mean it.'

'I think she must be part lesbo . . .'

'They're both a couple of sicko freaks,' Erin said. 'Let's just let it go at that, okay? You haven't gotta go and blab about every little perverted thing they've *done* to us.'

'Rupert doesn't mind. Do you, Rupert?'

'Well . . .'

'*I* mind,' Erin said. 'Jeez. So just cut it out. It's embarrassing. Rupert doesn't need to hear every disgusting detail.'

'Let him speak for himself. Do you want to hear what Thelma likes to do?'

I looked for a way out, and found it.

'She's dead, by the way.'

'What?' Erin blurted.

'I killed her. Over in the cove.'

'Wow.'

'Fan*tas*tic,' Alice said.

'Good going,' Erin told me. Something suddenly touched my thigh, so I flinched. Then I realized it was Erin's hand. It gave my leg a gentle squeeze. 'How'd you get her?' she asked.

'With one of those machetes.'

'Holy cow.'

'Fan*tas*tic,' Alice repeated.

Erin's hand slipped under the tatters of my shorts.

'So Wesley,' I said, 'is the only sicko freak we have to worry about.'

Her warm, small hand glided a ways up my thigh. It came close to my groin before reversing direction. I had to squirm.

'What about the bucket?' I asked. 'You said Wesley liked to take it up on top of the cages and dump water on you?'

'What about it?' Alice asked.

'If I can get my hands on a bucket of water, maybe I can take care of things if Wesley tries to set Billie on fire.'

Erin squeezed my leg. 'Yeah!' she whispered. 'That's a great idea.'

'Where do I find it?'

'I don't know.'

Alice said, 'I hate to embarrass you again, Erin.'

'Then don't.'

'The thing is, Rupert, we've each got a bucket in our cage. For you know what.'

I was surprised. It certainly made sense for them to have buckets in their cages, but I hadn't given the matter any thought. I hadn't seen any buckets, either.

Looking over my shoulder, I tried to spot one in Erin's cage. Too much darkness.

'Real nice,' she was saying to her sister. Even as she complained, her hand crept higher up my thigh.

'You think Rupert doesn't go to the bathroom?' Alice asked her. '*Everyone* goes to the bathroom. We just happen to do it in buckets.'

'Which won't do Rupert any good at all, because we can't exactly *hand* them to him.' In a more pleasant tone of voice, she said, 'My dumb sister seems to have forgotten that the buckets won't fit through the bars. Thelma has to . . . *used* to come in and take care of them.'

'Maybe we can *make* one fit through the bars,' Alice suggested. 'They're metal or steel or . . .'

'Doesn't mean they can't be bent.'

Erin's hand stopped moving. 'We'd have to fold one in *half* to get it through the bars. We'd have to, like, jump on it or something. And we're barefoot. Besides which, even if we *could* smash one small enough, the thing would make so much noise that Wesley'd probably hear us.'

'What about Wesley's bucket?' I asked. 'Where's the one he uses?'

379

'Who knows?' Alice said.

Erin's hand resumed caressing my thigh. 'It might be anywhere,' she said. 'Maybe back at the house, even. If you wanted to go back to the house, you'd be sure to find *some*thing. Cooking pots you could fill with water. Pitchers, waste baskets . . .'

'What about a fire extinguisher?' I asked.

'We keep one on the boat,' Erin said.

'Not in the house, though?'

'We've been in these cages for almost a month,' Alice pointed out. 'Who knows where anything is?'

'But I bet you could find something and fill it with water back at the house.'

'You'd *better* do it, too,' Alice said. 'I mean, Billie's gonna get burnt to a crisp if you don't have a way to put her out. She's all fueled up and ready to go.'

'Maybe I'd better do that,' I admitted.

Suddenly, I knew where to find a bucket. Back at the mansion, over near the veranda stairs. Earlier, I'd seen Thelma put out her torch in it.

I was awfully reluctant to leave, though. I felt sort of safe, hidden between the cages, the girls on both sides of me.

And Erin's hand kept roaming my leg.

Her hand was our secret. She was letting it stray pretty far up my thigh.

It was driving me a little crazy.

Anyway, I couldn't just stand up and walk away.

'What else should I get?' I asked, just to delay things.

'What do you mean?' Alice asked.

What if I reach between the bars and touch Erin?

'Back at the house,' I said. 'Is there anything else? Something I should get while I'm there?'

'Like what?' Erin asked.

If I try anything funny, she might quit. Just leave her alone. Let her do what she wants.

Where was I?

'Are there any guns in the house?' I asked.

'No way,' Erin said.

380

'That's one reason we left Los Angeles,' Alice said. 'To get *away* from things like guns.'

'I could sure use one now,' I said. 'What about bows and arrows?'

'No.'

'Just get the water,' Alice said. 'You'd better hurry, too. I mean, there's no telling. He might go ahead and light her up, just for the fun of it.'

Erin's hand eased up higher than ever. I flinched and caught my breath. Her hand flew off like a startled bird. And crashed against a bar of her cage with a low, ringing thud. She yelped.

'Jeez, I'm sorry,' I whispered. 'Are you okay?'

'My hand.'

'I'm really sorry.'

'What happened?' Alice asked.

'Nothing,' Erin told her. 'I bumped the bars.'

'What were you doing?'

'Nothing.'

'We were holding hands,' I explained. Which sounded better, I thought, than the truth.

'You shouldn't go holding her hand,' Alice said. 'You don't know where it's been.'

'Very funny,' Erin said.

'I'd better get going,' I said.

'Not so fast. Rupie? Come here.'

The Fire Storm

'Rupie? Come herrrrre.'

The voice made me cringe. For one thing, it was too loud. For another, it belonged to Connie, and she didn't sound much less crazy than last time.

381

'My God,' I muttered.

Alice was already scurrying across her cage, apparently hoping to shush her.

On my knees, I grabbed my spear and machete.

'What're you gonna do?' Erin whispered.

'I don't know. Make her be quiet.'

'I know you're there, Rupie! Now come on, pull your cock outa that bitch and come on over. I been waiting for you!'

I scrambled out from between the cages. On my feet but hunched low, I dashed through the grass behind Alice's cage.

'What is it with you, boy?'

'Be quiet!' Alice gasped.

'When you aren't fucking the old ladies, you're fucking the babies.'

'Shut up!' Alice pleaded. Her voice came from my left, and not far ahead. I slowed down.

'Why not me? You some kinda fucking geek?'

'Be quiet, Connie!' I snapped.

'RUPERT! GREETINGS!'

Wesley's shout slammed through me, knocking my breath out, stopping me cold.

It had come from far away.

From where he apparently still stood on top of Billie's cage.

Sounding cheerful, Connie sang out, 'Look who's fucked now.'

'Before you make any rash decisions,' Wesley called, 'let me advise you that the lives of the ladies are in your hands. I'm fully prepared to annihilate them all, Rupert, unless you give me your full cooperation.'

I felt sick and weak. I seemed to be trembling all over. My heart pounded hard and terribly fast.

'Do you hear me?' Wesley called.

I didn't answer.

'In that case, do you have any last words for Billie? I took the trouble of dousing her with gasoline. She'll make one hell of a torch. You'll be needing sunglasses, little buddy. Better put 'em on!'

I shouted, 'What do you want?'

'Go to the front of the cages,' he commanded.

'Okay.'

I found the bars at the back of Alice's cage. Keeping track of them with my left arm, I rounded the corner. I rushed between the cages. On one side, Alice said, 'Be careful.'

On the other, Connie hurried along with me. This much closer to Wesley's torch, the light was somewhat better. Connie's shape was fairly visible. Her eyes, mouth, nipples and what I took to be several injuries looked like holes or rips in the pale canvas of her skin. She seemed to be leaping sideways to stay with me.

As she leaped along, she ranted. 'See what you get? Huh? This is what happens, Rupie. This is what you get. You were mine. Mine! You blew it. Blew it big-time, boy. Now you're gonna pay. You're fucked. Big-time. Wesley's gonna ream . . .'

She ran out of cage. One moment she was springing along beside me, the next she wasn't. I heard the bars ring from the impact. She let out a grunt, sounding surprised and hurt.

I looked back and saw her prancing away from the bars as if she'd been hurled back by a giant, invisible spring. Then she slammed down on the floor of her cage.

She sounded like a slab of steak tossed onto a counter top.

Which made me realize the floor of her cage must be concrete. Until that moment, I hadn't given any real thought to the subject. I'd just assumed the gals must have earth and bars under their feet.

Not that it seemed to matter, either way.

Concrete was probably better when the cages needed cleaning. It would hurt you more, however, if you fell on it.

Connie appeared to be sprawled on her back. She wasn't trying to get up.

Had she knocked herself out?

I really didn't care, except to be glad that she, at least, might not be causing me any more trouble for a while.

God knows, she'd already caused enough.

After her crash, I slowed down but kept moving. For a couple of moments, I forgot about Wesley.

Then he called, 'There you are!'

I turned toward the sound of his voice.

And there he was. Standing on top of Billie's cage – legs spread, a blazing torch raised in his right hand, his left hand propped on his hip. In the firelight, his body gleamed like gold. A golden statue. Hercules gone to flab.

He'd lost the chest bandage; maybe in his fall down the stairs. The fall must've opened his wound, too. The split across the front of his left boob looked like a grim mouth, puffy-lipped and dribbling blood as if it had recently caught a fist. It made thin, dark streamers down his chest and belly, down to his leather belt. A few strands of blood had worked their way down his left thigh.

The wound obviously didn't bother him much. Neither did I. He was getting a charge out of the whole situation. Two things gave it away: his grin and his hard-on.

'Step right this way, little buddy,' he called to me.

As I walked toward him, I saw that Connie still lay sprawled on the bottom of her cage.

Knocked out or faking? I wondered.

Hope she split her head open, I thought.

The next cage over, Kimberly stood at her bars, watching me. Her raised hands clutched the bars to either side of her head. She didn't try to cover herself. Maybe she thought I couldn't really see her. I could, though. She was much closer to the torch than Connie. The air in which she stood seemed to be tinted with its dim, hazy glow. She looked almost distinct, but veiled. As if draped with a shroud of wispy black fabric that revealed her, but cloaked her with darkness.

I could actually recognize her face. I could see the entire front of her body – ribcage and breasts, the dark coins of her nipples, all the long slender way down past the dot of her navel, the hollows slanting down and inward from her hips to the smooth mound between the tops of her legs, and then her legs, parted and slim and sturdy. All visible, but darkly veiled.

All wounded. In spite of the murky light, I saw dark places where her skin should've been unblemished. I saw smudges, stains, patterns of narrow marks and stripes.

My throat turned thick and tight because of how she'd been hurt. I felt my eyes sting. At the same time, heat surged through me. It made me feel ashamed, but I couldn't help it.

'Don't let him get you,' Kimberly said as I walked by, staring at her. 'If he gets you . . .'

'Shut up, down there!' Wesley called.

'. . . he gets you, we're all sunk.'

'Hey!'

'Kill him, Rupert.'

'I'll try.'

'One more word and momma-bear's going up in flames!'

Kimberly's right hand slipped sideways between the bars. She raised two fingers.

I don't think she meant it to be the peace sign from the bygone days of the hippies.

I think she meant it to be Winston Churchill's V.

Hell, I *know* that's what it was. A Navy brat like her, Andrew's daughter, descended from a Sioux warrior, tough and proud.

V for Victory.

'Keep coming,' Wesley told me.

I gave Kimberly a nod, and walked on past the end of her cage. Up top, a ladder crossed the open space between her cage and Billie's. Just as the twins had said.

The ladder was extended to a length of about fifteen feet. Five or six feet at its middle bridged the gap. The rest of it overlapped the tops of the cages, maybe five feet on each side.

Wesley was standing away from the ladder, more toward the middle of Billie's cage. Near his feet, I saw the gasoline can and a cardboard box.

The box that held his 'bombardier' goodies.

'Okay,' he said. 'Stop right there.'

I stopped.

Billie stood almost directly beneath him, well-lit by his torch. The light wavered and shimmied on her body as if she was underwater. Her skin, copper in the shifting glow, gleamed with wetness.

The gasoline.

Her short hair was drenched, matted to her skull in tight golden coils.

Again, the gasoline.

And gasoline darkened the concrete under her bare feet. It had spread out around her, forming a shallow and lopsided puddle in the middle of her cage.

When I looked up from the puddle, she gave me a shrug.

Like a little girl who'd peed on the floor, couldn't help it, and was left embarrassed and resigned.

Why was she standing in the middle of the gas?

Wesley's orders, I supposed.

He must've commanded her to stand still while he poured the gasoline onto her head, while it ran down her body and made the puddle. Then he'd ordered her to remain standing in the same place.

Move a muscle, and I'll torch you.

And I had no bucket of water for her. Because I'd stayed too long with Erin and Alice, because of Erin's hand on my leg.

And because of Connie's roaring jealousy.

I should've had the water for Billie.

Her toilet bucket was off in a rear corner of her cage, upside-down. Apparently, she'd been using it as a seat. Obviously, it had nothing in it.

She's gonna burn!

I could think of only one way to save her: stop Wesley from setting the gas on fire.

'Look at you, look at you,' he said. 'You've gone quite native.'

'What do you want?'

'My first order of business is to neutralize *you*, don't you think?'

'I'll do anything you say,' I told him.

'Excellent. Drop your weapons.'

'Don't,' Billie said, her voice firm and clear. 'You're the only chance we've got.'

'Shut up, Billie darling.'

'He'll burn you,' I said.

'Let him.'

'No, I can't.'

Above her, Wesley bent over. He reached into the cardboard box with his left hand, and came up with a paperback book. He lifted it by a corner of its front cover, so that the book hung open. Then he lowered the torch and held its flame beneath the pages.

'No!' I shouted.

Fire crawled up the book.

'Don't do it!'

I threw down my spear and machete.

Wesley tossed the book underhand. It tumbled through the night, blazing. And dropped onto the grass near my feet.

'That was sure a close call,' he announced.

'Fucking bastard,' I said, stomping out the flames.

'Oooo, such language! You've been listening to Connie. A very bad influence, that girl.'

'What do you want?' I asked.

'Let me see. What do I want? I want you to step into your new accommodation, over there.' Swinging his torch, he pointed out the empty cage beside Billie's cage. 'Step right in and shut the door.'

With my first step in that direction, Billie gasped, 'No! Rupert, you can't, honey. If he locks you up . . .'

'I'm not gonna let him burn you.'

'Very wise, little buddy.'

'You have to take him down,' she said.

'Shut up with that kind of talk, bitch! I'll cook your cunt right now!'

Ignoring him, staring me in the eyes, Billie said, 'Kill Wesley. At least maybe you'll be able to save the others. Let him burn me, but kill him.'

'You asked for it!' Wesley yelled. He bent down and reached into the cardboard box.

'Wait!' I blurted. 'Wait a minute!'

He looked at me.

'If you burn her up, you won't have her to mess with anymore.'

He grinned. 'Oh, I don't know about that.'

'You get turned on by her pain, don't you? If she's dead, she won't even feel what you do to her. She won't flinch or cry out or bleed or anything. It won't matter how hard you whip her, or . . .'

'Who needs her?' Wesley asked. Even as he said it, though, he took his arm out of the box, no book in his hand, and stood up. 'I've got all the rest of them. And there'll be plenty more, once they start having babies for me.' Grinning, he shook his head. 'Good old Thelma, she always wanted babies. God save us all. Can you picture it? What if they came out looking like her? Who'd want 'em? Wouldn't be good for shit, girls ugly as that.'

'Billie'll have beautiful babies,' I said. 'Just look at Connie. That's *proof* of how her babies will look. And you want to burn her up? Are you nuts?'

'You've got a point there, little buddy. I tell you what, go on and step into that cage, and maybe we can give her a stay of execution.'

'Okay.'

'Wait,' Kimberly said. 'What happened to Thelma? Where is she?'

Wesley let out a harsh laugh. 'Gosh! I forgot to ask! How's my Thelma? I sure hope you didn't *hurt* my dear, sweet little wife.'

I looked over at Kimberly's cage. She stood at its nearest corner, facing me. 'I'm really sorry,' I told her. 'She was trying to kill me, and I . . . I'm pretty sure she's dead. She went down in the cove.'

Kimberly was silent for a moment. Then she murmured, 'It's all right. I mean . . .'

'All right?' Wesley blurted. 'It's fucking *perfect*! Thank you very much for ridding me of the ugly cow! She did have her uses, but . . . I do believe that we're all much better off without her. My God, what a pig! Three cheers for Rupert! Hip hip hooray!' On hooray, he thrust his torch high. 'Hip hip . . . hooray!' Up went the torch. 'Hip hip . . . hooray!' He rammed the torch at the sky.

Then, laughing, he performed a weird little dance on top of Billie's cage: stomping his feet on the bars, waving the torch, twisting and shaking, swinging his hips, thrusting with his pelvis. He probably would've jumped and twirled, but was afraid of stepping between the bars.

I *hoped* for him to slip and fall. I even thought about snatching up the spear and making a try for him while he danced. But Billie would burn if anything happened to make him drop the torch.

His wild gyrations sent sweat pouring down his body, flying off his hair and skin.

'So long, Thelma!' he yelled. 'Nice knowing you! Nice, my ass! Ha hah!'

Billie, looking straight up at him, suddenly blinked and ducked her head and rubbed her face.

Then *she* began to dance.

In silence, she swayed and turned, swung her shoulders, jumped from one foot to another.

Wesley noticed. He quit dancing himself, and bent over. Huffing for breath, he looked down at Billie through the bars. 'What the hell do you think you're doing?'

'Dancing.'

'Knock it off.'

She didn't stop. Though she remained in the center of her cage as if shackled there by Wesley's threats, she hopped from foot to foot, waved her arms, bowed, twirled, shook and leaped.

'You've got nothing to dance about,' Wesley said.

'Do, too,' she called out.

'Knock it off.'

'It's my rain dance!' she shouted. 'I'm calling up a storm!'

And her dance suddenly broke into a savage frenzy. It wasn't like anything I'd ever seen before. The way she leaped and writhed, she must've had manic drumbeats in her head.

Instead of ordering her to halt, Wesley stared down at her, captivated by the view.

I was captivated by the view.

It wasn't something you could look away from. Not if you were a guy.

My God, it was like watching some sort of pagan ritual, the way she cavorted naked in the firelight, bowing and rising, spinning, whimpering and grunting with the effort, her feet splashing in the puddle of gas, her shiny buttocks flexing, her glossy breasts jumping and bouncing and swinging, her face agleam and streaming as if dipped in oil, sweat leaping like melted gold off her hair and nose and chin and nipples and fingertips, sweat spilling down her neck and chest and breasts, down her back and belly, her buttocks, her pubis, her legs, sliding down like golden run-off from a torrent of rain.

A downpour.

A squawl.

It's my rain dance! I'm calling up a storm!

Spoken to Wesley.

Meant for me.

Dropping to a crouch, I grabbed the spear out of the grass. Wesley still stood atop the cage, bent over and watching Billie.

He didn't look at me as I straightened up, raised the spear above my shoulder and hurled it at him.

Wesley's Last Stand

He still had his head down when the spear struck him. It caught him near the top of his left shoulder, punched him there but didn't stick, bounced off the bone and leaped out of the thin covering of flesh, its other end whipping upward as if a pole-vaulter was taking off from his shoulder.

He roared.

The whole spear leaped off into the dark behind him.

He raised his sweat-slick, dripping face. His eyes bulged. He bared his teeth at me.

Straight below him, Billie had stopped dancing. She stood in the puddle of gas in the middle of her cage, her head tipped back. Her body gleamed and dripped as if she had just climbed out of a swimming pool. She whined with her struggle to breathe.

'You dirty little fuck!' Wesley shouted at me.

And jammed the torch down between the bars at his feet and let it go.

'No!' I yelled.

The torch fell.

A moment later, it touched off the gasoline. The gas erupted with a heavy *WHOP!* like a mainsail snapped by the wind. The sudden brilliance hurt my eyes. As I squinted, a hot wind rolled against my body.

Wesley had been right about needing sunglasses.

The cage looked as if a bonfire had erupted in the middle of its concrete floor.

I saw Billie in there. All firelit and bright and shiny, her back to me.

Running. Leaping onto her upside-down bucket. Using it like a step for leaping again. High up at the far back corner of her cage, she caught hold and latched herself to the bars, curled tight with her knees up.

Depending for her life on the sweat of her mad dance, sweat meant to sluice the gasoline off her skin and bathe her with saving moisture.

I didn't know if it would work.

Afraid to see her burn, I turned my gaze to the top of the cage.

Where flames leaped for Wesley.

They wrapped the cardboard of his 'bombardier' box, licked the sides of his gasoline tin.

With a squeal of alarm, he kicked the gas container and knocked it flying. The punt sent it well past the far side of Billie's cage, sprinkling gas from its spout. It clamored against the empty cage that he'd intended as my cell.

I looked back at Wesley to find him prancing across the bars like a ballerina as the flames tried to climb his legs. Just as he got away from them, he lost his footing. He crashed down belly-first on the ladder. It jumped and shuddered under him, raising a terrible racket.

Before the ladder had a chance to settle down, he shoved himself to his hands and knees and started crawling across it.

Away from the fire of his own making.

A fire that had already fallen to half its size.

But he didn't know that. He wasn't looking back. If he'd seen how the fire had diminished so abruptly, he probably wouldn't have been so quick to flee.

Billie still clung to the bars at the distant corner of her cage. She still had her hair.

From shoulders to buttocks, her skin looked ruddy, shiny wet, uncharred.

She'd made it!

Now the job was to kill Wesley.

I snatched up the machete and raced for him.

Halfway across the gap, he saw me coming. He let out a yelp and crawled faster, the ladder shaking and clattering beneath him.

I ran full-speed between the cages. With the ladder looming over me, Wesley almost to the other side, I leaped and reached high, slashing with my machete.

Missed him, the ladder, everything.

I'm not a tall guy. I must've missed the ladder by a foot.

Gave him a good scare, though. He'd squealed when I swung at him. As I put on the brakes, the clamor of the ladder let me know he was scurrying like mad.

The ladder noise suddenly stopped.

I turned around in time to see Wesley look for me over his shoulder and try to stand up.

He should've been watching his feet.

The right one stepped down between two of the bars. He cried, *'Yaaah!'* as his leg shot down. He flapped his arms. His other leg bent at the knee and scooted out from under him. His bare ass struck the bars.

And there he sat, his right leg hanging down into Kimberly's cage.

He made whimpery, frightened sounds.

Before he could even start to free himself, Kimberly jumped.

My God, what a jump!

'Yes!' someone yelled.

Billie.

She stood at the side of her cage, the fire behind her fluttering low, Wesley's blazing torch in her upraised hand.

Kimberly dangled beneath Wesley.

She hung with both hands from his right ankle.

Golden in the torchlight, arms stretched so high that her breasts were nearly flat – long, low slopes topped by hard and jutting nipples – her entire body taut and thin as if she were being stretched from both ends.

Wesley tried to kick free of her.

His leg hardly moved at all. Just enough to sway Kimberly back and forth with an easy, gentle motion.

'Let go of me!' he shouted.

Kimberly didn't answer. She just held on.

Wesley pulled a knife out of its sheath on his belt. He wouldn't be able to reach her with it. He could throw it, though.

'Look out!' I yelled, and ran between the cages.

Billie shouted, 'He's got a knife! Watch out!'

With an underhand toss, I flung my machete toward Billie's cage. It hit bars, but fell near enough for her to reach it. I faced Kimberly's cage just as Wesley let out a cry of pain.

Kimberly had started to swing.

Still hanging from his ankle, she flung her legs forward and up.

A kid on a swing, pumping for the sky.

'Stop!' Wesley wailed. 'Stop it! Fuck!'

I jumped, reached high, grabbed two bars, squeezed bars between my knees, and began my struggle for the top of Kimberly's cage. Slow going, awkward. I made progress, though.

As I pulled and scurried my way higher, Wesley's voice raged in my ears. 'My leg! Let go! Shit! You're gonna rip it off! Fuck! Let go! *Ahhhhh!*'

Kimberly no longer acted like a kid on a swing. The smooth, graceful pumping action was gone. She'd turned wild, bucking beneath him, twisting, kicking her legs toward the barred ceiling.

She had a knife protruding from her left thigh.

I hadn't even seen it hit her. Wesley must've hurled it down through the bars while I'd been looking somewhere else.

No wonder she'd gone wild.

She swung like a rabid Tarzan, a mad and naked Jane trying to ride her vine to the moon.

Through Wesley's shouts and shrieks, I heard a gristly, popping noise.

His thigh bone bursting out of its hip joint.

His scream gave me goosebumps.

'Don't kill him!' someone yelled.

A girl's voice from far off.

Erin.

'Don't kill Wesley!' she shouted. 'He's gotta tell where the keys are!'

And then my left hand caught hold of the crossbar at the top of the cage. I reached up with my right, grabbed hold and pulled myself up.

Wesley kept his eyes on me as I clambered over the edge. Suddenly, I found myself perched atop Kimberly's cage, my hands and knees on the roof bars, Wesley a distance to my right and just beyond the end of the ladder.

Though one leg lay across the top of the bars, he squirmed and swayed like a human torso – or like one of those inflatable punching toys that swings back and forth when you hit it, and keeps coming up.

'Help!' he blurted at me. His face was streaked with sweat and tears, tremulous with torchglow and shadows, twisted ugly with pain. 'Please!' he cried out. 'Make her stop! Please!'

Though he pleaded, he held his second knife high, its blade pinched between his thumb and forefinger.

'Put down the knife!' I shouted.

He couldn't seem to make up his mind whether to throw it at me or Kimberly.

Looking down, I saw her rising toward me on his leg. She seemed to be looking at me. In another moment, she was sprawled out beneath me like a lover. She lingered there, just below the bars, all shadowy and open.

Screaming, Wesley jerked the knife back toward his ear.

He'd made up his mind.

Kimberly.

His tormenter, and such an easy target inches below the bars, motionless, trapped in the moment before starting her downward course.

Yelling, I sprang.

Hurled myself – not so much *at* Wesley as *between* him and Kimberly.

I heard a thunk.

A grunt.

I landed flat and hard on the bars. They pounded me. They rang out. I slid on them.

Below my face was Kimberly's face.

Eyes squeezed nearly shut, mouth open, teeth bared.

Her face huge and beautiful but torn with pain.

Then shrinking.

At first, I didn't know why.

But as her face became smaller, more and more of Kimberly came into view.

Her neck, shoulders.

Her arms reaching overhead like a surrendering prisoner.

Her chest.

The knife handle jutting up between her breasts.

Her belly, her groin, thighs.

The knife handle jutting up from her left thigh.

Her long, spread legs.

All becoming smaller.

Then the shrinking stopped. She shook as if she'd suddenly been hit by a monstrous gust of wind. It shoved at the front of her whole body – spread her face, mashed her breasts, distorted her everywhere for a moment – then moved on.

I was vaguely aware of yelling.

Billie was yelling.

I was yelling.

Somehow, I missed the noise of Kimberly's body smacking the concrete. It must've been drowned out by our cries of shock and despair.

I don't know how long I lay sprawled on the bars, gazing down at her.

I couldn't believe this had happened.

I wanted it to be a dream.

Or a trial run. I wanted another chance, a way to try things differently.

A way to save her.

'The bitch was gonna rip my leg off,' Wesley said. 'I couldn't just let her rip my leg off, could I?'

I raised my head.

'Hey,' he said. 'Hey, look. Just settle down. It was an accident, okay? Accidents happen.'

In the Land of Pain

When the sun came up, Kimberly still lay sprawled on the bottom of her cage. A pool of blood had spread out around her, much like the gasoline that had puddled the floor of Billie's cage, but dark.

Billie and Connie stood at the front corners of their cages, facing me.

I faced Wesley.

Alice and Erin watched from their distant cages.

Four spectators, four witnesses.

One executioner.

One motherfucking son of a bitch about to die hard.

* * *

During the night, I had lowered him to the ground. Billie and I had belted him around the neck to a bar of her cage. Neither of us spoke to him. He cried and begged and made excuses and carried on about a lot of stuff. We didn't listen, though.

When we asked him about the cage keys, he said, 'I'm not telling. If I tell, you got no reason not to kill me. They're real bastards, these cages. Nobody's getting out, ever. Not without the keys.'

Billie stood guard over him with the machete while I went away.

I spoke briefly to Connie, who was conscious but confused. She'd been out cold during the action, and had no idea that Kimberly'd been killed. When I told her, she seemed to shrivel. She sank down in a corner of her cage and covered her face.

I went on to Alice and Erin, and explained what had happened. Then I returned to the mansion.

I searched all over the place, looking for the keys. While trying to find them, I came across a few sections of rope which appeared to be our old ropes, taken from the scene of the big battle at the chasm.

Also, I found Kimberly's Swiss Army knife.

I quickly hid the knife away for later. I didn't want to use it on Wesley, foul it with him. I wanted it as a keepsake, a reminder of Kimberly to be savored in times to come.

Downstairs, I gathered some food and water for my women.

I returned to the cages. After handing out the provisions, I took over with Wesley. He hadn't given Billie any trouble. She gave the belt to me, and I dragged him by the neck. He tried to crawl, but it wasn't easy because of his dislocated leg. He screamed and choked a lot.

It took plenty of effort, but I finally managed to stand him up and tie him to the front door of Kimberly's cage. He could only stand on one leg, the other being useless. I kept him upright by tossing two ropes over the crossbar at the top of the door and tying them under his armpits. Then I stretched his arms out to the sides and lashed them to upright bars. I took the belt off him, got rid of its two empty knife sheaths, and used it to strap his good leg to the bars.

By then, Billie's torch had burned itself out.

I wanted light to work by.

So I took a few steps backward from Wesley, and lay down on the ground. Billie called to me a couple of times. I didn't answer, though. I didn't want to go to her. She would hold me. We would weep. It would be comforting and nice. I would probably even end up with a hard-on.

I wanted no part of that.

I wanted no part of gentleness or sex or love.

It would ruin me for what I needed to do.

So I lay there on my back, in a position almost the same as Kimberly's. I pictured how it might look from the air: Kimberly and I stretched out like wings. Airplane wings. Angel wings. Eagle wings.

Wesley between us like the body between our wings. And what did that make us? What did that make him?

I'm starting to ramble.

No more of that.

I stayed on my back, not sleeping, until dawn arrived. Then I got up and went to Wesley.

Billie, Connie, Alice and Erin were already standing in their cages to watch. As if they'd all risen early, afraid they might oversleep and miss out.

Wesley watched my approach.

He was a wreck before I even got started. Aside from his dislocated, swollen leg, he had three spear wounds – the old ones in the boob and buttock, plus the one in the shoulder that I'd given him last night. He was also battered from falling down the stairs last night.

By the look on his face, he must've guessed that even worse was on its way.

Then he saw me pull the razor out of my sock.

When I flicked open its blade, he started to sob.

'Hey,' he said. 'Look. Don't. Don't hurt me.'

Billie called from her corner, 'Just tell us where the keys are, Wesley.'

His eyes were latched on the razor. He licked his cracked lips. 'I'll tell. Okay? Put that away. Put it away and I'll tell.'

I stepped up very close to him. Reaching down with my left hand, I grabbed him. His eyes bulged. I said, 'Where's your fucking boner now, tough guy?'

'Please,' he blubbered.

'Cut his cock off!' Connie shouted. 'Make him eat it!'

'Good thing *she's* locked up,' I said.

He nodded vigorously. His face dripped sweat and tears. 'Don't . . . do it,' he said. 'Please. I'm begging you. I'll tell where the keys are. Please.'

'Okay.' I let go.

'Thank you.' He sniffled. 'Thank you.'

'You're welcome,' I said, and sliced off the underside of his left forearm from wrist to elbow.

While he screamed, I stuffed it into his mouth.

'Eat *that*,' I said. 'You'll need snacks. This is gonna take a while.'

He wouldn't eat it, though. He gasped and choked and managed to spit it out.

'*The keys!*' he squealed.

Off to my right, Connie vomited. She was hunched over, face between bars, trying to get most of her mess to land outside the cage.

I looked at Billie. She stood with her arms up, hands gripping the bars. I saw where Wesley or Thelma or both of them had left marks on her, and I saw a fierce look in her eyes.

'It's not just for Kimberly,' I told her.

'I know that, honey.'

I faced Wesley.

'Tell me where the keys are,' I said.

'Bedroom,' he gasped. 'Upstairs.'

'Where in the bedroom?'

'Under mattress.'

'Liar,' I said, and sliced him across the left eye. My razor cut in through the closed lid, slit his eyeball and nicked the bridge of his nose.

It took him a long time to stop screaming.

I stood back and waited. Most of my audience had had enough. Making no complaints, they'd simply turned away and gone to far corners of their cages. Only Billie still watched.

When our eyes met, she nodded.

'I *told* you where the keys are!' Wesley blurted when he was finally capable of speech again.

'Not enough,' I said.

'What do you want? I'll do anything!'

'Apologize to Billie.'

'I'm sorry!' he cried out. 'Billie, I'm sorry! Forgive me!'

I took off one of his ears.

When he could speak again, he gasped, 'I did what you wanted!'

'Not enough,' I said.

'*What?*'

'You didn't apologize to Connie.'

'But . . . but . . .!'

I shoved my razor into the rip across his left boob, made so long ago by Kimberly's spear but reopened last night. I ran the blade through it, slow and deep.

When Wesley could talk again, he cried out, 'I'm sorry, Connie! I'm sorry, Alice! I'm sorry, Erin. Okay? Okay?'

'You forgot a few people,' I explained, and cut off his right nipple.

Had to wait.

Then, 'Who? Who?'

'Try to remember.'

I made him scream again.

Had to wait.

Then he shouted, 'I'm sorry, Andrew! I'm sorry, Keith! I'm sorry, Dorothy! I'm sorry, James!'

'Finished?'

'No?' he wondered.

'Who, then?' I asked.

'I don't know! You? I'm sorry, Rupert!'

I hurt him again.

Had to wait.

Then, 'Who? Please! Who?'

'Apologize to your wife. Don't you think Thelma deserves an apology?'

'Yes! I'm sorry, Thelma!' he cried out.

I sliced off a pretty good section down the front of his left thigh, and slapped him across the face with it a couple of times.

Had to wait.

Then, *'What? What? Who?'*

'You forgot Kimberly.'

'Kimberly? No, I . . . Yes! I'm sorry, Kimberly! I'm sorry, Kimberly! I'm sorry, *everybody! Everybody!'*

'Very good,' I said.

He hung there against the bars of the cage door, sobbing wildly, blood all over, and blubbered, 'Thank you. Thank you.'

Fool thought I was done.

'One more thing,' I said.

He shuddered. *'Yes! Yes! Anything! Please! Whatever you say! Anything!'*

'Make Kimberly be alive.'

'What? No! I can't! I would, but I can't! Please! I can't do that! She's dead! I can't bring her back to life.'

'Didn't think so,' I told him.

That's when I did what Connie had suggested in the first place. When his mouth was full, I clapped a hand across his lips and kept it there until he was dead.

Then I went over to Billie's cage.

Without being asked, she handed the machete to me.

I returned to Wesley.

'This is for Kimberly, too,' I said.

With one blow, I chopped off his head. It fell and thudded against the ground, and rolled. It came to a stop, face up, the tip of Wesley's penis peering out from between his lips like a curious passenger.

Then I chopped off his arms and legs.

I found a wheelbarrow in one of the storage buildings

behind the mansion, brought it over, piled it with Wesley, then rolled him off into the jungle and dumped him in some bushes.

Far enough away so we wouldn't have to smell him rot.

King of the Island

Almost three weeks have gone by since that morning.

My women are still in their cages.

Including Kimberly. After disposing of Wesley's body, I did what was necessary. I tried for a while to break into the cage. I couldn't get in, though. So she would have to stay.

There were sacks of concrete in the storage building where I'd found the wheelbarrow.

I mixed the concrete in the wheelbarrow with a shovel. I carried it in a bucket up the ladder, and dumped it through the bars. The heavy gray glop fell on Kimberly, bombed her, splatted her body and spread out, rolling like lava, some spilling down her sides to join the concrete of the floor.

I don't want to get into how I felt. Or which parts of Kimberly I covered first. Or last.

After many trips up the ladder with the paint bucket, none of her showed anymore.

Wesley's two knives, one in her thigh and one in her chest, stuck up out of the gray mass like miniature Excaliburs. But no hero arrived with the strength or magic to draw them out.

I gave the concrete a while to set, then mixed more batches in the wheelbarrow and hauled them up to the top and poured. I couldn't pull out the knives, but I could bury them.

When I finally quit, Kimberly's resting place was a long, low hill of concrete at the bottom of her cage.

Billie had watched all this from her cage. She'd given me

useful advice, from time to time. She'd spoken softly, sadly. It was good having her there. To Connie, Alice and Erin, I'd apparently turned into a leper. It didn't bother me, though. Mostly, I felt numb.

We didn't say anything over Kimberly.

Maybe we each did, privately. At least those of us who loved her.

Which probably included only me and Billie, when you come right down to it.

I thought about singing 'Danny Boy' for her. I couldn't do it, though. Maybe someday.

After cleaning up the tools, I returned to the mansion and took a long, hot shower. Then I stayed in. I went to where I'd hidden the Swiss Army knife. With the knife in my hand, I searched for a good bedroom. I picked Erin's, on the second floor. I flopped on her bed.

I stroked my cheek with the knife's smooth plastic handle, and remembered Kimberly. Next thing you know, I started bawling. I cried like crazy, like I'd never cried before. And then eventually I fell asleep.

I dreamed of Kimberly running on the beach. It was *our* beach on the inlet. She ran toward me, smiling. She wore her white bikini, and her husband's gaudy Hawaiian shirt. As usual, the shirt wasn't buttoned. It flowed behind her as she ran. And so did her long black hair. She was tanned, sleek, gorgeous. I couldn't believe my eyes. It must've been a mistake about her being dead. Maybe I'd only dreamed that she'd been killed.

She came into my arms, held me gently, kissed me on the mouth.

After the kiss, I murmured, 'I thought you were dead.'

'You think too much, Rupert.'

'You're not, then?'

Her smile. Her fabulous smile. 'Of course not. Do I look dead? Do I *feel* dead?'

No, she didn't. She looked and felt alive and very wonderful. Shaking my head, I began to weep in my dream. She kissed my tears away. 'Do you love me?' she whispered.

'Yes.'

'Would you like to marry me, Rupert?'

'Yes!' I blurted. 'Yes!' But suddenly I realized that I couldn't marry her, no matter how much I wanted to.

She saw the change in me. 'What's the matter?' she asked.

'I can't. I love Billie. I love both of you.'

Kimberly's smile beamed. 'Then marry us both,' she suggested. 'Why not? You're the king of the island, you can do whatever you want.'

'Okay, then. That's what we'll do.'

'Don't you think you'd better ask Billie, first?'

'Oh, yeah. Good idea.'

'I'll be back,' Kimberly said. She kissed me, whirled around and started running away down the beach.

'Wait!' I yelled. 'Don't go! Come back!'

I must've called out in my sleep, and I think that it was the sound of my own voice that woke me.

The room was dark.

I crept through the house and went outside. I walked across the front lawn, sad that the dream had lied about Kimberly being alive, but feeling less desolate than earlier. Wherever else her soul might've gone, it had found a home inside of me.

I would hold her in my heart forever.

Along with Billie.

Though I approached silently and invisibly in the full darkness, Billie touched me when I tried to find the bars of her cage. She took my hands and guided me forward. We hugged each other. Hard bars pressed against us, but couldn't keep us apart. We filled the spaces between them with our warm, bare flesh.

It was as if Billie had been waiting for me, needing me.

We didn't talk. We hugged and kissed fiercely. It started with the solemn urgency of two survivors finding each other after long and lonely wanderings. There was joy and relief, and a terrible sadness for all that had been lost.

Then that changed, shifted into an urgency of lovers. Hearts pounding, we explored each other with hands and mouths. Caressing, squeezing, delving deep, stroking. We licked each other, sucked and tasted. Gasping for breath. Moaning and sighing. Whispering no words except, 'Yes,' and 'Oh, there,' and 'God.'

I won't even try to describe all we did.

We were together for hours. Sometimes, we simply embraced and quietly talked. Then we would get started again.

Eventually, Billie managed a contortion that allowed us to make love between the bars. It was a hell of a trick, and took a lot of strength on her part. She couldn't hold the position for very long.

It drove me crazy to be inside her that way. I'd never felt anything like it. So soft and warm and tight and slidy. And how it made me feel as if we were almost the same person for a while.

We've done it plenty of times since. I've learned to help by reaching through the bars and clutching her. That way, she doesn't need to work so hard at holding herself up.

It has been wonderful.

Kimberly's concrete tomb gives us sorrow, but also reminds us that life is a gift and we need to savor every moment that we're given.

Though they've been imprisoned in the cages for three weeks now since the deaths of Wesley, Thelma and Kimberly, all four of my women are doing well. I have provided them with clothing, blankets and pillows, plenty to eat and drink. I clean them regularly by pouring water onto them from the tops of their cages. They have soap, washcloths, drinking cups, toothbrushes. They have hung blankets to make cubicles for privacy.

Their toilet buckets cannot be removed from the cages, so we came up with a system of lining the buckets with plastic bags. The used bags are passed between the bars for disposal.

I give my women whatever they ask for: combs, brushes, mirrors, sanitary napkins, books, magazines – even a Gameboy and a portable radio, both of which run off rechargeable batteries. I have become a fairly good cook.

The mansion has provisions enough to last us for a few months, so there is no need to worry about starving. I don't even ration the food.

My women want for very little, except their freedom.

It became obvious, after many tries during the first few days, that their cages were impregnable. I couldn't pick the locks. I couldn't force the doors or hinges. I had no saw or file capable of cutting through the bars. With a pickax, Billie tried to break out through her floor – only to find iron bars imbedded in the concrete.

Nobody treats me like a leper, anymore. Connie and the twins quickly got over their shock at what I'd done to Wesley. I couldn't be all that terrible, they must've supposed, since I was being so good to them. Besides, they knew that Wesley deserved everything he got.

The twins are great. They quarrel a lot between themselves, but they have become my great friends. Erin seems to be madly in love with me, which Alice thinks is ridiculous. They have been healing nicely (as have Connie and Billie). They are both incredibly beautiful, and continue to go around in their cages most of the time wearing few or no clothes.

Which certainly catches my attention. We don't fool around in any sexual ways, though. They are too young for such things. Also, I love Billie so much that I never seem to work up very much excitement over Alice or Erin.

As for Connie, she remained sullen and surly for about a week. She knew that she was to blame, at least partly, for Kimberly's death. She also found out, soon enough, that her mother and I were lovers. She gave us quite a hard time with that mouth of hers.

She seems to be over it, though. I think she has accepted the fact that it's stupid to be jealous over someone you never really liked that much in the first place. I was her boyfriend of convenience who'd stumbled into her life by an accident of the alphabet. I was not, and never had been, any great catch. So let her mother have me.

That's how I *think* she looks at it. We haven't actually discussed the matter.

It's hard to know what she feels. Lately, though, she has been a lot less snotty than usual. Eventually, we might even become friends. Who knows?

I could go on and on about Connie, Alice and Erin. And especially about Billie and me. I could write in lavish detail about all we've done, what we've said and how they've looked. The real story, though, pretty much ended with the death of Wesley.

Also, I've been spending too much time away from my women, writing in the privacy of Erin's room for hours each day.

Now that I'm caught up to the present, I'll be able to spend more time with them.

Eventually, I'll set them free.

The keys to their cages are bound to turn up, somewhere. Maybe under the mattress where Wesley said they'd be.

So long for now.

Quake

This book is dedicated
to
Mike Bailey

The sort of editor that writers hope for
but rarely find

Thanks, Mike

One

Twenty minutes before the quake hit, Stanley Banks was standing at his living-room window. Though he held the sports section of the *L.A. Times* at chest level, he only pretended to read it. He pretended, every weekday morning, to read it.

In case Mother should happen to wheel herself into the room and spy him stationed by the window.

Usually, she remained in the kitchen sipping coffee and sucking cigarettes and listening to the radio.

But sometimes she put in surprise appearances, and the newspaper made a good diversion.

By now, she knew that Stanley was in the habit of standing at the window to take advantage of the morning light while he studied the front page of the sports section.

That was what he had told her often enough.

It wasn't the truth, of course.

In truth, he stood there to watch the sidewalk.

He was watching it, now, over the top edge of the newspaper.

He hoped he hadn't missed her.

He glanced at his wristwatch. Eight o'clock on the nose. She ought to be running past the house within the next five minutes.

'Stanley!' his mother called. 'Stanley! Be a dear and fetch me some matches.'

Stanley felt his throat tighten.

'Just a minute,' he called.

'Do as you're asked, please.'

I'm gonna miss her!

Maybe not. Maybe not, if I hurry.

411

He slapped the newspaper onto the end table, then strode across the small living room to the fireplace, grabbed a handful of matchbooks from a wicker basket on the mantel and hurried through the dining room to the kitchen. He tossed them onto the table in front of his mother. They hit the surface hard, bouncing and scattering. One matchbook skidded off the edge and dropped to the floor beside her wheelchair.

Stanley whirled around. He managed only a single step of his escape before a harsh voice demanded, 'Stop right there.'

'Muh-therrrr.'

'Look at me when I speak to you.'

'Yes, ma'am.' Stanley faced her.

Alma Banks, squinting at him through her pink-framed glasses, jabbed a Virginia Slims between her lips and fired a match. She sucked its flame to the tip of her cigarette. She inhaled, then blew twin gray funnels out her nostrils.

'I asked you for matches, young man. Not for a display of temper.'

'I'm sorry. If you just could've waited for a couple of minutes . . .'

'Your time is so precious that you can't afford to do a small errand for your own mother?'

'No,' he said. 'I'm sorry.'

I'm going to miss her!

'Matches. That was all I asked for. Matches. Do I ask so much of you? You're a grown man. You're *thirty-two* years old. You live in my home. You eat my food. Is it so much to ask you to do a little something for me once in a blue moon? Is it?'

'No. I'm sorry. Can I go now?'

'*May* you go now?'

'May I? Please?'

'Go.' A flap of her hand kicked the smoke cloud coiling and twisting away from her face.

'Thank you, Mother.' He headed for the living room, forcing himself not to rush. 'I'll be back to do the dishes in a few minutes. I just want to finish the sports section.'

'You and your sports section. It isn't going to vanish, you know.' She wasn't letting up, but she wasn't following him. Her wheelchair remained silent. She was apparently content to pursue him with her voice. 'Your precious sports page isn't going to go up in a puff of smoke, do you know that? It won't go anywhere.'

He was already at the window.

'But it can't wait two minutes while you find your mother some matches?'

'I *got* you the matches,' he called.

'You threw them at me, that's what you did.'

'I'm sorry.'

'You *should* be.'

He checked his wristwatch. Three minutes past eight.

If I've missed her . . .

'I won't always be around, you know,' Alma reminded him.

Time for her to start pouring on the waterworks.

Stanley almost felt like crying, himself. He'd missed his chance for today, been cheated out of it by the selfish whims of . . .

And then she appeared.

Stanley thought, *My God.*

No matter how many times he saw her, no matter where, no matter what she might be wearing, a glimpse of Sheila Banner never failed to slam Stanley in the heart and suck out his breath and raise his penis.

'Oh, Sheila,' he whispered.

She came into view from beyond the oleanders at the left side of the lawn, long legs striding out, arms swinging at her sides with relaxed grace. Her white shoes and socks were so bright they flashed like sunlit snow. Her tawny legs gleamed, alive with shifting curves of muscle. They were bare all the way up to the golden trim of her shorts.

The royal blue shorts shimmered and flowed around Sheila as she ran. Stanley could *feel* how they caressed her. Slick as oil. Sliding over her thighs and buttocks, rubbing silken and warm between her legs.

She wore an old, faded blue T-shirt. Big and loose, it

413

fluttered and flapped around her. Its chest shifted up and down with the jouncing of her breasts. From their steady rhythm, Stanley could tell that she was wearing a bra.

She never ran without one.

Stanley actually glimpsed her bra when her right arm cocked back. Its side showed near the bottom of the T-shirt's armhole. It was white this morning.

The hole gaped enough so that he could see a lot of the bra.

Stanley wished she was not wearing it. Then he would be able to see most of her breast through the armhole. And the way her shirt was cut off at the waist, the way it hung down from her breasts, he would be able to look up from underneath and see them both. Their smooth round undersides . . .

Sure, he thought. If I'm lying on the sidewalk.

After noting that today, as always, she wore a bra, Stanley lifted his gaze to her face. A glorious face. At once smooth and hard, delicate and powerful, silk and granite, innocent and sophisticated. But altogether beautiful, the face of a movie queen and a warrior goddess melded into one stunning, incredible Sheila Banner.

Hair like a thick banner of gold flowed behind Sheila, and was the last Stanley saw of her when she ran past the bushes at the far side of the driveway.

Trembling, he took a deep breath.

Then he retrieved his sports section and stepped over to his armchair in the corner of the room. After sitting down, he pushed himself against the back of the chair so that it reclined and the footrest swung up. He raised the newspaper and stared at it.

He imagined himself going after Sheila.

Running out to the sidewalk after she passed, and following. At a discreet distance, of course.

It wouldn't be against the law.

Why *don't* I? he asked himself. Why don't I really *do* it instead of just sitting here and dreaming about it?

She'd be bound to notice me.

So what?

Plenty of so what. She sees Stan the Man, all six foot two inches of him, all two hundred and eighty pounds of him, all red and sweaty and lumbering after her, she isn't going to be exactly overwhelmed with ardor. She'll be disgusted or scared, one or the other. Or both.

And maybe she sees which house I came out of, so she changes her route and that's the last time she ever runs by.

And maybe she realizes it's *my* house behind her backyard fence, and maybe she starts to worry about what else I might be up to ... So maybe she starts being more careful about shutting the curtains, more careful about what she does in the yard. Warns the girl about me, too.

Lovely girl. Not in the same league as her mother, though.

To Stanley's way of thinking, *nobody* was. Sheila Banner formed a league of one.

He wished he had photos of her. He didn't dare sneak pictures of her with his good Minolta, though. He would have to send the film out to get it developed. People at the processing lab would see it. They might suspect something. For that matter, one of them might be a *friend* of hers.

Stanley just couldn't risk it.

He used to have a Polaroid camera. He'd bought it shortly after moving back into Mother's house, ten months ago. Because he just *had* to have photographs of the incredible woman who ran past the window each morning – who *lived* directly behind him.

He'd made the mistake of showing the new camera to Mother. Showing it to her before he'd even had a chance to use it.

She'd turned it this way and that, inspecting it. Then she'd narrowed her eyes at him. 'Do you suspect, for one minute, that I don't know what this is for?'

He'd blushed hot.

'What are you talking about?' he'd blurted.

'As if you didn't know. And who *is* it that you plan to take your dirty pictures of? Me?'

'No!' he'd cried out.

And watched Mother hurl the Polaroid. It struck the

fireplace bricks. Bits of plastic and glass flew like shrapnel. The demolished camera bounced forward a couple of feet, dropped, and crashed to the tiles of the outer hearth.

'I won't have it,' she had informed him. 'Not in my home. Not now. Not ever. I'm ashamed of you.'

Remembering the fate of his Polaroid, Stanley let out a sigh.

I'm such a gutless wonder, he thought.

I could've bought a new Polaroid the next day. I could buy one *today*, for that matter.

What Mother doesn't know won't hurt her.

But if she catches me . . .

If she catches me.

Stanley wished he had the guts to ignore that little refrain. *If she catches me.* Oh, the things he would've done if not for that. The things he would've seen. The wonderful opportunities . . .

He was thirty-two years old, and he felt as if he had missed his life.

Missed it because there had always been a woman watching over him like a prison guard. First Mother, then his wife Thelma, and now Mother again.

I shouldn't have moved in here, he told himself. *Stupid stupid stupid!*

After Thelma's death, however, Mother had begged him to come and live with her. It hadn't seemed like a bad idea at the time. For one thing, Mother possessed a considerable amount of wealth and a little stucco house valued at nearly $400,000. For another thing, Stanley's job had perished with Thelma.

Thelma was the only woman who had ever cared about him. So in spite of her age and size and face, he'd married her two weeks after his high school graduation. At that time, she had already been a fairly successful author of children's books, making enough money for both of them. With no need to find a job, Stanley had gone to work for his wife, answering her fan letters, handling such chores as photocopying and mailing manuscripts, and so on. He'd been her secretary, really. And not a very good one.

With her death, Stanley's prospects of finding a halfway decent job seemed remote. He doubted that he would be able to get by on her royalties.

So he'd agreed to move in with Mother.

And he'd missed his chance for freedom.

He had been like a prisoner whose guard had dropped dead while on duty, leaving his cell unlocked. He could've fled. All it would've required was an ounce of guts. But instead, he'd waited like a model prisoner for the new guard to show up.

But the cell has a great view, he told himself, and grinned. *Sheila.*

I would've missed out on her.

Stanley checked his wristwatch.

Seventeen minutes past eight.

Sheila would've been back inside her house for some time, by now. With all his meandering thoughts, Stanley had neglected his habit of tracking her movements with his imagination.

He considered pretending he hadn't missed out. He'd done that before, though, and it just wasn't the same. The thrill was to picture her at the *same moment* as her actions: finishing her run, taking out her house key . . .

Oh where, oh where had she kept it this morning? Tucked in a sock? Nothing so mundane as that. No no no. Slipped beneath the waistband of her panties, perhaps. Or maybe she'd kept it safe inside a cup of her bra where it had made an imprint of itself on her breast. So many places where the key might hide, a warm secret pressed to her skin. Places where she would need to delve with long fingers to . . .

Quit it, he told himself. *You missed all that. You've gotta catch up and make it simultaneous.*

By now, she had probably finished stripping off her sweaty clothes.

Stanley *loved* to picture that. How she started with a shoe, usually balancing on one leg while she raised the other, bent over slightly and clutched the shoe with . . .

Catch up, damn it!

Yes. Right. What's she doing now? At this very instant?

Stanley looked at his wristwatch.

Eight-nineteen.

Probably she was already standing under the shower, its hot spray splashing her naked body. Or perhaps she was sprawled out in her bathtub.

Stanley didn't know whether she preferred showers or baths.

Being such an athlete, Sheila was just the sort to prefer showers. But her more feminine and sensual side would relish lounging in a tub full of hot water.

So she did both, the choice depending on her mood.

On *my* mood, Stanley corrected himself.

This seemed like a shower day.

After folding the sports section and resting it on his lap, Stanley shut his eyes. And saw the shower doors through swirling twists of steam. They were sliding doors of clear glass. In spite of the steam, they were not fogged up. He could see through them as if they weren't there at all.

He could see Sheila standing beneath the nozzle, her back to the spray, her head tilted back, her elbows high as she pushed her fingers through her soaked hair. Her face gleamed with water. Shiny rivulets streamed down her breasts, which trembled ever so slightly with the motion of her arms. Drops like liquid diamonds gathered at the tips of her nipples and fell, one by one . . .

Stanley's chair jerked beneath him. In that instant, he thought that Mother had somehow caught wind of his dirty daydream and rammed him with her wheelchair. *Caught you, you filthy pervert!*

By the time he got his eyes open, however, he knew that Mother had nothing to do with the alarming jolt.

Because she wasn't in the room, and the room itself was juddering with such rough quickness that it blurred.

Beside him, the lamp pitched over.

He battered his newspaper aside and leaned forward, dropping the footrest. As he shoved himself out of the chair, he shouted, 'Earthquake!'

Of course, Mother already knew that.

Stanley could hear her scream over the sound of his own voice, the roar of the quake, the clamor of the front window shattering and the noises of things all over the house crashing to the floor.

A falling chunk struck his shoulder when he was halfway to the front door. Plaster?

The ceiling!

I've gotta get out of here!

He reached out and grabbed the doorknob, turned it and pulled. Only when the door refused to swing open did he remember that he needed to unfasten the dead bolt. He let go of the knob and tried to nip the brass turner between his thumb and forefinger. It dodged him as if it didn't want to get caught.

'Bastard!' he yelled.

Then he pinched it. He gave it a quick twist. A lurch of the house tried to hurl him backward. He grabbed the doorknob just in time, saving himself from a tumble.

'Stanley!' his mother squealed. 'Help me! Help me!'

He looked past his shoulder.

And here came Mother, hunched over and wheeling in from the dining room like a contender making a sprint for the finish line. Clods and slabs of plaster dropped all around her as the ceiling broke apart. White dust sifted down on her.

'Stanley!' she shrieked.

'I've gotta get the door open!'

He turned the knob, yanked. The door flew toward him. He had neglected to unhook the guard chain, but didn't notice his oversight until the chain and uprooted jamb plate lashed his brow.

He staggered backward, swinging the door with him. His grip on the knob began steering him sideways toward the demolished window, so he let go. His own weight shoved him back across the floor. The chair stopped him. It reclined, popped up its footrest, scooted with the impact and pounded the wall behind it.

Right back where I started!

Stanley hugged his head with both arms and screamed.

And watched his mother.

He stopped screaming.

Because, after all, this was serious but it was also pretty funny. Funny how he'd gotten thrown right back into his chair. And *really* funny how Mother had quit her bee-line for the door (maybe because the route was blocked with ceiling rubble?) and was wheeling herself around in frantic circles. She was no longer screaming, either. And she had ceased calling for assistance from Stanley.

Hunkered down and working her push rims like crazy, she circled and shouted, circled and shouted, 'Oh my oh my oh my oh my!'

A piece of ceiling plaster the size of a dinner plate dropped straight down in front of her. Either blessed with a good portion of luck or sensing the danger, she halted her wheelchair just in time. The plaster smacked the floor at her feet. 'Oh my oh my oh . . .'

'Hey, Ma!' Stanley yelled. 'The sky is falling!'

She didn't seem to hear him.

As if somebody had heard him, however, the house collapsed. Not all of it, though.

The part that collapsed did not include the living room.

From his reclined easy chair, Stanley only *saw* the cave-in that happened just beyond the dining room archway. A big cave-in that smashed the table flat against the floor and disintegrated the chairs and buried it all under a pile of plaster and wood and stucco. Through the thick fog of dust, Stanley saw sunlight shining down on the heaped debris.

He muttered, 'Holy fucking shit.'

He thought, I'd better get my butt out of here pronto.

He pictured himself making a detour on his way to the door. Scooping Mother out of her wheelchair and running with her, dodging this way and that as sundered support beams slammed down. Getting out the door and clear of the house even as the rest of it crashed down.

Quit thinking about it and DO it!

But what if I leave her?

What if I leave her and the house falls down?
Wouldn't that be a fucking pity?
Let's just get my own ass out of here – and quick!
As he leaned forward and shoved his heels against the footrest, the quake stopped.

The end of the roar left a great silence.

Mixed in with the silence were quiet sounds. Stanley heard the house creaking as its motions subsided. He heard the distant *wow-wow-wow* of car and house alarms. Somewhere far off, dogs were barking.

His mother's wheelchair was silent. So was her voice.

He looked at her.

She sat motionless, still hunkered over, head down, hands still clutching the push rims of her wheelchair.

'Mother?' Stanley asked.

She didn't move.

'Mother, are you all right?'

Stanley raised himself out of the chair.

'Mother?'

She lifted her head. White powder and flakes drifted off her hair and shoulders as she sat up. Her pink-framed glasses hung crooked on her face. She straightened them. She blinked at Stanley. Her chin was trembling. Spittle had dribbled down from her mouth, cutting moist streaks through the plaster dust.

In a shaky, piping voice, she said, 'It's over?'

'It's over,' Stanley told her.

He went to her.

'What ever will we do now?'

'Nothing to worry about,' Stanley said.

He crouched beside her wheelchair and picked up a chunk of plaster the size of a flagstone. He hefted it overhead.

He could see by the look in her eyes that she suddenly knew what was coming.

'Stanley!' She cringed away and started to bring up an arm.

The good, heavy slab of plaster broke in half when it struck the top of her head. It made a *thuck*. She made an '*Hunh!*' Her glasses hopped down to the tip of her nose, but didn't fall off.

Stanley held on to half the plaster slab. The other half fell, bounced off Mother's right shoulder and dropped to the floor.

She sat very still for a moment.

Stanley raised his slab.

While he considered whether or not to hit her again, her head slumped down. Slowly, she leaned forward. Her glasses fell. They punched her skirt, making a narrow valley between her thighs.

She leaned farther and farther as if hoping to peer down over her knees and find something wonderful hidden beneath her chair.

Stanley stepped back and watched.

She leaned so far forward that her knuckles brushed the debris on the floor. Then her rump lifted off the wheelchair seat. Her head thumped the floor. She did a clumsy, crooked somersault that showed off more of her gray pantyhose than Stanley cared to see. Her legs came down straight and fast. The heels of her shoes exploded glass shards from the demolished window. She bucked as if trying to sit up, then dropped down again and lay still.

Stanley gave her hip a tap with the toe of his moccasin.

'Mother? Mother, are you all right?'

She didn't stir. She didn't answer.

He gave her a good solid kick. The blow shook her, wobbled her head.

Stanley saw blood trickling out of her ear.

'That's a bad sign,' he said, and couldn't help but laugh.

Then his laughing stopped.

What killed it was the thought that Sheila Banner might be ruined, crushed beneath the rubble of her home.

Two

One minute before the quake hit, Clint Banner yawned and glanced at his empty coffee mug.

It was emblazoned with a portrait of John Wayne as Rooster Cogburn from *True Grit*. A birthday present from his daughter Barbara, who liked to insist that Clint looked 'exactly like Hondo.' She hadn't been able to find a mug with Hondo on it, however, so she'd settled for Cogburn. 'I know you don't look like *that*,' she'd said, making a face. To which Clint had responded, trying to mimic Duke's cadence and voice, 'Give me a couple more years and an eyepatch, little lady.'

He yawned again.

It was eight-nineteen on Friday morning. He had been up since four-thirty, his gimmick for beating the system. Jump out of bed, dress in the bathroom so you don't wake Sheila, and hit the road by a quarter to five for a forty-minute drive through the dark. A drive that would take you twice as long if you slept to a reasonable hour like six. Arriving so early, you had the offices to yourself for a few hours. That was nice. And you got to leave before two, ahead of the afternoon rush. Plenty of advantages.

Took a lot out of you, though.

Another yawn, then Clint picked up his empty mug, slid back his chair, and sidestepped clear of his desk. He planned to get a refill. But he only took one step.

He almost had time to wonder what that *roar* was.

But in an instant he knew what it was. Not an eighteen-wheeler or a freight train cannon-balling toward the building. Not a Boeing 747 about to take down the wall.

The roar came out of nowhere and before Clint could quite find time to wonder what it might be he knew it was a quake because it hit.

It sounded like a quake. It felt like a quake. This was

423

Southern California, land of quakes, so it probably wasn't a 747 crashing into the building. It wasn't a tornado inside the office with him. It wasn't the shock wave from a comet or a nuclear warhead striking ground zero a mile away; they might feel and sound a lot like this, but this was an earthquake.

First it roared.

Then it hurled a body block against Clint.

He staggered sideways, but kept his feet.

A quake had never hit him so hard before.

A *good one*, he thought. *A really good one. Maybe a six-point. Maybe bigger.*

Time for it to fade away now.

It didn't fade.

It grew.

It shook the window blinds so hard they clattered and jumped. It splintered windows. It killed the fluorescent lights. It wobbled the walls. It clawed acoustical tiles off the ceiling. It cluttered the air with the flying debris of papers, case files, pens, Rolodexes, staplers. Drawers of desks and file cabinets leaped open. Computer keyboards and monitors slid and dropped. Chairs on wheels raced across the wild floor.

Clint thought, *My God, it's the Big One! This is it!*

He wondered if this was his day to die.

Just stand your ground, he told himself. *It'll go away*.

Standing his ground was not easy. The office floor bucked and jumped. The carpet had *waves* in it – combers two feet high that raced for the wall.

Impossible, he thought.

He was seeing it, though – floor surf.

Clint pranced and stayed up.

And thought, *It's a race. Which calls it quits first, the quake or the building?*

If the quake wins, I'm dead meat.

He began his dash for the stairway. Knees pumping high, arms overhead. Dodging, jumping.

Get the fuck outa here!

As he ran, he recalled his years of glib wisdom. His quake

cracks. 'When your number's up,' pause for effect, 'it's an eight-point-five.' A little Richter scale humor. Or his favorite bit: 'No call to be afraid of earthquakes. A quake is completely harmless, never hurt anyone.' Pause for effect. 'It's the *shit that falls on your head* that'll kill you!'

Or taking a dive down the stairway, he suddenly thought.

At the top of the stairs, he reached for the handrail and missed. He reached again. This time, he caught the wooden rail. But it was jerked out of his grip.

No holding on.

The stairwell looked like a narrow tunnel. A steep one. A funhouse slide into a pit. It juddered and twitched down to where the light from above faded. The landing and door were somewhere below in the darkness.

Don't try it, Clint told himself. Wait till the shaking stops!

Sure thing.

He bounded down the stairs, leaping, taking two at a time, slapping the walls to help his balance.

Like sprinting down a mountainside, an avalanche on your tail. You'll probably take a headfirst dive, but it's worth the risk. Speed's the trick. Staying in front so you don't get buried, crushed. Staying in front, no matter what.

Gotta get outa this place!

Through the roar of the quake, he heard his own yell.

It occurred to him that a fellow with more panache might shout 'Geronimo!' in such straits.

But all Clint yelled on his stampede down the stairwell was, 'YAHHHHHHH!!!'

At the bottom, he crashed against a wall. He bounced off, fell against the stairs, scurried up and pawed the shuddering door until he found its handle. He levered the handle down. He pushed. Light from the foyer stung his eyes.

He rushed out of the stairwell, dashed across the reception area, flung himself against the front door, threw it open and ran outside into the morning sunlight.

The earth still shook. The quake still roared.

My God, Clint thought, *it's never going to stop!*

Covering his head with both arms, he raced into the street.

Into the middle of the street, away from falling glass and walls that might crumble.

He whirled around. The two-story building that housed the law offices of Haversham & Dumont, his employers, appeared to bounce and shimmy. Clint knew it couldn't possibly be jumping about so much without disintegrating. *It's jumping, but not as much as I am*, he thought.

He glanced up and down the street.

Saw several cars.

Couldn't tell for sure whether they were approaching or parked.

Probably just parked, he thought. Nobody would keep on driving through all this.

The cars were being tossed about like skiffs on a rough sea. And seemed to shriek with panic, their alarms set off by the quake.

A sound like the rip of tough fabric made Clint snap his head forward. He muttered, 'Jesus!' Moments before, the front of the office building had been intact except for several shattered windows. Now, it looked as if an oak tree had blasted its way through the stucco wall.

Got out of there just in the nick of time.

A horn blared. Its noise melded with the car alarms and the roar of the quake and a legion of other noises – a chaos of shatters and clashes and slams and sirens – so that Clint was only vaguely aware of the horn. The blare was like a sight glimpsed in his peripheral vision. Something barely noticed, vaguely troubling.

Until it wailed in his ears and he turned his head and saw a red Toyota pickup truck torpedoing at him through the road surf.

He yelled, 'SHIT!' and dived for the curb.

Airborne, he thought he'd done a halfway decent job of leaping clear. The bastard wouldn't kill him, probably just clip off both his feet at the ankles.

But he felt no pain until he landed. The pavement scorched his hands and knees, slammed his chest, knocked his breath out. For a moment, he felt as if he were sliding across a cheese grater. Then he stopped skidding. He thought, *Bastard!* and raised his head, wanting to shout at the crazy asshole behind the wheel of the Toyota. But he had no breath for shouting.

The asshole had painted out some of the big white letters on his tailgate. Changing the brand name to TOY.

Clint realized that he had actually been able to read the word TOY.

The word TOY was not a vibrating, pounding blur.

The quake's stopped!

Clint thought, *Thank God!*

Then he thought, *Oh, my God!* because the red TOY hadn't slowed down for the cross-street any more than it had slowed down for him, and this time there wasn't a man in its way but a gray BMW rushing into the intersection from the left.

Just short of the crosswalk, the TOY cut hard to the right. Maybe the driver thought he had cleared the curb at the corner. Maybe he figured a bounce over the curb would be better than getting broadsided by the BMW. But hadn't he noticed the power pole? Maybe he'd figured it would snap like a toothpick when he hit it, and he would speed merrily on his way.

The pole did snap.

But the driver didn't speed through a quick spray of splinters.

The pole didn't burst into splinters at all.

Instead, its stump bludgeoned its way through the front of the TOY.

The TOY stopped very fast.

Clint couldn't see what happened to the driver.

But the man in the passenger seat blasted headfirst through the windshield. He wore a blue baseball cap, a plaid shirt, and jeans. Obviously, he had not worn a seatbelt.

He soared over the TOY's crumpled hood. The crown of his baseballcap looked smashed flat. The bill of the cap dangled by one corner and flapped like a fractured wing. His blue jeans were at knee level as he shot past the collapsing power pole. They slipped lower, hobbling his ankles as he glided down for a landing on the far side of the corner.

The BMW, brakes shrieking, intercepted him.

He hit the passenger window headfirst.

The window burst.

His head went through it. The rest of his body didn't. The rest of his body snapped sideways and slammed the back door of the car, then dropped away. It tumbled and flopped, headless, as the BMW skidded to a halt and the power pole finished its downsweep and finally crashed against the street.

The TOY, its dented roof supporting one end of the pole, looked like a cheap metal parody of the Passion – a Jesus on wheels that had broken down on the way to Calvary.

Snapped lines, alive with juice, whipped and crackled high above the crossbeams.

Clint got to his feet fast, ready to bolt if any of the wires should try for him.

The way they leaped and sprang about, no telling . . .

The lines died. They went limp, sagged in midair, and dropped toward the pavement.

It's over, Clint thought. *Over. And I'm still here.*

He took a deep breath. He looked around.

Nothing was shaking any more. Most of the buildings along the street were still standing, but two on the next block had collapsed, piling the southbound lane with rubble.

No cars seemed to be moving.

I made it, he thought. *The Big One's over, and I'm still here. A few scratches, that's all.*

He glanced at the scuffed heels of his hands. Then at the torn knees of his trousers.

No big deal.

No problem at all with the quake, it was the Toyota that damn near creamed me.

He pictured himself saying that to Sheila and Barbara. It was the sort of crack they would expect from him, and he would have to remember to lay it on them when they all sat around and told each other their stories . . .

What if they're not okay?

They were in it, too, you dumb shit. A quake that strong . . . But maybe it wasn't so bad over on the west side. They're more than thirty miles.

Maybe it was worse.

For all you know, Sheila or Barbara might be . . .

He didn't allow himself to think the word, but he pictured them dead. Sheila at home, Barbara at school. Both of them crushed and bloody and dead.

Clint swung his eyes to the ejected TOY passenger, glimpsed a smear of red between the shoulders, noticed that the pants had disappeared entirely, along with both the shoes, and looked away fast to avoid seeing more.

They might be like him.

No. They're all right. They're fine.

I'VE GOT TO GET HOME. NOW. RIGHT NOW!

Clint ducked slightly. Close to the ground, the building had open spaces like long narrow windows. He ran his eyes along them until he spotted his old Ford Granada. Just the roof and windshield were visible.

His car looked fine.

So did the parking lot. Nothing had collapsed in there.

He was glad to see no other cars. He'd *assumed* nobody else had arrived at work by the time the quake hit, but he hadn't been absolutely certain. Several people who often showed up around eight-thirty worked on the ground floor, and he didn't always hear them arrive.

They're probably stuck in traffic somewhere.

Traffic's gonna be a bear. I'd better stay off the freeways, take sidestreets.

He raced for the parking lot entrance. As he ran, he dug the keys from his pocket.

He scurried down a short slope of driveway, stopped at the side of the rolldown security gate, and found the key to activate it. His hand shook badly. He used his other hand to help guide the key into the slot. He twisted the key.

Nothing happened.

'Come on come on come on.'

He twisted the key again.

With a quiet hum and metallic clatters and rattles, the gate should be lifting clear of the driveway.

There was no hum.

The gate didn't stir.

Clint looked over his shoulder at the intersection. The traffic signals weren't red, yellow or green. They showed no light at all.

He twitched the key, trying to *make* it work. Even though he knew it wouldn't.

Not with the power down.

He could get to his car easily enough. But the gate barred the only way out.

Bash through it?

Oh, sure.

'Movie crap,' he muttered. *This is real life, and you don't crash through a gate like that and speed merrily on your way. Even if you're lucky enough to live through the crash, your car bites the dust. No way.*

If he disabled his car with a stunt like that, it wouldn't get him home.

And that was all that mattered to Clint at the moment.

He had to get home. Had to make sure Sheila was okay. And Barbara.

Again, he pictured them crushed.

A quake never hurt anyone – it's the shit that falls on you!

Please, God, let them be all right.

Clint jerked his key from the slot. He kicked the gate.

Damn it!

His car was fine! His car was in great shape, safe and sound, just waiting to speed him home.

But useless! Trapped inside a goddamn parking lot!

Jailed.

What do I do now? he wondered. Start walking?

He climbed to the crest of the driveway. He scanned the cars scattered along the curbs. Though alarms still blared, nobody had come along to check on them.

Steal one?

How about a little grand-theft auto?

Hell, Clint didn't know how to go *about* stealing one. You pull the ignition? You cross some wires?

Sure thing.

Like which wires?

He frowned at the TOY pickup. He could take that and nobody was likely to make a fuss. It even, certainly, had the key in its ignition. But from the looks of the thing, it was as dead as its passenger, as dead as the driver who was inside somewhere out of sight beneath the smashed-down roof.

The BMW still sat in its lane just to the right of the intersection.

All right!

Bending over slightly, Clint could see the driver. A woman. She was sitting motionless, her head turned toward the passenger window. Clint thought she was staring at him.

I'm a witness, he thought. She probably wants to get my name and stuff.

He raised a hand at the woman. Then he hurried toward her. His legs felt weak and spongy. His head buzzed.

Too much action, he thought. Too much everything. But I'm still here. And so is she.

He almost called, 'Don't leave,' but stopped himself. He didn't want to give her any ideas.

She wasn't moving, though. Just staring.

Staring, but not at me, Clint realized as he neared her car. Her gaze was aimed lower. At the passenger seat.

Clint suddenly knew why.

'It's all right,' he said.

She didn't respond. She just kept gazing as if entranced by the sight of her odd companion.

A curl of brown hair draped her brow. Otherwise, she looked neat and prim in her white blouse and her matching gray jacket and skirt.

Clint guessed she'd been on her way to an office job.

She wore very little makeup. And needed very little. Too young and too pretty to require much help. Early twenties?

'It's all right,' he said again. 'It wasn't your fault. I saw the whole thing. You won't be in any sort of trouble. Okay?'

She didn't respond.

Okay, shit, here goes nothing.

Clint stepped forward fast.

The head was on the passenger seat. It still wore its baseball cap, but the cap had lost its bill completely, and was no longer Dodger blue. The head lay face up. It was as red as the baseball cap. It was staring at the ceiling, its stump of a neck aimed at the young woman.

No wonder she's freaked, Clint thought.

He grabbed the door handle and pulled, but the door was locked. Instead of wasting time trying to get the gal to unlock it, he reached through the broken window and found the lock switch. He flicked it, withdrew his arm, swung the door open wide, and suddenly surprised himself by stopping.

He'd thought he would just sweep the head off the seat, let if fall to the street.

He couldn't do it, though.

This wasn't garbage. It wasn't a spoiled sandwich or a dirty napkin. It was the head of a man who had been alive a few minutes ago.

A man who probably had a family and friends, a job, who was a Dodger fan, who maybe liked to take his kids to the stadium and eat hot dogs under the sunlight . . . Whose crime was being in the passenger seat of a guy who must've panicked when the quake hit.

Clint lifted the head gently by both sides of its face. It was slippery. It was heavier than he'd expected.

He stepped backward with it and carried it well in front of him so blood wouldn't get on his clothes. He took it to the body sprawled on the pavement. He set it down there, neck to neck, and had a sudden urge to fasten it on somehow – tape it or strap it or . . .

I've gotta get home!

The head rolled a little when he let go. Only an inch or so. Not far enough to matter.

Rising from his crouch, Clint spotted the dead man's blue jeans near the middle of the intersection. He hurried over to them and picked them up. They seemed clean. He used them to wipe the blood off his hands, then hurried with them to the BMW.

The driver met his eyes. She frowned.

So she's not catatonic. Is that good news or bad?

'It's all right,' Clint said. 'I'll just clean up this mess for you.'

She nodded.

He leaned inside the car and did his best to mop the blood off the seat cover. When it looked fairly clean, he tossed away the jeans and swung himself into the car and sat down.

He pulled the door shut.

'I'm Clint Banner,' he said, forcing his voice to sound calm. 'What's your name?'

She blinked a few times, frowned. Her lips moved, but no words came out.

'Your name?'

'Mary,' she whispered. 'Davis.'

'Were you on your way to work, Mary?'

A nod, barely perceptible.

'What do you do?'

'I'm a secretary. With an advertising firm.'

'Advertising.'

Her head bobbed, more pronounced this time.

'Okay, if that's your job, there won't be any work today. Do you understand? We've had a major quake. You don't need to go in to work. What you need to do is go home.' He glanced at her hands. They were clutching her thighs, fingers spread and pressing hard into the gray fabric of her skirt. She wore rings on both hands, but no engagement ring or wedding band. 'Do you have family?'

More bobbing.

'In L.A?'

'Chicago.'

'Then you don't need to worry about them. What you need to do, Mary, is get yourself safely home. Do you understand?'

'I . . . I don't know.'

'Where do you live?'

'Santa Monica.'

'Great!' The word burst out, and Mary flinched. 'Great,' Clint said again, speaking more softly. 'Look, I'll help you. I need to get home to my wife and daughter, and my car's . . . no good. I'm over in West L.A. It won't even be out of your way. All I need is for you to get me over the hills. And I'll help you. It might be a tough trip. A lot of traffic between here and there . . . traffic signals down . . . roads'll probably be blocked in places . . . no telling what we might run into. We can help each other. Okay?'

'What about my accident?'

'Don't worry about it.'

'But . . . that's hit-and-run.'

'Not today,' Clint said. 'You probably couldn't report this mess if you wanted to. And even if the phones *are* working, the police have business a lot more urgent than this.'

'I . . . I ought to *try* and report it.'

Clint put his hand on her shoulder. He squeezed firmly, but not hard enough to hurt her. 'We can't waste the time, Mary. Do you want to get home today?'

'Yes.'

'So do I. I want to get home so bad it hurts. So what we've gotta do is leave right now, and leave hard and fast. Do you want me to do the driving?'

'I . . . yeah, maybe so.'

Three

When the quake hit, the Chevy Nova rocked and swerved left and veered across the center line.

Barbara Banner's stomach gave a sick lurch.

Behind her, Heather squealed while Earl yelled, 'Hey!' and Pete muttered, 'What the . . . ?'

'Brakes!' gasped Mr Wellen, slapping the dash with both hands.

Barbara was already jamming her foot down on the brake pedal as she wrenched the wheel to the right. The car cut back into its proper lane, then nosed too far to the right and headed for the tail of a parked Wagoneer.

'You're over-correcting, Bar . . . Stop!'

'I *am* stopped!' she shouted back at her driver's ed teacher.

'Y'are not!' Earl yelled.

Barbara knew that she had stopped the car – braked it to a halt only an instant after it had taken the odd turn toward the Wagoneer. But it kept on shuddering and jerking and twisting its way closer to the Jeep's rear bumper.

'Look out!' Wellen scooted himself across the seat, grabbed the wheel with one hand, flung his left leg sideways, and stomped his shoe down hard on top of Barbara's foot.

'OW!'

He shoved against her foot as if trying to crush it into the brake pedal.

Barbara shot her elbow into his ribs.

Now I've done it, she thought. Oh, my God. What do they do to you for hitting a teacher?

But at least he quit mashing her foot.

'It's a quake!' Pete said. He sounded excited, like the only kid in class to come up with the answer to a teacher's trick question.

'No kidding,' Earl said.

A quake! Clenching the wheel, keeping her sore foot pressed to the brake pedal, Barbara for the first time looked beyond the nearby threats to the school car. She saw a stucco apartment building a short distance ahead and off to the right. It was a two-story building. Instead of a lawn, it had pavement sloping down to parking spaces beneath the ground floor.

The whole structure, the pavement below it, and the cars parked inside a few of its nooks, shook as if Barbara were watching through the viewfinder of a camera held by someone in the midst of a grand mal seizure.

She was looking directly at one of its high windows when

the glass exploded and a woman came out backward. An old woman with wispy white hair. Wearing a peach-colored terri robe that matched the stucco wall, a color that camouflaged her so that she was nearly invisible except for her head and small hands and bare white legs that kicked frantically at the sky.

'Everybody down!' Mr Wellen ordered.

The old woman dropped out of sight, rump first, scrabbling with both hands as if trying to claw a rung of air.

The wall of the next-door apartment building began to crumble. It was just sloughing down when Mr Wellen grabbed Barbara's upper arm. Clutching it, he fumbled at her hip.

'What're you . . .?'

She looked down. The safety harness, suddenly retracting, whipped its buckle at her face. She flung her head back. The buckle missed. Then Wellen was pulling her by the arm, dragging her from behind the wheel toward his side of the car. Then he was clambering onto her. Sitting on her lap. Squirming off. Scooting under the wheel. Taking the wheel with one hand, shifting to reverse with the other, and backing away from the Wagoneer's bumper.

'What're you doing?' Pete shouted from the rear.

'Getting us outa here!'

The car lunged forward, shoving Barbara back against the seat.

'Wait till the *quake* stops!' Earl yelled.

Wellen gunned it, speeding up Bedford, the Nova shaking and bouncing and swerving from side to side. A jaunt to the left skidded it toward the side of a parked Plumber John truck. Heather screamed. Barbara clutched the dashboard. Wellen fought the wheel, recovered, and swung them clear with inches to spare.

During the next few seconds, Barbara glimpsed apartment buildings on both sides of the street break apart as if struck by huge wrecking balls. Walls exploded. Roofs crashed down. One building only lost its front wall, while the next collapsed entirely, the next two appeared to be intact and the one after those dropped its north half to the ground while its south half remained standing.

This is really it, Barbara thought. This is the Big One.

She pictured her mother ducking and covering her head as their house on Swanson Street came down on top of her.

No! No, she'll be all right.

Maybe she's not even in the house. Maybe she's out watering the yard, or . . .

Please let her be all right. And Dad.

Dad's so far away, he might not even be getting this where he is. Or maybe just a little tremble.

'You ought to stop, Mr Wellen,' Pete advised. 'It isn't safe to be driving . . .'

'You'll kill us all!' Earl yelled.

'Shut your face, Jones! I know what I'm doing. I'm the teacher around here, right?'

'Doesn't mean you're right.'

'Shut up.'

Barbara released her grip on the dashboard, snatched down the passenger seat harness, swept its belts across her chest and lap, and felt for the buckle slot. Felt for it because she didn't dare look away from the destruction all around them.

The whole world's falling down!

But not on us, she told herself. Not so far, anyway.

Even the walls that toppled toward the road were too far away to reach them.

As long as nothing falls on us, we'll be okay.

And she heard her father. Kidding around, as usual. *An earthquake never hurt anyone. An earthquake's harmless. It's the shit that falls on your head that'll kill you.*

Or your driver's ed teacher freaking out and creaming you in a head-on . . .

She thrust the metal tongue into the buckle's slot, heard and felt it lock into place.

If he crashes now . . .

A bowling ball sailed down from high on the right and whunked the hood.

Can't be, Barbara thought. Not a bowling ball.

But it is.

She saw its finger holes, its pretty purple marbling . . .

It bounced, leaving a big dent in the hood, and the speeding car rushed at the airborne ball. In front of Wellen's face, the windshield dissolved into frosty chunks. Bits of it flew at him. Barbara expected the ball to come in. But it bounced off and fell away, leaving a hole no larger than an orange in the safety glass.

Wellen kept on driving.

'You okay?' Barbara yelled. And realized that her voice seemed strangely loud, that it seemed so loud because the roar was gone. Not only the roar, but the rough shudders and . . .

'I think it's stopped,' Pete said.

'Yes!' Earl blurted. '*All right, sports fans!*'

Heather was crying.

Barbara looked back at her. The girl seemed very small and fragile between Earl and Pete. She was hunched over, hugging her belly, head down, the sides of her face draped by long brown hair. Her shoulders hitched up and down as she sobbed.

'You okay?' Barbara asked.

Heather shook her head. The shrouds of hair swayed.

'We're all right,' Barbara told her. 'We made it. The quake's over.'

The car swung hard to the right. Barbara was thrust sideways toward Wellen, but the chest belt stopped her. In the rear, Pete caught hold of the door handle to keep himself upright. Heather fell across Earl's lap.

He cast his eyes down at her. Wrinkled his nose. Said, 'Hey, get off the merchandise,' and shoved her away with his forearm.

'Take it easy,' Pete said.

'Gettin' her cooties on me.'

'I'm sorry,' Heather murmured.

'Everybody knock it off back there,' Wellen commanded. 'Just knock it off!'

Heather, sitting up straight, leaned away from Earl. Which

438

pressed her right side against Pete. She glanced at Pete as if asking permission. He nodded. Then he slipped his arm across her shoulders. His hand cupped her left shoulder, gave it a squeeze.

And Barbara felt an ache deep inside her. Something like longing or regret. Which made no sense. She didn't even *know* Pete, just from driver's ed.

No sense at all. But it hurt a little, anyway, to see him holding Heather. So Barbara turned forward. She settled back into her seat.

What's wrong with Wellen? she wondered.

Hunched over the wheel, he was peering forward through the hole in the windshield. Barbara could only see his right eye. But it looked bulgy and wild. His red face glistened with sweat. He was gasping for breath. His lips were skinned back, baring his teeth.

It scared her to look at him.

So she looked forward.

Beyond the windshield, a wide road. Blocked here and there by stopped cars. Bordered not by apartment houses but by parking meters, shops, banks, businesses of all sorts – most in shambles. People stumbling about as if dazed.

We're sure not on Bedford anymore, Barbara thought.

No, of course not. That right turn we made . . .

She spotted the Shell station.

Our Shell station? she wondered. The one with Heinz who called the Granada 'your junk'?

Must be.

So we're on Pico, Barbara thought. And this is La Cienega just ahead.

Familiar territory. At least it would have been familiar if so much of it didn't look as if it had been leveled by bombs.

Barbara spotted the post office beyond the intersection, far ahead and off to the left.

We're going the wrong way!

'Mr Wellen?'

He didn't repond. Nor did he slow down as they rushed into La Cienega.

Car horns blared.

A Porsche bore in from the side, straight at Barbara.

'Look out!' Barbara yelled.

'Oh, Jeez!' Pete blurted.

The Porche missed, passing behind them.

Somebody's not obeying the . . .

The traffic signals at the far corners of the intersection were dark, dead.

No lights, and he's taking us . . .

You're supposed to stop and wait your turn!

'Wellen!' Earl shouted.

A moment later, they shot clear of La Cienega untouched.

'Stop the car!' Pete snapped.

Wellen picked up speed, weaving from lane to lane.

Heading east on Pico.

East.

Barbara jerked her head around to glance at the others. 'He's taking us the wrong way!'

Earl reached over the seatback. He smacked Wellen on the shoulder. 'Hey! Turn us around!'

'Don't touch me again, punk,' Wellen said.

'Mr Wellen,' Barbara said. 'Please! You've got to turn us around and take us back to school. We need to get *home*. Please.'

'I'll get you back to school,' he said, still hunched forward and peering through the windshield's hole. 'Just everybody quit your whining. I've gotta check up on my kid.'

'Your kid?'

'Yeah, my kid. My daughter.' His head jerked toward Barbara. A quick, fierce, hateful glare. Then he turned again to his windshield hole. 'Nobody stops me. Don't even think about it.'

'Oh, great,' Earl muttered. 'Terrific. So where the hell are you dragging us, you lunatic?'

'Shut your face,' Wellen said.

'Where *is* your daughter?' Barbara asked, trying to sound kind and sympathetic.

'Saint Joan's.'

'What?'

'Saint Joan's.'

'What's that, a church?' Pete asked.

'A school,' Wellen said. 'A Catholic girl's school.' He glanced again at Barbara. This time, his eyes didn't seem quite so mean.

'What grade is she in?'

'She's not in any grade. She's a teacher. Ninth grade English.'

At Fairfax, he slowed down only a bit. He drove onto a sidewalk to get past a line-up of waiting cars, bounced down from the curb, hit the brakes to avoid broadsiding a pickup truck, then gunned the engine and sprinted for the other side as cars in the way swerved and honked.

When Barbara could breathe again, she asked, 'How far away *is* that high school where your daughter works?'

'We'll be there pretty soon.'

'We won't get there at all if you kill us!' Pete yelled.

A tear was sliding down Wellen's face, alongside his nose.

'It'll be all right,' Barbara told him.

'It's such an old school,' he said. 'I think it's been reinforced to meet earthquake standards, but . . . Dear God, look at all this. How could Saint Joan's possibly still be standing after . . .' He shook his head. He was weeping outright, his face streaming.

'We're all worried about our families,' Barbara told him. 'They've gotta be worried about us, too.'

If they're not dead.

Don't even think about that. Mom and Dad are fine. They've gotta be.

'Your daughter's probably just fine,' she said.

'I don't know, I don't know.'

'Where *is* her school?'

He sniffed. 'On Pico.'

'Where on Pico?'

'Normandie.'

'*Normandie!*' Earl cried out. '*That's downtown!* That's *miles* from here.'

441

'I'll drive you back to Rancho Heights. Just as soon as I've picked up Katherine.'

'You won't be *able* to drive us back,' Pete said. 'Look at the traffic in that direction.'

'I'll get you back. Don't worry.'

'Just let us off here,' Barbara said. 'Just stop and let us out. We can walk back.'

Sobbing, Wellen shook his head. 'Can't stop. We're almost there.'

'Almost there, my butt,' Earl said. 'STOP THE CAR!' As he shouted, he leaned forward and swatted the side of Wellen's head. A hard smack. The car lurched to the left. Into the path of a gray Mazda.

Barbara braced against the dash. She squeezed her eyes shut.

Instead of a collision, she felt a sudden jerk to the right.

She looked, saw they were back in their own lane, safe for the moment, and glimpsed Earl's hand coming toward her about to launch another strike at Wellen.

She grabbed Earl's wrist. 'Don't! Leave him alone! You wanta make him crash?'

'Let go of me!' Earl wrenched his arm from her grip. But he didn't swing at Wellen. Instead, glaring at Barbara, he sank back into his seat. 'I could *make* him stop, you know.'

'I know. You're *so* tough.'

'You wanta see how tough I am, just keep it up.'

'Oh, I'm scared to death.'

'Everybody shut up!' Wellen shouted.

'If you don't like it,' Barbara snapped at him, 'stop the car and let us out.'

'I'll let you out when I'm good and ready, young lady. I'm still the teacher around here. I'm still in charge. So everybody sit still and keep your mouths shut. Is that understood? And as for you, Jones, you can look forward to criminal charges for assault and battery when all this is over.'

'Oh, yeah?'

'Yeah.'

Ahead, both eastbound lanes were blocked by stopped cars.

Wellen didn't slow down.

'Hey,' Barbara said. And cried out, 'NO!' as he poured on the gas. 'Stop it! Are you nuts?'

He cut to the left and they sped alongside the line of halted cars, straight toward the front of an oncoming RTD bus.

Four

'These'll come right down, *right* down,' Stanley muttered as he sidestepped between two of his mother's rose bushes. He hated them. He hated all of her rose bushes. They stood at the cinderblock wall like sentinels posted to keep him away.

Though they couldn't keep him away, they never failed to draw his blood.

No matter how often he trimmed back their thorny branches, no matter how much care he took to suck in his stomach and lift his arms above their reach as he eased through, their thorns always found him.

He'd paid with stinging wounds for his many trips to the wall.

Now, a nettle pricked the back of his shoulder. As he tried to escape it, another nicked his thigh. Both barbs snagged his pajamas and wouldn't let go.

Stanley almost wished he'd left his bathrobe on; its thick nap would've given him some protection from the thorns. But he'd left his robe in the house.

After all, why *should* he wear it? The morning was warm and luscious. Mother was hardly in any position to complain about his attire. *Nobody* was likely to complain, considering the circumstances.

Hell, the *house* had fallen down. What could they expect Stanley to wear, a tux?

He was glad he'd left the robe behind. He enjoyed being outside dressed in nothing except his moccasins and pajamas. He liked how the pajamas drifted lightly against his skin, caressing him. And he liked it that they were so thin; any woman he might meet would be able to see quite a lot of him through the lightweight fabric.

The heavy robe might have saved him from a few scratches, but it would've smothered him, hidden him.

After plucking his pajamas free of the thorns, he made it to the wall.

He braced his hands against the cinderblocks, leaned forward and lifted himself on tiptoes to see Sheila's house.

He moaned.

Beyond the lawn, beyond the concrete patio, the house was down.

It looked as if it had been kicked apart and stomped by a giant.

All that remained was a mess of junk corralled by broken walls – a litter heap of splintered wood, tattered patches of roofing asphalt, red tiles, crumbled stucco and plaster and sheetrock, tendrils of pipe jutting up here and there, a few wires leading to nowhere.

Maybe Sheila wasn't inside when it went down, Stanley told himself. Anything could've happened. Maybe she'd decided to run an extra mile or two. Maybe she'd gone on an errand.

Maybe she *was* inside, but she's still alive.

And if I save her, she'll be so grateful to me that . . .

If she was inside the house when it fell, she *has* to be dead.

Stanley squeezed his eyes shut. 'She's not dead,' he whispered. 'She's not. She's just fine, and I'm gonna save her.'

Opening his eyes, he clapped his hands down on top of the wall and jumped. He shoved himself higher, belly and groin and thighs scraping against the rough blocks. Elbows locked, he flung a leg up sideways and hooked the top with his foot. Seconds later, he was standing upright on the wall.

Nothing to it!

Should've done it months ago! Should've climbed right over the wall and enjoyed some close-up views.

But he'd never dared. Afraid of being caught.

By Mother. Or by Sheila's husband.

So he had never done more than peer over its top. At night after Mother had gone to bed. During the day, those occasional times when Mother was away from the house without him.

He'd seen a lot, but never enough. Never near enough.

From now on, there would be no Mother in his way. He could do whatever he pleased.

But now it was too late. The quake had seen to that.

It just isn't fair, Stanley thought.

From his height above the wall, he could see that the houses on both sides of Sheila's place still stood. They had broken windows, some cracks in the walls, and they might've sustained some serious damage beyond Stanley's view. But they hadn't collapsed.

Why her place?

Nobody even *lived* in the house to the left. It had been vacant for two months, a FOR SALE sign in the front yard. And the young couple who lived in the house to the right both held full-time jobs. So they probably weren't even home when the quake struck.

Nobody home at two out of three. The quake had dropped the only house with a person in it.

Not just any person. Sheila.

My Sheila.

Stanley leaped. In midair, he realized he should've lowered himself down from the wall instead of jumping. But it was a bit late for that.

His feet pounded the ground. Pain shot up both his legs. He stumbled forward, leaving one moccasin behind, and fell. He landed on his knees, dived from there, and skidded headfirst over the grass.

The grass felt thick and soft and very wet. Stanley lay motionless on it for a few seconds, then got slowly to his feet.

The front of his pajamas clung to him. Where the pale blue fabric adhered to his skin, it looked nearly transparent.

He went back for his moccasin, slipped his foot into it, then headed for the ruin of Sheila's house.

The sunlight on the concrete patio made him squint. The patio looked fine. Normal. Just the same as always. There was the Weber grill that often sent such wonderful aromas into the evening. There was the picnic table, a flower pot in its center, a long bench on either side. There was the lounger with its faded, green cushion.

Four times during the past few weeks, he had gazed over the wall and found Sheila stretched out on this very lounger. She had worn a skimpy white bikini. She'd rubbed her skin with oil, but hadn't been able to reach the middle of her back.

Only twice had he seen the daughter come out to sunbathe. Her bikini was orange. Compared to Sheila, she looked scrawny. Skin and bones. Cute, but not in the same league as her mother.

As if anybody could be.

Only last Wednesday, Louise Thayer had taken Mother to a bridge party and Stanley had visited the wall. Peering over the top, he'd spied Sheila sprawled bellydown on the lounger. She wore a baseball cap and sunglasses. She read a book. Her bikini top was untied, leaving her bare and glossy all the way down her back. A small white triangle draped the middle of her rump. A white cord crossed her hip. Except for that cord, her side was nothing but sleek skin all the way down from her shoulder to her foot.

Stanley had gazed at her, aching.

She's got to move sooner or later, he'd thought. She'll get up. And maybe she'll be careless about her top. Maybe she'll lift herself up, and it'll stay down there on the cushion.

Maybe she'll even turn over onto her back without it!

Yes!

She might! She just might!

And Stanley had suddenly remembered the binoculars in his bedroom closet.

He couldn't take a picture of her, thanks to the Bitch, but

he could damn sure get a good close-up look with his field glasses.

So he'd hurried away to get them.

Hurried so fast that he'd ended up with three nicks from the rose bush thorns.

No more than four minutes later, he'd returned to the wall, binoculars in hand, ready and eager.

No Sheila.

She was gone. Her book was gone. Her plastic bottle of suntan oil was gone.

She had gotten up, and he would never know whether or not she'd been careless about her top. He'd missed it. Gone for the binoculars and missed it!

In a rage, he had slammed the binoculars against the wall. Pounded them, smashed them.

Now, he realized that he had missed more than a chance to see Sheila rise from the lounger, possibly revealing her breasts.

He had missed his *last* chance.

Because now she was somewhere under all that rubble.

Crushed, ruined, dead.

Stanley walked over to the lounger. Its green cushion, faded in places so it was almost white, showed yellow and brown stains in the rough shape of a body. Run-off from Sheila, he thought. Some from Barbara, too, he supposed.

Crouching, he sniffed the cushion. Its dry, sweet aroma whispered to him of long summer days and sweltering beaches, the squeal of gulls, the rush of combers washing over the sand.

It's her suntan oil, he realized.

Suntan oil and sweat.

He pressed his face into the cushion. Eyes shut, he felt the warm fabric against his lids – and against his lips as he sucked, filling himself with the air from the cushion.

Sheila was right here.

He licked the cloth.

And sucked.

And thought he heard a voice.

The voice didn't startle him, didn't worry him. It hadn't come from someone near enough to observe what he was doing.

He hadn't been caught.

And he didn't *intend* to get caught, so he raised his head. A dark patch of wetness on the cloth showed where his mouth had been.

Glancing all around, he saw no one.

He heard no voice.

Maybe he hadn't heard a voice at all. It might've been something different. No telling what he had *really* heard through the awful clutter of noises: the wailing, blaring, hooting alarms from cars or houses; the sirens nearby and far away; the car horns beeping over on Robertson Boulevard; the whup-whup-whup of a helicopter that was out of sight but not very far away; the bangs and pops and blasts (none alarmingly loud) that might be backfires or slams, but were probably gunshots; a scream of car brakes; the sound of a crash; various other clamors and roars.

A regular chaos of noises.

Stanley heard such noises every day, but not so many of them, not all at once.

One of the neighborhood's normal sounds was missing, though. Probably the worst of all. The leaf-blowers. This morning, they were silent.

All the little crews of lawn workers must've decided to take the day off on account of the Big One.

Just three days ago, Mother had demanded that Stanley 'do something' about the Mexican gardeners who'd shown up across the street at seven-thirty and demolished the morning peace. First, they'd slammed the tailgate of their antique pickup truck. Then they'd gone into action with the power mower and the leaf-blower. The din of the blower had destroyed the last of Mother's restraint.

'You go out there right this minute and *do* something, Stanley!'

'What am I supposed to do?'

'Have a *word* with them. They've no right, no right in the

world, to be raising such a Godawful racket at an hour like this.'

'They'll be done in a while.'

'Stanley!'

'It won't do any good, anyway. They won't understand a word I say.'

Behind her glasses, her eyes narrowed. 'I suppose you're right. Damn wetbacks. They've got no business coming to this country if they can't learn to speak . . .'

'I know, I know.'

'Call the police.'

'The *police*? I'm not gonna call the police about a leaf-blower.'

'*I* will.' Scowling, she had wheeled herself toward the telephone. After passing Stanley, she'd looked back at him. 'You're totally worthless, do you know that? You've got no balls at all. Your father was a complete pervert and a moron, but at least he had balls. But not you. I've never seen such a worthless excuse for a man.'

Remembering, Stanley smiled.

Had the balls to bust your head in, Bitch.

As he thought that, he heard a voice again. This time, it seemed to find its way through a gap in the tumult of noise. A woman's voice. It called out, 'Hey!'

From somewhere in front of Stanley.

From somewhere in the rubble.

He felt an explosion of wild hope.

He shouted, 'Hello!'

'Help!' the voice called back. 'Helllllp!'

He stepped to the very border of the debris. Off to the left, a portion of the chimney rose out of the mess. The fireplace itself was buried, but a seascape still hung on a remnant of wall above the mantel. The painting looked only a little crooked.

No other artwork was visible. Nor could Stanley spot any piece of furniture, any book or garment, utensil or knick-knack. Except for the lone painting, the only signs that the house had been inhabited were the refrigerator and oven that still stood upright in what must have been the kitchen – near the right front corner. Every other possession of Sheila and her family was apparently entombed beneath the fallen walls and ceiling and roof. The scatter of mounds and slopes, he supposed, showed where there might be hidden sofas, beds, dressers, counters.

Under one of the piles might be Sheila herself.

'Where are you?' Stanley yelled.

'Down here!'

The sound seemed to come from an area somewhere ahead and to his right – near the oven? At the time of the quake, he had pictured her taking a bath or shower, but maybe she'd been in the kitchen.

'I'm on my way,' Stanley called. He reached out his leg, planted his foot atop of a tilted slab of stucco, wondered for a moment if it would hold him, then stepped aboard. The stucco wobbled, but he kept his footing.

From there, he surveyed the area ahead.

The tumbled remains of the house bristled with shards of window glass, with rows of nails. The thin leather soles of his moccasins might save his feet from cuts, but . . .

Just don't step on a nail, he warned himself as he risked another stride.

And for God's sake don't fall.

He spread his arms for balance.

He picked his route carefully and moved slowly, trying to avoid slabs or chunks or boards that didn't look stable. Some broke apart anyway. Many teetered. A few flipped and dropped him ankle-deep into laths or plaster.

'Are you there?' the voice called.

It *had* to be Sheila's voice. Though it sounded louder, more distinct than before, it was still battered by conflicting noises. Besides, he'd only heard her speak a few times. He couldn't be sure this was Sheila.

Must be, he thought. It's her house. Who else could it be?

'I'm coming,' he answered. 'Are you hurt?'

'I think I'm okay. But I'm trapped. I can't move.'

Her voice didn't actually seem to be coming from the

kitchen area – from that general direction, but not from that distance. Sheila was not so far away. Maybe ten or fifteen feet this side of the oven.

He couldn't see her, though. Between Stanley and the place where Sheila seemed to be, there stood hills of rubble and the low remains of a few interior walls.

Heading that way, he called, 'Was anybody else in the house?'

'No. Just me.'

'What's your name?'

'Sheila. Sheila Banner.'

Yes!

'I'm Stanley Banks. I live in the house behind you.'

'Sure am glad you showed up, Stanley.'

'I was checking around the neighborhood and saw the condition of your house.'

'You mean they didn't *all* go down?'

'Nope. From what I've seen so far, maybe one out of three or four got leveled.'

'My God!'

'Could've been a lot worse.'

'I just hope to God the school's okay.'

Careful, Stanley thought. 'Do you have a child?'

'Yeah. She goes to Rancho Heights High. Have you heard anything – any news?'

'None. It must've been a hell of a quake, though.'

'They always said we'd get it.'

'Yeah.' He began to climb a slope of wreckage. Until now, he had avoided anything so high. He could've detoured around this one, but knew there would be a good view from its top.

If I can just get there in one piece.

He made his way upward slowly, crouching, open hands down low so that he might catch himself if he should slip.

'How about your house?' Sheila called.

'It got . . .' His left foot suddenly triggered a small avalanche. He scrambled higher and found solid footing. Hunched there, he panted for breath. He was shaking, drenched with sweat. His pajamas felt sodden. His moccasins felt gooey inside, as if they'd been lathered with lard.

'Stanley?'

'Yeah?'

'Are you all right?'

'Fine.'

'Are you sure? Did you fall?'

'Some stuff . . . gave out under me. I'm okay.'

'Be careful. I don't want you hurting yourself.'

'Thanks.' Slowly, he straightened up. With a damp pajama sleeve, he wiped his face.

'What about your family?' Sheila asked. 'Are you married?'

'My wife died last year.' He resumed climbing.

As he gained the summit, Sheila said, 'I'm very sorry about your wife.'

'I appreciate that. Thank you.'

'You sound a lot closer.'

'Yeah, I . . .' He had been gazing at the debris under his face while he climbed. The moment he lifted his eyes, he saw the blazing house. And the handful of people gathered to watch it burn.

They were the *only* people he saw.

The burning house had apparently drawn every available spectator, leaving none to notice Stanley.

'What is it?' Sheila asked.

'A house fire. Over on the other side of Swanson. At the corner of Livonia.'

'Is the fire department there?'

'No. Not yet.'

'Police?'

'Afraid not. Just a few neighbors.'

'My God. What if it spreads?'

'Its pretty far away.'

'Oh God.'

'Don't worry.'

'I'm *trapped*.' Though the voice came to him along with a confusion of overlapping noises, he heard Sheila's fear. 'I don't want to burn up.'

'I'll get you out,' Stanley said. 'I'll save you. I promise.'

'Hurry? Please?'

'I'm coming.' Moving as fast as he could without taking reckless chances, he descended to the bottom of the mound without trouble. From there, he could still see the thick black smoke curling into the sky. But the burning house and the spectators were out of sight, blocked from his view by remnants of Sheila's walls.

I can't see them, they can't see me.

He liked that.

If they can't see me, they won't be coming over to snoop.

'Sheila?'

'You sound *very* close.'

He looked toward the sound of her voice.

It seemed to come from straight ahead – no more than a few strides away. But he could see only more tumbled, broken ruins of the house.

'I can't see you.'

'There's a bunch of stuff on me.'

He took a step. Another step. Halting, he studied the debris.

'Where are you?' he asked.

'You're almost on top of me.'

On top of you. Yes. Oh, yes!

'Can you see me?' he asked.

'Too much in the way. But you sound like you're somewhere above my feet.'

How could that be? The rubble in front of him looked fairly level and close to the floor. Unless Sheila'd been mashed – but she claimed to be unharmed. And she sounded fine. Scared, but not in pain.

'I don't get it,' he said. 'Where *are* you?'

'I think I'm in the crawlspace.'

'What?'

'The *crawlspace*. Under the house. I felt the tub drop. All this junk came crashing down, and the tub dropped out from under me. We must've landed in the crawlspace.'

'You're in your *bathtub*?' Stanley asked.

'Yeah. The luckiest break I've ever had.'

Me, too, Stanley thought.

'The stuff would've mashed me. But it's all across the top. Too much for me to budge.'

'Well, I'll start clearing it away.' He took off his pajama shirt. It felt good to be free of the wet, clinging fabric, to feel the air against his skin. He wanted to remove his pants, as well.

We'd both be naked.

Yeah, and what if somebody comes along? And what'll Sheila think? She'll be able to see me as soon as . . .

'How's that fire doing?' she asked, interrupting his thoughts.

Stanley twisted around for a look. Nothing had changed much. Black columns of smoke still climbed the sky. 'It isn't getting any closer. Don't worry about it. We've got all the time in the world.'

Five

Wellen had only avoided a head-on collision with the RTD bus by steering even farther to the left, *two* lanes away from their proper side of the road and into the path of a gray Mercedes. He swerved right. Filled in the space between the rear of the bus and the front of an oncoming Ford. Then again to the right, abandoning the westbound lane with an instant to spare.

And it had gone on like that.

Bursts of speed, lurches from side to side, skids and abrupt halts, near misses one after another. It seemed that Wellen would no sooner save them from a crash than still another car or bus or delivery truck would be rushing straight at them.

Barbara, belted into the passenger seat, sat rigid and squeezed her thighs and tried not to scream.

Heather, in the backseat, screamed plenty. And sobbed and pleaded.

Earl and Pete shouted.

Barbara barely noticed anything that wasn't a direct threat to their Nova. She was only vaguely aware of what they passed: collapsed buildings, fires, wrecked cars, sheared off fire hydrants spouting white geysers into the air, people sprawled on the sidewalk, all bloody, or hurrying somewhere or stumbling along like zombies. Such sights hardly registered on Barbara's mind. They didn't matter. They were background. They weren't real. Only the ride was real – the Nova piloted on its suicidal course by the driver's education instructor.

On and on and on he sped with his students.

Putting their lives at risk with every turn of the wheels.

Taking them farther from school and from their homes with every second.

A few times, Wellen made detours to avoid sections of Pico Boulevard that appeared to be completely blocked. He whipped around corners, sped down sidestreets, gunned his way through alleys. But always back to Pico.

Until finally, a few blocks past Western, he drove into a trap.

Ahead, all lanes were blocked, a solid row of vehicles side by side from one curb to the other.

Wellen cried out, 'No!' and mashed the brake pedal. The Nova skidded. It stopped less than a foot behind the rear bumper of a van. He shifted to reverse. Hit the gas.

The Nova jumped backward and bucked, slamming into something.

'Great move!' Earl yelled.

Barbara twisted her head around to look out the rear window. 'A bus,' she said.

Wellen glanced back.

At first, Barbara thought he was just curious to see what he'd bumped. From the way his eyes shifted, however, she realized he was looking for an escape route – a gap in the traffic that would permit him to speed backward and resume his mad rush for the school where his daughter worked.

'No way,' Barbara muttered.

She shot her arm out sideways and twisted the ignition key. Wellen didn't seem to notice.

He flung open his door, leaped out, threw the door shut and ran. There was a nice, clear path for him between the two rows of motionless traffic. Seconds after abandoning the Nova, he sprinted past a dumptruck and vanished.

He no sooner vanished than a lean black woman in a brown uniform – the RTD bus driver? – dashed by.

'Get him, lady!' Pete yelled. He sounded delighted.

Barbara laughed. She couldn't *believe* she could possibly be laughing, but there was no doubt about it. Her laughter had a certain frantic, crazy ring to it.

She looked back at Pete. He was laughing, too.

We've flipped out, she thought.

Heather was in no danger of laughing. She looked as if she might never stop bawling.

Earl opened his door. He climbed outside and stood next to the car for a moment, apparently hoping to see the bus driver catch Wellen. Then he looked to the rear.

'Did she get him?' Pete called.

Earl ducked into the car. 'Who knows?' he said. 'They're outa here. And so am I. You guys gonna come along? 'Cause I gotta tell you, the car's going nowhere. Traffic's backed up to hell 'n gone.'

'Just leave the car here?' Barbara asked, no longer laughing.

'It's *gonna* stay here. Don't matter if we're in it or not, it's *staying*. Guys're bailing out. Nothing's gonna move for hours. Maybe not all day.'

Frowning, Pete said, 'I don't think we're more than six or seven miles from school.'

'Walk it?' Barbara asked. 'Yeah. A couple of hours, it shouldn't take much longer than that. Four miles an hour.' The single mile from school to home should take an extra fifteen minutes. 'Let's do it,' she said. 'Better than sitting here. How about you, Heather?'

Heather sniffled. 'Okay.'

'Just in case Wellen comes back,' Barbara muttered, and plucked the key out of the car's ignition. She dropped the key ring into her denim purse, slipped the strap onto her shoulder, and shoved open her door.

The car had been air conditioned. Its windows had been shut. Except for the hole in the windshield, it had been sealed tight until Wellen, then Earl, had opened their doors.

Barbara had thought she would be glad to get out of the car. From the start of Wellen's mad race, it had seemed like a deathtrap.

She climbed out.

And wanted to climb back in.

'My God,' she muttered.

The deathtrap had been a haven.

Sanctuary from the heat, the stench, the smoke, the noise, the chaos and destruction.

The heat felt like the breath of an oven. Exhaust fumes and smoke from nearby fires stung Barbara's eyes, scorched her nasal passages. Her ears hurt with the blare of car horns.

Why does everybody have to honk!

Everybody wasn't honking. It only sounded that way. In fact, many of the vehicles in sight had nobody in the driver's seat. Some people were standing beside their cars, studying the situation. Others were sitting on hoods or perched atop their car roofs. In a few cases, people had banded together; strangers only minutes ago, they now stood in the midst of the traffic, chatting, nodding, pointing. Barbara supposed that plenty of people hadn't stuck around at all.

Everybody isn't honking, just every jerk still sitting in his car.

She longed to shut herself inside the Nova and lock its doors.

But I'll never get home if I do. This is the only way.

Heather had the right idea, plastering her hands against her ears.

'Let's get outa here!' Earl yelled. Without waiting for any

replies, he swung around and began to stride alongside the line of stopped cars.

Pete gestured for Heather and Barbara to go on ahead of him. Heather held back. She didn't want to go second. Hardly surprising. Barbara wasn't eager to be up there near Earl, either. The guy was a major creep. But she knew she was better equipped than Heather to handle him. So she hurried forward.

When she caught up to Earl, she called, 'Let's get away from Pico when we can! Take the first sidestreet! Get away from this mess!'

He frowned back at her, nodding.

At the first corner, they turned to the left.

They bypassed the sidewalk to avoid its collection of broken glass and other debris. This section of road had metered, curbside parking. All the spaces were taken.

They walked in the road, alongside the parked cars.

The vehicles to their right were moving no faster than those harbored at the curb to their left.

At least twenty were stacked up in the two northbound lanes because of the blocked intersection, but this road wasn't completely jammed. With cars plugging one side and rubble from a collapsed building piled in the other, no vehicles could escape onto it from Pico. The rubble was only at the corner, so the southbound lanes were clear. In a fairly orderly fashion, the cars at the rear were backing off, turning around and heading away. All those trapped here would soon be free.

The drivers were waiting their turns.

Without honking.

With every stride that Barbara took, the din of the car horns on Pico diminished.

So did the smoke. Several buildings had collapsed along this section of road, but none was on fire.

'This is a lot better,' Barbara said.

'Glad I thought of it,' said Earl.

She looked back. Heather, ears uncovered, was walking beside Pete, pressing herself against his side and clutching his arm as if her life depended on keeping herself attached to him.

Give the guy a break, Barbara thought. Maybe he doesn't *want* you hanging all over him.

He didn't look like he minded, though. In fact, he seemed pretty much oblivious to Heather. With a worried frown on his face, he glanced every which way as if he expected trouble and wanted to see it coming.

'Watch where . . . !'

Barbara couldn't stop in time. Head turned toward the others, she walked smack into Earl, ramming him with her right upper arm and breast.

'Geez!' he gasped, and shoved her away.

'Sorry.'

'What're you trying to do to me?'

'I *said* I'm sorry. If you hadn't *stopped* like that . . .'

'What's going on?' Pete asked.

'We had a little collision,' Barbara said. 'It wasn't anything.'

'Yeah, right,' Earl muttered. 'Ban-butt tried to flatten me with her Flying Tit Express.'

She was already so hot she could imagine steam rising off her skin. Earl's remark, however, boosted the temperature. A lot. 'Jerk,' she said.

The heel of his hand pounded her shoulder. The blow didn't hurt, but it twisted her torso and she stumbled backward.

Seething, she raised a fist.

'Oooo. I'm so scared.'

'Leave her alone,' Pete said.

'Leave *her* alone? She's the . . .'

'Let's not fight!' Heather blurted. 'It's stupid! Stupid! We're lucky to be alive, you people. Honestly! Just look around. The quake . . . Maybe thousands of people are dead, for all we know. We might get killed our*selves* before we ever make it back home through all this. We've *got* to depend on each other. We've got to be friends!'

'You're right,' Barbara said, amazed by Heather's outburst. The girl was new in school this year, but she'd been in three of Barbara's classes. In each of them, she had cowered at her desk, huddled in isolation. She had rarely spoken. Several times, she had burst into tears for no apparent reason. A basket case. But mostly a *silent* basket case. Until now.

'We don't have to be *friends*,' Pete said, 'but it is pretty stupid to fight among ourselves. We're in this together.'

Hugging his arm, Heather gazed up at his face.

Wonderful, Barbara thought.

She met Earl's eyes. 'Anyway, I should've watched where I was going. I'm sorry.'

'Yeah, sure. Okay. So the thing is, the reason why I stopped – I was thinking why don't we cross over to the other side, you know? Maybe we can hitch a ride.'

'Hitchhike?' Barbara asked. 'Are you kidding? That's a *sure* way to get ourselves killed.'

'What? There's four of us. Who's gonna pull something when there's four of us?'

'It's really asking for trouble,' Barbara said. 'Besides, these cars may be getting out of *here*, but they won't get far.'

For a while, they all watched the cars that were peeling away from the tail ends of the jammed lanes, making U-turns and heading south. The road was fairly clear for a couple of blocks. In the distance, however, Barbara could see a backup at Venice Boulevard. Cars going in that direction would be stopped again.

About half drove straight toward Venice Boulevard, but the rest turned off – taking their chances on little sidestreets.

'Maybe we oughta give it a try,' Pete said. 'If we can get any kind of ride at all, it'll save us time. As long as it's going in the right direction. Even a few blocks would be better than nothing.'

'I don't know,' Barbara said.

From the time she'd been a toddler, Mom and Dad had warned her against involvement with strangers. You didn't talk to strangers, you didn't believe anything a stranger might tell you, and you most certainly did not enter a stranger's car. On the subject of what might happen to her inside a stranger's car, Dad had frequently scared the wits out of her. *I can't even tell you how bad it might be. There are nuts out there who'll do things to little girls that you don't even want to think about.*

Barbara used to spend a lot of time thinking about it, wondering what Dad had meant by that.

He'd never come right out and explained. But Barbara had gradually figured out, from watching TV and listening to her friends, that the men who picked you up took you away and kept you. They made you take off your clothes, then they did things to you. They hurt you where you go to the bathroom. And then they choked you or shot you in the head or cut you into pieces and threw you away.

For years, that was how Barbara had imagined her fate if she should ever get lured or dragged into a stranger's car.

More recently, she'd read some books about serial killers. And found out, shocked, that her childhood version of the horrors had been almost charming compared to the real thing.

You were *lucky* if all they did was rape and murder you. If you weren't so lucky, they ripped at you with pliers, burnt you with matches or cigarettes, took off your fingers or toes or nipples with hedge clippers, jammed your vagina with screwdrivers or broken bottles or broom handles or God-knows-what. All that before you were dead.

Dad had been right: you don't even want to think about such things.

But there are *four* of us, Barbara reminded herself. And this is an emergency. And these are mostly just morning commuters. And . . .

'Okay,' she said. 'We can try it. But I won't get in a car unless the driver's a woman.'

'Yeah, right,' Earl muttered. 'Like women are a bunch of saints?'

'They're rarely homicidal rapists,' Barbara pointed out.

He huffed.

'Why don't we just ask somebody who's waiting?' Heather suggested as they walked alongside the line of cars. 'Wouldn't that be easier than trying to hitchhike?'

'Nobody's gonna go for it,' Earl said. 'Too many of us. Not

a chance. It'll scare 'em off. What we gotta do, we gotta use our heads.'

He led them to the end of the line. They waited while a couple of cars turned around. Then they hurried to the other side and headed south. While they walked, several cars sped by. Two turned right at the first cross-street.

'That's where we'll get one,' Earl said. He raised his eyebrows. 'You wanta be the bait, Heather?'

'Me? Huh?'

'Bait. You stand out in plain sight, charm a driver into stopping. The rest of us hide. You open up the door, and we all run out and jump in.'

'Cute,' Barbara said.

'I don't see why we need to be sneaky about things,' Pete said.

'Depends. Do you want to ride or walk? If you want to ride, this is how it gets done.'

They reached the corner.

To the right, 15th Street stretched into the distance.

This didn't look like a good place to be. On both sides of the street were two-story, woodframe houses with gables and bay windows and front porches. They looked as if they'd been uprooted from a quaint, midwestern town back in the days of the Great Depression, planted here in Los Angeles, and left to rot. About half of them were down. Barbara was surprised that *any* had survived the quake.

Every yard was enclosed by a six-foot chain link fence.

Protection against marauders.

Except for a lone derelict pushing his shopping cart down the sidewalk at the far end of the block, nobody seemed to be around.

No trees. No people.

'Where *is* everybody?' she asked.

'Maybe dead,' Heather said, her voice hardly more than a whisper.

'Dead, my butt,' Earl said. 'They're probably all off on a looting spree.'

'At least the cars are getting through,' Pete pointed out.

'Yeah!' For as far as Barbara could see – perhaps three blocks – the few cars traveling this street seemed to be moving fast.

We could make fantastic time.

Who knows? If we're really lucky, maybe the driver will take us all the way home.

But even a mile . . .

Dad probably won't be there, but Mom . . .

She might need me. Maybe just a few minutes could make all the difference.

'I'll do it,' she said. 'I'll be the bait.'

Heather looked greatly relieved.

'Fine,' Earl said. 'Just don't be picky. You don't gotta marry the guy, just ride in his car for a while.'

'No guys, remember?'

'Just do whatever you think is best,' Pete told her.

An old green pickup truck was parked at the curb. Barbara positioned herself beside its driver's door. The others ducked out of sight by the front bumper.

Seconds later, a white Honda rounded the corner. The woman behind its wheel was middle-aged, chubby, and wore rollers in her hair.

Perfect.

Barbara stepped away from the pickup's door, turned toward the driver, and waved her hands. 'Could you help me?' she called.

The woman gave her a glance, then turned her head forward very fast. As if afraid she might be caught looking.

It's the way people act with bums, Barbara thought.

I'm not a bum!

She supposed her hair might be a little messed up, but otherwise . . .

She looked down at herself. Her short-sleeved white blouse was clean, neatly pressed, buttoned almost to her neck, and tucked into the waist of her pale blue shorts. She fingered the zipper of her shorts. It was shut, of course. So the driver hadn't been put off by an open fly. Her shorts were clean. They weren't skin-tight short-shorts, either, but baggy-legged things that reached almost down to her knees.

Bending forward slightly, she inspected her socks and shoes. White crew socks, white athletic shoes. And a very nice tan between the tops of her socks and the hem of her shorts.

I look terrific, she thought.

Maybe the creepo just doesn't like teenagers.

Maybe she's afraid I'm *a serial killer. Like maybe I've got a chainsaw in my purse.*

The next car to turn onto 15th Street was a Mercedes convertible driven by a man. His hair was mussed. He wore sunglasses, a blue sport shirt and a necktie.

Barbara settled back against the door of the pickup. She folded her arms and gazed away.

The Mercedes stopped.

'Do you need a ride somewhere?' the driver asked.

'No. Thanks, anyway.'

'Are you sure? I don't normally give people a lift, but under the circumstances . . .'

'No, that's all right. I'm waiting for someone.'

'Is everything okay?'

'Yes. Fine. Thank you for stopping.'

He shrugged and drove on.

He looked like a nice guy, she thought.

Yeah, and so did Ted Bundy.

'What's the matter with you?' Earl called from the hiding place.

'I told you, no guys.'

But the next two cars that passed were driven by women, and neither stopped.

Earl yelled, 'Hey, got a great idea! Why don't you lay down in the road?'

Six

After trading seats with Mary and strapping himself in, Clint had reached out to turn on the radio. He'd needed news of the quake. And of traffic conditions.

Where a radio should've been, there was an empty space in the instrument panel.

'Where's your radio?' he'd asked.

'Gone.'

He had shaken his head and started driving.

He'd *really* wanted to hear some news!

The Valley had been hit hard, that was obvious. But what about the rest of Los Angeles? If the epicenter had been somewhere near here, maybe L.A. got off easy. Maybe at home there was nothing but a minor tremor, the sort of thing you might mistake for a big truck driving by the house. Maybe Sheila didn't know it was a quake until she saw the chandelier above the dining room table swinging.

The chandelier, their home earthquake meter.

Yep, that was a four-point-two on the Chandelier scale.

'It's the fourth,' Mary had said.

'What? What're you . . . ?'

'I've had four stolen. And they always break a window.'

Oh. Car radios.

'I even tried not locking the car at night. But they broke a window anyway. So I just gave up. I stopped buying new ones. After the fourth. They'd just get it, anyway. Why waste my time and money? Now I don't have a radio, but my window got broken anyway.' She'd glanced at it, but looked away fast. 'I love this car,' she'd murmured. 'And people keep . . . hurting it. Why can't people be *nice*?'

'People are fine,' Clint had said. 'Nine out of ten.' Two blocks ahead, the road had appeared to be jammed with traffic. Clint could avoid the mess with a detour. But which way to go? Probably right.

'Trouble is,' he'd continued, 'nine out of ten adds up to ten in a hundred who are jerks. They foul up the works for everyone else. Which is why my car's locked away in a parking lot and why *you* don't have a radio. I'd *really* like to know what the hell is going on with this quake. I've got a wife and kid over in West L.A. I'd *really* like to know if there still *is* a West L.A., damn it!'

He'd turned right.

'Where are you going?' Mary had asked.

'Laurel Canyon. I hope. You wouldn't happen to know how we might get there from here?'

'We need to get onto the Golden State, and . . .'

'Not today.'

South on the Golden State Freeway was Clint's usual route home. The Golden State south, then west on the Ventura Freeway to the Laurel Canyon Boulevard offramp – about a ten-minute drive on the freeways. Ten minutes to cover ten miles through smoothly moving traffic in the early afternoon.

But the quake had struck at eight-twenty when the commuter rush was at its peak.

Even without an earthquake, every freeway in the Los Angeles area was usually crowded at that time of the morning with bumper to bumper traffic that barely moved at all. The quake had probably turned the freeways into parking lots.

Clint knew enough to stay clear of them.

But he wasn't sure at all about which surface streets to take, so he'd picked his route at random – trying to avoid areas where the traffic appeared heavy, trying to keep a course that carried them south and west.

Some of his choices worked fine. Others didn't.

After swinging into a road that dead-ended, he turned the car around and asked, 'You aren't at all familiar with the streets around here?'

'Not really,' she admitted.

'Do you have a map?'

She shook her head.

'Are you sure?'

What kind of person doesn't have a map!

466

'It's just that . . . I don't normally go places when I don't know where they are. I'm sorry.'

'It's all right.'

'Do you have maps?' she asked.

'Sure, but they're in my car.' *Where they belong*, he thought.

'Do you think we should maybe go back and get them?'

Clint shook his head.

How long had he been driving? About ten minutes?

It would take at least that long to return for the maps – if he could even manage to find the office building.

'I don't think I could find my way back if I *wanted* to,' he said. 'Besides, it'd take too much time. Every minute . . . no.'

The minutes lost by backtracking might be the minutes that mattered, that delayed them just enough to make all the difference.

For want of a minute . . .

Clint *had* to get home. He had to be with Sheila, with Barbara. He had to see them with his own eyes, know they were all right, hold them in his arms.

Any delay could mean arriving at an intersection *after* it'd jammed.

They'd all be jammed soon. Most of them, anyway.

Because the traffic signals were dead.

People who believed in the rules would take turns crossing, but the few who were out for themselves would mess it up, trying to cross when they shouldn't. Every intersection that didn't have a cop directing traffic would soon be clogged, impassable.

It had to be happening already.

Five, ten more minutes, Clint thought. That's probably all we've got before the roads'll be totally screwed up. We've got to put some miles behind us while we can.

As long as we're heading in the right general direction, that's the main thing.

If we can just make it over the hills . . . as far as Sunset . . . we could walk from there . . . maybe four miles, five at most. Easy. We could cover that in an hour or so. Mary'll still be a long way from home, but . . .

467

Rounding a corner, he found the street ahead blocked by police cars and fire trucks.

He braked to a halt.

Halfway down the block, an enormous, two-story apartment complex was ablaze.

Forty or fifty people stood around, watching: few men, mostly women and small kids. Many were dressed in nightgowns or robes. One man, hair still slicked down from a bath or shower, wore nothing except a blue towel wrapped around his waist.

'Can you get around it?' Mary asked.

'Doubt it.'

Besides, a police officer was waving them off.

Clint shoved the gearshift into reverse. He started to back away, then noticed the woman. She was calling to someone as she hurried into the street.

Calling to us?

Her arms were busy hugging a baby to her chest. Her hair was wrapped with a pink towel. She wore a long, paisley robe and pink slippers.

Clint stepped on the brake.

'What does *she* want?' Mary asked.

'Guess we'll find out.'

'Let's not. Let's get moving.'

'We'd better wait and see what . . .'

'She'll want us to take her somewhere. I *know* it. We haven't got time. Every minute . . .'

'Yeah.' Lifting his foot off the pedal, he shook his head at the approaching woman and saw a look of despair crumple her face.

'Wait!' she called. 'Don't go!'

Mary squeezed his thigh. 'Do you want to get home to your wife and daughter or don't you?'

Clint backed up and swung the rear of the BMW into the cross street, retracing his course.

The woman was running, waving one arm, the baby jostling against her chest, the colorful robe open below its sash and flapping behind her. Her legs were very pale. Her pubic hair was a heavy black thicket, startling to see but not arousing. Disturbing, pathetic, and vaguely repulsive because somehow it reminded Clint of Holocaust pictures. 'No!' she yelled. 'Wait!'

He didn't wait.

He forced his eyes away from the woman and sped the car forward, leaving her behind.

Then he muttered, 'Shit.'

'Don't worry,' Mary said. 'It couldn't have been anything that urgent or she would've gone to the cops. That's what they're for, to help people.'

Good point, Clint thought. It made him feel better. Though not much.

'I just wish I knew what she wanted.'

'A ride. Either that or money. She would've given us some kind of a sob story and we'd still be sitting there listening to her.'

'You're probably right.'

'I know I'm right.'

But Clint wished he had waited, let the woman say her piece.

It would not have been the smart thing to do; speeding away had been the smart thing. He hardly needed a total stranger to be robbing time from him – time that he owed to Sheila and Barbara.

Lose a minute listening to some distraught woman, and maybe you end up on the wrong side of a crash that shuts your road.

Stupid.

But he wished he had risked it. He wished he had stayed to hear out the woman, then done whatever he could to help her.

Not the smart thing to do, but the right thing.

He felt a little bit sick inside.

Ashamed.

Not only ashamed of himself for fleeing from the stranger, but for allowing Mary to talk him out of doing what he knew was right.

Was he so used to letting Sheila and Barbara have their ways that he'd forgotten how to stand up to a woman?

Of course, mine're usually right about stuff.

The thought made him start to smile, but a terrible sadness suddenly swept through him.

If they're not okay . . .

Seven

Stanley savored the job of uncovering Sheila. He took his time at it, scooping up double handfuls of debris, lifting away a chunk of this, a slab of that, a broken beam, a section of fallen wall.

Though he simply tossed the smaller obstacles aside, he lifted each large piece, carried it a few paces, and set it down carefully.

Slow work. Exciting work.

When Sheila had asked if he could go any faster, he'd explained, 'It's awfully precarious up here. I don't want to start an avalanche.'

'I know you're doing the best you can.'

He *was* doing the best he could – to remove the material silently. Let Sheila think he was taking great care to prevent her from being injured by falling rubble; his actual purpose was to maintain the secrecy of his project. There would be an awful clamor if he started hurling the big stuff aside.

Though remnants of walls protected him from being seen by anyone who might pass in front of the house, loud noises might draw attention. The last thing he wanted was an intruder – a nosy neighbor coming along to investigate or help.

Sheila's mine.

He had cleared away rubble all the way down to floor level before she began to appear.

Low and out of reach.

The bathtub *had* apparently dropped into the crawlspace underneath the house, just as Sheila had told him. The rim of the tub seemed to be about two feet lower than the floor. And she was lower still, at the bottom of the tub.

Most of the scrap was jumbled atop the tub like a roof.

As Stanley carried it away, she came into view a part at a time. First a foot, then a knee, next a shoulder.

She was a wondrous jigsaw puzzle being assembled by Stanley, growing piece by piece as he removed the debris that concealed her.

A thigh, a hand tucked between her legs, her chin, a breast partly covered by a forearm.

Sunlit parts, dirty, powdered with dust, strewed with flakes and crumbs of wood and plaster. Stanley wondered why she hadn't brushed some of the litter off her skin. Maybe she appreciated the coating. Maybe it gave her the feeling that she wasn't totally naked.

Only when he worked near the foot of the tub could he see her face. From every other location, it was hidden beneath a wooden four-by-eight beam that lay across the far end of the tub like a wide, thick shelf.

He wondered how much *she* could see of him.

When I can't see her eyes, she can't see mine.

Still, just to be on the safe side, he took only small glimpses of Sheila. He tried not to stare. And he made small talk. 'We'll have you out in a jiffy, now . . . That one was heavier than it looked . . . I'm getting a pretty good workout here.' Talking as if he hadn't particularly noticed – or didn't care – that she was sprawled out naked below him.

She talked, too, as if unconcerned by her nudity. But she kept the hand between her legs and the arm across her breasts.

Stanley needed both hands for his work, so he couldn't use one to hide the jutting front of his pajama bottoms. Most of the time, however, he was bent over or crouching. Maybe she hadn't noticed the bulge.

She *might* have noticed, though.

Maybe it turns her on.

Stanley had a sudden urge to pop open the snaps of his fly.

Give her a good look.

No!

She might start yelling, and maybe somebody would come along to investigate . . .

Just keep it all normal and friendly, he told himself. Wait until just the right time.

Soon, Sheila was clear.

Except for the beams.

Stanley had saved them for last, knowing they would give him the most trouble.

Four-by-eights, both of them. He guessed they must be support beams that had broken and shifted under the house's floor. One lay across the far end of the tub, above Sheila's face. The other was jammed *into* the tub, braced up by the edge to her right, slanting downward and shoved tight against the left side. From its position, it looked as if it should've chopped off Sheila's left leg at the thigh. But she must have kicked upward in the nick of time.

Flat on her back, she had the beam between her legs – on top of her right, under her left.

The knuckles of the hand covering herself down there were less than half an inch from its rough wood surface.

Stanley supposed he probably *could* lift or shove the beams out of the way. If he got down and stood on the rim of the tub and really worked at it.

Moving them, however, might not be necessary.

He got to his hands and knees above Sheila's right hip. From there, he had a pretty good view of her. He hunched down so that he could see more of her face – chin, lips, the tip of her nose.

'Do you think you can work yourself out of there now?' he asked.

'I'll try.'

She raised her left leg off the beam. Keeping it high, she placed both hands on the beam. Her arms, nearly straight, pressed her breasts together. She pushed. Her skin suddenly writhed over flexing muscles and she slid toward the rear of the tub. But only a bit. An inch. Maybe two. Then the top of her head thumped the underside of the other beam.

She winced. Her muscles unbunched and she let herself slide back down a bit.

'You okay?' Stanley asked.

'Yeah, it just . . .'

'I should've warned you.'

'I knew it was there. Just didn't think it was so *close*.' Tilting her head toward her right shoulder, she again pushed at the beam between her legs.

Stanley watched the muscles come up in her arms and shoulders. She even had pecs that bulged near the tops of her breasts.

A moan growled out of Stanley.

A slip. But Sheila didn't react. Probably hadn't heard it through all the other noises.

She twisted herself and raised her left leg even higher and swung her arm from the beam to shove at the edge of the tub.

Though her right hand still thrust at the beam, Stanley could see past its wrist. Coils of golden hair. Pink, open flesh.

'*Damn* it!' Sheila cried out.

Thinking he'd been caught, Stanley flinched and looked away fast.

At once, he knew she hadn't seen where he'd been looking.

She was too busy squirming, straining upward, twisting herself, trying to work her tilted head out from under the other beam. Her face was red, teeth gritted, lips peeled back.

Abruptly, she quit that tactic. She flung both hands overhead and clutched the forward edge of the beam and thrust against it. Even as she shoved, her body made a quick slide toward the foot of the tub. She didn't get far in that direction before she was stopped by the lower beam.

Stanley grimaced when he saw it mash her.

She squeezed it between her thighs as if using it for a brace.

Then she struggled like a trapped savage.

Whether she was trying to force the beam out of her way or shove herself in front of it, Stanley couldn't tell. Either outcome would've worked. And she tried hard. Her whole body shuddered with the effort. Sweat poured, cutting skin-colored trails through her coating of powder and dust. Her muscles trembled. Her breasts shook.

At last, she let go and sank down against the bottom of the tub, panting for air. Her arms lay limp by her sides. She shook her head. 'Can't. The beams . . . not with . . . them . . .'

'They're sure in the wrong places, all right.'

'I can't . . . believe it,' she muttered.

'Yeah,' Stanley said. If the beams had fallen differently, she might've been able to squirm free – or they might've crushed her. But the quake had rammed them into the perfect positions to trap her.

If she were a few inches shorter, or the tub a bit deeper, she would be able to curl herself forward until her head cleared the four-by-eight that loomed above her face. Then, sitting up, she could slide clear of the beam between her legs. But she was too tall for that, the tub too shallow.

It's almost like a miracle, Stanley thought.

Everything had happened *just so* to pin Sheila naked and unhurt at the bottom of her bathtub.

Just for me.

She was put here for me.

Does that mean I'm supposed to *leave* her down in the tub?

It's not a question of *supposed to*, he told himself. She's like a gift. I can do whatever I want with her.

Right now, it seemed like enough just to *be* with her – to look at her and talk to her.

'Just relax for a while,' he said. 'We'll get you out, don't worry.'

She nodded, took a very deep breath, then blew the air out through pursed lips. Her arms still rested by her sides.

No more point in covering herself, Stanley realized. I've already seen what there is to see.

Or maybe she's just too distracted to care.

Thank you very much, my dear. Thank you oh so much.

'It's really a miracle you weren't killed,' he said. 'If you hadn't been in the bathtub . . .'

'I wasn't. Hadn't even started the water yet. But I was in leaping distance.'

'You *leaped* into the tub?'

'More of a dive. It was very impressive. Wish Clint had been here to see it.' She smiled in the shadow cast by the beam. But the smile lasted only a moment, then trembled and vanished. 'I just wish he was here, at all.'

'Clint's your husband?'

'Yeah. He works in Glendale. God only knows how long it'll take him to get home. If he *can* get home.' Her chin started to tremble. She pressed her lips together in a tight, straight line.

'I'm sure he's just fine,' Stanley said. 'Your girl, too.'

'I just wish they were here.'

'Yeah.'

'That's the worst part. Not knowing if they're okay. I don't mind the rest so much. You know? The house . . . As long as *they're* okay.' Her smile came back. 'Not that I'd mind getting out of this tub.'

'We'll get you out.'

'Maybe you could go and find some help,' Sheila suggested.

'Let's see if I can't move one of these beams out of the way for you.'

'It's no use. *I* couldn't budge them. They don't seem to have any give at all. I think they're wedged in, somehow.'

'Well, I could give it a try.'

'No.' She shook her head. 'Don't. You might hurt yourself. Or fall or something. Really, there's no point.'

'We might both try one together,' Stanley suggested.

'I doubt . . . Do you know what would work? A saw. I don't think even two or three people could manage to budge either of these beams, but . . . you could saw right through one. It'd be easy.'

'That sounds like a really good idea.'

'We've got saws in the garage.'

'Your garage went down. I'm sure I can find a saw

somewhere, though. Might take a few minutes, but . . .'

'Before you go, can you take a look around? I'd like to have *some*thing, you know . . . to cover myself with.'

'I'm afraid I already checked,' he lied. 'While I was clearing the stuff away. All the clothes must be buried under . . .'

She shook her head. 'What about curtains? Or a towel? A bedsheet. Maybe a pillowcase?'

'Unless you want a plank of wood . . .'

She let out a small, quiet laugh. 'No, that's all right. When you go for the saw, though, maybe you can find me something?'

'Sure,' he said.

When Hell freezes over, he thought.

He was glad he'd taken off his pajama shirt earlier. If Sheila had known about it, he would've had to toss it down to her as soon as she'd come into view. Either that, or risk making her suspicious. But nobody could be expected to give up his pajama pants. She hadn't asked for them, and she would think he was weird if he even offered to let her have them.

'Anything'll be fine,' she added. 'Just so I can . . . make myself decent. Even an old sack or a rug.'

'I'll find something.' He frowned. 'I just hate to leave you alone down there.'

'I'll be okay.'

'Yeah. It's just . . .' He stopped his voice.

'What?'

'Never mind. It's all right. The chances of someone coming along while I'm gone are pretty remote. And if anybody *does* find you, it probably won't be . . . anyone to worry about. It's just that you're so vulnerable down there. If the wrong sort of person . . .'

She smiled. A game smile, only a trifle nervous. 'Trying to cheer me up, are you?'

'Sorry. The thing is, I noticed a couple of strange characters over near where that house is on fire. They looked . . . unsavory, you know?'

'Terrific.'

'I didn't mean to worry you.'

'It's all right. How's that fire doing, anyway?'

Stanley glanced over his shoulder, but couldn't see much. In the way, near his back and about five feet high, was the remnant of an interior wall. 'Just a second,' he said. He crawled backward so Sheila couldn't watch him stand. On his feet, he turned around.

Off in the distance, beyond the low, ragged corner of Sheila's house, a column of smoke still surged into the sky.

'It doesn't look like it's spreading,' he said.

'Is the fire department there yet?'

'No,' he answered. 'No police, either.' He was guessing. The ruins of Sheila's house blocked his view of the street, and he wasn't about to climb a pile of rubble just to inspect the situation. 'There's hardly any breeze. I don't think we need to worry about the fire getting here.'

'So, as long as we don't have one of our own . . . I don't smell any gas. Can you smell gas?' she asked.

Stanley sniffed. The hot air made his nostrils sting. He smelled a faint aroma of smoke, a dry odor that might have been concrete or plaster dust, and a scent of suntan lotion that quickened his heartbeat and filled his head with images of beaches, surf, girls in bikinis, Sheila stretched out on her lounger.

Her lounger had smelled that way.

He closed his eyes, breathed deeply, and moaned with pleasure.

'Stanley?'

How wonderful to hear his name spoken by that sweet voice.

'I can't smell any gas.'

'Maybe you should turn it off at the main valve, anyway. It's what you're supposed to do after a big quake. And there almost *has* to be leaks.'

'Okay. I'll take care of that. Do you know where the shutoff is?'

'It's outside the house.'

'Okay.'

'It's near the chimney, on the outside wall. There ought to

be a special wrench attached. All you've gotta do is turn the wrench.'

'I'll find it.' He stepped close to the edge of the floor, leaned forward and looked down at Sheila. 'I'll turn off the gas, then go and find a saw . . . and something for your decency.'

'That'll be great, Stan. Thank God, you found me.'

'I'll second that.'

'Hurry back, okay?'

'I'll get back as fast as I can. You can bet on it.'

Eight

No matter what Barbara did – motion with her thumb, call out, jump up and down waving both arms – female drivers simply wouldn't stop their cars. Some scowled at her. Others pretended not to notice her.

It had taken Barbara a while to figure out why, but now she thought she knew the answer. It had little to do with how she was dressed. Nor was it because the drivers didn't like teenagers or were afraid she might be a criminal.

They weren't stopping, she decided, for the simple reason that women take an immediate dislike for any female they consider more attractive than themselves.

As Mom had put it, 'If you make them feel plain or ugly, they hate you for it.'

Mom knew from first-hand experience. She'd been a target for spite and envy all her life. Nearly everyone really liked her once they got to know her, but she seemed to be despised from a distance. By women. Barbara had seen it happen many times. Just as men gaped at Mom with wide eyes and sagging mouths, women glared, narrow-eyed, tight-lipped.

Barbara had been the object of such attention, herself. Not nearly as much as Mom, but often.

This has to be part of the same deal, she thought as one woman after another drove past her without stopping.

Men, of course, stopped even though she gave them no encouragement.

Not all of them, but several.

The sixth was in a black Pontiac. The passenger window slid down even before the car had come to a full halt. The driver leaned across the seat. He appeared to be about forty. He looked fairly prosperous and serious in his gray suit and necktie. His glasses had silver rims.

'Climb on in,' he said.

'Thanks for the offer, but I'm just waiting here for somebody.' She had used the line successfully with the other men who'd stopped.

But this one smirked. 'Hey, come on, don't give me that. It's no secret you're looking for a ride. I saw how you tried to flag down that Rabbit.' He nodded toward the white VW that had already gone some distance up 15th Street. 'Now all of a sudden you've lost interest? Come on, climb in here.' The passenger door swung open. Fast. Straight at Barbara's thighs.

She backstepped. The edge of the door made a whissing sound against the front of her shorts. It just missed her legs.

'Thanks for stopping,' she said. 'I appreciate it. But I'm waiting for . . .'

'Come on, where are you going? Do you need a ride home? I'll take you wherever you want to go. Traffic permitting. The streets are a mess, in case you haven't noticed. I'll be lucky if I can get home myself . . .'

'Don't you think that's where you *ought* to go instead of trying to pick me up?'

'Pick you *up*? You're *hitchhiking*. Christ!'

'I've got a policy not to ride with guys. Just women.'

'Just women,' he muttered. His thin upper lip lifted and stretched across his gums. 'Wonderful. Figures. Boy, how it figures. A gal looks like you, it just goes to figure she's a . . .'

The man's door flew open.

On *his* side of the car.

He'd been leaning sideways, braced up with a hand on the passenger seat, bright red face raised toward Barbara. At the sound of his door unlatching, he shoved himself upright and snapped his head to the left.

Earl sprang into the V of the open door.

'Hey!' the man yelled.

Earl grabbed him, tugged, brought the face close to his own and snarled, 'Hey yourself.'

'Earl!' Barbara yelled. 'What're you . . .?'

Her voice stopped as if her own breath had been smashed out. But it was the driver of the Pontiac who lost his air, lost it when Earl hauled him from the car and kneed him in the belly.

'Leave him alone!' she shouted, breaking into a run.

Pete and Heather both popped up in front of the old pickup where they'd been crouching along with Earl to wait for a ride. Pete looked confused, Heather excited.

'He's pounding the guy!' Barbara yelled.

By the time she reached the other side of the Pontiac, the driver was curled on the pavement, arms hugging his head, knees up close to his stomach. In a high, squealy voice, he cried out, 'Stop!' and 'Quit it!' and 'Please!' as Earl pranced around him, kicking him.

Barbara had already shouted for Earl to leave the man alone. Earl hadn't listened then. He wasn't likely to listen now.

So Barbara didn't waste her breath.

As Earl kicked his victim in the back, she threw herself over the squirming man. She went at Earl sideways, hunched low, head down. Her right shoulder bashed him in the chest.

He let out a grunt.

And another grunt when his back hit the street.

Barbara smashed down on top of him. The instant his body stopped skidding, she rolled off.

Earl lay sprawled on his back, eyes and mouth wide open. He made sucking noises.

On hands and knees, Barbara watched him struggle to catch a breath. His face was awfully red. He seemed to be having a very hard time. She frowned.

She hadn't meant to *hurt* him, just stop him.

'You okay?' she asked.

He glanced at her, said nothing, and kept on wheezing.

At the sound of quick footsteps, Barbara looked over her shoulder. Pete and Heather were rushing around the car. The man scurried for his open door. They gave him a wide berth, glancing from him to Barbara to Earl.

He clambered into his car and slammed the door. Through the open window, he shouted, 'Bastards! Fucks! I'm getting the cops!'

His car lunged forward, squealing and laying rubber, smoke rising behind its rear tires.

Barbara returned her attention to Earl just in time to see his arm shoot out.

'Watch it!' Pete yelled.

Before she could make a move to get away, Earl clutched the front of her blouse and yanked her toward him. Her arms went out from under her. She flopped on top of Earl. Twisting and bucking, he threw her sideways. He scrambled onto her, straddled her. Pinning her arms to the pavement, he bounced his rump on her belly.

'Get off her!' Pete snapped.

'You see what she did to me?'

'You were beating the hell out of that guy!' Barbara gasped.

'Yeah! Damn straight!'

'Get off her!' Pete said again.

Earl ignored him. 'We needed that car.'

'You aren't gonna steal a *car*,' Barbara gasped. 'Just 'cause we had a quake . . . doesn't mean all the *rules* are gone.'

'Oh yeah?' He bounced on her belly again, driving her wind out.

'Okay,' Pete muttered. 'Okay.' He rushed in from the side, ducked low, grabbed Earl's right forearm and jerked it toward him.

Earl lost his grip on Barbara's wrist.

The instant her left arm was free, she punched him in the face. The blow jolted his head. Spit flew from his lips.

He yelled and released her right wrist and grabbed her throat – and his right arm was loose, somehow. Barbara had time to think, *What did Pete do, let go of it?* before the fist struck her face.

The blow rocked her.

But she still had enough strength to tear Earl's hand away from her throat. As she shoved it aside, he punched her again. This time, he went for her jaw instead of her cheekbone.

Just as the punch landed, Pete kicked him in the head. The toe of the gray Reebok caught him in front of the right ear. His head snapped sideways. He tumbled off Barbara.

Propping herself up with one arm, she looked at him.

He was sprawled out, motionless.

'Geez,' she murmured.

They all stared at Earl. He lay on his back, arms and legs spread out, eyes shut, mouth open. His right cheek wore the rosy imprint of Barbara's fist. Otherwise, he looked okay. Except that he wasn't moving.

Barbara worked her jaw from side to side. It hurt on the left side, down below her ear. And a clicking sound came from there.

What did he do, break it?

Probably not, she decided. It doesn't hurt that bad.

The clicking noise made her nervous.

But it only came when she slid her jaw sideways.

So quit doing it, she told herself.

While Barbara worried about her jaw and experimented with it, she watched the front of Earl's shirt. Trying to see movement there.

Is he breathing? she wondered.

Heather suddenly let out a tiny, odd laugh. 'Lookit, lookit!' She pointed, and Barbara noticed a dark stain on the faded blue denim at the crotch of Earl's jeans.

Heather leaned forward, her face aglow with delight. 'He wet his pants! Jones! Mr Tough Guy! He peed in his pants!'

'Knock it off,' Barbara said.

Pete looked scared. 'What does it mean?'

'Wittow Err-owe need a die-dee,' Heather said.

Pete ignored her. 'Did I kill him?'

'I don't know,' Barbara said. Keeping her eyes on Earl, she slowly got to her feet. She felt dizzy for a moment, but it passed. She fingered her face. The jut of her cheekbone seemed twice its usual size, and the skin over it was tight and hot.

'God,' Pete muttered. 'I bet it means he's dead.'

'Maybe it's just 'cause he's unconscious,' Barbara said. 'I don't think he necessarily has to be dead to . . . you know . . . lose it.'

'I hope he *is* dead,' Heather said.

Barbara looked at her. 'I thought you wanted us all to be friends.'

'Yeah, but that was before.'

'Don't wish him dead, for Godsake,' Pete said. 'I'm the guy who kicked him.'

'He's such a creep.'

'Yeah,' Barbara said. 'He's a creep, all right, but that isn't a capital crime.'

Heather's lip curled up. 'Huh?'

'Nothing.'

Pete crouched over Earl. Bending low, he pressed his ear against the boy's chest.

'Is he okay?' Barbara asked.

Pete didn't respond. Barbara waited.

'He had it coming,' Heather muttered.

'Shhhh.'

Then the energy seemed to drain out of Pete. His eyes drifted shut, and he looked as if he might stretch out and fall asleep using Earl's chest for a pillow. Suddenly, he flinched. His eyes jumped open. He sprang to his feet. He pranced away from Earl and darted his glance from Heather to Barbara. 'Come on, quick. We've gotta get out of here.'

'He's really *dead*?' Barbara asked.

'All right!' Heather clapped her hands.

483

'Hell no, he isn't dead,' Pete blurted. 'Let's get outa here quick!'

Oh, Barbara thought. I get it.

Jeez!

At least he's not dead, she told herself. That's a good thing. Right?

Yeah, sure.

'Come on,' Pete said.

'Wait. We can't just leave him in the street. What if a car hits him?'

'You're right,' Pete said.

Heather rolled her eyes upward, shook her head, and said, 'Boy.'

Barbara and Pete each crouched over Earl and took one of his arms. They pulled until his back came up off the pavement. Then, side by side, they towed him toward the curb. He skidded on the seat of his jeans. He left a broad, wet trail like a mop being dragged across a floor. His head, hanging limp between his stretched arms, wobbled and swayed. Barbara watched it, hoping it wouldn't suddenly jerk upright, eyes open.

They pulled Earl over the curb. He still seemed to be unconscious when they eased him down onto the sidewalk.

'Good enough?' Pete asked.

'Good enough,' Barbara said. 'Let's beat it.'

'Should we tie him up, or something?' Heather asked.

'Are you kidding?' Barbara asked.

'What if he comes after us?'

'We took care of him this time, didn't we?'

'Yeah, but . . .'

'Besides,' Pete said, 'he'll have to find us first. Let's go! Let's haul it!'

Pete in the lead, Barbara taking the rear so that she wouldn't need to worry about Heather falling behind, they raced up 15th Street.

Nine

After making so many detours to get away from blocked streets, Clint hardly knew which way to turn. He couldn't go straight; the road dead-ended just ahead.

We're lost, he thought. Really lost.

Payback for running away from that woman back at the fire. We're getting the lousy luck we deserve.

'Which way do we go?' Mary asked.

Clint shook his head.

'We can't just sit here.'

From the angles of the shadows, he knew the sun was behind him. He'd been driving from east to west, so a turn to the left would head them south.

He turned left. 'At least we'll be going in the right general direction,' he said.

'Are you sure?'

'Yep. Left is right.'

He glanced at her. She twitched her lips to let him see that she wasn't much amused.

His choice had been good, though. It took them to Burbank Boulevard. He'd been doing all he could to avoid the major thoroughfares, figuring they'd be jammed, but on Burbank the traffic was moving along in a slow, steady flow.

A car eased back to let him in.

Clint waved a thank you to the driver and turned right onto Burbank.

Just ahead was Lankershim Boulevard. A police officer stood in the middle of the intersection, directing traffic.

'Fantastic!' Clint blurted. 'A cop!' A motorcycle cop, he realized when he saw the Harley parked at the corner. 'Wish we had one of those,' he said, nodding toward the bike. 'We could go just about anywhere.'

'Do you know where we are now?' Mary asked.

'I'm not positive,' he admitted. 'But doesn't Burbank go parallel to Ventura Boulevard?'

Mary frowned and shrugged.

'I think it does,' Clint said. 'And that'd mean it should run straight into Laurel Canyon.'

'Does Laurel Canyon go this far north?'

'Hope so.'

'Yeah, me too.'

And then Clint saw, up ahead, the Hollywood Freeway. Below the freeway, an underpass.

'Oh, have we lucked out!' He made no attempt to control his excitement. 'I didn't know *how* we'd ever get across the freeway, you know? Only the major roads go through, and they were bound to be totally jammed – but they're not! *This* one isn't! There's still the Ventura Freeway, but . . . hell, we'll worry about that when we come to it.'

They entered the shadows of the underpass.

They came out on the other side into the sunlight.

And brake lights.

Ahead, every westbound lane appeared to be jammed with traffic.

'Great while it lasted,' Clint muttered, and cut hard to the left. Just as he made it to the center lines, a break appeared in the stream of cars going east. He swung into the gap, jamming the gas pedal to the floor.

Mary gasped and grabbed the dashboard.

They shot through, untouched.

She let her breath out, let her hands drop to her lap. 'You're something else,' she said, and almost smiled.

'Just wanta get us where we're . . .'

He saw the girl.

She was striding down the sidewalk, head forward, her short hair shiny in the sunlight. She wore a big pink T-shirt that drooped down crooked over the seat of her white shorts. One pink sock hung lower than the other.

She reminded Clint of his daughter.

She was not as tall as Barbara, but just as slim. Though her hair was cut very short, it was Barbara's pale shade of blonde.

Like this girl, Barbara often wore T-shirts and shorts to school. And they both lugged huge, bulky book bags in just the same manner, slung over their right shoulder by one strap, the weight swinging against their backs.

This girl's resemblance to Barbara was enough to make Clint slow the BMW and stare at her.

He wouldn't have considered stopping because of it.

But she was also walking alone through an area that had been slammed by a devastating earthquake. And she was injured.

At least, Clint *thought* she must be injured. Behind her left shoulder, her T-shirt bore a brown-red stain that looked a lot like blood.

'She's hurt,' he said, and aimed for the curb a few yards in front of her.

'A *lot* of people are probably hurt,' Mary said. 'What're you doing?'

'I want to make sure she's okay.'

'Oh, for Godsake. No! Don't!'

'It won't . . .'

'Keep going! You don't even know her.'

'She's a kid.' He stopped at the curb and twisted around to look out the rear window. The girl, walking just as briskly as before, looked in at him and frowned a little.

'Damn it, Clint! This is *my* car.'

He said, 'Yup,' and plucked its key from the ignition.

'Clint!'

'Take it easy. I'll be right back.' Taking the key with him, he climbed out of the car.

The girl looked wary, but not frightened.

Instead of trying to intercept her, Clint stopped in front of the BMW.

The girl stopped on the sidewalk adjacent to the passenger door. She cocked her head a bit to the left, narrowed her left eye, and gnawed the left side of her lower lip.

At least she didn't have Barbara's face. For one thing, she was younger. Maybe thirteen or fourteen. Though she had sharp blue eyes like Barbara, her face was longer, more boyish, cute but not with Barbara's obvious beauty. She had the looks of a real tomboy – short hair mussed and hanging across her forehead, a sprinkle of freckles across her nose and cheeks, no lipstick or any other makeup.

She might have been mistaken for a boy except for the small, pointed breasts pushing out the front of her T-shirt.

A girl, all right.

Girls like this used to break Clint's heart when he was their age. Even now, something about her made his throat go tight.

'What's up?' she asked.

'I know you've probably been warned about strangers,' Clint said, 'but you look like you might be able to use some help. I'd be glad to give you a ride somewhere.'

'Clint!' Mary snapped from the car.

'Hi,' the girl said to her – the way she might speak to a growling dog, trying to soothe it. 'How are you?'

The treatment didn't warm up Mary. 'I've been better,' she muttered, and turned her eyes to Clint. 'We're wasting time, you know.'

'You're welcome to climb in,' Clint told the girl. 'We'll take you where you're going.'

With a nod, she hurried to the back door. She opened it and swung in her book bag while Clint returned to the driver's side. Their doors bumped shut at almost the same moment.

Plugging in the ignition key, Clint said, 'I'm Clint Banner. This is Mary Davis.'

Mary looked around at her. 'Where *are* you going?'

'Home?' she asked. 'That's where I was heading.'

'And where is that?'

Before she could answer, Clint said, 'Just point me in the right direction,' and started the car moving.

'Go straight for a while. My name's Em, by the way, in case you're wondering.'

'M?' Clint asked. 'Like 007's boss?'

'Cute,' Mary said.

'It's E-m. Short for Emerald. Emerald O'Hara. Could you just call me Em, though?'

'How old are you?' Clint asked.

'Thirteen.'

'I've got a daughter who'll be sixteen next month.'

'Do you live around here?'

'Nope. West L.A.'

'Guess I wouldn't know her, then. What about you, Mary? Do you have any kids?'

'I'm not married.'

'Do you have any kids, though?'

'Is that supposed to be a crack?'

'A crack? No. My mom isn't married. Never was. I've got a father, of course, but only in the strictly biological sense if you know what I mean. I don't have the vaguest notion who he might be. Mom won't tell me, either. He doesn't even *know* he's my father, can you beat that? All *I* know is that he was in her Chaucer seminar at UCLA umpteen years ago, and that isn't a whole lot to know about your own father. Mom doesn't believe in men, see. She only went with this one guy until he got her pregnant, and then she dumped him.'

'Your mother sounds like an interesting woman,' Clint said.

'Most people think she's a pain in the keister. I'd have to agree with them. Not that I don't love her, and everything, I do. But she's pretty hard to take most of the time.'

'Nice way to talk about your mother,' Mary said.

'I always try to be strictly honest about stuff. I mean, if you're going to tell lies, why talk at all?'

'Is your mother at home?' Clint asked.

'I hope so.'

'She doesn't work?'

'No. But that doesn't mean we're poor or anything like that, 'cause we're not. Mom calls it her sabbatical. But what it is, she won this huge lawsuit over sexual harassment at her previous workplace. I mean, it was a bundle. So she's staying home and writing a book. Like a handbook for women who are getting pestered at work?'

'Anyway, you're pretty sure she'll be at home?'

'Oh, yeah. I just hope the house hasn't fallen down or anything. Not that I'm terribly worried. It made it through the Sylmar quake okay. Not that we were living there at the time. Not that *I* was living anywhere, if you know what I mean. But I bet the house made it through this one. Not all that many went down, have you noticed? Just a few here and there. They're saying the Valley got off pretty easy. The epicenter's supposed to be over near downtown.'

'You've heard *news*?' Clint blurted.

'Oh, yeah. Mostly from this guy I walked for a while with. He had a Walkman that was picking up the Emergency Broadcasting Network. Think that's what he called it. They're saying it was an eight point one, but it wasn't on the San Andreas.'

Mary looked shocked. 'You mean this *wasn't* the Big One?'

'Big enough to suit me,' Clint said. 'What else did the radio say, Em?'

'Well, I only know what the guy told me. He said the power's out all over the place, and there're a lot of fires, a lot of buildings down, and whole bunches of people have gotten killed and hurt. They don't know how many yet. It's really supposed to be a mess. There're even some reports of riots and looting. The cops and firemen are having a real hard time getting anyplace because the streets are so bad. But it's not supposed to be nearly as serious over here on this side.'

'My family's on the other side,' Clint said.

'Yeah. Well, I sure hope they're okay. It doesn't sound too swift. I'm not even sure you can *get* there.'

'I'll get there.'

Em leaned forward. Her head appeared between the seatbacks. 'You ought to make a right when you get a chance. We'll need to go under the Ventura Freeway pretty soon. Maybe at Laurel Canyon would be the best place.'

'How far are we from there?' Clint asked.

'Just a few blocks. Once we get past the freeway, we're almost to my house.'

'We're almost to the freeway and Laurel Canyon?'

'Sure.'

He grinned at Em. 'This is great. I've got to tell you, we've been kind of lost for a while.'

'I can show you anyplace you want to go,' Em said. 'I do a lot of walking.'

'By yourself?'

'Sure. We get along fine, me and I.'

'It's awfully dangerous for a girl to be out on the streets alone.'

'You're telling me? I just got clipped by a *brick*. Not even during the quake, if you can believe that. I just happened to be walking by when half a stupid wall decided to fall. If *I* hadn't been so quick on my feet, it would've killed me. Only one brick got me, though. See?' She twisted her body to show Clint the back of her shoulder. Straining her head around in an attempt to see the damage for herself, she said, 'Is the cloth ripped? Can you tell?'

'Maybe snagged a little. It's not really torn.'

'I wonder if the blood'll come out.'

'What about *you*?'

'Oh, I'm okay.'

'You can't be *that* okay if that's your blood on the T-shirt.'

'It isn't bleeding now, is it?'

'I don't think so.'

'I just hope the shirt'll come clean. It's one of my favorites.'

'Were you on your way home from school when you got hit?'

'Yeah. We were supposed to stay and wait in the yard, but I'm not all that big on waiting around, so I made myself scarce.'

'You ditched?'

'Well, it's not like I'll be missing any lessons. I figured Mom might worry about me, and it's not *all* that long a walk to get home. Why should I stick around school, you know?'

Clint wondered if Barbara had seen things that way, too. The high school wasn't much more than a mile from their home. She could walk it easily.

No, Barbara wouldn't.

Not right away, anyhow.

She would know enough to wait at school.

You just stay put, Clint had told her when discussing what to do in case of a major quake. *One of us will come and pick you up. You're not to walk home under any circumstances.*

What if you can't pick me up? she had asked.

Stay at school.

They had never allowed Barbara to walk anywhere by herself. Too many perverts cruising around. Every day, the news brought stories of kids who disappeared a block or two from their homes, of frantic parents, of futile searches, of bodies being located. The bodies were almost always found naked, with evidence of torture and sexual abuse. Boys and girls both. Girls more often than boys, though.

Clint and Sheila had no intention of ever letting such a thing happen to their daughter.

So they walked with her, or drove her, anywhere she needed to go.

Overprotective. That's what some people called them.

Right.

No such thing as being overprotective in L.A.

Whatever it takes to keep your kid alive.

A cute kid like Em was lucky she had lasted this long. Breaks the most basic rules: walks alone, gets in a car with strangers.

I ought to have a talk with her mother, Clint thought.

Yeah, and she'll probably tell me to mind my own business. She's obviously some sort of radical feminist. She'll really appreciate a *man* telling her how to raise her daughter.

Forget the mother.

'All this walking around, Em, aren't you afraid you might run into the wrong sort of person?'

'You mean like a mugger?'

'Or worse.'

'He means like a psycho,' Mary explained. 'One of those guys who grabs girls like you and rapes them and cuts them into pieces.'

'Hey,' Clint said. 'That isn't necessary.'

'Isn't that what you were getting at?' Mary asked. 'I mean, if you've got an urge to warn her, *warn* her, don't pussyfoot. Just lay it out straight, tell her about all those guys out there who'd like nothing better than to get their hands on such a cute young thing – and how lucky she is that she was picked up by *you*, who's a gentleman and a father, not to mention a Knight of the Fucking Roundtable.'

Clint gazed at Mary, astonished. 'What's the matter?' he asked.

'Nothing. Not a thing.'

Em, very calmly, said, 'This is Laurel Canyon coming up. You'll want to turn left.' Then she patted Mary's shoulder. 'A couple more minutes and I'll be outta here. Then you'll have Clint all to yourself, and everything will be splendid again.'

Ten

While shutting off Sheila's gas, Stanley had wondered about the gas at Mother's house.

His house, now.

If only he'd taken care of the gas before coming over to look for Sheila! He hadn't *thought* of it, though. That was the problem.

Stupid.

He could lose everything.

Even though much of the house had collapsed, Stanley figured that he would be able to salvage plenty from the mess. If it didn't all go up in smoke first.

From the top of the cinderblock wall, he could see that his house was fine.

He grinned and shook his head. Hardly *fine*.

More like half a house, at this point. And no garage at all.

But at least there was no trace of fire.

Instead of leaping, he lowered himself down from the wall. At the bottom, he turned sideways to slip through the rose bushes. A thorn scratched his bare chest while another nicked his rump through the thin cloth of his pajama pants.

Gotta cut the bastards down, he thought as he jogged toward the house.

The earlier wounds felt itchy, like mosquito bites. The new ones stung. Cold water would sure feel good on them.

He saw the water spigot at the rear of the house, nothing covering it or blocking it, nothing to climb over. The back wall looked as if it had been battered away just below the roof, but the area beneath it was clear; the rubble must've all tumbled inward.

Better take care of the gas first, he thought.

What for? No fire, yet. Maybe there isn't even a leak.

He hurried over to the spigot. The garden hose was still attached. He unscrewed the hose and let it fall, then twisted the handle. Instead of the normal gush, only a few drops of water fell from the spout.

The disappointment clogged his throat.

'Stan?'

He almost cried out. The sound of his name felt like an icy spike being shoved into his belly. Cringing, he straightened up and turned toward the voice.

Judy Wellman stood only a few yards away, at the edge of the patio.

Nothing to worry about. Stanley hoped.

Judy lived next door. She and her husband, Herb. They seemed like nice people. Though they usually kept to themselves, they always had cheerful, friendly things to say whenever Stanley happened to run into them.

Last night, Stanley had seen Herb carry a suitcase out to the car. Judy had driven him away and returned an hour later without him.

Which meant, to Stanley, that she had delivered him to LAX.

He had flown somewhere, likely on a business trip.

So Herb was out of the picture.

This could be interesting.

Stanley liked the looks of Judy.

She was no Sheila Banner, of course. Nobody was in Sheila's league.

Still, she looked pretty good. Very good, in fact. Hard to believe she was old enough to have twins in college. Her tanned face had plenty of crinkles when she squinted or smiled, and a few threads of silver gleamed in her thick brown hair, but her body was trim. Though Stanley had never gone out of his way to spy on her, he'd seen her many times simply because she lived next door. He frequently saw her when she went out for the morning newspaper, when she went to her car, when she did yard work. He'd seen her last week wearing shorts and a bikini top while she hosed off her car in the driveway.

This morning, she wore a faded blue shirt so large that Stanley figured it must belong to her husband. Its sleeves were rolled up her tawny forearms. The top couple of buttons were unfastened. The shirt wasn't tucked in. It hung so low that it nearly covered her cut-off jeans. Her brown leather boots, ankle-high, looked very big and clumsy at the ends of such slender legs.

Had she been dressed this way when the quake hit?

Maybe not. Maybe she'd been in her nightgown.

If she'd changed clothes after the quake . . .

Stanley gazed past Judy. All he could see of her house was a rear portion of the side wall. The bedroom window was broken, but the wall appeared to be intact.

'Your house came through okay?' he asked.

She nodded. She looked very solemn. 'I'm awfully sorry about your mother, Stan.'

She knows!

He tried to hide his shock and fear behind a mask of sorrow.

She can't know I did it, he told himself. If she knew, she would hardly be giving me condolences.

'You saw her?' he asked.

'I came over to make sure everyone was all right. After I saw how badly your house . . .' She shook her head. 'Anyway, your front door wasn't locked. I knocked a few times, but . . . I hope you don't mind. I don't normally go barging into people's homes.'

'No. It was very thoughtful of you.'

'I guess you'd already left. Actually, I figured you were buried under the mess. You didn't answer when I called out. I looked around for a while. There wasn't any sign of you, so . . .'

'I went through the backyard to check on the Banners,' he explained.

Even as he heard himself speak the words, he wondered why he was giving such information to Judy.

Should've lied, damn it.

Why? he asked himself. Why bother?

From the vague expression on Judy's face, he guessed that she didn't know the Banners. 'They live directly behind us.' He nodded toward the wall behind the rose bushes.

'Oh. I saw you jump over.'

'The bushes got me pretty good.' He looked down at his sweaty chest, at the stripe of bright red blood above his left nipple. And he saw his pajama pants hanging so low that they looked ready to fall. Trying to appear embarrassed, he pulled the pants up above his hips. Then he folded his hands in front of his groin. 'Sorry,' he muttered.

'Don't worry about it. Why don't you come on over to my place? We'll patch you up a bit, and I'll find you something to wear.'

The offer made his heart pound quicker.

'Is Herb there?' he asked.

'Lucky dog, he flew to New York last night.'

She's asking me into her house. And she made it clear that Herb won't be showing up.

Oh, man.

Then he thought, Who do you think you're kidding? The last thing on Judy's mind is seducing a guy like me. She's just being friendly, trying to help. Probably feels sorry for me.

So what? The minute we step into her house, she's mine.

But Sheila's waiting, he reminded himself. Sheila's better than Judy – no comparison – and she's naked, and she can't get away.

Then he thought, *Judy'll keep.*

Her husband was in New York, some three thousand miles away. Sheila's was only about thirty or forty miles away in

Glendale. No telling how long it might take either husband to return home, but the one coming from Glendale was bound to arrive first.

Gotta get Sheila out and away to someplace safe, or I'll miss my chance.

'I don't think I should go into your house,' he said, 'if Herb's not there.'

Judy looked perplexed. 'What?'

'It wouldn't look good.'

'To whom? Are you kidding? Who would notice *or* care?'

'I don't know. It just . . . anyway, I've gotta get back. I only came around to find a saw and turn off the gas supply at Mother's.'

'I took care of the gas for you,' Judy said. 'I smelled a leak while I was inside looking for you.' The gloom returned to darken her face. 'It's . . . so awful about your mother. I'm so sorry.'

'It happened very fast. I don't think she suffered.'

'You saw it?'

'Yeah. A big chunk of ceiling dropped straight down on her head. She never had a chance.'

'But you're all right?' Judy asked.

'The quake never touched me.' He felt a corner of his mouth turn up. 'Just the damn rose bushes.'

Judy smiled slightly, herself. 'Well, why don't you come over? Under the circumstances, I really doubt that any of the neighbors are likely to tell on us. We'll wash you off and put some disinfectant . . .'

'That really isn't necessary. And I've got to get going.' Stanley frowned at the spigot. 'The water main must be broken, or something.'

'My faucets don't work, either.'

'I bet it's the whole neighborhood,' he said, realizing that Sheila's bathroom pipes probably would've sprayed all over the place if she'd had any water pressure. 'Maybe the whole city,' he added.

'I've got some water in the refrigerator,' Judy said. 'We can use that to clean your wounds. You're probably thirsty, too.'

'Maybe later, okay? But have you got a saw I can borrow?'

'What sort of saw do you need?'

'The best thing would be a chainsaw, I guess. It's a *thick* beam.' He held up his hands to show her the size.

'I don't know. We haven't got one of those. Honestly, I don't know of anybody around here who *does* have a chainsaw. Would a regular handsaw do you any good at all? We've got a couple of those in the garage.'

'Worth a try,' Stanley said.

'Come on.'

He followed Judy down his driveway and through the gate. As they started across her own front yard, she said, 'That beam you need to cut, did it fall on something?'

The question didn't surprise him much. After all, he had asked for a saw. It was only natural for a person to wonder why he needed it.

Very quickly, he tried to think of a lie.

But he had already told her about going to the Banner house. *Doesn't matter, anyhow.*

'It's got Mrs Banner pinned down.'

Judy looked over her shoulder, frowning. 'You mean she's trapped?'

'I'll have her out in a few minutes once I get back with a saw.'

'Is she hurt?'

'No, I think she's in pretty good shape. But I left her alone. I really need to get back to her as fast as I can.'

They headed up Judy's driveway toward her garage at the far end. Stanley walked slightly behind her, enjoying the view of her slim, dark legs. Threads dangled from her frayed cut-offs and brushed against the backs of her thighs.

He liked the look of the cut-off jeans, though he couldn't see much of them below Judy's hanging shirt tail.

Hardly anyone seemed to wear cut-offs anymore. Apparently, they'd gone out of style.

Too bad, Stanley thought.

'I haven't been into the garage yet,' she said. 'God only knows what kind of mess it'll be.'

'At least it didn't fall down.'

'Everything *inside* it probably did.' With that, Judy grabbed the handle and hauled the garage door sideways. It slid with a low rumble, rolling almost four feet before it thumped to a sudden stop. She looked around at Stanley, shrugged, and said, 'At least we can get in.'

She took one step into the garage before groaning, 'Oh, man. Maybe you'd better wait there.'

Remaining outside, Stanley watched Judy make her way deeper into the gloom. She kept near the wall and moved toward the back, nudging boxes aside, shoving a power lawn mower out of her way, stepping over long handles that Stanley supposed must belong to shovels, rakes, hoes, and brooms that had been propped up until the quake knocked them over.

Soon, she stopped and studied the wall. 'Ah. We're in luck. Right where it's supposed to be.' She stretched out an arm and lifted a saw down off the wall, where it had apparently been suspended by a nail.

She returned with it.

The saw in her hand looked shiny and new. It almost looked unused, but Stanley noticed some crumbs of yellow sawdust clinging to its teeth.

'Think this'll do the trick?' Judy asked.

'It should.'

She handed the saw to him. 'Maybe we should take her some water. It's awfully hot out.'

We?

'Right back,' she said, and hurried toward the rear door of her house.

Now what? Stanley wondered.

Judy's planning to come along, that's what.

The door bumped shut.

Why didn't I keep my big mouth shut?

Picturing Sheila sprawled out in the tub, he moaned.

Judy would ruin it all.

Oh, no, she won't!

The door flew open and slammed shut. Stanley watched Judy bound down the couple of stairs and stride toward him, swinging a plastic jug by her side. The jug was almost full. He could see the water through the frosted plastic, hear it sloshing. 'Have some?' she asked.

He wanted to be rid of her.

No, I don't want any of your fucking water. Get out of here and leave me alone!

But in his imagination, the water was as cold as a high Sierra stream spilling down from melting glaciers.

He clamped the saw handle between his knees, took the offered bottle, uncapped it, and raised it to his mouth. The water burbled out, flooding over his parched tongue, filling his mouth. Its sharp chill made his teeth ache. Cheeks bulging, he held the water in his mouth and capped the jug. He swallowed a small bit at a time until his mouth was empty.

'Thanks,' he said. 'That sure hit the spot. Want some?'

'Not just now.'

He took a deep breath. 'I've been thinking, Judy. Maybe you oughta stay here while I go over and take care of Mrs Banner. Her whole house is caved in. There's broken glass, all kinds of nails and stuff. I wouldn't want you to get hurt.'

'I'll be careful. Anyway, look at you. You're wearing moccasins. If it's that bad . . .'

'I made it okay last time.'

'I'd find you something for your feet, but you're so much bigger than Herb.'

'Doesn't matter. I'm fine. But look, I'd better get going.' He shifted the water jug to his left hand, then bent over and took the saw from between his legs. 'I'll bring these back to you as soon as I've got her free.'

Frowning as if she didn't understand, Judy shook her head. 'It's all right, I'll come with you. You don't need to worry about me. If I get hurt, I get hurt. The thing is, there's no point in you trying to rescue this woman by yourself. I'm not totally useless, you know. I might be able to help. If nothing else, I can keep the two of you company – give you some moral support.'

'I don't . . . just stay here. You must have a lot that needs to be done. Picking up, and . . .'

The look in her eyes stopped him. 'What's going on, Stan?'

His heart thudded. In spite of the drink he'd just taken, his mouth suddenly felt dry. 'Nothing,' he said.

'*Some*thing's going on.' She sounded more curious than suspicious. 'Why don't you want me to go with you?'

Think *think* THINK!

'Because . . . you make me nervous. The way you keep looking at me.'

'Looking at you? What are you talking about?'

'You know.'

'I don't know.'

'Let's just drop it, okay? The thing is, you're a very attractive woman. Very. But you're married. That might not mean much to you, but . . .'

'What?' She gasped out a single, strange laugh.

'I'm sorry. I just have a rule that I don't fool around with married women.'

'Hey, now.' Blinking, she shook her head. She looked astonished. 'Let's not get the wrong idea, here. You seem like a nice guy and everything, Stan, but if you think for one minute that I'm interested in . . .'

'You keep *looking* at me. You keep trying to get me into your *house*, and your husband isn't even there. What else am I supposed to think?'

'You're *supposed* to think we've just gone through a major earthquake, that we're neighbors and I want to help you. Because that's the truth. That's it.'

'Is it?'

She jerked her head up and down once, fiercely. 'Yes, that's it. My God, Stan, I realize we barely know each other, but how you could ever get it into your head that . . .' Her eyes, watching him with a narrow glare, widened a bit.

'What?' he asked.

'You didn't,' she said, her voice little more than a whisper.

'Didn't what?'

'Get it into your head. You knew good and well.'

'Knew what?'

Now, he saw fear in her eyes.

501

She shrugged her shoulders. She tried to smile, but her lips trembled. 'If you didn't want my help, you should've just said so. It's all right. Hell, I've got plenty of stuff to do around the house without butting in on your little rescue effort. So just go on ahead.' Still trying to smile, she began to step backward. 'You can bring her over later on if you want . . . or not. Makes no difference to me. If you need anything, you know where to . . .'

Stanley dropped the saw and water jug. Before they had time to hit the driveway's pavement, he sprang and grabbed the front of Judy's shirt. She started to yell as he jerked her toward him. He pumped his knee into her belly.

The blow picked her up.

She landed on her knees. Hugging her belly, she pressed her forehead against the pavement.

Stanley went to her side.

He bent over and swept her shirt up, baring the lower portion of her back. She wore no belt. The waistband of her cut-offs bulged upward slightly. He peeked into the gap and glimpsed shadowy skin, the cleft of her buttocks, the white of her panties.

He shoved his hand in.

Clutched the denim.

Hefted Judy off the pavement and swung her around and hauled her to the back door of her house.

Eleven

'I can't . . .' Heather gasped. 'Can't . . . gotta stop.' She'd done fine for a while, but her running had finally deteriorated to a stagger. Panting and hunched over, she held her stomach and grimaced.

Barbara, at her side, wondered if the girl was faking it.

They hadn't run all that far since leaving Earl unconscious on the sidewalk. Though they'd taken off at a very quick pace, they'd slowed down after turning the first corner. From then on, they'd merely jogged.

Only a few moments before Heather's first 'I can't,' they'd entered an alley that stretched westward behind house fences, garages, carports and garbage bins. Nearly every flat surface had been spray painted with gang signs. The alley ahead looked clear, though. No traffic, no major piles of rubble, no lurking strangers.

'Keep going,' Barbara urged the girl.

'Can't.'

'Just to the next street.'

'I . . . I'll try.'

Heather's agony almost had to be an act.

Barbara might've been able to understand the huffing, moaning and stumbling if it came from a fat slob. But Heather was thin, almost skinny except for her chest. For such a small person, she had awfully big breasts. Maybe being so top-heavy made it hard to run. Maybe that's what wiped her out.

Could be, Barbara thought. But also her legs aren't as long as ours. And she just isn't in very good shape.

Heather's strides shortened, slowed.

'Keep it up. Come on. Just a little farther.'

Shaking her head, Heather halted. She bent over, clutched her knees and panted for air.

'Pete!' Barbara shouted. 'Hold up!'

Pete jogged in a tight circle and came toward them. He didn't seem to be out of breath, but he was red and sweaty from the heat. He stopped in front of them.

'How you doing?' he asked Heather.

She shook her head and kept on panting.

'We did pretty good,' Barbara said. 'We might as well take it easy now.'

'I don't know.' Pete lifted the front of his shirt and wiped sweat off his face. He was smooth and tanned above his belt.

His gray trousers looked heavy, hot. 'Think we managed to ditch him?'

'I've been keeping an eye out. He isn't on our tail. Not that I could see, anyhow. That doesn't mean he won't find us, but we'd better quit running. Heather's pooped. And it's too hot.'

'Hot, all right.'

'You must be dying in those pants.'

'Yeah.' He smiled. 'Want to trade?'

Surprised, Barbara laughed. 'No, that's all right. I'll keep my shorts.'

'They wouldn't look as good on me, anyhow.'

When he said that, Heather let go of her knees and straightened up. She glanced from Barbara to Pete. 'We just gonna stand around, or what?'

'Are you ready to go?' Barbara asked her.

'I've *been* ready. I'm not a weakling, you know.' She switched her purse strap to her other shoulder. 'Just because *you* happen to be some sort of Amazon . . .'

'You've got the wrong Banner. The Amazon's my mom.'

Pete started walking. Heather hurried and caught up to him. Barbara hung back.

Let Heather fall all over him . . .

Pete looked over his shoulder, then stopped and waited. 'Are you coming?'

'Yeah. Sure.'

'Your mom's not really an Amazon, is she?' Pete asked when Barbara came up next to him. He studied her eyes.

And she studied his. They were pale blue, their whites like fields of sunlit snow. They seemed intelligent, earnest.

'She isn't *from* the Amazon, if that's what you mean. She doesn't throw spears.'

Pete smiled. 'Does she file her teeth into points?'

'Nope. And she hasn't cut off . . .' In mid-sentence, Barbara found herself reluctant to finish. 'She's just large, that's all. Large and strong. A bodybuilder.'

Pete looked impressed. 'You mother *pumps iron*?'

'So do I. Not like her, though. Compared to her, I'm sort of a pipsqueak.'

'You're not any pipsqueak,' Pete said. 'How tall are you?'

Can't you tell? she wondered, looking straight forward into his eyes. She decided not to answer his question. So she shrugged.

'I'm five-eleven,' he said, 'and you're almost as tall as me.'

She grinned. *Almost, huh?* 'Mom's six-one,' she said.

'Man, that is big.'

'If you ask me,' Heather said, 'it sounds pretty freakish.'

Barbara leaned forward and scowled at her. 'Watch it, okay? You don't even know my mom. How would you like it if I called *your* mom a freak?'

'My mom's dead.'

The remark worked.

It hurt. A lot.

It felt like the time last year when an elbow had rammed Barbara in the solar plexus during a basketball game. Not only had the jab knocked her wind out, but it had sent a cold ache radiating through her whole body. The pain had numbed her, driven her to her knees. Later, the coach had explained that the solar plexus was a nerve center, so sensitive that a blow to it would drop just about anyone. Later still, in the locker room, her friend Lynn had informed her that it was exactly like getting kicked in the balls.

Stunned now with pain from Heather's words, Barbara thought, *It's just like catching that elbow.* And then she thought, *What the hell did Lynn know about getting kicked in the balls?*

She muttered, 'I'm sorry.'

'I hope you're happy.'

'I'm not happy. I told you, I'm sorry.'

'Yeah, sure.' Heather returned to Pete's side and took hold of his hand.

He glanced at Barbara. He looked uncomfortable, downright squirmy. After the glance, he faced forward.

She stayed next to him, but kept her hands to herself.

Nobody said anything.

Beyond the end of the alley, the street appeared to be blocked solid with traffic. Barbara saw no people inside the cars. Some were milling about, others relaxing on their hoods or trunks.

'How did you lose your mother?' Pete asked.

I don't want to hear this!

'I didn't lose her. She killed herself.'

Barbara winced.

'She committed suicide?' Pete asked. He sounded appalled, impressed. As if he'd never heard of anything quite so astonishing.

Don't ask how she did it, Pete. Please.

'How . . . ? I mean, maybe you don't want to talk about it.'

Maybe we don't want to hear about it.

'No, it's all right.' Heather leaned forward to see past Pete. 'I bet *you* want to hear all about it.'

'Not really,' Barbara said.

'She jumped out a window, that's how. She checked into a motel, but there was only just one vacancy for that night and it was on the third floor. The third floor, right?' Heather laughed. The laugh was harsh, off-key. Barbara saw tears in her eyes.

Why is she telling us this?

'Mom went on ahead and jumped anyway, though. The thing was, three stories up wasn't really high enough. She landed flat on her back on the sidewalk, and it like split her open all over, but it didn't kill her. She was still conscious. And screaming. Her brains were oozing out, and blood was coming out her ears and eyes and *everywhere*.'

They had all stopped walking.

Pete and Barbara both gaped at the girl.

She was grinning and weeping as she talked. A long string of snot dangled from her nose.

Why is she telling us this? How does she even know all this yucky stuff? What the hell is going on?

'So you know what Mom did? She couldn't get up because she was too busted apart, so she wiggled across the sidewalk like a worm and dragged herself down into the street and a car ran over her head and popped it like a grape.'

With a look of frantic glee on her face, Heather sniffed and wiped her nose.

Whacko, Barbara thought. The girl's gone completely whacko.

Pete didn't seem to share that opinion. He looked stunned. 'That's . . . that's horrible,' he said. 'That's the worst thing I ever heard.'

Heather suddenly flung herself against him. She pressed her face to his chest, hugged him, and wept. With one hand, Pete patted her back. With the other, he stroked her hair.

Method in her madness.

She probably made up the whole thing.

At least Pete didn't seem to be enjoying the attention. As soon as Heather quit weeping, he eased her away. 'Are you okay?'

She blinked up at him and sniffed.

'Can we go now?' Barbara asked. She didn't wait for an answer. She walked to the end of the alley, then turned around. The other two were following, but farther away than she expected. 'Maybe we oughta make another turn,' she called. 'Just to make things tougher for Earl.'

'I don't know,' Pete said. 'Do you think we need to bother?'

'If he finds us, it won't be pretty.'

'Well, which way do . . . Watch out!'

Barbara glimpsed a quick motion to her left. Jerked her head toward it. Saw a bicycle speeding toward her, a kid hunched over its handlebars. He looked no older than twelve. He had a big grin. 'Beep beep, babe!' he called.

She leaped backward, yelling, 'Hey!'

The bike missed her.

As it shot by, out darted the kid's arm. He caught a handful of her blouse just below her right shoulder. Her blouse and the denim strap of her purse. She felt a quick tug. Buttons popped open. The right side of her blouse was tugged sideways and down off her shoulder before she could grab the kid's wrist. She kept the grip for just an instant, then lost it.

The kid raced away, Barbara's purse swinging at his side.

'You bastard!' she shouted. She swept her blouse shut and dashed after him.

The kid was moving off fast, butt up, head low, the bike wagging from side to side as he pumped its pedals.

Barbara sprinted after him.

A guy sitting on the hood of a car off to the side clapped and shouted, 'All right!' After him, a small group of people standing beside a long white car watched her run by. They made comments among themselves, a woman pointing at her, a man staring, another man letting out a hoot. Then two landscape workers drinking beer in the bed of a pickup truck whistled as she rushed by. 'Yo, baby!' one called. 'Marry me!' called the other. 'I make you smile all over!'

Creeps, she thought. So they can see my bra. Big deal.

Big men. Don't see any of *them* trying to stop Bike Boy.

Though Barbara ran at full speed, she didn't seem to be gaining on the kid. The sidewalk made a perfect getaway route for him: level and straight, unlittered by any debris from the quake.

Never catch him.

She kept on chasing him, anyway.

She tried to remember what she had in her purse – what she would lose: six or seven dollars; her house key and, oh yeah, the keys to the school car they'd left a long time ago somewhere in the middle of Pico Boulevard; her learner's permit; her library card, brush and comb, compact and mirror, lipstick, tissues, some bubble gum, and a few photos in her wallet.

Nothing really major.

Except maybe the pictures. Mom and Dad, and what if they've both been . . .?

Those snapshots might be all I ever have of them again.

'Damn it, you bastard! Stop!'

He glanced over his shoulder and showed Barbara a big, white-toothed grin.

'Give me my purse!'

He swung an arm out behind him and hoisted his middle finger.

I'll never get him. It's useless.

She staggered to a halt. Gasping for breath, she started to

fasten a button. The skin showing between the edges of her blouse was so sweaty it looked oiled. Her bra felt soaked.

She glanced back. Pete was coming toward her. He had Heather by the hand. He appeared to be towing her, trying to hurry but being held back. Obviously, Heather was in no rush.

Barbara took another look at the thief.

He was almost to the end of the block, still pedaling like mad, the purse swinging from his shoulder. And suddenly a man dressed like a banker leaped at him from behind a tree. The kid tried to swerve away. The man clubbed him in the face with a slim dark rod – a crowbar, maybe a tire tool.

The kid's head jerked back. He flung his arms out wide. Then he tumbled backward off his seat and fell. He smacked the sidewalk behind his bike. Barbara saw his head snap down against the concrete. His bike kept going. Riderless, it veered toward a lawn.

The man in the gray suit chased the bike. The moment it fell, he ducked and grabbed the handlebars. He dragged the bike to the sidewalk, tilted it upright, ran with it for a few strides, then mounted and pedaled away.

Nobody yelled. Nobody rushed from a house or from the street or from any of the waiting cars to stop him.

Maybe I'm the only one who saw it.

Hardly. They just don't care. Or they're scared.

The kid still lay sprawled on the sidewalk.

At his side was Barbara's purse.

The man sped around the corner at the end of the block and vanished.

Barbara looked back at Pete and Heather. They weren't much closer than before. She couldn't wait for them.

She ran to the kid and her purse.

The kid had a puddle of blood under his head. The blow had crushed a deep, leaky ditch above his left eyebrow. His eyes were open. One stared straight up and the other cast its gaze off low to the side as if nervous about something crawling toward his knee.

He wore tan trousers. They were wet in front.

Just like Earl's jeans.

He was sprawled out on the pavement like Earl. He was a creep like Earl, a thief like Earl, and he'd been bashed in the head and he'd peed his pants like Earl. But he was much younger than Earl and he was dead.

Barbara felt cold and numb and trembly inside.

Crouching, she lifted the strap of her purse. She was careful not to touch the kid as she slid the strap off his shoulder and out from under his arm. She stood up. She looped the strap over her head so that it crossed her chest like a bandolier, the blue denim purse at her hip.

She stepped aside for Pete. He stopped and looked at the body. 'Jeez,' he said.

Heather, holding Pete's arm, said, 'Wow!'

'Did you see it?' Barbara asked. 'Did you see how that guy got him?'

'I wasn't looking,' Pete said.

'You were in the way, anyhow,' Heather explained.

'A guy just jumped out and smacked him in the face. It was so weird. The guy was really well-dressed. He didn't look like someone who'd . . . kill a little kid.'

'Maybe he saw the kid snatch your purse,' Pete said.

'No. That wasn't it. He wanted the bike.' Her voice sounded far away as she spoke. 'That's all. He just wanted the bike. His car . . . it's probably stuck in the traffic somewhere.'

'You could really make time if you had a bike,' Pete said.

'Killed for a bike.'

Heather sighed. 'Let's not go feeling *too* sorry for the jerk. He was nothing but a purse snatcher.'

'He . . .' Barbara started.

'I know, I know. He didn't deserve to die for it. Well, he didn't – he died because some *other* jerk wanted his bike. Big loss.'

'Don't talk like that,' Pete told her.

Heather's face went red. She turned her head away.

'Let's get moving,' Barbara said, 'or we'll never get home.'

They stepped around the small body. Once past it, Barbara moved ahead of the other two.

'Can you imagine killing someone for a bike?' Pete asked.

Barbara turned sideways to watch him. 'It's crazy. This whole thing is crazy. You know? You always hear about how people pull together when there's a disaster.'

'You hear about looters, too,' Pete pointed out.

'Yeah, I guess so. But mostly it's acts of sacrifice and heroism, that sort of thing. They don't tell you about the people who go nuts. It seems like *everybody's* going nuts. Mr Wellen goes nuts with the car, Earl tries to *swipe* a car, that poor kid snatches my purse, some kind of executive breaks the kid's skull open for a bicycle. It's all like some kind of a huge, awful joke.'

'Maybe the quake released some kind of a nerve gas into the air,' Pete said, his mouth tilted by a crooked smile. 'It makes everybody go insane.'

Barbara found herself smiling. 'Right,' she said.

'I've read books about stuff like that.'

'Horror novels.' It wasn't a question.

'Well, yeah. It almost makes sense, though.'

Heather studied Pete. 'Could there really be a gas or something that makes people crazy?'

'I doubt it,' he said.

'Are you sure?'

'How could there be a gas like that?' Barbara asked her.

'Look at me and Pete. We haven't gone bonkers yet.'

'It's the quake,' Pete said. 'That's all. It shook everyone up too much.'

'Is that supposd to be a pun?'

'Everyone's scared.'

Barbara nodded. 'Everyone's scared and wants to get home and be safe.'

'Not me,' Heather said.

'Sure you do,' Pete told her.

'Oh yeah? How would you like going home if you didn't have any mother?'

'You've got a father, don't you?'

'Oh, sure.'

'He's probably at work,' Barbara said. 'Mine is. Though I bet he's trying awfully hard to get home right now.'

If he's okay.

'I don't know where my father is,' Heather said. 'And I don't care.' They walked a little farther before she added, 'Hope a roof fell on him.'

Pete frowned. 'You can't mean that.'

She didn't answer.

But Barbara saw the look in her eyes. 'I think she means it.'

Twelve

'Uh-oh.'

'What?' Clint asked.

'That's our house,' Em said. She stretched out her arm through the gap between the seatbacks, pointing. 'The one with that pickup in the driveway.'

'It looks all right,' Clint said. In fact, none of the homes along this quiet, dead-end street appeared to have been demolished by the quake. The only damage he'd noticed since turning the corner were a few broken windows and minor cracks in some of the stucco walls. 'Looks like your whole neighborhood got off pretty easy.'

'Yeah,' Em said.

Clint swung to the curb in front of her house.

'Bye-bye, Emerald,' Mary said. 'It's been a treat.'

'Yeah,' Em said again, still staring through the windshield.

'What's wrong?' Clint asked.

'It's that pickup. It shouldn't be there.'

Mary sighed. 'I thought we were supposed to be in a hurry, Clint.'

'That's where our Cherokee goes,' Em said. 'When Mom's

home, she leaves it right there in the driveway. We use the garage for storing stuff, you know? So Mom isn't home. And that pickup's got no business sitting in our driveway.'

'Have you seen it before?' Clint asked.

'I don't think so.'

The front door of her house opened. Out stepped a burly man carrying a large cardboard box. His hair stuck out in all directions. His eyebrows were black thickets. His jaw was shaped like a brick. Though much of his upper body was hidden behind the box, Clint saw that he wore a grimy white T-shirt. His arms were thick and hairy. The trousers that sagged around his hips showed, in a few places, where they used to be green. Just looking at them, Clint thought he could smell garbage.

'One of your mother's boyfriends?' Mary asked.

Em didn't answer.

A woman followed the man out of the house.

She, too, carried a box.

Her gray-streaked hair, parted in the middle, drooped straight down the sides of her face. With each step, her cheeks wobbled. Though Clint guessed he must be forty feet from the woman, he could see her bristly mustache. A cigarette hung from a corner of her mouth, its smoke crawling up her cheek and into her eye so she had to squint. The sleeves were missing from her old, plaid shirt. Her arms were thick and white and floppy. So were her legs. Her short skirt left them bare from mid-thigh all the way down to the tops of her red cowgirl boots.

'And I guess that's Mom herself,' Mary said.

'Oh, boy,' Em muttered.

The man carried his box down from the stoop and lumbered along the walkway toward the pickup truck.

'Do you know them?' Clint asked.

'I sure don't.' Em threw open the back door and leaped out. 'Hey! Put that stuff down!' She ran onto her lawn. She ran *at* the pair.

'Jesus,' Clint muttered.

'Is she nuts?'

Not totally, Clint thought. Because she'd stopped on the lawn at least ten feet away from them.

They turned and stared at her. The man looked confused, the woman annoyed. So far, neither of them had glanced toward the car.

'What've you got in those boxes?' Em demanded.

'Buzz off,' the woman said.

'Put them down!' Em snapped. 'Right this instant!' She planted her fists on her hips.

A grin slowly stretched the man's heavy lips. He turned his head to the woman. 'Let's take *her*, Lou.'

She guffawed.

They both twitched at the noise of the car horn.

Once he had their attention, Clint climbed out. The man's eyes grew wide. The woman's narrowed.

'You don't scare me none,' she said.

He stepped around the front of the car. 'I'm not here to scare you, ma'am.'

'Let's get outa here, Lou.'

The man hurried toward his pickup. Lou didn't budge.

'Put down the box, mister,' Clint said.

The man set it down on the grass, then waved his open hands at Clint and sidestepped away. 'I don't want no trouble. We're goin'. Come on, Lou.'

She ignored him.

Clint walked toward her.

She spat out her cigarette. Em did a quick prance to dodge it.

'Put down the box, ma'am, and leave.'

She put down the box. Then she stepped out from behind it. Leaning forward, she grinned at Clint. Her crooked teeth were brown. 'Come 'n get it.'

Off to the side, a door clanked shut. An engine rattled and wheezed. 'Less go, Lou!'

'Hold yer water!' she called.

'Why don't you just go away?' Em said to her.

Lou wiggled her fingers at Clint. 'Less tangle. You 'n' me.'

'I don't want to fight with . . .'

Lou lurched at Em. Her flabby arm swung out. Her fist struck Em like a hammer just beneath the throat.

Em flew backward off her feet.

Lou grinned at Clint. 'How y'like that?'

He'd only known Em for a little while. But he liked her a lot.

He took a step toward Lou. When she threw the punch at his jaw, he blocked it. His other hand chopped. He heard her collar bone break. Then all he heard was her squealing.

She was down on her knees, walking on her knees, waddling and squealing as Clint towed her by her greasy hair to the driveway.

He opened the passenger door for her.

Squealing and whimpering, she climbed up and fell into the passenger seat.

'Whad y'do to-uhr?'

'Get out of here. Both of you.'

The red cowgirl boot on Lou's right foot was still hanging outside when Clint started to swing the door shut. He stopped. 'Pull in your foot, Lou.'

When the boot was in, he slammed the door.

He glanced into the bed of the pickup. A dozen or so boxes were scattered about. They looked as if they'd been thrown in. Some lay on their sides. Clint didn't see any that weren't empty.

Must've been their first trip out with stuff.

The pickup sped backward to the end of the driveway, swerved out into the street, and sped off.

Em was already on her feet. 'Boy, you really *destroyed* her!'

'Are you okay?' Clint asked.

'Sure.' She rubbed her chest through the T-shirt. 'Not that it didn't hurt, but I'm okay.'

He looked into the box that the man had carried from the house. 'Looks like he cleaned out your mother's bar.'

Em bent down over the other box. 'Food here. Mostly stuff from the freezer.' She lifted it. 'Will you bring in that one?'

'You bet.' Clint picked it up. 'Watch when you go in,' he warned. 'I'm assuming there were just the two of them, but you never know.'

As he followed Em toward the stoop, Mary called from the car, 'Where are you going?'

'I'll be right back.'

'You're not going in, are you?'

'Just for a minute or two. I've got to make sure it's safe.'

'Oh, fine. Just fine. Wait for me.'

He didn't wait, but he left the front door open after stepping into the house.

Em stood in the middle of the living room, the box in her arms. She turned around slowly, surveying the mess, making a face. 'I guess it could be worse, huh?'

'A lot. If it doesn't get any worse than this, you're in great shape.'

'I don't know about *that*.' She wrinkled her nose. 'Those two were *in* here. Yuck.'

'I doubt they were responsible for . . .'

Mary hurried in. 'Everything all right?'

'Too soon to know,' Clint said.

'Who were those awful people?'

'Looters. They seemed to be after food and booze.'

'They sure looked like they needed it,' Mary said, and tried to smile. 'You really handled them well, Clint.'

She's trying to make amends, he thought. He told her, 'Thanks.'

Em started toward the dining room.

'Hold it,' he said. 'Let me go first.' As he walked past her, he asked, 'Are you pretty sure your mother's gone?'

'Oh, yeah. The Jeep isn't in the driveway. She's probably out shopping. She only goes shopping just about every day.' Em followed Clint into the dining room. 'Personally, I don't think Mom much cares for staying home. She's *always* looking for an excuse to go out for an excursion.' They entered the kitchen. 'She's probably at a mall. I suppose those malls are pretty sturdy, don't you imagine so?'

'Probably,' Clint said. 'She's just lucky she wasn't here.'

'Yeah. That's for sure.'

They set the boxes onto the kitchen table.

Mary, entering after them, stepped over some debris of

broken dishes and swung the refrigerator door shut. 'We really *should* get going,' she said.

'You don't need to rush off,' Em said. 'Maybe you'd like a drink?' She lifted a bottle of Jim Beam out of the box. 'Name your poison.'

'We really don't have time,' Mary said. Though she was speaking to Em, her eyes were fixed on Clint. 'The longer we stay here, the more trouble we'll . . .'

'I'll give the place a quick once-over,' Clint said. 'Then we'll go.' He left them in the kitchen and began to explore the rest of the house.

The walls and ceilings appeared to be intact. He saw no significant damage.

In the bathroom, the medicine cabinet door stood open. Toothbrushes, tubes of paste and creams, plastic bottles of pills and fluids were heaped in the sink, scattered about the floor. Maybe the looters had done it. More likely, however, it was the work of the quake.

In the mother's bedroom, a full length mirror on the closet door was cracked. Bureau drawers stood open, and one had dropped to the floor. The floor was an obstacle course of things that had been cast down from walls, shelves, the tops of the bureau and nightstands.

After checking under the mother's bed and inside the closet to make sure Em didn't have any hiding visitors, he went down the hall to the other bedroom.

Obviously, Em's room.

A poster on the wall showed Bart Simpson riding a skateboard.

Em's swivel chair had rolled away from her desk and stopped near the head of her bed. Two desk drawers were on the floor. All of her bureau drawers were open, but none had dropped.

Clint saw the jumble of books and dolls piled along the base of her built-in shelves. Like his own daughter, Em had a collection of Barbie dolls, a couple of Kens, and even Barbie's '57 Chevy. The big, plastic car must've been hurled off its shelf and hit the carpet bumper-first, throwing out Barbie. Its rear end was propped up high against an upright. Barbie lay in front of the Chevy, stiff, gazing at the ceiling.

As Clint crouched over Barbie, he heard footsteps. He picked up the doll. As he stood, Em came into the room.

She looked around, moaning and shaking her head. 'What a dump.'

'There's not much that didn't end up on the floor,' he said. He set Barbie on a shelf. 'I haven't spotted any particular damage to the house, though. And I haven't found any stowaways so far.'

'Are you sure you've looked everywhere?'

'Not quite done yet.' He opened the closet door. 'Nobody here. '

Em, herself, checked under the bed. Standing, she brushed off her hands. 'Actually, I just came in to grab a clean shirt.' She stepped over to her bureau, pushed the top drawer shut, then searched through a stack of T-shirts in the second drawer. She took a faded blue one from the bottom. 'No point wearing a good one on a day like this,' she said. 'I'll be with Mary in the kitchen,' she said, and hurried away.

Clint spent a few more minutes checking through the house for intruders, then returned to the kitchen.

Em was facing the sink, bare to the waist, while Mary stroked her below the left shoulder with a wet cloth. In front of Em, water hissed from the faucet.

'Glad to know there's water pressure,' Clint said.

Mary scowled at him. 'Hey. Get out of here. Can't you see she isn't dressed?'

'That's all right,' Em said. 'Just stay, all right? It's no big deal.'

'You shouldn't be . . .'

'Nothing *shows*, for heaven's sake. See?' She turned slightly, and Clint saw that she was pressing the blue T-shirt against her chest. The pink one was draped over the front edge of the sink. 'We're cleaning my wound,' she explained. 'You want to see it?'

Nodding, Clint stepped closer. Mary moved aside. The girl's back was white except for a few freckles and a very raw, red scrape where the brick had struck her. Most of the skin on her shoulder blade was ruddy and striped with fine, bright rows of scratches.

'Looks like it hurts,' Clint said.

'It stings, is all. It's not so bad.'

'Did you land on it when that gal knocked you down?'

She let out a soft laugh. 'Yeah. Now *that* didn't feel terribly swift, I must say.'

'You can put on your shirt now,' Mary said.

'Does it need a bandage?' Em asked.

'The air'll do it good.'

'Won't it stick to my shirt?'

'Here.' Clint sidestepped, pulled a square of paper towel off a roll suspended under the cupboard, and pressed it gently against Em's scrape to blot up the moisture. When he took his hand away, the paper adhered to her. It showed lines of pinpoint red dots. He took it away, tore off another square and folded it into a pad. 'Just leave this one against it loose under your shirt for a while,' he said.

He smoothed it against her, then turned away while she pulled the blue T-shirt over her head.

'Okay.'

He faced her. The T-shirt was printed with a dead cat, legs up, and the legend, I ONLY EAT ROADKILL AT J.R.'s, MOAB, UTAH.

'I guess it's time for us to get going,' Clint said.

'And then some,' Mary added.

'Will you be all right here by yourself?'

Shrugging, Em made a face that almost brought a smile to Clint. Her expression – lips curling, eyebrows writhing – showed a fine mix of deep thought, worry, revulsion and hope. 'What if somebody *else* comes along?'

'Your mother will probably be home soon,' Mary said.

'Yeah, but what if she isn't? *I* don't know where she went. Maybe she *can't* get back.'

'Is there a gun in the house?' Clint asked.

'Mom allow a gun in the house? I don't *think* so. The world's biggest pacifist?'

'Is there a neighbor you can stay with?' Clint asked.

Em shook her head. 'I don't know. I don't know much of anybody around here.'

'You don't know your neighbors?' Mary asked her. It sounded like an accusation.

'I don't know mine either,' Clint admitted. 'Just a few of them here and there. It was worth a shot.'

'I know everyone in my building,' Mary said.

'So do I,' Em said. 'Me and Mom.'

'What do you *want* to do?' Clint asked.

Her eyebrows climbed her forehead. 'Could I go *with* you?'

'With us?'

'I really don't want to stay here. Those people might come back. *Anybody* might come. I mean, I'd be all alone here. Maybe for hours. Or maybe even all day. Mom might not show up till tomorrow or something.'

She might never show up, Clint thought.

She's probably fine.

'And I especially wouldn't like to be here alone after it gets dark,' Em said. 'With no lights? And with no gun? And with no way to get any help?'

'The phone's dead,' Mary added. 'We checked.'

'Anyway,' Em went on, 'the point is that I'd much rather stick with you two, if you know what I mean.'

'No way,' Mary said. To Clint, she said, 'We're really losing a *lot* of time here.'

'I know, I know.'

'I'll leave a note for Mom so she won't worry about me.'

'Em, we're going all the way to West L.A.'

'And Santa Monica,' Mary said.

Em kept her eyes on Clint. 'That's okay. I'd sure rather go there than stay by myself.'

'We might not be able to get you back here tonight.'

'I don't *want* to be here. Not unless Mom gets home.'

'The whole idea's ridiculous,' Mary said. 'Her mother might walk through the door two minutes after we're gone.'

Clint nodded. 'She might.'

'You could wait here till she comes,' Em suggested.

'I've gotta get home to *my* family. And I have to leave now.'

'Is it okay?' Em asked him.

'No,' Mary said.

Em didn't even glance at her. 'What would you do if I was *your* daughter?' she asked.

He didn't need to think about it. 'Come on along. But you have to leave that note.'

Mary sighed and shook her head.

Em found a pad and pen beside the telephone.

Clint watched over her shoulder as she wrote, 'Mom, I'm fine but some sleezoids broke into the house. I can't stay. I've gone with Clint Banner. He lives at . . .'

Clint gave his address and telephone number.

'What else should I say?' Em asked.

'Tell her you'll stay with my family. I'll bring you back home as soon as conditions permit.'

When the note was finished, she stepped into the dining room. She folded the note in half and stood it upright on the table there.

'Are we ready?' Mary asked.

'Do we have a minute for me to use the john?' Em asked.

'We should probably all go,' Clint said. 'It might be a long and johnless day.'

Em laughed, then headed for the toilet.

When she was gone, Mary said, 'What is it with you and her?'

'We can't leave her alone here. She's just a kid.'

'You're not her father.'

'I'm aware of that.'

'You like her, don't you!'

'Sure I like her. She's a good kid.'

'A swell kid,' Mary muttered.

'We don't know where her mother is. We don't know if she's coming back at all. I hate to think what might've happened to Em if she'd been in the house when Lou and her pal broke in. They *might* come back. And there's absolutely no way for us to know how bad things are, how bad they might get. It's pretty obvious the cops won't be doing people a lot of good, not till the phone system is operating again and the roads clear. With a deal like that, you could end up with big-time chaos. A girl Em's age shouldn't have to face that sort of stuff alone.'

'I wonder if you'd be saying that if she was fat and ugly,' Mary said. Then came the sound of the flushing toilet. She left the dining room. She and Em crossed paths near the doorway.

Em looked at Clint, one eye narrowed. 'Don't you think maybe we should take some stuff with us? Water, for instance? And some food, at least something to snack on? Because we might very well need to walk part of the way. Have you considered that? I mean, I wouldn't be one bit surprised to find Laurel Canyon closed. Or totally jammed with traffic so we wouldn't be able to go an inch all day.'

'It's very possible,' Clint said.

'Maybe we'll be able to zip right over the top in the car, but we ought to be prepared for the opposite.'

'You're right. Let's take some food and water.'

'And maybe we should arm ourselves.'

'I thought you said . . .'

'Oh, we don't have any guns. But we could take along some knives.'

'Your mother allows knives in the house?'

Em smiled. 'She hasn't figured out how to get by without them. Not yet, anyhow.' As they walked into the kitchen, Em said, 'If we didn't eat meat, of course, I think we could manage without sharp knives. I'm certainly not about to tell her that, though – she'd turn us into vegetarians. Life is bizarre enough without that. I don't know what I'd *do* if I couldn't eat meat.'

The carving knives were on the floor, three still jutting from the slotted block of oak that served as their holder. The other five were scattered nearby. Em picked up the holder while Clint gathered the knives that had fallen out.

After setting the block onto the counter, she pulled its knives and arranged them beside those that Clint had spread out. 'Which should we take?'

'If we need any of them, we're in a whole lot of trouble.'

QUAKE

Mary came into the kitchen. 'Now what?' she asked.

'We're choosing weapons,' Em answered.

Mary stepped up to the counter. 'Terrific. You can count me out.'

'That's all right,' Em told her, 'I'll take two.'

'Take your pick,' Clint said.

'You go first.'

'Ladies first.'

'But you're in charge. You ought to . . .'

'Jesus H. Christ!' Mary snapped. 'Stop playing games!'

Clint quickly grabbed a paring knife with a four-inch blade.

'Is that *it*?' Em asked.

'Suits me. Shorter the blade, the less likely I am to cut myself. You go ahead and pick. I'll be right back.' He hurried to the bathroom. He urinated. Then he found the cardboard core of a toilet paper roll in the wastebasket. He took it out, mashed it flat, and slipped the blade of his knife inside. In the sink, he found a roll of adhesive tape that had apparently fallen from the medicine cabinet. He taped the end of the tube shut, then ran a strip down the knife handle and onto the cardboard to secure the knife within its makeshift sheath.

Keeping the roll of tape, he returned to the kitchen. Em, at the refrigerator, was stuffing food into a paper bag. Mary, at the sink, was filling a two-litre plastic Pepsi bottle with tap water.

Two knives lay side by side on the counter. The remaining knives had been put back into the holder.

'These the ones you want?' Clint asked.

Em smiled over her shoulder. 'I picked the biggest.'

'So I see. What I'm going to do is run a length of tape along their sharp edges. That way, you won't have to worry about slicing yourself open. If you need to cut something, you just strip off the tape.'

'Nifty.' She swung the refrigerator door shut. Crumpling the top of the bag, she came over to Clint.

Mary shut off the faucet. 'Okay, we've got three bottles. One each.'

523

Clint got to work taping the knife blades. 'You'll be a regular Jim Bowie,' he said.

'Didn't he bite it at the Alamo?'

'Well, yeah.'

'Real swift comparison, Mr Banner.'

'That's all right,' he said. 'We're nowhere *near* the Alamo.'

Em laughed. She laughed hard. She cracked up. She had never fallen apart like this in front of Clint, and he enjoyed seeing her so delighted.

After she regained control, Clint handed the knives to her. 'The trick with these is to keep them out of sight. They make an excellent secret weapon. Once the enemy becomes aware of them, though, they loose a lot of their effectiveness.'

Mary frowned. 'What is this? How do you know about that stuff? And I saw the chop you gave that woman. Who are you?'

'Bond. James Bond. And this is M.'

'Very funny.'

He glanced from Mary to Em. 'Are we all set? Are we forgetting anything?' They shook their heads. 'Then let's move out.'

He carried two of the water bottles for Mary. Em carried the bag of food and her two butcher knives. On the front stoop, he scanned the neighborhood. He saw no one. He saw no signs of trouble.

When Em finished locking the front door of her house, they walked across the yard toward Mary's BMW.

Clint was almost to the curb when he noticed that the right front tire was flat.

Shit!

Another delay. But as long as Mary's spare was okay . . .

He saw that the right rear tire was also flat.

His stomach dropped.

He rushed out into the street. Both tires on the left side of the car were flat.

Mary stood motionless and stiff, her mouth hanging open. 'Whuh . . .? What happened to . . . *to my car?*'

'That pair we chased off,' Clint said. 'I'd bet on it.'

'Lou and the guy,' Em explained.

'Did us a little payback.'

'My God! My Beamer! They . . . they *ruined* it!'

'All they did was slash the tires,' Clint said. 'Probably.'

'Why didn't you just let them take the goddamn boxes?' she blurted. 'Why did you have to *bother* them? Look what they did! Look what they did to my Beamer!'

Ignoring her outburst, Em asked Clint, 'What'll we do now?'

'Do you still want to come with us?'

'You must be kidding. They snuck back while we were inside. I'm not sticking around here.'

'If you people think for one minute that I'm going to leave my car on this street in the middle of God-knows-where . . .'

'Studio City,' Em broke in. 'And it's right in front of my house. It's not like it's *lost*. You can pick it up when Clint brings me back.'

'It might not even *be* here by then.'

'It'll be fine,' Clint said.

'It's not fine *now*!'

'Well, look, there's nothing we can do. Not with that many flats. If you try to drive it in that condition, you'll ruin the rims. In a day or two, after things have settled down, I'll bring you out and help you take care of it. Okay? But right now, we've gotta get moving or we'll never get home.'

'What're you planning to do, walk?'

'Yup.'

'Oh, fine and dandy. Have you forgotten about the *mountain range*?'

'It's just a ridge of hills. I've driven over it every day for the past three years. From Ventura Boulevard to the top, it's only two miles.'

'Two miles?' Mary grimaced.

'Two miles up, two miles down the other side to Sunset, and it'll be a level hike of about four miles from there to my house.'

'Right here,' Em said, 'we're about a mile from the bottom. So that'll make a grand total of nine miles.'

'I'm not going,' Mary said.

'You don't want to stay here,' Em told her. 'Besides, it'll be a cinch once we get to the top. The first part'll be tough. After Mulholland, though, no sweat.'

'And we'll take it easy on the way up,' Clint added.

'I'm not going. I'm staying right here.' She walked around to the other side of her BMW, opened the driver's door, and climbed in. She slammed the door shut.

Clint muttered, 'Women.'

Em gaped at him. 'Say again?'

'Just kidding. Women are terrific.'

'That's better.'

'Let's go, Em. *You're* still coming, aren't you?'

'Are you going to leave her?'

'It's her choice.'

He followed Em to the driver's window. The girl bent her knees and looked in at Mary. 'Are you sure you want to stay?'

'Buzz off.'

'It's not that far. Less than ten miles.'

'This isn't about walking.'

'What *is* it about?'

'What do you care? Just go. You've got Clint to take care of you now. Have a good time.'

'If you're really planning to stay, I'll give you my house key.'

'Don't bother.'

'You can at least go inside and . . .'

'*Fuck off!*'

Em lurched backward as if struck. Turning away, she glanced at Clint with startled eyes. 'Let's go.'

Mary was still sitting in her car when they reached the end of the block.

'What do you think's wrong with her?' Em asked.

'Plenty.'

'She certainly got upset about her tires.'

'I guess the car means a lot to her.'

'That's for sure. Not to mention she hates me.'

'Aah, she doesn't hate you.'

'Sure she does. That's okay, though. I'm used to it. People either love me or hate me – has something to do with my winning personality.' She grinned. 'Anyway, I didn't mean to come between you two, or anything.'

'Don't worry about it. We're probably better off without her.'

'I just hope nobody jumps her while she's . . .'

'Hey! Wait for me!'

Looking back, they saw Mary jog around the corner, waving. Her purse swung at her side by its shoulder strap. It was open, the top of her water bottle jutting out.

'Oh, joy,' Em said. 'Let's see if we can ditch her.'

Clint laughed. 'You have a cruel streak.'

Now that they had halted to wait for her, Mary slowed to a walk.

'Hurry up,' Clint called.

'Sorry.' She quickened her pace.

She looked different to Clint. Less formal and sour, somehow. And her suit jacket was gone.

'Change your mind?' Em asked when Mary stopped in front of them.

The woman nodded, shrugged, looked sheepishly from Em to Clint. 'I don't know what I was thinking,' she said. 'Honestly. I mean, how stupid can a person be? Guess I'll have to plead temporary insanity.'

'It's been a rough morning,' Clint said.

'You're telling me.' She fluttered the front of her blouse. 'Hotter than the dickens, too. Do you believe this heat?' She pursed her lips, blew, and fanned the air in front of her face.

'We'll take it slow,' Clint told her. 'We'll be all right.'

Thirteen

Stanley never meant to do any of this. He'd only wanted to borrow Judy's saw and hurry back to Sheila.

But Judy couldn't let it go at that.

Oh, no. Huh-uh. She had to stick her nose in. She had to push. She had to insist on going *with* him.

Stanley'd had enough of interfering women, women who butted into his business, women who wanted to control him and stop him from doing the good stuff.

Judy would've ruined his plans for Sheila.

So she had to be put out of action.

That was all Stanley had meant to do – take her out of the game. That's why he had driven his knee up into her belly. He'd meant to incapacitate her, haul her into her house, maybe tie her up and gag her, then hurry on back to Sheila.

But the moment Stanley felt his knee sink into her belly and heard her breath gush out, she'd stopped being an obstacle in his way. She'd suddenly become an unexpected gift.

An earthquake prize.

We'll just make it quick, he'd told himself as he lugged her into the house by the back of her cut-off jeans.

What if this ruins Sheila for me?

It won't, it won't. And anyway, who knows? The Sheila thing might fall through.

Shit, it probably will.

Something was bound to mess it up. Nothing ever turned out right for Stanley, and getting Sheila for himself wasn't likely to be the exception.

Anyway, a bird in the hand . . .

Even though Judy couldn't compare to Sheila, she was in his hands, in his power.

He'd never had a woman that way before.

They'd always held the power: he'd always been the beggar.

And he'd never even come close to having a woman who wasn't fat or ugly.

Sure, Judy was no Sheila. But compared to the few women who had allowed Stanley to touch them during his thirty-two years of life, Judy Wellman was incredibly gorgeous, breathtaking, stunning.

He *couldn't* just tie her up and go away.

So he'd carried her into the master bedroom, climbed onto the king-sized bed with her, swung her feet toward the ceiling while holding onto her cut-off jeans, and shaken her until she dropped headfirst onto the mattress, leaving the jeans in his hands. Panties halfway down her thighs, she'd flopped and rolled. Before she could get to her hands and knees, Stanley had pounced.

It seemed like ages ago.

I've gotta get back to Sheila, he told himself.

She'll keep.

Maybe not. Someone might come along. I've been here way too long.

He hated to give it up, though.

Judy had struggled in the beginning, but her resistance had caved in almost right away once he'd shoved into her for the first time. It was as if her only reason for fighting had been to keep him out of her body. After that, she'd cried a lot. Then, the crying had stopped. She'd let Stanley do whatever he wanted, and she'd followed orders.

Which had seemed great for a while.

He'd studied her all over, explored her, delved into her, caressed and squeezed her, kissed and licked and sucked her everywhere, commanded her to suck on him.

Absolutely great.

For a while.

After a while, however, Stanley began to feel cheated. Betrayed. Judy was letting him do whatever he wanted and she was doing everything he asked of her, but without *feeling*. As if her mind and spirit had taken a hike.

So long, Stan. Have a merry old time with the bod. We'll come back when you're done.

Thelma used to do that. Flop on the bed and gaze at the ceiling. As if he wasn't there at all. After a year of that, he'd quit bothering.

It made him feel a little sick inside to remember how it had been with Thelma.

And now Judy was pulling the same stunt.

Denying my existence.

'Fucking bitch!'

He rammed his cock up Judy, slamming his pelvis against her so hard that he jolted her whole body. Her breasts jerked and wobbled. Her teeth clashed together. But she stayed limp and kept her empty gaze on the ceiling.

'I'm here,' Stanley said. 'Hey!'

No response.

'Hey! Judy! Damn it!'

Nothing.

So then he pulled out of her. He slid down her body. She was slick and sticky. He scooted backward until his knees reached the edge of the bed. Then he slipped his arms underneath Judy's wide open legs and clutched the tops of her thighs.

He pressed his mouth against her.

He licked and probed.

His tongue got no reaction.

But his teeth did.

Judy shrieked and bucked.

Yes!

Stanley raised his face. He looked up from between her legs. She was all shiny and flushed, her belly pulsing as she gasped, her breasts shaking, her arms up, hands clenching the sides of the pillow under her head, her face crimson, her lips peeled back in agony, tears rolling down from the corners of her tightly shut eyes.

What a sight!

What a beautiful sight!

'Did you like that?' Stanley asked.

'No!' she cried out.

'Do you want more?'

'No! Please!'

'Who am I?'

'Please! Don't . . .!'

'Who am I?'

'Stan! Stanley!'

'Stanley who?'

'Banks! Stanley Banks!'

'Very good.' He kissed her. Not a bite, a kiss, but she flinched anyway as if scalded. 'Where am I, Judy?'

'Huh?'

'*Where?*'

'I don't . . . What do you want me to say?'

'Am I in outer space?'

'No!'

'Where *am* I?'

'In . . . in Los Angeles?'

'Yesss. But *where?*'

'On Marlene Street?'

'More.'

'What?'

'*Where?*'

'In my house!' she blurted. 'In my bedroom! In my bed!'

'*Where?*'

'Here! Right here!'

'Right! And you made a really big mistake when you decided to pretend like I wasn't.'

'I'm sorry.'

'Why?'

'Why what?'

'Why sorry?'

'Because . . .'

'Because you hurt my feelings?' Stanley asked.

'Yes! I didn't mean to. Honest.'

'Bull-fucking-shit.'

'I'm *sorry.*'

'Do you wanta know why? There's only one reason you're sorry, and that's because I'm in charge now. You can't make me go away. You can't make me stop. And you can't ignore me. You bitches think you own the fucking world. But you don't own me. Not today. Not here. It's *my* turn to be the boss.'

In a quiet and trembling voice, Judy said, 'I never did anything to you. I've always been nice to you.'

'Yeah. And I'm sure you're always nice to dogs, too.'

He made her scream again.

Fourteen

'You're not quitting?' Mrs Klein asked, alarm in her voice.

'Just taking a breather,' Barbara said as she climbed backward down the slope of rubble.

'A brief rest,' Mrs Klein said.

'Yeah.' Feet on the flat, safe surface of the alley, Barbara stood up straight. She stretched, arching her spine, twisting, thrusting her shoulders back. Then she bent over and held on to her knees and panted for air. Sweat dripped off her face. Her blouse was so wet that it hugged her back. A couple of the top buttons had come undone, so the front drooped open to her belly and let air in. Her bra felt sodden. Her panties were glued to her rump.

'Such wonderful young people you are,' Mrs Klein said.

'Glad to help,' Barbara muttered.

They'd hardly gotten away from the body of the kid who'd snatched Barbara's purse before they'd been waylaid by Mrs Klein. Actually, Barbara supposed they'd gone two blocks. Maybe three.

The woman had come stumbling out of the alley just in front of them, weeping, frantically flinging her head from side to side, then spotting them and calling out, 'Help me! Please! Help me!'

'Quick!' Heather had whispered. 'Let's get out of here!'

'Not me,' Pete had said. 'Sorry. I mean, look at her.'

About fifty years old, fashionably dressed, she looked like a woman who might've just been mugged on her way to a luncheon in Beverly Hills. Her brown hair was mussed, her face streaked with mascara as if she'd wept blue tears, her ivory silk blouse filthy and untucked, her stockings snagged and split with runs, her knees bloody beneath the hem of her skirt, her shoes missing.

'Are you okay, ma'am?' Pete had asked as she hobbled toward them.

'Am I okay? Is my outfit a ruin? Is my heart broken? Help me! Help me save my baby!' Without waiting for an answer, she'd dragged Pete into the alley. As Barbara and Heather had hurried after them, she'd gasped out, 'How could this *happen* to me? My poor Susie! I only left her for two minutes. Two minutes, not a second longer. I'd forgot my checkbook in the house. My checkbook! A checkbook I don't need. Do I have credit cards? Who doesn't? But off I go for a checkbook I don't need, and all God's hell breaks loose, do you know what I mean? The house? A shambles, but up it stays. The garage, down it goes like a bad stock. On top of my baby! My poor baby! You'll save her?'

'We'll do whatever we can,' Pete had assured her.

'Is she in the car?' Barbara had asked.

'Yes, yes. Such a fool I was to leave her alone. But only for two minutes? What can happen in only two minutes? An earthquake, for instance! The end of the world? Who knows! For two minutes I leave her alone. If I'd *known*! But we don't know these things! These things are rocks thrown at us – we're not paid to duck, if you know what I mean.'

Barbara had no idea what she meant. That didn't matter, though. It only mattered that her daughter was trapped. More likely her granddaughter, considering the gal's age – though Barbara supposed Mrs Klein might be the child's actual mother.

When they came to the ruin, Heather realized that more than a simple garage had fallen. 'Was it two stories?' she asked.

'An apartment up above. But it was vacant, thank God.'

'Your car's buried under all of *that*?' Heather asked.

'It's not so much. You should've seen it before. A mountain, that's what it was. Me, I've whittled it down. But I . . .' Shaking her head, she raised her hands. They were shredded and bloody.

'It's okay,' Barbara had said. 'We'll get her out.'

With Mrs Klein watching from the alley, Barbara and Pete and Heather had climbed the rubble and gotten to work. They'd made good progress for a while. Then Pete had gashed his forearm on the point of a nail. The wound not only took him out of commission while Mrs Klein hustled him into her house for first aid, but put a stop to Heather's half-hearted labors.

Crouching on the slope, Heather had watched the woman lead Pete away. Just when they were about to enter the back door of the house, she'd called, 'Wait! I'm coming, too!' and started to hurry down.

'You don't have to go with them.'

'I do, too. Anyway, I'm thirsty.'

'How do you think her *kid* feels?'

'She's probably dead.'

'Maybe not. The car could've protected her.'

'Yeah, sure. This is a big waste of time. I'm only helping 'cause Pete wants to. Anyway, I'm taking a break.' Then she'd hurried on to the house.

A while later, Mrs Klein had come back alone. Not only had she returned to the alley without Pete and Heather, but without a soda or even so much as a glass of water for Barbara.

That's when Barbara had decided it was time for a breather.

'Such wonderful young people you are.'

'Glad to help.'

Barbara raised her arms, one at a time, to wipe her face on the short sleeves of her blouse. 'What happened to Pete and Heather?'

'They'll be along. The poor girl overheated herself.'

'I'm pretty hot, myself.'

She suddenly seemed to *see* Barbara. 'Why, you're soaking wet.'

'I could sure use a drink.'

'A *drink*? You look ready to collapse, you poor thing.'

'No, I'm not that . . .'

'You shouldn't be standing out here, you'll drop dead from heat prostration. Into the house with you, right this minute. Find yourself a drink in the fridge.' She patted Barbara's arm. 'Sit, rest, cool off. I won't have you dropping dead from the heat. Come out when you're ready. You and your friends. But don't take too long. My Susie . . .'

With that, Mrs Klein staggered to the pile of debris, leaned forward, and picked up a chunk of stucco.

'I'll just get a drink and come right back,' Barbara told her.

'Cool off,' Mrs Klein said without stopping her work. 'A few minutes you should take to cool off.'

'Sure,' Barbara said, though she had no intention of relaxing inside the house. Maybe after they'd found Susie.

A narrow walkway led from the side of the demolished garage, through a neatly trimmed back yard to the patio of Mrs Klein's single-level, stucco house. The outside of the house looked undamaged.

A faded awning shaded the patio. Barbara let out a sigh as she stepped beneath it.

So great to get out of the sun.

On her way to the back door, she lifted the front of her blouse and wiped the sweat off her face. Then she fastened the buttons.

She pulled open the door and entered the kitchen.

Most of the cupboards were open, their contents thrown out and scattered on the counters and floor.

No sign of Pete or Heather.

'Hey, you guys,' Barbara called.

'In here,' Pete called to her. He sounded as if he were a room or two away.

'Be right there. What're you drinking?'

'She's got Pepsis in the fridge.'

The refrigerator was still standing, but looked as if it had been dragged toward the middle of the kitchen. Barbara headed for it. She stepped over a small pile of broken plates, kicked a can of Campbell's tomato soup out of the way, and tugged open the refrigerator door.

No light came on. But the kitchen was bright, so she had no trouble finding several cans of soft drinks lined up inside a rack on the inner side of the door.

She lifted one of them out. It felt fairly cold. But cool slime suddenly slipped onto her hand. She gasped, 'Uck!' and kneed the door shut.

'You okay?' Pete called.

'I think so.' Barbara looked at the top of the can. It was coated with a clear, mucous substance. Floating on the ooze, and embedded in it, were bits of broken eggshell.

'You oughta get in here,' Pete said. 'We wanta show you something.'

'Just wait'll you see *this*,' Heather added.

'I'll be right there.'

Barbara spotted a roll of paper towels beside the sink.

She made her way toward it.

She wondered if her kitchen at home looked this way: everything shaken off shelves, hurled out of cupboards – broken jars and bottles and cans and boxes and plates and glasses and mugs all over the floor – a strange jumbled mixture of containers, spilled ingredients, and utensils: as if a mindless dolt had hurled everything onto the kitchen floor in the hope of creating a surprise feast.

What a mess!

Maybe Mom'll have it cleaned up by the time . . .

Please, Mom, be okay . . . And Dad.

At the counter, she tore off a handful of paper towel and cleaned the top of her Pepsi can. Then she sidestepped to the sink, held the can underneath the spout, and twisted the cold water faucet handle.

No water came out.

Of course not.

No water, she thought, and here we are drinking up this woman's sodas.

Barbara raised the can to her face. She sniffed.

A lingering odor of raw egg.

She took the unopened can back to the refrigerator, opened the door, and set it into the rack.

She noticed there were five or six other cans.

It won't kill her if I drink one, she thought.

Ah, the can stinks anyway.

The egg couldn't have gotten them all.

But she left them all there, anyway, and shut the door.

At the end of a short, dim hallway, she found the living room. Pete and Heather were sitting on a sofa beneath a crooked watercolor of a Paris street in the rain. They looked dirty and sweaty. They each held a can of Pepsi.

'You didn't get yourself a drink?' Pete asked.

'Nah. I don't feel like one. Too sweet.'

'You need to get some liquid in you. You don't want to get dehydrated.'

'I don't know.' Barbara shrugged with one shoulder, and felt her top button slip out of its hole. Ever since the kid had grabbed her purse and tugged her blouse open, her buttons hadn't worked the way they should. Pete and Heather didn't seem to notice the problem, so she left the button alone.

On her way to the sofa, she looked around. Mrs Klein's living room had fared better than her kitchen. Except for a table lamp that lay on the floor with one side of its shade mashed in, there didn't seem to be any real damage.

'I bet you didn't find Susie,' Heather said.

'Not yet.' Barbara sat down beside Pete. 'How's the arm?'

He held it up, showing off the neatly taped patch of gauze on the underside of his forearm. 'Not bad. Doesn't even hurt. Mrs Klein, though, she said how I'd better check with my parents and make sure my tetanus shots and things are up to date.'

'Will you need any stitches?'

'Nah, it's mostly just a scratch.'

'Good thing.' She leaned back, and sighed at the wonderful feel of the soft cushion. She hadn't realized how sore she was: how much her neck and back and rump and legs ached.

I'll just stay here forever, she thought.

But suddenly realized that her sweaty hair and back might stain the upholstery.

So she sat up straight, and groaned.

'Why don't you take a drink of mine?' Pete asked. He held his can toward her.

'Well . . .'

'Go ahead. I'm done, anyway.'

'Well . . . Okay. Thanks.' She accepted the can. It felt half full.

'You'll never guess what we found out,' Heather said.

Barbara took a few swallows. The soda *did* taste too sweet. It's not too sweet, she thought. It's just not cold enough. Medium cool just doesn't do it when you're drinking colas.

Better than nothing, though.

She stopped herself from drinking more, and held the can out to Pete. 'Here, you finish it.'

'No, you go ahead.'

'I have to get back outside and help Mrs Klein.'

'I don't think there's a big hurry about that,' he said.

'What do you mean?'

'Get a load of this,' Heather said. Leaning forward, she stretched her arm past Pete. Her hand stopped above Barbara's left knee. It was holding a small tin of Whiskas cat food.

'What?' Barbara asked.

'Three guesses,' Heather said.

'We looked around,' Pete said. 'There's only one bedroom, and . . . no sign that Mrs Klein has any children.'

Heather, still leaning forward, gave Barbara a smug grin. 'Get it? Her Susie eats Whiskas.'

'Susie is her cat,' Pete explained, and shook his head.

'You're kidding,' Barbara muttered. 'Are you sure?'

'There's a plastic bowl on the kitchen floor,' Pete said. 'It has Susie's name on it.'

'Really?'

'And milk *in* it,' Heather added. 'Most of the milk's on the floor, but there's still *some* in the bowl. Susie's bowl.'

Barbara shook her head slowly from side to side. 'I don't believe this,' she muttered. 'Susie is her cat? We've been busting our butts out there, *cooking* in that sun, wasting God only knows how much time when we could've been on our way home to rescue that woman's *pussycat*?'

'It sort of looks that way,' Pete said.

'Terrific.'

Heather grinned. 'Cute, huh? I knew we shouldn't stop and help her.'

'We didn't know it was just a cat,' Pete said.

'She didn't exactly say it *wasn't*,' Barbara pointed out. 'She called it her baby, but a lot of people do that sort of thing.'

'She *wanted* us to think it's a person,' Heather said. 'She just figured we wouldn't help if we knew it was only a cat.'

'She would've been right,' Pete said.

Barbara shook her head. 'I mean, there are probably people trapped under buildings. If I'm gonna bust my butt trying to dig somebody out, I'm gonna do it for a human being.'

'I'd do it for my own dog,' Pete said. 'If I had one.'

'I'd do it for my cat, Mickey,' Heather said. 'Except that my father pounded his brains out with a claw hammer one time.'

'You're kidding,' Pete said.

'Huh-uh.'

'Why'd he wanta do that?'

Here we go again, Barbara thought. Another story of sickness and blight from Lady Cheerful.

'Mickey got into the Thanksgiving turkey.'

'Oh, man,' Pete muttered.

'It was right out of the oven and we were waiting for it to cool, and watching a rerun of the *Rose Parade* on the TV. Mom went in the kitchen to mash the potatoes, and she yelled – this was before she killed herself.'

Never would've guessed, Barbara thought.

'So then Dad went in, and he went totally ape. First off, he punched out Mom for leaving the turkey out where the cat could get to it.'

'Where'd she leave it?'

'On the kitchen counter.'

'Where was she supposed to . . .?'

'Nowhere. That wasn't the thing. Hell, *Dad's* the one who put it on the counter, anyhow. But that didn't matter. Mom was the one who got smacked for it.'

No wonder she killed herself, Barbara thought. Married to a guy like that . . . and with a daughter like Heather.

'Then he grabbed up Mickey by the tail and hauled him outside. I went running out after him, 'cause I knew he meant to kill him. But then he slugged me.'

A mad, gleeful look appeared on Heather's face.

No tears, this time.

Maybe because this one isn't about her mother, Barbara thought. And maybe she hadn't liked Mickey all that much in the first place.

'He slugged me in the stomach. He never hits me in the face, 'cause it'd show. But anyhow, he knocked my wind out and I was down on my back in the driveway, laying there and trying to catch my breath, when he came back from the garage. He'd gone there to get his claw hammer. So then he dangled Mickey right over my face and starting swinging at him with the hammer. It took him . . . oh, a long time. He kept missing. That's because of how Mickey was squirming around and everything. He didn't miss all the time, though. He'd wham Mickey in the back, and in the jaw . . . blood was flying, pouring down on me, getting in my face . . . but then finally he caught him a good one right on top of the head, and . . .'

'Could you knock it off?' Barbara said. 'You're making me sick.'

'Can't take it, huh? I bet *you* never had to take anything like that, did you?'

'My parents aren't a couple of lunatics,' she said.

Pete seemed to cringe.

Barbara stood up. Heather's grin looked crooked and

frozen. 'I'm sorry your mother's dead,' Barbara told her. 'I'm sorry your father's a crazy vicious madman. I'm sorry he killed your cat. I just don't wanta hear about it, okay?' To Pete, she said, 'I'm going back outside.'

'Me, too.' Pete crushed his Pepsi can. Leaning forward to set it on the table, he turned to Heather. 'You ready?'

'I guess so.'

They both stood up at the same time.

Heather took hold of Pete's hand. Her other hand, Barbara noticed, was out of sight behind her back.

'What've you got?'

'None of your business.'

'You're right,' Barbara said. And up yours, she thought.

On her way to the rear of the house, she looked back once. Heather's left hand was still behind her, and her right was still holding Pete's hand.

How can he stand her?

He can't. He's just being kind to her because she's such a loser.

After the cool shade inside the house, the sunlight was blinding, the air heavy with heat. Barbara squinted and lowered her head as she made her way across the back yard.

She wished she could've stayed inside.

Things seemed worse, now, out here.

She supposed that nothing had actually changed very much. Spending time in the house – though probably no more than ten minutes – she'd simply forgotten how bad all this was: the heat, the glare of the sun, the sour odor of smoke in the air, the sounds of sirens, amplified voices, shouts, screams, car alarms, and occasional bangs that were obviously gunshots.

'What I wouldn't give,' Pete said, 'for some air conditioning.'

Barbara glanced back at him. 'An air-conditioned movie theater.'

'Yeah. With a big old Pepsi full of chopped ice.'

'And an Eastwood movie on the screen.'

'You said it!'

'How about an ice-cold shower?' Heather asked. She bumped softly against Pete's side. 'With you and me in it.'

A grin spread across Pete's dirty face. 'Well, now.'

'Charming,' Barbara said, and turned away. She was already sweaty again. And her eyes burned. Lifting the front of her blouse, she wiped her face.

'Maybe somebody around here has a swimming pool,' Pete said.

'I wouldn't count on it,' Barbara said, not looking back.

She stopped and gazed at the piled jumble of the demolished garage.

'Mrs Klein?' she called.

No answer.

'Where is she?' Pete asked.

'Maybe around the other side,' Barbara said. Then she shouted, 'Hello! Mrs Klein! We're back!'

Still no answer.

'Well,' Barbara said, 'it's kind of noisy around here.'

'She should've heard that.'

'Oh,' Heather said, 'I sure hope nothing happened to her. Wouldn't that be such a shame?'

'Hey, cut it out,' Pete said.

'Don't give me that. You *like* the idea that she had us digging through this crap for her *cat*?'

'Not exactly.'

Barbara began to make her away around the fallen garage, eyes down, carefully watching each footstep to avoid stumbling or gouging herself on debris. She planned to keep going, and not check the pile again until she had reached its opposite side.

But Pete said, 'Oh, Jeez.'

Barbara stopped fast and snapped her head sideways.

And saw a pair of legs.

Like the legs of a clothes store mannequin that had been jammed headfirst into the side of the pile of rubble, jammed in so deep that only the legs stuck out.

It is a mannequin! Barbara thought.

Oh, Jesus, no it's not.

A mannequin wouldn't have bloody feet. Or torn stockings. Or varicose veins or cuts or scratches on its calves and thighs.

'Mrs Klein?'

Somebody'd stuffed her into the . . .

No, maybe not. Maybe she'd worked her way to the car and tried to squeeze her way in through one of the windows to reach Susie.

And gotten trapped.

And suffocated?

Suddenly feeling breathless and sick, Barbara rushed toward the protruding legs.

'Careful!' Pete shouted.

She didn't need to go far. She didn't need to climb at all. After staggering over a few scattered roof tiles and splintered boards, she grabbed the ankles.

'Mrs Klein!' she yelled. 'Can you hear me? Are you all right?'

Nothing.

'Dead?' Heather asked.

Barbara glanced back. Heather had forgotten to keep her left hand out of sight. It hung by her side. It was clinging to the can of Whiskas.

Apparently, she'd intended to confront Mrs Klein with the evidence of her treachery.

Pete was on his way.

'Here,' he said. He rubbed against Barbara's side, forced his way through more debris, and wrapped his arms around Mrs Klein's thighs. 'Okay,' he said. 'Let's try and ease her out. Gently.'

'Yeah.'

They both began to pull.

Mrs Klein came out slowly. When her rump was clear, Pete said, 'Wait.' He reached out and grabbed the hem of her skirt and pulled until the backs of her thighs were covered. 'Okay,' he said.

They resumed pulling, inching her out of her burrow in the side of the mound.

'Is she dead?' Heather asked.

'I don't know,' Pete called.

'Let's not worry about it till we've got her out,' Barbara said.

Above the waist of her skirt, the woman's back was bare. Barbara saw fresh, raw scratches on her skin. From crawling into the rubble? Or from being dragged out feet-first?

'Almost got her,' Pete said.

They pulled some more, and met resistance.

'Hold it. Let's not force her.'

They stopped pulling. She was bare halfway up her back.

'Something's stuck.'

'Her boobs are in the way,' Heather said.

'Try lifting,' Barbara suggested. 'Raise her as much as you can, and I'll pull.'

Hugging her around the belly, he pulled her upward. Barbara tugged her ankles and she suddenly came out so fast they both staggered, gasping with alarm and fighting to keep their feet.

As Barbara tried to stay up in a moment that seemed to stretch on and on forever, she glimpsed the broad, black cross-strap of Mrs Klein's bra . . .

. . . vertical straps that disappear under the ivory fabric of her rucked-up blouse . . .

. . . blouse rumpled high across her back, still clothing her shoulders and arms, shrouding the back of her head . . .

. . . speckled and splashed with shiny blood . . .

. . . arms still stretched out like a diver . . .

. . . blouse-hidden head coming out now . . .

. . . coming out of a dark gap in the mound . . .

. . . a squawling '*rrrroowwww!*' that races a shiver through Barbara . . .

. . . a cat leaping out of the darkness, pouncing on the shrouded back of the head – a cat so drenched in blood that a glimpse of it reminds Barbara of Carrie on prom-night – and then it springs away, blood flying from its fur.

The endless moment ended when Barbara heard herself cry out. Her own '*Yahhh!*' drowned out whatever noises might've come from Pete or Heather, but she saw Pete lurch aside and stumble and drop Mrs Klein.

Feet elevated by Barbara, the woman was about to smash her face into the alley pavement. Too late to help by letting go. So she flung the ankles at each other, made them miss, crossed them and thrust, twisting the body as it fell.

The shoulder, not the face, struck the pavement. Barbara was glad.

But not for long.

Mrs Klein flopped onto her back.

Barbara glimpsed her shredded, eyeless face, her ripped throat. Whirling away, she dropped to a crouch and squeezed her eyes shut and clutched her own face with both hands.

No no no no no!

Then she felt hands on her shoulders.

'You okay?' Pete asked.

She shook her head.

'I guess that was Susie.'

'Yeah.'

'What a way to go,' Heather said. She sounded far away, and impressed. 'Good thing it wasn't one of *us* tried to crawl in and save her cat. God! Look what it did to her. Just look at that, will you?'

Fifteen

Time to get back to Sheila.

Way past time, Stanley thought.

But he had to deal with Judy first.

She was slippery underneath him. Slippery and sticky, and motionless except for her breathing.

He got to his knees, and stared down at her.

Her skin was shiny with wetness. Smeared with a little blood here and there. Rosy where Stanley had used her roughly – places where there would soon be bruises.

'What a beaut,' he muttered.

Saying that, he felt a small rush of guilt.

'But not in Sheila's league,' he added. 'Not even close.'

He pictured Sheila in the bathtub.

Gotta get back to her, get her out of there. Clean her off . . .

But something had to be done about Judy, first.

Don't wanta kill her, he thought. That wouldn't be any good. Ruin her for later, in case something goes wrong with the Sheila thing.

Nothing better go wrong!

'Gotta get,' he reminded himself.

Not without taking care of Judy, though.

'First things first.'

He climbed off the end of the bed.

Bending over, he grabbed Judy by the ankles. He backed away, dragging her until her rump slid off the mattress. She bent at the waist and sat down hard on the carpeted floor. The abrupt landing made her breasts do a quick bounce.

Stanley pulled her away from the bed. When she was flat on her back, he lowered her legs to the floor.

She was unconscious now, or appeared to be. But she was sure to come out of it, sooner or later. He needed a way to secure her so that she wouldn't be able to run off and get help.

How about pinning her down in her bathtub?

The idea made him laugh.

But right away, he realized that it was a very good idea. Sheila had sure gotten trapped in her tub. The thing was almost as good as a cage.

Crouching, he shoved his arms under Judy's body. Her head dipped toward the floor and wobbled when he lifted her. He walked quickly across the bedroom toward a door that was open no more than a crack.

He hadn't looked behind the door, so far, but he suspected that it belonged to a connecting bathroom.

As he hurried along, Judy's limp body kept slipping through his arms, her hip sliding down his belly. Twice, on the verge of dropping her, he had to pause and give her a knee in the rump and readjust his hold.

He bumped the door with her head to make it swing open. Then he turned her sideways and carried her into the bathroom and was amazed by the aroma that engulfed him.

A rich perfume.

Vanilla? Marshmallow? Cotton candy? Sweet and mouth-watering, it teased him with old memories.

He squinted his eyes.

He sucked the wonderful scent in through his nose, filling himself with it.

Something from when he was a boy . . .

Carnival midways?

That's it!

Midways he'd walked a few times with his parents. Always with his parents, and always in daylight.

But oh, how he'd longed to explore them in the night, alone, with nobody to tell him no or stop him. Midways brilliant as Christmas with colored lights, dark and secret and mysterious in the shadows. Midways where forbidden rides could kill you with their thrills, where strange men promised to show you terrible wonders hidden in tents, where all the women seemed to be gypsies full of wild magic.

He had longed to sneak in all by himself at midnight and become part of it.

But, of course, he hadn't.

Hadn't dared.

What if Mother catches me!

Stanley inhaled deeply again. He felt a smile float on his face.

I've got my own carnival now.

'Step right this way, folks. See the Amazing *Limp* Woman. She jiggles, she shimmies, she shakes.'

He shook her, and smiled.

But suddenly she reminded him of Sheila.

'Sheila the Woman of Steel, who . . .'

Gotta get back to her.

Stanley glanced around the bathroom. Except for a crack in one large mirror, it looked unharmed by the quake.

It couldn't have gotten off this easily.

Judy had obviously spent time picking up whatever had been hurled out of its medicine cabinet and cupboards – including a bottle of wonderful perfume that must've broken or spilled.

I oughta check and see what's in the wastebasket, he thought.

Later, he told himself. For now, I've gotta take care of Judy.

He scanned the bathroom.

A very *nice* bathroom.

Twin sinks, counters that looked like marble, mirrors everywhere, a shower stall with a clear glass door (exactly like the one in his fantasy of Sheila when she showered after her morning runs), and a step-down tub.

The tub looked like a miniature swimming pool.

Only not all *that* miniature.

Stanley stood above it, gazing down past the body cradled in his arms.

Gleaming, royal blue tiles.

What a great tub. So much nicer than the one at Mother's house. So much nicer than Sheila's. He wished he could fill it high, right now, with cool clear water.

Damn quake.

It's not a damn quake, he told himself. It's my *friend* the quake. Yes yes yes. I wouldn't be here except for the quake. None of this great stuff would be happening. Just too bad it had to screw up the water system.

Oh, how I'd love to take a bath in this. Judy on one side of me, Sheila on the other. We'd be all cool and soapy and slippery . . .

Judy suddenly slipped down through his arms again. He planted his knee against the moist crevice of her rump, thrust her upward, and struggled to hold on while he hurried down the tile steps.

The bottom of the tub was as flat as a floor. He crouched and laid her down on her back, feet toward the faucets. Then he climbed out.

He looked down at her.

A tub this big wouldn't be much help in confining her. He

wondered if there might be a guest bathroom with a normal tub somewhere in the house.

I'm not gonna lug her around looking for one, he thought. This'll do. Long as she's tied up good and tight.

With what?

He doubted he would find anything useful in the bathroom, so he hurried into the bedroom. He glanced from the bed to the dresser to the closet, considering what they might have to offer: bedsheets, pantyhose, scarves, neckties . . . ?

I don't wanta be tying her with rags – nothing that's gonna stretch and rip.

Belts?

In the closet, he found a good collection of leather belts hanging by their buckles from a rack on the inside of the door. They were men's belts – her husband's, he supposed. He grabbed several and hurried back to Judy.

She didn't look as if she had moved.

Stanley dragged her closer to the faucets. The two chrome handles were slightly higher than his own knees, and about twenty inches apart.

He twisted both handles. As he'd expected, no water came out.

Would've been nice, though. Could've had a nice, cold bath.

Just as well, he told himself. I've gotta get back to Sheila.

He lifted Judy's right leg up between his own legs. He pressed its ankle against the side of the cold water handle, then squeezed his legs together to hold it in place. With both hands free, he wound a belt three times around her ankle and the faucet. He pulled it tight, then buckled it.

He did the same with her other foot, binding it to the hot water faucet with a second belt.

Legs elevated and separated as they were, she was probably secure. It would require a major effort to reach the belts, and Stanley doubted that Judy had the strength.

Bet she can't, he thought.

And he imagined how much fun it would be to watch her try.

He could just see it! Fabulous struggles and contortions!

Grunting and sweating and weeping, she would fight to sit up, strain to stretch her arms to the faucets and, failing, flop back down and resort to twisting and bucking and kicking.

It'd be great!

But Stanley knew he couldn't stay and watch. He'd already stayed too long.

Can't leave her this way, though. Not for real.

To leave her arms free would be tempting fate.

When you tempt fate, you get screwed.

He remembered seeing a straight-backed chair someplace. Returning to the bedroom, he spotted it in a corner. His pajama pants were wadded on its seat cushion, where he must've tossed them at some point – though he couldn't remember when.

He flung the pants to the floor and carried the chair into the bathroom. At the bottom of the tub, he set it down on Judy. Its back legs fit nicely above her shoulders. The rungs pressed against the fronts of her shoulders like the straps of a peculiar wooden bra, and the chair's front legs touched her sides just above her hips.

Squatting above her head, Stanley picked up another belt. He held it in his teeth, lifted both her arms over the padded seat, and forced her hands toward each other. Her arms weren't long enough. He couldn't get her hands to meet. Which meant he wouldn't be able to strap her wrists together with the belt.

If I just had some handcuffs . . .

He could change his plan, he supposed. But he really liked the idea of fastening her hands together above the seat as if she were clutching the chair against her chest. She wouldn't have a *chance* of sitting up and going for the ankle restraints – not while she was hugging the chair.

But a leather belt wouldn't work.

There must be some sort of belt or tie or strap that'll do, he told himself. Something handy. Don't wanta go rooting through the whole house.

Back in the bedroom, he returned to the closet.

Maybe two or three neckties . . .

Maybe Judy has a belt made out of rope, or . . .

Nothing useful near the front, so he worked his way deeper into the closet. He couldn't see much, and felt his way along. He liked the way some of the clothes rubbed against him.

Maybe I can find a robe, he thought. A terri-cloth robe like mine at home might have a belt that'll work.

As he felt among the blouses in search of one, however, his hand collided with several empty wire hangers.

Hangers!

He snatched a few out of the darkness.

Moments later, he was again squatting at the bottom of the tub. He swung Judy's arms up, pulled them toward each other above the seat of the chair, and slipped a hanger over both her hands. Then he forced them toward the sides until their wrists were wedged between the narrowing wires.

'Beautiful,' he muttered.

He collapsed the middle of the hanger, trapping Judy's wrists at each end, then bent and twisted the wires to make his trap secure.

Got her now, he thought. She'll never get out of this.

He tossed the unused belts and hangers out of the tub. On his knees, he smiled down at Judy. Her face was upside-down. It looked strange that way; her mouth was where her forehead ought to be, her eyebrows *under* her eyes. For the first time, Stanley noticed that she had a few freckles on her eyelids.

'Yoo-whooo,' he said. 'You still out?'

She didn't react.

'I'm going away for a little while. You gonna miss me? Huh? Anyway, I'll be back, so don't worry. Just stay here and relax.'

With his left arm for a brace, he eased down and kissed Judy's mouth. Her lips felt dry and scratchy, so he licked them. That seemed to soften them up some. He went on kissing her. While he did that, he reached his right arm around and under the chair and fondled her right breast. It was slippery and sticky, but he enjoyed squeezing it. He tried for the left breast. He couldn't get to it, though, so he stayed with the right.

551

He had his tongue deep in her mouth.

He was hard again.

He wondered what it might be like to fuck her the way she was tied like this to the faucets and chair.

'It'd be fuckin' impossible,' he muttered, and laughed.

He gave her nipple a final pinch, pulled his tongue out of her mouth, and struggled to his feet. He climbed out of the tub.

By the side of the wastebasket, he crouched. He sniffed.

Cotton candy.

But a perfume, really.

At the bottom of the plastic recepticle were wads of pink facial tissue, loose pills, pieces of broken bottles, a tooth brush.

Stanley scooped out a handful of the tissues. They were still moist. He lifted them to his nose. He gave them a small, careful sniff.

Yes!

He inhaled deeply, then rubbed his face with the tissues, smearing himself with the wonderful aroma.

When he was finished, he put the tissues back inside the wastebasket for safe keeping and headed for the bathroom door.

He stopped and glanced one more time at Judy.

She looked like the victim of an exotic, failed contraption.

'I shall return,' Stanley said, and left the bathroom.

He pulled the door shut, crossed the room and stepped into his moccasins. They felt mushy and slick under his feet, as if they'd been lathered inside with lard. Barefoot was better, but he had to wear *something* on his feet when he went outdoors.

He found his pajama pants, stepped into them and pulled them up. They stuck to him. They seemed to trap the heat against his skin.

He supposed he could probably find a pair of shorts to wear, instead. Something of Herb's.

But then Sheila's gonna know I found clothes.

'Can't have that,' he said.

He liked the idea of shorts, though.

So he went into Judy's kitchen to hunt for something sharp. He'd been through the kitchen when he carried Judy into the house, but he hadn't noticed much about it. Now, he realized that it seemed untouched by the quake.

Maybe Judy had already picked up all the things that had fallen. Sure, she had. Must've started scurrying around and cleaning house the second the quake stopped – even before rushing out to check on the neighbors.

Busy girl, Stanley thought.

Or maybe the kitchen had simply gotten off easy, the way some places do for mysterious earthquake reasons.

He started looking in the drawers for a sharp knife. But he found a pair of scissors, first. He took off his pajama pants, snipped off both the frail legs, and put the pants back on.

Much, much better!

He started to set down the scissors, then changed his mind. They might come in handy, later on.

What else? he wondered. There's a whole house full of stuff here, and it's all mine.

Food? Probably plenty of good stuff in the fridge.

He wasn't hungry yet. Besides, he could come back whenever the urge might strike him. Sheila shouldn't be needing food yet, either.

We'll have a little party after I get her out. Maybe even come over here. Yeah, bring her here.

Judy and Herb were drinkers, he knew that. He'd seen their empty bottles in the recycling bin that they put out to the curb once a week for trash day.

I'll offer Sheila a nice, tall vodka and tonic. We'll sip cocktails together on the sofa.

He pictured Sheila sprawled on the sofa, naked, smiling, sipping her drink, beads of icy condensation falling off the bottom of the glass and splashing her breasts, sliding down them, dripping off her nipples.

He groaned.

He wandered through the kitchen, checking cupboards. The cupboard doors had either stayed shut during the quake – which hardly seemed likely – or Judy had gone around and closed them afterward. She *must've* done some tidying of the kitchen: it couldn't have gotten off this lightly.

After tugging open the doors of several cupboards, he found the liquor supply.

'This'll be great,' he said. He shut the cupboard. 'Great.'

He hurried to the refrigerator. Planning to check for ice, he reached toward the handle of the freezer compartment.

No no no no no! Don't open it, you'll let out all the cold.

The voice inside his head sounded a lot like his mother, the Bitch. He grinned.

'Just can't get rid of you, can I?'

No no no no no.

In this case, however, he appreciated the warning. Judy and Herb were certain to have plenty of ice in their freezer, so there was no reason to look. The only question was how long the ice might last with the power down. It would last a lot longer if the door stayed shut.

Stanley turned away from the refrigerator.

'Okay,' he said. 'Anything else?'

Bet Sheila could use some sun block.

He laughed.

Then, with the scissors in his hand, he stepped outside. The sunlight made him squint, but he liked how it felt on his body. He took a deep breath. He smelled smoke, but he also detected a fresh scent of the ocean air, and the sweet candy aroma of Judy's perfume.

In the driveway, he bent down and picked up the saw and the plastic jug of water. The jug was dripping. It left a wet place that looked brown on the gray concrete.

With the saw and scissors in one hand, the jug in the other, he made his way down Judy's driveway. As he walked, he rubbed the jug against his chest. Its wet plastic was slightly cool. Too bad it wasn't ice cold, the way it had been when Judy brought it out.

That was a long time ago, Stanley told himself. I'm lucky the water isn't hot enough to boil eggs by now.

He crossed Judy's front yard. On his own driveway, he stopped and looked at the door of his mother's house.

My house.

He wondered if anything needed to be done inside.

Go in and give the Bitch a kick for good measure. One to grow on.

Laughing and shaking his head, he walked up his driveway. The garage in front of him was a collapsed ruin.

At least I've still got half a house, he told himself.

Too bad I can't change houses with Judy, he thought. Hardly fair, hers getting off with nothing more than a few broken mirrors and windows while mine is half destroyed.

I *can* change houses with her, he realized. At least for the time being. Who's gonna stop me?

When he came to the cinderblock wall at the back of his yard, he turned sideways and raised his arms and started to ease himself in between two of the rose bushes. A nettle snagged his shorts. He stopped.

He glanced at the saw in his hand.

'Ho! No time like the present!'

Backing clear, he set down his scissors and jug of water in the grass. Then he knelt in front of a rose bush. Bracing himself up with his left arm, just as he'd done in the bathtub to kiss and fondle Judy, he reached low with his right hand and pressed the teeth of his saw against the base of the stalk, no more than two inches above the garden's soil. The bush shook as he worked the saw back and forth. The teeth bit a deep slot into the stalk.

Sweat got into Stanley's eyes, making them burn. It dripped off his chin and the tip of his nose. It tickled him as it spilled down his body.

But soon, the bush keeled over sideways against its neighbor.

Stanley cut down that bush, too.

Then another.

He used the blade of his saw to drag and shove the three rose bushes out of his way. Then, breathless from the labor, he sat on the grass. He unscrewed the lid of the jug and took a swallow of water.

The grass felt prickly through the seat of his shorts.

He stood up, and rubbed his rump. With a slick bare forearm, he tried to wipe the sweat off his face. He wished he'd gotten himself a rag before leaving Judy's house: just something he could use for his sweat. His pajama legs would've been fine, but he'd left them in Judy's kitchen.

So he pulled down his shorts and stepped out of them. He wadded them and mopped his face and hair. The cloth felt sodden after that. He twisted his shorts into a tight stub and managed to wring out some of the wetness. Then he shook them open. He wiped his face once more.

He wished he didn't have to put the shorts back on. But Sheila might start screaming, or something, if he reappeared naked. Then he would need to hurt her, and he didn't want to do that until he had her someplace private – in Judy's house, maybe.

Gotta keep her thinking I only wanta rescue her, he told himself.

So he stepped into the shorts and pulled them up. They clung to him, but the elastic waistband seemed limper than before. He popped open the front, drew the slack out of the band, and resnapped so they didn't feel quite so loose.

Then he picked up his jug, scissors and saw. He carried them across the newly cleared strip of ground, and set them on top of the cinderblock wall. After that, he stepped to the side so they wouldn't be in his way when he climbed over.

He placed his hands on top of the wall and jumped. Braced high on stiff arms, the edge of the wall pressing against his waist, he got ready to swing a leg up.

But straight ahead, beyond the lawn and patio, a man was standing in the ruin of Sheila's house.

Stanley felt as if an octopus had suddenly wrapped its tentacles around his bowels and started to squeeze.

He groaned.

This is exactly what he'd been afraid of – someone else discovering her.

'I knew it,' he muttered. 'I knew it, I knew it.'

Shouldn't have stayed so long with Judy, he thought.

And then he swung himself over the top. He dropped to

the other side, stumbled, fell to his knees, then got to his feet and returned to the wall. Reaching up, he took down his jug of water, his scissors and his saw.

He headed for Sheila's place.

Sixteen

'Hey, all right, a *saw*, cool. Thata way to go.' The stranger hopped down from a pile of rubble and landed on a clear area of the patio.

He didn't look much older than twenty. His blond hair was almost white. Parted in the middle, it hung straight down past his bony shoulders. He didn't have a shirt on. His tan was so deep that Stanley suspected his pale hair might be a dye job. He was very skinny. Stanley could see his ribs. He wore faded old blue jeans. There was no belt, and the jeans hung low on his hips. He wore cowboy boots with pointed toes.

'You're Stan,' he said, head bobbing.

'That's me,' Stanley said, and smiled.

'Cool. We been waiting for you, me and Sheila.'

'Who are you?' He tried to sound friendly. It was easy; he'd been making himself sound friendly to people all his life, especially to those he feared or despised.

'I'm Ben.'

'Good to meet you, Ben. How's she doing?'

The young man bobbed his head some more. 'Good, good. Just scared, you know? Being stuck that way. She thought maybe you'd got hurt, or something, the way you didn't come back.'

'I had a delay. How long have you been here?'

'Aah. Five or ten minutes. I been going house to house,

you know, looking to see if anyone's needing help. She's my first trapped one. Now we got that saw, we'll have her outa there real fast.'

'Yep,' Stanley said. 'Let's go.'

Ben led the way. As he trudged into the debris of the collapsed house, he looked back at Stanley. 'Watch your feet. Stuff'll poke right up through them moccasins. What you need is a good pair of sturdy boots, like me.'

'Nice boots,' Stanley told him.

'Yeah, thanks.' Ben smirked. 'Where the hell's the rest of your clothes, anyhow?'

It wasn't much fun being almost naked with a *guy* around.

Embarrassed, Stanley managed a small laugh. 'What am I supposed to be wearing? The quake caught me in my p.j. pants.' As he said that, he wondered if Ben had stumbled across the shirt of his pajamas. He'd taken it off and thrown it down in the mess before starting to clear the debris covering Sheila. The shirt would make a liar out of him.

So what if he found it. What's he gonna do, report me?

'Then my house fell down around my ears,' Stanley added. 'I'm just glad I don't sleep in the buff.'

'Whatever,' Ben said. 'You can run around buck naked, for all I care.'

Asshole, Stanley thought.

Ben resumed picking his way through the rubble. Stanley followed. He kept his gaze down and stepped carefully.

They circled around the high mound that Stanley had climbed that morning when searching for Sheila. As they passed in front of it, she called out.

'Ben? Is that you?'

Her voice saying Ben's name gave Stanley a sick feeling. Jealousy?

No need to be jealous, he told himself. No need at all. Ben doesn't count. She's mine. I found her first, and I'm the guy with the saw.

The saw and the scissors.

'Guess who's here,' Ben called. Before she had a chance to answer, he said, 'Your old friend Stan.'

'Hey, Stan!' The greeting sounded almost cheerful. It soothed his sick feeling.

'Hi, Sheila. I'm back, and I've got a saw.'

'Great! Terrific!'

'Sorry it took so long. Had some trouble.'

Ben was first to reach the edge of the opening. Stanley moved in close to his side. Bending over, he gazed down at Sheila.

She was still sprawled inside her tub, pinned down by the four-by-eight support beams: one across the head of the tub and the other jammed down between her legs.

She looked exactly the same as Stanley remembered her.

Except for one detail.

From her breasts to her groin, she was draped with a faded green T-shirt.

Ben's shirt, no doubt.

The bastard!

'You okay, Stan?' she asked, frowning up at him.

'I'm fine,' he said. 'I guess.'

'You're sure a sight for sore eyes,' she told him.

You, too, he thought. What a wonderful sight. The most incredibly gorgeous, sexy woman in the world. But why did this bastard have to cover you up?

'I'd about given up on you,' she told him.

'Like I said, I had some trouble. I tried to get back sooner, but . . . How've you been doing?'

'Could be worse. It's not too comfortable down here. But mostly I was just scared. Not knowing, you know . . . And I'm not exactly used to being helpless.'

'You won't be down there much longer,' he said. He placed the scissors on a slat of broken board near the edge, then held out the saw so she could see it.

A smile spread over her face. 'My hero.'

'Brought you this, too.' With his other hand, he lifted the jug of water.

'Yes!'

'Do you think you'll be able to drink, lying down like that?'

'I'll sure give it a try.' She raised her arms toward Stan. Her hands waited, spread apart, fingers open. Below them, her chest was hidden beneath green fabric.

Stanley stretched his arm out above her and lowered the jug.

It remained well above Sheila's reach.

'I'll climb down,' he told her.

'I can catch it. Just let it go.'

'Drop it?'

'Sure.'

'Okay. Ready?'

'Bombs away,' she said.

Stanley let go of the jug, but gave it a slight push with his fingertips as he released it. The jug started to tumble. He gasped, 'Damn!'

Sheila almost caught it.

But she bobbled it, knocking it farther off course, and it fell between her hands. It landed on her belly with an impact that sloshed the water inside the jug and disrupted her carefully spread T-shirt.

As the jug slid, she grabbed it.

'Are you okay?' Stanley asked, trying to sound concerned. He realized, now, that she had tucked the T-shirt between her legs. That part of it remained in place. The rest of the shirt was now a rumpled heap beneath her breasts.

Oh yes, oh yes!

'I should've had it,' she said.

She picked up the jug with one hand. With the other, she pulled gently at the T-shirt and rearranged it to cover herself.

'I sort of lost my hold,' Stanley explained.

'No problem. It didn't hurt.' Holding the jug above her chest, she twisted off its cap. Then she sat up as much as possible, stopping when her forehead met the underside of the heavy beam. She tilted the round opening to her mouth. Some water slopped out and ran down her chin and neck. But then she had the opening tight to her lips, and she drank.

After a few swallows, she eased the jug away. 'Great stuff, water.'

'Why don't you hang on to that,' Stanley said. 'Ben and I have to leave you for a while.'

'What?' Ben blurted.

Stanley nodded, turned his head, and grimaced at the young man. 'I'm gonna need your help.'

'I'm not going anywhere. Not till we've got Sheila outa there.'

'I'm with Ben,' Sheila said. 'You're kidding about leaving, aren't you?'

'I wish I was. There's this girl I found. She can't be more than about four years old. I ran into her when I was looking for the saw, and I tried to get her out. That's what took me so long. She's trapped under part of a fireplace chimney that fell. I could just barely lift the thing. But I needed both hands for that, so there wasn't any way to drag her out from under. I need somebody else, someone to pull her out while I hold it off her.'

'You should've said something,' Sheila told him.

'Figured you needed a drink. Anyway, I wanted to make sure you're all right.'

'Thanks, but . . .'

'Give me the saw,' Ben said. 'I'll have her out of there in five minutes.'

'Is that what you want, Sheila?'

'No. For God's sake, get going. Both of you. Ben, go with him. Take care of that kid.'

Ben looked pained. 'Are you sure?'

'I'm fine down here. In fact, why don't you hand the saw down? Maybe I can cut myself out of this while you're gone.'

'That wouldn't be such a good idea,' Stanley said, rising. 'Just can't tell, those beams might be holding something up. You don't wanta start a slide . . . better just wait till we get back.' Before she could object, he turned away. 'Come on, Ben.'

'How long's this gonna take?'

Stanley shrugged. 'I don't know, twenty minutes. The house is a couple of blocks from here. It's a question of getting there and back – rescuing the kid shouldn't take any time at all. So I'd say we oughta be back in half an hour, at the most.'

Looking down at Sheila, Ben asked, 'Is that okay? Half an hour?'

'It's fine,' she said. 'Get going.'

'We'll hurry,' Stanley assured her, and headed through the rubble toward the rear of the house.

Ben followed him. He was silent for a while. He waited until Stanley had hopped down onto the patio, then said, 'I don't like this.'

'What don't you like?'

Ben jumped down. 'Leaving her.'

'Do you want the kid to die?'

'No, but I don't see how five minutes is gonna make a big difference.'

'Five minutes can make all the difference.'

'Yeah?'

'Yeah. Try holding your breath that long.'

'If this kid ain't breathing, she's dead already.'

'I didn't say she isn't breathing. I'm just saying five minutes can be the difference between life and death, sometimes. In this case, the kid *might* be bleeding. Down under the chimney where I couldn't see her? Do you want her bleeding to death while we saw on wood to untrap Sheila – who isn't in any danger at all and isn't even hurt?'

'Who says she's not in danger?'

Stanley turned around and walked backward, studying the distant sky. Smoke from the burning house across the street still drifted up, but it didn't seem as heavy as before. There were no other fires near enough to worry about.

'Long as a big wind doesn't come up and blow the fire this way . . .'

'It's not the fire,' Ben said.

'Then what?'

'You know. People. What if somebody finds her down there? I mean, she's buck naked.'

Not quite, Stanley thought, thanks to you.

'A lot of guys, you know, might get ideas. They might *do* stuff to her, you know?'

'You worry too much, Ben.'

'There's a lot of sick people in this world. Rapists and perverts . . .'

'I don't think Sheila is in much danger from a guy like that.'

Ben smirked. 'You don't, huh?'

'Nope. First, he'd have to *find* her. Then he'd have to *get* to her. A pervert's gonna be shit-outa-luck unless he's got a saw with him.' Stanley raised his own saw and waved it. 'Another good reason for taking this with us.'

'Yeah, right.'

'Can't rape her if you can't get to her. Can't get to her without a saw.'

'I guess you're right,' Ben said.

'Sure I'm right. Nobody's gonna touch Sheila till we get back.'

Seventeen

Though they walked slowly so that Mary wouldn't be left too far behind, they still made better progress than the traffic beside them on Laurel Canyon Boulevard. The cars and trucks in the northbound lanes moved very slowly. The vehicles in the southbound lanes, heading in the same direction as Clint and his companions, remained motionless for minutes at a time before creeping forward a few feet and stopping again.

'There must be some real trouble up ahead,' Clint said.

'I'll say,' Em agreed. 'Bet it's Ventura Boulevard. That street's a zoo, no matter what. It must be *crammed*.'

'Hey,' Mary called, 'wait up, will you?'

Turning around, they watched Mary saunter toward them.

She was even farther behind than usual. As she walked slowly closer, she stuffed her plastic Pepsi bottle down the top of her purse.

'Guess she stopped for a sip,' Clint said.

'Good thing we're not in a hurry,' Em muttered, and flicked a sly grin at him.

'Be nice,' he said.

'She's lost some of her *freshness*, hasn't she?'

Clint laughed softly. 'I'll say.'

Mary's hair hung in limp, damp strands. Her face was flushed and dripping. Her white blouse was twisted crooked from the pull of her purse strap. It looked drenched. It stuck to her skin and even to her bra, which showed through as if the fabric of her blouse had been melted thin by the heat. The blouse had come partly untucked from her skirt, and hung down sloppily. Even her skirt appeared to be crooked.

'Who won the wrestling match?' Em called out to her.

'Very funny. You're a million laughs, you little brat.'

'Part of my charm.'

'Em,' Clint said. 'Hey.'

'I know, "be nice."'

As Mary ambled nearer, she gave them an injured look. 'I sure wish you wouldn't walk so fast, you two.'

Em shrugged one shoulder. 'I don't know about Mr Banner, but I'm walking as slow as I can.'

'It's not my fault if I'm not a fast walker,' Mary said. 'And we wouldn't have to be doing this, at all, if we hadn't gone over to your house and gotten my car destroyed by that pair of throw-backs. It was being nice to you that got us into this mess.'

'Hey,' Clint said. 'That isn't necessary.'

'Yeah,' Em added. 'You oughta try being cheerful and polite for a change – or would that be too much of a strain on you?'

'Screw you.'

'That's sure a big improvement,' Em said.

'Up yours.'

'Do you know any *two* syllable words?'

'Fuck you.'

'No good. That's two words, one syllable each. Give it another try?'

Clint blurted out, 'Stop all this! Both of you cut it out, okay? Women! Bicker bicker bicker. Sometimes I think God created woman just to watch the bickering.'

'Whew,' Em said. 'That was certainly a sexist remark.'

'I'm allowed. I have a wife and daughter.'

'I'll forgive you,' Em said. Grinning, she bumped herself against him.

'Very cute,' Mary muttered. 'Anyway, it *is* her fault we lost my car.'

'It's just as well,' Clint said. 'I think they did us a favor, slashing the tires.'

'Oh, sure.'

'Saved us from getting stuck in all this traffic.'

'At least we wouldn't have to be walking.'

'I *would* be walking,' Clint said.

'We don' need no steenking car,' Em said, sounding very much like a Mexican bandito. 'Or badges.'

Mary glowered at her. 'Yeah? Well what about air conditioning?'

Em's head bobbed up and down a bit. 'That's another story,' she said. 'That'd be nice, air conditioning. I could sure use that. Or a swim. How would you like to jump into a swimming pool right now?'

'I'd rather jump in my car.'

'You don't like swimming pools?' Em asked.

'Not much.'

'I love 'em. You got a swimming pool, Mr Banner?'

'Nope.'

'We don't, either. We've gotta have about the only house in the valley without one.'

'Do you have friends with pools?' he asked.

'Sure. I'm in 'em a lot, too, but it's not the same. You've gotta be invited over, for one thing. You can't just hop on in any old time you feel like it. And your friend has to be there, so it's not like you can go in by yourself. And there're usually parents around. And maybe siblings. Thank the Lord, *I* have never been blessed with a sibling. I've *seen* them. They'll drop whatever they're doing if they spot an opportunity to pester you. Frankly, I would go buh-zonkers. Thank the Lord, my mom hates men.'

'But you don't,' Clint said.

Em grinned up at him. 'I don't hate *you*.'

'Thank you very much.'

'Very cute,' Mary said.

Still grinning at Clint, Em said, 'I think Mary believes I'd like to seduce you. That's ridiculous, of course. I mean, I'm thirteen. I'm way too young to even *think* about seducing someone.'

'Glad to hear it,' Clint said.

'Also, I have some fairly strong reservations about the entire sexual process.'

'You have *what*?'

'I mean – if what I've heard is true and I have every reason to believe that it is – it doesn't sound like something I would want to rush out and get done to me. I mean, really. I can't imagine anything grosser, if you want to know the truth.'

'Well . . .' Clint said.

'And talk about unsanitary.'

'I think it's about time to change the subject.'

'Bravo,' Mary said. 'I thought you'd never notice.'

'What should we talk about?' Em asked. 'Mary! Have you got a boyfriend?'

'A *boy*friend?'

'You know, a guy. A sweetie? A lover?'

'None of your business.'

'That's a no,' Em explained to Clint.

'Not necessarily.'

'It doesn't mean no,' Mary said. 'It means none of your business.'

'Maybe if you had a slightly more cheerful temperament, you'd have more luck with the fellas.'

Clint struggled not to laugh.

Mary's open hand smacked the back of Em's head.

Em yelped, 'Ah!' and flinched and staggered forward, ducking.

'Hey!' Clint shouted, whirling to face Mary. 'What the hell is the matter with you?'

'The little shit's got a big mouth!'

'That's no call to hit her, for Godsake! She's just a kid!'

'She's a little shit and I'm sick of her!'

'Then take a hike!'

'What?'

'You heard me, take a hike.' Clint turned to Em. The girl stood nearby, bent over, a hand clasped to the back of her head. She had dropped her paper bag to the sidewalk, where the two water-filled Pepsi containers inside had made it tumble over.

Clint curled a hand gently against the back of her neck. It felt moist, and very hot. 'Are you okay?'

'I seem to be getting knocked around an awful lot today,' she said, her voice quiet but steady.

Clint felt a thickness in his throat.

'Somebody oughta tell her it's not nice to hit people.'

He felt heat and wetness in his eyes, and Em's bowed blonde head went blurry.

'I hardly touched her,' Mary muttered.

'Do you want *me* to hardly touch *you* that way?'

'Don't,' Em told him. 'I don't want you hitting her.'

'I wasn't planning on it, but I'm tempted.'

'I'm sorry, okay?' Mary said.

'You sound sorry.'

'I won't do it again.'

'Just leave. Just get the hell out of here.'

Mary shook her head. She looked shocked, angry. 'I told you, I won't do it again.'

'You shouldn't have done it in the first place.'

'I'm sorry! Okay? I'm *sorry*!'

'So what?'

She raised her chin and stiffened her back. 'You've gotta give me another chance, that's what.'

'No, I don't.'

'Yes, you do. You can't just . . . send me away. You *have* to give me another chance.'

'In what rule book does it say that?' Clint asked.

'Everybody knows that.'

'Not me. I don't believe in second chances, apologies, or any of that crap – not when you pull a stunt like whacking my kid or . . .'

'She's not your kid!'

'She's *someone's* kid, and she's *my* friend, and if you *had* done that to my kid Barbara you wouldn't be talking back to me right now about second chances, you'd be on your ass on the sidewalk *bleeding*!' He took a quick step toward Mary and shouted in her face, '*DO YOU UNDERSTAND?*'

The color drained from her face. She staggered backward as if bludgeoned. Her lips twitched. Her chin quivered. Tears filled her eyes.

Em turned around and watched her.

'I'm *sorry*!' Mary blurted. This time, she looked and sounded as if she meant it.

'Who cares,' Clint said.

'You can't just leave me here!'

'Maybe we oughta tie her up,' Em suggested.

'See what a bitch she is! See!'

'She's *kidding*. Just stay away from us, that's all. Stay out of reach and keep your mouth shut, or else I *might* tie you up.'

Mary sniffed, rubbed her nose, and glared at both of them. Bending down, Clint picked up the sack that Em had dropped. 'I'll take this for a while.'

'No, that's okay. I don't mind carrying it.'

'It's awfully heavy. I'll carry it. What about the food?'

'What about it?' Em asked.

'Do you still want to share any of it with Mary, after what she did?'

Mary shifted her gaze from Clint to Em. 'Don't do me any favors,' she said.

Em pulled her head back and made a face as if Mary were threatening her with a fingertip loaded with snot. Then she turned to Clint. She made a crooked smile. 'She can have stuff. I don't care.'

'I don't want any of your damn food.'

'It'll be a long day,' Clint told her. 'You'll probably be getting hungry, so you'd better take something now. I'm not letting you anywhere near us once we start moving.'

'Big deal. I'm not gonna eat any of your precious food. If you're gonna leave me, go. Get outa here. Hope you croak.'

Clint nodded to Em. 'Let's go,' he said.

They started walking again. After taking eight or ten steps, Clint glanced over his shoulder. Mary was already following. She abruptly halted.

Sneering, she said, 'Do you want me to count to a hundred first?'

He shook his head. To Em, he said, 'Let's just pick up our pace a bit, and we'll leave her in the dust.'

They both began to quicken their strides. They walked side by side, Clint clutching the bag by its crumpled top. It was heavy. He felt bad about letting Em carry it for such a long time.

'You should've told me it was so heavy,' he said.

'It's not so heavy.'

'It weighs a ton.'

'I'll take it,' Em said, reaching out.

'No, you won't.'

'I don't mind. My book bag is a lot heavier, and I lug it around all the time.'

'That's okay. I'll carry this.' He kept hold of the bag, kept swinging it as they hurried along.

When he glanced back, Mary was chugging along at a fair clip. 'I can't believe it,' he said. '*Now* she's walking fast.'

Em looked over her shoulder. 'She's scared of being left behind.'

'Guess so. Knows we won't stop to wait for her any more.'

But they did have to stop. At Ventura Boulevard, the lanes they needed to cross were jammed with traffic. The signal lights were dead, just as Clint had expected. And nobody was out in the road, trying to direct traffic. Horns blared. People yelled. Cars and trucks, packed bumper to bumper, crept through the intersection while some inched off onto the crowded lanes of northbound Laurel Canyon and others struggled to turn right from Laurel and squeeze onto Ventura.

On the far side of Ventura, Laurel Canyon Boulevard was deserted. Its pavement stretched southward toward the hills, broad and sunlit and empty.

'What a mess,' Em said.

'It looks like they've got Laurel Canyon closed,' Clint told her.

'Yeah?' She stood on tiptoes, but shook her head. 'I can't see it.'

'There's no traffic at all over there.'

'Figures,' Em said. 'Laurel is always getting shut down. If it isn't a mud slide, it's a car crash . . . or a fire . . . or an earthquake. Always something.'

'*We'd* better be able to get through,' Clint said. He felt his lips pull back, baring his teeth.

'We could go over to Coldwater Canyon.'

'It'd be miles out of the way.' He shook his head. 'It has to be Laurel.'

'I'm waiting!' Mary called, her voice only slightly audible over the noises of engines and sighing brakes and car horns and radio music and shouts.

She stood about fifteen feet back, hands on hips, head tilted toward her left shoulder.

'Stay where you are,' Clint ordered.

'Are you gonna cross the street,' she called, 'or what?'

'Let's go,' Clint said to Em. 'Stay close to me, and keep your eyes open.'

For now, the lead cars on Laurel were motionless, waiting for small gaps between bumpers so that they might risk nosing out onto Ventura for their right-hand turns. It looked like it might be a long wait; the traffic on Ventura seemed to be at a dead halt.

With nobody likely to make a right turn and hit them, they only needed to worry about being crushed between cars that were waiting, going nowhere on Ventura.

Clint stepped off the curb. There was room for one leg at a time between the front of a Dodge pickup and the rear of a Mazda. He stopped beside the right front tire of the Dodge.

The driver behind the windshield wore a cowboy hat. A cigarette dangled from a corner of his lips. He gave Clint a wave. Clint smiled, called, 'Thanks,' and moved in front of the truck.

As he started to sidestep through the gap, he beckoned for Em. She gave the driver a big smile, and came in.

Mary failed to stay back.

Don't worry about it, Clint told himself. The thing is to get across the street in one piece. Forget about her.

She'd better just behave, that's all.

The Escort and Cherokee in the next lane were bumper to bumper. Clint walked through a narrow space toward the rear of the Escort, and found a Cadillac that hadn't pulled up all the way. The Cadillac's driver was a young woman who reminded him strongly of Mary. A career woman, severe in her business suit. Though she faced forward, she wore sunglasses. Clint couldn't see her eyes.

He patted the hood with his open hand, and saw her head jerk. Smiling, he gestured his intention to walk in front of her car .

She didn't respond.

'We're coming through!' he yelled.

Her lips seemed to tighten slightly.

She looks like a real bitch, he thought. But she might be a perfectly nice person. Anyway, it'd take more than a bitch to run into you on purpose. It'd take a complete lunatic.

It's probably safe, he told himself.

If you're wrong, you get your legs crushed at the knees.

He gestured for Em to wait. Then he stepped in front of the Cadillac. He took another step.

It'll be all right, he thought.

VROOOOOMMM!

At the roar of the engine, he sucked a shocked breath and jammed his left hand against the hood and thought, *This is it.*

Should've jumped!

A moment later, as the roar faded to a quiet idle, he realized that the car had not suddenly lurched forward and demolished his legs.

The gal had gunned it, all right. But she must've taken it out of gear, first. Gunned it in neutral, just to give him a thrill, and kept her foot on the brake.

He looked at her.

The pointed corners of her mouth turned upward.

Clint hurried through. Safe on the other side of the Cadillac, he glared in at the driver.

She continued to smile toward him.

Em still waited.

'Don't go in front of this idiot,' Clint called to her.

Em nodded. Then climbed up onto the hood and crawled across on her hands and knees, grinning toward the windshield.

The driver's smile quit.

Crawling by, Em smacked the glass hard with her open hand. The driver flinched. Then Em stood up and jumped to the pavement.

Clint shook his head as she came toward him.

She grinned.

'You're a little wild,' he said.

'I was gonna spit on her windshield, but I held back. Sometimes I've gotta hold back on these tendencies I've got. I could be a pretty unsavory person, if I let myself go.'

Laughing, Clint gave the top of her head a quick rub. Her hair felt soft and dry and very hot from the sun. It made him think about Barbara, the many times he had rubbed her hair – usually to her annoyance. *Cut it out, Dad!* It hurt him to think about Barbara.

What if she's dead?

She could be dead right now, mashed underneath the school or . . .

And Sheila might be dead, too. Buried under the house.

No!

Not both of them. I couldn't stand it if I had to lose both of them . . . Couldn't stand it to lose either *of them.*

They're both fine, he told himself. They've got to be. We'll all get through this just fine, and . . .

'Are you okay, Mr Banner?'

He realized that his hand was motionless on top of Em's head. They were standing in the narrow space between two lines of stopped cars, and she was gazing up at him with a worried look on her face.

'I'm fine,' he said. 'I was just thinking about my wife and kid.'

'I bet they're all right.'

'Yeah. I sure hope so.'

He turned his head and saw Mary. She still stood at the far side of the Cadillac. She was watching them.

'Are you coming?' Em called to her.

'After what *you* did?'

'Cheerio, then.'

Mary seemed to sag. She looked like a traveller who had arrived at a rushing stream only to find that the bridge had been washed away.

Clint could almost feel sorry for her. 'Let's go,' he said to Em.

Passing through a gap between two more cars, they reached the middle of Ventura Boulevard. As they headed toward the front of an eastbound RTD bus, Clint looked around for Mary. He couldn't spot her.

Em looked, too. 'Gone,' she pronounced.

'I'm sure it's a temporary reprieve. She's probably just *behind* something at the moment. Like that van way over there.'

'Maybe she got into a car.'

'That's possible.'

Em gave her eyebrows a playful wiggle. 'She sounded *very* fond of air conditioning.'

They made their way carefully through another lane of halted traffic, then scanned the area again for Mary.

'Maybe she *did* get in a car,' Clint said.

'You don't suppose something happened to her . . .?'

'Like what?'

Em bounced one of her slim shoulders. 'She might've gotten grabbed, I suppose.'

'Can't imagine who would want to *grab* her.'

'Someone who doesn't know her?'

Clint laughed.

'But really,' Em said, 'I'd hate for anything to happen to her. I mean, even though she is a major pain in the rumpazoid. It'd be my fault, you know?'

'Wouldn't be your fault,' Clint said. 'I'm sure she's fine, though. She's probably just taking a long way around. We can wait for her when we get to the other side.'

He led the way. A couple of minutes later, they hurried across the last lane and stepped up onto the curb. 'Made it,' Clint said.

Em pursed her lips and blew out a breath. 'Glad that's over with.'

'And no more major intersections to worry about until we get to Sunset Boulevard.'

'Which isn't till the other side of the hills, right?'

'Right.'

'By then, maybe they'll have the traffic lights working.'

'You never know.'

'What about Mary?' Em asked.

They both scanned the lanes of stopped traffic. No sign of her.

'I don't know,' Clint said.

'Do you think we should go back and look for her?'

'*No.*'

'Are you sure?'

'I'm sure.'

'What if something happened to her?'

'Nothing did. If she'd gotten nailed between a couple of cars, we would've heard the commotion. And I really doubt that she was grabbed in the middle of Ventura Boulevard on a day like this by a psychopath or serial killer or anything like that. Too many witnesses. Nowhere to go. My guess is, she made a big detour looking for better openings in the traffic, and she'll be showing up in a minute or two.'

'You think so?'

'Sure.'

'Maybe we oughta wait around for her,' Em said.

Clint smiled. 'This is our big chance to lose her.'

'I know, but then I'd have to go around feeling guilty about it.'

'Okay. We can wait for a while. Let's see what's going on over here.'

The entrance to Laurel Canyon Boulevard on this side of Ventura was blocked by two police cars and a cordon of bright yellow plastic that stretched across the entire road. The streamer was printed with black lettering that read, 'POLICE LINE – DO NOT CROSS'.

Clint stepped off the curb and walked behind it toward the patrol cars.

Two uniformed officers leaned against the side of one of the cars. A man and a woman, both with very young faces and short dark hair, both with their arms folded across their chests, both keeping their eyes on Ventura as they talked and smiled and nodded.

When Clint and Em approached them, they turned their heads.

'Can we help you?' asked the female. According to the silver tag on her chest, her name was Baker. She had a friendly, calm smile.

'How come you aren't out there directing traffic?' Em asked.

Clint gave her a dirty look.

'Not much point, is there?' Officer Baker said. 'Where would we direct it *to*?'

'We're just keeping an eye on the situation,' the man explained. Murphy was engraved on his nameplate. 'Making sure nothing gets out of hand. And keeping traffic off Laurel.'

'What's the problem with Laurel?' Clint asked.

'You can't get through,' Murphy said. 'This side of Mulholland, the pavement's buckled in several places. Down on the other side, they've got slides.'

'A real mess,' Baker said. 'We spent half the morning trying to clear out the vehicles that got stuck between here and the top. Were you hoping to get through?'

'I live in West L.A.,' Clint explained. 'I've got to get home. My wife and kid . . .'

'Who's this?' Murphy asked, nodding at Em.

'I'm his other kid.'

'Would there be a problem with *walking* over the top?' Clint asked.

'It'd be a tough hike,' Murphy said.

'We wouldn't stop you, though,' Baker explained. 'We just don't want cars trying to go up.'

'How is it on the other side?'

'A couple of slides,' Baker said.

'Probably nothing you wouldn't be able to climb over or walk around,' Murphy added.

'I guess we'll give it a try. Is it true that West L.A. got hit pretty hard?'

Baker shook her head. 'Not that much worse than over here.'

Murphy nodded. 'Moderately worse.'

'It's pretty bad everywhere,' Baker said.

'Pretty bad,' her partner agreed. 'But not catastrophic. I mean, this isn't India.'

'Or Afghanistan.'

'Or Mexico City.'

'This is L.A.,' Baker said.

'We're ready for this sort of emergency.'

'That's right.'

'I'd be surprised,' Murphy said, 'if we have more than a few hundred dead.'

'Four or five hundred.'

'If that.'

'It'd probably be a hundred thousand, any place but L.A.'

'Well, California in general.'

'Right,' Baker said. 'I was speaking in terms of a quake of this magnitude happening in an undeveloped place.'

'India, for instance.'

'Afghanistan . . .'

'Major loss of life.'

Baker frowned as she nodded. 'Not that four or five hundred is anything to sneeze at.'

Em nudged Clint. She glanced past him. Turning his head

to the left, he saw Mary step onto the curb half a block to the east.

'. . . makes you appreciate the building codes.'

'I'd sure rather be here than . . .'

'We'd better be on our way,' Clint interrupted the officers. 'Thanks for the help.'

Baker met his eyes. 'Hope everything turns out well for you, sir.'

'Thank you.'

'You, too,' she told Em.

'Thanks.'

'It'll be a tough hike,' Murphy pointed out, 'so take a break now and then. Don't over-exert yourselves.'

Mary, on the sidewalk now, noticed them and quickened her pace.

'Thanks again,' Clint said. 'So long, now.'

They turned away from the police officers, walked around the rear of the patrol car, and began to stride quickly up the empty middle of Laurel Canyon Boulevard.

'This is slick,' Em said.

'What?'

'No traffic. We've got the whole road to ourselves.' They both looked back in time to see Mary arrive at the corner. Murphy glanced at her. She ignored him, and started to walk up Laurel.

She looked angry. She didn't wave.

'Do you want to wait for her to catch up?' Clint asked.

'Not particularly.'

'Good,' Clint said.

Grinning, Em waved at her.

Mary scowled.

'She must be too tired,' Clint said, 'to give us the finger.'

Eighteen

'This is it, here,' Stanley said, leading Ben toward a house across the street and partway down the block from his own home. It was half-collapsed, as if one side of it had been stomped down by a monster.

He hoped nobody was inside.

He had thought about taking Ben into his own place. It was deserted except for Mother, so they would have plenty of privacy. But why litter up the place with another body? If he killed Ben there, he would have to dispose of the corpse; it would be idiotic to put himself to so much effort when the neighborhood had plenty of other houses to choose from.

He had also considered taking Ben into Judy's, but he planned to keep on using her house. Why mess it up and have Ben's remains lying around? If all went well, he might be staying there for several days. Ben would start to stink the place up.

No, he would have to take his chances with the house of a stranger.

'You sure this is the place?' Ben asked as they crossed the front lawn.

'Yeah, this is it.'

'But you said the kid's stuck under the chimney.'

'Huh?'

Ben pointed.

Stanley saw the chimney jutting above the section of the house that still stood. 'Oh,' he said. 'That's the part that didn't fall.'

'Huh?'

'You'll see. Come on.'

The front door was shut – probably locked. But most of the house at the other end of the porch had collapsed. 'This way,' Stanley said, heading for the wrecked area. 'Here's where I got in, last time.'

With Ben close behind him, he waded through the rubble. He made his way toward the section of the house that still stood. One of the interior walls had a doorway through which Stanley could see a shadowy carpet, a chair and a corner of a table.

'This is it,' he said. He leaned into the doorway. A dining room. Off to one side, he could see through an archway to the living room.

Both rooms looked as if they'd been kicked apart by a tribe of lunatics. But the ceilings and walls appeared to be intact, and curtains hid whatever damage had been done to the windows.

From where he stood, Stanley couldn't see the living room fireplace.

'Hello!' he called into the gloom.

No answer came.

'Hello! Little girl? I'm back! I went and got some help, just like I said I would.'

Still, no answer.

Either the house was deserted, or its occupant was in no condition to speak.

Stanley looked over his shoulder. 'Hope she's still okay.'

'Let's get this over with,' Ben said, and tossed his head to fling some stray hair away from his face. 'I wanta get back to Sheila.'

'Here we go.' Stanley stepped through the doorway. The floor creaked under his weight, but it felt firm. Holding the saw by the side of his right leg, he walked slowly around the end of the dining room table. As he approached the archway, the fireplace came into view.

It looked as if it hadn't been damaged at all.

When Ben sees this . . .

Stanley stepped through the archway.

Nobody else in the room. No way to see in from outside.

Perfecto!

'Oh, my God!' he blurted. 'Ben! Ben!'

'What . . .?'

Quick footfalls behind him.

He whirled around, bringing the saw up from his side, flipping it over to put the teeth forward and chopping it at Ben's neck in a clumsy, underhand swing. Ben yelped and flung up his arm to block the blow. He cried out as the teeth bit into him, then squealed as Stanley tugged the weapon, dragging its tiny steel teeth across the skin of his forearm.

'You nuts?' Ben yelled. He stumbled into the living room, clutching his wound and backing away.

'Nuts? Me?' Stanley raised the saw overhead. He walked toward Ben.

'Don't. Hey. Come on. Look. You don't gotta hurt me. Okay? What do you want? Just tell me. Okay? Whatever you want.' He kept backing away.

'If you go for the door,' Stanley said, 'I'll have to kill you.'

Ben stopped moving. 'Okay. I won't. I won't do anything, okay? What do you want me to do? There isn't any kid, right? Nobody's trapped. It was just to get me here, right?'

'Right.'

'Okay. Fine.' Letting go of his bloody arm, he reached back with his left hand and pulled a billfold out of the rear pocket of his jeans. 'This what you want? You can have it. I got almost fifty bucks in here.' He held it toward Stanley.

'Don't want it.'

'What *do* you want?'

'Make me an offer.' As he said that, he saw Ben's gaze slide down past his waist.

'Oh,' Ben said. 'I get it.'

'Get what?'

Ben smirked. 'Had me fooled. I figured it was Sheila you had the hots for.' He tucked the wallet back into his pocket. 'This is okay, Stan. This is cool. Shoulda just asked, though, if you know what I mean. You didn't have to go nuts and cut me.'

'What're you talking about?'

'Can we bandage my arm first?'

Stanley shook his head.

'I'm bleeding all over the place.'

'So what?'

'*Okay.* Okay. First things first, huh?' With an odd, slanted smile, Ben walked slowly closer.

Stanley stood motionless, the saw still raised. His heart was pounding and he had a hard time filling his lungs. 'What do you . . .?'

His voice died as Ben knelt in front of him.

Ben popped open a snap. The loose remains of Stanley's pajama pants clung to him with sweat, but only for a moment. Ben plucked them down.

'Oooo, look at you. You're a big boy, aren't you?'

Even without looking, he could feel that Ben was right. He lowered his gaze.

Can't be, he thought. No way. Must be some other reason. Not because of *him.*

But he squirmed with the feel of Ben's sliding fingers.

'Hey,' he said. 'Stop it.'

'You don't want me to stop.'

'Yeah. I do. I don't go for this kind of stuff.'

'Who're you trying to kid? Look at you. You're aching for it.' Head back, eyes tilted upward and staring directly into his eyes, Ben reached up behind Stanley and squeezed his buttocks. Kneaded them with slick, bloody hands and leaned forward.

His lips felt like a soft, moist O.

The pliant ring slipped forward and Stanley felt himself being sucked deep into Ben's mouth.

This is sick, he thought. This is perverted. The little rat's a fag and . . .

Gotta stop him . . .

Gotta . . .

But it feels so . . .

Judy's mouth had been a dry, unwilling hole doing what it had to do. Nothing like this.

But he's a guy! Can't let a guy do it to me! I'm not a fucking fairy!

'Stop it!' Stanley gasped.

Ben didn't stop.

I don't want him to stop.

Not yet.

Not till . . .

'No!' Stanley blurted.

He raced the toothed edge of the saw across the top of Ben's skull. Ben's mouth flew open. Stanley pulled out of it and kneed him under the chin. Ben fell backward and slammed against the floor, clutching his head with both hands. His face was twisted with pain. He cried out, 'Are you *insane*? Why'd you *do* that? My God! My God!'

'Shut up.'

'You wanted it! You *loved* it! Look what you've *done* to me!'

'Yeah. And just look what I'm doing to you now.' He scurried around to Ben's side and slashed down with the saw. 'No!'

Ben blocked it, but the blade ripped his hands. Squealing, he flung himself over. He tried to scurry away on hands and knees, but Stanley drove a foot down on his back, stomping him flat. As he pushed himself up, Stanley sat on him.

'No!' Ben shrieked. 'Get off me!'

Stanley grabbed the long, bloody hair with one hand and swatted Ben's rump with the flat of the saw. 'Giddy-up!'

Ben crawled. Stanley rode him, liking the slippery feel of the back underneath him.

Shouldn't be liking it, he told himself. Shouldn't be liking any of this.

But he looks like a woman. From up here. He's almost like one.

Yeah, but he isn't one. He's a guy.

You wouldn't know it from up here. The hair. The skin. You can't see she hasn't got any tits under there.

Not *she*!

He!

Trying to make a fag out of me!

Stanley jerked Ben's head back by the hair and sawed into the side of his neck. Blood flew.

The scream made his ears hurt.

Ben tried to buck him off.

Stanley planted his feet on the floor and clamped Ben tight between his thighs and hung on to the long hair and sawed and sawed.

Soon, Ben stopped struggling.

Stanley kept on sawing.

Nineteen

They walked slowly down the alley. Barbara knew that, if she turned around, she would still be able to see the fallen mess of Mrs Klein's garage.

She didn't look.

She wished they had never stopped to help the woman.

If they hadn't stopped, they would be a lot closer to home by now. And maybe Mrs Klein would still be alive.

Maybe we killed her by helping her.

It seemed like a crazy idea, but it made sense to Barbara. After all, they were the ones who had cleared away the really heavy debris. If Mrs Klein hadn't been able to make it through to her car window . . .

We can't exactly call it our fault, she told herself. We didn't rip her up, the cat did.

Barbara was a few strides ahead of Pete and Heather, so she turned around.

She couldn't stop herself from gazing past them.

The tumbled garage wasn't in sight, after all. Thank goodness for that, she thought.

Walking backward, she said, 'My dad claims an earthquake never killed anyone – it's the stuff that falls on your head.'

Pete smiled. 'Cool.'

'Stupid,' Heather said.

'I'll have to tell him quakes can also kill you with cats.'

'Man,' Pete said. 'Do you believe that? I've never heard of anything that crazy.'

'I have,' Heather said. 'I've heard of worse stuff.'

Of course you have, Barbara thought.

'I've heard about people getting *eaten* by their pet cats,' Heather explained. 'At least Susie didn't *eat* her.'

'I'm not so sure of that,' Barbara said.

'You didn't really look at her.'

'I looked at her plenty. I saw her better than you did. You didn't have to carry her around like me and Pete.'

'You didn't *have* to,' Heather said.

'Not if you'd helped, maybe.'

'It was your idea.'

'You still could've helped,' Barbara said.

'We should've just left her in the alley.'

'That would have been a lousy thing to do.'

'Yeah,' Pete said. 'I mean, I wasn't overjoyed about touching her, exactly, but Jeez . . . How can you just leave her there? If I got myself killed in some lousy alley, I think it'd be pretty nice if somebody'd take me back into my house.'

'Not me,' Heather said.

Pete looked as if he didn't believe her. 'Don't tell me you wouldn't rather have someone carry you inside and put you on a nice sofa in your own house so you don't have to lay out there in the sun and . . .'

'You think she *knows* she's on a nice sofa in her own house? Or that you two busted your humps hauling her in? You just wasted your energy, that's all. Dead's dead. Doesn't matter where you end up.'

'You'd like to get left in an alley?' Barbara asked.

'Sure, why not?'

'A car might come along and run over you,' Pete pointed out.

Heather shrugged.

'A cat might eat your face,' Barbara said.

'So?'

'A wino might come stumbling along,' Barbara added, 'and throw up on you.'

'Big deal.'

'Or rape you.'

'Sick,' Pete said. He wrinkled his nose at Barbara. 'That's really sick, Barbara.'

'It could happen,' she said. 'I've read about people who do stuff like that. Serial killers do it all the time.'

'Yeah, but . . .'

'So what if some wino came along and raped me?' Heather said. 'That'd be his problem, know what I mean? I'd be dead, so how's it supposed to matter to me? I'd sure rather get raped when I'm dead than when I'm alive. It's no picnic, getting raped. I'd rather be dead if it's gonna happen again.'

Oh, Jeez. She's been raped.

Big surprise, Barbara thought. Is there anything horrible that *hasn't* happened to Heather?

Pete looked shocked and embarrassed. 'You mean . . . somebody raped you?'

'Oh, do tell us all about it,' Barbara said.

Heather gaped at her. 'You think it's funny?'

'I didn't say that.'

'You oughta try getting raped and see how you like it.'

'Thanks, anyway.' As she said that, she saw how Pete was looking at her. 'Oh, give me a break. She's *dying* to tell us in great gory detail all about it, and I'm a little tired of hearing about Heather's endless stream of weird tragedies. My God, she makes Anne Frank sound like a lucky kid.'

'Who?' Heather asked.

'Look!' Pete blurted, pointing behind Barbara.

Barbara whirled around.

Out from behind a garbage bin strolled a husky cat. It stopped and stared at them. Its up-curled tail was golden brown with a white tip. Its eyes were amber. Its nose and muzzle must've been licked clean; the rest of the cat looked as if it had been dipped in a vat of blood. The fur was matted flat, clumpy, dripping.

'It's Susie,' Heather whispered.

Barbara stomped her foot down hard against the alley pavement.

The cat didn't so much as flinch.

'Don't scare it away,' Heather said.

Barbara looked back at her. 'What do you want to do, adopt the thing?'

'I don't wanta have it around *me*,' Pete said.

'Let's just keep going,' Barbara suggested. 'Maybe it'll mind its own business and go off on its own. Just don't do anything to entice it, Heather.'

As she walked forward, the cat turned away and began sauntering up the middle of the alley. It glanced back. Its jaw worked and it made a noise that sounded like '*Raw*.'

Barbara stomped her foot again.

The cat continued to stroll up the alley, staying a small distance in front of her.

'Great,' Pete muttered.

'The cat's meow,' Barbara said, and slowed her pace until Pete and Heather caught up to her. 'Think I'll just stick with you guys,' she said.

'She's probably just lonely,' Heather said.

'Me or the cat?' Barbara asked.

'Susie.'

The cat looked back again.

'Great,' Barbara said. 'Try not to say her name, okay? The thing's a psycho.'

They walked in silence, their eyes on the cat. It stopped looking back. Once in a while, its tail twitched. It crossed a deserted street and entered an alley on the other side.

'Maybe it'll keep going,' Pete said. He nodded to his left. 'Let's try *that* way.'

They turned and started up the sidewalk, but only took a few strides before Pete suddenly stopped.

Near the end of the block, four young men were coming out of a house, yelling and laughing, their arms loaded. One seemed to be carrying a television. Another had an electric guitar.

Before Barbara saw what the others were taking, Pete said, 'Uh-oh.'

'Let's get out of here,' Barbara whispered. Whirling

around, she found the cat staring up at her. She feigned a kick at it, then broke into a run.

Susie scampered ahead of them as they raced into the alley.

They sprinted past a hedge, past garbage bins and car ports and backyard fences. Pete kept looking over his shoulder as he ran. Soon, he slowed to a jog. 'I don't think they're coming,' he gasped.

Heather staggered to a halt. She bent over and clutched her knees and panted for air.

Barbara walked in slow circles, hands on hips, head back as she tried to catch her breath. She was dripping wet. 'We'd better . . . stick to the alleys.'

'Yeah,' Pete said. 'Yeah. Jeez.' He picked up the front of his shirt and wiped his face with it. 'Those guys . . . they had to be looting . . . don't you think?'

'Sure looked like it.'

'Man.'

Heather, still bent over and huffing, raised her sweaty red face. 'What if they . . . come?'

'They won't,' Pete said.

'But if . . .'

'They'd be here by now,' Barbara said. 'Probably. Anyway, they . . . had their hands full.'

'We oughta hide.'

Barbara shook her head. Sprinkles of sweat flew off her hair. 'We'll never get home if we . . . hide. Gotta keep . . .'

'We won't get home . . . if we get jumped by . . . guys like them.'

'Over here,' Pete said. He pointed, and walked toward a recessed parking area at the rear of an apartment building. Except for a few minor cracks in the stucco walls, the overhanging structure looked as if it hadn't been touched by the earthquake.

There were stalls for six vehicles.

Four were empty.

A pickup and a station wagon were parked side by side. Pete entered the narrow space between them. Barbara hurried after him, and Heather followed her. 'We'll just rest here for a minute or two,' Pete said.

They sat down. The concrete floor felt slightly cool. Barbara started to lean back, but the pickup's front tire was behind her. She was filthy enough already. Besides, how comfortable could a tire be? She crossed her legs, leaned forward, and propped her elbows on her knees.

The top of her blouse was wide open, thanks to the ruined buttonholes. Her chest looked dark and shiny. Her white bra had gotten smudged with dirt. The moisture from her sweat made the cups a little transparent. She could see the color of her skin through them, but her blouse wasn't open quite far enough to let her nipples show.

Pete had probably seen plenty.

Nothing I can do about it, she told herself. Not unless I wear my blouse backwards, and that'd look pretty stupid.

Pete hadn't exactly seemed to be overwhelmed by the view, anyway.

Why should he be? Next to Heather, I've got nothing to look at. A couple of humps. I've got mounds and she's got mountains. And maybe Pete's got a few things on his mind that don't include what's on my chest *or* Heather's. We'll be lucky if we make it home, and maybe home won't even *be* there anymore. If his mind is on boobs, he must be nuts.

Though *my* mind is on boobs.

She laughed softly.

'What?' Pete asked.

'Nothing.' There was no point in trying to fasten the buttons; they would only pop open again. Besides, she rather liked how she looked and felt with the blouse open this way. 'The shade's nice,' she whispered.

'If somebody comes,' Pete said, 'we'll sneak around in front of the pickup.'

'I just don't want to stay here long. We'll never get home if we keep stopping.'

'Should've thought of that,' Heather said, 'before you wasted all that time with what's-her-face.'

'Mrs Klein,' Pete said.

'Yeah. Her.'

'Let's not start in on her again,' Barbara said. 'Anyway, I was all set to leave as soon as we got her into the house. *You're* the one who made us sit around and drink her Pepsis.'

'Like the both of you weren't dying.'

'She was sure heavy,' Pete said. 'Jeez, that was awful.'

'I'm glad we did it, though,' Barbara said.

'Yeah. Me, too. I guess. Gross, though.'

'Well,' Heather said, 'I figure you wasted maybe an hour, and all because you wouldn't let her stay in the alley.'

'I don't think it was that long,' Barbara said. Then she wondered if Heather was wearing a watch. She didn't think so, but she wasn't sure.

She twisted around for a look.

But forgot all about wristwatches when she saw Heather leaning back against the pickup truck, legs stretched out straight, smiling at the cat by her right side as she stroked it with a gory hand.

'Aw! Jesus H. Christ!'

'What?' Pete asked.

'Look at her!' Barbara dropped back against the tire as Pete leaned forward. He gazed past her.

'Heather!'

The girl raised her eyebrows and continued to pet the cat. 'She's a nice kitty.'

'Have you lost your mind?' Pete blurted.

Barbara scrambled to her feet. 'I'm getting out of here.'

'Yeah,' Pete said. 'God almighty, Heather.'

Barbara leaped over the girl's legs and hurried toward the alley.

'You two sure freak out easy,' Heather said. She sounded amused.

Clear of the car port, Barbara felt the sun pound down on her. She squinted, and looked both ways. Nobody seemed to be coming. Except for Pete. He hurried forward, hunching down slightly when he left the shade.

In the car port, Heather was already standing. 'If you think I'm gonna *stay* here . . .'

'We just don't want that cat around us,' Pete said.

'It's a psycho,' Barbara repeated. 'It *killed* Mrs Klein.'

'That doesn't mean she's a bad kitty.' Heather came out of the shadowy car port, the cat swaggering along beside her. 'She felt trapped, that's all. She was only trying to survive. You can't go blaming her for that.'

'Just keep it away from us,' Pete said.

He and Barbara started walking, but they continued to look back. Heather and Susie were gaining on them.

'Just stay back there,' Barbara said.

'I don't wanta.'

'What *do* you want?'

'The front.'

'Okay, take the front.'

As Heather and the cat approached, Barbara took Pete by the arm and guided him toward the other side of the alley.

'It'd be funny if it weren't so sad,' Heather commented. 'Scared of a nice little kitty.'

Barbara wrinkled her nose when she saw all the blood on Heather. Not only was the girl's hand a mess, but the cat must've put a lot of effort into rubbing itself against her. She had blood on the side of her white sock and on her calf. The tan fabric of her baggy dress was smeared with blood on the right side from her thigh almost to her armpit.

'Look what it did to you,' Barbara said.

Heather looked, and shrugged. 'I'm not any dirtier than you.'

'Yes, you are. And I don't have *blood* all over me.'

'You oughta wash that off,' Pete said as Heather walked by.

'Doesn't matter. My dress is ruined, anyhow.'

'Maybe, but you don't want it on your hands all day.' He looked at Barbara. 'We need to find someplace where she can wash up.'

'Won't be easy,' Barbara said.

They'd both gotten blood on their hands carrying Mrs Klein into her house. Barbara had been frantic to get it off. It made her feel contaminated by the woman's death. She hated the rusty brown color and the tacky feel of the stuff.

She had hurried to the kitchen sink and twisted a faucet handle, forgetting that the quake had knocked out the water pressure – her memory returning when the faucet was silent and nothing came out. 'What're we gonna do?' she'd gasped. 'I've gotta get this off me!'

Pete had remained calm. 'Don't worry. We'll think of something.'

After a discussion that included searching for pre-moistened towelettes (good luck finding any), using Pepsi (sticky) or water from the toilet tank (gross), they'd pounced on Pete's idea of dipping paper towels into water from melting ice in the freezer compartment of the refrigerator. It had worked great.

Now, Pete came up with a fresh idea. 'Maybe we can find a garden hose that still has some water in it.'

'Can't get much out of a hose,' Barbara said. 'Besides, she'll just get bloody again messing with the cat.'

Heather suddenly looked pleased. 'Let's wash Susie. I bet we can find a swimming pool or something around here.'

Pete frowned, apparently thinking about it. 'Yeah,' he said after a few moments. 'You never know. This is sort of a lousy neighborhood, but if we start looking in back yards . . .'

'Courtyards of apartment houses have swimming pools,' Barbara pointed out. 'A lot of them do. Maybe even some around here. Couldn't hurt to keep our eyes open. One thing though.' She looked from Pete to Heather. 'If we do find a pool, I wanta have a crack at it before it gets screwed up with blood and cats. Okay?'

Pete smiled. 'Yeah. Me, too.'

'Let's find us a pool,' Barbara said.

Twenty

Stanley opened a curtain to let in more sunlight. Seeing nobody on the other side of the window, he gazed down at himself.

He looked as if he'd been wallowing in blood.

'Beautiful,' he murmured.

He rubbed his hands over his body. He liked where the blood felt slippery, but didn't care much for the sticky places where it was drying. He wished he could mix it with oil, so it would stay slippery everywhere.

A large mirror above the fireplace had survived the quake. He stepped close to it. His reflection was large, but the bottom of the mirror cut him off halfway down his chest. So he went to the far side of the room. From there, the mirror showed him only to the waist. So he stood on the sofa.

Able to see himself all the way down to his knees, he was stunned by how large and powerful and *savage* he looked. Like some sort of jungle warrior, naked and wild, washed in the blood of his enemies. The blood on his face was mostly around his lips and down his chin.

'Anyone might think I'd *eaten* him,' he said.

He laughed, but the grin made him look stupid, so he made a fierce face. Much better. He growled. He sucked in his belly and flexed his muscles.

'Oh, yeah,' he murmured.

It's me, he thought. This is how I oughta look *all* the time. Except work out better and build up some muscles. And let my hair grow. I can do that. Nobody to tell me no, anymore. Nobody to make fun of me. This *is* me. Naked and wild and covered with blood.

The blood made him a little itchy, but he could live with that. A minor nuisance. Like putting up with the itch of a wool shirt because the shirt makes you look like a lumberjack.

He stood on the sofa for a while longer, posing and watching himself in the mirror.

He wished he could go outside like this.

That'd be stupid, though. Hugely stupid.

Even if he was lucky enough to avoid meeting any strangers, he didn't want Sheila to see him drenched with blood. She might guess that it wasn't his.

He jumped down from the sofa.

Wandering through the rooms that hadn't been destroyed, he looked for water. He found no water, and no other liquid except for the blood on the carpet around Ben.

He had an urge to lie down there and squirm around.

'Gotta get back to Sheila,' he told himself. 'Had enough fun here.'

Instead of squirming in the blood, he sprawled on the sofa. He rolled and writhed, rubbing himself against the nubby upholstery. He left a great amount of blood on the sofa. After climbing off, he wiped himself with both of the sofa's pillows. The pillows worked especially well on his neck and armpits, his groin and the crease of his rump.

By the time he finished with the pillows, he was no longer wet. But he looked as if his skin had been stained with reddish-brown shoe polish. He felt sticky and itchy all over.

He looked at himself in the mirror and shook his head.

'Gotta do better than this,' he said.

He *had* to find water.

A swimming pool!

He knew just where to find one.

He'd seen it from the roof of Mother's house – *his* house.

Amazing what you could see from up there. Though the house was only a single story high, it seemed to tower above the neighborhood when he stood on it.

It's the standing that does it, he had figured out. Puts my eyes about six feet higher up than everything else.

He'd gone up there often. Not often enough, though. And he'd never dared to stay for very long. The problem was, his perch atop the roof not only gave him a great view of the neighborhood, but it gave the neighbors a great view of him.

The nearly flat plain of the roof, surrounded by knee-high walls, provided nowhere to hide unless he lay down. Not only that, but there were often helicopters in the sky. He didn't dare take binoculars up with him. Nor did he dare to spend much time looking down at the surrounding houses.

No privacy at all, up there.

He'd gone up, anyway, for a few minutes at a time – usually taking a bucket of asphalt 'roof patch' with him so he would appear to have a legitimate excuse. On those occasions, he'd relished the view: his mother's back yard; beyond the cinderblock wall to Sheila's yard and patio and back door and windows; the rear grounds of the houses to the right and left of Sheila's place; the back yard of the Taylor house, his first neighbor to the north; the Donaldsons' on the far side of the Taylors; Judy and Herb's house directly to the south, and the Benson place on the other side of Judy's.

It was the Benson place that had the pool.

Behind their small stucco house, with a redwood gate across the driveway and fencing around the borders of the back yard, the pool was like a guarded secret. Stanley supposed he would never have known of its existence at all, if he hadn't spotted it from his roof.

He had never seen anyone in the pool, or even sunbathing on the padded loungers beside it.

Not that he'd spent much time looking. Whenever he was on the roof, he occupied most of his time keeping an eye on Sheila's house. Hoping for a glimpse of her. Or a glimpse of Barbara. Though the girl was no match for her mother, she was still a great-looking piece, well worth watching. The best on the block, after Sheila. With Judy running in third place.

The Bensons had never interested him until now. He did know that they were a middle-aged couple and they rarely seemed to be home. Judy had once mentioned that they were school teachers. Stanley doubted if he could recognize either one of them, though he knew that he'd seen Mrs Benson and had judged she was nothing worth looking at.

He also knew that they had a fine-looking swimming pool in their back yard.

They're bound to be gone, he thought. Barbara's at school. That's what Sheila'd said. So if these Bensons are teachers, they'll be at school, too.

Probably.

'Doesn't matter,' he said.

He put on his cut-off pajama pants again. As he snapped the waistband shut, he saw that the front was spotted with blood. Not a lot of blood, though. He had enough scratches and minor cuts on his body to explain it away.

He thought about leaving his fly open.

That'd be stupid, he decided. You don't wanta look *too* conspicuous.

So he tucked himself inside the fly and fastened a snap in the middle. Then he stepped into his moccasins. He took his saw to a window and used a curtain to wipe the blood off its handle and blade.

That it? he wondered.

Think so.

Lifting the saw to his brow, he offered a salute to the dismembered corpse on the floor.

'So long, Ben – it's been good to know you. Been a treat. Been a hoot.' He laughed and went to the front door of the house. Opening it a crack, he peered out.

He saw no one, so he stepped outside. On his way across the yard, he looked all around. He saw a few people here and there, milling about in the distance. They were too far away to matter – so far away that they hardly seemed to exist, at all.

He heard distant noises, too: sirens and alarms, bangs, engine noises of cars and trucks and airplanes and helicopters, even a tinny voice amplified by a loudspeaker. But all these noises were far away, and the neighborhood itself seemed oddly quiet.

A ghost town, he thought. *My* ghost town. All mine.

From the curb, he looked across the street and down the block. Past the Taylor house, past his own house, past Judy's . . .

He wondered how Judy was doing.

Should he pay her a visit?

No no no. A waste of time. She's right in the tub where I

left her. It'd take Houdini to get loose, the way I had her tied to that chair and the faucets.

As he started to cross the street, he gazed at Judy's house. He remembered the look and feel of her.

It'd only take a minute to drop in and check on her, he thought. Make sure she isn't getting loose.

He laughed softly.

It'd take a *lot* more than a minute.

First, he would have to untwist the hanger and free her hands and take the chair off her. Then for the fun. But he wouldn't want to kill her, so he'd have to make her secure again after he got finished. Re-do the bit with the chair and hanger. Only *then* would he be able to go next door to the Benson's pool.

He wanted to do it.

He couldn't stop thinking about it.

He got stiff, thinking about it. He was stiff when he walked past his own house. He looked at the broken picture window and imagined Mother sprawled on the floor of the living room.

If she could see me now!

'Just what do you think you're doing, young man? Have you lost your senses? Get inside this minute and put on some clothes! What's got into you? You look like some sort of a pervert, galavanting around that way. You're positively indecent!'

By the time he had left his house behind, he was laughing regularly, and no longer aroused. He decided not to bother with a visit to Judy.

'She'll keep,' he said as he walked past her house.

Anyway, he'd already had her. She'd been terrific, but it would be a shame to use himself up on a third-rate gal like Judy when he had Sheila waiting for him.

What'll I tell Sheila about Ben? he wondered. Better come up with a good one. Maybe tell her they rescued the kid just fine, but she couldn't be moved, so Ben volunteered to stay with her.

Hell, he thought, I can tell her *anything*. Doesn't really matter. She's in no position to cause trouble. The worst she can do, stuck down there, is start yelling. If she tries that, I'll shut her up quick.

He pictured himself leaping down onto her.

What'll I do to her?

What a question.

What won't I do to her?

The real question is, where to start?

Start by making her shut up.

Stanley had to stop thinking about it, however, when he found himself in front of the Benson place.

It reminded him of house facades he'd seen during tram rides through the back lot of Universal Studios. The house's front still stood. It looked just fine except for the shattered picture window. He could see sky through the window.

Behind the front wall, the house was down.

'Perfect,' he said.

If the Bensons weren't away from home, they were no doubt underneath it.

Their driveway was empty, though. More than likely, the couple had driven off to work this morning and were marooned at a distant school or two.

Stanley crossed the front lawn to the driveway. The redwood gate at the far side of the house was padlocked shut, but the stucco wall to its right had been knocked down. Stanley detoured around the gate, climbing over broken stucco and lathe and plaster, then jumping to the pavement and continuing up the driveway.

As he walked toward the back, he scanned the ruin of the house. The roof had caved in completely, taking down most of the interior walls and crushing whatever else might have been inside the house. The front wall, of course, still stood. So did most of the northern exterior wall.

It had gotten off better than Sheila's place, but not by much.

He saw nobody.

He thought about calling out, but decided against it.

If there are dead Bensons in the vicinity, they aren't likely to hear me.

If a Benson is trapped, who cares? Not me.

Besides, someone might hear a shout and come to investigate.

I sure don't need that, he thought. All I want is a couple of minutes to wash off in the pool. Get myself all spiffy clean for my sweet Sheila.

Behind the wreck of the house, he spotted the pool. He halted, shocked.

Empty! No! Can't be!

He could *feel* the cold water. He *longed* to plunge in and glide through the chill. He *had* to wash the blood off his body. He needed to get clean for Sheila. And the itch was driving him mad!

'No fair,' he muttered, feeling his throat tighten. 'No fair!'

He had counted on the pool. He felt cheated, betrayed.

Everything had been going so well, until now.

Shaking his head, he shambled closer to the pool.

Do people drain the things in June? he wondered. For a spring cleaning, or something? No, that's crazy. This is the time of year when you'd want to be *using* them.

Maybe the Bensons are idiots.

He wished they *were* here, so he could kill them.

There must be other pools somewhere, he told himself.

He didn't know where, though. And he sure couldn't afford the time to go searching for one. Sheila was waiting. He needed to get back to her and cut her free and . . .

Stanley suddenly smiled.

At the shallow end, which was all he'd been able to see at first, the bottom of the pool was dry. But walking closer, he noticed that the blue tile floor sloped downward toward this end, the deep end. Partway down the slope, water glimmered.

He hurried forward and stopped at the edge of the pool.

Below him, the water looked blue and cold.

The Bensons *didn't* drain it, he realized.

And the pool looked undamaged, so the water hadn't leaked out through breaks.

The earthquake, he realized, must've done this – sloshed

QUAKE

out tons of water, tidal waves of it – leaving nothing but a few feet of water at the very bottom of the deep end.

He wondered where all the lost water had gone. There was no trace of it, now. During the hours since the quake, the run-off must've spread out, spilled down drains and onto neighboring property, been absorbed by the ground. The concrete apron surrounding the pool had obviously been baked dry by the sun.

Amazing, he thought.

He'd heard of earthquakes throwing water out of swimming pools, but he'd never heard of a pool being *emptied* by one.

It isn't quite empty, he reminded himself. It left enough water for me.

'Saved some for the fishies,' he said.

My luck hasn't gone bad, after all.

He couldn't get into the water from here. At this height, jumping into such shallow water would probably break his legs. Even the chrome ladder, over at the corner, didn't reach down far enough to let him enter the water without a risky drop.

So he hurried to the other end of the pool and stepped out of his moccasins. The concrete seared the bottoms of his feet. Quickly, he slipped back into the moccasins. He kept them on as he trotted down three tile stairs and walked on the bottom of the pool toward its deep end.

As the bottom slanted downward, the walls surrounding him seemed to grow. They were higher than his head by the time he stopped at the edge of the water.

He looked around at them.

This is great, he thought. Nobody can see me down here.

Nobody's *here* to see me, but even if people were around, I'd be out of sight. Unless they're right on top of me, looking down, they'd never know I'm here.

'Fantastic,' he muttered.

My own, secret place.

This, he realized, was even better than if the pool had been full to the brim with water.

A lot better!

I could even bring somebody here, he thought. Like Sheila, after I get her loose. We'd be outside, but still have all the privacy we need.

And we'd have water. I could wet her up. I could do stuff to her *in* the water, and that way she'd be all clean and cool and slick.

Holding images of Sheila in his mind, he stepped out of his moccasins and walked into the water.

Twenty-one

Heather stayed well ahead of Barbara and Pete. The cat pranced along beside her as she hurried through the alley with energy that Barbara had never seen in her. She rushed from side to side, peering over rear fences and gates, running up walkways to search for a swimming pool.

After ten or eleven tries, she bounded back into the alley from the shadows of an apartment complex's parking area and shouted, 'Found one!' Susie darted past her feet. 'Come on! Looks great!' She whirled around and rushed out of sight. The cat swiveled its head to watch her, then looked at Barbara. It blinked a couple of times, twitched its tail, then slowly turned and followed Heather.

'If she goes in that pool before us,' Barbara said, 'I'm not going in.'

'She'd better not,' Pete said.

'She found it.'

Pete made a face. 'If she goes in and gets it bloody, we'll just have to find our own.'

'I'm with you.'

From the rear, the two-story apartment building looked as

if it hadn't been damaged by the quake. Barbara didn't even see any cracks in the stucco wall or balconies above the parking area.

There were parking spaces for twelve vehicles. Three were occupied. If this was like most apartment houses, additional spaces could probably be found at the front.

Barbara wondered how many cars might be parked there.

Too bad we can't have the place to ourselves, she thought.

She followed Pete across the parking area and through a narrow passageway to a wrought iron gate. The gate was shut. Pete pulled it open, stepping backward, watching Barbara and nodding for her to go ahead of him.

'Thanks.' She stepped past him and entered the pool area.

Heather was waiting, just off to the side.

With Susie cradled in her arms.

She smiled at Barbara. 'How about *this*?' she asked. Her voice sounded too loud.

'Not bad,' Barbara said, unable to look at anything except Heather and the cat. The bodice of Heather's tan dress was smeared with rust-colored blood. So was the skin of her throat, as if the cat had been nuzzling her with its gory head.

The gate clanked shut, and Pete came to her side. He met her eyes, then looked at Heather. His lips peeled back. 'You're getting it all over you,' he said.

'No big deal. It's only a little blood.'

Mrs Klein's blood, Barbara thought. Blood from a dead woman. A woman killed by the very cat that Heather was hugging to her chest and caressing.

'You'd better hope Susie doesn't decide to rip *your* throat open,' Barbara said.

'Aw, she's a nice kitty.'

'My butt,' Barbara said.

'You'd *better* be careful with that thing,' Pete warned. 'Maybe it just went temporarily insane, or something, but it *did* kill her, and maybe it – you know – wouldn't mind doing something like that again.'

Heather gently kissed the top of Susie's head.

'Oh!' Pete blurted in disgust. 'Man!'

She grinned at him. Her lips now had more color than before.

Barbara grimaced. 'I'm going in the pool.'

'Same here,' Pete said.

She waited by his side.

He faced Heather. 'You'll stay out till we're done, won't you?' he asked.

'Maybe I will, and maybe I won't.'

'Hey. Please?'

'I found it, you know.'

'We know, but . . .'

'What'll you give me?'

'Let's not play stupid games,' Barbara said. 'Come on. Before somebody shows up and kicks us out of here and none of us gets to go in the water.'

'Susie and I *both* need a swim,' Heather explained.

'Just wait till we're out,' Pete told her.

'All right.'

'Thanks. It's not you. It's just that we don't want to be in the blood.'

'But I will require a small favor.'

Barbara considered punching her in the face.

If I slug her, I'll probably get some of that blood on my fist.

And that damn cat'll probably rip my face off.

'Okay,' Pete said. 'What do you want?'

'One favor.'

'What?'

Heather tilted her head. 'Anything I ask.'

'Let's just get in the pool,' Barbara muttered, turning her scowl toward Pete.

He ignored her. '*What* favor?'

'I haven't decided yet.'

'Oh, I'm supposed to . . .'

'The hell with all this,' Barbara said. She left them where they stood, and walked toward the pool. The surface of the water glimmered with sunlight.

At the edge, she stopped.

She turned slowly, scanning the windows and doors of the apartments surrounding the courtyard. All the doors were shut. The draperies appeared to be drawn behind most of the windows. Through a few windows, however, she could see the dim interiors of rooms.

Everybody can't be gone, she thought. Somebody almost *has* to be home.

Home, and watching us.

Why do they have to be sneaky about it? she wondered. *Maybe afraid of us. Scared we might be dangerous, or something. What if they're the dangerous ones?*

'Just stay out,' Pete said to Heather.

'I will. But you owe me.'

'Yeah, sure.'

Hearing Pete's footsteps behind her, Barbara slipped her purse strap off her shoulder. She set the purse down by her feet, then started to take off her shoes and socks. The concrete was very hot. After taking off her socks, she stood on them and twisted sideways to watch Pete get ready.

As he unfastened the buttons of his shirt, Barbara said, 'Did you bring your suit?'

He threw her a nervous smile and shook his head. 'Guess I'll just empty my pockets and go in the way I am.'

'Same here.' She nodded at the bandage on his forearm. 'You'd better try to keep that dry.'

'It's not really much of a cut.' He let his shirt fall, then started to take off his shoes.

'Oh!' Heather called, looking over her shoulder as she walked toward the far end of the pool. 'I forgot to tell you about the jacuzzi!'

Barbara saw it now – a low circle of tiles at the pool's corner.

'I wasn't even *gonna* get in *your* pool. Not till I was clean. So, ha! But you still owe me a favor, anyhow, Pete. A deal's a deal.'

'Fine,' Pete muttered. 'We'll see.'

'Watch this!' Heather called.

Still a few strides from the spa, she hurled Susie through the air. The cat cried, '*Rowwwwww!*' as it tumbled. In mid-air, it flipped over. It dropped paws-first into the spa. Water splashed high. Heather clapped her hands and hopped with delight.

An instant later, the cat sprang out of the spa. In a blur of speed, it scampered across the concrete away from Heather, away from the pool, and under the gate at the front entrance to the courtyard.

'Susie!' Heather shouted.

'Quiet down!' Barbara snapped. 'Do you wanta get us kicked out of here?'

'She's running away!'

'What did you expect? You don't throw cats into water like that.'

'Oh.' Heather looked agonized. 'I just wanted to wash the blood off her.' She glanced toward the gate, then turned to Barbara. 'Will she come back?'

'I doubt it.'

'Maybe you'd better go and find her,' Pete suggested. 'If you don't, that's probably the last you'll ever see of Susie.'

'Will you come and help?'

'We'd better not,' Barbara said. 'Cats get spooked awfully easily. If Pete and I come, we'd probably scare it off. You'd have more luck by yourself.'

'You'd better hurry,' Pete added.

Heather started jogging toward the front gate. She looked back. 'You guys won't leave . . .'

'We'll wait right here,' Pete said.

'Promise?'

'Cross my heart.'

'Okay, then.' She reached the gate, opened it, and walked quickly out of sight.

Barbara and Pete looked at each other. They both smiled. Barbara shrugged.

Pete said, 'Well . . .'

'Did you *see* her throw that cat?'

Pete laughed. 'I couldn't believe it.'

'I could. The girl's odd.'

Pete's smile vanished. 'Well . . . yeah. She's had a tough life, though. You know?'

'I know, I know. All she does is talk about it. Like she's *bragging* about it.'

'Yeah. Sort of. I guess she does get annoying but . . . I feel kind of sorry for her.'

'That's what she wants.'

'You think so?'

Barbara shrugged. She wished she hadn't started in on the girl. Now, Pete probably figured that she was heartless. 'I don't know,' she said. 'I've got nothing much against her, I guess. I'm going in.'

With that, she dived into the pool. It didn't look quite as full as it should be, so she didn't dive deep.

The water seemed to hit her everywhere at once, shocking her with its cold. She felt as if every inch of her body had suddenly been clamped by icy pliers. Almost immediately, however, the pain faded. She glided through the water, just beneath the surface, relishing the coldness.

It caressed her. It licked away her heat.

Surfacing, she rolled onto her back. She floated and watched Pete. He still stood above the other end of the pool. He was barefoot and shirtless. His pants looked big and hot. She wondered if he would change his mind and take them off.

No, not Pete.

Even if he was wearing perfectly decent underwear, he didn't seem like the kind of guy who would take his pants off in public, in broad daylight.

Not that I'd *want* him to, Barbara thought.

Not that I'd *mind*, as long as he keeps his underwear on. Might be kind of neat.

Maybe he doesn't even *wear* any underwear.

Of course he does, she told herself. Don't be ridiculous.

'What are you waiting for?' she asked.

He shrugged. 'I don't know.'

Lowering her legs, she found the bottom of the pool. She stood up. The water covered her to the waist.

Pete stood motionless and stared at her.

'Are you gonna take off your pants?' Barbara asked.

He didn't answer. He acted as if he hadn't even heard the

question. He simply stood there, mouth hanging open, and continued to stare at Barbara.

She glanced down at herself. Her blouse had come unbuttoned all the way. It was open, showing a lot of tanned, wet skin. And showing too much of her bra. This time, the cup on the right side was exposed. It held her breast like a white, flimsy pouch. It was almost transparent. Her nipple pushed at the clinging fabric like a stiff, dark cone.

Oh, my God!

Her heart slammed and heat flooded through her. She felt as if her breath had been stolen.

Her hand trembled as she raised it out of the water and fumbled with the right side of her blouse and covered her breast.

It's no big deal, she told herself. It's nothing. So what if he saw . . .?

'How's the water?' Pete asked. He sounded awfully nervous.

Sure he's nervous. He's been staring at my boob. And he knows I saw him.

'The water's fine. Are you coming in?'

'Should I?'

'Yeah. Come on.'

'Okay. Okay, sure.' Bobbing his head, he rubbed his hands together. 'Here I come, ready or not.' He dived off the edge.

Obviously, he was used to easier methods of entering pools. Barbara found herself grinning, but trembling, as he came down flat and smacked the water hard.

'Ouch!' she gasped.

Water from his huge splash rained down.

She stayed where she was, and watched him swim closer. He stopped just out of reach, and stood. The water was halfway up his chest. He blinked and wiped his eyes. 'It's *cold*!' he gasped.

'Yeah. Are you okay? You sure did a belly-whomper.'

He smiled. 'I'm not the greatest diver in the world.'

'You're okay, though?'

'Sure.' He nodded. His gaze darted down from her face, but he looked away fast.

Suddenly very aware that she was standing higher than Pete and in water just to her waist, she squatted down until the water lapped over her shoulders. Letting go of her blouse, she raised her arms away from her sides and moved them slowly to keep herself steady.

Pete went lower, too.

Only his head was above the water, but Barbara could see his neck and shoulders and arms and chest and belly below the surface. The way the water bent the light, his bare skin seemed to wiggle and shimmy.

Barbara supposed that she must look the same, to him.

Except I'm wearing stuff on top.

With her arms out, her blouse had probably drifted open. She didn't check to find out.

What I don't know won't hurt me.

Pete seemed to be sneaking glances and looking away fast, meeting her eyes for a second, trying to smile, looking all around, finding her eyes again.

'This is pretty neat,' he said after a while.

'It's probably the best place to be. Under the circumstances.'

'A hot day like this,' Pete added.

'Yeah. And safe. There's nothing much that can fall on us here.'

'And if nothing falls on you, you're okay.'

'Unless a cat gets you,' Barbara said.

He laughed softly, glanced down through the water at her, then turned his head away and appeared to study the upper level of the apartment building. 'I wonder where everyone is,' he said.

'It's kind of spooky.'

'Yeah,' Pete said. 'I'm glad, though. That nobody's around. I mean, we're sort of trespassing. We could get kicked out if anybody cared.'

'I know.'

'But where are they all?'

'Who knows?' Barbara said. 'Mostly at work, maybe. But there were cars back by the alley.'

'Yeah. Somebody must be here.'

'Probably spying on us.'

Pete wrinkled his nose. He slowly turned all the way around. His nose was still wrinkled when he faced Barbara again. 'Maybe we oughta get out of here.'

'We have to wait for Heather.'

'Yeah. But . . .'

'We might as well stay in the water till she shows up.'

'I guess so.'

She smiled. 'Scared?'

'Nah.'

'Let 'em spy all they want. As long as they stay in their apartments and don't come out to get us.'

'Oh, real nice.'

She started to scan the apartments, herself. As her gaze moved slowly past doors and windows, she noticed that Pete seemed to be looking straight ahead – at her.

Now that I'm not watching him . . .

Let him, she thought. It's fine.

It's nice.

Let him look all he wants.

'I really do wonder where everyone is,' she said, keeping her eyes away from Pete. 'It isn't just here, either. It's all over the place, ever since we got away from the main streets. I mean, it's not that *nobody* is around. But there just don't seem to be as many people as there *should* be. We're in the middle of Los Angeles. There oughta be people everywhere. They can't *all* be at work. Have they gone into hiding, or something? They can't be *dead*. I guess some are. Maybe a couple of hundred? But that's not so many. Even *thousands* wouldn't be enough to account for everyone being *gone* like this. It's sort of like they *vanished*.'

She glanced at Pete.

He was watching her, all right. Staring at her.

At her face, not at the areas below the water line.

She wasn't sure whether she ought to feel pleased or disappointed. And she found that she felt a little bit of both. 'What do you think?' she asked.

'It's sure funny,' he said.

'Maybe the monsters got them.'

His face broke into a smile. 'That's probably it.'

'I wonder where Heather is.'

'Maybe the cat ate her,' Pete said.

And Barbara laughed. 'Oh, that's real nice. A minute ago, you were sticking up for her.'

'Actually, I like it better when she isn't around.'

'Me, too.'

Pete's eyes seemed to be searching her eyes, almost as if trying to get *into* them. 'I really . . .' His voice quit.

'What?'

He shook his head and looked away. 'I don't know. It's . . . I just wanta . . . I mean, it's really awful, all this stuff that's happened. And how we're kind of stuck out here and things are sort of dangerous. And we don't know if our families are okay or anything. But . . . it's just that . . . I'm not glad any of it happened, nothing like that, but . . . I'm sort of glad we got a chance to . . . I've had a chance to, you know, *be* with you like this.'

'Me, too,' Barbara said.

Pete looked stunned. 'Really?'

'Really.'

'Oh, man.'

'Yeah,' Barbara said.

''Cause, what I mean to say . . . I really sort of *like* you, you know?'

'I really sort of like you, too.'

'You do?'

Barbara reached out through the water. Pete's arm swept forward and he took her hand. She gave his hand a gentle pull that brought him toward her, walking up the slope of the pool's floor but staying low and keeping his head level with Barbara's.

A single stride away from her, he stopped.

He had a very strange look on his face. Barbara couldn't tell whether he was terrified or ecstatic.

'Oh, man,' he said, his voice shaky.

Barbara's lips felt dry. She licked them.

'I can't believe this is happening,' Pete said.

'What?'

'This. You. Would it be . . . is it okay if I . . . Do you want to kiss?'

'Yeah.'

Still holding her hand, he put his other hand against the back of her head. His face came closer. It was sprinkled with tiny bright sparkles of water. His eyelashes came together in tiny, dark points. His eyes jumped a little bit from side to side as if he couldn't make up his mind which of her eyes to look at. He licked his lips. And Barbara shut her eyes.

And waited.

And wondered why he wasn't kissing her yet.

This'll be my first, she realized. My first *real* kiss – not Mom or Dad or a relative or a friend of the family or whatever but a *boy*.

A real boy kissing me.

And now she felt his mouth against her lips. Moist and cool, then warm, pressing gently as he held the back of her head.

This is it, she thought. This is really it. My first kiss, and I'm almost sixteen and it's Pete in a swimming pool on the day of the big quake. And here I am *thinking* about it instead of just *enjoying* it – but it *is* nice.

Nice because of how it feels, she wondered, or nice because it's Pete?

Stop thinking!

He's being very much a gentleman, she thought. Just a nice kiss, no funny stuff.

She wondered if anyone was watching.

From one of the apartments, maybe.

It's not like we're doing something wrong.

Our bodies aren't even touching, she realized. Just our mouths and hands, and his other hand back there in my hair.

It'd be nice to be up against him.

Just as she thought about moving in closer and maybe hugging him, he took his mouth away.

'Maybe we'd better stop,' he whispered. He lowered his hand from the back of her head. It went silently down toward his side.

'Okay,' Barbara said.

'Man.'

'What?'

'Nothing.'

'Come on, tell.'

'I never . . . that was sure a kiss.'

'In what way?' she asked.

He rolled his eyes. 'I don't know!'

'Was it a good kiss?'

'Are you kidding?'

'Felt pretty good to me,' she said.

'It was incredible,' he whispered. '*You're* incredible. I mean, *God*!'

'We'd better pretend nothing happened.'

'What do you mean?'

'Heather. She'd go nuts if she found out we kissed.'

Pete looked surprised. 'Do you think so?'

'Oh, sure. She's got a thing for you.'

'She does?'

'Of course she does. And you know it.'

'Yeah, I guess so.' Then he added, 'I'm very hard to resist,' and laughed as if he thought it a good joke.

'You are.'

'Right.' He laughed again, and shook his head.

'So anyway, if we don't want to see what Heather's like in a jealous rage, we'd better cool it.'

'I guess that means no more kissing.'

'She'd probably pop up right when we're in the middle of one.'

'Yeah. Like on TV.'

'We'll have to just save it for some other time,' Barbara said.

'Any time is fine with me.'

'I'll bet.'

'So . . . what should we do now?'

'Swim around?'

Pete looked toward the front gate. His smile slipped away. 'I wonder what's taking her so long.'

'She must be having trouble with the cat.'

'It's probably not extremely eager to get caught,' Pete said.

'No kidding. Cats hate water. One sinking was probably enough for it.'

After a moment, Pete said, 'I hope nothing's happened to her. She *has* been gone an awfully long time. I mean, if she couldn't catch the cat, don't you think she'd come back?'

'I don't know. She seems like the stubborn type.'

'Something really might have happened to her, though.'

'Do you think we should go and look for her?' Barbara asked.

'I don't much want to.'

'Me, neither. Besides, we said we'd wait here. What if she shows up while we're gone?'

'Can't let that happen.'

Barbara raised her eyebrows. 'Of course, one of us could go looking for her while the other stays here.'

'I'm not sure that's such a good idea,' Pete said.

'It's a *rotten* idea.'

He suddenly smiled again. 'It was *your* idea.'

'Figured somebody oughta bring it up. Doesn't mean I'm in favor of it. I'm totally against splitting up.'

'It'd be stupid to split up.'

'Exactly. Asking for trouble. Besides, she'll probably get back any minute.'

'If we're lucky, without the cat.'

Barbara laughed. 'Exactly.'

Twenty-two

Pete boosted himself up and sat on the edge of the pool.

Barbara, floating on her back near the other end, flipped over and swam to him. She stood up in the waist-high water and checked her blouse. It was unbuttoned and clinging and open a few inches. Just wide enough. Not so wide that it showed enough to be embarrassing.

She put her hands on Pete's knees. 'What do you think?' she asked.

'I don't like it.'

'I don't, either.'

'Where could she be?'

'We can't just stay here *all* day,' Barbara said.

'It hasn't been all that long.'

'Long enough. Between this and all the time we spent . . . you know, at Mrs Klein's . . . we could've been home by now.'

'I've sort of liked it *here*,' Pete said.

'Me, too. I feel about a million times better than I did.'

'That's what kissing me will do for you.'

She let out a laugh. 'Yeah, right. That wasn't bad, either.' She squeezed his knees, gave them a playful shake that jostled the water between his legs, then let go and moved sideways. She stepped forward to the wall of the pool.

Aware of Pete watching, she planted her hands on the concrete near his hip, and jumped. She braced herself up beside him, arms stiff, the edge of the pool hard against her thighs. Then she stayed that way – because of how Pete was trying not to stare at her. She didn't look down at herself. Didn't need to. Just by the feel, she knew that her arms, in tight against her sides, were pushing her breasts together and thrusting them forward. She took a deep breath. The smoky air made her lungs hurt, but she filled them anyway, expanding her chest to improve the view even more.

Pete turned his head away.

'I think we'd better go and find Heather,' Barbara said – just to make him look at her.

It worked. Pete faced her again. He met her eyes and nodded. 'Yeah. Guess we'd better.' He glanced down, began to turn away, then looked again and stared for a few moments before forcing his gaze away and studying the other end of the pool.

Barbara smiled. She swung a leg up, slapped a bare foot onto the ledge, and climbed out of the pool. She stood up straight, her legs apart. Water raced down her body and spilled off her clothes, splashing the concrete between her feet.

Must look like I'm peeing, she thought. So she took a few steps away from the pool. After turning around, she pressed her legs together.

Pete was already walking toward her. His soaked trousers dripped water. They were glued to his legs. Their front bulged, shoved outward by the knobs of Pete's fists which were jammed into the front pockets.

Why the fists? Barbara wondered. She felt a quick stir of worry.

'You okay?' she asked.

'What do you mean?'

'Planning to punch me out?'

'Huh?' He looked confused. Then he blushed and glanced down at the front of his pants. 'Oh, that. Nah. I wouldn't hit you. Are you kidding?' He smiled nervously and shook his head. But his fists remained in his pockets.

'Planning to punch out somebody else?'

'I'm not gonna slug anyone. I just . . . it's nothing, okay? You want me to bring over your shoes and stuff?'

'We can both go,' Barbara said.

Pete turned away. Taking his hands out of his pockets, he walked toward the corner of the pool. Barbara followed him past the corner, and along the side. His back was tanned and shiny. He left trails of water drops.

Halfway to the other end of the pool, Barbara looked into the water. She could see where the bottom began to slope downward.

That's where we were standing. That's where we kissed.

She wondered if she would be able to find this apartment complex again – this pool.

It'd be nice to come back with him some time, she thought.

What if we got married some day and came back to live right here in this building? And we could sneak into the pool late at night when everyone else was asleep, and go to our special place right there . . . ?

Wild, she thought. It'll probably never·happen. But it might. It might, if I want it to badly enough. Dad says you can make almost anything happen if you're willing to go for it.

This is a stupid time to even be *thinking* about stuff like that, she told herself.

No, it's not. As good a time as any . . .

Pete sat down on the concrete to put on his socks and shoes. Barbara sat nearby, but facing him. The concrete felt warm and rather nice through the wet seat of her shorts. She used one of her socks to wipe her feet.

'Maybe we can go somewhere,' Pete said, tying one of his Reeboks.

'Like where?'

'I don't know. Anywhere. How about the beach?'

'Are you crazy?'

'What do you mean?' Pete asked.

'The *beach*? I've gotta get home. And anyway, the beach is miles . . .'

'Not *today*,' Pete said. 'Jeez! That *would* be crazy. I meant like, you know, after all this is over.'

'Oh!'

'What do you think?'

He's asking me out!

'Yeah!' she blurted, and saw his face light up.

'Great! That's great!'

'I'm not sure about the beach, though. We'd have to figure out something that'll be okay with my Mom and Dad.'

If I'll still have a Mom and Dad.

Of course I will. Sure I will. They're fine. They have to be.

'They might have to go along, or something,' she said. 'Depending on what we wanta do. They're awfully protective.'

'That's okay. I don't mind.'

'Maybe you could come over to *my* place,' she suggested. 'You know, for starters. They'd go along with that. As long as one of them is home.'

'That'd be great,' Pete said. 'I don't care *where* we . . .'

A clamor of iron stopped his words.

They snapped their heads sideways. The front gate, flung open by Heather, squawled on its hinges and rang out as it crashed against the fence bars.

Barbara cringed at the noise.

She heard Pete mutter, 'Oh, man.'

Something was wrong.

Huffing and red-faced and streaming sweat, Heather ran toward them with her head thrown back, her mouth sagging, her arms swinging about wildly, her breasts jumping up and down as if trying to rip free of her clothes, her feet pounding down flat so that the soles of her shoes made heavy whapping sounds with each stride.

She was still bloody from the cat.

The cat didn't seem to be with her, though.

Maybe it's chasing her, Barbara thought.

Something must be chasing her.

But nothing followed Heather through the gate. It clanged shut as she chugged alongside the pool, hurrying toward Barbara and Pete.

They finished with their shoes. Pete grabbed his shirt and started to get up. Barbara reached for the denim strap of her purse.

She looked again at Heather.

No purse.

It had been hanging from Heather's shoulder when she left to go chasing after Susie, but now it was gone.

Does she know she lost it?

Maybe it got snatched, and that's why she's acting so weird and scared.

The kid who snatched mine is dead.

Maybe his ghost . . . yeah, right.

Pete and Barbara were on their feet by the time Heather staggered to a halt by the corner of the pool. Wheezing, she bent over and clutched her knees. She shook her head. 'Gotta get . . . outa here,' she gasped. 'They're coming.'

Barbara felt a sudden, sinking coldness inside.

'Who's coming?' Pete asked. 'What do you mean?'

'Guys. Whole bunch of 'em. Like a gang. I saw 'em . . . pulled people outa cars . . . Killed 'em . . . Can't let 'em get us . . . Can't . . . If they get us . . . Gotta hide.'

'Where are they?' Pete asked.

Still bent over, she let go of one knee and raised her arm. She flopped her hand in the direction of the front gate, then clutched her knee again.

'How far away?'

'Don't know. Couple blocks?'

'Are they coming this way?'

'Yeah.'

'Did they see you?' Barbara asked.

'Chased me.'

'Oh, my God,' Barbara said.

'Just two . . . came after me. Think I lost 'em.' Heather stood up straight. Still gasping for air, she wiped her face on a sleeve. Then she looked toward the gate. 'Lost 'em a few minutes ago. Over on . . . a different street. Hid. Circled around. But the main bunch is coming. Just saw 'em.'

'From right out in front?' Pete asked.

'Yeah.'

'Did they see you come in here?' Barbara asked.

'Don't know. Don't think so, but . . . Maybe. We gotta hide. Gotta hide quick.'

Barbara met Pete's eyes. He looked scared. 'Go for the alley?' she asked.

'No!' Heather blurted. 'They'll get us. I can't run. Can't. But I . . . I figured it out. We can hide here. All we gotta do is . . . get in a door . . . they'll never find us.'

'Break into an apartment?' Pete asked.

'Yeah! Yeah, it's perfect. They won't . . . know where to look for us.'

They'll know if they spot a busted door, Barbara thought.

'Upstairs,' Pete said. 'We'll try upstairs.'

Pete in the lead, they ran to the nearest stairway. He rushed up the stairs, taking three at a time. Barbara took two at a time. Heather grunted and wheezed behind her.

At the top, Pete raced along the balcony and stopped at the first door. He grabbed its knob, twisted it and shoved it.

'Nobody's gonna leave their doors unlocked,' Barbara said. 'Should I bust it in?'

'No. Not this one. Keep going.'

We don't want to hide in the very first room at the top of the stairs, she thought. Besides, maybe there *would* be a door that somebody hadn't bothered to lock.

They hurried on to the door of the next apartment. Pete tried that one, shook his head, and kept going.

Barbara followed him almost as far as the third door, then veered to the side and gazed over the railing. Nobody had entered the pool area yet. But she winced at the sight of the trails they had left on the concrete.

Huge, dark splotches of wetness showed where they had climbed out of the pool. A lot of water must've spilled off them there. Not so much where they had hurried along the side of the pool; only a few traces of dampness remained to show that trail. But plenty of water remained, undried, at the end where they had sat down to put on their shoes and socks.

From there, a weak trail of dribbles, barely noticeable from Barbara's position at the railing, led to the stairway they had used.

'They're gonna know we were here,' she said.

Pete lurched to the railing. He peered down. 'It's drying fast,' he said. 'In a couple of minutes, we oughta be okay.'

As if they'd both been struck by the same idea, Barbara and Pete suddenly turned their heads to see if they'd left a trail of water along the balcony.

Just a few drops.

'We'll be okay if we can get inside,' Pete said.

'In here!'

Barbara's heart jumped. She saw Pete flinch, heard Heather gasp.

She turned in time to see the door of the next apartment swing open wide.

A man stepped out.

He had a pistol, but it was pointed upward, not at them.

He was young – probably not much older than twenty – stocky and muscular. His hair was so short that the pale skin of his scalp showed through. His face looked handsome, but grim, with bright blue eyes and a broad jaw. He wore a white T-shirt, tight blue jeans and combat boots of gleaming black leather.

'Get in here,' he said. He gestured them forward with his pistol.

Pete looked back at Barbara and Heather. He shrugged, then turned again to the man in the doorway. 'Uh . . . Do we *have* to? I mean, what's going on? Are we supposed to be, like, your prisoners, or . . . ?' He shrugged again.

The man stared at Pete, eyes narrow.

After a moment, he said, 'You don't wanta see your day ruined, you'd better get in here fast.'

Twenty-three

On their way to the top of Laurel Canyon Boulevard, Clint and Em walked side by side up the middle of the road. Mary followed them at a distance. Sometimes, she gained on them when they stopped for a rest. But soon afterward, she would need to stop, herself, and they would leave her farther behind.

They stepped right over a few minor cracks that ran across the pavement.

When they came to the first of those, Clint had said, 'Watch out. Step on a crack, break your mother's back.'

Em had stepped over it, then given Clint a puzzled look. 'What was that about my mother's back?'

'An expression. "Step on a crack, break your mother's back." You've never heard it before?'

'Not that way. It was "step on a crack, snap a fella's back."'

'Bet your mom taught you that one.'

'You mean it doesn't go that way?'

'It's "break your *mother's* back."'

'I've been misled.' Grinning, Em had shaken her head. 'We used to chant it – Mom's version – and jump up and down on every crack we found.'

'I can't *wait* to meet your mother. I think I'll have to send you home in a taxi.'

'Oh, don't worry about her. She'll like you. How can she not, you know what I mean? You may be a man, but . . .'

'Hey, there's no "may be" about that. Please!'

'Anyway, you're not a jerk like most guys.'

'Why, thank you. I'm honored.'

They'd crossed several more cracks during the next few minutes. Though nothing more was said about the expression, Clint noticed that Em avoided stepping on any of them.

Higher up the hillside, they came upon a much larger break in the pavement. The jagged fissure crossed every lane of the road, but was never more than about two feet wide. Over to the right, several smaller cracks led away from it.

Em, striding along by Clint's side, suddenly halted and said, 'Wait wait wait. Whoa.'

'What?'

'Look at that thing.'

'The crack? It's no big deal. We can step right over it.'

'I'm not so sure about *that*. How deep is it?'

Clint walked closer to it.

'Be careful! Don't fall in.'

One more stride carried him near enough to see the bottom. 'It's not even three feet deep.'

'Are you sure it doesn't drop down into some sort of chasm or abyss?'

'Positive.'

'Okay. I didn't think so. Not really. But, you know, they *do* in the movies. I've seen movies where the ground opens up and swallows people whole – and like the crack goes all the way down to the center of the Earth, or something. Which is ludicrous. But one can't be too careful, if you know what I mean. I've never been in a quake of *this* magnitude, so who knows what might happen? Have you heard about "liquefaction"? Now *that's* pretty scary. And it's real, too. It's like the ground right under you can turn into quicksand? I've never seen that in the movies, though, have you?'

'I've seen quicksand in the movies,' Clint said, and crossed over the crack with one long stride.

'I mean liquefaction.'

Safe on the other side, he turned around and watched Em staring at the split. 'I haven't seen that in movies,' he said.

'Me, neither. I guess it's not as dramatic as falling into a bottomless chasm.'

'I don't know if liquefaction would swallow a person the way quicksand does,' Clint said. 'For that matter, I have my doubts that quicksand swallows people for real the way it does in movies.'

'You're probably right.' Em began to step toward the crack carefully, like someone walking on the frozen surface of a pond. 'The movies basically never get anything right, do they?'

'Mostly not.'

'I love 'em anyway, though.'

Clutching the grocery sack against his chest, Clint reached out his other arm. Em took hold of his hand. She clutched it tightly as she stepped across the gap.

'A cinch, right?'

'Right,' Em said. 'Thanks.' She let go, then turned around. She frowned down the road toward Mary, who was slogging her way slowly toward them. 'Maybe we oughta wait for her.'

'I don't see why,' Clint said.

'She might need a hand.'

'Tough tacos. She should've thought of that before she whacked you.'

'You aren't exactly brimming over with forgiveness, are you?'

'Nope. Come on, let's go.' They resumed walking. 'I am fairly forgiving of mistakes,' he explained. 'Screw-ups, accidents, errors in judgment . . . People should pay attention to what they do and consider what the consequences might be, but everybody makes mistakes. Meanness is something else. There's no excuse for it. There's no excuse for the way she hit you.'

'Does that mean you're *never* going to forgive her?'

'Not in the foreseeable future.'

'Whew. Hope *I* never tick you off.' As she said that, she looked back.

Clint looked, too. Mary was trudging up the road, the fissure behind her. 'See,' he said. 'She didn't need help, anyway.'

'Guess not.' They continued uphill. 'But you'll help her in case of *real* trouble.' It didn't sound like a question, more like a statement of fact.

'That remains to be seen,' Clint said.

Soon, they came upon a tree that had dropped across the road.

'The cops didn't say anything about this,' Em said.

'Nope, they sure didn't.'

The tree roots had left a dark pit in the hillside just above the road. The clump hadn't gone far; it rested at the edge of the hole like a ball joint popped from its socket. It was eight to ten feet high, and clotted with dirt. It elevated that end of the trunk.

'Your choice,' Clint said as they walked toward the fallen tree. 'Over, under, or around?'

Em turned her head, studying the tree from one end to the other. 'Looks like there's some room to crawl under it,' she said.

Still in the middle of the road, they angled to the left so they would reach the tree near its roots. Em took the lead. Stopping short of the trunk, she squatted down. She looked from side to side. Clint stopped behind her.

'Problem?' he asked.

'Maybe we'd better climb over, instead. It might not be the safest thing in the world, crawling under there.'

He walked past Em, placed a hand against the trunk, and shoved. The tree didn't budge. 'I don't think it's going anywhere.'

Em stood up. She made a face at Clint, and shook her head. 'I wouldn't want to be crawling under it if there's an aftershock. That would not be at all swift, if you know what I mean. A person could get squashed like a bug. And I think we're past due for an aftershock.'

'We're probably having them all along,' Clint said.

'Oh, I know. I'm sure we've had dozens, so far. Even hundreds.'

'I haven't felt any yet, have you?'

'I don't think so. But you don't have to feel them. They're there, all right. And we'll have a really big one sooner or later. Maybe even one as big as the first quake. Or bigger, though that isn't very likely.'

'You know your quakes,' Clint told her.

'Sure. How can you *not*?'

'I guess we all do,' Clint said.

'But I also did a paper on them in sixth grade, so I learned a lot then. It's only a matter of time . . .'

'That's close enough,' Clint called.

Mary, a few yards downslope from Em, stopped and uncapped her plastic bottle. She held the bottle of water by her side and panted for air, apparently too winded to take a drink.

Em turned around. 'The tree's in our way,' she said.

Mary found enough breath to gasp, 'No fooling.'

'We're gonna climb over it.'

'Be my guest.'

'In case of an aftershock.'

Mary smirked. 'What's an . . . aftershock . . . got to do with it?'

'Make it fall and smash you.'

'While you're crawling . . . underneath?'

623

'Yeah.'

'Right. You'd only be under the thing . . . couple of seconds. Wouldn't fall, anyway.'

Clint agreed with her, but he kept it to himself.

'You go ahead and crawl under if you want,' Em told the woman. 'But I'm going *over* it. Better safe than mashed like a bug.'

Mary raised the plastic bottle to her mouth and tipped back her head. She only took one swallow, then had to stop for a breath. After another swallow, she lowered the bottle. 'Do I have to wait?' she asked Clint.

He shook his head. As Mary stepped closer, he watched her.

'Don't worry,' she said, 'I'm not gonna *beat up* on anybody.'

'I'm not worried.'

'Just looking for an excuse to smack me, aren't you?'

'No.'

'Yeah, right.' She sidestepped past Em and Clint, then turned away and sank to her knees. She crawled under the trunk, the plastic bottle dragging against the pavement, her rump swaying from side to side. Clint noticed that she didn't have stockings on. Had she been wearing them earlier? He thought so. The lack of stockings made her legs seem strangely vulnerable.

Maybe I shouldn't be so tough on her, he thought.

But his moment of regret was pushed aside by the memory of Mary striking Em.

Don't go soft, he told himself, just because she looks a little bedraggled and pathetic.

'She'll make it,' Em said.

Mary must've heard her. 'The aftershock's waiting for *you*, sweetie.' A moment later, she cried out, '*OW! Shit shit shit!*'

Clint and Em crouched and looked.

Mary was only visible from the rump down. She seemed to be standing, hobbling away from the tree.

'Are you okay?' Em called.

'No!'

'What happened?'

624

'I wracked myself.'

'What happened?' Em asked again.

'As if anybody cares,' Mary said, and kept going.

'Wait!' Em rushed forward, dropped to her hands and knees, and started to scurry under the tree.

So much for climbing over it, Clint thought.

And realized that he wasn't concerned about the possibility of an aftershock – such a slim possibility that a huge one would hit at exactly the wrong time and drop the tree onto Em.

He found himself more interested in the look of her. She was crawling on her hands and knees, the same as Mary had done. Her white shorts were tight across her rump. Dirt smudges and grass stains on their seat reminded Clint of the fall she'd taken in front of her house – after being punched in the chest by that horrible, ugly woman named Lou. Lou the looter.

Even before that, before he had met Em, she'd gotten her back scraped by a brick. And finally, Mary had given her head a swat.

She'd been through plenty. A lot more than Mary. But there was nothing at all vulnerable or pathetic about how she looked as she crawled under the tree.

A kid on an adventure, eagerly crawling into the mouth of a cave.

Barbara.

This could've been Barbara, a couple of years ago. They're so much alike.

Em's a lot wilder, feistier, but . . .

'Watch it when you stand up,' Mary said. 'That's how I wracked myself. Stood up too soon and it got me in the back.'

She's warning Em. Good for her. Trying to get back in our good graces?

Doesn't matter why she warned Em, Clint told himself. Not much, anyway. She did it, and that's what counts.

Em stayed down. As she crawled a little farther, Clint got to his hands and knees. They were scraped raw. He winced and gritted his teeth. He thought about his dive to avoid the speeding Toyota pickup truck. The quake had still been going on when he'd thrown himself out of the way and skidded on the pavement. It seemed like a very long time ago. Days ago, not a few hours. So long ago that the abrasions on his palms and knees should've healed by now. But they hurt like hell.

Bracing himself up on his knuckles and thumbs, he scuttled underneath the tree on the balls of his feet.

No aftershock.

In probably no more than three seconds, he was on the other side. He started to rise, then remembered Mary's warning to Em and stayed down a few moments longer. To make sure that he was clear of the tree, he looked over his shoulder. And saw a broken limb jutting straight down from the trunk. A miniature stalactite, no larger than a thumb but sharp at its splintered end.

Em was lifting the back of Mary's blouse. Clint sidestepped for a better angle. He glimpsed blood on the fabric. Then Mary's skin was there. The gouge started just below the cross-strap of her bra. It was about three inches long, and looked as if someone had tried to plow a furrow down her back with a stick.

'Bet that hurts,' Em told her.

'God, what if it leaves a scar?'

'It won't,' Clint said.

'How would *you* know?' Mary snapped. 'This is all your fault!'

Of course, he thought. Should've known. As much as he loved Sheila and Barbara, they were usually quick to put the blame on him – no matter how remote his involvement might be in whatever mishap had befallen them. He had come to figure out that this was normal behavior for women.

'My fault?' he asked.

'You had me so upset,' Mary said, 'that I couldn't pay attention to what I was doing!'

'I had you upset?'

'Treating me like I'm some kind of a criminal.'

'Oh. I see.'

Em, still frowning at Mary's wound, said, 'We oughta put some water on it, maybe.'

Clint set down the bag. Em took out a water bottle and a paper napkin. She moistened the napkin. While Clint held up the back of Mary's blouse, Em gently dabbed at the wound.

'How does that feel?' Em asked her.

'Better.'

'Weird, huh? It wasn't all that long ago, you were doing this to me.'

'I liked it better that way,' Mary said.

Em laughed, and so did Mary. Even Clint found himself smiling.

'Now,' Em said, 'Clint's the only one who hasn't gotten screwed in the back.'

Looking over her shoulder, Mary gave him a tight smile. 'The day isn't over yet.'

'Real nice,' he said.

Em smoothed the wet napkin against Mary's wound. 'We'll leave it there,' she said. Guiding Clint's hand, she lowered the blouse. He let go of it. Em tucked it under the waistband at the back of Mary's skirt. 'That might hold it for a while.'

Clint looked at Em's back. Her T-shirt was clinging with sweat, spotted a little with blood near her shoulderblade. 'What happened to your paper towel?' he asked her.

'Oh, it fell out a long time ago.' She suddenly grimaced. 'Is there blood on my shirt?'

'Some.'

'Poop!'

'That's all right,' Clint assured her. 'Your blood goes nicely with the shirt's "road-kill" motif.'

She grinned. 'Hadn't thought of that. Speaking of road-kill, who's hungry?'

Mary turned around and faced them. She glanced from Em to Clint. 'I'll leave, now. Thanks for nothing.'

'You don't have to go,' Em said. 'Does she, Clint? Come on, tell her she can stay. I mean, I'm the one she whacked. And anyway, I might've gotten porked by the tree if it hadn't been for Mary.'

'If it hadn't been for Mary, you would've climbed over it.'

She grinned. 'Might've fallen and broken my neck. So see? That makes *twice* she's saved me.'

'Oh, sure,' he said.

'Anyway, don't you think she's been banished for long enough?'

Not really, he thought. It's asking for trouble.

But Mary *had* warned Em. That had to count for something. And she hadn't done any serious damage to Em by giving her the smack on the head. And Em herself wanted Mary to be given a second chance.

'Okay,' he finally said. He met Mary's eyes. 'Are you going to behave from now on?'

She glared at him. 'I guess so.'

'You guess?'

'I don't wanta be left behind any more.'

'This is sort of going against my rules, so don't blow it. Don't make me regret being nice to you.'

Mary's upper lip twitched.

'Why don't we all settle down and take a break and have something to eat?' Em said. 'This is as good a place as any.'

Gazing up the slope, Clint could see the unlighted traffic signals at Mulholland. They marked the crest of the ridge. Just beyond them, Laurel Canyon Boulevard began its long, curving way downward to Hollywood.

To Sunset Boulevard.

On the other side of Sunset, there would be no more hills to climb. The road would stop being Laurel Canyon and become Crescent Heights, and following it would lead him most of the way home.

Clint had wanted to reach the top before taking a break for lunch. But his bouts with Mary made him feel like a dictator. He didn't enjoy the feeling.

'Fine with me,' he told Em. 'Let's have lunch here. This looks like a great place for it.'

'Good, 'cause I happen to be starving.'

Twenty-four

The curtains behind the sofa were shut across the picture window, filtering out the sunlight, giving the room a murky yellow glow.

Barbara and Pete sat beside each other on the floor across from the sofa. Barbara figured that Pete had picked this spot because it was low and away from the big window. But maybe he'd avoided the furniture out of simple courtesy, because his trousers were wet. Either way, she liked where she was. She felt fairly safe down here. She had a wall at her back and she had a full view of the curtained window, the door, Heather and Lee.

Heather had taken a seat on the sofa as if she'd forgotten all about the blood on her legs and arms and hands. She sat sideways, one leg tucked under her, her hands resting on her thighs, her face toward Lee.

Lee was kneeling in the middle of the sofa, elbows on top of the back rest, peering outside through a bright sliver of space between the curtains.

His pistol was stuck down the waistband at the back of his jeans. Beside him on the sofa was a mean-looking, stubby rifle with a leather sling. It looked to Barbara like a military weapon. Just in front of its trigger guard, a big chrome magazine jutted downward.

A similar magazine was on the table in front of the sofa. At the open top of this one, Barbara could see a couple of slim pointed cartridges that were almost golden in the mellow light. A much smaller magazine was also on the table. Barbara figured that this one must belong to the pistol. The cartridge showing at the top was fat – its slug, a dull gray dome.

On top of the same table were several boxes of ammunition. And a pair of binoculars.

The first words out of Barbara's mouth, after being ushered into the apartment and glimpsing the collection, had been, 'Charles Whitman, I presume?'

629

'Lee Nolan,' he'd corrected her, grim-faced. Barbara's reference to the Texas Tower sniper had apparently gone over his head. 'I'm the manager here,' he'd said. 'Your two friends are Pete and Heather. Didn't catch your name.'

'Barbara. How do you know . . .?'

'Their names? You wouldn't believe the way sound carries in this place. From up here, I can hear the *ripples* in the swimming pool.'

'You were listening to us.'

'And watching.'

A heat of embarrassment had spread through Barbara as she pictured Lee at the windows, spying on her and Pete in the pool, treating himself to close-up views with the help of his binoculars. At such close range, it must've been like watching them from about two feet away.

'Terrific,' she had muttered, and glanced down to make sure that the top of her blouse hadn't somehow come open in spite of her left hand clutching it shut. The tight fist in the middle of her chest could only draw attention to the problem – and to her breasts. Especially how her left one stuck out and pretty much hid her wrist.

Still, she'd been determined to keep her hand there and hold her blouse shut.

'It's my job,' Lee had explained, 'to know what's happening in and around my facility. And to protect it.'

'We weren't doing anything,' Pete had told him.

'Sure you were. But you weren't doing any harm to my tenants or property. That's why I didn't interfere until you started trying to get through doors.'

'We don't normally do stuff like that,' Pete had explained.

'It's all right. This isn't a normal day. Sit down. Everyone sit down. Heather, start talking. I want every detail of what you saw out there.'

Heather then started in on an expanded version of the story she'd blurted to Pete and Barbara down by the pool. Lee didn't seem to pay much attention. He kept gazing out through the tiny gap between the curtains.

Barbara figured that he must've overheard the original . . . he'd heard everything else said down there.

Seen everything, too.

She'd been aware, all along, that people might be watching from the apartments. Peeking out from time to time, maybe. It hadn't occurred to her, though, that anyone would study them with binoculars – and listen to every word.

From where she sat, she could hear enough to know that the windows were open. She listened for the sound of ripples in the pool.

Not quite. There was a vague, hollow murmur that she thought of as 'pool noise' – a sound as faint as the whisper of a seashell held close to the ear.

But she couldn't hear ripples.

Though maybe if Heather weren't talking . . . Maybe if there wasn't that undercurrent of noises from outside the courtyard: faraway shouts and barks and sirens and bangs and horn blasts and engines . . . tires squealing . . . a scream now and then so muffled that she couldn't tell whether it belonged to a cat or a person.

Such background noises were barely noticeable unless you listened hard for them. Some of them must've gotten in the way a *little*, though.

Lee couldn't possibly have heard everything.

A lot, though.

She hated the idea that he might've heard Pete's shy, stumbling speech about liking her. Somehow, that seemed even worse than knowing he'd probably focused those damn binoculars in on her breasts.

He saw our kiss, too.

It really hurt that he'd watched that.

The creep.

'How many were there?' Lee asked, and Barbara realized that she'd been paying no attention to Heather's story.

'I don't know,' Heather said.

'Yes, you do. Think.'

'Well, maybe ten or twelve.'

He carefully shut the crack between the curtains, then

turned sideways on his knees and frowned down at Heather. 'How were they armed?'

'Some had guns.'

'How many guns did you see?'

Heather shrugged, then quickly said, 'Four? Maybe five. That I saw. Maybe they *all* had guns, but just weren't using them. I saw knives, too. And one guy had an axe.'

Pete grimaced at Lee. 'What'll we do?' he asked.

'There're too many to take on,' Lee said.

'Glad to hear it,' Barbara said.

Lee twisted his head around and gave her a sharp look. 'You find humor in this situation?'

'Not really.'

'I can do without your wise-ass comments.'

She tried not to cringe. 'I'm sorry, okay? I didn't mean anything.'

'Didn't mean anything by that Whitman crack, either, did you?'

She felt herself suddenly blush. 'Oh, that. Whoops.'

'Yeah, whoops.'

This guy had no sense of humor at all.

'It's just that . . . you've got these guns and you sort of look like you're itching for a shootout. So I was sort of surprised when you said that about not wanting to take on that mob, or whatever it is out there. That's all. Okay? I didn't mean to . . . you know, insult you.'

'Is that supposed to be an apology?' he asked.

Barbara shrugged. 'I guess so.'

'Never apologize. It's a sign of weakness.'

'Oh, for . . .' *What does he want?* 'Right,' she said. 'Whatever you say, sir.'

'Cut the attitude,' Lee said.

Heather grinned.

'*You* shut up,' Barbara told her.

'Me?' Heather asked, all innocence. 'What did *I* say?'

'It's your fault we're here in the first place, you and that damn cat.'

'Leave her alone,' Lee said.

And Heather glowed as if she'd been blessed.

Lee turned toward the window and parted the curtains.

Barbara bared her teeth at Heather.

Heather smirked at her.

'What *is* the plan?' Pete asked.

'We wait and see,' Lee said, peering out the window. 'If we're lucky, the marauders bypass us. There's a whole city out there. They can't hit everyplace.'

'What if they do show up here?'

'My first responsibility is to my tenants.'

'Tenants?'

'I have people in four of the units.'

'Right now?' Pete asked.

'You've got it. I made the rounds after the quake hit. Minimal damage, and no casualties. Most of my tenants had already left for work. A few are away on trips. But I've got people in those four units, like I said, and I have to protect them.'

'I thought you weren't going to take anybody on,' Barbara reminded him.

He didn't bother to look around at her. 'That only means I'm not planning an offensive operation. It doesn't rule out a defensive action.'

'Oh.'

'Maybe you think we should hunker down and hide in here while they slaughter my tenants.'

'I don't think that,' Barbara protested.

'I don't see why *we* should stick around, though,' Pete said. 'We aren't gonna be of much help if we don't have guns. I mean our idea was to lay low. But if you're planning to fight, maybe we oughta try and get away while we've still got a chance.'

'Fine with me,' Lee said.

Pete leaned closer to Barbara and said in a soft voice, 'What do you think? We could take off out the back and make a run down the alley.'

'Not me,' Heather said.

Pete's gaze stayed on Barbara. 'Whatever. We don't have to let that stop us.'

'Leave without her?'

'Go ahead,' Heather told them. 'I'm not going out there, not unless Lee *makes* me.'

'You're free to stay here,' Lee told her. 'It's your call.'

'Are you sure? That's so sweet of you. But are you sure you wouldn't mind? I don't want to get in your way, or anything.'

Barbara looked at her.

Obsequious, is that the right word?

Or fawning?

Or does she suddenly adore this guy?

Nah. She's gotta be faking it. Laying it on thick, so he won't toss her out.

Sickening, Barbara thought. The girl's pathetic.

'Stay,' Lee said. 'Or leave. Either way is fine with me. I'd think you might want to go with your friends, though.'

'Are you kidding? That mob's out there! I don't wanta get gang-raped and torn apart. Anyhow, I'm just in the same driver's ed class with those two – it's not like they're my friends.' When she said that, she cast a hurt look at Pete.

As if he'd betrayed her.

What does she know? Barbara suddenly wondered.

Maybe Lee isn't the only one who was spying on us.

No, she thought. Heather didn't see us, she's just mad because we didn't go with her to chase the cat.

'Even if we aren't friends,' Barbara said, 'we probably oughta stick together.'

'I don't see why.'

'How will you get home?' Pete asked.

Heather's shoulders bobbed up and down. 'I don't care. It doesn't matter.'

'Getting home,' Lee said, 'shouldn't be anybody's top priority at this point. Number one priority is survival.'

'Yeah,' Pete said. 'I agree.' He turned again to Barbara. 'That's why I think we should get out of here. With or without Heather. I think we'll stand a better chance if we're on the run. I mean, if anything goes down, Lee's planning on a shootout. It'll be like the OK Corral around here.'

Barbara nodded. 'I'm with you.' She glanced at the others.

Lee was peering out the window again. Heather met her eyes, and had a strange, sly smile. 'You're sure you want to stay here?' Barbara asked her.

'Why would I wanta go anywhere with you two?'

'Can't imagine,' Barbara said.

'I'll take my chances here, thanks anyway.'

'Okay.' Still holding her blouse shut with her left hand, Barbara shoved at the floor with her right as she drew in her legs and started to stand up. Her rump felt a little itchy. On her feet, she rubbed the damp seat of her shorts while Pete got up. 'So,' she said, 'I guess we'll be going.'

'You sure you don't want to change your mind?' Pete asked Heather. 'Once we're gone, it'll be a little too late.'

'Too late for you, you mean.'

They were almost to the door when the sound of a soft *clank* hit Barbara like a blow to the heart. She gasped and halted. Pete froze. Heather snapped her head toward Lee.

Lee's back stiffened.

'One of the gates?' Heather whispered.

Of course it's one of the gates, you idiot! They're here. They're down by the pool.

One eye at the gap between the curtains, Lee raised an open hand.

Nobody moved.

Nobody spoke.

My God, Barbara thought, what if we'd gotten to the door a few seconds sooner? We'd be out on the balcony in plain sight, and . . .

After a few moments, Lee reached behind his back and tugged the pistol out of his jeans.

'Oh, man,' Pete murmured.

'Who's out there?' Barbara asked.

'Visitor,' Lee whispered.

'Just one?' Barbara asked.

'So far.'

'What's he doing?'

'Shhh.'

Like Lee's little assistant, Heather frowned at Barbara and pressed a finger to her lips.

Barbara listened hard for sounds from the intruder.

He's sure being quiet down there.

She?

No, Barbara thought. Can't be a woman – Lee wouldn't have pulled his gun.

'Heather?'

Not a shout, but a soft call as if the person below knew how well his voice would carry to the surrounding apartments – knew, and wanted to make no more noise than necessary.

'Heather?' he called again.

The voice sounded familiar.

Barbara met Pete's eyes.

'It's Earl,' Pete whispered.

'My God. Where'd *he* come from?'

'*Earl?*' Heather asked. She looked stricken. 'What's *he* doing here?'

'He's calling your name,' Barbara said in a hushed voice.

'I didn't see him.'

'He saw you,' Pete said. 'Must've.'

'Great,' Barbara muttered. 'Just great.'

'Who is he?' Lee asked, not looking away from the window.

'He's a jerk,' Barbara said.

'He was in the driver's ed class with us,' Pete explained. 'He's kind of a trouble-maker.'

'Heather?' Earl called again. 'Are you here? Pete? Barbara? Where are you?'

'Right after the quake,' Pete said, 'he tried to steal some guy's car. We had a big fight about it, and we . . . sort of knocked him out cold and left him behind.'

'No kidding,' Lee said, still gazing out.

'Are you here?' Earl called. 'Come on, guys! I'm not gonna hurt anybody, I promise. I just . . . I don't like it out here by myself. There's scary shit going on. Okay? Can you hear me? Hey, I'm sorry I screwed up back there, okay? I wanta get back together with you. Please!'

Lee looked over his shoulder at Pete and Barbara. 'I don't like this. He'll give us away. Let's bring him in.'

'You sure you want to do that?' Barbara asked.

'I don't want him down there yelling, that's for sure. Pete, tell him to come up.'

'If you say so.'

'Do it.'

Pete slipped past Barbara, unfastened the deadbolt, and pulled the door open. He stepped over the threshold. Raising an arm, he called out quietly, 'Up here, Earl. Make it quick.'

'Hey hey, Pizzaria! My bud!'

'Quiet! Jeez!'

'Hey, hey, don't have a cow. Anybody else around here?'

'Don't ask so many questions. Just hurry up.'

'I'm coming, I'm coming. Hey, don't rush me. I've been in better shape, you know. It's not every day I get the crap beat out of me.'

Barbara heard Earl start pounding his way up the stairs.

'You got Banner with you?'

'She's here.'

'Good, good. Didn't see her. Or you either. Thought maybe something might've happened. Which'd be a real shame. Wouldn't want nothing happening to my old pals. You miss me?'

'Sure.'

'How'd you get yourselves a place?' Earl asked. From the sound of his voice, he had reached the balcony. 'Rent it? 'Cause knowing how fucking *moral* you and Banner are, you sure as hell didn't *bust* in.'

Not bothering to answer, Pete stepped backward out of the doorway.

A moment later, Earl strolled in. He grinned at Barbara. She felt her mouth drop open.

'Greetings and salutations, Banner-babes.'

'What happened to *you*?' she blurted.

'You oughta know.'

'We didn't do all *that*.'

The right side of Earl's face was puffy and smudged with dark bruises – damage, she supposed, that had been inflicted by herself and Pete. But the hair above his left ear was pasted down flat with dry blood. They hadn't done that to him. Nor were they responsible for his change of clothes. Barbara wasn't sure what he'd been wearing before, but not this: a white shirt so large that it hung down almost to his knees, pin-striped blue slacks that looked as if they might go with the business suit of an obese executive, and brightly polished black leather dress shoes.

Someone, probably Earl, had torn off the sleeves of the shirt so that his arms were bare to the shoulders. The shirt was unbuttoned, too, showing sweaty skin with bruises and scratches. Earl's huge, bulky slacks were cinched in around his waist with a striped necktie. The cuffs were rolled up. He had bare ankles above the fancy shoes.

'Greetings, Heather,' he said. 'And who's this?'

'Lee Nolan,' Lee said. 'I'm the manager of this facility.'

'No kidding. Figured maybe you was Rambo.'

'He's not amused,' Barbara said.

Ignoring them, Lee looked at Pete. 'Anybody else out there?'

'I don't think so.'

'Check again, then shut the door.'

When the door was shut, Lee got to his feet and faced Earl. He held the pistol low by his side. 'Tell us what's going on out there,' he said.

'What do you want to know?'

Heather spoke up first. 'How did you find us?'

'Just lucky, I guess. Heading for home, trying to stay out of trouble. And then I spotted you . . . You were like two blocks away. Knew it was you, though. You got yourself an unmis-takable figure.'

Heather blushed. 'Thanks,' she murmured.

'Think that was a compliment?'

The red of her face darkened.

Looking pleased with himself, Earl turned his attention to the others. 'Anyhow, I yelled. I thought she heard me, but she kept on going like she didn't. So then I chased after her, and saw her go through the gate down there.'

'What about the mob?' Lee asked.

'Huh?'

'Was that you yelling "Porky"?' Heather asked.

'Me, all right,' Earl said.

'You dirty . . .'

'Let's not get sidetracked, here,' Lee said. 'Heather reported that there's a group of marauders heading our way.'

'A what?'

'A wild mob,' Pete explained.

'Rampaging,' Barbara added. 'Killing people.'

'No kidding?' Earl asked.

'It wasn't exactly a *mob*,' Heather said. 'I mean, there weren't that many.'

'A dozen,' Lee reminded her. 'That's what you told us.'

'Well, it seemed like a dozen. Maybe it wasn't that many.'

Earl shrugged and made a face like someone faking perplexity. 'A wild mob of killers, huh? Only maybe just a few, but on a rampage?'

'Pulling people out of cars,' Pete said.

'Heather saw them raping and killing women,' Barbara added.

Earl's face lit up. 'Raping, huh? And to think I missed it.'

'What *did* you see out there?' Lee asked.

'I didn't see nothing like that.'

'I did,' Heather insisted. 'And some of them chased me, but I ditched 'em.'

'No kidding?' Earl asked. 'You sure about that? Looked to me like you was taking your sweet time, checking around under cars and stuff. What were you looking for?'

'A cat. But that was after those guys . . .'

'Hold it,' Lee broke in. 'I want to hear from Earl.'

Earl shrugged. 'I didn't spot any mob, that's for sure. Not around here. There was a whole bunch of looting over on Pico. A few fights and stuff, too. I saw some people who'd gotten themselves pounded pretty good – hey, you're looking at one.'

'We didn't do that to you,' Barbara said.

'Like hell.'

'I punched you in the face a couple of time, same as you punched me.' She realized that she had pretty much forgotten about her injuries. Reminded now, she noticed that she had a slight earache, probably from the punch in the jaw. She pressed her hand to her jaw. Not much swelling there. But the bulging skin over her cheekbone felt warm and tight.

'Be grateful, Banner,' Earl said. 'I improved on your looks.'

'Shut up,' Pete said.

'Screw you.'

'We didn't do that to your head,' Barbara told him. 'Not where your hair's all bloody there. That wasn't us. Maybe we should've, but we didn't.'

'I suppose you didn't steal my stuff, either.'

'We didn't steal anything. All we did was drag you out of the street so you wouldn't get run over.'

'Yeah, sure. What you did is strip me.'

'Did not.'

'We didn't do anything like that,' Pete said.

'Yeah, right.'

Heather looked as if she had made an amazing recovery from her embarrassment. She was beaming. 'Somebody took your clothes?'

'Yeah, and I know who.'

'Not us,' Heather said. 'You've gotta be kidding. You pissed your jeans.'

'Yeah, right.'

'You did,' Barbara confirmed, and found herself smiling.

'Bull.'

'It's true,' Pete said.

'That's three against one,' Heather pointed out. 'And you were out cold, so how can you say you *didn't*. Your little piggie went, "Wee wee wee wee." '

'Up yours.'

'Let's everyone knock it off,' Lee said.

'The thing of it is,' Barbara persisted, 'it wasn't us who did that to your head or stole your clothes. Somebody else must've come along and done it after we were gone.'

'What did they take?' Pete asked.

'What do you think?'

'Everything?'

'Yeah.'

'Jeez.'

'They take your *undies*?' Heather asked.

'My what?'

'Your underpants.'

'Who wears 'em?'

'And he calls *me* a pig. At least I wear underpants.'

'They left you naked?' Barbara asked Earl.

'Yeah, so what?'

'What did you do?'

'What do you mean, what'd I do? I wandered around in my birthday suit till I got this stuff.' He fluttered his fingers against the front of his shirt. 'Wasn't any picnic finding some new duds, I tell you that. It's not like people are real eager to part with what they're wearing, and I couldn't find me a clothes store that hadn't already gotten picked clean.'

'Let me guess,' Barbara said, 'you mugged a fat bank manager.'

'I don't know what he was. And I didn't mug him. He was already dead when I found him.'

'Dead?' Barbara asked, wrinkling her nose.

'Yeah, but I didn't do it.'

'I'm sure,' Heather said.

'Hey, I don't go around killing people for their pants.'

'This man you took the clothes from,' Lee said, 'did he look like he'd been assaulted?'

'Your mob didn't get him, if that's what you're getting at.'

'It's not *my* mob.'

'It's Heather's mob,' Barbara put in.

'My man was all in one piece. I mean, I don't think he was even cut. He probably died from a heart attack, or something. I'm surprised he still had his clothes, though. Every stiff in town has gotten itself stripped, from what I've seen. And this bozo's billfold was gone, but they hadn't taken his clothes. I can see why, too – the guy was an elephant. I had an awful time trying to . . .'

'Wait wait wait,' Lee said. 'What's this about stiffs? You mean corpses?'

'What do you think?'

'How many did you see?'

'I don't know. Hell, who counted?'

'How many?' Lee repeated.

'What do you think, I kept a scorecard? Aah. Let me think. Twenty? Maybe thirty?' He wrinkled his nose. 'It was pretty gross. Even the babes. Fact is, the babes were the worst, you know?' Something went out of his voice. He frowned down at the floor. 'You'd think it'd be sort of cool, seeing 'em all . . . with their clothes off like that. The way it turned out, though, it was . . . I don't know. It made me feel a little sick. The way they were dead. It didn't make me feel horny or anything, just sort of sick and depressed.' He suddenly seemed to cheer up. 'But hey, guess the good news is I'm not one of them necromaniacs.'

Lee didn't seem amused. 'These women you saw, did they look as if they'd been attacked?'

'Yeah. Attacked, all right. By falling buildings. Who knows, though? I don't know how they got killed. The men, either. I didn't go up and check 'em all, up close and personal. There were a couple I happened to notice with bullet holes, and one guy had a knife in him. But they were more like the exception. Mostly, they were sprawled around near places that'd gotten nailed by the quake. They were pretty messed up. Saw a lot of bashed heads. A lot of nasty cuts. One guy'd caught a big thing of glass right across his face. There was a gal, she didn't have any head at all. I sort of looked for it, too.' He turned to Barbara and raised a corner of his mouth. 'Fact is, thought she might be you. You know, she sort of had the same general shape and stuff. Could've been you.'

'Sorry to disappoint you.'

'Hey, I'm glad she wasn't.'

'Sure.'

'Really.'

'So,' Lee said, 'you think most of these dead people were killed by the quake?'

'Most of 'em, yeah.'

'And nearly all of them had been stripped?'

'Yeah, that's how come I had such a tough time finding myself something to wear. Fuckin' Los Angeles. The whole damn city's nothing but scavengers. Just look around on garbage day. I didn't catch any of 'em in the act, but you can bet there's gotta be all these creeps sneaking around taking what they can get off the dead people. Like the looters, only they're looting stiffs instead of stores. Maybe that's who got me,' he said. 'Took me for a goner.'

'From the look of your head,' Barbara said, 'they tried to help make you one.'

'You guys shouldn't've left me there like that.'

'You're the one who started it.'

'I was only just trying to grab us a car. If you hadn't messed it up, we'd all be home by now.'

'You can't go around and steal . . .'

'Let's not start quarreling again,' Lee said. 'It sounds as if the situation outside hasn't deteriorated quite as much as we thought.'

'I saw what I saw,' Heather said. 'I'm not a liar.'

'Nobody's calling you a liar,' Lee said.

'If Earl didn't see your mob,' Barbara said, 'then where is it?'

'He *had* to see it,' Heather insisted. 'He's lying.'

'Get real,' Earl said.

She leveled her eyes at him. 'Maybe you're *with* them!'

He smirked. 'Bull.'

'They sent you on ahead to find us, didn't they?'

'You're outa your tree.'

'Lee! He's one of them! He has to be. The rest of them are probably sneaking up . . .'

'I doubt it,' Lee said. Pistol in hand, he walked to the door, opened it and stepped out onto the balcony. He came back in, shaking his head. After shutting the door, he said, 'It's clear out there. Earl's not with that bunch you told us about, Heather. The rest of them would've been in here long before now.'

Heather shook her head. 'Maybe they're waiting for a signal from him, or something.'

'Give it up,' Earl said. 'You probably made up the whole damn thing.'

'Did not.'

'Then how come *I* didn't see 'em?'

'I don't know.'

'Why would she make up something like that?' Pete asked.

'Who knows? Maybe she likes the attention.'

'I didn't make it up!'

'Take it easy,' Lee told her.

'Maybe they all went inside someplace,' Heather said. 'You know? And took the bodies in with them.'

'That's a charming thought,' Barbara said.

'Sounds to me,' Earl said, 'like a crock of shit.'

Pete faced him. 'The thing is, we were just about to get out of here when you showed up.'

'Not me,' Heather said.

'Barbara and I. What about you? Do you want to come with us?'

'Yeah, sure, what do you think? I been out there on my own all morning, and it gives me the creeps. Yeah, I'll go with you. Damn straight.'

'Could you use a change of clothes before you take off?' Lee asked him.

'Yeah! Are you kidding? That'd be great. You know what else I could sure use? Something to eat. And a drink. You got some beer or something?'

Lee frowned. 'Beer? How old are you?'

'Know what?' Earl said. 'A guy's legal drinking age, it's supposed to be twenty-one around here, right? But the thing is, there's the *unwritten* law. The Quake Factor. Ever hear of it?'

'Afraid not.'

'Sort of like that wind-chill factor they talk about in places where they've got real winters? What you gotta do, you take a guy's real age and add on the Richter scale reading of the quake he made it through that morning. That's how you arrive at the Quake Factor. I'm sixteen, right? So you add about eight from the Richter scale to that. Total it up, and it makes me about twenty-three, twenty-four years old. Way past the drinking age.'

For the first time, Lee smiled. 'You convinced me. Beer it is. How about the rest of you? Could you use some lunch and a drink before you take off?'

'That'd be great,' Pete said.

'Yeah,' Barbara said. 'I'm all for that. Thanks.'

'Okay,' Heather muttered. 'I'm still not gonna leave, but if everybody's gonna eat . . .'

'How many beers?' Lee asked. 'Going by Earl's Quake Factor, you're all old enough. It might not be very cold, though.'

Twenty-five

When Stanley woke up, he knew right away where he was. Behind the Benson house, stretched out on one of the poolside loungers.

He'd flopped on it after climbing out of the pool.

He hadn't meant to fall asleep. He'd meant only to lie there for a couple of minutes and rest while the sun dried him. Obviously, though, he'd drifted off. Drifted off and sunk into a deep slumber.

Now, he couldn't move. He felt as if a huge, hot weight lay across his back, holding him down, pressing him into the cushion. It felt good, though, that weight. He knew it was only hot sunlight.

And the heaviness wasn't in the light, it was in him.

In his skin and muscles and bones. In his mind.

Gotta get up, he told himself.

But he didn't move.

He felt so heavy, so peaceful.

Vaguely, he wondered if anybody had found Sheila yet.

Doesn't matter, he thought. She won't get away. She'll still be there. Or somewhere. I'd better get up, though.

He couldn't bring himself to move.

Whatever you do, don't fall asleep again.

I won't.

The cushion under his face had a fresh, clean chlorine smell. He supposed it must've gotten doused by pool water during the quake. He wished it smelled like Sheila's lounger pad – of sunlight and tanning lotion, sweat and beaches and cotton candy.

Cotton candy?

This *is* Sheila's pad, he told himself. Let's just say it is.

Yes. I'm on Sheila's pad.

And he sees himself, as if from a distance, stretched out on the lounger behind the ruin of Sheila's house. His hands are crossed beneath his face. His back shines with sweat. The flimsy remains of his pajama pants cling to his buttocks.

Now he feels the soft, moist pad underneath him.

Sheila's pad. Soaked with her lotions and juices.

I've gotta get up. Gotta get back to Sheila before . . .

'What's the big hurry?' she asks, her voice low and teasing.

Stanley knew that it was only in his mind. And so were her hands. But in his mind, her hands are big and warm on his back. They press him down, massage his shoulders.

'You aren't going anywhere,' she tells him. 'Not just yet.'

Then she is pulling at his shorts, sliding them down and off.

She climbs onto him. She lies on him, all hot, heavier than the sunlight. He feels her thighs against the backs of his legs. His rump is tickled by her soft nest of hair. Her breasts, just below his shoulderblades, feel big and slippery and springy. As she licks and sucks the side of his neck, he squirms.

Stanley squirmed, imagining it.

He needed to roll over.

Then he imagined a hole in the pad. A hole in the pad and in the lounger directly below his groin. As big as a softball, maybe. Big enough to fit down into. With the hole there, he wouldn't be mashed and achy anymore. He wouldn't need to roll over. The hole would let him feel all loose and free down there.

And then he thought how it would be to have Sheila under the lounger. She squirms in on her back until her face is below the hole. Then she pushes herself up with her elbows. She takes him in her mouth.

But Stanley didn't have a hole in the lounger.

He flipped over, sweat sliding and spilling off him. Though his eyes were shut, he squinted as sunlight glared yellow through the thin sheaths of his eyelids. He flung a forearm across his eyes and tried to catch his breath. His heart was racing. He felt shaky all over – buzzing – as if his blood had gone fizzy in his veins and arteries.

Rolled over too fast, he told himself. Should've done it sooner, before things got so urgent.

I'll be fine in a minute, he thought. Just gotta settle down. Lie here and relax. It would help to stop thinking about Sheila, too. I can have her for real when I want, so it doesn't make any sense to get all hot and bothered daydreaming about her. That's for losers who can't get the real thing.

If I don't watch out, he thought, I'm gonna screw up and miss the real thing. Ben found her, didn't he? What if somebody else came along?

Then it'll be just too bad for somebody else.

Easy come, easy go.

But maybe the next person to find Sheila wouldn't be as easy as Ben. If he kept on wasting time, he ran a real risk of losing his chance at her.

He knew that he had to get up.

He was already feeling better – the tremors and pounding and tightness had subsided, along with the sizzling sensation in his bloodstream. But he waited a while longer. Then he sat up slowly.

Sweat poured off his face, streamed down his chest and sides and belly. He felt dizzy for a moment or two, but then his head cleared.

He swung his legs over the side of the lounger. His moccasins were waiting. He slipped his feet into them, leaned forward and pushed at his knees and stood up straight. Feeling a bit unsteady, he breathed deeply and didn't try to go anywhere.

Never should've laid down like that, he thought. Lucky I didn't get heat prostration, or something.

Who says I didn't?

No, he told himself. I'm fine. Maybe a little dehydrated, that's all. That's probably why I'm feeling weird. Too much sun. Sweated too much.

He wondered where he could get a drink.

Depends, he thought, on whether I mind a little chlorine and blood in my water.

He decided that he didn't mind.

The water at the bottom of the pool's deep end still felt chilly. He waded in until it wrapped around his thighs. Then he bent over and cupped some into his mouth. It didn't taste bad. He couldn't detect any hint of blood flavor. He drank some more. And some more.

Then he squatted until the water covered him to the shoulders. He dunked his head. He glided forward, leaving his feet, floating through the cool silence.

He felt wonderful as he climbed out of the pool. He felt *cold*. Which didn't make any sense at all. Never had. It was part of the magic of a swimming pool. The hot air cooks you before you get in. But when you climb out, it wants to freeze your butt off. The thing is, temperature of the air hasn't changed much at all. If anything, it's hotter than before.

Crazy, he thought.

He stood by the edge of the pool, shivering and smiling.

He wished he had a pool of his own.

I'll have one put in when I rebuild, he thought. Who's gonna tell me I can't? Mother?

'Oh Stanley, Stanley, Stanley,' he said in a whiny voice, mimicking her. 'We are not going to have a swimming pool.

What a ridiculous idea. I don't know what gets into you sometimes. Do you think we're *made* of money?'

'No, Mother darling,' he said in his own voice. 'I think *you're* made outa dead meat, you piece of shit.'

Laughing, he stepped into his moccasins again. He walked toward the lounger. He wanted to lie down on it. On his back, this time. Just for a while. Just long enough to let the sun dry him off and take away the chill.

'No no no no no,' he said. 'And zonk out again? Huh-uh, no way, no way.'

He went to where he had left his saw.

He bent down and picked it up, squinting as its shiny blade flashed sunlight.

'Excalibur,' he said, and waved it high.

He started walking toward the Bensons' driveway.

Why take the long way around? he wondered. So he changed direction and headed for the fence that separated their back yard from Judy's.

As he hurried along, he waved the saw and proclaimed, 'This is my sword, Excalibur. Not twenty-two caliber, not thirty-eight caliber, but *Ex*-caliber!'

He laughed.

He wished Sheila could've heard that one.

I'll have to tell it to her, he thought.

When he came to the redwood fence, he reached over the top and dropped his saw. Hitting the ground on the other side, it made a whangy sound.

Stanley gave the fence a shake. It creaked and wobbled.

Not climbing over *that*, he thought.

With both hands, he grabbed one of the upright slats. He jerked it toward him, throwing his weight backward. The board came with him. The nails near its top squawled as they were yanked out of the upper crossbeam. The lower set of nails only came out part of the way. They bent silently as he stomped the plank flat against the ground.

He ripped and smashed two more slats off the fence.

Then he crouched and tore all of them free at the bottom. He might be coming back this way later on. Maybe even after dark. It wouldn't be any good to leave the boards where he might step on them when he returned.

Not with those nails sticking up.

He made a small stack of the boards, off to one side and close to the fence. Then he returned to the opening, ducked and stepped through.

His saw had landed on a narrow, grassy strip that ran between Judy's side of the fence and the edge of her driveway. He picked it up.

He was only paces away from the spot where he'd been standing when Judy had brought the water to him.

He looked at the door to her kitchen.

It would only take a couple of minutes, he thought, to run in and check on her. Make sure she isn't getting loose.

We've already gone over that, he reminded himself. I go in just to check on her, and next thing I know I've gotta be feeling her, messing around with her, and then it's an hour or something before I get out.

Forget it. What am I, nuts? *Hunting* for ways to screw myself outa Sheila?

Judy isn't worth it. No way, no how. She's not anywhere close to being in the same league as Sheila.

But he wondered if he should make a quick trip into the kitchen. Sheila was probably awfully hungry, by now. She would be grateful for some food.

I could use a bite, myself, Stanley thought. Not to mention a drink.

'No,' he said.

We'll wait, he decided. We'll wait till Sheila's free, and then we'll come back here together and go in and have a nice party in Judy's kitchen. Vodka and tonic, maybe. And sandwiches made out of salami and cheese.

He hurried on, crossing Judy's back yard. At the far side, he placed his saw on top of the cinderblock wall. Then he boosted himself up. Crouching on the ledge, he took hold of the saw handle. Then he slowly stood, arms out for balance.

From this height, he could see down his own driveway,

over the top of the gate, all the way into the street in front of his house.

Where no cars passed.

Where no people roamed.

He gave no more than a glance to his half-collapsed house, his patio and back yard, his completely collapsed garage.

Nothing was on fire.

Nobody was snooping.

Everything looked fine.

He gazed out into the distance toward Sheila's house. If his garage were still standing, it would block his view. But it had gone down to rubble like a polite bystander crouching to let him see what he wanted.

At the sight of Sheila's house, he felt a quick thrill.

The ruins weren't aswarm with rescue workers.

He saw nobody.

Excellent, he thought. This is excellent.

Somebody *might* be there, of course, hidden from view, maybe hunched down behind a heap of debris or a broken wall. But the situation sure looked good from where Stanley stood.

What if Sheila's not there?

She has to be.

Somebody might've gotten her out. I've been gone for an awfully long time.

She's there, he told himself. She has to be.

The cinderblock wall, cracked in a few places by the quake but still intact, led like a narrow walk away from Stanley, along the side of his driveway, past his fallen garage to the corner where it joined the back wall.

I can do it, Stanley told himself.

It would be a lot easier than jumping down and cutting through his yard to the back wall, climbing over that . . . Quicker, too. And if he stayed up here, he wouldn't have to lose sight of Sheila's house.

His mind made up, Stanley turned and started walking along the top of the wall. He gripped the saw in his left hand. He held both arms out away from his sides to keep himself steady, and watched the block ledge just ahead of his feet.

I shouldn't be doing this, he thought. I must be nuts.

No. This is the best way to get to Sheila's. Long as I don't fall off.

I won't fall, he told himself. This is a cinch.

But what if someone's watching?

The thought sent a shiver through his stomach.

Here I am, up here in plain sight.

I shouldn't be up here, he realized.

But it was a bit late to change his mind. He couldn't jump down now. A drop to the right would land him in the rough debris of his garage where he was sure to get hurt. To the left, he would fall among Judy's rosebushes.

He quickened his pace.

They'll think I'm the Wild Man from Borneo.

Yeah, he thought. But what are they gonna do about it? Nothing, that's what. They spot me running around like this, they'll figure I'm demented. Won't come near me. I've got nothing to worry about.

'They're the ones better worry,' he muttered.

But he felt a great surge of relief when he came to the end of the wall. He was tempted to step out into space and drop.

Don't, he warned himself. It'll hurt too much. And what if I sprain my ankle?

So he sat at the corner where the walls joined, and lowered his feet over the side. The blocks felt rough and hot against his buttocks. He tossed his saw to the ground. Then he used both hands to shove himself away from the wall.

He didn't have far to drop. The landing was fairly gentle, and he managed to stay on his feet.

It was sure good to be down.

Here below the level of the wall, he felt hidden and safe.

He picked up his saw and jogged across the grass to the patio. There, he stopped to catch his breath. He gazed at Sheila's lounger.

Its green pad was faded and stained. He could almost feel the heat of its fabric against his face. He knew its aromas. He knew its taste.

If I need to take another nap, he thought, I'll do it right there.

Maybe I can fuck her on it!

He thought about that, pictured Sheila on the lounger underneath him, imagined the feel of her, all hot and slippery, and how the lounger would wobble as he thrust.

Wobble, then smash down.

It isn't strong enough to hold us, he decided. We'd probably bust the thing. Besides, we'd be out in the open. That wouldn't be any good. Somebody'd come along and try to save her.

I have to take her where we won't be bothered. Judy's place for a party. Then maybe over to the pool.

Stanley walked around the lounger. As he approached the remains of the house, he thought about calling out. If he called her name, Sheila might answer. Then he would know she was still here, still all right.

But what if somebody other than Sheila heard him?

Better to sneak in.

Go in silently and keep the element of surprise.

So he stepped over the broken back wall of the house and began making his way through the debris. He moved cautiously. He watched out for nails and broken glass. With each step, he lowered his feet gently, trying to make no noise. Every so often, he stopped and listened. He heard the usual background sounds, but nothing nearby.

The carcass of Sheila's house sounded dead.

What if *she's* dead? he wondered.

Why would she be dead? She wasn't hurt, and I left her with plenty of water.

If somebody came along and killed her . . .

Impossible, he told himself. Absolutely.

He found himself smiling as he remembered an old joke about an idiot who was caught carrying a bomb onto an airliner. The guy had carried it aboard as an act of self-preservation. 'What are the odds,' he'd asked, 'of there being *two* bombs on the same plane?'

Pretty much the same odds, Stanley thought, as two fellas like me happening to find Sheila.

No way has she been murdered. Impossible.

If anything, she got herself rescued while I was gone.

If that's what happened, he told himself, I'll find her. I'll thank her rescuer for saving me the work, and then I'll kill him with my little saw.

When he spotted the hole in the debris, he whispered, 'Please, please, please.'

It *looked* the same as when he'd been here before.

But he couldn't see Sheila yet.

He stepped closer.

The four-by-eight beam that had slanted down over the side of the tub and trapped Sheila's legs was still in place.

That's a good sign.

But he still couldn't see Sheila.

And then he did.

Yes!

Only the knee of her left leg that was hooked over the top of the beam, but enough.

If her leg's here, she's here. Unless she did like a trapped coyote and chewed her leg off, which she couldn't do anyhow, the way she was pinned down. Maybe she could've cut it off with a knife, but . . .

The rest of Sheila was there.

She lay motionless at the bottom of the tub, apparently unaware of Stanley's arrival.

Wanting the best view possible, he made his way to the section of floor above the foot of the tub. He squatted down.

When he'd last seen Sheila, her body had been draped from chest to groin by Ben's green T-shirt. Since then, somebody had pulled it higher. Now she was naked below the navel. The T-shirt still hid her breasts, but now it also covered her face.

They cover your face when you're dead.

That's why she isn't moving, he thought. She's dead.

Stanley saw no blood on her bare skin. No blood had soaked through the T-shirt, either. She didn't look hurt, just dead. He wondered if the sun had gotten to her. Or maybe she'd had internal injuries. A heart attack? An aneurism? Being muscular and full of energy didn't mean something couldn't go wrong inside and kill you.

Maybe someone had come along and strangled her.

He supposed that anything was possible. There were plenty of ways to die. And one of them had found Sheila.

Found her and killed her.

No fair! She was supposed to be mine!

She still is, he realized. She's here, isn't she? Dead, but here. Maybe it isn't such a bad thing, either. She was awfully strong. She might've given me some real trouble. This way, I won't have to fight her.

But I wanted to fight her!

Oh, well, he thought. That's the way the cookie crumbles. At least she didn't get away.

He wondered if he would still need to saw through one of the beams. Probably not. With her dead like this, he supposed he could simply pull her free. That'd be a lot easier and quicker than sawing through one of the beams. Use a little force and drag her out. Maybe have to break her neck or pop a leg out of its socket to help her clear the beams.

For that matter, it would be easy enough to saw off her head. With that gone, Sheila wouldn't have any problem at all clearing the overhead beam.

I don't wanta cut off her head. Not right straight off the bat, just to get her out. It'd ruin her looks.

Doesn't have to ruin anything, he told himself. I can take it with me. I can even set it up right in front of us so I can watch her face . . . all sorts of things I can do with it.

He got hard as he sat there and thought about uses for her severed head.

Plenty of time for that stuff later, he finally told himself. I oughta try to get her out in one piece, so at least I can start out with her whole.

Stanley set the saw aside, then lowered his legs toward the tub. He spread them wide enough to let him put his feet on the porcelain ledges.

As he started to stand, the tub wobbled slightly.

Sheila moaned.

Stanley flinched, then held still. He stood motionless on the sides of the tub and gazed down at her.

Gazed hard.

And detected the slight rise and fall of her bare belly, of the green T-shirt covering her ribcage and her breasts.

She was breathing.

Had she been breathing all along? How could Stanley not have noticed?

Unless maybe she'd been holding her breath?

Playing possum?

She wouldn't do something like that, he told himself. Not Sheila. That isn't her style. She's asleep, that's all, and I just jumped to conclusions about her being dead because she had the shirt on her face.

She had probably pulled it up there, herself.

Earlier, her face had been in shadow. But the sun had changed position during Stanley's absence, taking away the shade. She must've drawn the shirt up to shield her eyes from the direct sunlight.

Of course.

Now that he realized she was alive, he wondered how he could've possibly mistaken her for dead. The breathing was really pretty obvious. And her skin was shiny with sweat, ruddy from the heat or sunburn. Dead people might be red, he supposed. But they don't sweat, do they?

Sheila looked alive, all right. And very hot.

The water bottle that he'd left with her was empty. She or someone – had set it upright on top of the beam above her face.

Might need to go and get more, Stanley thought.

No. I'm not leaving again, no way. We'll just have to get by. We can drink all we want when we get to Judy's.

He wished he had thought to bring more water with him, though. He didn't want thirst to ruin his good time. Or rush him. He wanted to enjoy every moment of this, and make it last and last.

Still poised on the ledges of the tub, he squatted down. He placed his left hand on the beam that angled down across the top of Sheila's right thigh. Then he leaned forward.

This was the closest he had ever been to her.

He wanted to see her breasts. But she would wake up, for sure, if he reached out and snatched away the T-shirt.

There'll be plenty of time later for them, he told himself. For right now, enjoy what shows.

So he studied her.

And longed to feel her.

If he dared, he could reach down with his right hand and actually touch the smooth, sunlit curves of her left hip – stroke the skin of her belly – slip his fingers through her shiny curls and caress the fleshy lips that he could see down lower – even get a finger or two inside her.

But any sort of touch was likely to disturb her sleep.

She wakes up and finds me messing with her, Stanley thought, and she won't trust me anymore. The longer I keep her faked out, the better.

Even if she catches me hovering over her like this . . .

Very carefully, he uncrouched and made his way backward to the foot of the tub. Instead of climbing all the way out, he sat on the edge of the floor.

Not yet, not yet!

He was sticking up high out of the left leg hole of his pajama pants.

She sees that, he thought, and she'll know something's up.

He laughed softly.

He tried to cover it, but the flimsy fabric just fell away.

So he waited. Finally, he settled down. He adjusted his pajama pants.

There. He still showed. Sheila would be able to get a good look up through the leg hole, but he wasn't sticking out like some sort of exhibitionist.

Don't want her thinking I'm a pervert, he thought.

Then he laughed again.

Then he quietly called, 'Sheila? Sheila, I'm back. It's me, Stanley.'

Twenty-six

Sheila took a long time waking up. She groaned. She shifted her body slightly as if searching for a more comfortable position. The way she acted, she might've thought she was coming out of sleep on a fine morning in her own bed. But abruptly, she went rigid, snatched the T-shirt down from her face, and raised her head off the bottom of the tub. She squinted up at Stanley.

He gazed down at her, stunned. She was even better than he remembered. Her beauty wasn't diminished at all by her sweaty, flushed face and the tangles of hair glued down wet against her forehead. She looked as if she had just stepped out from under a shower.

In the brightness of the sun, her blue eyes looked like the summer sky on a clear day.

The specks of sweat above her lip looked like diamonds.

She licked her lips. Then she said, 'Oh.' After a pause, she said, 'Stan.'

'Are you all right?' he asked.

'I feel . . . wasted. Guess I'm okay. My butt keeps falling asleep.' One side of her mouth twitched as if she wanted to smile.

'I'll get you out of there, now.'

'You went off with . . . Ben?'

'Yeah. He might be back later.'

'There was a girl.'

'Right. We managed to pull her out. Ben and I. I couldn't have done it without him. Anyway, she was pretty banged up. One of her arms was broken, and she had some head injuries. But she could walk, so we decided I'd come back here to help you, and Ben'd take her over to the hospital. That one over on Pico?'

'Yeah.'

'So, here I am.' Smiling, he picked up his saw. 'Me and my trusty saw, Excalibur.'

'Excalibur?'

'Not twenty-two, thirty-eight or forty-five caliber. *Ex*calibur.'

Again, she tried to smile. 'I'm sure glad you're back,' she said. 'I was afraid you'd forgotten about me.'

'I could never forget about you, Sheila.' Even as he spoke the words, he regretted them.

'Guess not,' she said. 'The naked babe in the tub.'

The way she said that, Stanley knew he was all right; she hadn't picked up anything strange about his remark.

'Things might've happened to you, though,' she explained. 'That's what had me scared, really. I figured you'd come back if you could.'

'You figured right.'

'It just seemed like such a long time. Felt like hours.'

'We had a hard time getting the girl out. Did anyone come by while I was gone?'

Sheila shook her head. 'Don't think so. I dropped out of the picture, though. Fell asleep, I guess. Or passed out. I don't think anyone showed up, but . . . is anybody around?'

'Not much of anyone,' Stanley said. 'I spotted a few oddballs roaming the neighborhood. Like the ones I told you about before? Creepy types. But they didn't see me. I think we'll be all right as long as we don't make a lot of noise.'

'They're close enough to hear us?'

'Probably not. Just don't shout or something.'

'Okay. God. Thank God, *they* didn't find me.'

'We'd better get you out of there,' Stanley said.

'Yeah. Please.'

With the saw in his right hand, he stood up. He made his way slowly forward, sliding the soles of his moccasins along the smooth ledges of the tub. The beam across the other end blocked his view of Sheila's face, and she probably couldn't see much higher than his chest. He wondered where she was looking.

At least I'm not sticking out, he told himself. It isn't my fault if she sees something she shouldn't. Isn't my fault if I'm turned on, either. She's the one who's naked around here, not me.

'What about the fire?' Sheila asked.

What fire? Stanley wondered. Then he remembered the burning house across the street.

'Didn't see it,' he said. 'Must've burnt itself out.'

He tried to remember what he had seen over there during his return.

Nothing.

At the very least, there must've been smoke rising from the ruins.

He couldn't recall.

Too focused on Sheila, he supposed. But nothing of much importance could've been going on, or he would've noticed.

'Nothing left but smoking rubble,' he told Sheila – and wished he could remember.

What else did I miss?

Bending his knees, he leaned forward the same as before and placed his left hand on top of the beam that angled downward between her legs. Now, he could see Sheila's face again.

Gorgeous.

Was there a wariness in her eyes that hadn't been there before?

That ain't wariness – that's horniness.

It's probably nothing at all, he told himself. Don't go reading things in.

'What are you going to do?' Sheila asked.

'Cut right through it,' he said. He tapped the edge of his saw against the beam's front corner. It bit in, digging a tiny wedge into the wood. He began to pump it back and forth.

Pale sawdust torn from the gash spilled over the front of the beam and drifted down between Sheila's legs. She gasped. Her right hand darted down and she clapped it to her body.

A flurry of sawdust fell on the back of her hand.

'Wait, Stan. Wait.'

He stopped.

'It'll still be on top of my leg,' she said. 'Maybe you should try over there.' She nodded to her right. 'Do it over by the side of the tub, and we can take off the whole section.'

'I guess I could do that,' he admitted. He moved the saw seven or eight inches up the slanted beam. 'Here?'

'Perfect.'

He drew the blade back and forth a few times. Now, the sawdust drifted down between the wall of the tub and the side of her right thigh.

He met Sheila's eyes. 'If I cut it off here, you know, your leg's likely to get mashed pretty good when it drops.'

'Oh, don't worry about that. My leg's pretty strong.'

'You'd still be able to get out if I cut through the center where I was doing it before. Nothing would end up dropping on you, either, and we'd only have half as big a piece to deal with.'

'But I'd have to squeeze my way out,' Sheila said. 'I don't like it. God knows what'll happen when this thing isn't propped up anymore. You really should cut it off there. Please.'

'Your wish is my command.'

'Don't be angry.'

'I'm not angry. I'll cut it off anywhere you want.'

'Okay. Thanks.'

He resumed sawing. It was hard work: not so much the pumping of his right arm, but how he had to stand so precariously on the edges of the tub, knees bent, waist bent, torso twisted awkwardly so that he could reach the place where Sheila insisted that he make the cut. The sun felt very hot on his back. But he liked how his pajama pants were clinging halfway down his buttocks and how he felt so loose and free in front and how the sawing motion made him swing in there.

His body ran with sweat. The dribbles tickled. They felt odd when they got inside his ears. They stung when they got in his eyes. But he liked the way they dropped off his head and face and fell like small, shiny bombs onto Sheila. She still kept the hand between her legs. The sweat bombs hit the back of her hand, her wrist and forearm, and the nearby areas that the hand didn't cover. The tops of her thighs. Her curves and slanting hollows. The tender skin below her navel. Clear, gleaming bombs that hit and exploded with tiny splashes and mingled with Sheila's own sweat.

Her belly-button was full and shimmering.

Stanley's sweat fell all around it, but none wanted to land dead center.

He changed his position slightly, but still couldn't find the target.

Then he thought about how he would like to put his mouth down there, seal his lips around her brimming navel and suck it empty, and afterwards thrust the tip of his tongue down into the hole.

The tongue part would probably hurt her and make her squirm.

She would try to make him stop.

I oughta do it right now, he thought. What's she gonna do about it, pinned down like that?

What's she gonna do about anything?

A whole new ballgame, once she's loose.

He stopped sawing. As he forced his fingers to release the handle, he noticed how badly his left arm trembled from the strain of bracing himself above the beam. The muscles of his legs and rump also fluttered. His back ached. So did his neck.

'Are you okay?' Sheila asked.

'Yeah,' he huffed. 'Just . . .' He shook his head.

Leaving the saw embedded in the deep groove, he wiped his face with his upper arm. The arm felt as slick and wet as his face. It didn't seem to do any good at all. Blinking, he glimpsed the green of Ben's T-shirt.

'Can't see . . . what I'm doing,' he gasped. 'Need a rag.'

'Maybe you'd better rest a while,' Sheila said.

'You mind?' Leaning forward, muscles juddering, he stretched his right arm down over the beam toward the T-shirt.

'No!' While Sheila kept her right hand tight between her legs, her left forearm clamped the shirt against her chest. 'Don't,' she said, and shook her head. 'I need it, Stan. Please.'

'Okay. Okay. But I . . . I've gotta be able to see. But that's okay. I'll just . . . take a rest.'

He groaned as he straightened his back. When he was standing upright, he slid his moccasins along the ledges of the tub and slowly began to make his way backward.

He sat on the edge of the broken floor. With both hands, he wiped his dripping face. Then he interlaced his fingers behind his head, pressed his hands against his drenched hair, and arched his back.

'I'm sorry,' Sheila said.

'Sorry?'

'I shouldn't have . . . You can have it.'

'What?'

'The shirt.'

'No,' he said. 'That's okay. You need it.' He pulled his legs up, scooted backward and began to stand.

'What're you doing?' Sheila asked. Her voice sounded calm but worried.

He stood up. He couldn't see her face, though, so he squatted before answering. 'I'll go and . . . find a towel. It won't take long.'

'No! Don't leave! Please!' Her eyes shifted to the saw. 'You've almost got it done, Stan. Just a couple more minutes, and . . .'

'It'll take a lot longer than that. I'm only about halfway. And I'm all worn out. So damn sweaty, too – it hurts in your eyes. I'll find a towel somewhere, and maybe lay down for a while.'

'Don't! Here!' With both hands, she snatched up the T-shirt. She crumpled it and hurled the bundle at Stanley.

He watched how the sudden movement of her right arm made her breasts jump and shake. Then the unfurling T-shirt blocked his view. He grabbed it out of the air in time to see Sheila tuck her right hand down between her legs and fling her left arm across her breasts.

Bitch, he thought.

He wadded the shirt and mopped his face with it. When he rubbed his hair, he saw that Sheila was squinting up at him.

'This helps a lot,' he said. 'Thanks.'

She didn't say anything.

Stanley winced when he rubbed his shoulders and the back of his neck.

'We're both gonna have nasty sunburns,' he said.

'Yeah.'

'We'll put something on 'em when I get you out of here.'

He rubbed his arms with the T-shirt. Then his armpits. Then his chest and sides and belly. Then his face again. Done, he held up the sodden ball of fabric. 'You can have it back, now.'

'Keep it,' Sheila said.

'Are you sure?'

'I'm sure.'

She didn't sound very friendly, anymore.

Stanley stood up, his knees crackling as he straightened his legs. He couldn't see her face from this height, but that was just fine; she couldn't see his, either. He allowed himself to grin.

'I'll go and find us some water,' he said.

'No!' she blurted, shock and alarm in her voice. 'Don't! Please, Stan! You're almost done with the sawing. Don't go anyplace now. Just cut through the rest of the way. Please.'

'Why should I?' he asked.

Sheila didn't answer.

There seemed to be a great stillness.

Stanley stood motionless, staring down at her. She didn't seem to be moving at all, not even breathing. She looked rigid. Her right breast was tightly clutched by her hand, while her left breast was pushed down by her forearm. Because of the middle beam, he couldn't see much of her right hand. From the position of the wrist, however, he supposed that it was welded between her legs.

'Why should I do *anything* for you?' he asked.

After another long silence, Sheila spoke. Her voice sounded low and tightly controlled. 'What's going on?'

'What've you done for *me* lately? Huh? I'm out here in the hot sun working like a slave, and what're you doing for me?

Nothing. Giving me orders, that's what you're doing. Telling me what to do, like I don't know where I'm supposed to cut a fucking board. Giving me all kinds of stink when all I do is ask for your shirt so I can wipe my face. I've gotta *pry* the fuckin' shirt off you. And then you go and cover up like you're scared I'll catch a peek at your precious titties. Who do you think you are, huh? Who do you think's doing *who* a favor around here?'

'You're doing *me* the favor, Stan,' she said. She sounded as if she were trying very hard to sound calm and reasonable and sympathetic. 'I really and truly appreciate it, too.'

'Yeah? Well, you don't act like it.'

'I'm sorry. This is all very . . . difficult. My family . . . I don't know where my little girl is.' She suddenly started to cry. 'Or my husband. They might be dead, for all I know. I'm . . . I'm trying to hang on . . . don't mean to . . . to be bad to you.'

Except for her legs, her whole body seemed to be shaking and twitching as she sobbed there in the bottom of the tub. Stan watched, amazed and delighted. She was so sleek and shiny, all curves and hollows that rippled and throbbed and writhed, and the arm across her breasts couldn't hold them still.

The sight made him stiff and achy.

He glanced down. The front of his pajama pants jutted out so much that Sheila couldn't possibly miss it.

He thought about squatting down to conceal the bulge.

Why should I? She sees what she sees. She better get used to it.

Soon, Sheila's crying subsided. She sniffled a few times. She sighed. After a while, she said, 'Are you going to finish sawing the beam for me?'

'Maybe. Maybe not. What'll you do for *me*?'

Slowly, both her hands slid away from where they covered her. 'Is this what you want?' she asked.

Stanley grinned. 'I didn't say that.'

'You didn't have to.'

Her hands settled lightly on the smooth plain of skin below her ribcage. 'Okay?' she asked.

'Lovely.'

'Now get back to the saw,' she said.

'When I'm good and ready.'

Her hands slid, the right gliding downward while the left moved toward her breast.

'Don't push your luck,' Stanley said.

She didn't let the warning stop her.

'Okay, okay!' Stanley snapped.

'When you start sawing, I'll take my hands away.'

'Okay!' Once again, he lowered his legs toward the tub. He stood on its ledges and shuffled along until he came to the four-by-eight. Bending over, he braced his left hand against it. His right hand gripped the saw.

'Start,' Sheila said.

'Yeah,' he said. 'Sure.'

Tugging at the saw's wooden handle, he drew the blade out of its deep slot in the beam.

Sheila frowned. 'What're you doing?'

'You want me to start sawing. I always do what I'm told.' Her cry of pain split the quiet as Stanley ran the saw across the top of her left thigh.

Twenty-seven

'You'd better keep down,' Em warned, 'or else you'll pork your back.'

The man crawling underneath the tree grunted and stayed low until he was well clear of the trunk. His silver jewelry jangled as he rolled onto his back. Red-faced and huffing, he raised his knees into the air. 'You hear that, Loreen?' he called.

'I heard, Caspar,' a woman answered. She sounded irritated. 'I'm not deaf, you know.'

'Never said you were, baby.' He rolled his head sideways and blinked toward Em. 'Hello, miss.'

'Just Em,' the girl said. 'That's short for Emerald. These are my pals, Clint and Mary.'

'Pleased to meet you all,' Caspar said. He pushed at the pavement, struggling to sit up. 'Whew! That's a mighty steep old road back there. And I, for one, am not as young as I used to be.'

'How old were you then?' Em asked.

Caspar, done sitting up, scowled at her. He was as fat as Santa, but beardless. He had no mustache, either, but his black eyebrows were enormous, bushy, upswept to points, and more Satanic than Santa-like.

Though his scowl looked ferocious, Em smiled.

'Just my luck,' he said. 'A scamp. Beware of geeks bearing wit.'

Em's jaw dropped. She glanced from Clint to Mary. 'I think he just called me a geek. Did you hear that? He doesn't even know me.'

'He's psychic,' Mary said.

'Hardy har.'

'Psychic indeed,' Caspar said. He turned to the woman who was poking her head out from under the tree. 'Didn't see this one coming, did we, my dear?'

'Speak for yourself.'

'Watch your back, darling,' he warned her.

She kept crawling forward. Like Caspar, she was rotund, red-faced, and out of breath. She appeared to be twenty-five or thirty years old – about half his age. Her jet black hair was shorter than his, and shaped like a football helmet while his was a shaggy mane.

Clear of the trunk, she sat on the pavement next to Caspar.

What a pair, Clint thought.

They wore matching red blouses – loose, airy affairs that gleamed like silk, had billowing sleeves, and were gathered in around their waists with broad, golden sashes. Loreen wore a peasant skirt; Caspar, a pair of crisp blue jeans. They sported sandals instead of shoes. They each wore more jewelry than

Clint had seen on one person in a long time: enormous hoops that dangled from their ears, necklaces, pendants, bracelets, rings on most of their fingers.

Patting the woman's leg, Caspar looked from Clint to the others and said, 'My Loreen. What would I do without her? Smile more often, perhaps?'

She slapped the back of his hand. 'He finds himself amusing,' she explained.

'We just finished eating,' Clint said. 'We have some salami and cheese left over. Would you like some?'

'That would be splendid, I'm sure,' Caspar said.

'Help yourselves,' Em said, leaning forward and handing the bag to him. As he took it, she asked, 'What are your costumes for? Do you work in a Greek restaurant?'

'Scamp,' Caspar said.

'We're gypsies, my dear,' Loreen explained.

'Oh, delightful,' Mary muttered.

Clint gave her an annoyed glance. She smirked at him.

Em and the newcomers paid no attention. Em, sitting up straight, grabbed her knees and said, '*Real* gypsies?'

'What's real?' asked Caspar, peering into the bag.

'We're gypsy fortune-tellers,' Loreen explained.

'The Blotskis,' Caspar added. 'We're world famous in Studio City.' He took out a handful of cheese slices and the remains of the salami, and one of the knives.

'I don't think I've heard of you,' Em said.

'We won't hold that against you,' Caspar said.

'You're one among legions,' Loreen told her.

'Our parlor's in Studio City,' Caspar explained 'but our *lair* is in West Hollywood. The hike appears to be more than we bargained for.'

'Couldn't get through the traffic?' Clint asked.

'Ah. I took one peek at Ventura Boulevard and decided to leave our car in the parking lot.'

'My feet will never be the same,' Loreen said.

'The hike will do us good.'

'If it doesn't kill us.'

'You're almost to the top,' Clint said.

'Speaking of which,' Mary said, 'shouldn't we be going?'

'What's the hurry?' Em asked.

Though Clint hated to agree with Mary about anything, he told Em, 'We've been resting here too long already. I want to get home.'

'But these are gypsies.'

'Yeah,' Mary said. 'Sure thing.'

'I don't know about you, but I'd sort of like to have my fortune told.'

'What do you want to know, sweetie?' Loreen asked.

Em frowned. 'Don't you have to use a crystal ball or look at my palm or something?'

'Not Loreen,' Caspar said, cutting off a thick disk of salami. 'She's a face-reader.'

'I never heard of something like that.'

'A mug-inspector,' Caspar added.

'A fraud,' Mary muttered.

Clint had no doubt that everyone heard her, but nobody reacted.

Loreen said, 'Tell me what you want to know, Emerald.'

Em gnawed her lower lip. Then she said, 'To begin with, what's my last name?'

Caspar, chuckling, placed a slice of cheese on top of the salami piece. 'Such a scamp,' he said as he handed it to Loreen. 'A test! She wants to test you. How do you like that one?'

'I'm afraid I don't do parlor tricks,' Loreen told Em. 'Your last name is no mystery to you. I deal only in mysteries, in the dark secrets lurking in the mists of the future.'

'What a load,' Mary said.

Loreen didn't ignore that one. She turned her head toward Mary, smiled pleasantly, and said, 'The parting mists do show you, smart lady, coming to a very bad end in the very near future.'

Em cackled.

Smiling beatifically, Loreen chomped her salami and cheese.

'That's *real* funny,' Mary said. 'Ha ha ha. What am I supposed to do now, tremble? I'm *so* scared. Weirdos.'

Words muffled by her soggy mouthful, Loreen said, 'I just call 'em like I see 'em. So sorry. Rest in peace, honey.'

'Bitch.'

'Hey!' Clint snapped.

'She said I'm gonna die!'

'And soon,' Em added, laughing.

'That's really for shit!'

Clint tried not to smile.

'Oh, yeah, you think it's funny, too. You wouldn't think it was so funny if she said it about Em, though, would you? You'd be laughing out of the other side of your face, then.'

'I'm not laughing,' Clint explained.

'Maybe not, but you *want* to.'

'*I* am not laughing,' Caspar said. The grim tone of his voice shocked Clint. Em's laughter stopped as if crushed by a boot. 'You called my Loreen a bitch,' Caspar said, staring at Mary, his eyelids half shut. The salami was in his left hand, the knife in his right. He raised the blade of the knife. 'Perhaps I should remove your tongue?'

Oh, Jesus, Clint thought. 'She didn't mean anything,' he said.

'She called my Loreen a bitch.'

Clint turned on Mary. 'Tell them you're sorry. You didn't mean it.'

'The hell I will.'

'Do it!'

Her eyes suddenly shimmered with tears. 'You're just gonna let this asshole threaten me?'

Em rolled her eyes upward. 'Oh, wonderful, now she's called *him* an asshole. The fun never ends. Jeezle-peezle, Mary!' Leaning forward, she patted Caspar's knee. 'Don't let her get to you, okay? Sometimes, she's a *putz*. You know what I mean? You've just gotta basically ignore her.'

Caspar slowly nodded. 'For you, my little scamp, I'll let the woman keep her tongue.'

'Only because you're so nice,' Loreen added.

Mary wiped her eyes, then glared at Clint. 'Thanks a heap, He-man.'

'I'm not here to save your butt when you go running off at the mouth. I don't know what your problem is, but . . .'

'I'm a *putz*.'

Frowning, Em tilted her head and asked nobody in particular, 'Can a female person *be* a *putz*? Or is that a term that only applies in a strict sense to men?'

'It applies in Mary's case,' Loreen said, smiling.

Mary's face darkened and her mouth opened. But she shut her mouth fast.

'We're all friends again,' Caspar said. 'Aren't we, Mary?'

'Yeah, sure.'

He bared his teeth at her. 'Of course, I was kidding about cutting out your tongue. Just kidding. A little joke. I would never cut out the tongue of a pretty woman like you.'

Clint fully expected the next words out of Caspar's mouth to be, 'Of course, I would cheerfully *slit your throat* from ear to ear,' and mean it.

From the looks on the faces of Mary and Em, they seemed to be thinking pretty much the same thing.

Whoever this guy is, Clint thought, he's dangerous. Friendly and cheerful, but definitely dangerous. And probably no more of a gypsy than I am – just some sort of showman or con artist, or God knows what. Same with Loreen.

What's she, anyway? His wife? His daughter?

Ask?

Yeah, right, and risk the Wrath of Caspar? No, thanks. Leave that sort of thing to Em.

'Can we get going, now?' Mary asked.

'Let's wait till they're done eating,' Em said, 'and we can all walk together.'

'And why would we want to do that?'

'Well, for starters, it wouldn't be very polite to walk away and leave them. Also, I happen to find them very fascinating people.'

'Thank you, dear,' Loreen said.

'You're welcome.' She returned her attention to Mary. 'And also, it's a well-known fact that there is safety in numbers.'

'Excellent observation,' Caspar said, and stuffed his mouth with salami and cheese.

'Thank you,' Em told him. 'I'll just bet you'd be handy to have around if we should happen to run into a hooligan or two.'

Busy chewing, he nodded and twirled the blade of the knife.

'You can have some of that water, by the way,' Em added. 'You two are probably parched. I should've mentioned it. Those bottles in the bag there . . .'

'Ah.' He reached into the bag and pulled out one of the plastic bottles. Only about a cup of water remained in it. 'Thank you, my dear. You are a life saver.' He took a single swallow, then passed the bottle to Loreen.

Like Caspar, she restricted herself to one swallow. Then she licked her lips and said, 'Delicious.'

'Drink some more,' Em said. 'Both of you. That was hardly enough to wet your whistles.'

'Maybe later,' Loreen told her. She handed the bottle back to Caspar, who capped it and returned it to the sack.

'I think we could use a couple more people,' Clint said. 'Especially in case of trouble.' Eyeing Mary, he added, 'As long as we can all get along together. Are you going to behave?'

'I'll behave,' she said. Lowering her eyes, she muttered, 'Like I have a choice.'

'If you act up,' Em warned, 'we'll let Caspar cut your tongue out.'

'Oh, you're real funny.'

Clint sighed. 'That's no help, Em.'

'But fun.'

'Such a scamp,' Caspar said.

'She doesn't need any encouragement,' Clint told him.

'You're right. Emerald, be a sweetheart and stop pestering Mary.'

'Thanks,' Clint said. 'Anyway, what do you think about joining up with us?'

'Which way are you heading?' Loreen asked.

'Some psychic,' Mary muttered. And quickly added, 'Sorry.'

'They're heading the same as us,' Caspar told her. 'You didn't see them on the way up?'

'I wasn't looking up.'

'I saw them. I saw *someone*. It was you?'

'Probably,' Clint said. 'Nobody else seems to be up here.'

'I didn't see anyone,' Loreen said.

'We know that,' Caspar told her. 'Tell us something we don't know.'

'We're in for big trouble,' she said in a very casual voice, as if commenting on bland weather.

Clint felt his stomach sink.

'Wonderful,' Mary muttered.

Em curled her upper lip. 'Is that a prediction?' she asked Loreen.

The woman didn't answer, but Caspar said, 'I'm afraid so.' Then he asked Loreen, 'What sort of trouble?'

'Big trouble.'

'Is she getting this from someone's face?' Em asked Caspar. 'You said she's a face-reader.'

'From the face of the day,' Loreen said. 'I see blood on the face of the day.'

Mary let out a huff of air. She said, 'This is such . . .' But she didn't let herself finish.

Everyone stared at Loreen.

'Tell us more,' Caspar said.

'I see death at sunset.'

Something down low inside Clint seemed to shrivel.

'One of us?' Caspar asked.

'All right,' Clint said. 'That's enough. Just cut it out. I don't know who you people are, but I don't want to hear any more of this. Nobody can predict the future . . . and you're giving me the creeps. So knock it off, okay? I don't want to hear this kind of stuff. Just keep it to yourselves, or . . .'

'I don't want to be *around* them,' Mary protested, standing up. 'Okay? Let's just go.'

'If you leave now,' Em said, 'you won't find out who's going to die at sunset.'

'As if I didn't know. Who do you *suppose* the fat lady's gonna finger? She's got it in for me. You've *all* got it in for me.'

'No, we don't,' Em said. 'That's silly.'

Mary frowned down at Clint. 'Are you coming?'

'Is everybody ready?' he asked, glancing at the others.

'Those two don't have to come with us, do they? Come on, Clint, they're . . . they scare me.'

'I'm done with banishing people.'

'You oughta be happy about that,' Em told her.

'As far as I'm concerned,' Clint said, 'the Blotskis are welcome to come along.'

'You're a fine and decent man,' Loreen said.

'True,' Caspar added. 'And that's not a prediction, it's a fact. Mind if we eat while we walk?'

'Go ahead. Just lay off this fortune-telling stuff. Nobody wants to hear it.'

'Or maybe,' Em suggested, 'you could tell us just the nifty stuff, and leave out anything that's ooky.'

'No,' Clint said. 'Any more predictions, nifty, ooky or otherwise, and *I'm* going to take off and leave everybody behind.'

'Same here,' Mary said.

'Those are the ground rules.'

'Fine by me,' Caspar said. 'Loreen?'

She pressed a forefinger to her greasy lips. 'Mum's the word,' she said.

Clint got to his feet. 'Let's get moving,' he said. 'We're almost to the top, so the worst is behind us.'

Twenty-eight

They had eaten a lunch of barbeque-flavored potato chips and peanut-butter-and-jelly sandwiches. Barbara had tried a beer, but she'd given up on it after one taste, and switched to Dr Pepper. The others had seemed to enjoy their beers.

Leaving Heather to keep watch out the window, Lee had taken Earl into the bedroom for a change of clothes. Barbara and Pete had sat beside each other on the floor while they were gone. Barbara could hear quiet talking from the other room, but she couldn't make out the words.

'Cool, huh?' Earl said as he swaggered into the living room. He'd kept the dead man's huge, white shirt. But the pin-striped slacks had been replaced by a pair of camouflage trousers and he now wore white socks and faded blue running shoes. He fluttered a baggy leg of the pants. 'Gets all his stuff at Supply Sergeant.'

Heather looked over her shoulder and smirked. She said nothing, though.

'All I need's like an M-16, or something, and I'd be all set to rock 'n' roll.' He grinned at Lee. 'Anyway, thanks for the duds. I'll get 'em back to you, promise.'

'No hurry,' Lee said.

'Thanks for feeding us,' Barbara said, getting to her feet.

'Yeah,' Pete said. 'It sure hit the spot.'

'Glad I could help,' Lee told them.

'Now, if you *really* wanta help,' Earl said, 'how about letting us borrow one of your guns?' He said it smiling, as if it were a big joke, but Barbara knew he meant it.

'No can do.'

Earl made a mock-pouting face. 'Hey, I thought we were pals.'

'I don't loan out my weapons.'

'You don't need both of 'em, do you?'

'Yes.'

'Hey, come on. How am I gonna protect Banner if I don't have a gun? Look at her. She's a beauty, isn't she?'

Lee glanced at Barbara. His eyes darted from her face to the hand that held her blouse shut, then back to Earl. He said nothing.

'Don't you care what happens to her?'

'I care.'

'All we gotta do, you know, is run into the wrong sort of guys out there on our way home, and . . .'

'Stay here,' Lee said. 'Nobody's pushing you out the door.'

'I have to get home,' Barbara told him. 'My parents . . .'

'Same here,' Pete said.

'But we don't need one of your guns,' she added.

'Speak for yourself,' Earl said.

'I just did. I don't want one.'

'I do.' Earl frowned at Lee. 'Come on, you've got that *assault* rifle.' He nodded at the carbine that was leaning against the sofa near Heather. 'What do you need the pistol for? It might save our lives. Might save Banner from getting herself reamed by a gang of drooling maniacs.'

Barbara scowled. 'Shut up.'

Heather smirked over her shoulder at Earl. 'You said there *isn't* any gang of maniacs out there.'

'Yeah, well, who knows? Just 'cause I didn't see it . . . I sure saw plenty of poor jerks who'd gotten themselves trashed real good. It ain't exactly a picnic out there.'

'Then don't leave,' Lee said. He looked at Barbara. 'I know you want to get home. I know you're worried about your parents . . .'

'And it has to be killing them, not knowing if I'm okay.'

'Same here,' Pete said.

Lee nodded. 'I understand. But you'd be better off playing it safe. Do you think that your parents would want you to risk your lives, just in order to get home a little bit sooner? Not a chance. The National Guard'll be on the streets tomorrow.'

'The Guard?' Pete asked. 'Really?'

'How do you know?' Barbara asked.

'Heard it on my radio,' Lee said.

'You've got a radio that works?'

'Down in my car.'

'Sure!' Pete said. 'Car radios. They'll still work.'

'What else did you hear?' Barbara asked.

'Not much. I had to get back into the building. The car was no good as a defensive position, so . . .'

'But they said for sure the National Guard will be here tomorrow?' Pete asked. He seemed very excited.

'That's right.'

'Jeez, Barbara. Maybe we *should* stay here. You know?'

'Not me. I can't wait till tomorrow. Besides, how do we know the Guard will really show up when it's supposed to? It'd be crazy to wait that long on the chance that things'll be safer. I mean, we're only a few miles from home. An hour or so, that's all it'll take.'

'On the other hand,' Lee said, 'you might not make it at all.'

'I'll take my chances,' Barbara told him.

'See that?' Earl said. 'She's going, with or without a gun.'

'I don't want a gun,' Barbara repeated.

'I do,' Earl said. 'Come on, Lee. You afraid I won't bring it back?'

'That's not . . .'

'I'll *buy* one of 'em off you? Okay? I'll give you five hundred bucks for the forty-five.'

Lee shook his head.

'Six hundred.'

'We both know you don't have any money, Earl.'

'Maybe not on me . . .'

'I'm going,' Barbara said. 'Thanks again for the lunch, Lee.'

'Welcome.'

'Pete, are you coming?'

'Just hang on a minute,' Earl said. 'Nobody's going anywhere. We're in the middle of some negotiations here.'

Barbara smirked. 'Negotiations, my butt. You haven't got any money.'

'How much have you got?'

'Not nearly enough. Maybe five bucks.'

'Pete?'

'Six or seven, I guess.'

'Heather?'

'I'm not paying nothing,' Heather told him. 'I'm staying right here.'

'Okay,' Earl said. 'Okay. So, we don't buy it with money. What'll you take for the forty-five, Lee?'

Lee was beginning to look annoyed. 'I won't take anything for it. I'm not selling.'

'What'll you take to let us *borrow* it just for . . . say, three or four days? I mean, we only need it for an hour or two, but I'm not sure when I'll be able to get it back to you.'

'Forget it,' Lee said.

'How about an hour with Banner?' Grinning at Barbara, Earl patted her shoulder.

She swatted his hand away.

'Hey! Watch the merchandise!'

'Keep your hands off her!' Pete snapped.

'Yeah, yeah, sure, don't wet your pants. How about it, Lee? Look at her. A fair trade – you get an hour in the sack with Banner, and we get the loan of your forty-five.'

Lee met her eyes.

My God, he's thinking it over!

'No,' she said. Her voice sounded hollow and seemed to ring in her ears.

'How about it, Lee? A deal?'

'She said no.'

'What if she changes her mind?'

'Cut it out,' Pete warned.

'Shut up.'

'She isn't gonna do something like that.'

'Maybe she is and maybe she isn't. Lee's gonna let us have the gun if she comes across.'

'No.' Lee shook his head. He seemed less sure of himself than before. After a moment, he added, 'Not unless she wants to.'

'Look at him, Barbara. He's a handsome guy, isn't he? A real hunk. Wouldn't you like to have him put it to you?'

'Stop it,' she said.

'I'm pretty sure she must be a virgin, Lee. Everything in mint condition, if you know what I mean.' He faced Barbara. 'Is that the problem? You wanta save it for . . . ?'

'She asked you to stop,' Lee said. 'So stop. I'm not going for this. I'm not about to have you brow-beat her into doing something against her will.'

'Ah, don't be such a Boy Scout.'

'Knock it off, Earl!' Pete yelled.

'*I'll* do it,' Heather said.

The room suddenly went silent.

Everyone turned to Heather, who was kneeling on the sofa, looking at them over her shoulder. 'I'll do it,' she said again. Then she climbed off the sofa and turned around and faced Lee. A corner of her mouth trembled. 'How about it?'

Lee looked flustered. 'I'm sorry. This is all . . . don't know how this got started, exactly, but I don't want any part of it. Earl's crazy if he thinks I'm going to trade one of my guns for . . . for sex . . . with you or anybody else.'

Heather gaped at him. She blinked. She looked as if she couldn't believe her ears. Then she muttered, 'What's so wrong with *me*?'

'Nothing. Nothing's wrong with you. This is all a mistake.'

'Wasn't a mistake when it was *Barbara*.'

He shook his head. 'I wasn't going to . . .'

'She didn't *want* you, or you would've.'

'That's not true,' he said.

The hell it's not, Barbara thought. If I'd said yes . . .

'So why not me?' Heather blurted. 'Am I so ugly and disgusting . . . ?'

'You're not. You're very attractive.'

'Screw it,' Earl said. 'He's just trying to spare your feelings. It's Banner or nothing. Right, Lee?'

'It's nothing,' he said.

Barbara gripped Pete's arm. 'Let's get out of here. Right now.'

Whirling around, Earl blurted in her face, 'We need that gun, Banner! You wanta get us killed out there? Fuck the guy and we walk out with a gun! What's your pussy worth, for . . .!'

Pete grabbed Earl by the front of his shirt.

'Stop it!' Lee shouted and reached for Earl.

The blast of a gunshot slammed through the room.

Lee's head jerked as if it had been struck in the side by a baseball bat. His lips flopped. Spit flew from his mouth. The bullet came out the left side of his head an inch above his ear, throwing out a heavy red splash. He went sideways as if chasing it, tripped on his own feet, and crashed to the floor.

Heather took aim with the rifle and put another shot into him.

'No!' Barbara yelled.

'Good job!' shouted Earl. 'Way to go, Heather! Now we get *both* his guns.'

'The dirty rotten son of a bitch,' Heather muttered, scowling at Lee's sprawled body.

Still holding Pete's arm, Barbara staggered backward on flimsy legs. She stopped when her buttocks bumped softly against the wall.

Oh, God, she thought. Oh, my God. Oh, my God.

She gonna shoot me next?

'Got just what he deserved,' Earl said. 'You're terrific, Heather. Not only beautiful, but damn smart!' He knelt beside the body. 'Don't know what we would've done without you,' he said. Nodding and smiling at her, he pulled the forty-five out of the back of Lee's jeans. 'Thanks to you, Heather, we'll have a real fighting chance out in the streets.'

'Is he dead?' Heather asked. Her voice sounded strangely flat, as if she was speaking from a trance.

'You killed him deader than hell,' Earl said. 'I couldn't have done better myself.'

'He was a rotten son of a bitch,' Heather said.

'Yeah. Sure was. Who else do you think we oughta shoot?'

'Her.' Heather swung the muzzle toward Barbara.

'No!' Barbara yelled.

She heard Pete yell, too, and felt him shove her out of the way.

As she stumbled, she watched Earl jab the forty-five at Heather and fire. The noise was low and heavy and didn't stop. He was pulling the trigger very fast. The black pistol jumped in his hands, spitting brass out its side, smoke and fire out its front. Slug after slug punched Heather. They hit her in the chest and breasts, poking holes through her blouse, flinging out gouts of blood, shoving her backward. She dropped the rifle and sat down hard on the sofa.

Barbara's ears rang.

Shreds of white smoke drifted silently through the air.

'God!' Earl cried out. 'I had to do it! Did you see her? Did you see what she did? I had to do it!' Earl's voice sounded very far away. Barbara could barely hear it through the ringing. He was standing in front of her, looking from her to Pete. 'You're my witnesses, right? You saw what happened. I had to shoot her. She flipped out. No telling who she was gonna shoot next. Right?'

Pete muttered, 'Guess.'

Barbara nodded her head.

'Damn right,' Earl said. Pointing the pistol toward the floor, he pushed a button to release its magazine. His hands started to shake. Badly. Then more than his hands. He stood there with his shoulders hunched, arms tight against his sides, chin jumping up and down – shuddering all over like a wet, naked man standing in a blizzard. Finally, the magazine came sliding down out of the pistol's handle. He fumbled it and it fell to the floor.

He stared down at it.

'Why'd she do it?' he asked. He looked at Barbara. 'She *shot* him. He was a good guy. He helped us. What the hell did she want to go and shoot him for? Does that make any sense? Was she nuts?'

'You . . . said he deserved it,' Barbara muttered.

'Yeah. That was *after*. Anyway, I didn't mean it. Had to say something.' He held the pistol toward her. 'You want this?'

'No. Huh-uh.'

'I'll take it,' Pete said. Earl handed the pistol to him.

'Better reload,' Earl said, and turned away. Turned toward the sofa. 'Jesus,' he muttered. 'Jesus, look at her.'

Heather sat slumped against the back cushion, her mouth hanging open, her arms limp by her sides, the rifle across her lap, her legs apart and stretched out underneath the coffee table. Her face was spattered with blood. From the shoulders down, her dress was sodden. She looked like she'd caught a bucket full to the brim with red paint square in the chest.

There's that woman's blood under all that somewhere, Barbara thought. The woman the cat killed.

She couldn't think of the woman's name.

She couldn't think of the cat's name, either.

That's Heather, though, she told herself. I know that's Heather. But what's her last name?

Doesn't matter, she decided. I don't have to know.

'I did that to her,' Earl said. 'Can you believe it? Jesus. I did that to her.'

Pete bent over the table and picked up the full magazine. He shoved it up the handle of the Colt, then jacked a fresh round into the chamber. 'She flipped out,' he said. 'Maybe we all had something to do with it, I don't know.'

'We did,' Barbara said.

'Yeah, I guess so.'

'One way or another.'

'Yeah,' Pete said.

Earl shook his head. 'I'm the one that blew her out of her socks.'

'We helped,' Barbara said. 'She was . . . so jealous. Of me.'

'It's almost like we led her right up to the brink,' Pete said.

'I think she saw us in the pool.'

'What'd you do in the pool?' Earl asked.

'Kissed,' Barbara said, looking him in the eyes.

'That's all?'

'It was plenty,' Pete said. 'We wouldn't have done it with her watching. Not if we'd known.'

'She had a thing for Pete,' Barbara explained.

'Maybe she didn't see us.'

'But what if she did? And then, on top of that, Lee won't . . . sleep with her.'

'She just lost her marbles and I had to shoot her,' Earl said. 'That's all there is to it. She went nuts. Doesn't make any sense to blame anybody but her.'

'Maybe not,' Barbara muttered. 'God, I don't know.'

'What should we do about . . . all this?' Pete asked.

'Nothing,' Earl said. 'Let's just get out of here. Get the rifle, Barbara.'

'I don't want it.'

'Shit. I'll get it.' He stepped toward the end of the coffee table. 'Just don't shoot me, Pete. You aren't gonna shoot me if I go for it, are you?'

'You aren't gonna try and shoot *us*, are you?' Pete asked.

'Gimme a break.'

'So we can't testify.'

'Are you kidding? I'm gonna *want* you to testify. You can tell 'em how it was self-defense.'

'Yeah,' Pete said.

'It *was* self-defense,' Earl said, and picked up the rifle. 'No telling who she was gonna shoot next. I had to put her down. It was her or us. Isn't that so, Banner?'

'I guess so. Yeah.'

'Okay. Okay. Now let's take whatever we need and get the hell out of here.'

'Take what?' Barbara asked, frowning.

'The ammo, for starters. And anything else we want.'

'We can't steal from him.'

'If you think we're walking outa here without the guns and ammo, you're crazier than Heather.'

'I'm not a thief,' she said.

'You don't have to be. Leave it to me and Pete. Anyhow, it isn't really stealing – he's dead.'

'It's still stealing.'

'Right, sure. Screw that. You and your morals, Banner. If you weren't such a damn prude, Lee'd be balling you right now in the other room instead of lying here with his brains on the floor. And Heather'd still be alive.'

'Oh, suddenly now it *is* my fault?'

'Not saying it's your fault. Just saying none of it would've hit the fan if you'd done what I said and let him fuck you.'

'Go to hell.'

'Leave her alone,' Pete said. 'You had no business trying to push her into something like that in the first place.'

'He was gonna go for it.'

'We didn't need a gun that badly.'

'Oh, no? You might just be singing a different tune, Pizza face, if we get out there and run into trouble. Anyway, we've got 'em now. No thanks to Banner. Now, let's get what we need and hit the road. Startin' to stink in here.'

Twenty-nine

He'd made Sheila call out that they should go away, that she was fine and didn't need help and wanted to be left alone. But they had come, anyway.

Two men and a woman.

Earlier, Stanley had warned Sheila about 'oddballs' and 'creepy types' he'd seen roaming the neighborhood. It had been a lie to keep her from shouting for help. But these three fit the bill perfectly.

Too perfectly.

They *are* real, aren't they? he wondered.

I might be nuts, but I don't hallucinate.

They've gotta be real, he told himself as he watched their approach from his hiding place in the rubble.

Not only could he see them, but he could hear them: their voices, the crunch of their footsteps, the heavy breathing of the big guy. He could smell the woman's cigarette.

If that wasn't enough to prove they weren't some sort of

phantoms concocted by his imagination, he'd heard Sheila calling to them, answering them, telling them to go away. So she was aware of them, too; they had to be real.

Unless I'm imagining *all* of this, Stanley thought – including Sheila.

The notion made him smile. Then it sent a chill through him.

What was that story?

An Occurrence at Owl Creek Bridge.

Shit! This better be nothing like that!

It's not, he told himself. This is real. I know what's real and what isn't.

If this *isn't* real, he thought, when did it *stop* being real? Maybe I never got out of my house – the quake brought the place down on top of me and I'm out cold and I never did any of this stuff, none of it, everything's been in my head.

Or maybe I'm still asleep by the pool over at the Benson place – in which case the *early* stuff really happened but this about coming back to Sheila is only a dream, and . . .

'Watch out,' Sheila called. 'There's a guy named Stan. He was just here a few minutes ago. Do you see him?'

He ducked as the three strangers raised their heads and scanned the area.

'We don't see nobody,' one of the men said. 'You included. Where are ya?'

'Make sure Stan isn't around. I don't think he's too stable. He . . . he cut me on purpose. That's why I screamed like I did.'

'Don't look like he stuck around for us,' the same guy said.

'Can't say I blame him,' said the woman who was with the men. 'Where are you?'

'Follow my voice.'

'Keep talking.'

Stanley raised himself enough to see past the side of the pile. The three were walking slowly through the debris, side by side but spread out.

'I'm down through a hole in the floor,' Sheila said.

They were making their way through what was left of

Sheila's kitchen, so it wouldn't be long before they found her.

When she sees what they look like, Stanley thought, she'll wish she'd kept her mouth shut in the first place.

The big one looked like a grizzly bear masquerading as an outlaw biker. He wore a black Harley-Davidson T-shirt and sagging blue jeans. A great, hairy loaf of fat hung out below the bottom of his T-shirt.

In spite of his size, hair and filth, however, he didn't seem nearly as strange as his smaller friend. That one was hairless. From what Stanley could see, he didn't even have eyebrows. He wore high, black leather boots and black leather pants. Instead of a belt, he had rusty strands of barbed wire wrapped around his waist. He wore no shirt. His skin was dead white, and his tiny eyes looked pink.

What fucking rock did *he* crawl out from under? Stanley wondered.

While the big one lumbered through the ruins of the house, the smaller one walked lightly and fluidly as if he were performing some sort of slow, weird ballet.

He made Stanley's skin crawl.

The gal looked skinny and mean. She might've been as bald as the spook a few days ago, but now her scalp was a sloping field of black stubble. Her eyebrows looked like black, upturned slashes. Her small eyes seemed to crowd the sides of her nose. Her thin, sneering lips pinched a cigarette. Her chin came to a point.

She's not so bad, Stanley thought, and smiled. Just get rid of the head, she's fine.

Drooping from shoulder straps was a gray tank top that ended at her midriff. She had a good, dark tan. Her breasts weren't much larger than tennis balls, but they had a nice bounce to them when she moved, and Stanley liked how her nipples pushed out against her shirt. The shirt was cut off just below her ribcage. She looked flat and sleek below it. She had a golden ring in her belly button. Her jeans hung very low, and she didn't wear a belt – barbed wire or otherwise.

They'll tug right down, Stanley thought.

He watched her, and she was the one who found Sheila.

'Over here, boys.' Squatting down, she tossed her cigarette aside. 'Fine time to take a bath,' she said. It sounded like a complaint, not a quip. Turning her head, she called, 'You boys are in for a treat.'

They came up on each side of her.

'Hey, now,' the big one said. 'Ain't this a pretty picture?'

'Will you help me get out?' Sheila asked.

Stanley thought she sounded a bit tense.

'That's what we're here for,' the man said. 'Why else'd we be here, if it wasn't to help?'

'Go on and climb down there, Crash,' the woman said. 'Give her a hand.'

'You bet.' Before he could move, the hairless one clapped a hand on his shoulder.

'What's the hurry? Know what I mean?'

'Please,' Sheila said. 'Help me. I can't get out. I've been down here . . . ever since the quake. These two beams . . . I just can't get out from under them.'

'What's your name?' the hairless one asked.

'Sheila. Sheila Banner.'

He squatted by the edge, and grinned down at her. 'Sheila,' he said. 'Sheeee-lah. I'm Eagle. My big buddy here, he's Crash. Our main bitch here, she's Weed.'

Fucking freaks, Stanley thought.

'Nice to meet you,' he heard Sheila say.

'Why are you down there?' Eagle asked her.

'The quake.'

'But *why*?'

'I . . . thought the tub would save me.'

'Did it?'

'Yeah. I think so. I didn't get crushed.'

'But you're trapped.'

'Yes.'

'Why?'

'What do you mean?'

'Delve.'

Sheila was silent for a few moments. Then she said, 'I just need someone to help me get out of here. Please.'

'Is it a punishment?' Eagle asked her.

'What?'

'A punishment being visited upon you.'

'No!'

'It's gotta be,' Weed chimed in. 'Everything happens for a reason.'

'And,' said Eagle, 'the punishment *always* fits the crime.'

'Always,' added Weed. 'It's karma.'

'Okay,' Sheila said. 'This probably *is* a punishment. You're absolutely right.' She sounded wonderfully calm. She's trying to humor them, Stanley thought, and smiled.

'But maybe it's time for my punishment to end,' she suggested. 'I've been down here a long time. I'm . . . really sore. I hurt all over. And look at my leg. Look what he did to it. He did that with his *saw*. Like my leg was a board. You know? That's when I screamed. So don't you think all that's enough, and you can help me get out now?'

'That would all depend,' Eagle said.

'On what?'

'The nature of your offenses.'

'Gotta confess 'em,' Weed said.

'Confess,' Crash said as he sidestepped, probably hoping for a better view. He bent over and picked up the saw that Stanley had left behind for the strangers to find. Then he sat down where Stanley himself had preferred to sit – above the foot of the tub.

Can't see her twat from there, Stanley thought. But she's probably got it covered with a hand, anyhow. Probably has her tits covered, too. She isn't gonna give freebies to these three freaks.

'If I confess,' Sheila asked, 'you'll help me get out?'

'If you're deserving,' Eagle told her.

'What do you want me to say?'

'The truth.'

'You *know* why you're there,' Weed pointed out.

'Sure I know!'

Temper, temper, Stanley thought.

And Sheila shouted, 'The goddamn earth shook like hell and

the goddamn house fell down, that's why! Wrong time, wrong place, that's why. It's what I get for living in L.A., that's why.'

'That's not why,' said Eagle. His voice was slick, oily. 'Tell us the truth.'

'Stan!' she suddenly shouted. 'You oughta get over here, Stan! You'll love these jerks – they're as buggy as you are!'

'We're here to save you,' Weed explained.

'Then do it!'

'You haven't confessed yet,' Eagle said.

'If I confess, you'll get me out?'

'If you *don't*, all hope is gone.'

'Okay. Okay. It's gotta be poetic justice, right? Some sort of payback that got me pinned in the tub?'

Eagle's strange, white head bobbed up and down. He continued to squat by the break in the floor, but Weed – on the side of him closer to Stanley – sat down and lowered her legs over the edge. 'Tell us,' she said. 'We're all ears.'

Something about that made Crash chuckle, but he didn't say anything.

'Okay,' Sheila said again.

Stanley wished he could see her, gaze down at her wonderful body, watch her face as she tried to con these three weirdos into helping her. But he couldn't see Sheila at all. From where he crouched, he had a great view of Crash's broad back and maybe half the face – all black, greasy hair and beard.

Over Crash's left shoulder, he could see Weed and Eagle in profile.

He wished he could see them better.

But he liked knowing that they couldn't see him – not without turning their heads.

'I'm trapped,' Sheila said, 'to punish me for being too independent. Okay? I like my freedom too much. I never allow myself to be restrained from . . . doing whatever I want to do. Even if it means . . . going against the wishes of other people . . . people who want to hold me down.'

'You're held down now, aren't you?' Weed said. She was nodding, rocking back and forth, hands on her knees. '*Really* held down.'

'That's right.'

'No good,' Eagle said. 'You don't get punished for being independent.'

'Sure you do,' Weed objected.

His hand flashed sideways. The back of it struck Weed's cheek. Stanley heard the sound of a clap, and saw her flinch.

Yes!

'What'd you hit her for?' Sheila demanded.

'You got a problem with it?'

'Yes!'

The back of his hand smacked Weed's face again.

'Damn it!'

'Just shut the fuck up down there,' Weed said. 'I'll jump on ya.'

'Give us something else, Sheee-lah. Tell us why you're being punished.'

She was silent for a few moments. Then she said, 'I wouldn't have the foggiest idea.'

'Betcha *I* know why,' Crash said. He hoisted the saw like a kid eager to be called on in class.

'Don't tell,' Weed said. 'She's gotta figure it out for herself.'

'What's *wrong* with you people?'

'Nothing wrong with us,' Eagle told her. '*You're* the one stuck in a bathtub.'

'You want us to set you free, don't you?' Weed asked.

'My God,' Sheila blasted. 'People are supposed to pull *together* in times of crisis. *Help* each other. All I'm getting are a bunch of sadistic *lunatics*!'

'What goes around comes around,' Eagle told her.

'It's your karma,' Weed added.

'My karma's just fine, thanks. Why don't you all just get out of here and take a flying leap!'

Stanley wanted to laugh, wanted to clap, but he only allowed himself a grin.

'You don't want us to leave,' Weed said.

'I want you to get one of these *beams* off me, but you keep playing your stupid games.'

'We only want the truth from you,' Eagle explained. 'As

soon as I hear the truth, I'll let Crash jump down with the saw and set you free.'

'Just confess,' Weed told her.

'Yeah,' said Crash. 'I *wanta* cut ya loose, but you gotta play along.'

'Okay.' A few moments passed. 'Okay,' Sheila said again. 'We're looking for . . . my biggest sin, is that it?'

'Sin has nothing to do with it,' Eagle said. 'Sin is mythical nonsense.'

'You're full of it,' Sheila said.

Eagle grabbed up a handful of debris, stretched out his arm, and let go. As his hand opened, Stanley saw dust, grit, a few chunks of stucco or plaster, and a small triangle of broken glass fall out.

'Hey!' Sheila gasped.

'Confess,' said Eagle.

'What am I *supposed* to confess?' she blurted. 'If it can't be a sin . . .'

'How about if we torture it out of her?' Crash suggested. 'If she won't cooperate . . .'

'Pride!' Sheila cried out. 'My pride! That's what put me here! "Pride goeth before a fall," right?'

'Go on,' Eagle said.

'I . . . take too much pride in my appearance. I tell myself that I'm more attractive than anyone else. That I'm beautiful. And I work on it. When I should be doing other things. When I could be . . . I don't know, doing something useful . . . helping others . . . instead, I concentrate on my body. I run, I work out with weights, I admire myself in mirrors, I pamper my body. Pride. It's too much pride. That's why I'm being punished.'

'Good,' Eagle said. 'Very good. Go on.'

'That's it. What do you . . .?'

'Explain the justice of your punishment.'

'Isn't that obvious?'

'Tell us.'

'I'm stuck here naked. Where everyone who comes along gets a chance to inspect this body I'm so proud of.'

'Very insightful,' Eagle said.

'And where everyone who comes along gets a chance to *damage* it.'

'Yes?'

'And where all my muscles aren't doing me any good at all, and all my beauty is working against me because every creep who comes down the pike only wants to *mess* with me instead of help. Except maybe for that one guy, Ben, and he pulled a disappearing act.'

'Yes?'

'Isn't that enough?'

While Eagle seemed to be thinking about a response, Crash asked, 'How come you got naked?'

'I don't take baths with my clothes on.'

'Oh. Me neither.'

'You don't *take* baths,' Weed told him.

He laughed, then said, 'Yeah, I do.'

'You don't *smell* like it.'

'How about sawing me out of here, now?' Sheila asked. 'I did what you wanted.'

'What'd you think of her confession, Crash?'

'I liked it. Yeah. I really liked the part where she says how she's so beautiful everybody wants to mess around with her. You know? 'Cause I think it's true. I mean, I know *I* wanta mess with her.'

Nodding, Weed said, 'It wasn't too bad a confession. I've heard worse. But I bet we could get some *good* stuff out of her if we kept at it.'

'I wanta get her out,' Crash said. 'You know?'

'We know,' Weed said.

'Can I?' he asked Eagle.

'Go on down and do it.'

Stanley waited while Crash climbed down, saw in hand, and scooted along the sides of the tub. When the big man bent over the beam, Stanley stood up and hurled a clump of stucco at him. The stucco was the size of a small brick.

He aimed at Crash's head.

And didn't wait for the results.

As he launched the stucco, he charged Weed and Eagle. They both turned their heads and looked surprised. The stucco hit the back of Crash's neck.

Weed, seated with her legs hanging over the edge, started trying to get up.

Stanley swung his board with both hands. It whapped her across the back, just below the shoulders, bashing her forward. She grunted. She flung her arms out. From the look of things, she would land on top of Crash, who'd fallen across the beam and onto Sheila. Stanley didn't have time to watch.

Even as he'd struck Weed, Eagle had leaped up and whirled to face him.

Grinning.

Slowly writhing, swaying, undulating.

Hissing.

Stanley lurched forward, going for Eagle's head with the backstroke of the swing that had knocked Weed from her perch. Eagle seemed to have all the time in the world. He swept downward, bending at the waist and knees. As the board passed above him, he stroked the top of his right boot. His rising hand showed Stanley what it had discovered there – a straight razor. The blade flashed blinding sunlight.

Stanley lurched backward as the razor slashed up. It slit air instead of his belly and chest.

Eagle's odd, white face looked puzzled as if he couldn't believe that he had missed.

Stanley brought the board down from overhead with both hands. It broke in half across the top of Eagle's head. His eyes bulged. For an instant, the dead white skin of his face seemed to jump loose. It was still shimmying when his knees struck the floor in front of Stanley. The straight razor fell. He wavered on his knees, his arms hanging limp by his sides, the pupils of his eyes almost out of sight as if he were inspecting the undersides of his upper lids.

Stanley glanced toward the tub. Weed was trying to climb off Crash.

Nobody there needed urgent attention.

Stanley tossed his broken board aside. As it landed with a

clatter in the rubble, he took the scissors from between his teeth. He slipped his thumb into the ring handle, his first two fingers into the bow handle, then opened the scissors until their twin points were about an inch apart and punched them into Eagle's eyes.

He drove them in deep.

He expected a scream, but there wasn't one.

Hope bird-boy ain't too stunned to appreciate this, Stanley thought.

The bridge of Eagle's nose forced the blades farther apart. Stanley kept pushing until the crotch of the scissors met the bridge. Then he shoved hard enough to tumble Eagle away. As the silent body flopped backward, Stanley jerked the scissors out.

One down, two to go.

He faced the tub.

Weed had her left knee in Crash's back, her right foot on the edge of the tub, her back to Stanley as she reached up about to grab the floor at the far side of the break. Crash, folded over the beam, was struggling to rise.

Stanley jumped down. He landed with both feet on Crash's back. He heard a grunt from the man, a moan that must've been Sheila. As he flapped his arms, trying to catch his balance, Weed vaulted upward. She seemed to rise in a quick blur of tank top and tan back. Stanley tried for her with the scissors. They stabbed at the faded seat of her jeans. But somehow they missed and suddenly his wrist was pounded upward by her escaping foot. He kept his hold on the scissors. About to fall over backward, he dropped to his knees.

He glimpsed a blur of vanishing boots.

No!

Can't let her get away!

But he couldn't give chase. Not yet.

The body under Stanley's knees started to rise. Teetering, he reached down fast with his left hand and grabbed a fistful of Crash's thick, greasy hair. He dragged at the hair as he fell. He landed on his side. Elbow digging into Crash's back, he reached out with his right hand and stabbed the scissors as hard as he could into the side of Crash's neck.

Crash shrieked. His body lurched rigid.

Stanley tugged out the scissors and stabbed Crash again and kept on stabbing him, over and over, going for the neck and mostly getting it but knowing from the feel that sometimes he was hitting jaw or teeth or cheek. Crash shrieked and grunted and bellowed while his body shuddered and bucked, and blood flew.

Stanley wanted to stop.

Wanted to leap from Crash's back and chase down Weed. But kept on stabbing Crash.

Die die die, you dirty hunk of lard! She's gonna get away!

At last, the blood stopped shooting and Crash stopped making noises and Stanley realized that the huge body was flinching underneath him only because he was punching it so hard with the scissors.

He was worn out, breathless, dripping. But there was no time to waste. Without pausing for even a moment of rest, Stanley pulled the scissors out of Crash, pushed himself up, and climbed onto the floor. He struggled to his feet.

He blinked, trying to clear his eyes of sweat – and maybe blood.

Then he gazed out over the ruins of Sheila's house, her patio and back yard. Weed had taken off in that direction, but there was no sign of her now.

Was she hiding nearby?

Had she made her way clear of the rubble and run away across the yard?

Had she circled around to the front?

'Weed!' Stanley yelled, trying to make his voice sound gruff. 'Weed, it's Crash! I got the guy! Nailed the sum-bitch! Where'd you go off to? Hey, Weed!'

She didn't answer.

She didn't show herself.

She'd have to be an idiot, he thought, to fall for a gimmick like that.

Probably too far away to hear it, anyway.

'Weed!' he called out, louder than before. 'Weed! It's Crash! Get back here, bitch!'

'Get him off me, Stan – please?' The soft, muffled voice came from behind him, came from Sheila.

He turned around. She was down there somewhere, underneath Crash and the beams and all that blood. But he saw nothing that he could recognize, for sure, as Sheila.

'Stan?' she said again.

'Shut up.'

'You've gotta get him off me. Please.'

'I don't gotta do shit. It's your fault these freaks came and found you in the first place, you and your big fucking mouth. Now I gotta go and find the one that got away.'

'No! Don't leave me here under him! Stan! You can't! He's dead.'

'You'd better just shut up,' Stanley said. 'Unless you wanta have more visitors and get them killed, too. I killed that Ben fella, by the way. Your pal, Ben? There wasn't any girl trapped under any chimney. That was just a story to get him where I wanted him. And then I sawed his head off. Thought you oughta know.'

He wiped the scissors on the side of his pajama shorts, turned around, and began his hunt for Weed.

Thirty

The sudden pounding on the bathroom door startled Barbara. She gasped, then asked, 'What?'

'You gonna take all day?' Earl complained. 'What the hell're you doing in there, taking a bath?'

'I've got the trots,' she said.

'Well, shit. Get a move on. We got stiffs out here. It ain't pretty.'

'Wait outside if you want,' she told him.

'Oh yeah, sure. So the neighbors can get a good look at us. Come on, would you? Let's get going.'

'I'll come out as soon as I can.'

'We oughta leave without you.'

'Feel free,' she said, knowing they wouldn't.

'This whole fuckin' mess is your fault.'

'I know, I know. Go away and quit bothering me, or I'm *never* coming out.'

'Leave her alone,' she heard Pete say. His voice was quiet, barely audible. 'I think she's pretty upset about all this.'

Damn right, she thought.

'Yeah, yeah, yeah,' Earl muttered. From the sound of his voice, he was still standing just outside the bathroom door. 'Wipe your butt and get outa there, Banner, or I'm coming in after you.'

'Don't talk to her that way, Earl.'

'I'll talk to her any way I want. What're you gonna do, shoot me?'

'Just be nice, okay?'

'Woos.'

'Quit it, you guys,' Barbara called. 'And no talk about shooting anyone. Calm down. I'll be out in a minute.'

'We don't have all day,' Earl said, then walked off.

I shouldn't have stayed so long, Barbara told herself. Should've just peed and gotten out.

But she'd peed, and stayed.

Maybe it was having her pants down.

Maybe it was the feel of the toilet paper.

Fuck the guy and we walk out with a gun . . .

Lee'd be balling you . . . instead of lying here with his brains on the floor . . .

About to get up from the toilet, she'd suddenly been pounded by the knowledge that Earl had been right: if she'd agreed to his deal and gone to bed with Lee, she would probably still be with him in the bedroom.

Nobody would've shot anyone.

Lee and Heather would still be alive.

What's your pussy worth?

Not their lives.

Nobody's life.

I should've said, 'Yeah, sure, why not, a gun'll come in handy and what does it matter anyway?' But I didn't, and now he's dead and Heather's dead and it's all my fault . . .

And then she'd come apart there on the toilet, shuddering and crying, making too much noise. To muffle her noises, she'd reached out and pulled a bath towel off the rod where it was hanging, and she'd buried her face in it.

The towel had been slightly damp.

Still damp, she'd guessed, from a shower or bath that Lee must've taken before the quake.

Back when he'd still been alive.

She'd imagined him rubbing his wet body with it – maybe humming or whistling a cheerful tune – and had cried all the harder.

By the time she'd been able to quit, her throat and lungs had felt tired and achy, and she'd had the familiar, tinny odor behind her face that comes from crying too hard or catching a fist in the nose.

She'd lifted her face, checked the wadded towel for blood, found none, and pushed her face into it again.

I've gotta get up, she'd told herself. Get up and get going. They're gonna think I fell in.

I'll say I've got the trots.

Cute, she thought. Real cute.

So, who cares?

What'll Pete think?

Who cares?

I do.

The hell with it. Just tell the truth – you fell apart. You got Lee and Heather killed because you wouldn't give up your stupid virginity, and so you fell apart.

Earl would love that.

Anyhow, I *didn't* get anyone killed. Not really. That's Earl's big idea, and it's a big damn lie. It was the quake and everything else that made us end up in Lee's apartment, and it was Earl with his stupid plan for getting the gun, and it was the bad luck of having a crazy, jealous lunatic like Heather with us, and it was Lee's own fault for leaving a loaded weapon in her reach.

Not my fault.

Too bad for Lee and Heather, but not my fault.

Just the way the ball bounces.

The way the cookie crumbles.

Any one of a thousand things might've gone differently, and they'd still be alive.

A couple of 'em had to do with me.

Yeah. True. And I'll live with it, but I'm not gonna let it ruin me.

I'll try not to.

Sitting up straight on the toilet seat, she'd wiped her face a final time with the towel, then taken a deep breath. And flinched, startled by the sudden pounding on the bathroom door.

'What?' she'd gasped.

'You gonna take all day?' Earl had demanded.

Barbara found Pete and Earl waiting in the kitchen. Pete, leaning back against the refrigerator, was holding a can of Pepsi. Lee's forty-five made a big bulge in the right front pocket of his pants, and most of its handle stuck out the top of the pocket. Earl had a beer. The rifle was hanging by its leather strap behind his right shoulder.

'Everything come out okay?' Earl asked.

'Very funny.'

'Are you all right?' Pete asked her.

She saw concern in his eyes. 'I'm okay,' she said. 'It's just, you know . . . what happened.'

'The poop hit the fan,' Earl said.

She turned on him, glaring. 'There are two dead people in

the living room, you creep! And *you* killed one of 'em. You think there's something *funny* going on?'

He smirked. 'Give it a break, Banner. I saved your life. The crazy bitch was gonna pop you next.'

'Thanks to you.'

'Let's quit arguing,' Pete said. 'We oughta get going, now.' He asked Barbara, 'Do you want a can of something to take with you?'

'No. Thanks. I'm not taking something that doesn't belong to me.'

'Lee would've let you have whatever you asked for,' Pete told her.

'I guess.'

''Sides which,' Earl said, 'he's dead.'

'I'm not thirsty. Let's just get out of here.'

Earl tipped his head far back to finish off the beer, then stepped across the kitchen and smacked his empty can down on the counter next to a stack of brown paper bags. 'We're wearing these,' he said to Barbara, and picked them up.

He handed one to her, another to Pete, then pulled the last bag over his head. He adjusted it until the side-by-side holes were in front of his eyes.

'We made these while you were in the john,' Pete explained.

'Masks?'

'People might see us leaving.'

'They had plenty of time to see us when we were down at the pool.'

'Not me,' Earl said.

'You think nobody spotted you when you were down there yelling for us?'

'Who knows? But that was before all the shooting. Everyone in the whole joint must've heard that. We're lucky nobody came over. Probably scared to. But you can bet some idiot'll be looking out a window to see who comes outa here.'

Pete nodded. 'I think it's a good idea. Why take chances? Anyway, we can take them off as soon as we get away from the building.'

'You and I didn't do anything wrong,' Barbara said. 'We don't need to hide our faces.'

'Shit on you, Banner!'

'Cut it out!' Pete snapped.

'I go down, you go down.' Earl's breath shook and wobbled the bag. 'Both of you.'

Pete put his bag on, and looked at Barbara through its eye holes. 'It'll be better if you just wear it,' he said.

'Okay. Fine. It's not worth fighting over.' She shook open her bag and slipped it on. It was only slightly larger than her head, and the sides of it rubbed loudly against the rims of her ears. It had a slight musty odor like damp cardboard. Twisting the bag, she found the eye holes. One was lower than the other.

'Is it okay?' Pete asked. 'We had to guess where to put the holes in yours.'

'They're all right.'

'You can see out?'

'Sort of. I'll hang on to you.'

Earl led the way. Pete followed, Barbara behind him with her right hand on his shoulder. She couldn't see much except his back.

Which was fine. There was nothing in the kitchen that she needed to see.

In the living room, she was very glad to have the bag over her head. Some of the bad odors reached her nose, but she didn't catch so much as a glimpse of the dead bodies.

She could see them without her eyes – Lee sprawled on the floor, Heather slumped on the sofa – but she watched Pete's back, glad that the tiny eye holes allowed her no fresh view of them.

She heard the door open. A moment later, Pete moved forward beneath her hand and she followed him onto the balcony. The afternoon was so bright that she had to squint. She thought that she could feel the heaviness of the sun's rays pressing down on top of the bag and on her shoulders.

They walked to the left.

'So far so good,' Earl said.

The air inside Barbara's bag grew warmer and began to smell vaguely of smoke. The paper felt hot where it touched her ears and face. Her blouse seemed hot enough to burst into flames.

Don't be ridiculous, she told herself. The sun can't set clothes on fire.

The bag'll go first, she thought.

And pictured it suddenly combusting, saw herself stumbling along the balcony with her head ablaze.

Can't happen, can it?

If it does, I'll jump in the pool,

I might wanta do that anyway, she thought.

'We're coming to the stairs,' Earl said.

'Is anybody watching us?' Barbara asked.

'Don't think so,' Earl said.

'It'll be okay,' Pete said, 'as long as they don't try to stop us.'

'Here we go,' said Earl. 'Watch your steps, boys and girls.'

Afraid of stumbling and knocking Pete down the stairs, she let go of his shoulder and found the railing. The painted steel scorched her hand. She released it fast, then glided her hand along the top of the railing as she descended, barely touching it but ready to grab hold if she should start to fall.

Turning her head, she could see the pool below and to the right.

'I'm going in,' she said, speaking softly. 'How about you?'

'In the pool?' Pete asked.

'Yeah. Feel like I'm gonna go up in flames if I don't.'

'I don't know,' Pete said. 'I've got this gun.'

'A little water won't hurt it.'

'Nobody's going in no pool,' Earl said.

'Right,' Barbara said. 'Whatever you say.' The railing ended. As she stepped off the bottom stair, she plucked the bag off her head. Without it, the hot afternoon air felt almost cool against her face. Earl, a few strides beyond Pete, was walking toward the rear gate of the courtyard.

On her way to the pool, Barbara pressed the bag against her belly to flatten it so it wouldn't blow away. Then she folded it in half and dropped it.

At the edge of the pool, she tugged off her shoes. She let them fall. They clumped against the concrete.

'Banner!' Earl yelled.

She dived.

The water was wonderfully, shockingly cold – icy silk sliding over her body as she glided through. She wished she didn't have clothes on. They slowed her down, dragged at her, bound her, came between her skin and the water's caress.

Some other time, maybe.

Sneak back here some night, she thought. Me and Pete, slipping into the water naked, long after midnight . . .

I wouldn't dare.

Oh, yeah?

Maybe I would, maybe I wouldn't.

Opening her eyes, she saw the blue tile wall just ahead. She surfaced, snatched a quick breath, flipped, rammed her feet against the wall, shoved off, and submerged.

Earl's gotta be royally pissed, she thought.

Tough toenails. He shouldn't be so bossy.

Why'd I do it?

I had to, that's why. The hell with him.

Yeah, right, we're trying to get away from a double-killing, and I decide it's a nice time for a dip. What's wrong with me?

I was cooking, that's all.

And he has no right to control my life.

And what're we talking about, anyway – two minutes? Big deal.

Angling upward, she swept her arms back and did one more scissor-kick. Her head broke the surface. She reached up and slapped her hands on the concrete edge of the pool.

'Now!' Earl's voice, loud and rough. 'Right now, bitch!'

Barbara thrust herself up.

Earl had the rifle to his shoulder, had it aimed.

But not at Barbara.

Braced up on stiff arms, she snapped her head sideways and saw a woman standing in the open doorway of a ground level apartment. One of Lee's tenants? A gaudy redhead, probably fifty years old, built like Marilyn Monroe, wearing a shiny black kimono that was sashed shut and only reached halfway down her thighs.

'Where's Lee?' the woman demanded. 'That's all I want to know. What did you do to him?'

'Nothing! Get back inside and shut your door.'

'We'll see about that!' She strutted toward Earl, angry and apparently fearless. 'What'd you do to him? I heard those shots.'

What took you so long? Barbara wondered. Had to wait and see who came out?

And *we* look like people you wanta mess with?

The woman's bare feet made slapping sounds on the concrete. She swaggered and bounced so much that her sash loosened. The front of her kimono was flung apart by her leaping breasts, but she didn't seem to care.

Is she totally nuts? Barbara wondered. What does she want to do, take Earl's gun away? Slap his face? Throw him down and make a citizen's arrest?

She's gonna get killed!

'Go back!' Earl shouted.

'Not on your life, buster!'

'Don't shoot her!' Barbara yelled.

'Earl!' Pete yelled.

The rifle still at his shoulder, Earl used his firing hand to snatch the paper bag off his head. He let the bag go. As it slowly fell, he returned his hand to the rifle.

'I'm warning you, lady!'

'Don't!' Barbara shouted. Out of the pool and on her knees, she scurried toward Earl, waving an arm at him, yelling, 'Don't shoot! Damn it, don't! Don't do it!'

Earl looked ready.

The woman kept on coming, almost to the corner of the pool, no more than thirty feet from the muzzle of Earl's rifle, marching, swaggering, the black kimono open completely now, hanging from her shoulders, fluttering behind her like a cape.

Caped crusader.

My what big boobs you have – look at 'em go!

Is everybody nuts today?

Barbara hurled herself, shoulder first, against the woman's hip. Even as the collision jolted her, she glimpsed Pete thrusting the forty-five against Earl's temple. She heard Pete say, 'You shoot, I shoot.'

The woman went down sideways, letting out a whimper as she fell.

Barbara landed on her.

The woman went, 'Umph!'

'Watch out with that thing!' Earl yelled.

'I'll blow your head off!'

'Hey! Hey! Take it easy.'

Instead of lying still, the woman rolled onto her back. Barbara had no time to climb off or struggle. The body flopped, and her face went down in a pad of soft hair. With a gasp, she lifted her head. The woman was pushing at the concrete and starting to sit up.

'Stay down!' Barbara gasped.

The woman thrashed her legs. Her knee pounded Barbara under the armpit.

'Nail her, Banner!'

She glimpsed Earl and Pete standing side by side, their eyes fixed on the action. Pete's mask was gone. Both the weapons were lowered.

Thank God, she thought.

'Offa me!' the woman gasped, and kneed her again.

'Nail her! What're you waiting for?'

'You can take her,' Pete added.

She didn't know whether to feel proud or betrayed. But she suddenly knew that she wouldn't let this woman get the better of her.

The knee caught her in the breast. This time, it hurt.

Damn it, all I did was try to save you!

She drove her forehead down. The woman's belly was soft. Barbara's brow and face sank in, and she heard a huff of breath blow out of the woman. Pushing at the hot concrete, she raised her head.

The woman's eyes were bulging, her mouth wide. She was

fighting to suck in a breath. As Barbara watched, her straight arms folded at the elbows. She sank down slowly, then lay flat, gaping at the sky and wheezing.

'Give her another one!' Earl urged her.

Barbara shook her head. She climbed off the woman and stepped clear. She was breathless, dripping. Bending over, she clutched her knees. She knew that her blouse hung open, but she didn't much care.

They've got her to stare at, she thought.

The woman was sprawled there, arms and legs flung out, everything showing. And the guys were both gazing at her.

Maybe this is what she was after, Barbara thought. Who knows? Why the hell did she come out like that? Could've at least gotten dressed.

Earl approached the woman.

Barbara stood up straight and said, 'Leave her alone.'

'She ain't a natural redhead, is she?'

'Do you always have to be such a pig?'

Grinning at Barbara, Earl let out a couple of snorts. Then he cradled his rifle, stepped between the woman's legs, squatted down and ducked his head for a closer look.

'Cut it out,' Pete said.

'Looks like somebody already did.'

'Bastard,' Barbara muttered. Wiping her face with the front of her shirt, she stepped around the woman's head and hurried toward Pete. 'Let's get out of here.'

He nodded. 'Come on, Earl.'

'We ain't finished yet.'

Barbara whirled around. 'We're finished! Come on!'

'She saw our faces. And she knows your name, Banner.'

'So what do you want to do, shoot her?'

'We don't want her telling tales, do we?'

'You idiot. Do you think she's the only one? Lee said there're tenants in four apartments. *Four*. This gal only accounts for one. What do you wanta do, go through the whole building and shoot everyone?'

'It's a thought,' Earl said.

Reaching down by Pete's side, she took hold of the forty-five. He made no attempt to keep hold of it. She pulled it from his hand, raised it, and aimed it at Earl's head.

He looked disgusted with her. 'Gimme a break, Banner.'

'Set the rifle down and stand up.'

'Yeah, sure.'

'Do it!'

'Like you're gonna put a bullet in me. I'm sure.'

'I've had enough. Put the rifle down and stand up.'

'Fuck you.'

She fired. The pistol boomed, leaped in her hand. She'd aimed for a near miss. From Earl's reaction, he must've felt the slug's wind in his hair. He flinched so hard that the rifle hopped out of the crooks of his elbows. He bobbled it for a second or two. It started to fall, stock first, between his arms. With his left hand, he caught the sling. He sprang up and turned toward Barbara, the rifle dangling by the strap, a sick look on his face.

'Fine,' she said.

'You stupid fucking bitch!'

'Don't try anything with the rifle, or the next round goes in your chest.'

'Fuck you.'

'Yeah, right. Pete, go up and take the rifle from him.'

'Just try it,' Earl said.

'Just do it,' Barbara said, trying to soften the tone of her voice for him. 'If Earl goes for you, I'll put him down.'

Pete started walking toward Earl.

The woman on her back, head turned, stared at Barbara. She was breathing hard, but looked as if she'd mostly recovered from the blow that had knocked her air out. She also looked terrified.

'It's all right, lady,' Barbara told her. 'Nobody's gonna hurt you.'

The woman didn't seem reassured.

She has every reason to be scared, Barbara realized. I'm the one who flattened her and pounded her. I just fired in her direction. And here I am, all set to empty my pistol at the jerk standing between her knees.

As Pete walked closer, the woman started to shove at the concrete with her elbows and heels, started to squirm and scoot her way out of the line of fire. Her breasts were lurching around as if they had minds of their own.

Barbara hoped Pete wasn't watching them – or trying to get a good look between her legs.

She almost warned him to keep his eyes on Earl. Then she realized that she was the one who had better pay attention to Earl and stop worrying about the woman or what Pete might be looking at.

She concentrated on Earl's left arm, on the hand gripping the leather strap, on the rifle swaying by his side.

She held the pistol the way her father had taught her to hold his revolver: right arm bent slightly, left hand supporting her right like a platform, legs apart, knees bent.

The weapon shook quite a lot because she was trembling badly, but for the most part she was able to keep the sights on the center of Earl's chest.

Pete approached him from the right.

Good.

He would be able to take the rifle without getting in the way of a clear shot.

Almost within reach of Earl's weapon, he stopped and looked over his shoulder at Barbara.

Waiting for the go-ahead?

The woman was clear, but making no attempt to get up. She lay flat on her back, gasping for air, gazing at Barbara.

'Earl!' Barbara snapped.

Earl flinched.

'Pretend you're a statue.'

The corners of his mouth twitched. He didn't say anything.

'Get it, Pete.'

Pete hurried forward and grabbed the barrel and pulled. Earl let go of the strap. The rifle swung like a pendulum, and Pete trotted backward with it.

'Earl,' Barbara said, 'put both hands on top of your head and intertwine your fingers.'

'You're really asking for it, Banner.'

'Do it now.'

He did it.

'Lady, we're leaving here now and we're taking him with us. You can go back into your apartment. Everything'll be fine. Only next time, don't stick your nose in. You came damn close to getting yourself killed.'

The woman didn't try to get up.

'Should we tell her about Lee?' Pete asked.

Barbara nodded. 'Lee's dead, lady.' The woman showed no reaction to the news, just lay there gasping for air and gazing at Barbara. 'I'm sorry about that. He seemed like a nice guy. We didn't kill him, though. Heather shot him.'

'Heather?' The woman narrowed her eyes. 'The girl that threw the cat in the water?'

She watched everything,

'Yeah, her. She went nuts and shot Lee. Then we had to shoot her in self-defense. They're both up there in his apartment.'

'She shouldn't have done that to a cat,' the woman said.

Barbara frowned. 'Shouldn't have done that to *Lee.*'

'He was no great shakes, anyhow.'

'What's the matter with you, lady?'

'Nothing. None of your business. Why don't you just go away and leave me alone?'

'The National Guard's supposed to show up tomorrow,' Pete told her. 'You oughta stay inside and not get mixed up in anything till then.'

'Let's go, Earl,' Barbara said, 'This way. We'll take the alley.'

Thirty-one

They'd gotten past the other slide without any trouble at all – simply climbed over the loose mound of dirt and rocks near the right side of the road, where it was only a few feet high, then continued on their way down Laurel Canyon Boulevard.

This slide, scattered with fallen trees, boulders and parts of a house or two, covered the entire road to a height of at least sixty feet.

'Now what?' Mary asked, gazing up at it.

Em hurried back from the right side of the road. 'There's like a gigantic ravine over there,' she said.

Caspar grinned at her. 'First step's a big one, is it?'

'First step's a fatal one, if you get my drift.'

'I guess we'll have to climb straight over the top,' Clint said. He was glad they had nothing left to carry; after using the last of the food and water, they'd gotten rid of everything except the knives. 'It won't be so bad,' he said. 'We'll take it slow.'

Loreen put a hand on Caspar's arm. 'I see trouble, Papa.'

Ah, Clint thought. So, he *is* her father. Thought so.

'Trouble of what sort?' Caspar asked her.

'Hey!' Mary blurted. 'No predictions. That was the rule. We don't want any of that gypsy shit around here.'

'Take it easy,' Clint warned her.

'Sure, take *their* side. You're the one who made the rule – no predictions. What're you gonna do now, just let her say any damn thing that . . .'

'The walking dead woman has a lively mouth,' Loreen said.

'See! See! Did you hear that!'

'We don't want that kind of talk, Loreen,' Clint said. 'Please.'

'She is so skinny and aggravating,' Loreen said.

Caspar chuckled softly.

Mary opened her mouth, then shut it and glared at him. Her lips formed a tight, hard line. Clint supposed she must be thinking about Caspar's threat to cut out her tongue.

'Let's everyone try to be considerate,' Clint said. 'Okay? Fighting among ourselves doesn't solve anything.'

'I need to warn Caspar . . .'

'There she goes again!' Mary blurted.

Clint turned on Mary. 'Would you shut up for half a minute!'

Her eyes widened and her jaw sagged.

'Let the woman finish her sentence!'

'Thank you,' Loreen told him, then squeezed Caspar's arm. 'Papa, you don't want to climb this. You're not young. You're not strong.'

His eyes flashed. He jerked his arm from her grip. 'I'm not young?' he bellowed. 'Not strong? Piss on you!'

She greeted his sudden anger with calm. 'It's a very large hill to be climbing,' she said.

'For you, maybe!'

'I'm not an old man,' she said.

'*I'm* not a fat *cow*!'

Her calm collapsed. 'You're calling me a fat cow?'

'You are what you are.'

'Hey!' Clint said. 'Let's stop . . .'

Loreen's hand swung out and slapped Caspar hard across his face. 'You don't call *me* a cow.'

'Cow!' Caspar slapped her.

She slapped him again.

Mary, grinning, began to clap. Clint clutched one of her hands. She quit clapping, quit grinning. She looked at Clint and didn't try to take her hand away from him.

Caspar again smacked Loreen across the face.

Em whistled.

No purse-lipped, mild whistle of amazement or appreciation. Certainly not a tune.

She had her thumb and forefinger jammed in her mouth for this high and ear-blinding shriek.

Clint flinched and gritted his teeth.

'Jesus!' Mary cried out, covering her ears.

Caspar and Loreen seemed to forget all about their slapping contest. Looking shocked, they gaped at Em.

Then came silence like the inside of a vault.

Em, smiling slightly, rubbed her spitty thumb and finger on the front of her T-shirt. 'One of my mom's girlfriends showed me how to do that,' she said. She seemed very pleased with herself. 'It sure hurts the ears, doesn't it? Anyhow, I don't want to make a nuisance out of myself, but I really can't stand this rowdy behavior. I think we should all keep our hands to ourselves, especially when it comes to the slapping department. Does that suit everyone?'

'Loreen struck me first,' Caspar explained. 'I give what I get.'

'You called her a cow,' Em reminded him.

'She insulted me, I insulted her.'

'She was only trying to keep you from climbing the hill and dropping dead from a heart attack. That's because she loves you. You called her a cow because she's worried you'll kill yourself.'

His chest seemed to swell. 'I do what needs to be done.'

'Jeez, and I thought you were a nice guy. It was cool how you stood up for Loreen when Mary called her a bitch . . . but now you end up treating her worse than Mary did. I think probably you must suffer from what my mom calls "a case of macho bullshit."'

'Stupid child,' Caspar said.

'Oh, that's nice,' Em said, looking rather amused. 'I thought I was supposed to be a charming scamp.'

'Let's stop all this right now,' Clint said. 'Em, quit trying to push him, okay? Caspar, be careful who you call names. You want to treat your daughter like crap, that's your business. Em and Mary are *my* business, so you'll treat them decently.'

'The cow is no daughter of mine,' Caspar said.

'Whatever.'

'Granddaughter,' Mary suggested.

Caspar, growling, lunged at her. With a yelp, she staggered away. Clint shouted, 'Hold it!' He hurled himself in front of

712

Caspar, but was shoved aside. As he stumbled, Mary scurried backward up the steep slope of dirt, Caspar rushing for her.

'Caspar!' Loreen yelled.

One foot planted in the dirt, he leaned toward the slope, reached high, and grabbed Mary's left ankle. Then Em crashed against his side, throwing him over sideways. For a moment, he kept his grip on Mary's ankle. Her leg was jerked out from under her. She sat down hard, then skidded downhill on her rump, skirt climbing her thighs.

Caspar struck the slope with his shoulder and flopped onto his back. As he started to sit up, Clint stepped on his chest. 'Stay put,' Clint said. 'I don't wanta hurt you.'

'Keep him away from me!' Mary cried out. She was on her feet again, now at the bottom of the slide, rubbing her buttocks with both hands.

Em sat in the dirt, her knees up, frowning as she glanced from Mary to Clint and Caspar.

'I don't want any more trouble!' Clint snapped. He kept his foot on Caspar's chest. 'From either one of you! I've had it with you, Caspar. You pushed it one too many times. Mary, you've been nothing but a pain in the ass from the get-go!'

'Fuck you.'

Em frowned up at her. 'Cut it out, would you?'

'Fuck you too, you little twat.'

'Hey!' Clint yelled.

'Fuck all of you!' Mary whirled around. She threw herself at the slope and scurried upward, gasping. The filthy tail of her blouse draped the seat of her skirt. The skirt swished across the backs of her thighs. Her shoes sent down tiny avalanches.

Em stood up, turned around, and watched Mary climb. After a few seconds, she glanced at Clint. 'She's not a very happy camper, is she?'

'She'll probably be back.' He looked down at Caspar. 'Don't even think about going after her. Just stay down till I tell you otherwise.'

'Behave yourself, Caspar,' Loreen said, approaching. 'If

you try to sit up, the *cow* will sit on you. That is no prediction, but a promise.'

Clint lifted his foot off the man's chest, and stepped away.

Caspar stayed on his back. He was gasping for breath, but he managed a smile for Loreen. 'I've misbehaved, haven't I?' he asked.

'You've behaved atrociously. These people are our friends – with the exception of Mary. As for Mary, she is to be pitied. Her end will be very bad, very bad.'

'Do you have to say that?' Em asked, wrinkling her nose.

'I only say what I see.'

'Just because you see it, you don't have to say it. For one thing, it gives *me* the creeps. And I don't think you really improved Mary's disposition with all that kind of talk. I've gotta admit she isn't any prize, but that's no reason to tell her horrible things are supposed to happen to her, you know?'

'She gets what she deserves,' Loreen said.

Clint looked over his shoulder and found that Mary was more than halfway to the top. She had apparently stopped for a rest. She was bent over slightly, holding herself steady with one hand on a section of brick chimney that protruded from the soil just to her right.

Could almost feel sorry for her.

But she's done all this to herself, he thought. Nobody's been holding a gun to her head and forcing her to act so obnoxious all the time. All she had to do was act decent. What's so hard about that?

'Does she get killed because she isn't with us?' Em asked.

'That's entirely possible,' Loreen said.

'May I get up, now?' Caspar asked.

'Yeah,' Clint told him. 'But behave.'

'He will behave,' Loreen said.

Caspar struggled to sit up.

'Maybe we should tell Mary to wait for us,' Em suggested.

'We're better off without her,' Clint said. 'Anyway, it's her choice. This isn't like before. We didn't force her to go running off like this.'

'But we can't just let her get killed.'

'You don't believe that stuff, do you?'

'I don't know.'

'She is right to believe,' Loreen said.

'Don't give me that,' Clint said, turning to face her. 'You two are just a couple of con artists, and you know it. You make a business out of tricking suckers. So don't fall for it, Em. Loreen doesn't know any more about what's in the future than you and I do.'

'The fellow doth protest too much,' Caspar said. On his feet at last, he brushed off the seat of his jeans and nodded at Clint. 'You believe. Oh, yes, you do indeed. And you're frightened by what she . . .'

Mary cried out, 'Eeeeeeee!'

Clint ripped his gaze away from Caspar and swung around in time to see Mary, arms flapping, stagger backward as if to get away from the horrible *thing* crawling above her on the crest of the hill.

He thought, Shit! It's happening already!

Should've stopped her.

It's my fault.

What the hell is that?

A person? Not a person!

He only glimpsed it before his gaze seemed to sheer away from the ragged, crimson creature and find Mary as she lost her footing and toppled backward. Grabbing at the air with her hands, she teetered and fell.

Clint thought of ski jumpers.

How their skis seemed to fly for a long while just above the snowy slope before touching down.

Mary glided downward, head-first and face up, her body stiff and straight except for her waving arms – plunging but not quite touching the ground.

Someone was squeezing his arm.

Em?

Em, by his side, was yelling, 'Marrrry!'

Then Mary touched down, but not with the smooth landing of a ski jumper. Her back slammed the tilted earth – off a bit to the side of the chimney where she'd been resting not so long ago – and her legs bounced up. The impact flung them high. Clint saw a shoe fly off and sail away. Then both her legs were pointed at the sky like a V – tall and slender bare legs, a patch of bright pink fabric where they joined at the bottom. They came forward and down as Mary folded at the waist. Her pink panties turned out to be a thong. Her naked buttocks quivered when her knees pounded the slope.

For a moment, she looked as if she might be kowtowing in homage to the beast at the top of the landslide. Then she raised her head and shoulders. She was upright on her knees, then tumbling backward again. She hit the slope quicker than before. Her legs swung toward the sky. This time, the V looked a little crooked.

Clint jerked his arm free from Em's grip and charged up the face of the landslide, arms pumping, shoes chunking into the loose soil, eyes on Mary.

Her body had turned. Instead of pitching down the slope heels over head, she was now rolling, flipping over and over. Her limp arms and legs were tossed about in a way that made Clint sure she had no control over them. She was unconscious. Or dead.

And tumbling fast down the hill straight at him.

Just as they were about to collide, he braced himself, twisted his body and rammed his right shoulder forward. It caught Mary in the hip. Her weight slammed into him. He grunted. His feet scooted a few inches, then held. But Mary had already flipped over, flinging herself onto his back and knocking his forehead into the dirt.

He shot his left elbow up. It struck her and almost stopped her, but she began to slip. He realized there was no way to stop her from falling off his back.

So he lowered his elbow.

She rolled off him, striking the slope with one shoulder. As she tumbled onto her back, Clint reached down and grabbed her upper arm.

And stopped her.

He knew he wouldn't be able to hold her for long; his own position was too precarious.

But Em was on the way up.

In a moment, Em was kneeling just below Mary. She leaned forward and pushed against the woman's shoulder and hip.

'Got her?' Clint gasped.

'Yeah.'

He let go, then started to get up. As he raised his head, he tried to spot the thing that had startled Mary into falling.

It was nowhere in sight.

He scurried across the slope until he was clear of Mary's feet, then crawled backward past her sprawled body and made his way over to Em. On his knees beside the girl, he pressed his hands against Mary's hip and thigh.

'What now?' Em asked.

'Depends,' Clint muttered.

'She isn't dead, in case you were wondering. Just *really* messed up.'

She lay sprawled on her back, tilted as if all set to roll down on them the moment they let go. She had lost both her shoes. Her skirt was twisted around the tops of her legs. Her filthy, torn blouse was spread open. The left shoulder strap of her bra had broken. A few inches of the strap, along with the flimsy silken pouch, hung beneath her breast. The breast had a few minor scratches. It had fared better than most of Mary.

From her face down her torso, from her thighs down to her bare feet, she was smudged with dirt, blotchy with ruddy contusions, puffy with welts, scuffed raw with abrasions, striped by bright scratches, bleeding here and there from deeper wounds.

But Clint could see the slow rise and fall of her chest and the throb of a pulse at the side of her neck.

'Mary?' he asked.

She didn't react.

He called her name again, louder this time.

Nothing.

With both hands, Em gently shook her. Mary's body wobbled a little bit, but she didn't wake up.

'What'll we do?' Em asked.

'We can't leave her here,' Clint said. 'I guess that means I'll have to carry her.'

'Too bad we can't just call 911.'

'You're telling me.'

'How is she?' Caspar called from below.

'Out cold,' Clint answered, not looking back. 'We're going on to the top.'

'We're coming, too,' Caspar called. 'Do you need a hand with her?'

'No thanks.'

'I'm sorry she fell.'

Yeah, right, Clint thought. But he didn't answer.

'You go on,' Loreen called. 'Take care.'

Em turned her head toward him. 'What *was* that up there?'

'I don't know.'

'Did you see it?'

'I just caught a glimpse. I couldn't tell what it was. I thought it might be a dog – maybe a mastiff, but . . .'

'It didn't have a snout like a dog or anything,' Em said. 'Maybe some kind of a monkey or . . . I don't know . . . I think it might've been a guy, but it looked so bloody and weird.'

'Guess we'll find out,' Clint said.

'Whatever it was, I sure hope it's gone by the time we get up there.'

'I just hope I *can* get up there.'

'I'll help.'

'Why don't you start by fixing her blouse. I'll hold her.'

With Clint bracing Mary to keep her from rolling, Em leaned forward. She plucked up the blouse where it hung off Mary's far shoulder and lifted it and pulled it toward her until she could reach it with her other hand. Then she held the entire side of the blouse at an angle, taut like the slanting wall of a lean-to.

'Last look at her chooch?' Em asked.

'Her what?'

'Her chooch. You know, her boob.'

'Just go on,' Clint said. 'Twerp.'

'I'm a scamp, not a twerp.' She lowered the side of Mary's blouse and let go.

It settled smoothly on the mound of her breast. The dark of her nipple showed through. Moments later, spots and streaks of blood began to appear here and there on the soiled white fabric.

Em reached down in front of herself for the right side of the blouse. She had to tug it out from under her knees before sweeping it forward over Mary.

'Want me to fasten the buttons?' Em asked.

'Yes.'

'You sure?'

'Quit clowning, okay? I'm not interested in her chooches or anything else.'

'You're not?' Em asked as she started to work on the buttons. 'Really?'

Not much, anyhow.

'I'm married,' he said.

'So?'

'Just wait'll you see my wife. It'll be pretty obvious why I can't get all that worked up about Mary. They aren't even in the same league.'

'You talking nautical?'

'Baseball.'

Em smiled. 'I knew that.' She finished with the buttons. 'All set.'

The blouse clung to the wetness of the sweat and blood on Mary's skin.

'Okay,' Clint said. 'Now, let's see if I can pick her up.'

'Want me to take her legs, or something?'

'I guess what you'd better do is stand clear. Just be ready to grab her, maybe . . . in case I drop her.'

Em crawled aside, then moved slightly downslope and got to her feet.

'What're they doing?' Clint asked.

'Just watching,' she said. Then she called, 'Stay down there till we're out of the way, all right?'

'Fine,' Caspar called. 'Don't worry about us.'

Clint stared at Mary.

He didn't like the idea of carrying her to the top of the hill cradled in his arms – all her weight would be in front of him – and it'd be hard to climb fast without nailing her in the back with his knees.

Just sling her over your shoulder, he told himself.

Just?

'Here goes,' he said. He moved sideways a bit, shoved his knee against her hip to keep her from slipping, then reached up with both hands and grabbed her shoulders. He jerked her to a sitting position. As she started slumping forward, he caught her by the sides, just under her armpits.

Lifted her.

Pulled her.

Turned her.

Muscled her up and onto his left shoulder and clamped his left arm across her rump and dug his shoes into the dirt and hurled himself at the slope.

'Yes!' Em yelled.

Go go go go go, his mind shouted as he dashed for the top.

Go go go. Don't stop for anything. Go go go.

Get it done, get it done, get it done!

Go go go!

Get to the top and you can put her down.

We'll roll her down the other side.

The other side of the landslide.

I'm a poet.

My feet show it.

Longfellows?

Go go go!

I think I can, I think I can.

Heart attack, heart attack!

Ha!

Shit!

Go go go!

Don't stop, don't stop!

Almost there!

Go go go go go!

And grunting, dragging air into his hurting lungs as his heart slammed, he gained the crest of the hill.

The thing was sprawled in front of him.

Before he could halt himself, his foot hooked under its shoulder.

He plunged forward.

They almost landed on the body.

They landed just beyond it, instead. Mary's rump hit the ground first, taking the brunt of the impact. Then she flopped forward off Clint's shoulder.

He lay on top of her, too spent to move.

Em had arrived at the top and finished vomiting by the time Clint was able to push himself up. He crawled backward off Mary's unconscious body. On his knees, he looked down at the thing that had tripped him.

'It's a man, isn't it?' Em asked. She sounded very calm. She was standing up straight, but facing away from Clint and the body.

'I'm not sure.' The hips and rump didn't seem to flare out. He supposed this was probably a man, not a woman. But there was no way to be sure without turning it over. 'I guess so.'

'How did he get that way?' Em asked.

'I don't know.'

'Earthquakes . . . they don't scalp people.'

'No,' Clint said. 'They don't.'

'Or skin them alive.'

'No. Earthquakes don't . . . skin people, either.'

'Did humans do that to him?'

'Somebody did.'

'He came up over here. I can see where he . . . he must've crawled up all the way from the road. How could you do that, if you'd been . . . wrecked like that?'

'I don't know,' Clint said. 'Willpower, I guess.'

Em's head swiveled slowly from side to side. She seemed to be scanning the area below the landslide – the remains of Laurel Canyon winding down toward Sunset Boulevard.

'Some awfully bad stuff must be going on down there,' she said.

Clint struggled to his feet.

Em looked over her shoulder as he approached her.

He stopped beside her. He reached across her back and gently squeezed her shoulder. 'I don't have any choice about going on, Emerald. I've got to get home to my wife and daughter.'

'I know.'

'You scared?'

'I guess so.' He felt her shrug. 'I'm sure not eager to end up like that guy, if you know what I mean.'

'We'll take care of each other, okay?'

'Okay.'

Letting go of her shoulder, Clint stroked the back of her head. Her short hair was dripping wet. 'Yuck,' he said, and wiped his hand on her T-shirt.

Em turned, put her arms around him and pressed her face against his chest.

He wrapped his arms around her.

They were still embracing when Mary called out in a shaky voice, 'Clint?'

He turned slowly, Em in his arms, and saw Mary raise her head off the ground. 'Just lie there and relax,' he called to her. 'You took a bad fall.'

Lowering her head, she shut her eyes and started to cry.

Em squeezed herself harder against Clint. 'Stay with me,' she murmured.

'I will.'

'I'm not . . . too good at being scared.'

'You're doing fine.'

'Stuff doesn't usually get me, you know?'

'This sort of stuff would get anyone.'

After a while, she said, 'Maybe we'd better go and see Mary.'

'There's no hurry,' Clint said.

'Maybe we can stop her so she doesn't see the guy.'

'I guess that'd be a good idea.'

'I'm ever the thoughtful type,' Em said.

That brought a smile to Clint. He eased away from her, gave her shoulders a gentle squeeze, then let go.

As they walked side by side toward the place on the ground where Mary lay quietly sobbing, Caspar and Loreen trudged into sight.

Thirty-two

Earl walked up the alley with his hands folded on top of his head while Barbara and Pete followed, side by side, about ten paces behind him. They held their weapons pointed in his general direction, but kept their fingers off the triggers.

Earl had been cooperating nicely and without complaint since leaving the apartment complex. But now he stopped and turned around. 'Come on, Banner, my arms are killing me.'

'Tough.'

'Just let me put 'em down, okay? I'm not gonna try nothing. What do you think I wanta do, run back and strangle the old bat? I probably couldn't even *find* that place again.'

Barbara looked at Pete. He shrugged. 'Okay, Earl,' she said. 'You can put your arms down. But stick your hands in your pockets.'

'In my *pockets*?'

'You heard me.'

'It's hotter 'n' a mother-dog, 'n' you're telling me I gotta stick my hands in my pockets? No way!'

'Then keep them on top of your head.'

'Shit!' He spun around and resumed walking. A moment later, he called, 'Okay if I just stick 'em up?' Not waiting for an answer, he raised both his arms straight overhead. 'Don't know what you're so afraid of, anyhow.'

723

'You with a gun,' Barbara said.

'Yeah, right. I saved your ass, Banner. Don't you forget that.'

'We don't think you're very particular about who you shoot,' Pete explained. 'Not to mention, you threatened Barbara.'

'Did not.'

'"You're really asking for it"? Sounds like a threat, to me.'

'I was pissed. Didn't mean nothing by it. What're you gonna do, keep me covered all the way home?'

'If possible,' Barbara said.

'Yeah? Well, I'm putting my arms down, so go ahead and shoot me.' With that, he lowered them. Barbara felt an urge to fire past him – give him a good scare. But she'd already fired a warning shot, back at the pool. That one had probably been necessary, but a shot now would be a waste of ammo. Stupid, she knew, to fire if you didn't absolutely have to.

The round you save may save your life.

So far, they had run into no real trouble except for Earl (and Heather, don't forget poor Heather), but they still had a few miles to go.

If those blood-thirsty marauders were more than just a figment of Heather's imagination . . .

Sure hope that's all they were.

Just ahead, most of the alley was blocked by rubble from the collapsed rear of a two-story apartment building. Earl angled to the right and started to go around it. He kept his arms partway up. He kept his head down and seemed to be watching his step until he was past the side of the pile. Then he looked to his left.

And jerked to a quick, rigid stop.

'What?' Pete called.

For a moment, Earl didn't move. Then he grinned back at them. 'Nothing. No problem. Thought I saw a snake. Just a piece of rope. No sweat.'

He walked on, but watched over his shoulder.

There wasn't room to walk side by side past the edge of the

debris heap, so Barbara went first. She didn't like the way Earl kept watching her.

Something's going on.

Maybe he *had* spotted a real snake. The things were rare in Los Angeles, but the quake might've let a few pet pythons get loose. And she knew there were rattlers in the hills around the city.

Who knows?

But it wasn't a snake that had startled Earl. Nor was it a piece of rope.

Stepping carefully past the fan of broken stucco and glass, Barbara turned her head to the left and saw the bodies. She flinched and caught her breath.

'Surprise, surprise,' Earl called out.

She glanced at him. 'Bastard.'

Pete came up behind her. 'Oh, man,' he muttered.

Earl had walked on past the bodies in order to pull the gag on Barbara and Pete. Now that his trick had succeeded, he came wandering back.

'What're you doing?' Pete asked him.

'Just want a closer look. Come on over. They don't bite.'

Barbara suddenly found herself approaching Earl and the bodies. She thought, This is nuts. I don't *want* a closer look.

Sure you do.

No big deal, anyway, she told herself. It's not like these are the first of the day, or something. Oughta be pretty used to this stuff, by now.

The three bodies were stretched out on their backs, side by side: two young men, a slender blonde woman between them.

Barbara, standing near the feet of the woman, flanked by Earl and Pete, didn't like the similarities.

They could almost be our shadows.

They aren't, she told herself. They're dead people, and it's just a coincidence they're lined up this way and they sort of look like us.

They *do not* look like us.

The guy stretched out at Earl's feet was fat, for one thing.

Pete's dead counterpart was very tall, probably six-three, and had a crew cut. The blonde between them was probably ten years older than Barbara, had much bigger breasts that stood up solid with implants, slick bare skin where her pubic hair should've been, and a tan that seemed to have no boundaries.

Also, one side of her head was caved in.

The fat guy's guts showed through a deep slash across his belly.

The tall guy was missing most of his right leg.

'They weren't murdered, were they?' Pete asked, his voice quiet and shaky.

'Nah,' Earl said. 'The quake got 'em. I've seen plenty the same way. Some scavengers probably dragged 'em outa the shit and left 'em here.'

'Stripped them like this?' Pete asked.

'Less maybe the babe was catching some rays on her roof-top when we started to rock 'n' roll. She got one a them all-over tans. See that?'

Pete nodded.

'You got one a them all-over tans, Banner?'

'Knock it off,' she said.

'Betcha this babe's a stripper, or something. Maybe does porno flicks. Look how she's got her pussy shaved. You got your pussy shaved, Banner?'

'Shut up.' This time, the warning came from Pete.

Earl chuckled softly. He bent over and planted his hands on his knees and squinted. 'What do you think, they do her?'

'Earl!' Pete snapped.

'Ah, cool your jets. Just kidding around.'

'Real funny,' Barbara muttered.

'Yeah, well, it happens. Don't think it don't. Not that *I'd* be interested. Not me. I like my babes alive and moaning.' He stepped between the bodies of the fat guy and the woman. Turning toward the woman, he squatted down.

'What do you think you're doing?' Barbara said.

Casting an innocent smile at her, Earl squeezed one of the breasts. 'Honk honk.'

'What's the matter with you?' she muttered.

'Silicone job. Yuck. I like the *natural* feel. Don't ever get no silicone job, Banner. Love ya just the way you are.'

Feeling a little sick, she nudged Pete with her elbow. 'Let's get out of here.'

'Hang on, hang on,' Earl said. He reached down to the woman's face.

'Earl!'

'Just wanta check out a little something here. Look how she's bloody around her mouth.' Holding the woman's mouth open by the jaw, he hunched down lower and peered in. He turned her head a bit from side to side. 'Yeah. Shit. Just what I thought.'

'What?' Pete asked.

'She's missing a couple of her pearly whites.'

'What are you talking about?' Barbara asked.

'They been pulled. Outa the back.'

'Maybe they got knocked out by the quake,' Pete suggested.

'Yeah, right.' He turned around and inspected the fat guy's mouth. 'This one's okay – least if you overlook his *obvious* problems.'

Pete stepped forward, crouched, and looked into the mouth of the tall guy. 'This one's got all his teeth.'

'It was just the babe, then,' Earl said. 'What happened, some fucking street-vulture yanked her gold crowns.' Shaking his head, he stood up. 'Not enough, they strip every damn body down to the skin and rip off everything – now they're going for the teeth. Ain't seen that before. Beware of trolls bearing pliers, know what I mean? You got any gold in that mouth-hole of yours, Banner?'

'No.'

'Me, neither,' Pete said.

'Guess I'm the only lucky one.' Earl opened his mouth wide and pointed in. Barbara didn't bother to look. 'Three of 'em. Cost my step-dad a fortune. Bet he never figured he was marrying into no dental disaster.' Earl laughed sharply, then scowled. His eyes shifted from Pete to Barbara. 'Something happens – don't let nobody take my teeth, okay? Shit. I go down, I wanta go down in one piece.'

'Don't worry about it,' Pete said. 'Nobody's going down.'

'Right. That's probably what *they* thought.'

'Let's get going,' Barbara said.

Earl took the lead again, but he neither raised his arms nor kept his hands in his pockets.

Might as well let him do what he wants, Barbara thought. He could've jumped us or made a getaway while we were with the bodies. Would've been a cinch to take us by surprise, grab one of the guns . . .

'I wonder if we should get out of the alleys,' Pete said.

Barbara saw that they were coming up on a street. No cars were going by. The alley on the other side of the street looked much the same as this one and the others – a narrow lane of old, crumbling pavement bordered by dumpsters, parking stalls, fences, occasional hedges, and the rear ends of several apartment buildings.

All the apartment buildings that Barbara could see along the alley were standing. She saw no major damage. She saw no bodies. She saw no scavengers. She saw nobody.

'I don't know,' she told Pete. 'It doesn't look bad up ahead.'

Earl turned around and walked backward. 'Hey, the alleys are better. Believe it. I been in the streets. You don't wanta get mixed up in the looting and shit. Here, all you got're the vultures. And they ain't interested in us till we're toes up, know what I mean? Hell, you don't even see 'em. You seen any? They're like invisible. You only know they're around 'cause you can see what they done to the stiffs. But we go out in the streets, and we're asking for trouble. Some of them looters spot you got guns, they're gonna want 'em. Fact is, you oughta put those babies outa sight till we get across the street. We been lucky so far nobody's spotted 'em and come for us.'

Pete and Barbara looked at each other.

Then Barbara opened her purse. The Colt was too large, but she managed to stuff it in. The purse suddenly felt very heavy against her hip. The strap, slanting down from her shoulder, pulled taut.

No way, she thought.

Grimacing, she removed the pistol from the purse and reached behind her back. She lifted the tail of her blouse and pushed the .45 down under the waistband of her shorts. The shorts became a bit more snug, but not uncomfortable. As she inserted the gun, the muzzle or front sight caught on the top of her panties, shoving them down a few inches. The steel felt thick and slightly cool against the crease of her buttocks.

Not bad, she thought. Beats keeping it in my purse.

'What am I supposed to do with this?' Pete asked, gesturing with the rifle.

'Do like Banner and stick it in your pants,' Earl suggested, grinning.

'Sure,' Pete muttered.

'Just carry it by your side so it isn't so obvious what you've got,' Barbara suggested. 'Nobody's bothered us yet. And you go trying to hide something that big in your clothes, you won't be able to get it out if we need it.'

'Want *me* to carry it?' Earl asked.

'Thanks, but no thanks.'

'Your funeral,' Earl said, and walked on out of the alley.

Barbara and Pete followed him, staying close together, the rifle between them, clamped under Pete's arm and pointed downward.

Barbara looked from side to side as they crossed the street.

In both directions, cars and pickups and vans were parked along the curbs. A few were double-parked and seemed to be abandoned.

To her right, she could see a lot of stopped traffic in the distance – no doubt where the street approached one of the main east-west roads. Quite a few people seemed to be milling about. She supposed they were drivers and passengers who'd decided not to leave their vehicles behind. She'd seen such groups a lot.

She'd come to think of them as 'the waiters.'

Not doing anything, just waiting around for the traffic to clear so they could drive on home.

Between the waiters and where she was crossing the road, Barbara saw nobody except a pair of women standing together on the sidewalk in front of an apartment building, chattering and gesturing, probably sharing their quake adventures.

To the left, far off, Barbara could see traffic stopped at another major east-west artery. She could barely make out the tiny shapes of the waiters.

Between those distant waiters and where she walked across the street, she saw nobody.

Nobody at all.

A street of empty vehicles. Sunlit air, yellow, adrift with haze and smoke. A few trees that didn't give much shade. Patches of green here and there, but mostly the gray of concrete and the pastels of painted stucco walls of homes and apartment buildings.

Cracks in walls and pavement.

Crumbled stucco.

Shattered windows.

Fallen chimneys.

But nobody.

No people at all.

Just as well, Barbara thought. The main quake's all over and you got through it without getting your head bashed in, so now all you've got to do is worry about getting killed by the survivors.

She was glad that she and Pete had guns.

She thought about the revolver at home, and hoped that Mom had thought to grab it.

Maybe Dad's home by now, she thought.

If only they're home and all right and the house is still in one piece . . . then we'll all be together and fine.

If I can get there.

It felt good to get out of the street and into the alley, where they were not so exposed. Pete quit trying to conceal the rifle. He carried it at port arms, ready. Barbara decided to keep the pistol down her waistband. She liked having her hands empty.

She figured that she could probably pull it out fast enough if trouble started.

From the feel she had in her stomach, she was expecting trouble to come soon.

So do they, she thought. Just look at us.

All three were walking much more slowly than before.

Earl, in the lead, kept swiveling his head. Pete, by Barbara's side, was constantly glancing over his shoulder. Barbara, herself, couldn't stop turning this way and that to make sure nobody was about to creep out from behind a dumpster or pounce on them from the shadows of a car stall.

We look like we're walking into an ambush and know it, she thought.

It's just that we're spooked because of the bodies.

Hope that's all it is.

On the other side of the alley, a Dodge pickup truck was parked in the car port beneath the second story of an apartment building. Beside it stood a Jeep Wrangler. The Jeep didn't bother her; it was a convertible and she could see that nobody was in it. But the pickup bothered her a lot.

It was a big pickup truck, not one of those sporty little foreign jobs. The bed behind its cab had high metal sides. From where she stood in the middle of the alley, Barbara couldn't see over its tailgate.

'I'm taking a look over there,' she whispered.

'What?' Pete asked.

She nodded toward the pickup. 'Don't want any surprises. Just keep an eye on me, okay?' She stepped past him. As she walked closer to the pickup, she reached under the tail of her shirt and drew the Colt.

When she did that, Pete said, 'Wait for me.'

He hurried to her side.

Earl looked back and frowned. 'What's up?'

'Just checking,' Pete told him.

'For keys?'

Pete shook his head.

'Didn't think so. Couple of weenies.'

With each step, Barbara could see more of the pickup's bed. So far, it seemed to be empty except for a rumpled blue tarp near the cab.

Doesn't look like anyone's . . .

'Shit!'

The yelp was high and girlish and didn't sound like Earl. But Barbara whirled and it was Earl back-pedaling, Earl turning around with his eyes wide and his lips skinned back, Earl blurting out, 'Hide!' and breaking into a run.

As he sprinted past them, Barbara snapped her head sideways.

And saw what he'd seen.

A scavenger pushing a shopping cart. Pushing it on the run, the cart bouncing and swerving on the rough alley pavement. Inside the cart sat a naked man. He looked as if he'd been tossed in, rump first. His arms and feet hung over the high edges of the wire basket, and flopped about as the cart bounded along. His head bobbed and swayed.

Running hard behind the cart, shoving it along, was a filthy thing in a huge soiled overcoat and boots. The derelict's hair was long and straight, the color of pewter.

A witch, a hag.

But maybe a guy.

A 'street vulture' for sure – racing along with its cargo of dead man, taking him God-knows-where for some ungodly reason Barbara didn't want to think about.

No wonder Earl had lost his cool and . . .

Barbara suddenly spotted the mob.

She knew, at once, that Earl hadn't lost his cool and lit out and blurted the warning because of the horror pushing the shopping cart.

It was the mob giving chase to the vulture.

One glimpse of it was enough. Barbara elbowed Pete and gasped, 'Here,' and vaulted the tailgate of the pickup truck.

Inside, she dropped flat. Pete sprawled beside her. He was breathing very hard.

'Think they saw us?' Barbara whispered.

'Jeez, I hope not.'

'They were pretty far away.'

Letting go of the pistol, Barbara pushed herself up with both hands. She peered over the corner of the tailgate in time to see a thrown hammer bounce off the back of the derelict's head. He or she lost the shopping cart and flew head-first toward the pavement. The cart went scooting and bouncing forward, then veered aside and tumbled, throwing out the dead man.

The laughing, hooting mob engulfed the derelict.

They seemed to be mostly teenagers, mostly boys. But there were girls, too – girls who seemed no less fierce and gleefully wild than the guys.

Barbara sank down beside Pete.

Her heart throbbed as if it were being hammered to pulp.

'Jesus,' she gasped.

'What?'

'They'll tear us up.'

'Not if we blast them.'

'Fifteen or twenty of 'em?'

'We can do it.'

'But they're just kids. Younger than us, some of 'em.'

'Better than letting them . . . Maybe they won't find us, but . . . We could pull the tarp over us . . .'

'Wait. No. I've got it. Get your clothes off.'

'What?'

'They won't kill us if they think we're dead.'

As the mob squealed and laughed and hooted over the scavenger they'd downed fifty or sixty feet away, Barbara and Pete in the bed of the pickup truck stayed low and struggled out of their clothes.

Barbara glanced at Pete a few times. He was making good progress, and he wasn't staring at her.

He kept mumbling, 'Jeez,' and, 'Oh, God,' over and over again.

The stripping seemed to take forever.

'Okay,' Pete finally gasped.

Barbara looked. 'Underwear, too.'

'Oh, man.'

On her back, Barbara tugged her panties down as far as she could without sitting up, then worked them the rest of the way down with her legs. Her foot shoved them under the loose wad of tarp.

She rolled onto her side.

Her purse and most of the clothes were heaped between their bodies.

Pete lay on his side, facing her, holding the rifle against his body, the shoulder stock pressed to his genitals. He looked red and shaky.

'Everything goes under the tarp,' Barbara whispered. 'Except the guns. And this.' She plucked her denim purse away from the pile.

Working together, they shoved the pile of clothes down past their waists, past their thighs. Then they used their knees and feet. Soon, everything was out of sight beneath the tarp.

'Roll over and hide the rifle under you. If the crap hits the fan, we'll open up on 'em. But not unless we have to. I don't wanta kill anyone.'

'Me, neither,' Pete said. 'But we'll do it if we have to.'

'Right.'

'I'm not gonna let anyone hurt you.'

She felt her throat thicken. 'Turn over.'

He rolled toward Barbara, lowering his body onto the rifle and resting his forehead on the metal floor of the pickup's bed. His head was turned slightly toward her. The single eye that she could see was gazing at her face.

She pushed herself up on one elbow. For a moment, she thought how smooth and nice he looked. He had a deep tan on his back and legs. His rump was white.

This is so nuts I don't believe it, she thought. Got a mob of crazy weirdos gonna be showing up, and . . .

She looked at his face.

Caught him staring at her breasts.

His eye shifted quickly to her face.

'Sorry,' he whispered.

'It's okay. But turn your head the other way. Get your hands out from under your body. And you're too stiff. Limpen up. Get your legs apart. Bend a knee. You gotta look dead.'

She waited until he had turned his head the other way, then reached into her purse. She found her makeup compact and pulled it out. She popped it open. With a fingernail, she pried the mirror loose. She jammed the compact back into her purse and scooted the denim bag toward the tarp. It stopped short. She shoved it out of sight with her foot.

Still braced up on her left elbow, she held the mirror with both hands and snapped it like a cracker.

'What're you doing?' Pete whispered.

'Taking care of business.'

'You better stop messing around and play dead.'

'I know. Yeah. Almost done.' Holding half the mirror in her right hand, she pressed a corner of its broken edge against the underside of her left forearm. She gritted her teeth and held her breath, determined not to make a sound.

Then she ripped a gash.

In her mind, she cried out, 'YOW!'

But she stayed silent.

Blood flooded from the slit.

Setting down the piece of mirror, she cupped the spilling blood in her right hand. She dumped it over the back of Pete's head. He cringed. The bright red blood matted his hair and dribbled down the nape of his neck.

'What is that?'

'Shh.'

She dumped another handful in the same place.

She wanted to be facedown, herself, but didn't see how she could manage the blood that way. So she turned onto her back. She twisted herself crooked. She swung her left leg sideways and draped it across Pete's buttocks.

Then she tucked the pistol under her body, just above her right hip where she would be able to reach it fast.

Finally, she raised her cut forearm and moved it slowly back and forth, letting blood patter onto her chest and neck and face.

With her right hand, she smeared the blood over her skin.

That oughta do it, she thought.

Let 'em come.

From the sounds of laughter and voices and wild outcries of delight, the mob didn't seem to be any nearer than before.

Still messing with the scavenger?

What the hell could they be doing?

Don't want to know, she thought.

Turning her head, she looked at Pete. She stretched her arm over him, and bled for a little while onto the back of his neck and shoulders.

'Just hope they don't think the blood looks too fresh,' she whispered.

'You gashed yourself, didn't you?' Pete said without moving.

'Yep.'

'That's what I thought. Jeez.'

'Don't worry, my blood's good and healthy. Won't give you AIDS or anything.' She swung her arm away from Pete, lowered it across herself, and pressed the wound tightly against her belly. 'Now,' she whispered, 'long as I don't bleed to death . . .'

'Whooo-eee! You need a bath!'

Though the stranger's voice came from some distance away, it made Barbara flinch.

'Too hot for this shit,' said a girl who sounded annoyed.

'Find us a pool,' said a different guy.

'Fuck that,' said another guy. 'I wanta rip more ass!'

'You see how I done her?' asked a guy who sounded like a braggart.

'We saw, we saw,' said a girl.

'Gonna have to disin*fect* your sorry ass,' said someone else. A lot of people laughed and hooted at that one.

The voices were getting louder. Barbara could hear the scrape and shuffle of a great many shoes coming closer, closer.

She willed herself to relax. She quit pressing the cut to her belly. She shut her eyes and made her mouth sag open. She slid her right hand nearer to her side until her fingertips were less than an inch from the pistol tucked beneath her back.

This is it.

She realized she was shaking.

Gotta stop, gotta stop.

She couldn't stop.

Won't fool anyone! They'll take one look in here and see me shaking like a damn leaf.

Please, she thought. Go away. All of you, just go away. Nobody here but us chickens. Please, please.

Thirty-three

'Here I am, ready or not.'

Sheila didn't answer, and Stanley couldn't see any part of her body from where he stood over the bathtub. He wasn't worried, though. She had to be down there – under the huge body of Crash and under the beams.

'Snug as a bug in a tub?' he asked.

He sat down and hung his legs over the broken edge of the floor. He still wore only his moccasins and the flimsy, cut-off pants of his pajamas, but he had grabbed a towel while roaming through a house in search of Weed. He used the towel to mop the sweat off his hair and face, his neck and chest. Then he draped it over his shoulders.

Now that he was sitting, he could see Sheila's arms at the far end of the tub. They looked as if they were folded, one on top of the other, above the crown of Crash's bloody head. From elbows to hands, they were sleeved with dark, drying blood. Her face had to be under them, but Stanley couldn't see any of it. All he saw of her head were a few wisps of golden hair above the crossed arms.

'Did you miss me, darling?' he asked.

She didn't answer or move.

'Playing possum?'

Nothing.

'Won't do you any good, you know. I'm not going anywhere. Not till I've got you.'

He supposed that she might've passed out. After all, she had been down there a long time. And for quite a while, she'd been down there with a huge dead guy on top of her.

Crash was slumped over the beam, the top of his head at Sheila's chin. His arms were up as if he'd died trying to protect the back of his neck. They looked like thick, bloody wings spread out to shield as much of Sheila as possible from Stanley's view.

It didn't seem likely that the body was mashing her too badly, or had suffocated her.

'You didn't faint on me, did you?'

Still nothing.

'No,' Stanley said. 'Not you. You're a tough one. You just figure to keep your mouth shut for a while and see what happens. Right? You been down there so long, maybe you figure it's high time for the Cavalry to show up and save you. Just stall a while longer, and everything'll work out fine.'

He wondered if she was listening.

'Maybe you're thinking Weed made a getaway and she'll be charging over the horizon at the head of a SWAT team.'

He wondered what had made him say that, of all things.

Maybe because it's what I'm afraid of.

'Isn't gonna happen,' he said. 'She almost got away, but she was more interested in trying to jump me. Want to hear what I did to her?'

Sheila didn't answer.

'Maybe I shouldn't tell,' he said. 'I plan on doing the same to you, so this way it'll come as a surprise. You like surprises, Sheila?'

'Did you kill her?' Sheila asked.

'Ah, she speaks.'

'Did you?'

'You bet. Eventually. But we had a lot of fun, first. I did, anyway. Did you hear her screaming?'

'You bastard.'

'Did you *hear* her?'

'No.'

'It was lovely.'

And it would've been lovely, too, he thought – if only I'd caught her.

Over and over again, while roaming through neighborhood yards and ruins and abandoned houses, he'd imagined what he would do to Weed when he caught her. Leave the tank top on her – what there was of it – but hang her by the hands from something so she'd be stretched and the bottom edge of the shirt wouldn't quite reach down enough to cover her breasts. Tug those jeans down off her skinny hips, down her skinny legs.

That would've been for starters.

Just to get her in the best position and looking good for the rest of it.

While searching for Weed, he'd come up with many ideas about what to do with her after that. He'd lived them in his head, excited by them, relishing the images for their own sake but also knowing that sooner or later he would find her and get to make his fantasies come true.

He hadn't found her, though.

She must've either run far away or found herself a terrific hiding place.

Stanley had been very reluctant to give up the search. She *might* go and find help and come back with cops or something, but that wasn't what bothered him most.

It was missing out on her.

She was no Sheila. Nowhere close. Sheila was in a league of her own. But something about that harsh, skinny girl really made him want her. Want her strung up by the wrists and helpless so he could look her over good and feel her up and down and *do* things to her – things to make her writhe and twitch and scream.

After giving up on the search and starting back toward the ruin of Sheila's house, he'd felt a terrible emptiness.

Would've been so great. Now I'll never get her.

But I'll have Sheila, he'd told himself. I can do all kinds of things to Sheila. It'll be just as good – better.

No, it won't! I want Weed!

That's crazy, he'd thought. There's no comparison.

God, why did I let her get away!

He'd realized that he could keep on searching for her;

there was no law that said he had to quit and go back to Sheila. Why not give it another hour? And another? And as long as it takes?

It's hopeless, that's why. I would've found her by now if I was gonna.

And a bird in the tub, he'd thought, is worth two in the bush.

Nothing so special about Weed, anyway. She's nothing compared to Sheila. A skinny, ugly, vicious witch. Sheila's a goddess, a gorgeous Amazon. Better Sheila any day of the week than Weed.

And here we go.

'Are you ready for me?' he asked.

'Just do what you're gonna do,' Sheila said.

'Golly, you used to be so *eager* for me to get you out.'

'Maybe I'm getting used to it down here.'

'Would you like me to go away?'

'I'd like you to drop dead.'

'Gosh, that isn't a very nice thing to say.'

'I'm sick of being your game. I'm everybody's game.'

Stanley laughed, then lowered himself down to the bathtub. He stood on its edges and gazed at Crash's body.

The legs hung against the bottom of the tub. The broad, faded jeans were halfway down Crash's butt. At the hips, he was slumped over the four-by-eight that was pinning Sheila. Some of his weight, Stanley supposed, had to be resting on her left leg, pressing it into the beam.

'How's your leg?' he asked.

'Which one?'

'The one getting mashed.'

'Numb. Thanks for asking.'

'I'm a very considerate guy. Shall we see what I can do?' Stanley set the scissors aside, then bent down and grabbed the back of Crash's jeans.

He remembered how he'd grabbed Judy the same way.

Only this morning, but it sure seemed like a long time ago.

He thought now that he should've checked on her while he was out looking for Weed . . . made sure she hadn't gotten loose. He hadn't even thought about her, or he would've done that.

And maybe taken a few minutes to have some fun with her.

She'd been a real treat, right after he'd hauled her in from her driveway.

Hauled her in by the back of her jeans. Which had been nice, in its own way. He remembered how much he'd enjoyed it. The feel of her rump against his knuckles as he'd stuck his hand down there. The look of her butt and her white panties.

But Crash was a guy. A dead guy, at that. His rump was wide and fat and ugly. The feel of it made Stanley want to wash his knuckles.

When he tugged at the edge of the jeans, Crash didn't budge.

'Hate to say this,' he said, 'but we might have to wait for a crane.'

'Very funny,' Sheila muttered.

He decided that part of the problem was his precarious perch on the rims of the tub. So he stepped down, placing his feet on the porcelain between Crash's ankles.

He crouched and hooked both his hands into the seat pockets of Crash's jeans.

When he pulled, the pockets tore away. He stumbled but managed to stay up.

For his third try, he shoved both hands down between the top of the jeans and Crash's buttocks. He clutched the denim waistband and threw his weight backward. *Pupp, zzzz!* Crash stayed put, but the jeans went loose and seemed to leap toward Stanley. As he fell, they were tugged down almost to Crash's knees.

He landed hard on his rump.

'Shit!'

'What's going on?' Sheila asked.

'I'm having . . . problems.'

'Try getting him from this end. You lift and I push . . .'

'Yeah. Yeah, good idea. If nothing else, there's gotta be a better view.'

He stood up, climbed again onto the edges of the tub, and made his way forward. Just beyond the beam was the saw. It stood upright between Crash's body and the left side of the tub, where the big man must've dropped it after being knocked down by the chunk of stucco Stanley had thrown.

'Guess what I see,' he said.

Sheila didn't answer.

'The answer to our little difficulty.'

Bracing himself with a hand on Crash's back, Stanley bent low, reached down for the saw, and caught a glimpse of Sheila's bare right side. It was gray with shadow. It was way down there, almost blocked from view by Crash's overhanging bulk.

The sight of it dragged a moan out of him.

In his mind, he suddenly saw *all* of her. Crash vanished and there was Sheila on the bottom of the tub, one leg hooked over the beam and one leg under it, her hands folded under her head, all of her body there for Stanley to see – smooth and golden – and his.

She's mine, he thought.

Get this fat slob *off* her!

'It won't be long,' he said.

Keeping his left foot on the rim of the tub, he crouched and planted his right knee in the middle of Crash's back. He set down the saw. Using both hands, he forced Crash's arms down to the sides. The arms had been covering Sheila's breasts, just as he'd thought.

Stanley felt his penis rise stiff and poke out through the slit of his pajama pants.

'Oh, honey,' he muttered.

With his left hand, he lifted Crash's head by the hair. With his right hand, he picked up the saw began to cut through the neck.

'*What're you doing?*' Sheila cried out.

Her hands were suddenly up, gripping the edge of the beam that crossed above her face.

Stanley stopped sawing. He smiled at her.

She looked so lovely. It didn't matter that her face was

streaked with sweat and filth and old blood, that her lips were cracked, that her features were twisted with horror and disgust.

'*My God! Stop it! You can't . . . No!*'

'I don't hear him complaining,' Stanley said.

'*Please!*'

'You want out, don't you?'

'*No! You can't . . . do that to him!*'

'Sure I can. Just watch.' He pushed again at the saw, running its blade through the shallow, raw groove on the side of Crash's neck.

'*No!*'

'Shut up! Look what you've already done with that mouth of yours. I wouldn't have to be doing this, at all, if you'd just kept it shut in the first place.'

She gazed up at Stanley, gasping and jerking her head from side to side.

'That's better.' He started sawing again, and grinned when Sheila squeezed her mouth shut. 'Good idea,' he said. 'You wouldn't want to swallow some of this.'

Soon, she covered her face with both arms.

Stanley kept a good grip on Crash's hair. The sawing took a while; he had to keep the angle of the blade just right and use very short strokes to avoid gouging Sheila. At last, however, he severed the spinal column. He pumped the saw a few more times. Then he hoisted the head. A few remaining shreds of tissue were still connected to the stump of the neck. They stretched and wouldn't let go, so he ripped through them with the saw.

He flung the head away. It tumbled high, vanished beyond the broken flooring, and thumped into the debris with a sound like a hurled brick.

'I bet you feel lighter already,' Stanley said.

'You . . . you sick bastard,' Sheila said from underneath her crossed arms.

'Let me just take care of his arms, then we'll see if we can't haul him off you. Sure hope so. If I've gotta saw him off at the waist, we'll have an incredible mess.'

One at a time, he sawed off Crash's arms and flung them away.

'That's got him whittled down pretty good,' he said.

Sheila uncovered her face. She glanced at the remains of Crash, whimpered and shut her eyes tight.

'I did it with my little saw,' Stanley said, and laughed.

Then he made his way forward on the rims of the tub, turned around, and sat on the beam above Sheila's head. Reaching out to set aside the saw, he smiled and lowered the flat of its blade onto the eyeless face of Crash's buddy, Eagle.

Then he bent at the waist and peered through his spread legs. Sheila's face was upside-down. She looked up at him from the shadows.

The pulpy stump of Crash's neck was still leaking onto her, spilling red fluid through the valley between her breasts.

'You *are* a mess,' Stanley said. 'But don't worry, we'll wash you squeaky clean as soon as we've got you out of here. I know where there's a swimming pool. Now, let's see you stick your hands under this boy's chest and shove him up.'

'What if I don't?'

'Do you think I was bluffing when I said I'd cut him in half? I wasn't, you know. You either give me some cooperation here, or I'll saw him off at the waist. You think things are messy *now* . . .'

'Okay,' she muttered. 'Okay. But I won't be able to do much. The leverage is all wrong. Don't think I haven't already tried.'

'Just do your best. That's all that we can ask, isn't it? You shove him up, and I'll do the rest with my feet.'

'Why don't you just come down and *lift* him off me. All you'd need to do is bend over and pick him up by his shoulders. It'd be easy.'

He thought about her suggestion.

After a few moments, he said, 'Nah.'

'Why not?'

'Because I say so.'

'But it'll work.'

'So what? It'll be more fun *my* way. Anyhow, I'm all done with women giving me orders. We do it my way. You gotta push him up, and then I'll shove him off.'

She glared up at Stanley.

'Do it. Now.'

'Okay. Okay.'

Watching her, Stanley saw what she'd meant about the poor leverage. With the tub against her back, she had no way of lowering her elbows far enough; she couldn't simply shove Crash up like a barbell.

Even if she'd had the elbow room, Stanley supposed that the position of Crash's body might've given her trouble. The massive shoulders, just below her breasts, were too low for a straight upward push.

Sheila didn't waste much time with awkward thrusts – just made a few tentative tries to see whether Crash's sudden loss of weight had improved the situation.

Then she brought her arms in close to her sides, elbows bent, fists in front of her own shoulders. She took a few deep breaths. Gritting her teeth, she drove her elbows upward against the front of Crash's shoulders.

The headless torso started to rise.

Stanley didn't care about that, cared only about what was happening to Sheila.

Oh, look at her! Look at her!

Bulges of straining arm muscles, shoulder muscles, chest muscles. Breasts so much larger than before, squeezed together by her arms, the valley between them gone, a long sloping crease where they met.

Her skin bloody and sweaty.

And the tremors!

Look at her shake!

Magnificent!

Her right breast suddenly lurched free as she chopped her forearm down over the top of it and into the space under Crash's chest. Her lips peeled back. Grunting, she thrust at the body and rammed her left arm down beneath it.

Stanley couldn't see her forearms, now. But he knew they

must be crossed in the space between her lower ribcage and Crash's upper chest.

And they were *raising* him.

'Thata way!' Stanley blurted.

'Do it!' she gasped through clenched teeth.

'Get him higher.'

She pushed the body higher.

'Do it!'

'Higher.'

There was no need for more height. But Stanley didn't want this to end.

Sheila the Magnificent.

Struggling, suffering, sweating, muscles and veins and tendons all there and showing under her shiny skin, and every part of her shuddering, shaking, trembling, quaking.

'Do it!'

'Here goes.'

He raised his feet off the edges of the tub, leaned back and braced himself against the broken floorboards, then bent his knees and shot his feet forward. They slammed the tops of Crash's shoulders. A red gob leaped from the neck stump.

The headless and armless torso teetered backward, rising from the waist. Then it dropped. For a moment, it seemed to be kneeling behind the beam. Then it tumbled away and smashed against the other end of the tub.

'Bravo!' Stanley yelled.

Below him, Sheila panted for air.

'Get . . . me out,' she gasped.

'We still have the small matter of sawing through the wood.'

'Do it.'

He pursed his lips. 'Oooo. Are you telling me what to do?'

'No.'

'Good. We wouldn't want that.'

'Do . . . whatever you want.'

'Thank you. I think I will.'

He brought up his feet, one at a time, and peeled off the moccasins. Then he lowered his bare feet toward

Sheila's chest. Before they could touch her, she clutched his ankles.

'What do you think you're doing?' he asked.

'You're not doing that.'

'I do whatever I want.' He grinned. 'You told me I could.'

'I lied.'

'You'd better let go.'

She didn't let go.

Stanley shot his arm out, grabbed the saw by its handle and swept it down between his legs. He jabbed the steel tip into Sheila just below her sternum.

With all the blood down there from Crash, he couldn't tell whether the point broke her skin.

But she flinched.

And tightened her grip on his ankles.

'Let go, damn it!'

She didn't.

And Stanley suddenly imagined Sheila giving his ankles a tug that would drag him off the four-by-eight. He could almost feel the heavy beam scraping the skin off his back as he fell. He would land rump-first on her chest. And there he would be, sitting on her, his back braced up by the beam, his arms nearly useless because she would be under him and so hard to reach.

With her strength . . .

She could kill me!

Scared, Stanley shoved the saw. It gouged a shallow furrow down toward her navel.

Crying out, she let go of his ankles and tried to snatch the blade. He jerked it clear. He kicked his legs high as she grabbed for them. She kept trying to catch them as he drew them back, but he battered at her hands and arms with the saw, striking and cutting her, finally planting his heels on the top of the beam, springing up and leaping to safety.

Thirty-four

Barbara felt Pete's buttocks flex underneath the calf of her outstretched leg. Neither moving nor opening her eyes, she whispered, 'Lie still.'

'They're gone.'

'Let's give it a little longer.'

'Okay.'

They probably *are* gone, she told herself.

Some time ago, the gang had wandered down the alley, laughing and jabbering and arguing, and gone on by without any mention or inspection of the pickup truck where Barbara and Pete were hiding.

Which had seemed too good to be true.

So Barbara hadn't allowed herself to believe it.

Must be a trick, she'd thought. They know we're here. They're just pretending to leave. Wanta see what happens.

So wait, just wait.

If we think the coast is clear and show ourselves, it'll blow any chance of playing dead. We'll end up dead for real.

Maybe they're sneaking up on us.

They startle us, she'd thought, and we'll probably both jump and that'll be it.

Not that our little dead act is gonna fool someone, anyhow.

A long time had gone by since the footsteps and voices of the gang had faded and vanished. It seemed like at least an hour. But Barbara knew how time had a way of stretching, slowing down, when things were bad. It probably hadn't been an hour, at all.

At least *half* an hour, she told herself.

They've gotta be gone by now. They wouldn't have that much patience. They never had any idea we were here and they just kept walking.

We could've kept our clothes on, she realized.

I didn't need to cut myself.

Now we're both naked and bloody and I've got a nice gash on my arm.

And if we stay here long enough, someone *else* might come along.

Earl, for instance.

She wondered what had happened to him. He must've seen the gang come running into the alley on the heels of the scavenger. Either they hadn't spotted him, though, or they hadn't cared. Maybe they *had* seen him, but were more interested in nailing the scavenger.

They'd sure spent a lot of time on her.

On *them*. Don't forget the guy in the shopping cart.

Another good reason to stay here, Barbara told herself. Who wants to see those bodies?

But I sure don't want Earl showing up and finding me like this. Even if he did warn us, he's still a major creep.

Better get a move on.

She opened her eyes. Seven or eight feet above her was the dim, raftered ceiling of the parking stall.

Nothing up there to worry about.

She glanced from side to side. Nobody leered down at her over the truck's side panels.

Raising her head, she checked the rear window of the cab. Nobody there.

So she tipped her head back. The area above the tailgate was upside-down. She saw no one.

'Maybe it *is* safe by now,' she whispered.

'I think they're long gone.'

'And if they aren't, we've got our guns.'

'Yeah,' Pete whispered.

'Okay.' She looked at him and saw that his head was still turned away from her. 'Stay like that, okay? I'll tell you when to look.'

'Sure.'

'Thanks.' She pulled the Colt out from under her back, then shoved herself up with her elbows and studied their sprawled, naked bodies.

Maybe we could've passed, after all.

The back of Pete's head and neck, where she'd dumped a couple of handloads of blood, looked as if he might've suffered some sort of fatal wound. Not much blood lower down, though – and the tan on his back seemed too glowing for a dead guy.

Guess we'll never know, she thought.

Her own body was good and bloody, but she could see hand and fingerprints in the brownish-red smears that might make it pretty obvious she'd spread the blood around, herself. And she'd entirely neglected the area below her waist.

Her legs were wide apart, one draped across Pete's rump. Between them, she'd spread no blood, she had no tan, and her tuft of blonde curls was too sparse to hide the skin beneath it.

A sudden heat rushed through her body.

Thank God, nobody saw me like this!

'What're you doing?' Pete asked. He sounded curious, not annoyed.

'Nothing,' Barbara said.

'Just looking?'

She hesitated.

'You are, aren't you?'

'Sort of.' She raised her leg and swung it away from Pete. It left behind a ruddy hue. 'I just wanted to see if we looked all right. You know, bloody and dead.'

'How *do* we look?'

'Pretty good.'

'Too bad we didn't get a chance to see if it worked.'

'We're really lucky, is what we are.'

'I thought you said we look pretty good.'

'Yeah. We just don't look especially dead.'

Pete laughed a little.

'I guess the whole thing was a dumb idea,' Barbara said.

'It was sure extreme. How's your cut?'

She looked down at the gash on the underside of her forearm. All around it, the skin was stained with dry blood. The wound itself was a raw, dark slit two inches long. 'It isn't bleeding anymore,' she said. 'But it's kind of sore.'

'That was really a brave thing, cutting yourself like that.'

'Naw, just stupid.'

'No, it wasn't. It was heroic. You might've saved our lives, doing that.'

'Might've. Except nobody even looked at us.'

'Including me,' Pete said, and made a soft laugh.

'Including you?'

He wants to look! Oh, my God!

'I'm . . . never mind,' he muttered. 'I just thought . . . you know, we're playing dead in the back of a pickup truck. It doesn't, like . . . happen every day.'

'That's for sure.'

'It's all right,' he said. 'I mean, I know I can't look.'

The pounding of Barbara's heart quickened. 'Do you want to?' Her voice sounded shaky.

'Me? No. Jeez!'

Heart pounding very hard, she sank down against the floor. She couldn't believe she was planning to go through with this. And she couldn't believe how much she wanted it. 'Yes, you do,' she said.

'No, really.'

'Wait a second. I'll make it the way it was.' She swung her leg onto Pete's rump, stuck the Colt beneath her back, and ran through the position in her mind to make sure it was the same as before.

The same except for her head and eyes.

Because she had to watch Pete.

'Okay. You can look now.'

'No, really, I . . .'

'Come on. It's okay. I *want* you to.'

I almost sound sort of calm, she thought. Amazing.

'Like you said,' she went on, 'we don't go around playing dead every day. We've got all this blood on us . . . I don't want you regretting how you blew your chance to see . . . how we looked.'

'Are you kidding?'

'I mean it. Come on.'

She watched Pete raise his head and turn it toward her. He pushed himself up with his elbows. He stared into her eyes.

Then his gaze moved slowly down her body. He licked his dry, cracked lips. He blinked a few times. Barbara could see that he was shaking slightly.

She wondered if her own shaking showed.

More than likely.

Bracing himself up with his right elbow, Pete twisted his torso and peered back at her.

He can see everything!

She thought about trying to cover up – flinging an arm across her breasts, clapping a hand between her legs.

But she stayed on her back and didn't move her arms and found breathing a very hard thing to do.

'A lot of blood,' he said, his voice quiet and trembling.

'Yeah.'

'You're right, though. We don't look very dead.'

'Not very.' Lifting her head, she looked at Pete. The way he was turned and holding himself up, she could see the red imprint that the rifle had made on his chest and belly. The rifle was on the floor beneath him, its stock pinned down by his left thigh.

If the rifle wasn't in the way . . .

Glad it is, she told herself. Who'd wanta see something like that, anyway?

She turned her attention to his face. He almost looked as if he were in pain. His eyes kept jerking this way and that as if he couldn't make up his mind about what he would rather stare at.

'Hey,' Barbara whispered.

He flinched, then met her eyes.

She couldn't help but smile. 'Are you all right?'

'Oh, man.'

She lifted her leg off his rump, then turned onto her side. Facing Pete, she pushed herself up on one elbow. His gaze flicked to her breasts, but quickly returned to her eyes.

'Sorry,' he muttered.

'It's okay.'

'I've never seen . . . you know . . . a *girl* . . . a real one without, you know, clothes on.'

'Do I look okay?'

'Are you kidding? You're . . . God, nobody would believe this!'

'You aren't going to tell anyone, are you?'

'No! No way! I'd never tell *any*one.'

Reaching out with her right hand, Barbara caressed the side of his face. His cheek felt wet and hot. Her fingertips, curled over the edge of his ear, stroked through dripping hair. She slid her hand down the side of his neck, and up over the solid mound of his shoulder.

His eyes never strayed from her face.

'This'll be our secret,' she said.

'Yeah.'

She followed his arm to the wrist, wrapped her fingers around it, and guided his hand to her breast. She gasped when he touched her. She went rigid and moaned when he squeezed.

He let go fast. 'Did I hurt you?'

'No. No, no.'

His hand returned. But it was more gentle this time. His fingertips brushed lightly over her breast. She felt her skin go crawly with goosebumps, felt the nipples of both breasts squirm and rise hard. She shut her eyes.

When the hand went away, she thought it was going to her other breast. Instead, it pressed against her back.

The bed of the pickup wobbled slightly. For a moment, she thought there was an aftershock. Then she realized that the motion came from Pete scooting toward her. The rifle made scraping sounds.

Pete's hand went away again.

'I'll put this behind you,' he whispered.

Not such a hot idea, she thought. The rifle oughta stay between us . . . we oughta keep *something* between us.

It clamored against the floor behind her back.

Then Pete's arm was on her back, his hand curling around the nape of her neck, urging her closer to him.

His lips found her mouth.

Just like in the pool, she thought.

But different.

Very, very different. Because in the pool they'd had clothes on, and now they didn't, and she wasn't ready for this sort of thing, not at all, and it scared her but she wanted it. His mouth was wet, exciting. She didn't want to stop kissing him. She just wished she didn't have to be scared about the rest.

Maybe not *all that* scared, she thought, realizing that she was squirming on her side closer to him. Closer until she felt her breasts push against his chest. Closer until she felt his penis bump against her belly.

The shock of its touch pounded her breath out.

Oh, my God!

It felt slippery and smooth and enormous.

With a sudden gasp that was almost a whimper, Pete pushed himself away from her. He flopped over, rolled quickly onto his other side, and curled up.

Barbara gaped at him, stunned.

A little frightened.

What's going on?

She waited for a few moments. He seemed to be shuddering.

Oh, God, he's not crying, is he?

'Pete?' she asked. 'Are you okay?'

He didn't answer, just kept shaking and gasping for air.

'Pete?' she asked again.

'Uh?'

'What's the matter?'

'Nothing.'

She reached out and caressed the side of his arm. 'Something has to be wrong. You sure got away from me fast.' When he didn't respond, she asked, 'Was it my breath?'

He blurted out a short laugh. 'It wasn't your breath.'

'What did I do?'

'Nothing. Forget about it, okay?'

'Forget about it?'

After a moment, he said, 'It wasn't anything you did.'

'Something I *should've* done?'

'No.'

'I mean, I don't know much about this sort of stuff.'

'You and me both.'

'I just know that I like you an awful lot,' she said, gently rubbing his arm. 'A *real* lot.'

'Same here. I've never . . . liked a girl this much.'

She scooted toward him and gently curled herself against his back. She kissed the nape of his neck, which was a little sticky with her own blood. Then she reached over his side and started to caress his chest.

'I don't think we'd better get started again,' he said.

'I'm not starting anything.'

'I mean it, Barbara. It got . . . so out of control.'

'Okay.' She took her hand away from his chest, and rested it on his arm. 'It did get out of hand awfully fast, didn't it?'

'That's for sure.'

'It was great.'

'It was great, all right,' he said. 'Man.'

'But I guess it's a good thing we stopped . . . *you* stopped. I don't think I could've. I've never . . .' She patted his arm. 'Now what?'

'Why don't you go ahead and get dressed?'

'Okay.' But she didn't move. 'You aren't mad at me or anything, are you?'

'No! Are you kidding?'

'So, it's not like we won't . . . do stuff . . . again sometime.'

'No. I sure hope not.'

'Me, too.'

'Get dressed now, okay?'

'How about a kiss first?'

Pete shook his head.

'You don't want to kiss me?'

'Sure, I want to. Let's just wait till we're dressed. Just so nothing . . . happens again.'

'Okay. Sounds good to me.' She gave the side of his neck a quick nibble that made him cringe and hunch his shoulders. Then she rolled onto her back.

And smiled and filled her lungs.

She felt wonderful. Wonderful and strange. Shivery and warm, empty and full, frightened and very excited.

You'd think we'd *done* it, she thought.

Yeah, right. How would I know?

Maybe I'd *really* feel incredible if we'd done it. But who knows? It's supposed to hurt, the first time. And there'd have to be all kinds of guilt, not to mention worries about a few little matters like getting pregnant or . . .

'You don't have AIDS, do you?' she heard herself ask, and couldn't believe that she'd asked.

'No! Jeez!'

'I mean, the way you . . . just stopped everything all of a sudden like that. I mean, you really got away from me fast, like there was a big emergency, or . . .'

'There *was* a big emergency,' he muttered.

'Uh-huh.'

'But it didn't have anything to do with AIDS.'

'I'm glad of that.'

'Or any other disease.'

'Okay.'

'It wasn't anything you need to worry about.'

'Okay.'

'It was a guy thing.'

'A *guy* thing?'

'Never mind. Okay? Jeez, I don't wanta get into it. I thought you were gonna get dressed.'

'I'll get dressed,' she said. 'Excellent idea,' she added, and sat up.

She quickly twisted from side to side, looking both ways and behind her.

She saw nobody.

Then she spotted the overturned shopping cart far down the alley to her right. She looked away fast, but not quickly enough to miss a glimpse of the two shapes on the pavement near the cart.

Her stomach went squirmy.

Why did I have to look?

'Coast is clear,' she said.

'Good,' Pete said.

She crawled toward the front of the pickup's bed. At the edge of the tarp, she glanced back at Pete. He still lay curled on his side, legs together, knees drawn up. The ruddy imprint of her calf had almost faded from his buttocks.

'You can turn around if you want,' she said.

'That's okay.'

'You'd rather stare at the side of an old pickup truck than at me?'

'I just think it's better this way.'

'Okay.' On her knees, she peeled back the tarp. Her clothes were mixed together with Pete's. 'Toss you your stuff?' she asked.

'I'll get dressed when you're done,' he said. 'Thanks, though.'

'Welcome.'

She looked around to make sure nobody was in sight. Then she stood up. Staying low, shifting from foot to foot, she stepped into her panties and shorts. She sat down to finish.

'Your turn,' she announced. Leaning back, she stretched out an arm and picked up her forty-five.

'Okay,' Pete said. But he didn't move.

'You want me to leave?'

'Maybe you could, like, stand guard in the alley.'

She grinned and shook her head, uncertain whether to be amused or worried by Pete's behavior. All she knew, for sure, was that she didn't want to give him any trouble. So she slipped her purse strap over her shoulder and stood up. She walked past him, climbed over the tailgate, and hopped down.

Standing with her back to the pickup, she lifted the tail of her blouse and slid the Colt down the rear of her shorts. The muzzle shoved her panties down an inch or two. The cool steel felt good.

'I won't look, I promise,' she said. 'But I don't much wanta go out and stand in the middle of the alley, if it's all the same to you.'

'You're fine right there.'

She heard thumps and shuffling behind her back, as if Pete

were racing to reach his clothes and get into them before Barbara might change her mind and look at him.

'No big hurry,' she told him. 'Nobody's coming, and I promise not to peek.'

'Fine.'

She dug into the bottom of her purse. A lot of junk down there: crumbs and gum wrappers, an old Bic pen, several paper clips and rubber bands. She came out with two rubber bands. Holding them between her lips, she reached again into her purse. She took out a small packet of facial tissues, tore away their cellophane wrapper, and folded the tissues in half. She placed the thick square against the gash on her arm, then took the rubber bands out of her mouth and slipped them over her hand. They caught and pulled at some hairs as she rolled them up her forearm, but she got them around the makeshift bandage.

That oughta hold it, she thought.

Hearing a thump of shoes, she turned around in time to see Pete swoop down for the rifle. He came up holding it by the leather sling. His shirt was on, but hung open. It billowed behind him as he planted a foot on top of the tailgate, leaped, and dropped. He landed on his feet and took a few rushing steps past Barbara before stopping himself. As he turned to face her, he hooked the sling over his shoulder.

'Ready?' he asked. He was standing in the sunlight, squinting at her.

'Come here,' she said.

'Shouldn't we get going?'

'You owe me a kiss, remember?'

'Sure, I remember.'

'Now that we're dressed.'

'Yeah.'

'So, come and get it.'

Pete suddenly hurried back to her, out of the sunshine and into the shadow of the car port where she waited, smiling.

He slipped his arms around her. He pulled her against him, gently, and kissed her.

She eased her mouth away. 'Got something for you,' she whispered. Stepping back from him slightly, she thrust a hand down a front pocket of her shorts. 'Something,' she said, 'to help you remember about us in the pickup truck on the day of the big quake.'

'I'm not about to forget about it. Are you kidding?'

'Well, I think you should have a souvenir.' She pulled the crumpled wad of fabric out of her pocket and shook it open in front of him.

He glanced at the dangling bra, then stared at her chest. 'Oh, my God,' he muttered.

'Take it.'

'Thanks. Jeez.' He took it, and stuffed it into a front pocket of his trousers. 'You sure it's all right?'

'Huh?'

'You don't . . . you know, need it?'

'Not much. Nobody'll even know it's gone.'

'I sure know.'

'You're supposed to. You'll cherish it, right?'

He grinned.

'Just don't wear it.'

'Barbara!'

'Except on special occasions.'

He laughed.

'What've you got for me?' she asked.

'Uh . . .' He shrugged and looked helpless.

'I need a souvenir, too.'

'What would you like?'

'Oh, maybe . . .'

'Should've given her a twat-load of come when you had the chance, Pizzaman.'

Pete suddenly looked sick.

Stomach coiling tight, Barbara whirled around.

Earl came strolling out from the far side of the Jeep Wrangler that was parked beside the pickup truck. Smirking, he sniffed and rubbed his nose.

'You watched?' Barbara asked.

'Had to. Oooo, Banner. Ooooo.'

759

Nobody could've been watching! she told herself. I looked!
I looked everywhere!

You glanced around a couple of times, that's all.

It's like some kind of damn conspiracy, she thought. Lee
watched us in the pool, and now Earl . . . Is somebody *always*
spying on us?

'Where?' she muttered. 'Where were you?'

'Here, there.' Grinning, he halted a couple of paces in
front of her. 'Close enough to touch you most of the time.'

'No, you weren't.'

Pete stepped up to Barbara's side. He held the rifle low by
his hip, its muzzle toward Earl. 'Maybe you'd better get out
of here.'

'Oh, sure. What're you gonna do, shoot me? Gimme a
break. First off, you haven't got the guts to shoot anyone.
Second, that old mob would've had your asses except I saw
'em coming and warned you. Not to mention I stuck to the
alley and ran off so as not to give you away. You owe me
plenty, both of you.'

Grinning, he rubbed his chin and glanced at Barbara's chest.
She knew that she'd left the top two buttons of her blouse
undone. Without looking, she started to fasten the top one.

'Nothing you gotta hide from me, babe,' Earl said. 'I seen
it all.' He raised his hand as if to stop her from protesting.
'But you got no reason to blame me for looking. Shit, I
thought you were dead, both of you. I came circling back
around, once everything looked safe, and I figured they'd
gotten you. I mean, I took a look in back of the pickup, here,
and you're both stretched out starkers and bloody. What was
I suppose to think?'

'You took us for dead?' Pete asked.

'Sure.'

Pete bumped Barbara softly with his arm. 'Guess it
worked.'

'It worked fine,' Earl said, 'till you sorta twitched your ass,
and then Banner tells you to stop it. That was a pretty good
giveaway.'

'You were here *then*?' Barbara asked.

'Standing right there.' He pointed at the tailgate.

'How come we didn't hear you?' Pete asked.

'I was being quiet, what do you think?'

'Oh, God,' Barbara muttered. 'You saw . . . you watched everything?'

'Ooooo, yes.'

'Could you hear us, too?' she asked.

'Every word.' Shaking his head, he laughed. 'You two are a real pair.'

Barbara groaned.

'Hey, don't take it so hard! You oughta be glad it was *me* caught you at it. Could've been a lot worse. A lot. All I did was watch, know what I mean? Didn't join in. Didn't take the guns. Didn't kill you. I was a real gentleman. All I did was enjoy the show.'

'Well,' Pete said, 'the show's over. Now how about getting out of here?'

'No, I don't think so. I'm sticking with you all the way.'

'What the hell for?' Barbara blurted.

He grinned. ''Cause you're such a babe, Banner. And it's a kick to be around a couple of lovebirds like you and Pizzaboy. And you guys have all the guns.'

'Why didn't you take them when you had the chance?' Barbara asked.

'Too busy watching the fun.'

'Sure.'

'You want the honest truth, soon as I found out you two weren't dead, I figured on sticking with you. So I figured why not let you keep on carrying the things?'

'I've got news for you,' Barbara said. 'You *aren't* sticking with us.'

Grinning, Earl glanced from Barbara to Pete, and back to Barbara. 'How would you like your folks to find out all about what you guys were up to? I mean like a blow by blow description, know what I mean?'

A terrible flood of heat surged through Barbara.

'If you tell on us,' Pete said, 'we'll tell on you for shooting Heather.'

761

'Oooo, I'm scared. Big fucking deal. You tell what you wanta tell, and I'll tell what I wanta tell. No way you could stop me, unless you shoot me, and we already know you aren't about to do that.'

'Don't count on it,' Barbara said.

He laughed.

She thought she might throw up.

It was so easy to imagine Earl telling her parents every little detail of what she'd done with Pete in the back of the pickup truck. And it would sound so bad, so dirty. They wouldn't understand. They'd blame Pete, no matter how much she tried to explain that it had all been her idea. They'd figure it was Pete's fault, and they'd hate him for it.

And Pete's parents would probably figure she was some sort of slut, and hate her.

Or maybe they all got killed in the quake, so there's nobody for Earl to tell.

She felt a moment of relief at the thought, then despised herself for it.

I didn't mean it. I want everybody to be fine. Please.

'Okay,' she said. 'Let's all decide, right here and now, that we'll stick together and keep our mouths shut about everything. Is that how you want it, Earl?'

'You got it.'

'Pete?'

'Yeah. Fine. But what if he tells on us, anyway?'

'I won't,' Earl said. He grinned again. 'I might be an asshole, but I got my principles. I don't never go back on my word, no matter what.'

Pete met Barbara's eyes, and nodded.

'One more thing,' Barbara said to Earl. 'No more cracks about what just happened here. Pretend you never saw us or heard us. Erase it from your memory. This has been a real funny day, and I have a feeling that it wouldn't take much to make me go ahead and shoot you. I know you don't think I'll do it, but *I'm* not so sure.'

Earl started to grin again.

But only one corner of his mouth curled up, and it wouldn't let him look amused.

'Okay,' she said. 'Let's get moving.'

Thirty-five

Mary had blubbered and sobbed and whimpered all the way down from the top of the landslide – a trip she'd made like a terrified kid, feet first and scooting on her rump. 'Don't touch me!' she'd blurted when Clint had offered to give her a hand. 'I can't be touched! Nowhere! Nowhere! I hurt! I hurt! Everything hurts!'

Matters had improved once they'd left the landslide behind. On the paved surface of Laurel Canyon Boulevard, Mary had continued to shuffle along, trembling and wincing, but she'd cut out the worst of her crying and complaining.

Clint walked ahead of her, Em by his side. For Mary's sake, he was careful to keep his pace slow.

Very slow.

He tried not to resent it.

Mary and her damn fall.

It wasn't her fault that she'd been startled by 'Mr Gooey' (as Em had taken to calling the poor guy), but she shouldn't have gone stomping up there in a huff ahead of everyone else. Clint was sure that the fall wouldn't have happened if she'd behaved herself.

So much time wasted, because of it. Because she'd refused again and again to get off her back and start moving. Because, when she was finally ready to get up, she'd insisted on someone retrieving her shoes, so Em had gone back down the other side to find them. Then because she'd taken forever sliding down the hill on her rump. And finally because, reaching the road again, she'd been holding them back by hobbling along like an old lady.

I could be home by now, Clint thought.

Maybe not *all* the way there, but close. Except for Mary. She's such a bitch, but I've let her hold me back this way. It isn't right. Sheila or Barbara might be hurt or trapped or something, needing me. I should be there for them!

Still, he wouldn't quicken his pace.

Have to stick with her, he thought. Have to see her through this. God knows why.

I wouldn't have gotten this far without her car, he reminded himself. It gave us a good start, way back at the beginning of it all. Maybe that's why.

Or maybe it's just because she's a woman. If you're a guy, you've gotta take care of the women. It's just part of the deal, no matter what the feminists say. They're the damsels and you're the knight, whether you like it or not.

He could see, just down the road, an intersection with dead traffic lights and lanes leading off to the left.

'We're almost to Sunset,' he said.

'Is that it?' Em asked.

'That's Hollywood Boulevard. See the street sign? Sunset's just a little farther.'

'That little thing is Hollywood Boulevard?'

'Where it starts.'

'Sure doesn't *look* like Hollywood Boulevard.'

'Not much at this end. Just some apartment houses, condos. But you keep going, and you'll run into all the tourist stuff. The Chinese, the Walk of Fame . . .'

'So, how far are we from your house?'

He grimaced. 'Not far. From here, if we walked at a pretty good clip, we could be there in an hour.'

'Hey, that isn't bad!'

'The rate we're going, it'll be more like two or three.'

She gave Clint her nose-wrinkled look as if something smelled vile. Then she glanced over her shoulder.

'What's your problem?' Mary muttered.

Em shrugged and shook her head and returned her gaze to Clint. 'Wanta ditch her?'

'It's crossed my mind. Can't do it, though.'

'Yeah, I know. She might end up *Ms* Gooey.'

'That's right.'

'Course, you could put Caspar and Loreen in charge of her.'

Clint let out a laugh. 'That'd be a sweet thing to do.'

'Serve her right.'

'A lot of stuff might serve her right,' Clint said. 'But she's already paid a pretty high price. I wouldn't want anything else happening to her.'

Em squeezed his hand. 'You're such a *gentleman*. My mom would absolutely despise you.'

'No, she wouldn't.'

'You're right. But she'd *let on* that she did.' The mischief suddenly fled from Em's face. 'I sure hope nothing's happened to her.'

'She's probably fine,' Clint said. 'Everyone's probably fine.'

'Mr Gooey didn't end up so fine.'

'But he's just one person out of . . . what, twelve million? The odds are in our favor. Your mother, my wife and kid . . . They're probably all just fine.'

'Yeah. I guess so.'

'We'll be fine, too.'

'Except maybe for Mary,' she added, and a glint returned to her eyes. 'Who may or may not be dead meat, depending on whether you're a believer, or . . . '

'Loreen doesn't know beans.'

'If Mary *is* going to meet a bad end, I wish it'd happen soon so we can stop all this dawdling.'

Clint scowled down at Em.

She laughed and bumped her shoulder against his side.

'Such a scamp,' Clint said.

'I'm glad *somebody's* enjoying themselves,' Mary called from behind them.

Em let go of Clint's hand and turned around. Walking backward, she said, 'How're you doing?'

'Horrible.'

'Is there anything I can do for you?'

'Yeah, turn around and leave me alone.'

'Well, that's a sweet thing to say.'

'How much longer is this going to take, Clint?'

He looked over his shoulder at her. 'We're almost to Sunset.'

'Oh. Just great. Loreen'll be happy about that.'

Clint saw Loreen and Caspar walking side by side, probably fifty feet behind Mary. They were facing each other, gesturing and moving their mouths.

'Nothing is going to happen at Sunset,' Clint said.

'If you don't count me getting killed.'

'Including that.'

'Like, you're gonna save me.'

'Like, nothing's gonna happen. Stop worrying about it, okay?'

'You'd be worried, too, if some fucking gypsy bitch said you were gonna die at Sunset.'

'Nobody's gonna die at Sunset,' Clint said.

'We'll see about that.'

A few minutes later, Sunset Boulevard came into view. Em tightened her grip on Clint's hand, and halted.

'Let's keep going,' Clint said, trying to keep his voice steady.

Em shook her head. She made a high-pitched humming sound, not quite a moan, not quite a whine.

'It's all right,' he said. But he knew it *wasn't* all right. Not at all. He knew why Em wanted nothing to do with the intersection ahead, and why she was making such a frightened noise. He had a quick urge, himself, to squeal, 'Let's get outa here!' and whirl around and run away.

It was the first major thoroughfare they'd encountered since Ventura Boulevard on the other side of the hills.

Like Ventura, every lane was jammed with traffic.

But the other boulevard had been alive.

Not Sunset.

Here, the vehicles didn't try to inch forward. None moved. Some had been turned onto their sides, others upside-down. Many were smoky, smoldering husks.

766

No horns honked.

There was nobody to honk them.

Most of the cars and trucks and vans looked abandoned, as if their drivers and passengers had thrown open the doors and run for their lives.

Many hadn't made it.

There were bodies. Fifteen or twenty of them, at least, that Clint saw from where he stood looking down on the scene. Several bodies were slumped across car hoods. Most of the others were sprawled on the pavement, just this side of the traffic, as if they'd been slaughtered while trying to flee toward Laurel Canyon.

Mr Gooey must be the one that got away, Clint thought.

But he didn't exactly get away, did he? They took what they wanted from him, and let the poor guy go.

Who the hell could've done all this? Clint wondered.

He saw nobody down there roaming among the cars. Nobody at all who didn't look dead.

Mary staggered to a halt by his side. She didn't say anything. She stared straight forward and trembled.

Soon, Caspar and Loreen arrived.

Everyone stared at Sunset Boulevard.

After a while, Loreen muttered, 'Blood on the face of the day. So much blood. I saw . . .'

'Stop it,' Clint said.

'There's a police car,' Em said, pointing.

Clint nodded. Like the patrol car at the other end of Laurel Canyon, this one had been parked broadside – stationed there to prevent vehicles from turning off Sunset onto the closed boulevard.

Clint remembered the two cops at the other end.

A young man and woman. They'd been friendly and helpful. He hoped they were still all right.

These cops were probably not all right.

Probably among the dead.

None of the bodies scattered on the street near the patrol car wore uniforms.

None wore much of anything.

At this distance, the figures seemed to be made of bare skin and blood. Clint could see that some, at least, had been scalped. Several had been dismembered to one extent or another.

'Shoot 'em full of arrows,' he muttered, 'and it'd look like an Indian massacre.'

'We can't go down there,' Mary said.

'I have to,' Clint said.

'Not me.'

Em squeezed Clint's hand. 'I go where you go.'

'Whatever happened,' Clint said, 'it looks like it's over. Whoever did this might be long gone, by now.'

'They're waiting for us,' Loreen said.

Clint scowled. 'Don't say it if you don't mean it.'

'Don't say it, anyway,' Mary told her.

Loreen shrugged her thick shoulders. 'I only tell what I see.'

'Well,' Clint said, 'please don't. Unless you literally *spotted* someone down there. Did you actually *see* someone?'

'With the eye of my mind.'

'Then we don't want to hear about it,' Clint told her.

'When Loreen sees something "with the eye of her mind,"' Caspar said, 'it's usually there. We'd better turn back.'

'No!' Loreen blurted. 'We cannot turn back. Going back is far worse than going forward. This, I know.'

'Terrific,' Mary said. 'We can't go forward, we can't go back, where the fuck are we *supposed* to go? Not that it matters a hell of a lot, far as *I'm* concerned, seeing as how I've been pronounced dead already by this fat tub of . . .' She cut off her words and eyed Caspar. 'This delightful psychic,' she added, then gave Loreen a grin that looked more like a snarl.

'I only tell what . . .'

'Knock it off!' Clint snapped at Loreen. To Mary, he said, 'I know you're scared. We're all scared. I don't wanta go down there any more than you do. But my home is on the other side of Sunset, so I'm going across.'

He reached into a front pocket of his pants and pulled out the paring knife he'd taken from Em's kitchen. 'Time for these,' he told Em. As he drew the blade from its cardboard sheath, the girl lifted the hanging front of her T-shirt and removed two butcher knives from the pockets of her shorts.

'Give me one,' Caspar said.

She shook her head. 'I don't think so.'

'You don't need the both of them.'

'One's for Mary. If she wants it.'

'That makes no sense,' Caspar protested.

'I hate to say this, Mr Blotski, but I'm not sure you're someone I'd trust very much with sharp objects, if you know what I mean.'

'Me?' Eyebrows leaping up in shock, he pounded an open hand against his chest. Shiny waves of red silk rippled the front of his blouse. 'Me?' he blurted again. 'You don't trust *me*?'

'You've made some threats,' Clint explained.

'Besides which,' Em said, 'Mary was with us first. And she's the one Loreen says is in the most trouble around here, so she oughta have something she can use for defending herself just in case things get hairy.' She held one of the knives out toward Mary. 'You can have it if you want it,' she said.

Mary looked from the knife handle to Em's face. 'Thank you,' she murmured. 'You . . . You really . . . want me to have it? After everything . . .'

'Sure.'

Mary's chin trembled. Tears spilled from her eyes and dribbled down her cheeks. 'Thank you.' She took the knife. 'You're so nice to me. I don't deserve . . .'

'You *don't* deserve!' Caspar assured her. Pounding his chest again, he gaped at Clint. 'I am a *man*. I should get a knife!'

'Go find one,' Clint told him.

'This is outrageous! This girl, this *child*, she has no right to decide who gets what! Are you mad?'

'They're her knives,' Clint pointed out, 'so knock it off.'

'Fool!'

'Settle yourself down, Caspar,' Loreen said, and placed a hand on his shoulder. 'Look at you. And you wonder why little Em doesn't want to give you a weapon?'

'She's a child. She knows nothing.'

'Child,' Clint said, 'rip the tape off your blade. You too, Mary. Then try to keep your knives out of sight when we go in. With any luck, you won't need to use them. If you do get attacked, though, don't let your assailant see your knife. Let him *feel* it before he sees it. Shove the blade in as hard as you can, then twist it, rip with it. Do as much damage as you can, as fast as you can.'

Mary nodded and sniffled.

'Where'd be the best place to stab somebody?' Em asked.

'Wherever you can get to. Just get that knife into him as fast and hard as you can. And don't worry . . . either of you. I'll be there to help.'

'What a *mensch*,' said Caspar.

Clint faced him. 'We'll all help each other. There're five of us. We oughta be able to take care of trouble.'

'I go first,' Loreen said.

'What?' Caspar blurted.

'You heard me, Papa. The madness cannot touch me. My aura will act as my shield. Those who would do us harm will be struck numb with awe. Thus will I settle the turbulence and make the passage safe for you who follow.'

Em wrinkled her nose, glanced at Clint and rolled her eyes.

Mary made a snorting sound.

Caspar said, 'I forbid it.'

'No harm will come to me,' Loreen told him, smiling with gentle confidence.

Maybe she knows something I don't, Clint thought. Or maybe she's just nuts.

'No,' Caspar said. 'Let *them* go first, the Three Stooges. We'll wait and see what happens to them. If they get to the other side without . . .'

'My way is best,' Loreen said.

She took a step, and Caspar blocked her way. They both

stood motionless. Caspar glared into her eyes, but slowly his fierceness faded and vanished. He moved out of her way, then turned and watched her walk past him. When he started to follow her, she raised her hand. He halted.

She kept on walking, her peasant skirt swishing from side to side with the sweep of her broad rump.

'Loreen!' Caspar called.

Without looking back, she waved him forward.

Caspar hurried after her. He gained on her for a few moments, then slowed his pace. He stayed about twenty feet behind her as they made their way toward Sunset.

'Let's do some catching up,' Clint said. Holding the knife inside his right pocket, he gestured Mary forward with his other hand.

She started to hobble.

With her left hand at her chest, she held her torn blouse shut. She carried the knife in plain sight by her right hip, blade to the rear.

'Better hide the knife,' Clint reminded her.

Without argument, she swept it upward. The knife and the hand that held it disappeared inside the front of her blouse.

'Move it along, now,' Clint said. 'Come on, you can do better than that. Pick it up, pick it up.'

Mary quickened her pace.

'Em, you go now.'

Em hurried past him.

Her right arm, bent at the elbow, hitched up the back of her T-shirt so high that a swath of bare skin showed above the top of her shorts.

Clint felt a sudden ache, glimpsing the skin. Not arousal, exactly. Partly that, but more a strange mix of desire and envy and loss. And a great, awful tenderness.

Can't let anything happen to her. Can't. No matter what. She's what's best in the world, girls like her and girls like Barbara. Have to take good care of her.

He had a thickness in his throat, but he smiled about the back of Em's Roadkill T-shirt.

The cloth was so thin and clingy that it took on the shape

of her forearm, her fist, and the broad tapering blade that stood upright over her spine. The point of the knife was midway between her shoulder blades.

The knife's almost bigger than she is, he thought.

Such a toughie.

And damn it, she shouldn't have to be going around in this world with a knife in her shirt like some sort of pint-sized Saint Joan.

Thirty-six

'What're you doing?' Sheila asked.

'Nothing,' Stanley told her. He had exhausted himself earlier by hoisting the remains of Crash out of the tub. Breathless, drenched in sweat, heart slamming, he had sat down in his favorite place beyond the foot of the tub. It had only taken him a few minutes to recover. But he'd stayed where he was, sometimes mopping himself with the towel while he stared at Sheila.

'Are you just going to sit there?' she asked.

'I guess so. It's a nice view. And this way you can't get your hands on me.'

'Sure,' she muttered.

'You look like you're sweating blood. All shiny red, and dripping. Do you want to rub it off?' He raised his towel.

'Please.' She lifted a hand to catch the toss.

But Stanley laughed and draped the towel over his shoulders. 'Nah. You look beautiful just the way you are. You look like a wild woman. A gorgeous, naked, wild woman.'

'You wanta do more than look, Stan. You know it and I know it.'

He grinned. 'But what are we going to *do* about it?' he asked.

'*You* have to finish sawing through this beam.'

'Uh-huh.' He bobbed his head. 'But what happens to me when you're no longer pinned down? There's the rub, so to speak. The sad fact is, you're not only gorgeous but extremely powerful. Muscles, muscles, everywhere. If I set you free, you might try to take me apart.'

She stared up at him. Her face was bloody. In the shade of the beam above it, the whites of her eyes had a pale blue tint.

'Maybe we can make a deal,' she said.

'What sort of a deal?'

'You help me get out of here, and . . . I won't do anything to you. I won't try to hurt you.'

'Will you let me fuck you?'

She pressed her lips into a tight, straight line, and nodded. 'Yeah,' she said. 'Okay. If that's what it takes to get out of here.'

'No fighting? I get full cooperation?'

'Yes.'

'Promise?'

'I promise.'

'Liar, liar, pants on fire! Woops! *What* pants?'

'I'm not lying, Stan. Quit the games. Just let me out of here. I'll do anything you want.'

'Why is it that I don't believe you?'

'Believe me.'

'Maybe if you hadn't grabbed my ankles when all I wanted to do was play a little footsies with your tits . . . '

'I'm sorry. That was a mistake.'

'A big big big mistake.'

'What do you want me to do?'

'There might be something.'

'What? Name it.'

'Because, the thing is, I've got half an inclination to just leave you down there, call it a loss, and wait around to see who else shows up. Maybe your husband, for instance. You've seen how easily I kill people. But do you know who I think is bound to show up sooner or later? Barbara. Wherever she is, I'll bet she's on her way home right now. I've seen her in her bikini. She's got a sweet, young body. Is she a virgin? I'll bet she is. I'll bet she has a . . .'

'You don't want her,' Sheila said. Her dry, husky voice sounded fairly calm, but Stanley heard a tremor in it. 'I'm the one you want. She'd be a lousy substitute, and you know it.'

'But she hasn't got your muscles. If she fights me . . .'

'*I* won't fight you. I'll do anything you say.'

'Will you? We'll see about that.'

'You'll see.'

'At the first sign of resistance, it's over. You're history, and I nail Barbara.'

'I won't resist.'

'And you'll do exactly what I tell you to do.'

'Exactly.'

'Very good. We'll see how it goes.'

With that, Stanley got to his feet. He made his way alongside the hole in the floor and crouched over Eagle's pale, hairless body.

The barbed wire was wound four times around Eagle's waist, its ends twisted together in front.

Why on earth anyone would wear a barbed wire belt . . .

Maybe so he'll have some handy, Stanley thought, for occasions like this.

Or maybe it's just a fashion statement.

After untwisting the ends of the wire, Stanley used Eagle's straight razor to slash the belt loops. Then he nudged the ring of wire higher, past the top of the leather pants, so the four loops encircled Eagle's bare waist.

Holding one end, he stood up and stepped to the other side of the body. Then he pulled hard.

By the time all four loops had unwound, Eagle looked as if he wore a frayed, red ribbon around his waist.

Stanley coiled the wire. It was slippery. There were bits of skin on some of its sharp little points.

He stepped over the body and placed the wire on the floor near his saw, scissors and straight razor. Then he climbed down onto the edges of the tub. When he leaned over the middle beam, his leg and back muscles began to tremble.

'Boy,' he said, 'am I ever gonna be sore tomorrow.'

Sheila didn't open her mouth.

'Okay, now let's see if you're as good as your word.'

'I am.'

'Give me your hands.'

She raised her arms from her sides and stretched them toward him.

'Put them together.'

She did, and Stanley watched the way her breasts got squeezed between her upper arms.

'Very nice,' he said. 'Keep them that way.'

He reached out and grabbed the coil of barbed wire. When Sheila saw it, her eyes opened wider. But she said nothing, and held her arms up toward him, hands together.

He began to bind her wrists, winding the wire around them, drawing it between them, bending it, twisting it, pulling it tight. Sheila twitched a few times when barbs dug in, but she never protested or struggled.

Finally, her hands seemed securely bound together and Stanley had his 'lead' – five or six feet of leftover wire that extended from between her wrists.

'So far, so good,' he said.

'You didn't have to do this,' Sheila told him.

'Sure, I did. You may now put your hands down, but be careful where you put them. You don't wanta poke yourself.'

He paid out the lead and watched her. Wrists bound so tightly together with the barbed wire, she had trouble finding a new position for her arms. Finally, she swung them up and rested them against the edge of the overhead beam. Face between the undersides of her arms, she looked as if she were about to perform a high dive.

Sans diving board.

Sans swimsuit.

Sans pool.

Stanley moaned with delight, then set aside his end of the wire and anchored it down with a chunk of plaster.

He picked up the saw. Its blade was smeared with Crash's

blood. He shook it. The wide blade shimmied and made whangy sounds.

'Shake for me, Sheila,' he said. 'Shake like the saw.' She pressed her lips together. Keeping her arms up, she shook her body from side to side.

'Harder!' He shook the saw harder. 'Hard as you can!'

She shook so hard that sparkles of bloody sweat skittered over her skin. Her breasts flung off a crimson spray.

'Oooo, beautiful. Beautiful. But that's enough.' He quit shaking the saw.

The rough shudders of Sheila's body ceased. Stanley watched how her breasts continued to sway. Then the only movement came from her hard breathing.

Stanley twisted himself awkwardly to the left and fit the saw blade into the cut of the beam. He worked it into the slit until it would go no deeper, then began to pump the saw back and forth. Wood dust began dribbling down into the narrow space between the wall of the tub and Sheila's right thigh.

He remembered how she had talked him out of making the cut in the middle.

Seemed like years ago.

Who's giving the orders now?

He glanced at the old cut. Shallow. Awfully shallow. She had stopped him before he'd made much progress at all.

I could go back to it, anyway, he thought. Just to show her. *Screw that. I'm almost done.*

But he was winded again, wheezing for breath, sweat spilling down his body. Every muscle in his neck and shoulders and arms, in his back, in his buttocks and legs seemed to be jumping and twitching out of control.

He stopped sawing, climbed down backward into the tub, and stretched. With the towel, he mopped his hair and face. He plucked the clinging seat of his pajama pants away from his rump, but it stuck again the moment he let go.

'Almost done,' he gasped. 'Hot work.'

'I'll bet.'

'But don't worry . . . I'll have you . . . outa there.'

'Looking forward to it,' Sheila muttered.

'Sure you are.' He wiped his face again. 'Tell you something . . . *I* am. Looking forward to it. You've got no idea . . . I've been watching you . . . Never thought I'd . . . get a chance at you, but . . . thanks to the quake . . . my lucky day. Thank God for earthquakes.'

Sheila's right foot suddenly jerked. Her knee shot upward and her thigh slammed the underside of the beam. Stanley flinched at the quick blast of exploding wood. The saw jumped from its slit. As it lifted into the air, the slit spread wide at the top. Sheila's thigh came punching up through the bottom. A spike of splintered wood leaped after the saw.

'No!' Stanley yelled.

Her blow knocked the beam on end. It stood upright between her legs like a two-foot post.

Stanley looked around, trying to spot the saw.

It didn't seem to be in the tub.

With the fists of her wired hands, Sheila rammed the post near its top. It scooted toward Stanley and tumbled. As it fell toward him, he hopped backward. It thudded against the bottom of the tub, skidded and pounded the toes of his left foot through the soft leather of his moccasin.

Yelping in pain, he saw Sheila shove at the overhead beam. She slid forward. The moment her head was clear of the wood, she sat up.

But she can't *stand* up, Stanley told himself.

She drew her legs in, crossing them, leaning forward.

The hell she can't, Stanley thought. Damn it, she'll get up even if she *can't* use her hands.

He thought about leaping onto her.

That might be just what she wants.

Can't tangle with her, she'll destroy me.

She was suddenly on her knees.

Stanley squatted and grabbed the sawed-off chuck of four-by-eight at each end. He stood up with it. As he raised it overhead, he saw that Sheila already had her feet on the bottom of the tub. She was still crouched, but rising.

She had her eyes on him.

She looked fierce – but wary.

'This'll bust ya!' Stanley yelled.

She froze.

'It'll bust ya good! Don't make me do it!'

'Don't,' Sheila gasped. She shook her head. 'Put it down. Just put it down.'

'I'll bust ya with it!'

'You've got me, Stan. Okay? I'm not going anywhere. You don't have to use that.'

'I'll cave in your head!'

'No. Please.'

'On your knees,' he said.

She sank to her knees and stared up at him.

He hurled the heavy stump of beam.

It crashed into the debris on the floor beyond the far end of the tub.

'Thank you,' Sheila said.

'You're welcome,' said Stanley.

Then he crashed his knee into her forehead. Her head jerked backward. She flopped away from him. The other beam caught her across the back, just below her shoulders. It stopped her with a massive jolt. As she started to slump, Stanley crouched in front of her.

The leftover length of barbed wire dangled from between her hands. He picked it up.

He pulled.

Raising Sheila's arms from where they hung in front of her body.

Tugging them toward him.

She opened her eyes and gave him a lazy look. She hardly seemed aware of what was happening.

He continued to pull.

She toppled forward.

He pulled hard enough to straighten her arms so that she wouldn't be able to break the fall with her elbows. Her torso made a nice moist slapping sound when it landed on the bottom of the tub.

'Are you gonna give me any more trouble?' he asked.

She groaned.

'Is that a yes or a no?'

She didn't answer.

'Who are we kidding?' Stanley asked.

She squirmed a little.

'You'll keep on giving me trouble as long as you've got a breath left in you.'

The sound that came from Sheila was more like a rough growl than a voice. But Stanley was pretty sure of what it said: 'That's right.'

He forced himself to laugh, but he felt an odd little shiver race up his spine and tingle his scalp.

Thirty-seven

Clint didn't see Loreen go down.

She'd entered the jam of abandoned vehicles on Sunset with her arms outspread as if ready to embrace all comers. Caspar had followed her in, but stayed well behind her, apparently realizing that his presence might disrupt Loreen's protective aura.

Caspar must've had his eyes on her.

Clint had been sidestepping through a narrow space between two cars, facing a Mazda where the body of a man was sprawled across the hood. The man's throat had been slashed. Not only was he naked and scalped like most of the other bodies, but someone had spray-painted his genitals black.

Em, moments ago, had turned her head away fast after a glimpse of the man.

Clint was wondering if he should say something to her. But what *could* he say? *It's all right?* It's *not* all right, not even close. Some sort of madness happened here, he thought, and we're walking through what's left of it, and maybe it isn't over yet.

This sort of stuff doesn't happen.

Not even in L.A.

It's like some kind of . . .

'Loreen!' Caspar suddenly cried out.

Clint saw him, two lanes ahead, scurrying sideways between a couple of cars, struggling to get through like a man trapped among theater seats and desperate to reach an aisle.

'Answer me, Loreen!'

'What happened?' Mary called, herself in an open area just ahead of Em.

'I don't know!' Caspar shouted. 'Loreen!' He looked back. 'She just went *down*. Maybe fell?'

'Where?' Clint asked.

Caspar pointed, the red silk sleeve of his blouse fluttering in the hot breeze. 'Behind that van.'

The gray van was in the next lane over, and about fifty feet to the left of where Caspar stood.

Though Clint hadn't been paying much attention to Loreen, he supposed she must've gone that way in search of a good passage. Since starting across Sunset, she'd done a lot of meandering to avoid areas where burnt cars still smoldered, or where there was little or no space because of vehicles that were bumper to bumper. They had all followed her lead.

What the hell happened to her?

It's my fault, Clint told himself. I should've led the way.

None of this hunting for good places to cross; except for avoiding a few smoky wrecks, he would have taken them straight to the other side of Sunset, simply climbing over hoods or trunks when there were no spaces between vehicles.

Should've done it, Clint thought. Might've been a little rough on Mary and the Blotskis, but we'd be finished with all this by now and nobody'd be missing.

'Loreen!' Caspar called again. Staggering clear of his narrow pathway between the cars, he ran toward the van.

'Wait for us!' Clint shouted.

Caspar paid no attention.

Mary, ahead of Em, had stopped between the lanes and seemed to be watching Caspar's dash for the van.

'Mary!' Clint said. 'Stay put.'

As if sensing the need for quickness, Em leaped out of his way. He stumbled free of the bumpers and caught a glimpse of Caspar's head beyond the next two lanes. 'Follow me,' he gasped at Em and Mary. As he started to give chase, he shouted, 'Caspar! Wait for us!'

Caspar didn't even slow down.

Clint poured on more speed. But didn't get far before Mary called, 'I can't . . .!'

He glanced back. Em was only a stride behind him, arms pumping, the big butcher knife jerking up and down in her right hand.

Mary wasn't keeping up.

No wonder, Clint thought.

Like Em, Mary ran with her knife out. Her other hand was busy clutching the front of her blouse shut. The sodden blouse clung to her. It was torn, soiled with dirt, streaked and stained and blotched with blood from the injuries that it covered. Her torn skirt showed legs that were dirty and scratched and bloody.

Mary's red face was swollen, scratched, dripping sweat, twisted with pain.

She's a wreck, and I'm making her run like this. She oughta be in a hospital bed.

Clint stopped running.

He turned forward again and looked for Caspar.

Couldn't spot him.

But cars and pickups were in the way. Maybe the old man had simply crouched or bent down.

'Caspar!'

No answer came.

Clint called out again.

'They got him, too?' Em whispered.

'I don't know,' Clint said. 'Just be ready for anything. You, too, Mary.'

Mary sleeved sweat out of her eyes, and nodded.

Clint took the knife from his pocket. He started moving again, but slowly. Every few steps, he glanced back to make sure that Em and Mary were staying close behind him.

All around them, nothing seemed to move.

It's like sneaking through a graveyard, Clint thought. A hot, smoky graveyard. Where mad killers might be lurking, waiting to pounce.

Someone *must* have pounced on Loreen and Caspar. What else could've made them disappear?

Clint tried to think of a good explanation that didn't involve murder.

He had no luck.

And we're heading straight for where it happened.

Maybe this isn't such a good idea, he thought.

It's the only way we'll ever know. Besides, what if they aren't dead? Maybe they need help. We can't just run off and forget about them.

Deciding to approach the van from a different direction than Loreen and Caspar, Clint stayed two lanes away and walked on past its front. Then he climbed onto the hood of a Mustang. He got to his feet and looked for the Blotskis.

No sign of them.

He couldn't see much, though; a large pickup truck blocked most of the van from his view.

Nor could he see down close to the street.

The Mustang wobbled slightly under him. Turning, he watched Em climb onto its hood. He took hold of her arm and helped her up.

Mary came next.

The three stood together atop the Mustang's hood and surveyed the area.

'Caspar?' Clint called again.

'How could they just vanish like this?' Em asked, speaking softly as if afraid there might be strangers trying to listen. 'They never even yelled or anything, you know?'

'It must've been awfully sudden,' Clint said.

'Could they be playing a trick on us?' Mary asked.

'Why would they do a thing like that?'

'They hate me, for one thing.'

'I doubt if it's a trick,' Clint said.

'What *do* you think?'

'Somebody got 'em.'

'Oh, God.'

'Whoever got all these others . . .'

'It was by the van over there?' Em asked, pointing with her knife at the bit of van that showed beyond the pickup.

'Apparently,' Clint said.

'So that's where the killer is . . . or where he was up till a couple of minutes ago, anyway.'

Clint nodded. 'But probably more than one.'

'They're probably watching us right now,' Mary muttered. 'Or coming.'

'Maybe we oughta hide our knives,' Em whispered.

Clint almost smiled. 'Don't worry. When they show up, they'll be on us so fast . . . just keep your knives ready.'

'Aye-aye, sir.'

'Where the hell are the cops when you need them?' Mary asked.

Clint shook his head. Why bother trying to answer? The pair of officers who belonged to the patrol car were either gone or dead. All the other cops were probably scattered over Los Angeles. Many, he supposed, must be fighting to regain some order. Some were certainly dead.

'Where the hell is *anybody*?' Mary added.

'Who knows,' Clint said.

Em smiled. 'There's still us.'

'Not for long,' Mary said. '*I'm* supposed to get killed, remember?'

'You know what I think?' Em asked. 'I think Loreen wasn't much of a fortune-teller, after all. You know? I mean, the way things are starting to look, she's the one who bit it. And Caspar . . .'

'Let's go,' Clint said. He stepped to the edge of the Mustang's hood, glanced both ways, saw nobody, and jumped. Keeping watch, he waited for Em and Mary. Em leaped and landed on her feet with a springy bounce. Mary sat down, then lowered herself to the street like a timid child easing into a swimming pool.

'This way,' Clint whispered.

Unwilling to turn his back on them – afraid that Em or Mary might suddenly vanish like the Blotskis – Clint sidestepped alongside the pickup truck toward its rear. He glanced all around, but never let his vision stray from his companions for more than a few seconds at a time.

They looked scared, but alert, as if they expected an attack but had no idea where it might come from.

The bed of the pickup truck was empty.

Clint thought about climbing in. The bed would make a good observation platform; from the far side of it, they'd be able to look directly at the place behind the van where Loreen and Caspar had apparently gone down. But this was a bruiser of a pickup with big wheels, an elevated chassis, and high side panels. There would be no easy way to climb in. It'd be a major struggle, especially for Mary.

'We going up?' Em asked.

Clint shook his head. 'Too high.'

'It isn't so high.' She stood on tiptoes to peer over the panel. 'I bet we'd have a great view.'

'Let's just go around.'

'I could hop up there for a second, just to see.'

Her suggestion gave Clint a sick feeling. It was a way he had felt watching Barbara, on their vacation in the mountains last summer, when she'd wandered too close to the edge of a cliff.

'No,' he said. 'You're not going up there by yourself. Not a chance. We stick together. And we watch out for each other. Nobody goes anywhere alone.'

Nodding, Em shrugged with one shoulder.

Clint sidestepped the rest of the way to the rear of the pickup. The Porsche behind it had left a good, wide space that led like a corridor to the driver's door of a Mercedes that was stopped behind the van.

He saw no one.

'Stay close,' he whispered, and started through the gap.

'Wait,' Em whispered. She tugged the back of his shirt. 'Just a second.' She stepped around him, dropped to her hands and knees, then bent her elbows and lowered her head to the pavement. She peered underneath the pickup truck.

A kid on her knees, butt in the air, checking under her bed for boogeymen.

Clint dearly hoped she wouldn't find any.

He watched her head swivel very slowly, stopping sometimes, then continuing to turn. Soon, she was gazing straight forward at the area under the Mercedes. After a pause, her head resumed its slow movement to the right.

Things must be okay, Clint told himself. She wouldn't still be down there looking around if she'd spotted anything terrible.

At last, she was gazing past her right shoulder at the space beneath the Porsche.

'Anything?' Clint whispered.

Em slowly pushed herself up. When she turned around, Clint felt his stomach sink.

Mary moved in beside him and clutched his arm.

They both stared at Em.

'They're under there,' Em whispered.

'Oh, no,' Mary murmured.

Em's lips twitched as if she were making a Bogart face.

'What do you mean?' Clint asked very quickly, very quietly. 'Who's down there? Where? Loreen? Caspar?'

'Not them. I'm pretty sure. People, though, and they're underneath . . .'

'Dead people?' Clint asked.

'I don't think so.'

Mary groaned.

'How many?'

Em raised and dropped her shoulders. 'Nobody under these,' she said, nodding to either side at the pickup truck and the Porsche. 'Nobody under that, either.' She pointed her knife at the Mercedes in front of them. 'But there's like, I think, maybe *four* people under the van. Maybe more. There were tires in the way. I couldn't really tell . . .'

'Did they see you?' Clint asked.

'Maybe. I only saw a couple of actual faces. And it's dark under there. I couldn't tell what they were looking at. Maybe their eyes weren't even open, for all I know.'

'What makes you think they were alive?'

'Some of 'em were moving.'

'Oh, God,' Mary muttered.

'Coming out?' Clint asked.

Em shook her head. 'Just, you know . . . fidgeting, squirming, like that.'

Mary gave Clint's arm a quick tug. 'Maybe they're just hiding! They might be scared, and . . .'

'Then what happened to Loreen and Caspar?'

'I don't know, but . . .'

'These people got 'em,' Em said. 'I'd bet anything. Killed 'em, maybe threw their bodies in the van, or something. This bunch isn't just hiding, I can tell you that. I saw what they look like.'

'You said you *couldn't* see them very well,' Mary pointed out.

'I saw enough.' Em lifted her gaze to Clint and stared into his eyes. 'What're we gonna do?'

Before he could answer, Mary tightened her grip and said, 'We've gotta get out of here.'

'No,' he said. 'We have to get *through* here.'

'They're just waiting for us,' Em said. She looked as if she were trying hard not to cry.

'They won't get us.'

'But I don't think they're the only ones,' she told him.

'What do you mean?'

'It doesn't make any sense, you know? That Loreen just happened to go straight to the only place where a bunch was waiting to grab people. I think maybe . . . they might be all around us. And we've just been lucky so far?'

Mary made a quiet groan.

'It's possible,' Clint muttered.

What the hell isn't? he thought.

All this at Sunset Boulevard seemed like madness. One person, alone, couldn't have committed such slaughter and mutilation; Em had supposedly seen at least four people lying in wait for them. If that many had reverted to savagery, why not twenty? Why not a hundred?

Or a thousand.

A thousand wild savages, banded into tribes.

Lurking everywhere.

Don't even think about something like that, Clint told himself. There can't be that many.

Can't be that many people so messed up that they'll let a little thing like an earthquake – not even a major quake – knock apart every civilized restraint and turn them into barbarians.

Not even in Los Angeles, he thought.

And a voice in his mind said, *Oh, yeah?*

'What'll we do?' Em asked.

Clint faced Mary. 'Are you with us?' he asked.

'Have I got any choice?'

'You could go back.'

'By myself?'

'I have to go on ahead,' Clint said. 'You know that. I have to get home.'

'Even if it kills you?'

'It won't.'

Mary smirked. 'Famous last words.' She frowned at Em. 'What about you?'

'I'm sticking with Clint. No matter what.'

'He's already married, you know.'

'It's pretty amazing to me,' Em said, 'that you can find it in yourself at a time like this to still be such a snot.'

'Both of you stop it,' Clint said. 'Are you with us, Mary, or not? That's all I wanta know.'

'I'm supposed to go off by myself . . .?'

'It's up to you. If you go back, you go back alone.'

'Or plug on ahead with you on your big odyssey home and get myself killed. Some choice.'

'It's your choice,' Clint said. 'Now, make it.'

'I'm staying with you.'

'Okay.'

'So, now what?'

'I'm not sure yet.'

'Terrific.'

Em dropped again to her hands and knees, lowered her head and scanned the area underneath the nearby vehicles. A moment later, she sprang up. 'Still there,' she said.

Mary sneered at her. 'What did you think, they'd go away?'

'I was afraid they might be sneaking closer.'

'They're staying put?' Clint asked.

'So far.'

'Just waiting for us to walk by.'

'And then they grab our feet?' Em asked.

'Something like that, I guess.'

'Let's just make a big detour around them,' Mary said.

Clint shook his head.

'*Why not?*'

'A lot of reasons.'

'Name one.'

'We know where these are.'

'So?'

'That makes 'em easier to deal with. I don't wanta waste time making a detour just so we can get jumped somewhere else. Come on.'

They backtracked out of the space, and Clint led them alongside the pickup truck. When he came to the driver's door, he stopped and faced them. 'Okay,' he whispered. 'We need a plan. Any ideas?'

Em raised her eyebrows. 'They're hiding underneath vans and cars and stuff, right? So they can grab us when we go by? It's kind of like this movie I saw, only there was this giant monster worm-thing that came up out of the ground to get you. So what Kevin Bacon did – he and the others – they like got away from it by *pole*vaulting from boulder to boulder. That way, they stayed off the ground and the thing couldn't get them. *Tremors*, that was the movie.'

Mary said, 'Do you see any *poles* around here?'

'No, but . . .'

'Yes!' Clint blurted. 'That's it! Em, you're brilliant!'

'It was just a movie I saw.'

Scowling, Mary muttered, 'Who knows how to polevault, anyway? Even if we *had* poles, which we don't.'

'We don't need poles,' Clint said. 'Everything's parked so close together, we oughta be able to make it across just by jumping – never have to touch the street at all. We stay high, move fast, and . . .'

'Wait, wait,' Mary said. '*Jump?* You mean like from car to car? From their *roofs*?'

'Roofs, hoods, trunks.'

'I can't do that.'

'Sure you can,' Em said.

'No. No way.'

'It'll be easy.'

'We're wasting time,' Clint said. 'Come, or don't.' He pushed his knife back into its makeshift sheath in the right front pocket of his pants. Then he turned around and climbed onto the hood of the pickup truck. On his feet, he approached the other side. The space between the lanes looked clear. So far, nobody was coming out from under the van or any of the nearby cars.

He waited for Em and Mary to join him on the pickup's hood. Then he stepped up onto the roof of the cab. It seemed to be about the same height as the top of the van.

The two vehicles were separated by a gap that looked about five feet wide.

Not bad, he thought.

Turning around, he offered a hand to Em. She took it, and he gave her a pull as she came up onto the roof. She smiled, squeezed his hand, and stepped out of the way.

Mary halted at the base of the windshield. She glanced over the side, then gazed up at Clint.

He held his arm toward her, and nodded. 'Come on,' he mouthed, not speaking the words.

Looking scared and miserable, Mary stopped clutching her blouse shut. She switched the butcher knife to her left hand, and raised her right toward Clint. They clasped hands. She planted her right foot at the top of the windshield.

Clint pulled.

She bounded up. The left side of her blouse flapped open. Her breast was bare above the flimsy triangle and broken strap of her bra.

Clint glimpsed it, looked away, then felt its firm, warm pressure against his chest as she stumbled into him.

The moment Mary seemed steady on her feet, he stepped back from her. She hadn't covered herself yet. He turned away and faced the gap.

The area below still looked safe.

Maybe they aren't even under there anymore, he thought. Maybe they've moved on, and all this is a waste of time.

Who you trying to kid? They haven't gone anyplace. Just fall, and see what happens.

There's no reason to fall, he told himself. Just one good stride and you'll be across. It won't even take a jump. Not a real jump. Just give it a little oomph on the take-off, then try like hell not to let the momentum run you off the other side of the van.

He stepped to the edge of the pickup's roof.

He swung his right leg out over the chasm and shoved off with his left. His stomach dropped away as he went airborne. For a moment, he hung above the gap. Then his right foot landed on top of the van. A couple of quick staggers, and he halted himself.

He turned around.

Em and Mary stood side by side atop the pickup's cab. Em, smiling, gave the blade of her knife a twirl. Mary, knife clamped between her teeth, was using both hands to tuck the bottom of her blouse into her skirt.

Clint gestured for them to come over.

Em mouthed something to Mary that looked like, 'You go first.'

Mary shook her head.

Let's not dawdle, ladies! Let's move it before the creeps crawl out!

He beckoned again.

Em nodded. She took a couple of backward steps to give herself a running start. She switched the butcher knife to her left hand, didn't seem to like it there, and returned it to her right hand. She took a deep breath. She wiggled her eyebrows at Clint. Then she rushed toward the edge.

She kicked out over the gap.

As she shoved off, her left foot slipped.

Thirty-eight

Clint glimpsed a look of disbelief on Em's face.

In midair, she tilted backward.

No!

Her arms thrashed. Her knife waved. For a moment, she looked as if she were trying to slide into base, right foot reaching for the edge of the van's roof.

Clint was going to be there to catch her.

But he knew she wouldn't make it. She was coming in almost horizontal.

Dropping to his knees, he bowed over the edge and reached for her foot.

Caught it!

The sole of her sneaker pounded the van.

Gasping, she bent at the waist and swiped her left hand at Clint. It didn't even come close. She was already dropping.

Clint braced himself.

A moment later, Em's back slammed against the metal side of the van.

Clint didn't let go. He held her right ankle in a solid, double-handed grip.

She hung upsidedown directly beneath his eyes, her free leg waving about as if she didn't know what to do with it, her panties showing through the wide and drooping leg holes of her shorts, her body bare below her shorts, her arms outstretched to the sides, her face hooded by her fallen T-shirt.

Clint strained backward, trying to raise her. 'Somebody's got my hair!' she yelled.

No!

Had an arm reached out from under the van? He couldn't see it, but he couldn't see much of anything; the Roadkill T-shirt had flopped down until stopped by Em's armpits. It shrouded her face – her entire head – concealing whatever might be happening between her neck and the street.

They could scalp her . . .

Slash her throat . . .

I wouldn't even know it.

He saw that Em still had hold of her knife.

'Use your knife!' he called.

She started stabbing at the area hidden under the loose tent of her shirt.

Someone cried out as if wounded.

Clint tugged at her ankle. He couldn't raise her at all.

She kept on stabbing. With each jab, her body jerked and twisted.

Clint felt a freezing sickness in his bowels as three people came squirming out from under the van.

They came out on their bellies. The hair on the backs of their heads was matted with blood. Their arms, shoulders and backs were smeared and blotched with it.

Two men and a woman.

One of the guys appeared to be a boy, skinny, small enough to be ten or twelve years old. He wore a T-shirt. He held a claw hammer in his right hand as he scurried out from under the van.

The other guy, possibly his father, was much larger. Husky. Like the boy, he wore a T-shirt. He clutched a Bowie knife. Its broad, stained blade was as long as his forearm.

The woman, as bloody as the others, had her hair in a ponytail. She wore some sort of top that left her back bare except for strips of cloth that tied behind her neck and in the middle of her back. In her hand, she held a hunting knife.

Is this the mother? Clint wondered.

We've got a family here?

The family that kills together, stays together.

Clint tried again to pull Em up by her ankle.

This time, she started to rise.

Yes!

But a pair of red arms suddenly shot out from under the drooping shroud of her T-shirt, swung up off the pavement, reached high and swept down. Their hands hooked into her armpits.

Clint held on.

He knew he could keep holding on.

But he couldn't bring Em up. Not with someone hanging on to her like this.

The man was still squirming out, but the boy and woman were already clear of the undercarriage and getting to their knees.

I can't do her any good up here, Clint thought. I've gotta let go.

Drop her on her head?

I can't!

Gotta!

As he was about to release Em's ankle, he glimpsed a quick plunging movement directly in front of him. Someone leaping down from the other side?

What, more of them?

He looked.

Mary!

He couldn't believe it.

Not Mary, leaping down to help Em.

But that was certainly how it looked.

Hair and skirt hoisted high by the wind of her descent, she landed on her feet beside the cab of the pickup truck. Her shoes struck the pavement with a clatter. The impact seemed to jolt her whole body.

She staggered forward, and Clint thought she was falling.

She *was* falling.

She fell to her knees by the head of the man as he tried to shove himself up from the pavement, and slammed her butcher knife into his back.

He squealed.

Mary tugged out the knife and stabbed him again.

The woman and boy started to rise.

Still hanging onto Em's ankle with his right hand, Clint let go with his left. He used his left to brace himself while he bent down fast over the edge of the roof and reached as low as he could.

He opened his right hand.

Em dropped.

As she plummeted down the side of the van, he sprang.

He sprang for the boy, who was just to the left, standing but still bent over.

Both Clint's feet landed on his back, driving him toward the street. He rode the kid down. He knew what he was doing. He hated it, but not enough to leap off.

The boy's face struck the pavement. The sound of it made Clint wince. He stumbled off the kid's back.

The woman, halting her rush at Mary, looked over her shoulder. She glared at the sprawled body. Shrieking, 'Randy!' she whirled around, raised her hunting knife overhead and ran at Clint.

Her top seemed to be made of bandannas. She wore cut-off jeans with slits up their sides.

From her leather belt, several thatches of hair dangled and swayed.

And dripped.

Scalps?

Clint crouched and snatched up the boy's hammer.

She sprang at him, screaming, and her right arm swept down, plunging the knife toward his chest.

He knocked her arm aside.

With the hammer, he smashed the side of her face. Her eye bulged and popped out of its socket. Leaving the hammer embedded in her temple, he turned quickly and plucked the knife from her hand. He jerked its blade across her throat. As blood shot out, he jammed the blade deep into the center of her throat, then hurled her down on top of the boy.

He leaped over them and rushed toward the place where

Em had fallen – where two bodies now struggled on the narrow alley of pavement between the van and pickup.

Mary was already there, on her knees and stabbing.

Fresh blood flew up, splattering her face and neck.

The way the bodies were tangled, Clint couldn't tell *who* Mary was driving her knife into with such fury. He couldn't tell one from the other.

'Stop!' he gasped.

Mary stopped. Huffing for air, she backed away on her knees, then rested her knife-hand on her thigh and gazed at the two bodies.

The one on top was completely shirtless and had a dozen gashes in its back. It wore jeans, not shorts. As Clint told himself this couldn't be Em, the body rose, tipped sideways, and tumbled. When it rolled onto its back, he saw that it was a boy.

Randy's brother, he supposed.

The handle of a butcher knife protruded from his side, just below the left armpit.

Em's knife?

Em lay on her back, panting. Knees up, limp arms outspread, she looked like a long-distance runner after the end of a race.

But bloody.

So much blood.

Her hair, skin and shorts were splashed and spattered with it.

Can't be hers, Clint told himself. Not much of it, anyway. *She's gotta be all right. Gotta be.*

Em raised her head enough to see what she looked like. Without comment, she fumbled at her T-shirt and drew it down to her belly. Then she propped herself up on her elbows. She turned her head toward Clint, then toward Mary. 'We're all still alive?'

'So far,' Clint said. 'Thanks mostly to Mary.'

'Thanks, Mary,' Em said.

Mary raised her bloody face. She stared at Em. She shrugged her shoulders.

'Are either of you hurt?' Clint asked.

Keeping her elbows on the pavement, Em lifted her right hand and wiggled its fingers at him. 'Somebody dropped me,' she said.

'Sorry about that. I had to.'

'I figured. It wasn't so bad, though. Mostly, I ended up on top of the guy. I think I hurt him pretty good. Not as much as when I stabbed him, though. Boy, that sure took the wind out of his sails, the dirty rat.'

Nodding, Clint turned to Mary. 'How are *you* doing?'

'Okay. I guess.'

'You really saved our bacon. I couldn't believe it when you jumped down like that.'

'Neither could I.' She struggled to her feet. 'Are we gonna get going?'

'We'd better.'

'Yeah,' Em said, sitting up. 'Let's am-scray before we have to kill *another* bunch of loonies.'

Clint stepped over to the dead man, crouched and picked up the Bowie knife.

'What do you want *that* for?' Mary asked. 'You didn't use the knife you had.'

He looked at her and saw a smile.

Not a smirk, an actual smile – weary, but friendly.

He waved the Bowie knife at her and said, 'This one's bigger. Want it?'

'No, thanks.'

'The gal has a good hunting knife,' he pointed out.

She shook her head.

Em, squatting and about to pull her butcher knife out of the boy's side, looked up at Clint. 'Yeah?' She stood up and turned around. 'Her?'

'It's in her throat.'

Em walked toward the woman, and abruptly halted. 'Oh my God,' she muttered. 'Her eye.'

'You don't have to study her,' Clint said. 'Just grab the knife.'

Her back to Clint and Mary, Em crouched beside the

woman's body. She reached out. Suddenly, her back went rigid. She leaped up and staggered backward.

'What?' Clint asked.

'She's got . . . !' Shaking her head, she continued to back away. Then she turned around. Her face, still painted with blood, was twisted with disgust. 'Did you *see* what she's got?'

'The scalps?'

'Yeah!'

Mary grimaced. 'Scalps?'

'She's got 'em,' Em said. 'Five or six of 'em, anyhow. They're hanging off her belt.'

'God, how sickening.'

'I wonder . . .' Em reversed her direction. She approached the woman's body slowly, knees bent, back hunched, like a kid trying to sneak up on someone.

'What're you doing?' Clint asked.

'I want to see if she's got Caspar's hair. Or Loreen's.' Standing over the body, Em shook her head. 'Doesn't look like it. Looks like she preferred blondes.'

All of a sudden, Em crouched, grabbed the hunting knife by its handle and jerked the blade out of the woman's throat. She hurried backward. Then, turning around, she met Clint's eyes. 'Okay,' she said. 'I'm ready.'

'Okay,' Clint said. 'Let's start by seeing if we can find the Blotskis.'

'Might be in there,' Em said, and nodded toward the van.

'I'd bet on it,' Clint said.

He glanced at the bodies. From the look of things, a family had been massacred here. No one was likely to realize it had been a family of savages.

Not without a close inspection.

A glimpse of the woman's trophy belt should set the record straight.

'Okay,' Clint said.

He led the way to the rear of the van, and stepped behind it. The double doors were shut. Each had a rectangular window near the top, but he could see curtains on the other side of the glass.

Clint switched the Bowie knife to his left hand. With his right, he reached for the door handle.

'Wait,' Em whispered.

For a moment, he thought she might be planning to drop down for another look under the nearby vehicles. But she stayed up, stepped quickly past the corner of the van, and swung her head to the left. She gazed in that direction for a few seconds, then glanced the other way before returning.

'First off,' she whispered, 'nobody's over there. So, you know, it's not like we're about to get attacked. Unless it's by somebody hiding *under* something, if you know what I mean. Anyway, the thing is, I mainly wanted to check on the van. There aren't any windows over on that side. What there is, there's one of those big sliding doors.'

'Is it open?' Clint asked.

'Huh-uh.'

'Guess I'll try this one,' he said.

Mary put a hand on his arm. 'Maybe you shouldn't,' she said. 'What if somebody's in there? Not just Loreen and Caspar. Maybe more of *them*.'

'I don't think so,' Clint said, and pulled open the door.

He was wrong.

Thirty-nine

Barbara had tried not to look at the remains of the scavenger and the body from the grocery cart, but there'd been no way, short of shutting her eyes, to avoid catching peripheral views of the gory messes.

There'd been no way to miss Earl's comments, either.

'Oh, Lordy, look what they done to him. Ouch! Oooo,

makes me hurt just looking... Watch out there, Banner, don't step in her... Ugh, those guys musta been hard up. How'd you like'm doing that to *you*?'

'Hey,' Pete had said, 'shut up.'

'Ha! Sorry, sorry.'

There had been more bodies, later on. Whenever Barbara spotted one in the distance, she fixed her eyes on the pavement at her feet. But she saw enough, and heard enough from Earl, to know that the people had been stripped naked, robbed of everything, and usually mutilated in horrible ways: breasts and genitals had been cut off, eyes gouged, scalps taken, patches of skin peeled off (for the tattoos, Earl had suggested), teeth torn from mouths.

According to Earl, *everybody* had been raped. Men as well as women.

But maybe he was exaggerating, just to make things sound even worse than they really were. After all, he was the only one who went up close to the bodies and studied them. Pete and Barbara stayed together, dodged the remains and never paused to inspect them.

Several times, Earl had said, 'Come on over and look at this,' or, 'You gotta get a load of *this*!' or, 'You don't know what you're missing, folks.'

But they'd refrained.

Though Barbara didn't keep score, she guessed that they had probably walked past at least twelve bodies – and that was *after* leaving the scavenger and shopping cart guy behind.

Earlier in the day, the alleys had seemed like fairly safe havens. Now, she hated them.

But she knew that the streets were much worse.

Each time they came to one, they hid and checked carefully before crossing. At the end of almost every block, the streets were jammed with halted vehicles. Most of the cars and trucks appeared to be abandoned, but a few people always seemed to be sneaking among them.

They saw bodies in the streets, on the sidewalks, on lawns, sometimes dangling from tree limbs or tied to fences. They saw looters hurrying out of houses and apartment buildings with full arms. They saw armed gangs that looked like hunting parties in search of prey.

Not long ago, they'd watched a fat, bald man get surrounded. The gang had closed in on him, and his screams had been joined by wild shouts and laughter.

Though the alleys were awful, the streets were insane.

Barbara dreaded the end of every alley and what she might have to see when she came to the street. But she especially dreaded the sprint to reach the alley on the other side; you just never knew who might spot you dashing across.

Who might come after you.

So far, they'd been lucky.

But she was afraid that the luck wouldn't last.

It doesn't have to last much longer, she told herself. We're almost to the school. Just a few more blocks. Could be home real soon. Half an hour, maybe.

Earl, in the lead, turned around and walked backward. Barbara quickly glanced over her shoulder. Nothing. Just fifty feet of alley, and the street they'd raced across a couple of minutes ago.

'What is it?' she asked.

'Nothing.' He grinned at her. 'Enjoying the view.'

She looked down at herself. Her blouse was untucked, and she hadn't bothered to refasten any of the buttons that had come undone since she'd handed over her bra to Pete. Only the button at her waist remained fastened. Plenty of her skin showed between the blouse's open edges. Not her breasts, though. Nothing showed that should be of much interest to Earl, especially since he'd seen everything when she was in the pickup truck.

'Made ya look,' he said.

'Go to hell.'

He grinned. 'We're there.'

'You're not kidding,' Pete muttered. He was walking close to Barbara's side, the rifle across his back. He looked tired and feverish. He also looked as if he might be getting ready to throw up. 'I don't get it,' he said.

'What?' Barbara asked.

'It's been getting worse. It wasn't like this . . . none of this *really* bad stuff was happening . . . just since . . . about when we were at Lee's.'

'It was pretty bad before,' Barbara said, remembering way back to the kid who'd snatched her purse, who'd shortly afterward been killed for his bicycle.

'It wasn't like this,' Pete told her.

'That's right,' Earl said. 'I'm the living proof. Back in the good ol' days – like this morning – all they did was beat you shitless and steal your clothes.' He grinned. 'I didn't get screwed or killed. I still got my scalp, my teeth and my dick. The difference a few hours makes, you know? I tell ya, we're in hell.'

'Are not,' Barbara said. She didn't like to hear that kind of talk. 'That's bull, and you know it.'

'*Something* is sure going on,' Pete muttered.

'Yeah,' she admitted. 'God knows, I've noticed.'

'It's like they aren't human, any more – the ones doing this stuff.'

'I bet they weren't any great prizes to begin with,' Barbara said.

'They probably didn't go around *butchering* everyone in sight,' Pete said.

'Or bangin' everything that has a hole,' Earl added.

Barbara scowled at him, then met Pete's haggard gaze. 'I think what's happened, is that they're just . . . doing what they wanted to be doing all along. Only they just *didn't*, most of them, because there was stuff in the way. But now there's nobody to make them stop. The quake . . . it knocked all the barriers down. You can't exactly dial up the cops, you know? So anything goes. And more and more of them are taking advantage of it. Doing whatever they wanta do, and the hell with everything.'

'Welcome to hell,' Earl said.

'It's *not* hell,' Barbara insisted. 'It's a bunch of your typical everyday assholes doing what comes naturally. The only thing is, now they're running amok because they figure they can get away with it.'

Pete was staring at her. He looked as if his weariness and nausea had receded. He looked almost amused.

'What?' she asked.

He shrugged. 'Where'd you get *that*?'

'Where'd I get what?'

'What he means, Banner, is he's amazed by your analysis of the situation. Like he didn't know you had such depth. Me, I always knew you was deep. You're a regular *hole*.' He laughed.

'Shut up,' Pete snapped at him.

'Relax. I called her a hole, not a twat. Don't you know a *compliment* when you hear one?'

'Just knock it off. And why don't you . . .'

Three quick booms stopped Pete's voice.

Earl flinched. 'Shit! Those were shots!'

They hadn't come from very far away.

Barbara whirled around and reached under the back of her blouse. As she pulled the forty-five out of her shorts, Pete unslung his rifle.

Instead of more gunshots, she heard engine noises.

The loud, blatting thunder seemed to come from somewhere up the last street they'd crossed.

When a white car skated sideways and leaped into the alley, Barbara knew it wasn't the source of the thunder. The car was long and low and wide. A Lincoln? After the squeal of its tires, it rushed forward with an urgent but well-muffled roar.

Behind its windshield, a woman gripped the steering wheel with both hands. She was looking back over her right shoulder.

Someone grabbed Barbara's arm and yanked it so hard that she stumbled sideways and almost fell.

But she kept her eyes on the mouth of the alley.

The thunder came.

Bikes.

Fat-wheeled hogs – two of them side by side, three more, two after that – seven choppers kicking up gravel and tilting as they turned, their riders hunched low, some with firearms aimed at the fleeing Lincoln.

Outlaw bikers.

Barbara stumbled sideways, dragged by the hand. But it stopped pulling when a big metal dumpster blocked her view of the action. With a glance, she saw that it was Earl clutching her arm. Pete, his back against a garage door, was sinking down to a squat, scowling fiercely and swinging the muzzle of his rifle toward the alley.

She heard two more gunshots.

She jerked her arm free and rushed forward, halting at the corner of the dumpster and peering around it as the Lincoln came speeding up the middle of the alley.

It'll miss us, Barbara thought, unless the gal swerves in the next second or two . . .

The two bikes at the head of the pack were tight on the Lincoln's tail.

'*Back* here,' Earl gasped, and yanked her by the hair. This time, she did fall. As the Lincoln sped past, she dropped against Earl. He caught her under the armpits, and held her up.

Struggling to stand, she watched the gang blast by.

The lead biker raced up alongside the Lincoln and snapped off two quick shots.

But not at the driver, though she would've made an easy target. At the front tire.

Though the bullets missed, whinging off the alley pavement inches away from the tire, the big car suddenly swung out of control. Brakes shrieking, it cut hard to the left. It skidded sideways, then smashed through an old aluminum trash can and slammed into the corner of a garage. The stucco corner caved in. The front of the car crumpled. The driver lurched forward, then rebounded. Barbara couldn't tell whether she'd hit the steering wheel or been saved by her safety belt. She seemed to be all right, though. She turned her head to glance over her shoulder, made a terrified face at what she saw, then turned her attention to the dash.

Her car must've died, Barbara thought. 'Come on,' she muttered. 'Get it going. Go!'

But the car just sat there as the bikers flanked it and dismounted. When they shut their engines off, the stuttering thunder abruptly stopped. Barbara heard the whinny of the car.

It had died, all right. The woman was trying to start it up again so she could get the hell out of there.

But one of the bikers, the one who'd shot at her tire, was already striding toward her door. He was lean and walked like a cowboy. He wore a shiny, black Nazi helmet. On the back of his denim jacket was a skull-and-crossbones emblem. His jeans hung low on his rump. He held a revolver in his right hand, down by his side.

Barbara felt a dull punch against her upper arm. She looked back.

'Come on,' Earl whispered. 'We're getting outa here.'

Pete, nodding at her, was standing again, his back to the garage door.

'We'll cut through,' Earl said.

He led the way, hunching low, rushing past Pete and apparently heading for a gap on the other side of the garage.

Pete waved her to get moving.

I'm coming. Just hold your horses. Gotta see what's . . .

With the other bikers close behind him, blocking some of Barbara's view, the lanky one demolished the side window of the Lincoln. Moments later, the door swung open. The woman was pulled out, screaming, and vanished completely as the pack closed in and took her down.

'Leave her alone!' Barbara yelled.

Yelled as she broke into a run.

Ran because she knew she was too far away, had to get closer to take control and save the woman – near enough to hit what she aimed at if it came to that.

'Barb!' Pete shouted. 'No!'

Yes, she thought.

As she charged at them, she wished she hadn't yelled. The yelling hadn't stopped anything.

At first, she thought that nobody had even heard her. Then a couple of the bikers at the outside of the cluster looked back, saw her, and turned around.

One of them, with a face a lot like the skull on the back of the leader's jacket, grinned at her. He was missing teeth.

The other was fat and bearded, and wore a Viking helmet that looked like a tin bowl with horns. His eyes seemed to light up when he saw Barbara dashing toward him. He rubbed his hands together.

I'm coming at them with a gun, she thought, and they look like they're glad to see me.

'Cause your shirt's wide open, idiot.

Just as she thought that they might not try to shoot her – wouldn't want to ruin her looks – the cadaverous one brought up a weapon that looked like a sawed-off shotgun.

Barbara had no time to halt and take aim. Stretching out her arm, she pointed her pistol at him and fired.

And watched the Viking helmet fly off the head of the fat guy.

At least Skull-face was distracted. Looking surprised, he glanced at his fellow biker, who was now stumbling backward into the others, a hole in his forehead.

Barbara skidded to a stop. She braced herself and took aim for another try at Skull-face as he leveled his shotgun at her.

Before she could fire, a sharp *blam* pounded the air.

She pulled her trigger.

At least I take him with me.

Waiting to be hit by the blast from the shotgun, she realized the shot had come from behind her. Skull-face fired into the air as he was knocked off his feet.

She risked a quick look back.

And there was Pete by the garage door. He hadn't gone anywhere. What he'd done was shoulder the rifle and join the battle.

A battle that ended very fast.

The other side got off a few shots.

As many as Barbara, maybe.

She had hardly begun to fight when the slide of her Colt locked back and nothing would make it shoot any more. But Pete had Lee's rifle, some sort of military thing that could be fired very fast and held a lot of ammo.

A lot.

The storm of bullets tore down all the remaining bikers very fast. Incredibly fast – before they could do much more than quit brutalizing the woman and turn around to see who was killing them and throw back three or four quick, wild shots.

When it was done, all she could hear was a high-pitched ringing sound as if someone had struck tuning forks and held them to her ears.

Those in front of her were sprawled about in positions that mostly looked awkward and uncomfortable. A few were moving slightly: here, a knee lifted; there, a head turned, a foot kicked; one man, in a fetal position, twitched and jerked. Nobody was crawling or trying to get up.

'You okay?'

She turned. Pete was now standing beside her. She nodded. Looking him up and down, she saw no sign that he'd been injured in the abrupt gunfight. But she asked, 'How about you?'

He shrugged. 'Okay.'

'My God, you sure got 'em.'

He wrinkled his nose and said, 'Yeah. I tried not to hit the woman.'

'We'd better check.'

Pete nodded. He started walking forward, and Barbara stayed at his side. As they stepped between a couple of the Harleys, he muttered, 'I can't believe I did this.'

'You did fine. We couldn't just let them kill her.'

'I couldn't just let them kill *you*. What were you trying to do, commit suicide?'

'I just wanted to stop them.'

'You stopped 'em, all right.'

'There she is.'

The woman, surrounded by the dead or badly wounded bodies of her assailants, was sprawled face-down on the street. Her arms were crossed over the back of her head. A biker had fallen forward across her rump.

Halting near the shotgun dropped by Skull-face, Barbara called, 'Lady?'

The woman didn't move.

'Lady? It's okay, now. We're here to help you.'

Still, she didn't respond.

'Oh, man,' Pete muttered. 'I bet I shot her.'

'I don't think so,' Barbara told him. The back of the woman's cream-colored blouse was spattered with blood, but not sopping. Though a sleeve had been ripped from the blouse's shoulder, Barbara could see no holes.

'Why don't you wait here?' Pete suggested.

'I'll come with you.'

'Some of these guys aren't dead.'

'I know. What'll we do about them?'

'Just make sure they don't try anything, I guess.'

She glanced at the Colt in her hand. 'I'm all out of ammo. How about you?'

Pete shook the rifle slightly as if testing its weight. 'I'm not empty yet.'

'Are you sure?'

'I've got one ready to go, I'm sure of that. It might be the last, but . . .'

'Yo! *Compadres!* My oh my, what *have* you done?'

Glancing back, Barbara saw Earl come striding toward them. She quickly fastened a middle button of her blouse. Then she crouched and picked up the sawed-off shotgun.

'Fine shooting, Pizzaboy.'

'Why didn't you just keep running?' Pete asked. He was watching Earl's approach, so Barbara kept her eyes on the bikers and the woman.

'I *waited* for you, but then I heard all the gunplay so I came back to help out.'

'Yeah, right.'

Earl laughed. 'Not really. Just wanted to see who won. And see who was doing what to who, if you know what I mean. Looks like you sure cleaned house. Hey, Banner.'

She looked at him. He had halted on the other side of Pete. Grinning, he raised a hand in greeting. 'Aren't ya glad I'm back?' he asked.

'Thrilled.'

'Now you guys're killers, just like me. Feels good, don't it?'

'Shut up,' Barbara told him.

'Looks like ya missed a few.'

'They aren't missed,' Pete said.

'Aren't dead, either. Want me to take care of 'em for you?'

'Just leave everyone alone,' Pete told him, and walked in among the bodies.

'Give you a hand,' Earl said, starting after him.

'No,' Barbara said. 'Stay where you are.'

'What's your problem?'

She ignored him. 'Pete, why don't you take all the guns and stuff away from them? I'll keep you covered.'

Nodding, he slung the rifle behind his shoulder. 'What about the woman?'

'She can wait. I don't want you getting killed by a "dead" guy. It happens all the time in the movies.'

He looked back and smiled at Barbara. 'You're some kind of an expert on playing possum, aren't you?'

Though she returned Pete's smile, the reminder of their time in the pickup truck made heat rush to her face. 'Yep, that's me.' In a loud voice, she said, 'Any of you animals can hear me, I'll blast anyone who makes a sudden move. Got it?'

Nobody answered. Nobody moved.

She wondered if all the live ones had either passed out or died in the past couple of minutes.

Not likely.

'Careful,' she said.

Wandering slowly among the bikers, stopping over each, Pete crouched again and again to pick up weapons. He only went after those in plain sight: handguns and knives that were still clutched in hands or had fallen to the pavement; knives sheathed on belts. He stuck the guns into the pockets of his trousers, and pitched the knives away.

But he disturbed none of the bodies. He seemed reluctant to touch them at all, much less frisk them or turn them over.

Not exactly a thorough search, Barbara thought.

I wouldn't wanta touch them, either.

But, my God, if one of them comes up with a gun . . .

'Do you want to go in and help?' she asked Earl.

'Thought you'd never ask.'

'Turn 'em over, make sure they don't have anything.'

'Never fear, Earl is here.' He pointed at Skull-face. 'Dead.' He pointed at the Viking. 'Dead.'

Pete, now standing above the woman, looked up and asked, 'What's going on?'

'Earl's double-checking things.'

'Maybe dead.' Earl kicked a body in the head.

'Hey!' Barbara yelled.

'My way of checking.' He smiled down at the corpse and pronounced, 'Dead.'

'For the love of God,' Pete said.

'Just turn them over, Earl.'

'If they're dead anyhow, why bother?'

'Stop kicking them in the head!'

'Okay, okay. Don't wet your pants.' The next biker was face down. Unlike the two that Earl had kicked, this one still wore a helmet. The back of the black T-shirt had a few holes in it and looked awfully bloody, but Barbara noticed that one arm was tucked out of sight beneath the body.

'Be careful of that one,' she warned.

She worked the shotgun's pump action, and took aim.

'Okay, turn him over.'

Earl stepped to the other side of the body and glanced at Barbara. 'Make sure you don't shoot *me* with that thing.'

'I'll try not to.'

Crouching, he reached over the body. He grabbed it by the shoulder and hip. Then he pulled. It came up, rolling onto its side.

The hand had a gun in it.

Big surprise, Barbara thought.

She saw the pistol start to come up, muzzle rising toward her.

She yelled, '*No!*'

And fired.

Blasting apart the face guard and the face behind it, blowing the helmet off.

The pistol leaped out of the biker's hand. It fell, clattered against the alley pavement, and Earl snatched it up.

Barbara cocked the shotgun. 'Put that down,' she said.

'Yeah, right.'

'Do it,' Pete called. His rifle still hung down the back of his shoulder by its strap, but he'd already pulled a revolver from one of his pockets and pointed it at Earl.

Earl glanced back at him, then faced Barbara and shook his head. 'Hey, this sucks, you know? All this shit going down, and *I'm* not supposed to have a gun?'

'Put it down,' Pete said.

'Come on!' Though keeping his eyes on Barbara, Earl spoke loudly enough to be heard by Pete, too. 'I could've had *yours* back at the pickup, and you know it. I could've taken *both* of 'em and even shot off both your asses if I'd wanted to! But I didn't. 'Cause I'm not the bad guy around here, you know what I mean? I'm on *your* side.'

Pete tilted his head to one side and shrugged at Barbara.

'Okay,' she said. 'We'll let you keep the gun.'

'Thanks. You're a champ, Banner.' He stood up, turned away, and walked to the next biker. 'Dead,' he announced. He stepped around it. Bending over another sprawled body, he said, 'Maybe dead.' He bent lower, shoved the muzzle of the pistol against the nape of the biker's neck, and fired. 'Dead now.'

'Earl!' Barbara cried out.

He grinned. 'Better safe than sorry.'

'Don't *do* that!'

'Okay,' he said. Standing in place, he aimed quickly and fired into another body. The biker flinched and cried out. 'Live one!' Earl yelled.

'Damn it!' Barbara shouted as Earl fired twice more. The body jerked with each impact, then went limp.

Earl lowered the pistol. He grinned at her. 'I won't do it any more. I promise.'

'That was the last of them,' Pete pointed out.

'Ah, then,' Earl said, 'I guess we don't have to worry about any surprises from them, do we?'

'You're such a bastard,' Barbara said.

'Me? A bastard?' Laughing, he shook his head. 'I'm not a bastard. How can you possibly call me a bastard? If I was a bastard, I might do something like *this*.'

His arm came up fast.

Laughing, he shot Barbara and she fired back as he pivoted and shot Pete.

The thunder of the gunshots crashed through the alley. Blood exploded from punched flesh.

All three went down.

Forty

'We're almost there,' Stanley said. 'The pool's just on the other side of this fence.'

Sheila didn't respond. She hadn't spoken at all, or resisted in any way, since her small rebellion in the bathtub.

After slamming her down on the bottom of the tub, Stanley had let her rest. He'd needed time, himself, to recuperate before starting the journey to the Bensons' swimming pool.

So he'd stepped around her body and sat on the remaining beam and tried to be patient. The view was nice. This was his first chance for a good, long look at her backside.

Her hair wasn't much to see, the way it was dark and ropy and plastered to her head. Though her skin glistened, it was filthy, stained with blood, sprinkled with dust and crumbs of plaster that had adhered to the moisture. But her *shape* – her shape was lovely. Even with her arms stretched overhead, Stanley could see how broad and strong she was across the shoulders. She tapered down from there, smooth curves of muscle showing where he'd never seen them before on any other woman; not on a flesh-and-blood woman, just on superhero types in comic books, on body-builders pictured in magazines and sometimes on television. Never on an actual woman sprawled in front of him.

And her *ass*.

He'd seen it many times before, full mounds flexing under shorts or sweatpants. He'd seen it in jeans. He'd seen it in little bikinis that didn't cover much at all. But never like this, never naked so he could study the twin, bare globes, linger on them, run his eyes down the curve of their crack.

Near enough to touch.

To kiss.

Mine. She's mine from head to foot.

I could go ahead right now and fuck her, he'd realized. She isn't trapped anymore, and she's sure in no condition to fight me. Just step down, spread her legs, and have at her.

'No no no no no.'

That'd ruin everything.

His heart was set on taking her to the swimming pool, getting her all washed up so her skin would be shiny, wrestling with her in the cool water . . .

'What are we waiting for?' he'd said.

No answer from Sheila. She lay on the bottom of the tub, and all that moved were her back and ribcage, just barely rising, expanding, lowering, shrinking with the in and out of her breath.

'Sheila? We're leaving, now, so get up.'

Her head had lifted slightly.

'We're leaving right now. I'm taking you to a nice, cool swimming pool where you can wash up and get all squeaky clean. You can even wet your whistle, if you don't mind the chlorine. Any questions?'

She hadn't answered.

But from that moment on, she'd followed every order: climbed out of the tub while he'd watched from below; waited on hands and knees for him to climb out; made no fuss when he'd knelt behind her and steadied himself with a hand on her rump while he ducked down and reached forward between her thighs to find the loose end of the barbed wire. Suddenly hard again, his face so close to her, he'd been tempted to mount her without any more delays.

No no no, he'd told himself. You've waited this long. A few minutes more won't kill you, and you'll be able to have her all clean and wet in the pool. Don't spoil it. There's no hurry. Stick with the plan.

Why wait for the pool? I can lick her clean.

'No!'

Just a little bit, and then I'll stop. What can it hurt?

So he'd stuck out his tongue and begun moving his head toward her, but then his hand, groping through the rubble under her torso, had found the barbed wire.

Was the timing of the discovery a signal that he should hold off?

In a high-pitched mockery of his mother's voice, Stanley had said, 'No snacking, boy! Do you want to go and spoil your dinner?'

'How about just a little taste?' he'd asked in his own voice.

'You go and do that, boy, you'll shoot your squirt and spoil your appetite same as if you'd whanged her.'

'Hmmm. Good point. No snacking for me.'

With his left hand, he'd picked up the scissors and straight razor. Then he'd pushed at Sheila's rump and raised himself, holding on to the long strand of barbed wire with his right hand.

'Up.'

Offering no objection, Sheila had gotten to her feet.

'Now. A few simple instructions. You're going to walk ahead of me. I'll be holding the other end of this.'

Lifting his hand, he'd pulled the dangling wire up between her legs until it met her flesh. She'd flinched a bit and gone up on her tiptoes. After a moment on tiptoes, however, she must've figured out a better course of action; bending forward at the waist to lower her bound wrists and *her* end of the strand.

'If you give me any trouble,' Stanley'd gone on, 'I'll be forced to give it a yank. Which is bound to hurt, don't you think? I don't care how much you bend over, I give it a good pull and you'll be sorry.'

After the warning, he'd given the wire some slack so Sheila could stop bending over so much.

813

'Okay. Start walking.'

She had begun to make her way slowly through the ruins, walking ahead of Stanley. She didn't stand up completely straight, but Stanley couldn't blame her for that; the lower her hands, the less chance of catching the wire in sensitive areas. She kept her legs apart to spare them from the barbs. As a result of her precautions, her gait was more a waddle than a walk.

She'd flinched and winced sometimes when she either stepped on something with her bare feet or allowed the barbed wire to scratch or poke her.

It had taken a long time to get through the ruin of her house, but she'd picked up her pace after that. They'd made fairly good time crossing her patio and back yard, but they'd been stopped for a while by the cinderblock wall at the rear of her property.

'How do we get you over this?' Stanley had asked.

She'd simply stood facing the wall, neither speaking nor gesturing.

'It's going to be a problem, since I'm not stupid enough to undo your hands.' Frowning, he'd swept the wire gently from side to side, watching it swing below her buttocks like a wicked jump-rope.

'We can't exactly go around, can we? I suppose we *could*. Take the front way, and we wouldn't have to worry about any walls at all. But I think we'd probably attract a wee bit of attention, I walk you around the block like a dog. What a dog, huh? What a leash! Ho! Can't you just see it? It'd almost be worth a try. But somebody'd come running out of a house, sure as hell, and try to save you. Wouldn't want that. I'd have to kill 'em, and I'm too pooped for any more of that. Gotta save all my energy for you. So I guess we'll have to go *over*.'

He'd let his end of the wire fall to the ground, then shoved her toward the wall. 'Give you a boost.' After setting down the scissors and razor, he'd crouched behind her and cupped his hands. 'Put a foot in the stirrup, my dear.'

Sheila had raised her arms, placed her bound wrists against the upper edge of the wall, and planted her right heel into the cup of his hands. Then she'd straightened her leg, thrusting herself upward, rising toward the top of the wall. As Stanley had uncrouched, he'd looked up and watched Sheila swing out her left leg and kick it high.

'Oh, look at you,' he'd said.

Too bad there aren't ten walls between us and the pool. Or a hundred. I could look at that all day!

As her foot started to rise out of his hands, he gave it a sudden upward thrust that sent Sheila hurling over the top.

'Surprise!'

No complaint had come from Sheila. Just a squeal of alarm as she went head-first over the wall, feet kicking at the sky. Not waiting to hear her land, Stanley had snatched up his scissors and razor, tossed them over, then hurled himself at the wall and clambered up.

From the top, he'd looked down at Sheila.

She had apparently not landed on her head. Perhaps she'd hit the ground arms-first and done some sort of somersault. She was lying on her back, head toward the wall, hands on her belly, knees up.

'You're lucky I cut down the rose bushes,' he had called to her. Then he'd lowered himself to the ground, retrieved his scissors and razor, and squatted beside Sheila to pick up the end of the barbed wire. 'Fall down go boom?' he'd asked in baby-talk.

No answer from Sheila. Just a narrow-eyed glare.

She was gasping very hard for breath, so Stanley had spent a while watching her chest heave, lifting and lowering her breasts. They were shiny with sweat and blood. They were speckled with goosebumps, and the nipples stood erect.

'You turned on? You *can't* be cold. Maybe you like all this. Do you? Do you like *pain*?'

She'd blinked her eyes, then crossed her legs and sat up.

'Ah. You'd rather get going. Scared I'll start on you, I bet.'

The momentum of her quick sit-up had carried Sheila to her knees. From there, she'd gotten to her feet. Instead of bolting, she'd only stood there, her back to Stanley, the wire hanging between her legs to the grass.

At her back, Stanley had ducked and reached between her knees and grabbed the wire. He'd drawn it up behind her.

'Welcome to my back yard. That's my house right there – what's left of it. Of course, it fared better than yours. Mine is only *half* down. Over here is my garage, which fared even worse than my house. Mother's in the house. Deader than shit, as the saying goes. And a good thing, too. She would not approve of my behavior today. Wouldn't approve in the least. The old bat always *did* think I was a pervert.'

Laughing, he'd given the wire a couple of quick upward tugs that made Sheila jump and gasp.

'Giddy-up, horsey.'

Bending over, Sheila had started to hobble forward.

'To the right, to the right. Our next obstacle is the block wall there by my driveway. But I think we'll go around it. Would you like that? You took such a nasty fall at the last wall, so we'll try to spare you, this time. I think we can probably make it to the gate without drawing undue attention to ourselves, don't you? We'll just go down my driveway.'

She'd led the way, and Stanley had kept a sharp watch as they approached the front of his house. Making her wait, he had stepped past her and opened the gate that shut off Judy's side of the cinderblock wall.

Then they'd gone in and made their way alongside her house to her back yard.

'This is the home of my friend, Judy. I don't believe you know her. Me, I've gotten to know her *quite* well since the quake. It was her saw we used to get you out. A lovely woman. Not in your league, of course. *Nobody* is in your league. Perhaps we'll visit with her, later on. You two have a lot in common. Me, for one thing. And guess what – she's *still* in her bathtub. Not that her house fell on her. Her house didn't fall at all, the lucky bitch. But *I* fell on her. Ho! Maybe we'll let her out, later on, and ask her to join us for cocktails and hors d'oeuvres. Why not? It'll be her stuff.'

Stanley had kept the monologue going all the way across Judy's back yard, smiling at Sheila's backside, sometimes chuckling, wondering if she was at all impressed by his wit.

Under the circumstances, he'd thought, I can hardly expect her to be amused.

'We're almost there,' he said. 'The pool's just on the other side of this fence. See where I made a doorway for us? We won't have to climb over this one or go looking for a gate – we can walk straight on through. But watch your head.'

Hunching down, Sheila stepped over the lower crossbeam and slipped through the gap in the redwood fence. On the other side, she halted. Stanley stepped through. He ducked, but not quite enough. The upper beam scraped the top of his head.

'Ow!'

Sheila ignored him.

'I hurt myself.'

She acted as if she were deaf.

'Say you're sorry.'

'I'm not sorry,' she muttered.

'You're not being very nice to me.' Stanley flipped the wire from side to side, switching it against her thighs. 'But why *should* you be? All I did was rescue you.'

She didn't look back, didn't make a comment.

'Get moving.'

She waddled toward the pool.

'Go to the right. We're going to the other end. That's where the water is.'

She followed orders.

As they walked alongside the pool, Stanley said, 'Bet you can't wait to get in. I've been in. Not a whole lot of water down there, but it's plenty good for washing off blood. And it's really quite refreshing. I'm sure we'll both enjoy it. Okay, stop here.'

Sheila stopped.

'Face the pool.'

She turned and looked down.

This is it! Stanley thought. Suddenly, he was trembling.

He could hardly believe that he'd actually freed Sheila from the bathtub and brought her to the swimming pool – that they were finally here, exactly as he'd hoped.

This is my day! The greatest day ever! And the best of it hasn't even started yet!

Dreams *can* come true, he told himself. All you've gotta do is reach out for them and not let anything get in your way.

Stanley peeled the clinging remains of his pajama pants away from his rump. He crouched, lowering them to his ankles. While still down, he placed the scissors and razor on the concrete. Then he straightened up. With a few quick, silent movements, he stepped out of his moccasins and the scanty rag that draped his feet.

Sheila seemed to be unaware of what he'd done. 'We can't go in here,' she said.

'Sure we can.' The concrete felt awfully hot under his bare feet. He was glad to be naked, though. He wished Sheila would turn around and look at him.

See how big I am? It's all because of you.

Just tell her to turn around.

No no no. I want her right where she is.

'It's too shallow,' she protested.

'This is the *deep* end, moron!'

With that, he used both hands to jerk upward on the wire. Sheila cried out. The barbed steel vanished in the crease of her rump, but she bent down and it came out fast. Still tugging the wire, Stanley took a quick step backward.

The pull made Sheila fold as if broken at the waist. Her bound hands came swinging toward him between her calves. Her elbows struck the inner sides of her knees. Her face appeared, upsidedown, hair hanging.

Stanley yanked the wire upward as hard as he could.

Sheila shrieked.

For a moment, Stanley thought he might be able to drag her whole body, arms-first, through her widely spread legs.

Make her kiss her own ass!

But suddenly her legs flew up, bare feet almost kicking him as she flipped over. Her back, just below the shoulders, struck the edge of the pool. The blow jolted her body, straightened her out. Stanley strained at the wire as if he hoped to drag her from the brink.

Propped up at only one end, Sheila was stretched out over the pool like the naked and bloody victim of a demented magician more interested in torture than levitation.

The wire lurched in Stanley's hands.

Letting go, he watched his end of the wire leap high.

Sheila's legs dropped out of sight and the fulcrum of the pool's edge seemed to launch her upper body forward.

Stanley rushed to the edge.

At first, he thought she would hit the water flat, a real belly-whomper. At the last instant, however, her body twisted and curled. Her side hit the surface. A geyser of white, sparkling spray shot up and she was submerged in a roil of froth.

The spray sprinkled down.

The froth vanished.

After her impact with the water, Sheila must've rolled over. She was face down, bound hands hanging toward the bottom, legs spread apart. Submerged in water tinged with pink, her body seemed to waver and shimmer.

As Stanley watched, she glided slowly upward.

The surface of the water slid away to make room for her back.

Her back became a slick, clean island that gleamed with sunlight.

But it was the only island.

The rest of Sheila stayed down, a layer of water rippling over her buttocks, the hair on the back of her head rising and swaying.

She's faking it, Stanley told himself. Wants me to think she's drowning so I'll let my guard down. She'll come up for air any second.

But the only movements of her body seemed to be those made by the gentle shifting of the pool water buoying her up.

What if she's out cold?

What if she drowns?

'Sheila!'

Nothing.

She can't drown! That'd ruin everything.

But even as Stanley leaped from the edge, he wondered if this was exactly what she wanted him to do.

He was on his way down when he realized that his hands were empty. He'd set down the scissors and razor . . .

'Shit!' he yelled.

His feet slapped the water. A moment later, they struck the bottom of the pool and he felt as if his legs were being rammed up through his hips. His knees folded. He tumbled forward through the rising spray of his splash and slammed onto Sheila's back.

He drove her down.

He felt a slight jolt when she hit the bottom of the pool.

No struggle came from under him.

No good, he thought. No good at all.

What if she drowns?

He knew he should act quickly to save her, but he wanted to savor the moment – the silence, the mild and heavy coolness of the water, the slick feel of Sheila's skin against his chest and belly, the way he was pressed against her rump with his penis snug between her buttocks.

Why they call 'em buns, he thought.

Could do her right now. Go just a little lower, and shove it in . . .

And she'll drown for sure, he warned himself. Don't want that. She's gotta be alive and kicking, or it won't be any good at all.

So he clutched her just below the armpits and slid himself backward. On his knees, he leaned away from her and pulled. She glided up with him. As her body rose, her arms descended and slid over the backs of his hands, pressing them against her sides.

Their heads lifted out of the water.

Stanley gasped for air.

Sheila didn't. She hung limp in his arms, her head drooping.

Stanley shook her. 'Hey!'

Nothing.

He stopped shaking her.

She didn't seem to be breathing.

Doesn't mean anything, Stanley told himself. Maybe she's just holding her breath.

From his position at her back, hands clamped to her sides, he couldn't tell whether she had a heartbeat. So he shoved his hands forward, forcing them through the tight spaces under her arms.

When they came out the other side, they met her breasts. Which ended his quest for her heartbeat.

He filled his hands. The breasts were wet and slippery, heavy. He squeezed them. They were soft, firm, springy. He swirled his hands around them. The nipples under his moving palms were stiff, rubbery nubs.

Breathless, he grew so hard that he ached.

'Can you feel it?' he whispered, pushing against her.

She didn't respond.

'Answer me.'

She didn't.

'This is a test,' he whispered. He clamped both her nipples between his thumbs and forefingers. 'Tell me when it hurts.' He squeezed.

Not gently.

She didn't flinch rigid and scream with pain, as Stanley thought she might. But she did moan. She did squirm slightly. As if disturbed in her sleep. Then she started to cough. A wet, rattling cough.

Stanley cupped her breasts loosely so he could feel them lurch and bounce, slapping against his hands as she was wracked with spasms of coughing.

Don't wait till she stops! Get her now while she's screwed up!

Clutching her breasts, he pulled her backward until she was tight against him, then put his feet on the bottom and stood up, lifting her. The water was almost waist-high. He glanced over his shoulder and spotted the chrome ladder fixed on the side of the pool, near the corner. It didn't extend down very far – was intended for use when the pool was full. He wondered if he would be able to reach the lowest rung. Hoped so.

Wading backward, he dragged Sheila toward the ladder. She twisted and writhed, and couldn't stop coughing.

821

At the corner of the pool, he swung her around and shoved her at the wall. She didn't bring up her arms in time to stop the collision. Her body made a wet, smacking sound when it hit the tiles. Her forehead thumped. Stanley's hands felt pleasantly trapped between the wall and her breasts. He kept them there while Sheila coughed a few more times. Then he slipped them free.

He stepped away from her back, grabbed her upper arms, and spun her around to face him. She tried to push him away. The effort was feeble.

So much for our Amazon, Stanley thought. Bash her around enough, she ain't so tough.

He thrust her bound arms high.

Her wrists reached almost to the ladder's lowest rung.

Pinning them to the wall with his left hand, he caught the dangling strand of barbed wire with his right. Though he jabbed himself a few times, he drew the wire up and wound it around the side rail and bottom rung of the ladder. With a few twists, it was secure.

He stepped back.

'Fabulous,' he muttered.

In his wildest fantasies, perhaps Sheila had almost looked like this.

But perhaps not quite so beautiful, so vulnerable, so ready for him.

Most of the filth and blood had been washed away. Except for a few bright red trickles sliding down her forearms from fresh wounds on her wrists, her skin looked clean and glossy. It ran with streamers of silver water. It dripped diamonds.

Arms raised high, she stood straight and tall, her head tipped back.

Each time she coughed, her body shook. Between coughs, she panted for air. The shaking and panting did wonderful things to her breasts.

The ruffled surface of the water encircled Sheila's waist like a fluid, transparent skirt, vaguely pink. Just below it, the fine curls of her pubic hair sparkled like gold. Stanley could see through them as if they weren't there.

Her legs seemed to blush in the sunlit, blood-tinted water. Stanley knew they weren't moving, but they appeared to undulate.

My Sheila, Stanley thought. Just the way I always dreamed, only better.

While he was gazing at her, she lowered her head. She grimaced at him, eyes squeezed almost shut, teeth bared. She coughed a couple more times, then sniffed.

'Are you all right?' Stanley asked.

She didn't answer.

'You *look* spectacular.'

He moved closer. He dipped his hands into the water by her hips, then slid them up her sides to the smooth hollows of her armpits. Then he explored the sleek muscles of her upraised arms before sliding his hands down to her breasts.

He watched her breasts as he fondled them, hefted them, pressed them together, squeezed them. Sometimes, Sheila moaned.

She likes it, Stanley thought.

She squirmed and made quiet wincing sounds when he pinched her nipples. When he pulled and twisted them, her back seemed to stiffen and she hissed through her teeth.

He caught one of her nipples between his lips. He flicked and wiggled it with his tongue, then opened wide and sucked in her breast until his mouth was full of the slippery, cool flesh. He tested its springiness with the edges of his teeth.

What if I bite it?

Bite it off and eat it?

She wouldn't look so great afterwards, but imagine the scream! And the taste! And she'd turn into part of me, flesh of my flesh . . .

Sheila attacked him with her knee.

Stanley felt it thrust in and slide up between his thighs.

A groin shot – sapped of its power by the weight of the water.

If we hadn't been in the pool . . .

But we are! Yes yes!

As the knee rushed upward, Stanley shut his legs to trap it. But the water slowed him. By the time he clamped his thighs against the sides of Sheila's knee, it was already touching his scrotum.

Instead of crashing into his testicles, her knee simply stopped, barely touching him, and hoisted Stanley upward. His feet lifted from the bottom of the pool. His mouth lost hold of her breast, which popped out with a squelchy, sucking noise.

Rising out of the water, he saw the fierce look on her face. The agony.

And despair, because she could obviously see that her attack had failed. Stanley was riding her knee like a pony, grinning, pointing at her with his stout penis.

He didn't even fall off.

He simply rode her knee up, and rode it down.

'Wanta try again?' he asked.

She glared at him.

'You could've hurt me, you know. You could've ruined everything.'

'That was the point,' she said.

'I know.'

Stanley punched her in the stomach. There was no water in the way to slow down his fist, so it landed good and solid just above her navel. It sounded like smacking wet meat. Her breasts jumped nicely. Her legs jerked upward as if she wanted to double over but couldn't. Her breath blasted out and she was smashed backward against the side of the pool.

Stanley punched her once more in the same place.

Not only did her breasts bounce like before, but this time her eyes bulged wildly and her knees broke the surface of the water so that she hung there by the barbed wire around her wrists. Hung there and squeaked as she tried to haul air into her lungs.

Fabulous!

Stanley shoved his hands into the creases behind her knees. Clutching her there, he pulled the knees wider apart and drew them toward him and stepped between them.

As he lifted them above his hips, her dripping cleft came up out of the water and tilted toward him.

He plunged into her.

He thrust up hard, rising on his tiptoes to reach high and deep, staggered by her tight, gripping slickness.

It had never been like this for him.

Not even close.

This was better than he'd thought possible.

I'm in her! Sheila! I'm fucking her! Yes!

Sliding his hands up the backs of her thighs, he clutched the solid globes of her buttocks. He clung to them and tried not to move.

Don't move a muscle, he told himself. Don't, or you'll lose it. Hang on. You're in her. In her as in as it gets. Hang on. Make it last. Try to think of something else.

That'd be a neat trick.

Suddenly, the hug of Sheila around his shaft was too much.

Or maybe the knowledge that he was inside her, inside Sheila, finally, was more than he could stand.

He felt himself swelling tight with a massive urgency. Even if he didn't move, he was past being able to stop. Even if he tried to think of something else.

No use holding back.

Go for it!

Gripping her ass, he quickly slid almost all the way out. When only his tip was still embedded, he rammed hard into her again. He felt as if he were being clutched and sucked up.

Torn from his throat was a noise he'd never made before.

'RAWWWWWAHHH!'

And he was pounding inside her, throbbing, pumping, grabbing her by the hips and trying to shove himself higher and deeper, jolting her so hard that he had trouble hanging on.

Slam it to her, slam it to her, slam it to her!

Yes yes yes!

'Stop it! Leave her alone!'

He heard the shout – a woman's voice from somewhere close behind him.

But the voice couldn't stop him. He kept thrusting, kept squirting.

'Get away from her right now!'

Someone I know, he thought. But who?

Judy! Sounds just like her.

How the hell did Judy get loose?

'Get away from her or I'll shoot!'

Shoot?

He quit thrusting. He was done with Sheila, anyway – at least for now.

'I'll stop!' he gasped. 'Don't shoot!'

'Put your hands up!'

He let go of Sheila's hips and raised his arms. Though no longer supported by his hands, she stayed against him, still impaled.

'Judy?' Stanley asked, not looking back.

'You better believe it.'

'Don't shoot.' He took a few quick breaths. 'I give up.'

'Get away from the woman.'

He nodded. Then he tried a couple more thrusts. *Look, Ma, no hands!* He watched how the thrusts made Sheila jiggle. Great. But not nearly as great as how she felt on him.

I could do her all over again.

'You fucking bastard!' Judy cried out.

And a new voice said, 'Here, give it. *I'll* shoot him.'

He pulled out fast and turned around.

When he'd last seen Judy, she had been naked at the bottom of her bathtub, feet bound to the faucets, a chair on her chest, her arms wired together with a hanger.

Now, she stood directly across from him, looking down on him from the edge, only the width of the pool away. She wore cut-off jeans and an old blue workshirt with rolled sleeves. They looked like the clothes she'd been wearing that morning.

Her arms were straight out in front of her. She was using both hands to hold the revolver that was aimed at his chest.

The revolver was big and shiny. It looked like something Dirty Harry might use.

Standing by Judy's side, tugging the sleeve of her shirt, was Weed. 'Give it to me,' Weed said. 'I'll blow his fucking head off.'

Judy shook her head. 'Don't do that.'

Weed. She looked exactly the same as Stanley remembered her: skinny and mean, her scalp hairless except for black stubble like a two-day growth of whiskers, her eyebrows pointed, her eyes tiny, her chin sharp. She still wore the gray tank top that was cut off just below her ribcage. The golden ring in her navel glinted in the sunlight. Her jeans looked ready to drop from her lean hips.

She held a butcher knife in her left hand.

Stanley'd had big plans for her. If only he could've found her.

Seeing Weed with Judy, a lot of things suddenly made sense.

He *hadn't* searched for her in Judy's house. But that was obviously where she'd gone to hide from him. And while there, she must've found Judy in the bathtub and set her free.

Two of his victims, joining forces.

And coming for him.

Shouldn't have cut through Judy's back yard.

Shouldn't have made Sheila scream so much.

Tipped 'em off, and now they're here like a couple of fucking harpies.

It's like some kind of a nightmare, Stanley thought.

Maybe it is a nightmare. Maybe none of this is real, and I'm asleep. Or in a coma. Maybe I never even got out of my house this morning, and I'm trapped there under . . .

Bullshit, he thought. Forget the 'Owlcreek Bridge' bullshit, this is real. It better be real, or I was only dreaming I fucked Sheila.

It's real, he told himself. So deal with it.

'I surrender,' he called. 'Don't shoot. You don't wanta hit Sheila. I mean, that's a *big* gun. It'd shoot right through me and right through her, too. You don't wanta kill her, do you?'

'Of course not,' Judy said. 'Just you.'

'I give up. See?' He raised his hands even higher. 'I won't try anything. I promise. Just tell me what you want me to do.'

With the barrel of the revolver, Judy gestured to her right. 'Move that way.'

He looked back at Sheila. She was still panting for air, but her head was upright between her raised arms. She was watching him, her eyes narrow.

He faced Judy again. 'She won't be in the line of fire if I move over there. What's to stop you from shooting me?'

'I could shoot you where you stand.'

'And kill Sheila.'

Hand on Judy's arm, Weed leaned closer to her and spoke softly. Stanley heard the murmur of her voice, but couldn't make out any of the words.

Judy nodded. Keeping the revolver aimed at Stanley, she sidestepped to the corner of the pool and started walking toward him.

Oh, no, he thought.

Then he gasped, 'Shit!' as Weed, straight in front of him, leaped off the edge.

She dropped toward the water, the bottom of her tank top gliding up. Her breasts were tanned as dark as her belly. They had wonderful nipples that stuck out, and Stanley wanted to feel them in his mouth.

She vanished for a moment in the middle of a splash. When Stanley could see her again, she was soaking wet, her tanned skin gleaming, her tank top clinging to her breasts. She waded toward him. The water was high enough, on Weed, to cover the ring in her belly button.

The blade of the knife in her left hand was at least twelve inches long.

Should've kept after her, Stanley thought.

Stupid, stupid, stupid. Could've taken her down and had her. And taken her out of the picture.

Now she's gonna kill me.

If she doesn't, Judy will.

As Weed sloshed closer, he looked over his shoulder. Judy stood at *his* corner of the pool, not far from the shiny chrome arches of the ladder's rails. From there, she had a clear line of fire at him; her bullet would pass high over Sheila's head.

'I could've *killed* you!' he shouted at Judy. 'I spared your life! You owe me!'

Her upper lip twitched. 'I owe you dick,' she said.

'I saved your life!'

'You raped the shit out of me!' she yelled. With the thumb of her right hand, she hooked back the revolver's hammer.

SNICK-CLACK

The black tunnel of the muzzle pointed at Stanley's face.

Oh, God, I'm dead.

He didn't want to see the gun go off, so he turned his face.

And found himself looking at Weed. A stride away, she swung the butcher knife at his neck with a hard sideways sweep as if she planned to lop his head off.

The earth shook.

Forty-one

The afternoon roared, and the alley shuddered under Barbara's back. Startled out of a dream, she thought, *Christ, a quake!*

She thought she was at home, so she tried to hold on to the mattress of her bed. Her groping hands met pavement.

She jerked open her eyes.

Sky above her. A lurching, shimmying garage to the left, nothing nearby on the right.

Nothing to fall on me. I'll be okay. It's the stuff that falls on you . . .

Suddenly, the roar faded. The earth stopped jolting and pounding her, but seemed to continue swaying slightly.

An aftershock, she told herself. That's all it was.

All? Had to be better than a six-point.

But not like the big one, not even close.

Now that it was over, Barbara realized that she was hurt. From the feel of things, something had clobbered the back of her head. The alley, maybe. Had the quake knocked her down? She couldn't remember, but it seemed likely. Her head felt as if it had been smacked a good one.

Grimacing, she raised her arms to clutch her head. And let out a cry as the movement stoked a fire in her left side.

The starkness of the pain frightened her.

What happened to me?

She suddenly remembered the gunfight.

Pete!

She'd seen Pete go down, shot by Earl. She'd been hit first, herself, but she'd stayed on her feet long enough to shoot Earl while he'd been spinning around to fire at Pete. He'd gotten off his shot at about the same moment that Pete had fired at him – an instant before the blast from Barbara's shotgun had slammed into his back. While Earl was going down, so was Pete.

Then me, Barbara thought. I stayed up long enough to watch them both get shot. Probably bashed my head when I fell.

The pains tore a cry out of her as she shoved herself up on her elbows.

Below her left breast, her blouse clung to her side like a sodden, red rag.

That's where he shot me, she thought. Jesus H. Christ. Shot. I'm actually shot.

Forget it. It didn't kill me. Worry about it some other time.

She quickly checked for other wounds. Her blouse was open a few inches, and the bare skin between its edges looked okay. The right side of her blouse wasn't too bloody. She looked okay from the waist down.

So she raised her eyes and tried to spot Pete.

Maybe he's alive. Maybe he was only wounded, like me.

Beyond her outstretched body, she saw motorcycles and bodies. A couple of the bikes had fallen over, but most of them still stood upright. Something didn't look . . .

The Lincoln.

The huge, white car was gone.

Explains how the bikes got knocked over.

Who drove off? she wondered. The woman? Some scavenger? Not Earl, that's for sure. That's him, there.

The guy on his back.

How'd he get on his back?

Doesn't matter, she told herself. Where's Pete?

She couldn't see him. But a lot of dead bikers were sprawled and piled in the alley. Pete had been standing beyond most of them at the time of the shootout.

I just can't see him 'cause of all the bodies in the way.

'Pete!' she yelled.

No answer came.

She decided not to call out again. The wrong sort of person might hear her.

As gingerly as possible, she sat up. The effort made her tremble, and the pain filled her eyes with tears. Blinking to clear them, she looked about for the shotgun.

Gone.

'Hell with it,' she muttered.

Then she struggled to stand, whimpering, flinching at times with sudden stabs of pain. When she was up, she swayed and almost fell. Spreading her feet, she kept her balance. Her side felt as if it had been scorched with a white-hot rod.

She wiped tears from her eyes.

She began staggering toward the bodies.

They hadn't been stripped.

What's with the vultures? Barbara wondered. They don't like biker duds?

Just haven't gotten here yet, more than likely.

She changed her mind, however, when she halted above Earl's body. Maybe he'd still been alive after she'd blown him off his feet and he'd made a face-first dive at the pavement. She supposed it was possible that he'd turned over by himself. More likely, though, he'd been rolled onto his back by someone else.

Someone wanting to get at his mouth.

His mouth, wide open, brimmed with blood.

Using her foot, Barbara pushed against his cheekbone. His head turned sideways, the blood dumping out. With the edge of her sneaker against his ear, she managed to tilt his face upright again.

She peered into his mouth.

Gory in there, but she couldn't see well enough to tell whether or not his gold crowns had been removed. To do that, she would need to hunker down over him and take a long, hard look.

The way her head ached and the way her wounded side throbbed with pain, she didn't want to do that.

Doesn't matter anyway, she told herself.

I promised him I wouldn't let any damn scavenger yank his teeth.

So what.

He shot me. He shot Pete. We killed him. Some asshole took his teeth, tough tacos.

She glanced around, searching for his pistol. It was nowhere near his body, nowhere to be seen.

Gone, just like Barbara's shotgun.

Looks like somebody took the guns, she thought.

She moved on, walking in among the bodies. Several had bloody mouths.

Someone had been at them with pliers, she was sure of it.

Didn't take their clothes, scalps, tattoos or motorcycles. Maybe stole their wallets; she had no intention of checking.

Scavenger specialists.

Not my field, honey. I deal only in guns and crowns.

How about knives and bridges?

Never touch 'em, sweets.

I'm losing my mind, Barbara thought.

She tongued her own teeth.

And wondered if some filthy, jibbering vulture had searched her mouth while she was out cold. Stuck fingers in. Poked around with pliers.

She began to feel as if she might throw up.

But forgot her nausea when she saw that the woman who'd been dragged out of her car was gone, for sure. Here was the biker who'd fallen across her rump. And here was the sleeve of her cream-colored blouse.

Pete apparently hadn't shot her, after all.

A possum player, same as me.

After all the gunplay, she'd simply gotten to her feet, climbed back into her car, and driven away.

Maybe.

Or maybe someone took her.

Threw her in the car and raced off with her.

None of the bikers could've done that; all of them had been dead before the final gunfight.

Maybe a scavenger snatched her.

Guns and crowns and ladies.

Then how come he didn't take me?

Thought I was dead?

Quit stalling, she told herself. You've gotta find Pete.

She moved her gaze to the bodies that she hadn't yet studied – that she'd been avoiding, knowing Pete would be among them and not wanting to see him dead. So long as she didn't see him, she could keep her hope that he'd survived the gunshot.

Just turn around and walk away, she thought.

Don't look. You don't want to see him dead.

If you don't see him, you can remember him the way he looked when he was alive.

How he looked in the pickup truck.

How he felt.

Sobbing, she wiped her tears away.

If you don't see him, you can pretend he's still alive and you'll meet again someday, and he isn't gone forever, and you'll kiss him again, and you can go off somewhere secret in the moonlight and make love all night long.

Clint heard the approaching roar. Before he could say anything, the road began to jump and shake under his feet.

'Holy Samolie!' Em yelled.

Mary cried out, 'Oh, God!'

Tugged from both sides, Clint stumbled and capered about like a blind man at a square dance, torn between two partners.

'Aftershock!' Em shouted. Was there triumph in her voice? She'd been predicting a big aftershock, and here it was.

Clint hated that he couldn't see. He knew that they were somewhere on Crescent Heights, and they'd crossed Wilshire a while ago. But he couldn't see what buildings might be near enough to collapse on them, couldn't see what might be overhead about to fall and crush them, couldn't see anything at all except for the blackness.

As he pranced sideways, Mary cried 'Wah!' and his right arm was suddenly dragged downward. He stumbled and fell, not knowing whether he would land on hard pavement or soft Mary.

He landed on Mary.

Em, still gripping his left arm, was pulled down on top of him.

The quake stopped.

From the feel of things, Clint supposed that his fall had been cushioned by Mary's chest. She was gasping for air as if she'd just finished a sprint.

Em seemed to be pressing down against Clint's left side, straddling his hip as if it were a saddle. He felt her chest working like a bellows against his upper arm, her breath brushing the side of his neck.

After a few moments, she said, 'That was a good one.'

'Are we okay?' Clint asked.

'Bet it was a six-point-five. Maybe better.'

'Can everybody climb off me, now?' Mary asked.

'Nothing's going to fall on us?' Clint asked.

'Nope,' Em said. She squirmed and pushed. Her weight went away from him. 'We're in the middle of the street.'

'Is anything coming?'

'Nope. No cars. No nothing. Give you a pull?'

'Maybe you'd better let go.'

Em let go, and Clint suddenly felt as if she had vanished.

'Don't go anywhere,' he said.

'Right here.'

As he tried to climb off Mary, she helped by pushing at

him and rolling. He seemed to skid across her body. When she was out from under him, the hard flatness of the pavement pressed against his back. He started to rise, but was held down by a hand on his chest.

'Don't.' It was Mary's voice. 'Don't move. We gotta rest. I'm dying.'

'You're long overdue,' Em said. 'You were supposed to bite it at Sunset.'

'So much for predictions,' Mary said. She sounded grim.

'God almighty,' Em muttered.

Clint wondered if she was thinking about Loreen. The fortune-teller had sure predicted death at Sunset, but she'd missed by a mile on who would die.

The single advantage of losing his eyesight: he hadn't been able to see the remains of Loreen and Caspar. By the time the big battle was over and Clint had gotten around to opening the rear door of the van, the guy inside had apparently already stripped off their clothes, scalped them both and gotten into some sort of vile, intimate surgery that Em and Mary had refused to give details about.

The guy had greeted Clint with a can of spray paint – a blast of black paint full in the face.

Full in the eyes.

Clint remembered hearing giggles through his own outcry. But the giggles had stopped very fast.

Must have been a nasty surprise for the guy: taking out the big tough man who had the Bowie knife, only to be killed within seconds by two women.

A real 'team effort,' according to Em.

While Clint had stumbled backward away from the door, Em had hurled her hunting knife. 'Got him right in the throat,' she'd bragged.

'Sure,' Mary'd said. 'With the hilt.'

'But it knocked him down, didn't it? I had it planned that way, so you could get all the glory.'

'So I could get the dirty work, you mean.'

They'd sounded mighty cheerful for two gals talking about how they'd subdued a man and slashed his throat. But Clint supposed they had every right to feel proud of themselves. They'd done a hell of a job.

If they hadn't found the bodies of Loreen and Caspar, they probably would've started a party right there in the rear of the van.

With water she'd found inside the van, Mary had washed out Clint's eyes. The water had taken away some of the burning sting, but hadn't restored his vision. Em had tied a cloth around his head – a blindfold to protect his eyes from the sunlight.

Then they'd each taken one of his arms and guided him across lane after lane, weaving through a tangle of stopped vehicles until they reached the other side.

'Guess what,' Em had said, shaking his arm. 'We made it. We got all the way across Sunset. And Mary's still alive.'

'Maybe that *was* the only bunch of killers,' Clint had suggested.

'Maybe,' Em had said. 'But maybe what happened, the other gangs, they saw how we totally demolished that bunch of weirdos and so they figured us for *bad news* and hid when they saw us coming.'

Mary had made a quiet chuckle. 'That's us, bad news. Two babes and a blind guy.'

'You know what, Mary?'

'You're gonna tell me, Em.'

'Looks to me like adversity agrees with you. You were a major sort of pain in the old rumpazoid a few hours ago, and now you're almost human. Why do you think that is?'

'Better not look a gift horse in the mouth.'

'Yeah. Good point. Maybe you just like killing people.'

'I think it might be the other way around,' Clint had said. 'She likes *saving* people. And she's been doing a damn good job of it, too.'

After that, they'd continued on their way. Em on one of his arms, Mary on the other. Guiding him around obstacles, describing what they saw: the collapsed buildings, the fissures in the pavement, the abandoned vehicles, an occasional small group of people digging through rubble in search of those buried or trapped beneath fallen walls.

There seemed to be few people wandering about. Though Mary and Em reported seeing no roving gangs, they found plenty of dead bodies. Most of the bodies had been stripped and maimed.

Clint wasn't able to see them, which was fine with him.

He was glad that he couldn't look at the bad stuff, but he hated not being able to keep watch for trouble. He felt as if he'd betrayed Em and Mary. He was supposed to be their guardian. How could he protect them when he couldn't see the dangers?

What if I don't get better? he wondered. How can I take care of Sheila and Barbara . . .?

Maybe they're dead.

No!

It occurred to him, lying there on the street with Em and Mary beside him, that he might already have found himself a replacement family.

Don't want replacements! I want Sheila and Barbara!

He elbowed the pavement and sat up. 'We've gotta get going. I have to get home.'

He raised his arms. He reached out to each side.

Mary clutched his right hand and said, 'I'm ready.'

His left hand, searching for Em, found her face. She didn't say anything, or move. He felt her forehead and eyebrows under his fingers, her nose pressing against his palm, her lips soft near the heel of his hand.

They kissed him.

Wouldn't mind keeping you around, he thought. If your mother didn't make it . . .

Stop it.

He gave Em's nose a gentle twist. Then she took hold of his hand. 'We better hit the trail,' she said. 'Time's a-wastin'.'

Instead of chopping into the side of Stanley's neck, the butcher knife only nicked his throat as the quake shoved Weed backward. She staggered away from him through the pitching, raging water.

Mixed in with the hurricane roar of the quake was the crash of a gunshot.

Stanley, thrown off his feet and falling, didn't feel a hit. He twisted around.

For a moment before the water blurred his sight, he glimpsed Judy above the corner of the pool. She looked like a terrified sailor dancing the Hornpipe, her revolver jabbing at the sky.

Water closed down over Stanley's head.

He was tossed, shoved, rolled over.

Gonna drown!

Shit!

It rushed through his mind that the aftershock had come like a miracle, just in time to save him from Weed's knife and Judy's .357 magnum or whatever it was – but it had been a big joke, a false save, a dirty trick. It had saved him from the harpies only to drown him.

Gonna drown in three feet of water.

Should've fucked Sheila in her safe, dry tub.

But the vicious currents of the pool suddenly loosened their grip on Stanley. He splashed and thrust his face into the sunlit air. His feet found the bottom. He stood up.

Judy was no longer standing at the corner of the pool.

Had she fallen in?

If she's in, I'll take her. Get that gun . . .

But he could've spotted her easily if she had fallen into the pool; the water was only waist-deep and almost clear.

She wasn't in it.

She must've fallen backward.

He glanced at Sheila. She still hung from the bottom rung of the ladder. She looked freshly splashed, glossy, gorgeous.

I'll nail you again after I get rid of these two . . .

Judy came stumbling to the edge of the pool, looming high above him, the revolver in her hand.

Stanley glanced at Weed.

Out of reach, still submerged.

Try to get to her, use her for a shield?

She'd probably cut my balls off.

Do something quick!

Stanley flung himself sideways, splashed down, kicked and battered his way through the shallow water until the bottom slanted up under him. He scurried along, leaving the water behind, racing over the slick tiles toward the stairs at the end of the pool.

Gonna catch one in the back.

'Stop!' Judy shouted from behind him. 'Stop or I'll shoot!'

'Don't shoot!' Stanley yelled, and kept on running.

'Stop!'

'Don't shoot!'

She fired.

Off to Stanley's right, a blue tile exploded. A flying chip from it slashed his calf.

He bounded up the pool stairs.

Judy fired again.

Forty-two

Dad's old blue Ford wasn't in the driveway. It wasn't parked out front by the curb, either. It was nowhere to be seen.

Beat him home, Barbara thought.

Then she saw that the house was down.

She muttered, 'Oh, my God,' but could hardly hear her voice over the rumble of the Harley's engine.

She steered into the driveway, coasted to a stop, and put down her feet to hold the huge motorcycle steady. The vibrations of the bike made the house seem to shake.

She shut off the engine and dismounted.

She stared at the ruins.

If Mom was in there when it fell down like that . . .

She's gotta be all right, Barbara told herself. Gotta be. I

made it, didn't I? Mom made it, too. Somehow. Please. We've all gotta be all right – Mom and Dad – Pete, too, wherever he is.

Standing in the driveway, she yelled, 'Mom! Mom?'

She listened for an answer.

None came.

She knew that she would have to enter the demolished house and search for her.

Gonna find her crushed.

No! She's fine.

Barbara felt a sick reluctance to start the search.

She decided to fix her bandage.

Back in the alley, after checking all the bodies and not finding Pete, she had pulled the T-shirt off the biker who'd worn the Viking helmet. Somehow, his shirt had escaped most of the blood from his shot head. She'd folded it into a long pad, placed it against the raw furrow on her side, then strapped it in place with the guy's wide, leather belt.

The makeshift bandage had worked fine for a block or two, but then the rough vibrations of the motorcycle had started shaking it down her ribcage. She'd caught the T-shirt in time to save it, and tucked it under the front of the belt.

Now, the belt drooped around her waist, the T-shirt hanging from it like a loincloth.

She started to take off her blouse, then changed her mind.

This wasn't some alley far from home; this was the driveway in front of her house. Neighbors might be watching.

Her back to the street, she peeled the sticky blouse away from her side. She slipped the T-shirt underneath, placed it gently against her wound, and strapped it secure with the belt.

Then she fastened a couple of buttons to hold her blouse shut.

She took a deep breath. It made her lungs ache the way they usually ached when she got home from the family's annual visit to the L.A. County Fair in Pomona – a day of breathing badly polluted air. She guessed that the ache, now, came from too much smoke and dust.

She wondered if she would ever again go to the Fair with her mom and dad.

Wondered if she would ever again see them alive.

She swallowed. Her mouth and throat felt very dry.

Go on and get it over with, she told herself. Stalling won't make it any better. And what if Mom needs help?

She decided to check around, one more time, before starting into the house.

So she turned slowly and scanned the neighborhood. Near the far corner, a house had burned down. A couple of other homes had been destroyed, some had major damage, and a few looked almost unharmed. She saw no one.

No one at all, dead or alive.

If a gang had come through, she told herself, there'd be a lot of bodies around.

That's good news, at least. But where is everyone?

At work, she supposed. Or at school. Or staying inside their houses – cleaning up the messes, or hiding.

She wondered if any of her neighbors had turned wild.

Turned wild and gone on a rampage.

Some must've, she thought.

Damn near everyone she'd encountered had been nuts, one way or the other. As if the quake had released a virus buried in the depths of the earth – a virus that turned people into savages.

Barbara doubted that anything like that had happened, though.

Nobody'd gone nuts because of a virus or a gas or space invaders.

It seemed to be more like everyone had a drooling, wild-eyed lunatic walled up inside, eager to get free, and the quake had broken apart the walls holding them in.

Everyone but me and Pete.

Pretty much.

Maybe we went nuts, too, and just didn't happen to notice.

Who knows, who knows, who knows?

Quit stalling.

She wished she still had a gun. Or a knife. Or any weapon at all.

She had nothing.

Doesn't matter, she told herself. Nobody's around.

Not yet, anyway.

She started walking toward the remains of her home.

She was only vaguely aware that she no longer had a house to live in, that everything she owned was probably broken or ruined, that her life would never be the same as it had been before the earthquake.

She supposed that, later, such things might really hurt.

For now, though, all she really cared about was the safety of her mother and father.

If they're okay, she thought, everything else'll turn out all right.

And if Pete's okay, too.

But she'd seen Pete go down, shot. He might've crawled off, she supposed. But why would he do that? Maybe the woman had driven him away in her Lincoln. Or his body could've been rushed off in a shopping cart by some filthy scavenger who wanted him for reasons too awful to think about.

Just don't think about him.

Barbara climbed the front stoop.

The house looked like a bombed-out ruin.

I've never *seen* a bombed-out ruin, she reminded herself. Well, in documentaries.

But she'd seen something that reminded her . . . Places burnt during the L.A. riot of '92.

Those places had been black, though – smoked and charred. No fires, here. Just everything torn apart, shattered, busted, smashed, splintered, crushed.

'Mom?' she called out. 'Mom! Are you here? Mom?'

She stood motionless and held her breath. Nearby, everything seemed very quiet. The only sounds came from far off: sirens, car engines, bangs that were probably gunshots, shouts, helicopters.

The activity was elsewhere.

Los Angeles was a place of troubles, but her own

neighborhood had always been spared – a tranquil island surrounded by raging seas and sharks.

It was tranquil now.

Tranquil, but devastated.

'Mom?' she called again. 'Where are you? Can you hear me?' She listened again.

And heard a groan from somewhere in the debris.

It seemed to come from her left, from someplace near the area where the kitchen used to be.

'Hello?' she called. 'Mom?'

'Buh – Barrrr?' It was barely a murmur, but she heard it.

'Yes!' she cried out, tears flooding her eyes. 'It's me, Mom! It's me! I'm home! Where are you? Talk to me. I'm on my way.'

She started trudging through the rubble, stepping carefully to avoid nails and broken glass.

'I'm okay,' she explained. 'Basically. I got shot a little bit, but I'm okay. We got stuck downtown 'cause Mr Wellen went nuts. The driver's ed teacher? He flipped out . . . who didn't, though? God, you're lucky you were here. It was like a horror movie downtown, you wouldn't believe it. Are you okay? Could you say something?'

She went silent and halted.

Heard nothing.

'Mom?'

'Baaa . . . bath . . .'

'You're in the bathroom?'

'Tub.'

'You're in the tub? Great! I'll find you. That's probably what saved you, the tub. I saw what the house looked like, and I figured you . . . I just hoped you weren't in it, that's all. I hope Dad's all right. He's probably stuck in traffic somewhere. You wouldn't believe how crazy it is out there. Everyone went nuts. People are getting murdered right and left . . . The good news is, the National Guard's supposed to get here tomorrow. That's what I hear. Won't be a minute too soon, if you ask . . .'

The head stopped her voice.

It was staring up at her from the cluttered floor behind the refrigerator.

A head of tangled black hair and shaggy beard and blood and plaster crumbs.

Its neck, near Barbara's foot, was an ugly raw stump.

She took a quick step backward to get away from it.

'Mom? Who's this?'

No answer came.

'There's a head over here.'

She was answered by a groan from somewhere not far beyond the half-buried stove.

Approximately where the bathroom should be.

She hurried toward it.

When she got past the stove, she found a body stretched out alongside a place where the floor was missing. A man.

All his clothes were gone.

He had his head, though.

A gang got here, after all. Scavengers, too. But they missed Mom.

Barbara stepped past the head of the naked man and peered down into the hole in the floor where she expected to find the tub.

The tub was there.

But not her mother.

The body at the bottom of the tub was a man, a skinny little guy in black leather pants and boots. He had no shirt, but he had his head. It was hairless. He didn't even have eyebrows.

He didn't even have eyes.

His sockets were dark, gooey pits.

Barbara jerked her gaze away from them and raised her head. Turning, she scanned the broken remains of the house.

'Mom?'

She glimpsed a pair of feet sticking out from behind a nearby pile of rubble, but the feet wore black boots.

'*MOM!*' Barbara shrieked. '*MOM, WHERE ARE YOU? WHAT'S GOING ON?*'

'Here I am, dearie.'

She flinched. The voice came from just behind her, and sounded like a man mimicking an old lady.

She turned around fast.

The dead man she'd found stretched out naked on the floor wasn't dead.

He was no longer stretched out.

He was squatting, leering up at her.

'Surprise,' he said.

Barbara felt chilly prickles on the back of her neck.

I was right, she thought. One of the neighbors *did* go wild.

He didn't have on a stitch of clothes. His eyes were as wild as any she had ever seen. From the fiery redness of his skin, he must've been out in the sun all day. Hands on his wide-apart knees, he made no attempt to hide his erection; it looked as if it were pointing at Barbara's face.

'Hi, Mr Banks,' she said.

His leer slipped. 'You know me?'

'You live behind us. Over there.' She dipped her head in the direction of his house. 'With your mother.'

He frowned. 'How do you know that?'

'We've gotten your mail by mistake. I've walked it over to your house a few times. And I've seen you around. Are you all right?'

Good one, Banner. Sure he's all right. Slipped a few cogs, that's all. And any second he's gonna pounce on your sorry ass and do God only knows what to you.

'I'm hunky-dory,' he said. 'And you?'

What'd he do to Mom?

Ask?

I don't think so.

'It hasn't been the best day ever,' Barbara said. 'For one thing, I got shot.'

His eyes widened. He suddenly looked eager and gleeful. 'Shot? Is that so?'

'Do you want to see?'

His gaze latched on the bloody side of her blouse. 'Under there?'

'Yes.'

845

'Show me.'

Hands trembling, she started to unfasten the two buttons that kept her blouse shut. 'That was a good trick,' she said. 'Playing dead? I've used it myself.'

Shouldn't have fallen for it.

She opened her blouse.

Banks nibbled his lower lip. He was still squatting, hands on knees, but now his lower end was swaying a little from side to side. 'What's that?' he asked.

'A belt.' She reached for the buckle that was just beneath her right breast, and started to unfasten it. 'I took it off a dead biker. It's what holds my bandage on.'

'Ah.'

'You want the bandage off, don't you?'

'Sure. I want *everything* off.'

She tugged, and the belt went loose around her chest. The rag against her wound started to slip. She pulled some more, and the belt fell out from under her blouse. She kept hold of its buckle. As the leather strap swayed by the side of her leg, she shook herself slightly. The sodden T-shirt still stuck to her wound for a moment, then let go. It dropped and landed by her foot.

'It's sure bloody,' she said.

'That's all right.'

'Do you want it?'

'Show me where you were shot.'

'Okay.'

He gazed at the bloody side of her blouse. 'Show,' he said. 'Off with the blouse.' He wiped his mouth with the back of a hand.

'First, you have to tell me where my mother is.'

He grinned. 'Dead. Deader than shit. Like all good mothers.'

The words made a sick, cold hardness grow in the center of Barbara, somewhere just below her chest.

'I fucked her to death,' Banks said. Rolling his eyes upward and hanging his tongue out, he made quick thrusting motions with his pelvis.

Barbara whipped the belt at him. He jerked his hands up

to block it, but wasn't quick enough. He cried out as the leather strap smacked the side of his face.

Barbara leaped away from him, twisted around, and ran.

'You're dead!' Banks yelled.

She glanced back. He was already up, already chasing her. He flapped his big arms and brought his knees up high like a crazed man charging through surf.

Barbara had a good headstart.

She knew that she would be fine if she could make it as far as the patio. Clear of the debris, she would be able to pour on the speed. Banks wouldn't stand a chance of catching her.

Not far from the remains of the rear wall, she glanced back again.

He was huffing along, staggering, farther behind than before.

Not gonna get me!

She leaped over a small pile of debris, right leg stretching out, foot pounding down.

Driving a spike of pain up the middle of her foot.

She squealed.

Looking down, she saw the point of a nail come up through the top of her sneaker.

Oh, my God!

She didn't stop running.

Her left leg stretched out and went down and landed on nothing horrible, but the pain in her right foot turned to ripping agony. Looking over her shoulder, she saw it kicking up behind her, a plank attached to the bottom of her shoe like a short wooden ski.

The toe of the plank stubbed a block of plaster.

Barbara fell headlong.

Stanley hooked his right hand under the waistband of her shorts and lifted her out of the rubble where she'd fallen.

She swung her arms, kicked, squirmed and squealed.

A few strides, and Stanley was clear of the ruined house. He hauled her across the patio.

Barbara squirmed and twisted so much that she started to

come out of her shorts. When they were halfway down her rump, Stanley lowered her to the concrete and let go.

She tried to scuttle away.

Crouching, he caught her shorts by their sides and yanked them down to her knees. Her panties went down with them. Though they hobbled her, she kept on crawling.

Stanley grabbed them and tugged them the rest of the way off. They took a shoe with them. He glimpsed the bloody bottom of her right sock.

And stomped on it.

Barbara shrieked.

The pain seemed to freeze her on her hands and knees.

Stanley grabbed the back of her collar. He jammed his other hand between her legs. With both hands, he picked her up. He carried her to the lounger.

The lounger where she liked to stretch out and sunbathe.

Where Sheila did, too.

Both of them nearly naked in their bikinis – their bodies long and tawny and gleaming.

He swung Barbara into position above the faded green pad, and let go. She dropped onto it. He peeled the blouse off her shoulders and down her back. He flung it away.

She was facedown on the pad, naked except for her socks, one sneaker, and a pad of tissues attached with rubber bands to one of her forearms.

Good enough, Stanley said.

He spread her legs.

No no no no! Turn her over. The best stuff's on the other side! You haven't even seen her tits yet!

Standing by the side of the lounger, he bent and reached across her body. He grabbed her upper left arm and hip, then pulled. The lounger suddenly tipped toward him.

Barbara was holding on to the aluminum frame under the pad.

'Let go!' Stanley yelled.

'No!'

He released her hip and jammed his thumb into the pulpy groove of her bullet wound. Her body jerked rigid and the blast of a gunshot crashed through the noise of her scream.

Stanley jumped.

He stood up straight.

Judy again.

Standing atop the cinderblock wall at the rear of the yard, her revolver pointed at the sky.

Weed stood on one side of her, Sheila on the other.

The three women looked the same as before, except that Sheila wasn't naked anymore. She wore a shiny, royal blue kimono that probably belonged to Judy. It was much too small for her. It wouldn't shut all the way, in front, and reached only a few inches down her thighs. Its sleeves barely reached to her elbows.

Both of Sheila's wrists were wrapped with broad, white bandages.

'Don't move a muscle!' Judy called.

Stanley shook his head.

This'd be funny, he thought, if it wasn't such a pain in the ass.

She thinks she can hit me! She couldn't hit me at the pool, and this is three times the distance. At least!

But he didn't see how he could enjoy a good time with Barbara – not with them here.

Why the hell hadn't the bitches stayed away?

For a while after escaping from them, he'd thought they would try to hunt him down. He'd hidden in the ruins of Sheila's house and waited, frightened but eager, planning to take them by surprise when they came looking.

Take 'em by surprise and take 'em down.

Have myself a ball.

But they hadn't come.

Barbara had showed up, instead.

He glanced down at her.

Her head was raised. She was looking toward the three women on the wall.

Probably surprised to see her mother there, alive after all.

'Get away from her,' Judy called. 'Get away and walk toward us.'

'Go ahead and see if you can hit me!'

She took aim at him.

'Sure thing,' he called.

With a laugh, he bent over, grabbed Barbara and flipped her onto her back. The noise of a gunshot made him flinch. But he didn't bother looking up, because he knew that Judy wouldn't have risked hitting the girl.

He gazed at Barbara's slick body.

Not in Sheila's league, he thought. But close. Close enough to make him ache to have her.

He squeezed her breasts. They were smaller than Sheila's. Very hot and slippery and firm. The nipples felt like tongues probing the palms of his hands.

Judy fired again.

You're hurting my ears, you bitch. I'll drive nails into your ears, when I catch you.

Forget about Judy, you've got Barbara.

A bird in the hands.

Birds. A couple of tits.

She was gasping for air, gazing up at him with very wide eyes.

Scared to death, hurting bad.

Turned on?

'Love it!' Stanley blurted.

And thought, maybe I *have* got time. Just a quick one. In and out. Once, maybe twice.

The way he felt, just once should be enough.

I'll blow the roof off the joint!

It could get me killed, he thought.

And laughed, and jerked her legs apart and climbed onto the pad and knelt between them. The lounger wobbled, but held.

Another gunshot.

Was it nearer than before?

If Judy's off the wall, running . . . She gets close enough, I'm dead.

He looked at the wall.

Judy was still on top of it, and Weed still stood at her side. But Sheila was in midair, dropping toward the ground.

850

The breeze of her fall lifted the bottom of her kimono and spread it open to the sash at her waist.

My honey, Stanley thought. *Come to me!*

Her feet hit the ground. Her legs bent. She did a very fast somersault and came out of it sprinting over the grass straight toward Stanley.

He glanced down at Barbara.

Do it! One quick one!

But he couldn't stop his eyes from being pulled back to Sheila. The sash of her kimono had come loose. The silken blue robe shimmered and flowed behind her like a cape.

She raced toward him, long legs striding out, arms pumping hard, fists clenched. Her legs gleamed, alive with shifting curves of muscle under their sunburn and scrapes and welts. She had a long white bandage high on her thigh where Stanley had cut her with the saw. Except for the bandage, her legs were bare all the way up to her wispy tuft of golden curls.

Her breasts lurched and jumped with the rough motion of her running.

Stanley had always hoped to see her running without a bra on.

Getting my wish, he thought. *At last, at last.*

No wonder she always wore one!

Look at 'em go!

They looked splendid.

She looked splendid.

Not just her body, but her face. As weathered and battered as it was, it still looked glorious to Stanley. At once smooth and hard, delicate and powerful, silk and granite, innocent and sophisticated. But altogether beautiful, the face of a movie queen and a warrior goddess melded into one stunning, incredible Sheila Banner.

My naked, caped crusader.

Wonder Woman.

Super Sheila.

MIGHTY MOM COMING TO SAVE HER KID AND SHE'S UNCHAINED, UNWIRED, ON THE LOOSE, COMING FOR ME – SHIT!!!

Suddenly, watching Sheila dash toward him, Stanley was scared.

Scared to death.

Gotta get the fuck outa here!

He was kneeling between Barbara's legs.

He started to scoot backward.

Barbara reached out fast and grabbed him, one hand wrapping tight around his penis.

'Let go!' he shrieked.

She tightened her grip.

'No!'

He jerked his head sideways.

Sheila, dashing full speed, bare feet smacking loud on the concrete of the patio, stretched out her arms and took to the air.

She dived into Stanley.

Hugged him.

Tore him down sideways off the lounger – from the feel of things, Barbara held on too long – and smashed him against the concrete.

He had Sheila on top of him.

Sitting on his belly.

He was in agony, too breathless to scream.

But he could feel the slippery heat of Sheila's buttocks against his skin. The tickle of her bush. The sharp iron blows of her fists against his face. He watched how her breasts bounced and jerked as she punched him. He watched her face, too.

She had such fury in her eyes.

Banner, Barbara
English 11A
September 23

THE QUAKE AND I

I guess that a subject like 'what I did on my summer vacation' would make a fairly lame assignment, considering that we all went through such an incredibly bad earthquake just before the end of last semester.

It turned out to really be the end of last semester.

Anyway, I am glad to be back in school, even though I'm not exactly filled with joy about having to write about the earthquake.

It was like Charles Dickens said: 'It was the best of times; it was the worst of times.'

I was out on the streets in the driver's education car with the teacher and three other students when the earthquake struck. Mr Wellen took over driving, and took us on a detour to downtown, where we ended up getting stranded. We had quite an adventure trying to get back home.

When I finally did get home, I discovered that our house had been completely knocked down by the earthquake. My mother, inside the house at the time of the collapse, lived through it by jumping into our bathtub. The bathtub saved her life.

My father was at work in the Valley when the quake struck. Like me, he had all sorts of adventures trying to get home. He arrived about an hour after I did, and had a couple of strangers with him. The strangers were a grownup woman named Mary, and a thirteen-year-old named Em, short for Emerald. Dad was blind when he arrived home, having been injured by getting some paint in his eyes. It was a good thing he had Mary and Em with him, because they are the ones who led him home. Fortunately, Dad has since regained his eyesight.

As our house was destroyed, we all lived in the home of our neighbors, Judy and Herb. All of us stayed there together for about a week – and what a week it was! Judy and Herb were really neat people. Mary got to be very annoying, but Em and I became very good friends. We've gotten together quite a number of times since then, and we always have a fine time. Em's mother is a real character, and sort of fun.

Anyway, my parents and I found ourselves an apartment and are living there while our new house is being built, which is supposed to take about a year.

The worst thing about the quake is that so many people got injured and killed. Stuff fell on some of them. A lot of people, however, slaughtered each other during that first day, before the National Guard showed up. People can be so horrible when they think they can get away with things.

The best part about the quake is that I learned a lot about things such as courage and loyalty and love.

I just hope that when the next major earthquake hits Los Angeles, I am out of town on a vacation.

the end

'Jeez, you left out a few things.'

'Yeah? Like what?'

'Like me.'

'Oh, you want me to tell what we did in the back of the pickup truck? That'd be cute. I'm sure Mr Kling would *love* that.'

'You could write about how we saved the woman

from the bikers, and how she drove me to the hospital and saved *my* life.'

'I don't wanta write about that. I mean, it's great that she saved you, but . . . I sure wish she'd left me a note, or something.'

'She thought you were dead.'

'I know, I know. A very observant lady. But I spent like *weeks* thinking about all the awful things that might've happened to you. I figured maybe one of those street-vultures had probably eaten your pancreas for dinner.'

'Can someone eat a pancreas?'

'If someone's hungry enough. Sure. Why not?'

'Anyway, you're just gonna leave everything out of your paper?'

'I didn't leave *everything* out.'

'Almost everything. And all of the bad stuff.'

'If I put all *that* in, my report'd be like hundreds of pages long and I'd never get it done. Besides which, I'm not about to go telling some teacher about that nut trying to rape me. And, God knows, I don't want to incriminate anyone. It isn't as if we didn't kill quite a bunch of people, you know?'

'It was in self-defense.'

'Yeah, but you don't go around admitting to that sort of thing in an English paper.'

'Your mom really *beat* that guy to death?'

'With her fists.'

'God. It's hard to imagine her doing something like that. I mean, she's so . . .'

'Beautiful?'

'Well, you know, yeah. But *nice*, too. I mean, she's one of the nicest people I've ever known.'

'Just don't get her mad at you.'

'Great.'

'And my dad can be even worse.'

'You're sure they know I'm here?'

'*Why?* Are you worried? I mean, we're just doing our *homework* together, right?'

'Yeah, I guess so.'

'My homework's done. How about yours?'

'As if I had any.'

'What do you want to do, now?'

'I don't know.'

'The apartment house across the street has a pool in its courtyard.'

'It does?'

'I've never seen anyone using it, either. I bet we could sneak in and have it all to ourselves.'

'What if we get caught?'

'What're they gonna do, *shoot* us?'

'What time are your parents supposed to get home?'

'The movie gets out at ten, so we've got almost a whole hour. And by the way, they *don't* know you're here.'

'I could sure go for a swim, about now.'

The Richard Laymon Collection Volume 2

Richard Laymon

THE WOODS ARE DARK

In the woods are six dead trees. The Killing Trees. That's where they take them. Innocent travellers on the road in California. Seized and bound, stripped of their valuables and shackled to the Trees. To wait. In the woods. In the dark . . .

OUT ARE THE LIGHTS

The Vampire movie came first, then the story of the Axeman. This was the horror movie series to end them all. Cinema buffs admired the grainy, amateur camera work – it suggested the action was the real thing. But it couldn't be – could it?

'If you've missed Laymon, you've missed a treat' Stephen King

'A brilliant writer' *Sunday Express*

'This author knows how to sock it to the reader' *The Times*

0 7553 3169 9

headline

Coming soon in the **Richard Laymon**
Collection and available from your bookshop
or *direct from his publisher*.

FREE P&P AND UK DELIVERY
(Overseas and Ireland £3.50 per book)

Volume Twelve:
Body Rides & Bite   £7.99

Volume Thirteen:
Fiends and After Midnight   £7.99

Volume Fourteen:
Among the Missing & Come Out Tonight   £7.99

TO ORDER SIMPLY CALL THIS NUMBER

01235 400 414

or visit our website: www.madaboutbooks.com

Prices and availability subject to change without notice.